I0590337

A
Dreamer's Fervor

A Novel

Vladimir Konecni

A Dreamer's Fervor is the author's translation into American English of his novel *Жудећи за Ољом—Далеки ртови љубави и сазнања* (*Seeking Olya—Remote capes of love and insight*), published in Serbian Cyrillic by Prometej, a major publishing house in Novi Sad, Serbia, in 2022.

Corniglia Press
Santa Monica, California, USA

ISBNs: 979-8-9940415-0-5 (hc/j); 979-8-9940415-1-2 (hc); 979-8-9940415-2-9 (pb); 979-8-9940415-3-6 (ebk)
Library of Congress Catalog Number: 2025925091

Cover Design by Vladimir Konecni
Book design and typesetting by Mayfly Book Design and Publishing Services, Minneapolis, MN

First Printing: 2026

TO MIRJANA-MIRJAM, MY WIFE, DUŠAN, OUR SON,

AND

HERMAN MELVILLE
(1819-1891)

Note. Our son Dušan Konecni drew the picture on the front cover in 2004, when he was nine years old. In 2021, at the request of the novel's author, Dušan added "OdQ 81" to the drawing. He did it with a smile, in postmodern style, implying that the fictitious Odile de Quernevelle was the artist when she was nine.

Contents

PART ONE

Odile and Célestin Above Earth's Heart

1.

The little girl wriggled on the hard seat but kept looking through the dirty window of the compartment: Only some yurts were visible. However, a quarter of an hour later, she was surprised to see a Ferris wheel emerge from the blazing sand of the Gobi. Placing pink sunglasses on her tiny nose, she determined the wheel was stationary. "It looks like it will never turn again," thought Odile. The train slowed down and a modest station appeared. She looked at her father Célestin questioningly as he explained: "Ulan Bator, *ma chère fille*, the capital of Mongolia—the 'Red Hero' city, as it says in Russian on that building. Here we won't get off. We're very far from Peking, one thousand five hundred kilometers."

Odile and Célestin were alone in compartment № 4, car № 1, in the half-empty international train № 3. On the small semi-oval table next to the window, there stood two empty tea glasses in metal holders and a juicy, knobbly, pale-yellow pear. The girl was tired from days of travel, and the plastic sandals pinched her feet. Her father bought them for a crumpled five-yuan note at a market in Peking shortly before their departure when it was too late to find better ones. She did not like the noisy city filled with black-haired children who observed her inquisitively with their huge eyes.

Célestin took off his daughter's sandals and lifted her small feet into his lap. He kissed both ankles and after rummaging in a bag, found band-aids. Then he diverted her attention: "In this desert country, they are masters of horseback riding, as you'll be one day. They've always had fabulous horses. Riding them expertly and furiously, and fighting fearlessly and cruelly, the Mongols, together with their Manchu neighbors, subdued all of the enormous country of China. Imagine that! A Manchu dynasty by the name of Qing ruled China for three hundred years—until the beginning of our century. You'll learn all this much better when you grow up and return here. I hope you will because northern China and Mongolia are otherworldly."

He then pointed through the window: "The two men over there, on a placard the size of the station building, are Leonid Brezhnev, the Soviet president, and a Mongol leader in his employ. The words are quotations from their speeches, with letters so big they can be read from here."

She did not want her father to stop gently massaging her feet so she tried to keep him at it by asking: "Those two, *cher Papa*, they are probably very important, right?" While he was carefully returning the sandals to her feet, Célestin responded: "Those people, *ma douce*, are very different from us, and their time will pass much quicker than ours." Odile had other questions: "Papa, why is this 'city hero' red? Does it have a carrot for its nose like our snowman last winter or tells lies like Pinocchio?"

2.

Seven-year-old Odile and her father, a handsome, vigorous man, spent the previous winter on their spacious, opulent estate near the city of Metz in Lorraine, in the northeast corner of France. Sitting comfortably for many centuries by the Moselle River, the manor was Célestin's birthplace.

Winter began early that year, 1979. Around the time of his thirty-fifth birthday, at the end of October, it snowed incessantly for days. One radiant morning after the long snowstorm, he set Odile on the faithful and slow but strong mare Pasha, as the girl had named the horse affectionately, and walked for a long time leading the animal through deep snow. The girl firmly gripped Pasha with her thighs, having been taught by her father to ride without a saddle. Sometimes, she would lay her rosy cheek on Pasha's neck and drift off in the winter sun holding the mane. She trusted her father and the mare absolutely. No name other than Célestin would suit her papa, Odile mused: He was a parent gifted to her by heaven.

Besides, she had no one else in the world. Her mother Patrizia did not survive the birth of twins. That happened on the tragic 18th of January 1972 in Koblenz, a pretty old German city surrounded by vineyards; like Metz, it lay on the banks of the Moselle. Odile's twin brother lived only several hours longer than their mother. Had he survived long enough to be christened, his name would have been Patrice. Because she had been born first, the girl long thought she had lost a younger brother. Much later, she learned that in China she would be considered Patrice's younger sister—since he had been conceived first.

In the joyous period when they awaited the birth, not knowing about the number of fetuses or their gender, Patrizia and Célestin decided, by pulling cards from a deck, the son's name would be the mother's choice and the daughter's the one the father preferred. He chose Odile—the name of a young heroine in an old French novel with whom he had been infatuated as a boy of thirteen. Patrizia had laughed and declared she was not jealous of someone fictitious and over a hundred years old.

Patrizia and Célestin were born in 1944 in two neighboring countries at war with each other and cities only two hundred kilometers apart. His parents Anne-Louise and Joseph died together in early 1945 in one of the last Nazi bombings of Lorraine. The opinions and behavior of Patrizia's German parents in Koblenz, her native city, provoked the deepest contempt possible for a daughter to feel for her parents. For sound reasons, they forever ceased to exist in Patrizia's kind and just heart. Later, these people seemed not to grieve his wife's death, and he could not forgive it despite subjecting himself to self-examination.

That evil war. Célestin didn't know how to speak about it to his little angel. He took her out of school for an extended period mostly because he had found out what despicable lies about the war were fed to children in both countries. He obtained permission to teach Odile at home by virtue of his high education and international standing as a comparative linguist.

The two of them flew from Paris to Peking on the 2nd of July 1980 and their adventure began.

3.

The girl and her father sometimes communicated in their mixture of French and German, although both had perfect command of both tongues. From early childhood, Odile had a great desire to learn everything that came her way, including how the same thing was called in various languages. When the train stopped in a small place two hundred fifty kilometers north of Ulan Bator, the girl immediately inquired about the name of the station. Célestin answered: "You can't read that yet, but it's written: 'Кяхта' and 'Хиагт.'

"Let me explain. We entered Mongolia from China in a town called Erlian. On the station building, there was a square clock set in green neon light—remember? We waited on the platform for two hours while the axles on the cars of our train were being changed—because the width of the track in China is intentionally different from the USSR." The girl nodded. "You see, Mongolia is now almost a part of the USSR. Our travel permit is valid for both countries. Take a look at our passport: Here's our visa № 64471, which we got at the Soviet Consulate in Peking in the ugly brown house. Then we crossed all of Mongolia from south to north and stopped in the capital." Odile jumped in: "Yes, it was Ulan Batr!" "Precisely, *ma chérie*, Ulan Bator. But now we've officially entered the USSR."

He continued: "In the Mongolian language, this town is called 'Хиагт'; they use Russian letters, and it would sound 'Hiyagt.' But that's not pleasing to Russian ears, so they say 'Kyachta'—there, in Russian letters, 'Кяхта.' You know how Germans say 'Koblenz' for the lovely city in which you were born whereas the French for the same city..." "... say 'Coblance,'" she interrupted cheerfully. "Yes," he carried on, "different tongues, linguistic habits, even the desire to hear one thing and not another. *Hélas,* people all over the world tend to appropriate all they can and impose their own as something superior on others, often by force."

She observed her father attentively as he spoke: "We have for the first time in our lives stepped into Russia, the USSR, a truly enormous country, much bigger than China and all of Europe. We'll spend some time here so it would be useful to teach you Russian words and how to write and pronounce Russian letters. We can begin with 'Кяхта.' But before that, let's come out on the platform and stretch our legs on Russian soil."

As the train traveled another three hundred kilometers northward, father and daughter occasionally visited the restaurant car. It was without luxuries, but they enjoyed drinking black tea, reading, and writing in diaries. When hungry, they ate tasty red borscht with rich cream, salad with cucumbers and onions, and sausage with thickly cut dark bread.

Before the train arrived at Ulan–Ude, the capital of Buryatia, one of the numerous republics comprising the USSR, the passengers—all of whom were foreigners—had received a notice in Russian and French it would be forbidden to descend to the platform at the next stop: Ulan–Ude was a "closed city." Upon arrival, a line of armed soldiers wearing tense expressions stood next to the train. Célestin found it difficult to explain to Odile the reasons for firearms confronting a harmless international train. She had seen soldiers with rifles and machine guns on Tiananmen Square near the scary, huge Forbidden City in Peking but was astonished by the presence of scowling young soldiers after so many hundreds of kilometers of untouched nature. From the train one could see a square, in the middle of which was a monument: It consisted of a massive glass cube on which was set a bronze likeness of Lenin's head the size of a smallish house.

Because she was the only child on the train, Odile attracted the attention of other passengers. They stopped by to give her an apple or sweets and talk to her father in various languages. One visitor was a young Pole who intended to leave the train at Irkutsk and fly from there to Warsaw on a ticket he had bought for eighteen dollars on the black market in Peking. Several times two young Germans came to their compartment to talk and exchange jokes, usually bringing chocolates and bottles of warm beer—the only kind available from the train bar. One was a philosophy student from Cologne, the other a novice car salesman from Munich. The Bavarian made the girl laugh by exaggerating his southern German accent while the philosopher complained in French about being unable to sleep at night because of the smoke produced by the salesman. However, the smoker was polite to the child while visiting: The pipe stayed cold between his teeth.

She liked having visitors except when someone spoke to her father only in English, a language in which she was still not proficient. For that reason, among others, a cute youngish redhead from San Francisco was a problem. Lisa first appeared at their compartment before the border of Mongolia to banter and ask for a loan of forty dollars, the price of the Mongolian-Russian visa at the border in Erlian. "She's not sincere," thought Odile, but Célestin readily gave the cash and received Lisa's check. Even though the transaction was simple, the girl was not mollified. Inwardly, he debated: "Is my daughter protecting me from a possible trickster or just jealous—not of any person's attention but a young woman's attention?"

Soon after the train crossed into Mongolia, Lisa appeared again and returned the money. "Goody, we're getting rid of her!" Odile concluded happily. However, just then, the tall redhead firmly embraced Célestin to thank him in the California manner, pressing her sizable breasts against his chest. It turned out that she had crossed the border without a penalty. Lisa then kissed Odile noisily, gave her a slightly melted Swiss chocolate, and made herself comfortable, long legs propped on the seat across— as the girl peevishly noted. Then she took two cold beers from her bag and gave one to Célestin. "For a clever manipulator, there is always fine chocolate and cold beer," Lisa's hosts mutely surmised, the child with inborn intuition.

"Sure, red female hair and charming freckles are a rarity in Mongolia, whereas high cheekbones and glittering black eyes certainly are not," he teased Lisa while they drank, laughed, and sang Lou Reed's song "Lisa Says." Célestin understood what was happening in Odile's heart. At the time, however, he didn't know how to help his jealous little daughter.

4.

After Ulan-Ude, the train continued north along the Selenga River but then turned westward and traveled for many hours through the taiga—the magnificent forests of conifers bordered by the tall and slender white birches. Although they had painted marvelous Russian landscapes with their pen and brush, Ivan Turgenev and Ilya Ryepin never eyewitnessed the yellow, red, and purple colors of Siberian deciduous trees. Nor did they gaze, through air pure as crystal, at Buryatia's mountain peaks etched in the deep blue sky. Célestin and Odile had long been standing by the window on the right side of the train as it ran westward when he told her they would soon see a color described by many as astonishingly beautiful.

The girl did not know what to expect, but she was a thoughtful, sometimes mysterious child, quite capable of not bothering her father with incessant questions even when impatient. Then, near Babushkin, it was Odile who first saw the magical Baikal. Carried on the wings of the splendid blue-green color and the huge size of the magnificent lake, she exclaimed not like a child but like a painter. Both knew it was her first experience of genuine aesthetic awe.

"We are almost there, *mon bijou!* As you already know, at your age, I had an atlas and read a lot. Lake Baikal was one of the places that fascinated me. To see it—the oldest and largest freshwater lake on Earth—was one of my boyhood dreams." Odile stared at the lake, motionless, unblinking. "It's so, so gorgeous, Papa! I didn't expect ever to see something so wonderful." Célestin had pressed the girl, his gentle motherless child, so firmly against his side that it seemed he had squeezed out the tears running down her cheeks.

The train wound its westerly way some two hundred kilometers along Baikal's southern shore to Slyudyanka but then turned sharply to the northeast and, rounding the lake's corner, traveled another hundred kilometers to Irkutsk. Finally, after two thousand five hundred kilometers and sixty-five hours on the train from Peking, Célestin and Odile reached the city in the heart of Siberia. It was 3:30 p.m. on a sunny autumn day, the 26th of September 1980. By train from Irkutsk to Moscow, in the northwesterly direction, there remained over five thousand kilometers via Krasnoyarsk and many other cities. Metz, Koblenz, and Paris were on a different planet.

5.

In Irkutsk, they had a spacious room with two separate beds on the tenth floor of the hotel Intourist. The reservation, obtained at an astronomical price, was necessary for them to leave the train at all. Their main immediate problem was that the water from the faucet and shower was viciously hot, and there was no cold water. There were also some stern, strange rules, one being that it was forbidden to use the stairs—only the slow, always busy elevator. They became used to it and much else.

Odile charmed female members of the staff in part because her father had taught her how to pronounce many Russian words. When he occasionally sent her to the front desk to exchange money, women who worked there gave her fifteen rubles for five dollars, instead of one ruble for a dollar and twenty cents, which was the official rate. The transaction was usually accompanied by the girl's hair being stroked and words of endearment, so numerous in Russian for children, spoken. Célestin could probably accomplish the same through the hotel doorman, but a child is a child, so everyone emerged lily-white.

Playing the child card worked well even with the police and their permit to stay in Irkutsk was extended from three to thirty days because the girl had allegedly experienced stomach upsets. Célestin, as a matter of principle, never offered bribes; besides, no one in Irkutsk ever asked for one. He and his daughter were an unusual traveling couple, a pair of genuine innocents. By their obvious mutual love and closeness, they won over the tough bureaucrats and policemen of the Brezhnev era, at least in Siberia.

Every morning, they had breakfast at the hotel: hard-boiled eggs, thick sausage, cabbage salad, dark rye bread, and the superb thick yogurt to which Odile was slowly getting used. She had also become accustomed to Russian black tea but unlike the locals, took it without sugar—which was her father's health-minded preference. He also made sure she never drank fake fruit juices or any type of cola.

The only other guests in the breakfast room were two groups of seven or eight men each. One consisted of Azerbaijanis who created clouds of smoke and spoke Russian fluently. In the other group were Yugoslavs, who spoke some sort of bogus Russian, yet addressed the staff loudly and self-confidently, akin to the style of some Nebraskans at a Paris bakery. Most of the men in both groups appeared unwashed and unshaven. They clearly did not solve the problem of scalding water in their rooms or were simply lazy, perhaps because they traveled without women.

In contrast, Célestin traveled with an impressionable child and never permitted himself any self-neglect. Odile had been taught proper hygiene from a very young age, which was easy because she rarely whined. That, in turn, must have been due to her inborn nature but also to the self-restraint instilled by the respect she felt for her dad. After all, in their life together, there were many occasions when she could have been willful, yet these were opportunities of which she scarcely availed herself.

The two often took long walks along the calm, shady streets of Irkutsk, with few cars around. For Célestin to enter the city museum cost four times what it did Soviet citizens, while Odile did enter free of charge after a protracted consultation with the museum director. The girl did not like the 1875 statue of Tsar Ivan IV the Terrible, but her father nevertheless explained how important that ruler was. They stood for a long time in front of Ryepin's tender 1874 painting entitled *The Beggar Girl* (*Nishchaya*): A destitute young girl in a patched-up blouse, with a sweet face and a tangle of blond grubby hair, forlornly looks at the ground. Tears filled Odile's eyes. "Look, *Papa chéri*, how poor and sad she is— and what a pretty face! She looks my age..." Célestin embraced her head and whispered: "Yes, she is a child like you and has lovely eyes and face like you. The master painter succeeded in showing how poverty-stricken she is... and probably hungry."

In the evening, they went to a concert where a musician called Olga Schiller performed several J. S. Bach's suites for solo violoncello exceptionally well. The youngish blond woman received prolonged applause and bouquets from the audience— middle-aged women dressed in their provincial best. Odile had heard Bach's music live in Metz but never for solo cello. She listened carefully, often looked at her father, and applauded when he did. At the end, Célestin said: "The cellist is from the city of Tomsk, one of the oldest in Siberia, and her surname is written 'Шиллер' in the program. Undoubtedly, she's Russian of German descent and probably speaks at least some German. Would you like to say a few kind words to her? No, better not, I'll explain later." While they were walking back, he gave a tactful lecture about the horrific war the Nazis from the country of Odile's birth had waged against the country in which they were visitors.

Before reaching the hotel, he noticed that two urchins of twelve or thirteen were following them. At a street corner, the boys funnily gestured a plea for chewing gum. He denied in Russian having any, adding boringly that gum was bad for teeth. The boys tittered and disappeared.

The next day, they were denied entrance to the city library. The doorman gruffly claimed all the books were in Russian. That Célestin spoke Russian well enough did not help—it had a contrary effect. However, father and daughter managed to spend almost three hours in the biggest bookstore in Irkutsk. The nosy security person and his arrogant female boss repeatedly imposed themselves but failed to kick them out. At the checkout, the callous woman invented that the foreigner had to pay four times the stated price of a children's book and a pocket atlas, haughtily telling the security guard in the visitor's hearing, that it was a new rule she had instituted. He made the purchase smiling.

From the post office, they sent postcards to European countries, hoping they would arrive. Another rule prevented them from having lunch at the nearby hotel Angara, only at their hotel. At one point, three young men asked Célestin about jeans for sale. He rebuffed them unceremoniously, worrying about a police or petty-bandit trap; that, too, he explained to Odile, who was learning fast how to interpret odd situations. He was not pleased to be teaching his daughter suspiciousness and cynicism but hoped that for each scoundrel, she would meet many kind people in the USSR.

Marvelous days of autumn ensued. They walked next to the fast-flowing Angara River, along the wide boulevards named after Marx and Engels, and around the obelisk and massive statue of Lenin—yet were glad to discover a quarter where renovated houses from the beginning of the twentieth century stood. The streets were quiet and tree-lined, impeccably clean except for the fallen leaves, although many, in numerous nuances of yellow and red, still adorned the trees. The passersby were well dressed, with an occasional woman in a short fur coat and tall leather boots. A few people sent the pair invariably friendly or just curious looks. However, no one addressed them.

Odile confided she enjoyed being in Irkutsk because they were, unlike in Peking, surrounded by people similar to themselves—and the locals were few! Célestin decided to leave for some later time a serious talk about groups and races, differences and similarities, and the justified and unjustified likes and dislikes. With her warm hand in his, walking slowly on the softly rustling or sharply crackling leaves, he was at peace and happy.

6

It was the beginning of the fourth week of their stay at Baikal. As soon as they could, they had left the hotel Intourist in Irkutsk. By a local bus, they traveled fifty kilometers to the south, up the Angara River to where it flowed out of Baikal near the village of Listvyanka. "The Angara is the only river that dares to abandon beautiful Baikal," exclaimed Célestin. They were sitting on a rock, stunned by the enormous quantity of water. "You see, *mon ange*, many rivers flow into something but few flow out and have the strength to go somewhere else. The Angara is powerful in front of our eyes, yet from here, as it flows to the north and then west, it gradually becomes even more mighty, until it finally enters the gigantic Yenisei River that itself disappears, far, far to the north, in the Arctic Ocean..."

After being quiet for a while, Odile opened her backpack and took out a pocket-size book. "In this atlas you bought for me in Irkutsk, I've already found Angara, Yenisei, and some cities through which one or the other river passes, like the one called Bratsk. Also, I read two other rivers flow all the way to the North Pole. One is called something funny like 'Ob' and the other is called 'Lena,' like the lady who changes money at our hotel."

At Listvyanka, they had the final scheduled encounter with the claws of the ubiquitous Intourist agency: They had previously booked a one-day excursion with a guide, car, and driver. The automobile was a large, gray, comfortable Volga, while the driver, Pyotr, was a serious, balding Siberian in his early fifties, who, as it turned out, said only a dozen words the whole day. The guide, Oksana Eduardovna Grigoryeva, was a blue-eyed and pleasantly plump young woman with shortish blond hair and very light skin. As a third-year student of English and German literature at Irkutsk University, she had a fine command of English and an acceptable one of German. When Oksana and Célestin spoke English for a while, a tiny frown of displeasure sometimes appeared on Odile's face despite her effort not to show it, so they would switch to German.

The Russian woman's parents were engineers who lived in the populous Siberian city of Krasnoyarsk, the place of her birth twenty years earlier. Oksana was an open person, and he felt certain her behavior was natural, regardless of the instructions she may have received from the local KGB. During the conversation, she addressed Odile in a friendly manner and produced a pretty Baikal pebble as a gift. Slowly she managed to melt the girl's heart, so after a while the two even teased each other. Célestin knew his daughter's sense of humor, but that was the first time during their trip she revealed her gay side to someone else.

Instinctively trusting each other, the guide and the visitor pursued serious themes out of Pyotr's earshot: from politics and religion to their families, Oksana's studies, and her boyfriend Alyosha. She divulged having long shared with her young man a feeling of belonging to Orthodox Christianity, unlike their parents, who firmly accepted the communist doctrine. "Alyosha and I attend services at the Irkutsk Cathedral, though only on feast days. My father insists I take a university course entitled 'Atheism,' but I won't do it, I know what those lectures would claim."

Pyotr asked them to return to the car when he thought they spoke too long, while Odile listened to every word, often holding her father's hand. In the vehicle, Oksana recited facts about Baikal: "Elevation 445 meters; the greatest depth 1,620 meters; length 636 kilometers; width 25–80 kilometers; the coastline measures over 2,000 kilometers. Baikal is the deepest lake in the world, with the most transparent water; 336 rivers flow into it, and..." Odile interrupted with a giggle: "And only the Angara flows out of it!" Oksana was also omniscient: "Yes. But do you know, Odilichka, the lake freezes five months of the year, from the beginning of January to the end of May? People ski and skate on the ice and snow, a wonderful thing to do; but the Angara is so fast-flowing she never freezes!"

They drove in the northeasterly direction from Listvyanka, along Baikal's northern shore, passing through typical Siberian villages. Several times, Célestin asked Pyotr to stop for half an hour and thus placed the driver into a dilemma: He would not hear what was talked about but be able to smoke, which was not permitted in the car. On those occasions, the three of them climbed a hillock or, passing through a grove, descended to a narrow beach. In one case, they did not return to the car for an hour. Sitting on rocks above small waves, Oksana sweetly spoke to Odile in German, with many Russian words added, as if she were a kind auntie: "Dear Odilichka, you must return to Baikal when you grow up, it's a wondrous place. This huge body of water has a sensitive soul and a volatile temper. It has its own climate, its ebb and flow, its storms and tempests. And its own winds: Barguzin, Sarma, Kultuk... Waves can be as high as five meters. Last summer, the mighty Sarma sank a boat full of scientists.

"Unfortunately, I know Baikal only from my twelfth year so I was quite a bit older than you when I first came. You're lucky your dad brought you here early in life and you two are alone. I came with my school: Clamor, non-stop chatter of my girlfriends, stern teachers. It prevented me from appreciating this beauty and reflecting on it." Célestin waited, and what he was hoping for indeed happened. In German words and phrases he had never heard her use before, Odile described to Oksana how she felt when she saw Baikal for the first time from the opposite shore, standing next to her father in the train that eagerly clattered through Siberia—endless and eternal.

7.

Célestin repeatedly brought up Soviet citizens' inability to travel abroad. When Oksana got to know him better and realized that far from despising her native land he loved it, she decided to confide: "Yes, I find it hard I can't travel to other countries: To see, to feel the places about which I've read so much! For example, you flattered me by saying my name, Oksana—together with the related 'Aksinya,' and there are other variations—is famous in Russian literature from Gogol' to Sholohov. You showed me you hold our extraordinary literature in high regard. And while caring for a young daughter, you came to visit Siberia where you met a girl with a name known to you from Russian novels.

"I have read a modest amount of German and English literature and even some French. I'd love to travel to those countries, meet the people whose names I know from books, and flatter them a little by showing I'm familiar with their names from some good novel. Perhaps it's a superficial example although I think I'm not a superficial person. Now I have Alyosha, it's even more important we see something of Europe. Please understand we'd never live somewhere else: This is our country, the one and only. We Siberians are the most sincere Russians. Why are we not believed we'd return?"

He did not know what to say and was proud of his daughter for grabbing Oksana's hand: She sensed the young woman spoke of something with which she struggled. After a few moments, it was as if Oksana came to and continued in a different voice: "Of course, even if we were to receive passports for foreign travel, how would Alyosha and I pay for the trip? Although I receive a small stipend from Irkutsk University, it's my parents' support on which I depend; Alyosha is in the same situation. To be a guide at Baikal, I passed a course but am hired infrequently. And in a few days, I'm returning to the university, the summer is over. I don't do this job for money but to practice foreign languages and indirectly get to know the world a tiny bit. As for money, during the entire peak season, the month of August, I earned only twenty-nine rubles! For today's work, I'll receive, believe it or not, two rubles; and Pyotr, as far as I know, will receive ten. Your cost is probably sixty dollars."

When they stopped in Bolyshiye Koty, a big village, Oksana recommended a restaurant for lunch. Célestin naturally invited her and Pyotr, but the driver joined the locals in a corner while the trio sat at a large round table. Before lunch, an excellent juice of cranberries and other rare Baikal berries was served; the Frenchman also drank a shooter of Moskovskaya vodka. Oksana fondly described the customs of the Buryats, a people of Mongol origin who lived on the southern shore of Lake Baikal and subsisted by breeding sheep, goats, and camels. They practiced Shamanism and Tibetan Buddhism. Their yurts were different from the Mongolian ones and Oksana skillfully drew one. After writing "For my dear Odilichka" and adding her name and address in Russian below the drawing, she gave it to Odile with a dazzling smile. The girl leaped up and kissed Oksana on the cheeks.

They all had a small steak with fried potatoes, cabbage, and red beet salad. Célestin sipped an indifferent Moldavian red wine, which Oksana declined. For dessert, they enjoyed a fruit compôte and coffee prepared in the Mongol-Turkish style, Odile drinking from a tiny children's porcelain cup. The lunch cost eight rubles—twelve dollars by the official rate of exchange, less than three by street rate. Célestin was pleased his daughter witnessed a young woman's table manners as polite as Oksana's. Ever since Odile was old enough to sit at the table, etiquette was gently but firmly instilled.

After lunch, they went for a walk and ran into small groups of Russian teenagers in sports clothes—decent, good-looking, gay, with much blond hair flying. He photographed gorgeous specimens of listvenitsa, Siberian larch. Oksana explained the leaves of that tree, although a conifer, became yellow in autumn and fell. Also, its cones were turned skyward. It was very hard, resistant to dampness and even fire. Therefore, Russian pioneers in Siberia used larch logs to build their cabins. Members of the trio then took photos of each other with elegant larches and Baikal in the background. Odile used her father's faithful Nikon more assuredly than Oksana.

Pyotr honked, but Oksana ignored him and led them uphill to Saint Nicholas. The small old church, unlike so many others, had not been turned into a warehouse. Several murmuring Russian tourists and two sextons of advanced age were in the quiet church. The walls were covered with beautiful, well-preserved icons. Célestin first showed his daughter how Russian Orthodox believers cross themselves, and then they both did so in front of the icon of Jesus Christ. He intentionally did not look at Oksana to see whether she crossed herself. After all, who could tell for whom the sextons worked?

Oksana then brought them to the spacious, almost luxurious home of the head priest, by far the biggest in the village. "I wanted to show you the modest old church but also the head priest's house," she mumbled. Célestin thought: "Is she simply following instructions, or is she truthfully of two minds about the contradictions in the Church she so fervently wishes to join? Hmm... I should speak to Odile and point out that greed can be found in other Churches, including ours."

Other thoughts crossed his mind. Most were inspired by the otherworldly beauty of Baikal and the absurdly short time they had to experience it. Near the church, out of Pyotr's sight, Célestin finally reached a brave decision and immediately acted. Holding Odile's hand firmly, he said to Oksana with a serious expression on his face: "Listen, dear Oksana. You are a wonderful person, and I don't want to cause you any harm, but please try to understand us. We don't want to return to Irkutsk with you and Pyotr. The grim Intourist hotel is not our Russia. We have a valid visa for several more weeks, and it's not written where we must be. We'll be here, around Baikal. People are good-hearted and like small children. As for our suitcases, we'll pick them up at the hotel before taking the train to Moscow. The agency has a lot of our money prepaid for services we won't use."

Oksana's eyes and brow darkened for a moment, but soon a broad, pretty, Slavic smile emerged on her face. "*Horosho!*" She briefly considered the situation and led them down narrow, unpaved streets to the door of an ordinary house. After a rapid exchange with the host, she said: "You can stay here tonight and then you'll see. They'll help—these are awfully good people. The host is my dad's best friend from their army days. The lake is a stone's throw away."

She squatted in front of Odile and hugged her forcefully, receiving juicy kisses on her face in return. Then she kissed Célestin on the mouth. He clumsily attempted to give her one hundred

German marks, but Oksana waved the gesture away and kissed him again on the mouth, lightly that time.

8.

At the village market, they bought a jacket, two blouses, a skirt, long trousers, shorts, and a thick woolen sweater for Odile. All the items were second-hand, but they liked her new look of a Russian lass from Siberia. After several days, they left the house of their kind hosts and traveled, holding fast to Baikal's shore, to the northeast, in the direction of Bolyshoye Goloustnoye, a village some forty kilometers away. The buses often broke down, but the local people with whom Célestin and Odile shared them were friendly and helpful. They bought vegetables, cheese, sausages, and apples wherever they could, and the tasty dark bread seemed to grow straight from the earth. In some unlikely humble inn, they ate freshly caught Baikal sturgeon prepared in a rustic way. On one occasion, they were even served a first-rate omul, a salmon endemic to Baikal. Before long, he quit shaving and apologized to his daughter. At first, she found her father's wild look a little scary, and the beard scratched her face when she kissed his cheeks. The lake was always with them, day and night, with its fabulous colors and sea-like temperament. In front of others, they spoke French, with some Russian words, never German.

One evening, they were on a small sandy beach gazing at the full moon above the mighty lake. Célestin lay on his back while Odile, snugly beside him, counted his heartbeats. He spoke softly: "The lake is so deep because it sits above an enormous hole, a huge rift created in ancient times by a cataclysmic earthquake caused by the collision of two vast plates—they are called 'tectonic' plates—unimaginably deep below us in planet Earth. Moreover, the rift grows constantly, bit by bit, each year about this much." With his thumb and forefinger, he showed three centimeters.

Odile sat up on the sand, thought for a while, and asked: "Does that mean Earth has a crack in its heart?" Her father responded: "A smart question, but don't worry: Earth's heart is much deeper than the rift. There are rifts elsewhere on Earth. In the southeast of Africa, there's a big lake called Tanganyika. It's similar to our Baikal geologically but somewhat younger and therefore shallower." She lay on her back again and thought aloud: "So, Earth's heart is deep below us and the Moon is much farther above us..." They both laughed and Célestin added, "yes, and much farther is our only star, the Sun!"

They found out from the locals that Baikal's water was the warmest at that time of the year. The ideal spot to enter the lake was the nearby cove where Baikal was shallow, and no rivulets were flowing in. The cove was only two kilometers from Bolyshoye Goloustnoye, their adopted village, in the direction of Bugulydeika. That's where they would feel Baikal on their bodies.

Their sunlit morning walk along the tranquil lake was pleasant, and the cove was "deserted and magical," as Odile exclaimed. The weather was mild, so they took off their clothes. Célestin had experienced cold sea-water temperatures when wintering in Bretagne, so it was clear to him, as soon as he stepped into the lake, that the temperature was about thirteen degrees Celsius. That was not discouraging for what they wished to do—acquire a new experience and perform a ritual. "The bottom is sandy and you may enter safely but only to your ankles for now."

Odile was a brave girl who seldom shrieked, nor did she then. Her father walked into the crystal-clear water to his waist, squatted with his head bent, and jumped up, hands high in the air, yelling "divine!" Returning to his daughter, he asked her if she wanted to do the same or preferred to submerge only her head in the water sacred to the Buryats. "I want to be all wet like you!" was the determined answer. So Célestin took the girl's hand, and they made half a dozen steps together before he let her squat in the chilly water and jump out by herself. How happy and proud she was while the water ran down her face and she received a loud kiss on her forehead! "Quickly run out and dry yourself with my shirt."

She watched him from the narrow beach as he plunged into the water and swam in a furious freestyle he would use when competing for the ball at the beginning of a water polo match. Then he dived and looked through the water. Down there, at a depth of perhaps eight meters, Baikal was blue-green. While he swam back, he saw Odile gaily applauding him.

When they were both sitting on the sand, Célestin reminded the girl what Oksana had told them about the Buryats' beliefs: "Oksana said that by pouring Baikal's water over your head, you become ten years younger, and when you enter the lake with your whole body, you lose twenty years. So, I am now around fifteen years old, and you... you still have to be born—in thirteen years!" The girl first giggled happily and then, with a mixture of Baikal and tears in her eyes, firmly hugged her father.

Several days later, they decided to say goodbye to the spectacular lake and travel from Irkutsk far to the west, to Moscow. Before leaving, Odile sent a postcard to Oksana. She thanked their guide in German for her kindness, but everything about splashing in the lake and being born in thirteen years was the girl's charming attempt at jokes in Russian.

9.

The seemingly endless taiga followed by forests; dense trees followed by steppe and an izba here and there; incredibly broad rivers; populous Siberian cities; more taiga, forests, and log izbas scattered in the steppe. A sunny, late fall. Magnificent Russian land. God!

At the station in Irkutsk, around nine in the evening, the train № 1 from Vladivostok had been running twenty minutes late, but after it arrived—mighty, self-important, with a flushed face, exhilarated—Célestin and Odile quickly found themselves alone in a compartment of the deluxe car. Both beds were already made. On that train, everything was known ahead of time: who sleeps in which bed, at which station he gets on, and at which off. Soon, they were invited to the adjoining compartment for tea, chocolate, and Moskovskaya; they contributed yellow Antonov apples, the best available in Irkutsk. The hosts, Cathryn and David, a couple of sixty-year-olds from the London southeastern borough of Bromley, had boarded the train in Vladivostok after a holiday in Japan. They were worldly people who headed a small Asian ethnographic museum in Dulwich, five kilometers from the Greenwich Observatory.

After Odile had brought out her new Russian pocket atlas, Célestin conveyed to the Londoners through laughter that in Irkutsk they were indeed very far from their home near Greenwich—on the hundred-fourth meridian East, or more accurately 104°17'0" East. Cathryn and David looked through the atlas, and she congratulated the girl for writing her name on the first page in Russian script. Odile blushed: Even though these people did not speak the languages in which she was fluent, she sensed their thoughtfulness. The conversation continued, and already before Célestin half-carried the sleepy girl to their compartment, the adults agreed they could not stomach Margaret Thatcher, the British Iron Lady.

Father and daughter were lulled to a long sleep by the sounds, rhythm, and rocking movements of the train. She never woke up through the whole dark night, whereas he was sometimes touched by the deep Russian voices when the train stopped at one of the rare stations. They were in the middle of—certainly not of nothing: In the vast Siberian space, there were human beings right outside their window. The Russian language had stopped being alien and had become a melody he welcomed.

Other thoughts then arose in his half-awake mind and conscience: Primeval, beautiful Siberia, but also odious Siberia, accursed by so many suffering souls. He was aware that not long ago, somewhere not far, on the bank of a crazily powerful river in the wilderness, there could have existed a gulag for people like himself. Was it too early for Odile to be told, to be subjected to the horrific truth? Not yet, there would be time, Célestin assured himself, though feeling vaguely ashamed that he avoided delivering the painful lesson.

The next morning, he woke the girl with kisses on her nose and head, whispering "your tea is getting cold." Then he led her to the tiny restroom nearby and helped her wash her face, neck, and arms in the miniature sink. While he waited in the corridor for Odile to complete her ablutions, sentimentally observing the endless row of white birches streaming by, suddenly, as in a spy movie, he was mellifluously addressed in French by a blond woman in her late twenties: "Good morning, neighbor! Is the toilet free?" Behind her lumbered down the corridor an overweight middle-aged Russian man of intelligent countenance who said quickly, in comprehensible English, he realized the blond lady had arrived first, but he was in an awful rush, so... Thus began new acquaintanceships in the deluxe car of train № 1.

Odile, everyone's favorite, was at the center of the emerging sociometric behavioral pattern. No one dared to be anything less than inordinately friendly with her, yet she preferred to be alone with her father, so he could read to her in Russian and English, both of which she was eagerly learning. When after eighteen hours on the train from Irkutsk they arrived in Krasnoyarsk, he gave his camera to the girl to take a picture of the station, saying: "Maybe you remember Oksana was born in this city. You might send her a photo. If I understand her, she'll cry when she receives it or laugh merrily or both—and she'll think about you. It's nice when people you meet think of you fondly." She jumped to embrace him.

The English couple tried repeatedly to behave as if Odile were their grandchild, and Célestin was tickled to observe their well-meaning clumsy attempts. She opined: "They are nice but treat me as if I were a little girl because I don't speak English properly—yet that's all they speak!"

The two amiable, blue-eyed, thickset Russians from the compartment down the corridor invariably spoke warmly to Odile, often making jokes at their own expense. Vasiliy and Pavel were hydroengineers who worked on dams and power stations on the enormous rivers Amur and Ussuri near Habarovsk in the Russian Far East. They managed to stroke Odile's head a little after several evenings. Célestin was teaching her to play chess by mercilessly defeating their hosts in game after game, although there was one unfortunate draw with Pavel. She noted the outcomes in a notebook, radiating delight but saying nothing—aware that chess was an ancient, noble game of kings, quite dissimilar from kicking a ball in front of a screaming crowd.

Hanna was a mysterious blonde from Warsaw. She sat alone in her compartment, having paid for both beds. Except for one on which she languorously reposed all day, the entire space was filled with numerous boxes of various sizes containing technical products. Despite being a prideful woman, Hanna's Slavic nature prevented her from showing excessive vanity in front of Odile, a child she very much liked. In the Polish style of the nineteenth century, she spoke fluent French, so the girl became fond of her and chattered about Metz and Baikal. Hanna and Célestin taught her how to play *préférence*, a card game for three players, which allowed the adults to study each other innocently. Odile sensed an extra motive for the game but pretended not to notice.

The travelers soon spoke frankly. Once, when his daughter fell asleep, he admitted that Patrizia's death was devastating and that taking care of the girl was the main reason for his gradual recovery. He spoke of the beginnings of his and Patrizia's young love: They belonged to a group of Franco-German Catholic leftists in the Moselle region, which forever estranged Patrizia from her ultraconservative parents.

Hanna's marriage of five years was to a man she met at the best Warsaw high school. Afterward, both were involved in various failed liaisons, so their eventual marriage was mostly a business convenience of two disappointed twenty-year-olds who had recast their idealism into greed. From a starry-eyed, would-be political dissident, Hanna's husband converted into an ambitious communist functionary with useful connections in the Polish diplomatic service. Meanwhile, she contributed to the family business by reselling in Poland the goods she brought from the Far East without paying customs duties. In short, Hanna was a smart, stylish young woman—and a proficient smuggler.

When Célestin asked where she got suntanned, Hanna breezily explained how she had spent the previous four weeks: "First, I stayed a fortnight at a luxurious beach hotel in Tunisia, where my husband joined me for a few days. After that, I flew alone to Tokyo and there, in the Akihabara quarter, bought these computers. I boarded a ship in Yokohama and traveled north along the entire east coast of Honshu Island, then westward between Honshu and Hokkaido near the city of Hakodate, and eventually across the Sea of Japan to Nahodka in Russia—a port two hundred kilometers east of Vladivostok. There, I finally boarded the train № 1. And here I am confiding in you!" She smiled charmingly, while Célestin was dumbfounded but not admiring.

Hanna shamelessly continued the description of her trip: "In Moscow, I'll stay at one of the Polish Embassy apartments for visiting dignitaries and then travel by train to Warsaw. My husband and his diplomat cronies will meet me at the border. They'll send the goods to us in Warsaw by special channels without paying duty." She was proud of her undertaking: "This is my third trip. Everything always works out. In Poland, there's nothing of quality to buy, and Japanese copies of technical goods are much cheaper than American originals."

Odile slept on. As always when she felt protected, she was lying with her head in her father's lap and sweetly snoring. Hanna and Célestin looked at each other silently for a longish time, both wearing a smile. His was French, subtle, with shaded mockery. He was an ethical person, which was not based on religion: The loss of Patrizia at childbirth, when trying to bring new life into the world, had destroyed many of his Catholic beliefs. He simply regarded Hanna's behavior as coarse. "She has no scruples. All right, she doesn't lie, but that's only in this situation where she feels safe and is trying to show off her clever independence. Odile seems dear to her; however, if she wants a child, why doesn't she bear one instead of smuggling stuff from Japan to Poland across the entire USSR?"

Hanna's smile was supposed to be mysterious, but the sexual thirst in the woman was recognizable even to the inexperienced

Célestin—inexperienced by choice because he had loved profoundly and lost horribly. He was attractive to Hanna as a man and an exceptionally devoted single father of an exquisite female child. She felt like shutting the compartment door and kissing him passionately, regardless of the sleeping child. But foxily conscious that she did not comprehend the half-smile of his, she gave up the impulse. Perhaps he did not find her pretty enough? How could it be? Was he pious or ridiculously devoted to a wife who had died seven years earlier?

In the end, she mistakenly undertook a roundabout but pathetically transparent maneuver: "I'm a little tired and sleepy. On Thursday morning at 8:20, we'll arrive in Moscow. You said you'd never been there and would like to see it with Odile. Stay with her at the National, the best hotel for foreigners. It's close to Red Square. I'll first go to my Poles to take care of business. However, I'll be free around eight to buy you a drink at the Metropol, which is also a luxurious and historic hotel. Of course, I thought about our little one, and it's not a problem. The embassy has on its extensive staff some educated Polish women, one of whom could come to your hotel and read to Odile, as Soviet television isn't worth a mention. She'd watch over her, if necessary, all night. These women are trained as little spies, but it doesn't matter. Listen, you've been a perfect traveling companion, and I wish to thank you properly. So, I'd love to treat you to everything the Metropol has on offer." She laughed youthfully, freely, quite singly—*à la madame Bovary*: "In that hotel, things don't go by the Soviet but by Parisian rules!"

With a broad smile, Célestin lifted Odile into his arms and walked through the door. In the corridor, he turned around: "You, Hanna, are very generous, but I don't wish that your Mr. Hubby, the esteemed diplomat, turns bandit to settle accounts with me. However, if he would like, out of jealousy, to challenge me to a duel, let it be on horses, with swords, bludgeons, or golf clubs at my manor, ha, ha!"

Afterward, they rarely saw Hanna. Célestin played countless chess games with Vasiliy Ivanovich, the wise, even-tempered chess fanatic. During these evenings, father and daughter learned about Moscow, ancient and contemporary. Odile effortlessly learned Russian, chess rules, and much else. She never had to say she was hungry or tired because her papa always had the correct hunch about what she needed.

10.

Days and nights, cities and rivers, forests after the steppe... They crossed the Yenisei at Krasnoyarsk, the Ob at Tyumen, and the Irtysh at Omsk, while at Perm—where the train would have already passed through the Urals—they would be crossing the Pechora River. When they left Tyumen, Célestin told his daughter that the next important station would be Sverdlovsk, once called Yekaterinburg. He then recounted the Bolyshevik execution of Tsar Nikolay II Romanov and his entire family in the cellar of the merchant Ipatiev's confiscated house in that city. While she listened to her father's sorrowful but measured voice, her velvet eyes teared up.

At Sverdlovsk station, they were the only passengers who descended the steep metal steps to the platform. The station was somber, enveloped in drizzle, but he purposely took photos in the gloom. Six p.m. Sverdlovsk time, four p.m. Moscow; three time zones west of Irkutsk, more than the width of the entire non-Soviet Europe from west to east.

Vasiliy flew into their compartment at 6:40 p.m. to announce that in a few kilometers, the train would pass the middle point of the Ural Mountains and thus leave Asia. Indeed, they soon saw a massive stone tablet on which was engraved ЕВРОПА. The sign disappeared quickly, though not before Célestin took a bad photo, while Odile squealed merrily. They knew from her atlas they were 7,493 kilometers west of Vladivostok but still 1,777 kilometers east of Moscow. God...

On the way to the restaurant car, they saw Hanna sitting disinterested in her compartment: just another business trip. While they drank tea, he spoke about the invisible frontier and the many peoples who had crossed it—Russians, Mongols, Tatars, Turkmens, Turks, Uzbeks, Slavs, even Vikings—and about their own Frankish and Germanic peoples somewhere far in the mist toward the west.

For the celebratory party at the compartment of their Russian friends, Célestin and Odile bought at the restaurant three bottles of Soviet champenoise wine, uncooled of course, as well as Gruziyan mineral water and half a dozen Russian chocolate bars. On the way back to their comparative luxury, they passed again through two ordinary cars—crowded, smoke-filled, almost suffocating—and immediately met some Romanians. One of them offered them a delicacy from his native Transylvania: He had cut a long pepper sausage into small rings and artistically stacked them into a slightly crooked tower, like the one in Pisa but thirty centimeters tall. Despite the shaking of the train, the tower stood. From another compartment emerged a middle-aged Armenian with a hanging mustache yellow from tobacco. In a fatherly manner, he offered Odile a chocolate from Yerevan, "from my dear Hrazdan River," as he put it. To Célestin he offered a glass of orange liquor, which could not be refused. Wishing them good health, the man explained: "This was a gift from my father-in-law. A homemade 'armagnac' or something like that. But it's excellent rather than poisonous, a miracle!"

These people were inhabitants of the Soviet Empire and spoke Russian fluently. Célestin was courteous, even friendly, with most of them. His honest face and strange errors in Russian helped in simple dealings with people, some probably traveling crooks. However, his main trump in most encounters was Odile's disarming poise. He was teaching her not to be vain but also not perilously naive. The girl was maturing, and he was certain that nothing could have accomplished it better than their complicated trip.

When they finally managed to reach the chess compartment with bottles intact, Vasiliy and Pavel ensured the explosion of warm fake champagne was heard throughout the deluxe car. Cathryn and David soon arrived at Pavel's invitation, but Hanna politely declined Celestin's while giving him a folded sheet of luxurious paper with a phone number in Warsaw and words in French: "If you come to Poland, call me... Hanna Kotowicz, fellow passenger, train № 1." A civil ending to Hanna.

China, Mongolia, Erlian, Buryatia, and magical Baikal were inconceivably far. To celebrate their arrival in Europe, Vasiliy put on an old jacket from his suitcase. On its front, there was a long row of military medals. He got them in 1944/45, when, as an eighteen-year-old, he fought the Germans near Wrocław in Poland. Impressed, Cathryn and David suggested that Vasiliy show the medals to Hanna. He was offended: "No, not to her! She is Polish but a new sort. She's not one of those Poles who died courageously fighting with us against the heinous Nazis. These medals—and those my brother-in-arms Pavel has for bravery in battle—mean nothing to her and her thieving diplomat husband."

Everyone in the compartment, including the London couple, took a long gulp from the bottle of vodka that emerged from Pavel's bag. Odile was briefly neglected but did not mind. She did miss Auntie Hanna... a little.

Minutes from midnight, they arrived in Perm. The girl slept, as did most of train № 1—except Célestin, who wandered on the muddy platform, bypassing other men with restless minds. Wet snow was falling.

After leaving the city, the train clattered and gnashed its teeth like an angry man on the bridge over the broad Pechora, flowing north to the Barents Sea, south of the archipelago of Novaya Zemlya in the Arctic Ocean. Vasiliy, a little tipsy, confided to Célestin: "North of Perm, on the bank of the Pechora, there's a big gulag. For a long time already, a war comrade of ours has been imprisoned there. He too has medals for bravery unless they tore them off his chest."

Early the next morning, the first of October, they arrived in the city of Kirov, in the last time zone before Moscow's. "Snow!" exclaimed Odile when she woke up. Hugging each other, they looked outside; the window's corners were covered by cobwebs of ice. Siberian white birches and conifers had disappeared in the endless steppe. Instead of the frost the day before, the ground was covered by snow.

Cathryn arrived to stand beside them as if they had known each other for years. She looked at the endless whiteness and murmured: "Imagine the German soldiers' growing dread as they marched through this wasteland—day after day, farther and farther to the east." Célestin was long silent and then said with a catch in his voice: "Wasteland, Cathryn? People live here even if it's in izbas! In their literature, Russians admire the winter steppe while their breath freezes and snow creaks underfoot—which one cannot experience in Greenwich. And the steppe in spring, fragrant with flowers. I hope Odile and I will smell that and also have our nostrils burn from summer's hot air. Maybe we'll find a shady willow grove by a cool stream." He looked at the girl, whose English was still patchy, and whispered in French: "I'll explain, *ma chère*."

The Englishwoman tried to apologize but Célestin interrupted her: "There's no need. About the German soldiers' fears... I'm incapable of commiserating with them nor am I willing to preach forgiveness and compassion to my daughter based on what you've said. Not all of them were Nazis, for sure, but even the dumbest knew the enormous steppe, thousands of kilometers away from Munich and Berlin, was not their land. Still, they trampled it and mercilessly killed the people living there. 'They had to do it,' some would say. But was it only because they'd been ordered, my deceased wife Patrizia and I ask you, or out of an undeserved, revolting sense of superiority?"

Silence from Cathryn. "You know my Patrizia was German. But apart from how fervently anti-Nazi she was, Koblenz and Moselle are certainly not Prussia and Bavaria. Listen: It'll be very bad for Europe if Germany is reunified."

She grabbed Célestin's arm: "Please forgive me! I was thoughtlessly shooting my mouth off. You're absolutely right and feel it all in your heart even without being Russian! I'm lucky Vasiliy and Pavel haven't heard me.

"We in England think only of ourselves. Now the Thatcher woman is setting our teeth on edge. Even though David and I are

Londoners, we are aware that the Iron Lady is sadistically destroying the elementary rights the miners of northern England had acquired through a decades-long struggle for their families' decent lives.

"And it wouldn't surprise us if our country started a war with Argentina because of the trivial Falkland Islands in the South Atlantic. With America's approval and help, of course. It's depressing to watch how Thatcher's England has submissively clung to America's skirts to maintain the illusion of colonial power. Already De Gaulle pronounced us American poodles although that expression was actually thought up by us—about us! It was invented by people like David who, even though an ethnographer, has for years been writing hilarious critical articles for the weekly satirical magazine 'Punch.' It's existed for hundred and fifty years, poking fun at the august 'Times' and other conservative bastions. When we hear Thatcher's arrogant, combative voice on the telly, we are nauseated. Please excuse me, I've been talkative, but believe me, it wasn't an attempt to camouflage what I said at the beginning. I am genuinely sorry."

Around noon, David appeared in the corridor grumpy and disheveled, "due to sleep that doesn't bring rest," as he put it. "You should've woken up earlier, darling, to look at the boundless steppe and hear what the three of us have been talking about," said Cathryn, stroking Odile's hair. David knew his wife and mentally got going without washing his face. He ran to their compartment and returned with a business card with their address. "Célestin, you two must come to London and stay with us as long as you wish. We'll go to the Greenwich Observatory, which sits on the prime meridian. Odile will be able to talk about it to her great-grandchildren!" Célestin showed the card to his daughter, thanked David, and said such a visit may take place.

David had woken on time. Almost exactly at noon, the train № 1 crossed the Russian "little mother Volga" and entered the station of the ancient city of Yaroslavl'. There remained two hundred fifty kilometers to Moscow. When the train was leaving the city,

Célestin pointed out to the girl the historic churches erected with stunning red bricks. However, when he spoke about David's invitation, her immediate disconcerted reaction ensued: "So I can tell my great-grandchildren? Which means I'll bear children? *Non, non, cher Papounet*, I don't want that! *Maman bien aimé* died doing it!" She choked and hugged her father who held her close.

He was speechless. That topic has never been tackled before. "Listen, *mon trésor*, when the time comes, it'll be your decision. What's more, I don't want to lie: I don't know, I really don't know whether your *maman* would've wanted to give you life at the cost of losing her own. Excuse me, *mon ange*, but I hope she wouldn't have! She loved life, she loved me, we loved each other, and you were a completely unknown, unfamiliar being, only something cherished in her belly. Can you understand me?"

They were silent for a long time. "But Papa, *cher Papa*, you *do* know me! Would you choose that I was not born, that I don't live?" An even longer silence ensued. Then he gently grabbed her face with both hands: "You're torturing me, *mon ange*! Again, I dare not lie to you: If it were me deciding on that fateful day at the hospital in Koblenz I would have chosen your mother." He finished the painful utterance softly, embracing his daughter and adding almost inaudibly: "Please understand, *mon âme*, these are questions for God alone."

They sailed embraced into Moscow's Yaroslavl' station under a wintry, agitated sky.

11.

In their room № 420, on the sixth floor of the famous hotel National, Odile and Célestin were relaxing in deep armchairs, drinking excellent fruit juice and cold German beer. Earlier, to stretch their legs, they had sauntered to the nearby Red Square. They were astonished by its size, visually augmented by the massive, tall walls of the Kremlin towering along one entire edge. And there was the indescribable architecture of the Cathedral of Saint Vasiliy the

Blessed, standing wondrously alone on the slope toward the Moskva River. "I read in this book that the cathedral has been unique in the entire world of Christian Orthodoxy since the Byzantine era. There are nine small churches around the central one. To many believers, the cathedral resembles enormous flames rising into heaven above the sacred fiery stake," reported Célestin.

Odile silently stared at Saint Vasiliy and nodded: "Yes, when I close my eyes, I see something like a giant fire above those beautiful domes shaped like onions with stripes of various colors. Let's go closer." While they were passing by Lenin's tomb, adjacent to the wall of the Kremlin, her father explained: "The cathedral is no longer a church open for prayer and service but only a museum—in part because of the godlessness of the man whose mummy lies in this pompous granite structure, modeled after something from ancient Egypt; it's called a mausoleum."

The girl asked when they would visit the Saint Vasiliy museum. "We won't go there," he said decisively. "My principle is not to accept the politicians' base behavior by which they intentionally destroy something holy, something in the soul of their people. You see over there, next to the building called GUM, which we passed when entering Red Square—it's a huge department store, the best in the USSR—there used to stand Kazan Cathedral, smaller than Saint Vasiliy but equally beloved by the Russian folk. It had an even worse fate. In 1936, the Soviet communist leader Stalin, Lenin's heir, ordered that Kazan Cathedral be demolished. The name of the church was 'Cathedral of Our Lady of Kazan'; my book says the holy icon of the Kazan Virgin had nevertheless somehow been saved, but no one knows where it is."

They circled Saint Vasiliy and descended to the river. The Moskva was dark and flowed mysteriously to the east along the southern walls of the Kremlin. Farther to the southeast, it would join the Oka, and their waters would flow into the Volga and far southward to Astrahan and the Caspian Sea.

Before going to sleep that night, they watched television. There were four channels. On the first, there was a program about the "freedom-loving communist writers in Italy," while the second was showing a chess game from some important tournament between the world champion Anatoliy Karpov and Svetozar Gligorić, the top Yugoslav grandmaster. Célestin, a solid club player, was amazed that the five-hour game was carried live on television, without breaks for advertisements and saccharine-cute vignettes about the private lives of the players—so common in the West. Most of the time, one could see only the wall chessboard showing the position of pieces in front of the players. Nothing disturbed the silence ruling in the hall where the game was played. Now and then, the players' table was shown. They thought long, sometimes for twenty minutes, before making a move, which would be manually replicated by a "demonstrator" on the wallboard. When a move was unexpected, Célestin heard in his mind the simultaneous sighs and exclamations of the millions of chess lovers throughout the vast Soviet space from Kaliningrad to Chukotka.

The picture on the screen would occasionally be a close-up of the rivals in profile—both bent over the board, with foreheads no more than half a meter apart. Their bodies were tense and motionless, resembling an ancient sculpture of two wrestlers' eternal embrace.

Célestin promised Odile he would buy her a traveler's chess set and teach her the game more diligently than he did on the train. "I should've done it earlier. After all, I was only four when my grandfather Olivier, your great-grandfather, taught me how to play. Later he abandoned the lessons because, I think, he wasn't overjoyed to lose against a kid. You and I have much to learn together."

The fourth channel showed live an exciting ice hockey game between the Moscow clubs Spartak and CSKA. Odile knew how to skate but had never seen that sport. She was surprised by the lightning-fast skaters who used, with admirable skill, their strangely curved sticks to guide and accurately pass a small black rubber disk called a puck. On both sides of the ice-covered rink with rounded ends, there was a wire cage in which a masked and thickly dressed man-walrus squatted; he tried to prevent, with his body and stick, the puck from entering his cage. That was amusing, but she nevertheless chose, relying on her father's facial expressions, to return to the third channel. There they watched and listened to the extraordinary piano concert from the Bolyshoy performance hall, which marked the occasion of the sixty-fifth birthday of Emil Gilels. He was a Jew from Odessa, widely regarded as one of the most brilliant pianists in the world.

Two evenings later, Célestin took Odile to the same Bolyshoy hall for a performance in Italian of the opera *Pagliacci* by Ruggiero Leoncavallo. They were dressed in the new clothes bought at the GUM on Red Square—he in a dark-blue suit and she in a cute green dress, suede jacket, and black patent-leather shoes. The girl was pleased she now had not only Baikal village attire but also clothes for the opera in Moscow. While the usher led them down the aisle to their seats in the middle of the seventh row, Odile, feeling pretty and proud like never before, gracefully descended arm in arm with her father.

12.

Volga cars on the streets, attentive driving, and many faces similar to those one could see in Metz and Koblenz. When she inquired, Célestin explained that for political and economic reasons, the Soviet authorities had strictly controlled immigration from the provinces to Moscow and Leningrad, especially from the never-quite-tamed Caucasus, where the people generally had darker complexions than the Northerners.

Tirelessly, they walked around Moscow. In various parts of the city, there were almost identical skyscrapers, each topped by a big red star brightly lit at night. Six of these monstrous giants, including Moscow University, allegedly stood for Stalin's six slaps to New York, Chicago, Hitler, Roosevelt, Churchill... and a mysterious one other.

Atop many handsome buildings sat gigantic signs, ugly advertisements for communist leaders and ideas. "This awful practice has spread all the way to Mongolia and the train station in Ulan

Bator," Célestin reminded his daughter. He then switched to an internal monologue: "Although George Orwell, the left-winger and fighter against Franco in Spain, had never been to the USSR, he would have heard about such insults to architecture and the human spirit before writing his dystopian novel *1984* in 1949. It's premature to talk to Odile about it. Besides, are these signs truly uglier than the giant advertisements for hair shampoo and facial cream in the West and Westernized Japan?"

No less than her father, she admired the pictures at the Tretyakov Gallery and the Pushkin Museum of Fine Arts. However, at the Museum of Ancient Russian Culture and Art, Célestin spoke even more enthusiastically about the works of Andrey Rublyov, the greatest medieval painter of Orthodox icons and frescoes. His eyes teared before an icon at which he had long looked, disclosing he had never seen such humanity in something merely painted, such sincerity and depth of belief. Odile looked closely at Rublyov's icon and then at her dad's face. Understanding him better day by day, she was no longer surprised by the emotion he openly displayed to a work executed by human hand, a creation far surpassing mere beauty.

They spent long hours ambling in Red Square and the older parts of the city near Gorkiy Street and Kitay-gorod. From the Old Arbat area, with its throng of shoppers, idlers, and policemen, father and daughter would descend to the embankment below the Kremlin and then cross the river on the Great Stone Bridge. When they were tired of walking, or simply for a change, a bus ride was usually handy and cheap: five kopeks into a little box, no conductor necessary. Passersby readily provided information when sought. The foreigner's young daughter allayed any fear Muscovites may have felt from the ubiquitous police.

Of course, there were splendid small museums dedicated to individual composers: Mihail Glinka, Pyotr Chaikovskiy, and—just down the street from the American Embassy—Fyodor Shalyapin, the most celebrated Slavic basso profundo. "What a voice in opera and song he had," enthused Célestin; "we have gramophone records at home and will listen to him together, *ma mignonne.*" Then, there were museums of Dostoyevskiy and Tolstoy: To all of them, he introduced his daughter with *élan.*

In the restaurants and cafés of the hotels National and Metropol, Célestin and Odile met other guests at various times. One was Jonathan Brown, a correspondent of an important newspaper from Boston, and another a metallurgical engineer called Unai Larrazabal, a Basque from San Sebastian. There was also a lawyer, Annette Vankonich, employed at the International Labor Office in Geneva. Not being excessively naive, Célestin concluded that such people were in Moscow despite Brezhnev's hard-line stance. Both allies and enemies of the USSR apparently expected major changes in the country's course. Ensconced in expensive Moscow hotels, they were on alert, vigilant. There was little doubt they worked for various Western agencies as some sort of spies—political, military, or economic.

It was curious that all three mentioned individuals approached uninvited, with a lame excuse, the table at which the pair was sitting. Maybe they could not decipher the identity of the well-to-do Frenchman endowed with a young face, refined profile, broad shoulders, and fingers shaped not only for the piano but also for the reins and an ax. Why was he in Moscow conversing with an air of raillery in four languages with his daughter as if she were an adult? "And the girl, when she grows up, will be stunning," thought all of them.

The interest expressed by Annette Vankonich, an unmarried, childless woman in her thirties from Nova Gorica in Slovenia, was honest rather than sinister; however, the transparent calculation made it fruitless. Odile looked her over, skillfully evaded the predictable questions, and soon ignored the young woman by opening a German-Russian grammar. She thought grumpily: "This woman is talking to me only because of Papa. But the lady for him must be tender and very beautiful, as I know *Maman* was. This one has thin lips and keeps tilting her head toward her shoulder to make herself look interesting and vivacious." Her father observed it and accurately read her mind: "Has this trip prematurely aged my daughter and made her overly fault-finding? No, she tends to judge fairly and likes and accepts good people, good women. At Baikal, she became close to Oksana; we should write to her soon."

The next day was painted with all the colors of the Moscow autumn. In the early evening, when the girl was a little tired and sat with her dad in the almost empty bar Vostok on the second floor of the hotel National, to Odile—so often suspicious of young females—suddenly happened Dinara Alimova Naratovna. And to her father.

An elegant phantom, though neither a ghost nor a figment of the imagination, glided into the bar and without a smile waved to the bartender from afar. The young woman seated herself in a corner and calmly observed the guests without seductiveness. She had a serious, all-seeing face of delicate beauty. What noble bearing and exquisite body! Célestin surmised she might be from the world of theatre, but also that she led a double life, whereas Odile had the presentiment that the beautiful lady would be a rival who... Perhaps one who would teach her? She did not quite know what. Something vaguely feminine and admirable?

On second thought, he regretted that the girl, woman, lady— who came alone to the hotel bar and knew the bartender—was probably an escort or a call girl, if not a prostitute. Is there a difference, he wondered?

PART TWO

Dinara a.k.a. Olya

1.

A month later, when Odile and Célestin had been a week in Leningrad, Dinara arrived from Moscow to visit them at their ten-story high Pribaltiskaya on the Gulf of Finland, over ten kilometers from the city center. The hotel was only two years old and had five, admittedly Soviet, stars. As they had done themselves a week earlier, Dinara traveled eight hours by a comfortable train from Moscow. She called Célestin as soon as she arrived in Leningrad and asked him to meet her at the hotel entrance. She was aware that Soviet citizens, especially young women, had difficulties being allowed to enter hotels where many foreign guests were staying.

The KGB doormen were astonished to witness the joy, warmth, and unabashed familiarity with which a lovely Russian woman embraced the two waiting foreigners when she ran out of a taxi: a handsome, slender man and his daughter who jumped up and down childishly and clapped her hands.

It would be hard for anyone to divine how long a life journey those three people had traveled during the three short weeks of their acquaintanceship following the threefold epiphany they had experienced at the Vostok bar of the hotel National. The path was woven out of delicate feelings in the hearts of three different, strong personalities whose attractions and emotional needs were miraculously in harmony. The eight-year-old girl, with her pure soul and inner strength, was not a weak link in the triangle—the precise opposite was true.

Around eight o'clock in the morning of the tenth day after their inexplicable, momentous meeting at the Vostok, he awoke to the hushed sounds issuing from the kitchen where breakfast was being prepared. Even softer was a woman's voice singing a Neapolitan song. Driven by the first thought that flashed through his mind, Célestin jumped out of bed naked and ran to find his daughter. Near the oven in which something tasty was baking, he encountered broad smiles on two faces and heard "*Cher Papa!*" and "*Tino, dorogoy!*" before escaping to the bedroom for clothes. He then ran back to embrace the two cooks. Later, while shaving, he listened to Dinara teaching the song to Odile and was moved by how sweetly the girl followed. That morning and the previous night remained forever in the memory of all three.

Dinara's small apartment was on the third floor of an older building in a pretty and quiet corner of central Moscow near the Patriarch's Ponds. As she unnecessarily explained to Célestin, it was the area where the beginning of Mihail Bulgakov's novel *Master and Margarita* took place. Her flat consisted of a bedroom and a kitchen big enough to contain a sofa for Odile. Breakfast abounded in laughter and jokes in several languages, though mostly Russian.

Word by word, they returned to their meeting at the Vostok at which Dinara had dubbed him "Tino." She had bravely approached their table and asked for permission to sit down. He had looked at Odile and they wordlessly agreed it would be rude to refuse the request. Softly speaking English, the young woman had addressed Célestin: "Don't worry, Sir. I know what you think of me and you are right. However, I don't want anything from you. It's obvious you are a decent man, and it would be a pleasure to make your acquaintance, but your real trump in my eyes is your daughter. I love children, but there are none in my family. Your girl is in the period of childhood dearest to me. I rarely have the chance to speak to a child her age." While her father was translating, Odile studied his agitated face, throwing now and then looks at the young lady—looks that were neither harsh nor unwelcoming.

Never before had Célestin met a woman so beautiful, shockingly beautiful, with a voice so melodious and a gracefulness so natural. Finally, with a shy smile, he said: "My daughter, this is Odile, agrees it would be our pleasure if you would join us." When he turned to the bar to hide he was blushing and to order something, she interrupted: "No, please don't order anything for me. I don't want our chance conversation to cost you a single ruble. There is no pressure on me in this bar. Besides, take a look at this." From a miniature purse, she took something out. He noticed her hand was trembling as she gave it to him.

Célestin had been staring at long fingers on narrow hands—fine and girlish but in their shape and proportions similar to his own strong and masculine ones. Opening the student identification document with a photo, he discovered that Naratovna, Dinara Alimova, a citizen of the USSR, was of mixed Tatar-Russian ethnicity; that she was born on the 17th of May 1958 in Kazan, the capital of the Tatar Autonomous Soviet Socialist Republic; that she was a fourth-year full-time student of the Gnessin State Music-Pedagogical Institute in Moscow; and that she studied in the Departments of Vocal Art and Stage Direction, with a specialization in Musical Theatre.

He was amazed, for he knew the Gnessin was a high-level, world-famous institution and that he should regard Dinara, their guest, with a new and different kind of admiration. While Odile was studying the name and photo in the document, he told her Dinara was a serious artist. Then he recovered his senses and became cross with himself. To prove he was not a naive greenhorn, he spoke to Dinara in a no-nonsense voice when returning the document: "Yes, impressive. I congratulate you on the talent and work habits you possess, but what then are you doing here?" He used an almost severe tone, at least he imagined it was, not realizing to have fallen in love like a pimply boy.

Of course, he had been sufficiently long in Brezhnev's USSR not to be aware of the dark-gray social reality and the dramatic shortages the inhabitants were experiencing. He suspected such facts could lead to major unwanted changes in the behavior of ordinary people. But... Célestin persisted in not wishing to see himself as a pathetically sentimental man. He was too old and worldly to act like an immature, infatuated male who had become smitten by feminine charms. He had suffered and experienced much. Above all, he was a responsible father to Odile.

Dinara returned the document to her purse and was long quiet. It seemed she was making every effort to conceal her distress. Yet she refused to be perceived as currying favor with Célestin and his daughter by emotionally breaking the uncomfortable silence. Finally, in a voice that rarely quavered, she said: "Listen, please understand I am not a trollop from a public house. My mother and her parents live in Kazan where I was born. It's an ancient Tatar city on the Volga, some eight hundred kilometers east of Moscow. My dad was called Alim Naratovniy. He was a Tatar, a bridge-construction engineer, killed in a horrible accident at some building site when I was five. I can barely see him in my mind's eye; he was away so much at work, but I remember he was always gentle with me. My mama is Russian, as a girl she was called Olga Shevtsova. When I was twelve, my mom, grandpa, and grandma took me to a church to be baptized; my Russian name, after my mother, is Olga with the nickname Olya."

She smiled at the girl: "So, Odile and Olya! Since our names start with an 'O,' it will be easy to remember. Or more difficult?" The girl, who the entire time could not take her eyes off the young woman, gratefully relaxed. She felt honored by the attention and responded in an innocently endearing way: "I will always remember you—with an 'O,' for Olya, and with a 'D,' for Dinara." Dinara-Olya was surprised. "Gosh! What a wonderful child! How she remembers everything," she whispered. Célestin observed the first interaction between his daughter and the stranger, and there was warmth in his heart.

Olya continued: "The pension Mom was receiving after Dad's awful demise was reduced year by year, and the small piece of land my grandparents owned was 'expropriated' by the thugs from the neighboring kolhoz, the local collective farm. So, my mother provided food for four mouths by doing minor accounting jobs at the invariably failing enterprises. And I—even when I was fifteen years old—I wasn't permitted by my elders to do anything for money. The three of them have always loved me very much and love me now more than their own eyes. Do you understand? Mine was only to study. I was a good child. Perhaps I was a girl similar to Odile. From the first to the last, eleventh grade, I was the best pupil in my class in all the subjects. And when Mom heard from the local choirmaster that I possess a voice that can be schooled and even have 'absolute pitch,' she almost starved to save money to pay for my voice, piano, solfeggio, and music-theory lessons. So, I was promptly accepted at the Gnessin, and up to now, my fourth year, I've had excellent grades. That's not easy. During all of my Moscow years, Mom naturally had to stay in Kazan with grandma and grandpa, so we rarely saw each other. That's also not easy."

Father and daughter attentively listened to Olya, as her despondent, confession-like monologue became lighter: "You won't believe me, but in addition to my affection for children—and it's clear Odile is smart and lovable—there's something else. Maybe I wouldn't have approached you if not for a comical, quite silly, coincidence. I came to your table wishing to ask you if you were by chance a Corsican." He was startled and grinned: "No, I am not, but they too are French. Well, supposedly French; some prefer to be Italians, although most don't like anybody except themselves!"

Olya also laughed: "You see, yesterday evening I saw on television an old French film, I think from 1934, with the title *Les Nuits Moscovites*. They sometimes show harmless films from Western countries, mostly those with singing and dancing, to entertain our stupefied 'broad masses,' as ordinary people are called here. Well, in the film, the star is someone by the name of Tino Rossi, and his role is 'Neapolitan singer.' He does a few charming songs in the style of 'See Naples and Die,' which is how you say it, right? I remember the melodies of a few of the songs, that's easy for me. Anyway, have you heard of this Tino Rossi?"

"Of course! Rossi has long been known in France. He is still alive, very alive, though probably over seventy years old. And on Corsica—he was born in Ajaccio, the capital—he is lionized." Olya was also quick: "Napoleon Bonaparte was born there also." "Indeed he was," said Célestin, and went on seriously: "Napoleon was a larger-than-life man, or so he thought, someone who long divided the French people. Some idolized and almost deified him, others feared and abhorred him. But now, when it's safe, they all love him. The French adore grandiose feats—they couldn't care less for their countless countrymen who perished of hunger and frost in your country. After all, it's clear those alive now aren't the direct descendants of those who died far from home, in the Russian snow."

Olya disagreed: "You've disappointed me a little. I think the point isn't whether some now living Frenchman had or didn't have after the Battle of Borodino some great-great-great-grandfather ancestor dead in the snow, with wolves on his corpse, but that the French people love to build monuments to their military leaders, actually to themselves! I hear Paris is full of them. As is, after all, Moscow. But here, in my country, even the most intelligent people say, 'we are more righteous, we were only defending ourselves.' The Tatars would not agree. And yet, the Tatars themselves, arriving from Central Asia, were brutal and ghastly when they had the upper hand and ruled Muscovy. According to Mom, Dad had often admitted it."

"May I continue? So, I watched the film and listened to those songs—songs created by temperamental, poor people, born under a hot sun and azure sky, next to a sea of all the nuances of blue, from aquamarine to dark blue to the color of red wine blind Homer saw. The star, Tino Rossi, had good taste and musical sense, he didn't push beyond what his voice allowed. Besides, Tino was very handsome. In the film, he seemed thirty years old, about your age. Also, his features and the shape of his eyes were similar to yours." Célestin was speechless, while Odile sensed something important was happening.

Olya said: "Obviously the young Tino Rossi wasn't resurrected in the Vostok bar. But I thought of how indescribably marvelous it'd be if a phantom à la Tino Rossi suddenly appeared in my often miserable life—even if I became only slightly acquainted with him during an ordinary evening. Yes, even if our meeting is to end this moment, I'll always dream I've met an exceptional man called Tino."

3.

"In response to your question about what I'm doing here," Dinara-Olya went on, "I come rarely but charge two hundred dollars for two hours. I never accept a whole-night proposal. The... thing happens here in the hotel and nowhere else. Always with a man who is polite, decent, and sober. No orgies, never with two men or such. Eighty-five percent of my income from these disgusting activities I send home to Kazan. Without me, Grandma and Grandpa would starve, they'd have a horrible, primitive end to an honest, hard life. Listen, this is no melodrama, this is the horror of life in Russia in these times. Fortunately, schooling and medical care are free for outstanding students. From the remaining fifteen percent, ten are for healthy food, which is hard to find and expensive. And the remaining pittance goes for clothes—otherwise, I couldn't enter here. Besides, most of my seemingly expensive wardrobe consists of cheap goods Mom and I painstakingly alter.

"Let me mention something tragicomical: Occasionally, I hear a wise thought from a client, and some of them, I think, leave Moscow having learned a wise tidbit from me. But not once have I given my phone number or address to anyone. I don't want either my own or their dependence. I see in your eyes the query about how many clients I've had. I won't say. The question would reveal more about you, and I wouldn't be believed anyway because the number is far smaller than what you're imagining in your male mind."

During the monologue, Célestin-Tino and Odile breathlessly watched Dinara-Olga-Olya. He briefly told his daughter in German: "I'll try to explain everything later. But now, be good, please, to this young woman." He apologized for speaking in German and continued: "Olya, I believe you and understand your situation. I am not condemning you, nor would I have any right. But Odile—as far as I can guess—she knows what sex is and believes sex is love. Or the other way around. It's not clear to me, nor probably to her, what she thinks or thinks she ought to think. However, I'm certain sex for money is unimaginable to her so she and I need to have a talk tonight. I don't in the least wish to insult you and it seems—looking at the expression in your, if you permit me to say it, beautiful eyes—you believe me, but she's a child, and it'll be hard to explain it all to her."

Olya blushed crimson and said indignantly: "It's not hard to understand what you're saying, and you're certainly a father one doesn't meet every day, especially a father of a female child. What I don't understand is why you'd waste time in Moscow explaining to your little daughter who I am and what I am doing in this hotel. Why wouldn't you instead of talking about sex, which may be premature for her—although you know best—why wouldn't you teach her about the history of ancient Moscow and our Mother Russia?"

Célestin felt ashamed and long searched for an answer looking alternately at Olya and Odile. Finally, he sighed: "*Mademoiselle... Naratovna*, Mademoiselle Dinara, dear Olya, if I may: Please be assured that for me talking to my daughter about you won't be a waste of time. I'd like her to understand you as fully as I wish to accomplish myself." There was another long silence before his face and body relaxed, and he went on: "Now it's your turn to ask us anything you wish: who we are and from where. We'll tell you everything, my Odile and I."

4.

The trio was inseparable every day and every evening during the three weeks following the first meeting. Olya took them to the renowned *MXAT*, the Moscow Art Academic Theater, and to the two apartments once long occupied by the outstanding theatre directors Konstantin Stanislavskiy and Vladimir Nemirovich-Danchenko—apartments that have been turned into lovingly maintained mini-museums. At four addresses in various parts of Moscow, they visited Anton Chehov's abodes and examined, under Olya's guidance, the invaluable artifacts and mementos kept there. With emotion and knowledge, Olya spoke of the sea, flowers, and trees of Yalta, nestled under Crimean hills, where the beloved Anton Pavlovich lived toward the end of his life, hopelessly trying to resist the onslaught of tuberculosis. She described the old town of Taganrog, on the Sea of Azov, where Anton was born and attended high school. When not in school, he worked in his father's store for "oriental" goods. Chuckling, Olya talked about his first literary attempts signed "Antosha Chehonte." And she spoke at length of the huge island of Sahalin, far to the east, in the Pacific Ocean north of Japan, where Chehov visited a prison camp in 1890 and wrote a book about it. To reach Sahalin, he passed through all of Siberia, traveling in the direction opposite Célestin's and Odile's—and did it before the endless iron road of the train № 1 was completed.

Not anymore as wandering tourists but with Olya as their music guide, father and daughter again visited the Shalyapin museum. In the great singer's intact study, Olya softly sang in her fine soprano a familiar Russian song accompanying Shalyapin's voice on a crackling record brought from the archive by the courteous, middle-aged museum director. They listened thoughtfully, standing without the slightest movement next to the lady. She was the one who shed a tear first, followed soon by Odile—who did not know why she was crying, for her heart was joyful. "*Gospodi! Mon Dieu!* What voice and music sensitivity you have!" exclaimed the lady to Olya. Célestin was proud as if his daughter had sung and been praised. "Even though you're French, Sir, and love music," added the lady, "perhaps you aren't aware Shalyapin was buried in Paris: yes, in 1938, in the Russian Cathedral of Saint Aleksandr Nevskiy. It was built and consecrated long ago, in 1861, under the patronage of Russian Tsar Aleksandr II, the Liberator—of the serfs, that is." He warmly thanked the lady and made a conscious effort to remember these facts.

On an enjoyable sunny afternoon, Célestin and Odile again admired Count Lev Tolstoy's house in the Hamovnik Quarter. They arrived with Olya from Gorkiy Park, crossing the Moskva River by the Crimean Bridge. She explained everything along the way tirelessly, with love. Odilichka often grabbed the adults' hands while hopping, skipping, and prancing between them, fond of their bond.

Olya showed them the opulent and hospital-clean interiors of some Moscow Metro stations and the startlingly lavish, ornate decor of the Yeliseyev store on Gorkiy Street: It sold the finest Russian and foreign comestibles, although the peak of its fame and quality of food items had been reached long before, during the tsarist times. They infrequently ate together at the National in the evening, but on one occasion father and daughter brought Olya to their room. All three, sitting on the carpet, with their backs against one of the beds, watched the painful Soviet film *The Flight* about the war between the Whites and the Reds in 1917-1918. The excellent 1970 cinematic work was based on the motifs from Bulgakov's novel *The White Guard,* and his stories "The Flight" and "The Black Sea." Odile successfully chased sleepiness away and watched the film to the end. Her father and Olya then tucked her in lovingly. Célestin promised to be back as soon as he had placed Olya in a cab, which brought a smile with closed eyes to her angelic face.

On some afternoons, they waited for Olya near the Gnessin. The instant she saw them, Olya carelessly ran across the street, where Odile flew to embrace her. One evening, they took the metro to North Moscow to visit a girlfriend of Olya's. Lena was a hard-working student of child psychology, a sweetly chubby woman with smiling brown eyes. She was also from Kazan, the same age as Olya, and worked with children in the laboratory of a professor at Moscow Lomonosov University. That man was a brilliant researcher and Célestin knew he was described in France and Switzerland, with some pique, as the main, though much younger, rival to the professor who had formulated an influential approach to developmental psychology in Geneva. Lena lived alone in a decent apartment thanks to her parents—mid-level communist party members in good standing—whose "dogmatic opinions" she nonetheless dared to oppose. She disclosed that the professor she so much admired could not stand "dutiful and compliant party cadres."

Earlier, on the way from the metro station to Lena's flat, while Odile was skipping behind them and ahead, Olya had explained that Lena was lucky never to need to visit hotels but was fully aware of Olya's behavior. Then she reddened violently: "I meant to say 'aware of what I *had* been doing'!" They gazed at each other wordlessly for an eternity. Much of importance was thus conveyed—and promised. Célestin thought cautiously: "Very well, but one step at a time, I'm not naive." However, Lena's kindness and openness, her winsome closeness with Olya, and the utterly normal atmosphere were so disarming that he had wholeheartedly begun to trust what Olya had told him on the street.

Adults drank Soviet champenoise, Odile a juice, and all four savored the fancy candied fruit Lena had purchased at the Yeliseyev. The hostess put on a classical music record, while the girl took several thick books with reproductions of Russian and French paintings from the shelves. One volume contained only Ryepin's works. Kneeling on the carpet, she leafed through the book, when suddenly *Nishchaya* appeared: "Papa, look! This is the picture of the pretty beggar girl we saw at the museum. *Tu te souviens, Papa?*"

Célestin sat on the floor beside Odile, gently saying: "*Oui, ma douce,* you're right, we saw this painting at the museum in Irkutsk. You were sad because of the plight of the destitute girl in tatters—you almost cried. Now you're older and have seen much that's beautiful, ugly, and sad, but I hope you haven't changed and are still sorry for the innocent child. It's only an excellent, realistic painting, although such girls exist, as we speak, and they are your age! So you shouldn't be ashamed if you feel like crying even now, *ma chérie.*"

Sergey Rahmaninov was playing his B minor Prelude, the young women were watching father and daughter affectionately, and Odile's eyes glistened with tears. Lena jumped and ran to a distant shelf, saying: "I also feel like crying when I see that picture, but now I'll show you some paintings of ships in agitated seas off the coast of southern Russia." She brought a book with the marvelous seascapes by Ivan Aivazovskiy. "This painter, Odilichka, was born and always lived by the sea—in the far south, on a gorgeous peninsula called Crimea, in the small town of Feodosiya, where long ago lived the ancient Greeks. Your dad must take you there one day." Célestin added: "Feodosiya must be close to Yalta. Olya told us Chehov stayed there for the clean sea air when already very ill." He looked at Olya and noticed how pleased she was that he had remembered her words.

The proud hostess wanted to entertain her guests with the many records and cassettes of Western rock and roll she had acquired. First, she put on *Rumours* by the group Fleetwood Mac, then music by Bruce Springsteen, Neal Young, and Joni Mitchell, and finally records by Bob Dylan from the sixties, *Like a Rolling Stone*, and seventies, *Blood on the Tracks*. Célestin was familiar with all that music—nothing new, unusual, or rare but still first-rate. He and Lena closely listened, while Olya, by talking to Odile about paintings and showing her funny knick-knacks, ensured the girl was not bored.

Then Lena announced brightly: "And now something you almost certainly haven't heard before. I got this cassette from a girlfriend who has just returned from a tour of England with the choir in which she sings. The music had recently been recorded and is not pleasing—on the contrary, it's intentionally savage, ugly, raw. It's a new trend, in London they call it 'punk.' You'll be shocked by the rage of the vocals." Thus did Célestin and Odile in the middle of Moscow, in late 1980, for the first time hear punk music—from the band Killing Joke. "I don't know how to translate the name of the group into Russian so it makes sense—but why look for sense in punk?"

When the music started, father and daughter frowned, whereas Lena smiled sheepishly, and Olya showed signs of unease. Célestin thought he was too old-fashioned, too ancient for something so rebellious, or else too innocent, childlike.

He therefore inquired about the original Russian rock and roll because he had heard from Oksana in Siberia that it existed. The answer came from Olya. While Lena was showing Odile various drawings done by children her age, which she had brought home from the laboratory to analyze, Olya searched through Lena's collection until she found what she wanted. "Let's leave Russian rock for another time and instead listen to the music of our Vladimir Vysotskiy. He passed away at only forty-two earlier this year."

She gave the cassettes to Lena, sat on the couch next to Célestin, and spoke softly: "Millions of people in Russia have these cassettes. Ordinary folk know Volodya was an honest man, truly his own. Maybe you've heard of him, his music is available in France." He had not and felt very small in that enormous country, in the presence of those astute women. Lena started a cassette and added: "He was a poet, actor, and singer who composed and sang hundreds of songs." Father and daughter sat spellbound, listening to the longing, all-knowing, smoker's voice of Vysotskiy— Olya's and Lena's Volodya. Somehow, it was a voice both soulful and distant.

Olya drifted around the room with a serious expression: "He sang sad ballads about our life. Listen, here he's accompanying himself on a Russian guitar with seven strings. He was sarcastic about Soviet power and paid dearly. As a protest, out of spite, he sang what we call '*Blatnaya pesnya*,' 'Song of Thugs,' about renegades and lawless people. What you hear is not an agreeable voice to coddle listeners but one belonging to a talented man with unblemished integrity." Lena added: "For us, Volodya surpasses Dylan. He suffered more, together with us."

At the request of Odilichka and Tino, Olya took them to Lena's again the following evening. The story about Russian rock and roll began with Lena sharing her impressions of the first rock and roll festival in the USSR, which took place earlier that year in the middle of March. It was held in Tbilisi in Gruziya with the cryptic name "Spring Rhythm." There, for the first time on the big stage, appeared the group Akvarium, led by Boris Grebenshchikov, the prime mover of Russian rock and roll. Lena said: "Borya's rock is good, and his music has long been known in our so-called underground here in Moscow and also in Leningrad, where he is from. Before this festival, Borya's band went to play in youth clubs in the provinces by jumping onto freight trains.

"He is only twenty-seven. At the festival, I heard the story that he lives in the garret of an old building on Vasilyevskiy Island in Leningrad, the sort described by Dostoyevskiy and Andrei Biely. So, he lives in the attic, and on all the walls of the staircase below, some three floors, his female fans have written, drawn, and painted their love, sufferings, and offerings."

Olya felt uncomfortable, so she hugged her friend and explained: "You must forgive Lenochka. Rock music and festival atmosphere do it to young people all over the world. She doesn't care that Borya isn't handsome—he is talented! Moreover, he isn't stupid and has managed to complete studies of physics despite countless two-liter bottles of the cheapest wine and illicit drugs. Such news quickly spread here. Immediately after the festival, they kicked him out of the Komsomol—the Communist Soviet Youth organization... But now I remember I didn't see Lena for a few days last March. Perhaps she was in Leningrad writing a psychological message on Borya's staircase!" The two friends hugged again and laughed, while Célestin felt like an old youngish man.

They listened next to Borya's music from 1974, the *Temptation of Saint Aquarium*, recorded in someone's flat—authentically, primitively, memorably. He got up, bowed to Odile, and asked her for a dance. He was not tipsy, only young. Olya and Lena rocked and rolled in their way, almost gracefully. The acoustic album by Borya and Mike Naumenko *All Brothers are Sisters*, recorded three years earlier, and Borya's new *Blue Album*, followed. She enjoyed dancing with her dad to weird rock and roll. "Things happen to her daily for the first time, how wonderful it is to witness it," he thought.

When their turn finally came, the lovers danced passionately, barely moving, regardless of the music. It was his first chance to feel her slender young body pressed close. They were both excited, breathless, tempted—but not daring to kiss. With a smile that looked almost knowing, Odile watched attentively, never taking her eyes off them no matter how eagerly Lena tried to distract her. Célestin thought of Olya: "How gentle she is, what a lovely face. Thank God, I'm not in the least repelled by her body. But will I be able to forgive?"

Less than a dozen days after the first meeting at the National, when Olya was also Dinara, father and daughter went to her apartment by the Patriarch's Ponds and spent the whole night there.

5.

For fun, Lena took Odile to her professor's laboratory and introduced her to eight-year-old girls who had come with their parents for cognitive testing. She found it intriguing, while her new girlfriends were surprised by how quickly she had learned to communicate in Russian. But when Lena a few days later offered to take her to the puppet theater for a matinee performance, she was again delighted, whereas her father hesitated, wondering if it were selfish to agree so he could be alone with Olya. In the end, he decided minor risks were necessary for the normal development of a child. Permission was given, and he spent an afternoon with Olya.

Célestin spoke about most things with Odile, trusting his judgment about what she should know, and the girl responded with confidence in his discernment. While becoming very fond of Lena, Olya remained for her a lovable, exceptional woman. Which child, especially motherless, could resist such warmth, true goodwill, and natural kindness?

On one important day, the sweethearts spent hours in the beautifully manicured Aleksandrovskiy Gardens near the Kremlin. They walked, sat on a bench, then walked again. Olya finally spoke to her lover about a long phone call with her mother Olga in Kazan. "I called Mama yesterday and told her I'd stopped working some weeks ago, that I'm done with the sordid business. Mama was delighted, but I sensed anxiety in her voice. At first, I felt bitter, thinking she regretted that I wouldn't be sending money to Kazan any longer. It turned out something quite different was bothering her: Without my saying a word, she assumed I'd fallen in love with a well-heeled foreigner. But I've never had any relationship, any liaison, with a foreigner outside of the horrid 'job'! You must believe me, and Mama knows it. However, it seemed the most likely scenario to her."

She did not choke up or sob or snivel. Lips trembling, she wrung her gloves and looked into the distance at the National—only about three hundred meters away. Célestin's heart beat madly. He waited for her to continue as if a crucial judgment was about to be passed on him, on them. Yet it seemed he was not absolutely certain which judgment he preferred.

"I told Mama in detail about our relationship: We were not intimate in the hotel, I didn't take a single ruble from you, and I truthfully disclosed everything in the first ten minutes after we met. I convinced her my love for you was sincere and deep, and you felt similar emotions. I described Odile to Mama and conveyed how much I care for her in a motherly way." They were silent for a while. Célestin knew he genuinely and intensely loved Olya but still commanded himself, with merciless willpower, not to express it as the moment was not yet right.

"I then sensed an immense relief in Mama. Apprehension disappeared from her voice. She said: 'Olyechka, I'm very happy for you and your man. I'll tell you why I wasn't more pleased when you told me you wouldn't any longer make hotel visits: Because, *moya dorogaya doch*, I was afraid that now, instead of receiving money from several men, you'd be receiving it from only one—but again without love, with impure motives.' And then we both cried."

In Aleksandrovskiy Gardens, Olya could no longer endure the turmoil in her heart and openly wept, embracing Célestin with all her might. He responded in kind and knew that the judgment he heard pronounced was indeed the one he had fervently desired. Whom was he fooling by trying to hold back? He felt boundless love, passion, and tenderness toward her.

It took time before Olya collected herself: "Even before I had a chance to ask Mama, she told me not to worry about Grandma and Grandpa—she would find an additional job. Then she begged me not to neglect my studies nor accept any money from you. Finally, through tears, she wished us to be happy, happy!"

Three days later, on the twelfth of October, Olya saw Célestin and Odilichka off from Leningrad Station in Moscow to "Peter": Some people, not too secretly, called the city of Lenin by Sankt-Peterburg's nickname. The parting was not painful because Olya had already at Aleksandrovskiy Gardens joyfully accepted Tino's invitation to join them in a week.

6.

By the time Olya embraced them in front of the hotel Pribaltiskaya, Odile and Célestin had become thoroughly acquainted with the stunning city on the Neva River. They spent an entire day in and around the Hermitage Museum intoxicated by art, and Odile made friends with the knowledgeable ladies in charge of a gallery with artworks related to children. Having visited famous and less famous city quarters during their tireless walks, they confidently oriented themselves, feeling able to guide Olya.

Because their hotel was flooded with agents, it was best that she did not stay there. Luckily, thanks to the Gnessin card, Olya found a room at a student hostel belonging to the Nikolay Rimskiy-Korsakov Conservatory and close to Nevskiy Prospekt. "It's a pleasure and honor," she said, "that I can enter the magnificent edifice, talk to students-musicians, and attend orchestral rehearsals. Many composers—Chaikovskiy, Prokofiev, and Shostakovich no less—were once students there."

They walked for hours up and down the Prospekt, or Boulevard, along its four and a half kilometers from the Admiralty of the tsarist era on the Neva to Saint Aleksandr Nevskiy Lavra, or

Monastery. Its wooden predecessor was consecrated by Pyotr I the Great in 1710 near the site on which—it was thought at the time—a major defeat of the Swedes at the hands of Prince Nevskiy took place in 1240. (*The Neva Battle actually occurred twenty kilometers away.*) The Sankt-Peterburg of the tsars was for most purposes Nevskiy Prospekt. At the time of Pyotr the Great, it was the beginning of the road to two ancient cities: Novgorod and Moscow. In 1980, the width of the part of the Prospekt nearest to the Neva, from the Admiralty to Green Bridge, by which it crosses the tiny Moyka River, was only twenty-five meters—as in the time of the tsars; elsewhere it was much wider.

During one of their first walks, Odile recounted to Olya: "Every day, Papa and I walk from our hotel across the whole Vasilyevskiy Island to Nevskiy. We found the building in which the singer Borya lives. As you know, when we listened to him at Lenka's, she said his staircase was full of drawings and messages from adoring girls. So, Papa and I came to the staircase. He was against it, but I made him climb with me to the attic. I looked at all the kisses and drawings and scribbles, and Papa studied them also. Ha, ha!" Odile was out of breath, while Olya and Célestin looked at each other smiling.

"Then I found a small empty space on the wall. It was on the second floor, the right side, wasn't it, Papa? I used my thick pencil to write in French: '*Je t'aime beaucoup, je t'aime vraiment, mon B!*'" Because Odile was half-serious, Olya and Célestin stopped tittering as the girl went on: "Well, then I signed our Lenka: '*Lena, jeune fille de Moscou*'! Papa was surprised, but he laughed and didn't forbid it. He only looked up and down the stairs to see if someone was coming."

"That's nice," chuckled Olya, "we'll tell Lena she has become Borya's fan, whether she wants to or not." These words returned the girl to reality: "Lenka isn't going to be annoyed with me, is she? Well, he'll probably never see the message. And how can he find her in Moscow?" Winking at Olya, Célestin asked: "Should we go back there and add Lenka's phone number?" She had long had a sense of humor even at her own expense. So, instead of going into a sulk at her leg being pulled, she shrewdly said: "We can't do it without Lenka's permission, but let's leave our number!" Olya prevented further complications: "That would be fine if you had signed yourself. Then he might have called you because your name is rare and pretty. But what then, what would you say to Borya on the phone?" Odile was befuddled for a moment but did not become vexed: "I'd say to him, I'd say, 'Zdravstvuy, Borya!' and 'Ciao, do svidaniya!'"

7.

One morning, the pair took Olya to the Cathedral of Our Lady of Kazan. She was touched: "I know you brought me here because of the name of my native city, and I'm grateful. However..." her voice trailed off. Odile was perplexed, but he immediately said: "I think I understand what bothers you." Olya explained: "When this cathedral was erected at the beginning of the nineteenth century, the Kazan Icon of the Mother of God—sacred to every Russian man and woman regardless of their religion—was placed here for safekeeping. And now, who knows where it is? One doesn't even dare inquire! Does it still exist? Already in the thirties, a 'Museum of Atheism' was opened here; can you believe it? One hopes that at least the tomb of our eminent military commander, Prince Mihail Golenishchev-Kutuzov, Count of Smolensk, has been preserved. We talked about the bloody Battle of Borodino against Napoleon in 1812 and Tolstoy's *War and Peace*. Well, near Kutuzov's tomb, Pushkin wrote unforgettable verse."

Father and daughter were touched by Olya's sad face. She continued: "But much more bothers me about this cathedral. Consider the gargantuan size of the edifice and the bulky, prodigious dome. There's very little Russian in it. The chief architect—I forgot his name, something starting with V., maybe Voronihin—used the Papal Basilica of Saint Peter in the Vatican as his model and applied the French *Empire* style. What's the logic? Our people suspect the architect managed to 'sell' to the young Tsar Aleksandr I, with the help of ambitious courtiers, the idea of Sankt-Peterburg, rather than Moscow, as the Third Rome."

It was apparently necessary to stand in front of the church, once home to the Kazan Icon—and be aware it might still be there hidden in a vault—for Célestin to hear Olya's opinion of the Soviet system, as she went on: "Moreover, the Church of the Savior on Spilled Blood was also forcibly shut down in this city. I'll tell you about the incredible history of that church in connection with the assassination of Tsar Aleksandr II in 1881. Tino, the lady director of the Shalyapin Museum said Aleksandr II was responsible for the building and consecration of the Russian Cathedral in Paris... Well, although I'm not truly familiar with Leningrad, I do know about its history, architecture, and churches from high school and the Gnessin. What did I want to say... Yes, we'll look at the Church on Spilled Blood for the sake of all of us, but mostly Odilichka's, whom we've neglected through my talkativeness. You see, in many photos, the church resembles Saint Vasiliy the Blessed, near the Moscow Kremlin, of which she was so fond. Remember, darling girl, the church with onion-shaped domes?" She did, plunging her face into Olya's bosom.

Stroking Odile's cheek, Olya spoke again: "They also shut down Saint Isaac's Cathedral. I don't find that ponderous neoclassical edifice attractive either, but this city is celebrated for buildings in such style—it's completely different, as you've certainly noticed, from ancient Moscow. These here are overly embellished buildings, at least for my taste, less than two centuries old. But Saint Isaac, which is now probably also a museum, perhaps of 'Bolyshevism,' was named for St. Isaac the Confessor, also known as Saint Isaac the Dalmatian, a monk from the fourth century, I think. He wasn't from Dalmatia but from Syria, yet he started a monastery with the name 'Dalmatian' in the Constantinopolis of his day. However, what's important—here I go again talking like an expert about a city I don't know well—what's important is that the birthday of Pyotr the Great, the 30th of May, 1682, fell on St. Isaac's Day, so Pyotr chose him for the Patron Saint of the Romanov Dynasty." Holding hands or hugging each other, the trio rambled from the Moyka to the Griboyedov Canal and then to the historic Anichkov Bridge on which the Prospekt crosses the Fontanka, a minor left branch of the Neva.

Later that evening, in their room on the eighth floor of the Pribaltiskaya, from where one had a spectacular view of the Neva delta and the Gulf of Finland, Célestin asked his daughter: "It's just crossed my mind—do you wish to write to Oksana? We can buy a picture postcard. She would be glad to hear from you." Instead of a quick "yes, I'll do it," which he expected, Odile observed her father before responding: "Oksana was good to us and a real girlfriend to me, but *cher Papa*, what do you think? Would I be hurting Olya? Because Olya is like a... I don't know how to tell you. I love her very much, awfully much, and she loves me the same."

"I'm really pleased, *mon ange*, that you care about Olya's feelings," he said. "But listen: By continuing a friendship with a fine Russian girl, you won't in any way imperil Olya's place in our hearts. The two of them are not in a competition. You won't offend Olya by writing to Oksana. Our friend from Irkutsk deserves it." Relieved, Odile embraced him: "I'll write to her tomorrow!"

Thus ended their evening. Pyotr the Great built Sankt-Peterburg for Russia to acquire a window toward Europe, particularly to the shipbuilding and seafaring nations like Holland, a country he knew well by working there. In the twilight, father and daughter looked through the window in their room at the peaceful Gulf of Finland and, in their minds, much farther west, to Metz and Koblenz.

8.

Early the next day, Célestin and Odile met with Olya in the magical Summer Garden, which occupied an islet: On its three sides flowed the Neva, Fontanka, and Moyka, while along the western edge, bordering the Field of Mars, shimmered the charming Swan Canal. Although it was almost the end of October, the weather was sunny and windless. All three were in a relaxed mood. They strolled for a long time through the magnificent deserted garden, for which, according to legend, Pyotr the Great himself drew the plan at the beginning of the eighteenth century.

Olya announced she had a surprise and would act as a guide. They crossed the Neva on the famed Dvortsovy Most, Palace Bridge, to Vasilyevskiy Island and then walked almost two kilometers along the Little Neva to Tuchkov Bridge. Once across it, they were in the Petrograd Quarter and after a stroll of twenty minutes arrived at the monumental, light-yellow Cathedral of Prince-Saint Vladimir. "I found out from students that this cathedral had also been shut for years, but had recently again begun to function as a house of prayer," said Olya happily. "I wanted to surprise you. What's more, the Kazan Icon of the Mother of God, about which we spoke, is purportedly safeguarded here."

Before they entered the cathedral, Olya covered her head with a dark kerchief. Although the modest piece of cloth was supposed to reflect humility, it made Olya even more feminine. They spent a long time in the church, each pursuing private thoughts while admiring exquisite icons—many were on view but not the Kazan Mother. Célestin brought Odile to the altar and reminded her of their visit to Saint Nicholas Church on the shore of Lake Baikal with Oksana, which seemed unimaginably far in the past. They crossed themselves together in the Russian way as they did then, by the enormous, distant, mystical lake.

And Olya? She crossed herself several times and, while praying, lit two beeswax candles. As she explained later, one was for her father and all the departed members of her family, and the other for the living who were dear to her but also for good people everywhere. Shyly, she told father and daughter they had been lovingly mentioned in her prayers. Célestin intimately squeezed her arm above the elbow, whereas Odile—even though she had until then behaved hesitantly—could not resist and embraced Olya in her unrestrained way.

There were only a few people in the cathedral. Almost all were old women praying devoutly on their knees. However, in a remote corner, Olya detected a sacristan the age of Methuselah. A grayish beard reached to his waist, and the whites of his eyes were bloodshot. After Olya asked him about the Kazan Icon, he was silent for a while, suspiciously peering at her face. "My daughter," he began, in a voice at the same time hoarse and squeaky, as if he were in puberty, "yes, our most sacred Mother of God is here, in the church, but you can't see her. We're protecting her in the cellar, in the vault, hidden from the red devils. I am sorry, dear daughter." And he stroked Olya's bowed head with trembling, gaunt fingers.

9.

It was late afternoon when they returned to the Pribaltiskaya thirsty and tired. The girl did not complain, having been taught good manners unwaveringly by her devoted, though far from spineless, father. The entire hotel, from chambermaids to waiters, receptionists, and porters, fell in love with her. However, Olya's striking appearance and very existence were something else.

By that time, Célestin had acquired a fair knowledge of the hotel. On each floor, there were café-restaurants and bars among which there were few differences. All became nightclubs after eight and accepted only foreign convertible currencies. The colorful blend of people resembled that found in an oriental bazaar or Rome at the time of Caesar Augustus soon after the birth of Christ.

Everywhere could be seen the exotic Party cadres from the often remote regions of the Soviet Empire. Not lagging in numerousness were apparatchiks belonging to the "brotherly" communist parties located in South America and Cuba, as well as North Africa, Italy, France, and Spain, not forgetting Bulgaria, Poland, Yugoslavia, and others. Most of the time, Célestin could identify them by language, clothes, and skin color. Here and there, one could see Swedes and Finns, often stumbling drunkenly. They worked for companies that routinely received lucrative engineering and building contracts in the USSR—including for hotels like the Pribaltiskaya—because Nordic countries were allegedly neutral.

Sometimes, father and daughter would walk in the cafés through a multitude of men—there were almost no women. The duo was therefore a startling sight. For his part, Célestin was discreetly engaged in an educational lesson by interpreting for his daughter what was on view: Attire; languages; the loudness of arguments; the degree of inebriation and boorish manners; and conspicuous examples of well-fed self-satisfaction. The child absorbed it all, knowing not to stare nor to condemn—at least not visibly. They were sophisticated, but not conceited, Franco-Germans.

Americans were also represented. Some attempted to befriend the pair, judging them to be "their Westerners." One group was called the "Ancient and Honorable Artillery Company of Massachusetts." It was a so-called fraternity of moneyed lawyers, medical doctors, engineers, and pilots, who traveled together somewhere far once a year, "to get away from our wives, learn something new, and moderately raise hell," as one member confided to Célestin. Most of them were amiable and courteous people. Odile got a small gift from a lawyer called Rodney—a pin inscribed with "I love you, Pete," which referred to Pyotr the Great. She thanked him but declined his offer to attach the pin to her.

"Absence of women" was correct except for *filles de joie*. On each floor, in each café-bar, there was a woman, usually two, colleagues of sorts. All were elegantly dressed and pretty, some exceptionally pretty, and very young—from sixteen to twenty-something years old. They could operate by tipping porters and bartenders, including the KGB operatives among them. As it happened, these same men insisted on giving sweets to Odile. Following her dad's diplomatic advice, she accepted the gifts with a polite smile.

So when that afternoon, after their long visit to Saint Vladimir Cathedral, the three of them returned to the hotel, Olya had to show her document at the front desk and was told she needed to leave by eleven: being Célestin's guest made no difference to the usually pleasant lady receptionist. The reason for Olya's entering the hotel was his and her stubbornness, with a sprinkling of anger. Father and daughter took Olya to their floor because he surmised the people who worked there would be decent.

But as soon as they entered one of the cafés, and Olya looked around, she quickly led her hosts out, distressed and briefly unconcerned with Odile: "Forgive me, Tino, I simply can't stay there. Did you see what I saw? Those are girls sixteen or seventeen years old. Beauties, the future of Russia. *Gospodi!* How wrong I was, stupid, disgusting."

In their room, Olya sat down in an armchair and dejectedly looked through the window. He did not know how to cheer her up, but Odile did. She climbed into Olya's lap murmuring: "Don't be sad, Olyechka, embrace Papa instead. Tomorrow is his birthday!" They both threw themselves on the astonished Célestin. The girl then ran to the cupboard, while Olya continued to hug him: "Darling, I didn't know... I wish you everything the best in the world!"

He was deeply moved, as his daughter produced a birthday card she had designed: "*Cher Papounet*, I was planning to congratulate you tomorrow, on the correct date, the 27th of October. Still, because Olya is here and so sad, I want us to rejoice together." Célestin and Olya then embraced Odile and forgot the "valuta" café.

He ordered a chocolate cake, fruit juice, and Soviet champenoise by phone. The day waitress Katya arrived and explained the bottle was the coldest she could find, adding that the juice was a gift for the girl. Odile smiled, but shyly turned her head aside when the waitress tried to kiss her. On Célestin's request, Katya promptly returned with proper champagne glasses and happily wished him "*S dnem rozhdeniya.*"

Twenty minutes later, just as merriment filled the room, a knock sounded on the door. It was Polina Andreyevna, the kind chambermaid, delivering their ironed laundry. Especially Odile had a good rapport with her. Polina certainly did not choose the moment and must have been ordered to check the goings-on. Scoundrels! She shamefacedly deposited the laundry, mumbled "... *rozhdeniya,*" and left without a single look at Olya. All three felt sorry for her.

The cheerful mood resumed and lasted until about half past seven when Odile claimed she felt sleepy, although that was not her usual bedtime. The day had indeed been long, but it was more likely the girl wished to leave them alone. Olya and Célestin tucked her in and switched off the light. She was a healthy child without night anxieties.

Back in the living room, they found themselves in a passionate lovers' clinch. Olya interrupted it after a while and turned on the radio. A song was heard. She murmured, "It's better like this, maybe there's a microphone in the room." But after another period, she whispered again: "I have something to show you." From her purse emerged a booklet containing some forty pages of typewritten text with *K. Sepuhova—Verses* on the cover. Olya explained: "Katarina spent six years in a gulag, sentenced for 'anti-Soviet agitation and propaganda,' and now she is under house arrest somewhere in the provinces. There she wrote down the verses she had created in her mind in the gulag. She managed to give the manuscript to some students who typed and reproduced it. We call it *samizdat*. Volodya Vysotskiy and Borya Grebenshchikov also did such things.

"I think you know Russian enough to understand these poems. But listen, Tino, please read the verses tomorrow in a park, don't leave the booklet in this room. And when you've finished reading it, destroy it while you are still in Peter. Please, please don't take it to Finland with you the day after tomorrow. They'll meticulously go through your luggage at the border. Even if you like the poems and feel they are important, don't try to take them abroad and publish them in France or Germany. Darling, I don't want you to be a hero and put Odile and yourself in danger: They have people in the West. Promise you won't, please!"

Célestin vowed to obey Olya's ardent request. He then leafed through Katarina Sepuhova's tiny volume. It was probably a pseudonym, but he decided not to embarrass Olya by inquiring. On the seventeenth page, he came across a poem in five short stanzas entitled *"Only The Sun."* He read it three times, occasionally asking Olya for clarification. When urged to read it, she did it with poise and feeling, without excess. Célestin was moved to his core and courageously read the verses aloud. He did his best to mimic Olya's gentle phrasing:

ONLY THE SUN

Even to my father I won't admit
they kicked me like a pierced ball.

To my mother I'll claim amnesia
about the scars on my frost-bitten toes.

That I pulled hairs from my scalp,
even my brother will never know.

About my hair turning gray,
one-time friends won't dare to crow.

Even with my lover I'll never walk
on the shady side of the street.

Only the sun.[1]

He sighed: "Darling, thank you from the depths of my heart for trusting me with this. What horror!" They looked at each other. Amplifying the sound on the radio, he said: "I'm not going to ask from whom you got this amazing collection of poems. Nor with whom you associate regarding politics. Nor whether and how Lena is involved. I don't have the right to ask such questions—not yet." He sat next to Olya on the couch. Several hours remained for passion. They somehow managed to put out of mind that their rapid breathing was occurring near the flimsy wall separating them from the sleeping girl.

---

1. Inspired by Irina Ratushinskaya's poem "I Will Live and Survive," which she wrote at a gulag in 1983. (I. R.: 1954-2017).

At five minutes to eleven, Célestin sneaked into the bedroom, lightly kissed Odile on the forehead, and placed a note on the pillow next to her sweet head. The note said in French: "*Mon ange*, I left to see Olya off by cab. I'll return in a jiffy. *Je t'aime, mon bijou, Papa—Mille bisous*, Olya." It was unprecedented that he would leave her alone at night, even briefly. From the bedroom door, Olya blew a silent kiss to Odilichka. The girl was loved not only by her father but also by a wonderful young woman.

While the cab hummed across Vasilyevskiy Island, Olya was fiercely clinging to her Tino. She had never loved like that if she ever loved at all. He was immeasurably happy and for no particular reason said to Olya in English: "I don't know why, but I remember something about the human soul and our souls. In a book by the American writer Pearl Buck, the rich middle-aged Chinese heroine, 'Lady Wu,' says to her ascetic and wise French mentor: 'So the soul is that part of our being that's neither male nor female'."

10.

Despite it being their last day in Leningrad, Célestin and Odile were in a good mood as they crossed the entire Vasilyevskiy Island on foot. The day was again sunny. While they were passing Borya's building, her bungling father asked the girl: "This is your last chance to add something to Borya's wall. Do you want to?" She pretended to become peeved: "*Mais Papa*, enough of that joke! And why the last chance? Aren't we going to come back soon? When will we see our Olya again? Of course, we'll invite her to visit us—wherever we are. Won't we, *cher Papa?*"

He did not know what to say or how to explain that his life was in a vortex. "*Ma petite fille chérie*, Olya and I must decide." Odile studied him, understanding that her future would also be deeply affected. So many children had both parents, and she...

As soon as they sat down on a bench at the Senate Square, by the statue of Pyotr the Great and a stone's throw from the Admiralty, Olya appeared. What a young woman! They watched her admiringly as she approached. He mumbled: "What a face she has, what a noble high forehead and graceful bearing... And what a radiant smile directed at me—at my daughter and me!"

He got up and walked toward her. They hugged each other tightly, as lovers—there, in front of Pyotr, the famous *Bronze Horseman*. Sensitive as she was, Odile remained on the bench, looking at their embrace with shining, loving eyes.

After they sat down, Olya said to him: "I have a modest birthday gift for you, something quite personal. I hope you won't think it's too flaunting—I didn't know what to buy because you'll be traveling." She then produced a nicely wrapped square object, which turned out to be a framed black-and-white photograph under glass. "This is me at age nineteen. Mama took me to a photo studio in Kazan just before I left for Moscow to study. She also has one like this." He could only embrace her wordlessly.

Olya turned to Odile: "I didn't buy any toy. I noticed you don't play with dolls and trinkets so I brought you a book of art drawings of objects in this city: There are churches, monuments, and mansions." As she did in the hotel, the girl sat in Olya's lap—although she felt too old—and begged: "Olya, Olyechka, come with us, please!" Olya was moved. Also, she felt guilty for having made love rather noisily the previous evening. "Odilichka, darling, I would love to, but..." A great closeness and gloomy silence ensued.

Still hugging Odile, Olya waved toward the bronze Pyotr and said to Célestin: "You see, my dear, Soviets build all kinds of gigantic eyesores—they think huge size is great art that brings appreciation and love—but in all of mother Russia, there isn't a statue cherished like this one. I don't know about Kamchatka and the Caucasus, nor what the psychopath from Gruziya-Georgia thought, and it doesn't matter. Without shame, the Soviets are lying about the whole history of Russia."

They were silent for a while, and then Célestin, to lighten the mood, asked Olya: "I know the sculpture is made of bronze, yet in Russian it's called *Myedny vsadnik*, which means *copper* horseman. Well?" Olya laughed but then held back her mirth: "Tino, now you've put your finger, without meaning to, on something very Russian. The monument is indeed constructed of bronze, but in his poem 'Myedny vsadnik,' a hundred fifty years ago—a poem taught to every Russian—Pushkin wrote 'Myedny'! Perhaps it rhymed better? So, you see, Pushkin is more important to Russians than metallurgical details."

All three looked across the Neva toward Vasilyevskiy Island. Above them, the incomparable gilded spire of the Admiralty rose to a proud height. It was topped by the beloved *Korablik*, a weathervane shaped like an old warship with sails. The magnificent edifice was erected at the beginning of the nineteenth century in the Empire style that so much bothered Olya on the Kazan Cathedral. What about the Admiralty?

There was no time to talk about it because Célestin was bewildered: What to say to Olya in the maybe crucial moment of their lives? He had no experience with such decisions ever since the time, more than nine years earlier in Koblenz, when Patrizia and he agreed to get married and have children. The wedding took place. The progeny was right next to him but Patrizia and Patrice...

Odile instinctively understood her father's dilemma: The best parent imaginable. She decided to step aside and leave him alone with Olya. "Papa, please give me the Nikon, I'd like to take pictures of the horseman and the sharp golden spike. You know I can." He knew she could and gave it smiling, for he had taught her back on the Great Wall of China how to use the complex camera. There was little about her that he did not admire. Olya respected that.

She and Célestin sat reading Katarina Sepuhova's poems. There were tears in their eyes: "I think, dearest Olyechka, *you* wrote these poems. Perhaps you identified, body and soul, with a real or fictitious poetess who had a tragic fate in a gulag. This is you. I adore and cherish you, but please tell me the truth." She did not move even an inch away from him. "I was hoping you'd guess, hoping you know me. I wrote these poems whenever I felt pitifully sad, depressed, and alone. Sometimes I'd do it immediately after returning to my little flat from the National. I don't wish to defend myself in an easy way, but shame and self-hatred played a part. I embraced and absorbed someone's much deeper, *innocent*, suffering and added it to mine, of which I was the cause. Despise me for my behavior in the National and for stealing the pain of an imaginary woman—although she probably exists somewhere in Siberia. But now you know everything. And remember, you and I share souls."

It had been a long time since he ceased to despise her—if he ever did. There was no doubt they genuinely loved each other, the extraordinary Tatar-Russian and the gentlemanly Frenchman. Their foreheads were, and were held, equally high.

Odile was somewhere nearby with the camera, and he returned the poems to Olya: "I wrote a few lines in Russian for you. Please destroy after reading." The two grieving souls stayed on the bench. After a long time, she said: "I know I'm not lying to myself that we love each other passionately. And I'd be a good mother to Odile. But when will we see each other again, even if I were to receive the Soviet exit visa? I don't wish to live in the West! This here, and in Moscow and Kazan, is my country, my home." She whimpered: "Come with Odile to Kazan and get to know Mamochka. The girl would acquire a gentle babushka, a granny..."

Célestin was not able to comprehend what was happening. It crossed his mind that he was a good-for-nothing person, impotent and indecisive. Yes, he loved his daughter and would do anything for her, but was that truly all he could offer Odile, Olya, and himself?

While returning to their hotel, father and daughter wore long faces. He was silent and disgusted with himself. "That's precisely what Olya said about herself, wasn't it?" he thought.

On the table in their room at the Pribaltiskaya, they found a pair of pink woolen gloves knitted by hand. A note said: "For my Princess Odilichka—from Auntie Polina Andreyevna."

11.

They arrived at ten in the morning at Finlyandskiy vokzal, Finland Station. It was located in the Kalinin Quarter, not far from the Arsenalynaya Embankment of the Neva. V. I. Ulyanov, Lenin, had arrived at that station from Switzerland, Germany, Sweden, and Finland on the 3rd of April 1917—by the Julian calendar, then still used in Russia—to destroy the three-hundred-year-old Romanov dynasty and introduce the "dictatorship of the proletariat." It was a historical fact that Lenin, an unrepentant traitor, was sponsored by Germany, to which Bolyshevik sabotage was invaluable in the war against the Russian Empire. Célestin sensed Olya's opinion.

She wore a modest dark coat and a tiny hat. By agreement, Odile and Célestin arrived only half an hour before the train's departure. Everything that could be promised already took place—mostly tearfully—the previous day. They did not wish to create a satisfyingly sorrowful scene for the observers. Olya and Tino appeared to be talking calmly, barely touching, until departure was imminent; then, their embrace was violent, almost painful. In contrast, Odile had clung tightly to Olya the entire time and whispered through tears. The serious, precocious girl was just a small bawling child.

The train for Helsinki was leaving the station. Father and daughter stood at the window in their compartment. Olya was waving to them through tears, and they responded zestfully. But unlike Odilichka's white hankie, his thoughts were black. "Is this the last time I'll see her? Is it possible? *Adieu, adieu! Proshchay, proshchay!*"

Just then, while the train was still crawling, they saw two tough men in long coats grabbing Olya, one by each arm, and pulling her roughly from the platform. She looked at Célestin over her shoulder with desperate eyes, and he knew what those eyes were telling him: "That's what they are like..." People on the platform, who had been furtively studying the beautiful young woman, suddenly turned their gaze. Olya's little hat had fallen on the ground but was not worthy of a glance because it had become diseased. Hugging the blubbering Odile, who had understood everything, he pursued a horrifying thought: "My darling Olyechka, my soul, have you destroyed the book of poems?"

For the first time since the passing of Patrizia, he knew he was deeply concerned not only about Odile's safety but also someone else's, his Olya's. The fear became linked with rage, an emotion not an inherent attribute of his personality. On top of the wicked treatment, which would doubtlessly be Olya's lot, they delivered a gratuitous slap to him and his little girl: Olya could have been easily grabbed later and elsewhere. But no, they did it in the middle of the platform, in front of his and Odile's eyes, to humiliate them. "Damn them and damn Finland Station!" thought Célestin angrily.

12.

Father and daughter long sat in somber silence. The expensive compartment had two made beds for a day trip of five and a half hours—a final Intourist machination. Absently, they watched the suburbs. Bare trees, only a few with yellow and red leaves. Then, dense woods of conifers, with small lakes and white birches between them. Célestin opened the window and murmured: "What a spectacular, enormous land, but... Let's breathe this air, *mon ange*, we shall long remember it."

He had to tell Odile something important but did not know how. Finally, words flew out: "Listen, *mon coeur*! This is hard for me to explain and for you to understand, but I must try. Our Olya is not guilty, she isn't responsible for what happened. Those evil men probably dragged her to prison. They were like policemen, only worse. What will happen to her and how long she won't be free... there's no way to know. I am angry beyond measure. They are punishing her because she was close to us, which means we—without the least intention—have contributed to what happened."

Odile moved slightly away so she could see her father's face better. "But why, why?" she asked piteously. Célestin tried to explain: "It's called international politics. I often don't understand it, nor will you be able to. The bosses of those policemen don't like the countries from which we come. And one must admit the behavior of our countries toward this one has in the past been truly ugly. And so, the rulers here consider us enemies, while those at the station only did their dirty job, with more or less pleasure."

A long silence. "But why should Olya be the victim and not we?" stubbornly asked the girl, with an enviable sense of justice. "Why? Because they can get away with it. Olya is a Soviet citizen like we are citizens of France and Germany. Besides, she wrote poems against those rulers. Understand? They don't think of her poems as art but as hostile pamphlets. But everything she did was just and courageous. That's why they don't like her. People like Olya are a thorn in the eye of those people.

"Don't imagine we are safe, not after our intense relations with Olya. We aren't safe, although we haven't done anything forbidden by their strict laws. But they probably aren't certain and so will try to find something for which to blame us—justifiably, they'd claim, and thus not provoking an international incident. Because of this, our crossing from the Soviet Union to Finland will be unpleasant. They will go through your things and ask you questions in a fake-friendly way." By chance, a waiter in a white shirt knocked and cheerfully served them orange juice and tea.

Unflustered, Célestin went on: "When the border officials show up, we'll speak only French to each other. I'll need to speak English but will refuse any communication in Russian. You'll speak only French because they aren't likely to be comfortable with it. We'll open our suitcases when asked and answer reasonable questions, but that's all; we won't help them pry. We'll not be polite in our normal manner, let alone ingratiating. I don't enjoy asking you, but please be a little surly and brusque! They are in cahoots with those who arrested Olya." Odile looked at her father baffled. "*Oui, mon ange*, get ready to become a sulky, peevish child when they come, although it's far from your nature." He held her close and kissed her forehead.

Then he spoke about the people they had met while traveling in the USSR, reminding her of the kindness of so many. "Never forget we aren't enemies to ordinary people, nor are they to us. Think of Oksana and the family of her father's army friend, who hosted us generously and courageously in the village of Bolyshiye

Koty on Baikal. And of Polina, who knitted the gloves for you. Not to mention Lenka. Even the popular Borya would become our buddy if we met him!" He tried to wink at her. On Odile's face, for the first time since the arrest of Olya, there appeared a trace of a smile.

"So, remember the good in people. It would be a great pity if all your memories from our magnificent trip were polluted by two nasty policemen. Or that in your mind there's lodged the sight of our tender Olya—who so much loves us—between thugs dragging her." She steadily looked at her father and then hugged him wordlessly. And he? He was unable to erase from his mind's eye Olya's forsaken little hat swirled by the wind on the platform of Finland Station.

The train traveled one hundred twenty kilometers from Leningrad and arrived in Vyborg, thirty kilometers from the border. A multitude of men and women in uniforms poured out of the gray station building and climbed on the train. The pair sat motionlessly, Odile with a stony expression and lips compressed. Defying his will, a shiver ran down Célestin's neck and spine. A young border officer mounted their car, locked the toilet and windows, and took their passport. Father and daughter watched officials checking the roof of the train and its belly above the rails. "What are they doing?" asked the girl and received a scathing reply: "It seems they are checking whether someone so maniacally wishes to escape from the USSR, regardless of danger, that he has climbed on top of the train, or hidden under it, to cross the border unnoticed."

Soon the train left the station only to stop half a kilometer farther. "The middle of a desolate field," thought Célestin, "is a more discreet place for interrogation and search." A three-member team arrived in front of their compartment. His chills were quickly replaced by disdain, and he encouraged Odile in French, pretending not to notice the trio. Asking her to sit by the window, he took a stubborn stance with resentful darkness on his face and hardly budged when the leading inquisitor pushed into the compartment. The man had clear steely eyes and a strong square jaw of the type Americans like to see on their fearless film heroes. "This one is arrogant like Solyony," Célestin found a nickname for the man in Chehov's play *Three Sisters*.

Due to his obstinacy, the other two team members were compelled to remain in the corridor. A good-looking woman in her thirties was near the door. She had thick brown hair and a ringing voice in which she greeted the compartment occupants. But there was no response, even from Odile. "This one is sly," decided Célestin derisively, "I won't let her enter our house using friendly pretenses, as Nataliya Ivanovna did to the three sisters." Nevertheless, as a Frenchman, he had to admit the woman had a fine face and elegant fingers for the keyboard. She spoke fluent English and interpreted for Solyony. The third man, Chehov's sub-lieutenant Fedotik, was older, with a polite expression on his intelligent face. He quietly stood in the corridor, observing the scene in a seemingly benign manner. "That must be a psychologist, a specialist in the interpretation of nonverbal behavior's subtle details. He won't outsmart us either, the police hound. Perhaps he isn't a psychologist but a gofer—the rules of the border KGB Workers Union might demand three comrades on the job," thought Célestin cynically.

Nataliya Ivanovna spoke softly in Russian: "But you speak our language, don't you?" That sounded like an invitation to an amorous glass of champagne. Or, in Célestin's grim literary mind, to Vladimir Nabokov's *Invitation to a Beheading*. The response arrived sharply: "*Nyet!* Only a few words—and only to decent Russian people. As if she had not heard him, Nataliya turned to Odile with words flowing like honey: "And you, my dear, how are you? What a sweet girl you are! You surely understand both English and Russian?" Odile could not avoid throwing a long curious glance at pretty Nataliya but blurted out: "*Je ne parle que français.*" Then she abruptly turned to the window.

The inquisitors realized the French pair would be uncooperative, so the temperature in the compartment rose. Solyony tried to open the biggest suitcase, which had complicated locks and lay on the upper bed, not far below his face. He asked Nataliya to demand the keys, which she did. With half a smile, Célestin showed the little trick necessary to open the lock, making the man's face as red as Solyony's in Act III, and said to Nataliya: "The suitcase was unlocked. Unlike this window. Perhaps you locked it so my daughter and I wouldn't jump out before the border of Finland!" He caught the corners of Nataliya's mouth in a smile and maybe something similar on Fedotik's face. Odile remained haughty and pouting, obeying the instructions.

While Solyony rummaged through the suitcase, where the travelers had intentionally mixed their clothes, Nataliya asked Célestin to show the dollars-to-rubles exchange receipts. He lay in ambush for such a request. Without an apology, he removed Solyony's paws from the suitcase and took out a folder overflowing with pieces of paper. A huge mass of receipts, bills, and other documents protruded from it. He said: "I know all that's here and have copies. Be sure to return every piece of paper, comrade border official—or Miss, as you like."

Suddenly, he snarled at Solyony: "What are you looking at? Just continue, as you've been doing, to plow through my little daughter's clothes!" Nataliya seemed to redden. Untroubled, Solyony took Olya's framed photograph from the suitcase, studied it, and showed it to Nataliya. "Russian?" asked she. Célestin grabbed the photo, passed it to Odile, and scornfully spat out: "You know well she's an innocent woman."

Solyony again did not react. Instead, he victoriously pulled out of the suitcase a cotton pouch on which was imprinted the name of the laundry at a renowned Peking hotel where father and daughter had "borrowed" it. It was filled with round black boxes containing rolls of film. When Solyony opened a box, Célestin calmly said: "This film has not been developed, one of thirty-nine rolls. Traveling as tourists, we took photos in China, Mongolia, and Russia. One of these rolls was shot only yesterday. My daughter photographed the statue of Pyotr the Great. And Admiralty. Maybe the naughty girl even took a photo of me with a Russian acquaintance. Your agency knows who that is and surely has pictures. As for the innocent acquaintance, you brutally arrested her today as this train was leaving Finland Station!" Nataliya naturally did not respond; instead, the female fox's question was: "Just an acquaintance?

A discussion among the inquisitors ensued in the corridor. Célestin was intrepid and followed Solyony. He snatched the pouch, saying loudly: "These are tourist photos. You are allowed to look at them, but you have no right, without a court order, to develop or destroy them. There are courts in the USSR! Even for the KGB and the three of you. The films are my property, and you would be breaking international law." They looked at him astounded. "Besides, what's the matter with you? It's as if you are eagerly trying to smash my eight-year-old daughter's love for Russia, which I and our Russian friends have been cultivating in her for months." He returned to the compartment and threw the pouch into the suitcase. Then he stroked Odile's cheek, mumbled they were winning, and faced the trio again: "Continue!"

Having somehow recovered his command of English, Solyony pointed to the second suitcase that lay on the floor next to Odile's legs and ordered: "Open!" Célestin was furious but kept his composure. He urged his daughter not to worry and still sitting, turned to Nataliya: "Please tell this rude gentleman he is behaving insultingly." She calmly translated. Then Solyony heard in English something to which he had never been exposed in his stimulating career as a border KGB intimidator, tormentor, and bully: "You want to explore that suitcase too? Fine. I have nothing to hide but won't help you. The suitcase is also unlocked. Open it yourself." Solyony looked at Célestin with hateful disbelief similar to Staff Captain Solyony's nasty emotion when he challenged Baron Tuzenbach to a duel knowing how easily he would kill him.

But when Solyony angrily bent down and opened the suitcase—which Odile had previously pushed toward him with her foot—the operative had a shock: Father and daughter had acquired an incredible pile of letters, diaries, business cards, handwritten addresses, and notes in Chinese, French, Japanese, German, English, Korean, Russian and other languages and scripts. In the sea of paper, Solyony's attention was drawn to a sketch pad, but as soon as he opened it, Odile got up and took it from him: "That's mine!" She returned to the corner by the window, pressing the pad to her chest together with Olya's photograph.

The man raised himself from the suitcase to his full height and width, but in front of him again stood Célestin—plucky and sarcastic. In an almost friendly tone, Solyony said: "Do you think I am stupid? It's my job." Without a second's hesitation, the Frenchman retorted: "You are silly. Do you really think I would have something incriminating you could find? To bring shame and disgrace on myself in front of my daughter? Are you people sane? But to calm the KGB man in you, I am telling you honestly: We have nothing illegal by Soviet law."

Changing tack, Solyony looked at Célestin civilly and spoke as man to man: "Yes, I believe you and your angry little girl who has traveled through our country and bathed in Baikal. Have you noticed, my friend, we haven't taken a peek inside her little shoes? We are cordial people. In America, you would have it worse!"

Pressing home the momentary advantage, Célestin followed Solyony as he joined the others in the corridor and pounced: "Telephone the KGB in Leningrad. Tell them my daughter and I are clean. And free Dinara Alimova Naratovna! We love her and she loves us. Good heavens, she is a better Russian than any of you."

Solyony and Fedotik ignored him and exited the car. Nataliya, however, stayed. Bringing her face close to his in a bogus-seductive way, she said: "That's precisely the problem, Tino—yes, we recorded in Olya's apartment how she coos to you—we don't like people who are more Russian than Soviet. If you wish to love this country, you must love not only Russia but the entire Soviet land and our Soviet system. As for me, I'm Tatar from Kazan, like your Olya—although she's that only through her father. Maybe you and I will meet again somewhere. I'm returning your folder with receipts; the passport will arrive soon."

She thought she had managed to leave victorious, but Célestin caught her: "So, comrade," he spoke through his teeth, "if a citizen doesn't adore the Soviet regime, she must go to prison? Is that Soviet law and Soviet justice, comrade self-righteous?" He waited for Nataliya to respond, but she was defeated: He had chased the intruder out of the three-sisters' home.

Embracing Odile, Célestin questioned the political system that tried hard to make departing visitors despise it. It took an hour and twenty minutes for the authorities, aware that Olya was arrested, to check two suitcases and humiliate the travelers. They prayed for departure. But Olya! She remained behind—alone in prison, without help.

The train began to move. Emotionally exhausted, they looked at the barren fields. Then steps, perhaps the passport? But no, another *Schweinerei*. The young KGB official swiftly entered without knocking and asked them to rise from the made beds. Confused, they got up. And what did the aspiring apparatchik do? He lifted the lid of the bench under the bedsheets, looking for a human being concealed there. How much would all three souls hate him had Olya been hidden in that space?

After a few minutes, the passport finally arrived: Fedotik. And he—by Célestin's initial guess either a psychologist or a KGB flunky—smartly saluted, clicking his heels in the sharp military manner. With a good-natured smile. Everything was surreal.

Célestin checked the passport. The yellow piece of paper with the visa had disappeared—it was as if they had never been in the USSR. He hugged Odile again, joking unconvincingly, "Now you can stop sulking." He reassured her: "*Tout est bien, mon ange, regarde, la frontière est ici!*" Indeed, the train was crawling through Brusnichnoye, passed through a corridor of barbed wire, and arrived in another tiny village, Vainikkala.

An elderly official in a blue uniform knocked on their door. Unnecessarily, Célestin asked him: "*Suomi?*" The man answered gaily: "*Joo!* Welcome to Finland!" He hardly looked at their passport and exclaimed in an amiable salesman's voice: "Welcome to our restaurant car! Because you are in an expensive compartment, coffee, tea, and juice will be free!"

The relentless tension in their minds and bodies diminished when they sat in the restaurant, startled by the sunny beauty of Karelia sparkling after the recent rain. But when they looked at each other, Olya remained in the love and guilt of their eyes. Everything was understood.

He groused in French: "This Finnish tea is not as good as the Russian. And your juice?" A young woman sitting with a girlfriend nearby merrily addressed them in beginner's French: "Oh, you're French! I like the French language and culture but can't speak well. We are Finnish, from Lahti. Where were you in the USSR?"

They were young, fashionably dressed, and brimming with sound health and self-confidence. Having taken stock, Célestin said in English, to make communication easier: "My daughter and I were in Siberia on Lake Baikal. And you two?" The second girl, self-possessed and speaking accentless English, took over: "We were at an international congress in Moscow and attended political seminars in Leningrad. Especially for me, the trip was very significant." When Célestin questioningly raised eyebrows, she continued proudly: "Last year, I was elected in Helsinki as the Secretary General of the Finnish Youth Peace League and this was my first international appearance in that capacity."

He gestured to Odile to finish her juice and spoke to the girls: "Let me guess. In Moscow, you probably stayed at the National or the Metropol, and in Leningrad at the Pribaltiskaya. As did we. Wonderful hotels, aren't they?" A youthful, self-satisfied giggle was heard from the young women: "*Joo*, luxurious hotels and the food—much better than in Finland!"

As Odile and Célestin got up from their table, she furtively looked at the Finnish girls with distrust. He said goodbye but interrupted their departure: "Yes, luxury in the land of hammer and sickle. I'm certain that not your parents, but the Soviet organizers paid for your top hotels, excellent food, and first-class trains—and gave you ample pocket money for shopping in the GUM." Both women's faces first lost all color and then became red. The girl who first spoke French reluctantly nodded. The Secretary-General quickly switched her glance from Célestin's face to her professionally manicured nails, not quite a communist worker's.

PART THREE

Rimbaud and Christo on Rive Gauche

1.

They did not find Helsinki particularly interesting, except for the squares and churches from the time of Aleksandr II, when Finland was a Grand Duchy within the Russian Empire. For a time, Célestin pondered their further travel and decided that neither he nor his daughter should be knocked off the mystical, though sometimes brutal, heights of China, Mongolia, and Russia, down to the plains of the commercial and banal Nordic Lutheranism of Sweden and Norway.

Therefore, after less than two weeks in Helsinki, they boarded a fast ferryboat and arrived in Germany—in Travemünde near Lübeck, the city of Thomas Mann, one of Célestin's favorite authors. On the highest point of the oval island that is the city of Lübeck, they found a hotel across the street from the ancient Marienkirche; at the same square, sat the house of Mann's family. Each morning, Mary's sublime bells awakened them, and on most days, they spent time in the splendid church, moved by the ageless grace and sanctity of her heart.

Repeatedly, they visited Mann's house and spent afternoons walking around the entire island. He affectionately held his daughter's hand, or Odile took her father under the arm like a young lady. They talked about the times with Olya in Moscow and Leningrad, and she was always "our Olya," a beloved family member. During these recollections, not only were sorrow and longing present, but it was inevitable that they would recall the painful sight at Finland Station.

During the month they spent in Helsinki and Lübeck, he wrote thrice to Olya at the address of her mother in Kazan, and

Odile added loving words to each letter. Making a genuine effort never to sound hopeless, Célestin was also learning about himself. It became clear that he loved a woman more profoundly than ever since Patrizia. What's more, he loved Olya not only crazily like a youth but on many levels, as a mature man and responsible father.

He knew it was essential to attend to his girl's emotional needs and was also conscious of how much her support meant in his relationship with Olya. Odile's warmth toward his lover contributed to him being less selfish and more humane.

On the twenty-sixth of November, they left Lübeck by train for Paris.

2.

Their elegant hotel was on Île Saint-Louis in the middle of the Seine, about two hundred meters from Cathédrale Notre-Dame. They often crossed by a small bridge to Île de la Cité on which the famous edifice was the undisputed sovereign.

One evening, father and daughter were reading in their beds. A long illustrated article in an English magazine about the Bulgarian artist Christo Vladimirov Javacheff caught Célestin's eye. The odd-sounding title was "Christo wraps it up!" What could that be, he wondered—but then examined the incredible photographs of several Christo's works. Using an undisclosed material, the man wrapped the entire Kunsthalle in Bern in 1968. Then, three years later in Milan, he used tarpaulin to wrap two statues. One, at the square in front of Duomo di Milano, represented no less a personage than the King of Italy, while the other, in front of La Scala, was of Leonardo da Vinci. "The city fathers who gave him permission must be both brave and visionary, for the fellow might not be mad but a genius," decided Célestin.

Earlier that evening, Odile was reading in French a police novel by Georges Simenon entitled *L'écluse № 1, The Lock at Charenton*, a thin volume which she had found in the hotel library. The hero—the bulky and seemingly sluggish Commissioner Inspector Maigret—was someone she found *très sympathique*. Born and raised in the provinces, Jules Maigret loved to eat—a lot! He looked sly in an amusing way, more so when he would stick his worn-out pipe between his powerful teeth. Madame Maigret was pleasantly old-fashioned, liked to cook and knit, regretted not having children, and had a kind heart.

The next day, Odile and Célestin discovered coincidences concerning both the location of their hotel and their reading materials. The person who explained it all was *une belle Parisienne* who lived in the neighborhood.

3.

The name of the new female phantom in their lives was Mathilde LeClercq. Before they were married, Patrizia and Célestin met a young French woman in Koblenz. She was their age, born in 1944, and on her way to study German at the Hamburg branch of the Goethe Institute. Her parents were from Cadillac, a wine-growing area on the Garonne River, some thirty kilometers south of Bordeaux. It was a three-way friendship at first sight, without ulterior motives, something about which mere mortals could only feel resentful. Of course, suspicious individuals tried to find a hidden problem to feel better—but failed. The sincerity of the friendship was undoubtedly helped by Patrizia's feminine beauty being at least equal to Mathilde's. No rivalry had existed, but life and distance led to irregular correspondence.

When Célestin wrote to Mathilde informing her of the tragic demise of Patrizia and Patrice, and Odile's miraculously healthy birth, two years had passed since these events. Mathilde wrote she was offended—why so late? She added: "How is your daughter? She must be a magical two-year-old when she survived such a birth." Afterward, letters were exchanged more often. Mathilde even received a postcard from Baikal; Odile signed it, not knowing who the recipient was.

Knowing Paris, Célestin realized Mathilde lived close to their hotel, half a kilometer away. He found her phone number and called. C.: "*Mathilde? Célestin parlant. Oui, bien sûr, avec Odile.*" M.: "*Mais où? Vraiment? C'est magnifique! J'arrive immédiatement!*" Nevertheless, it took her forty minutes to arrive. Somewhat sarcastically, he commented while they were waiting in the foyer: "Being a woman and a *Parisienne*, Mathilde must apply at least the basic cosmetics, although she doesn't need them—you'll see." She readily responded: "I'll never 'applicate' lipstick and rouge, let alone mascara. They are so ugly!" "Oh, yes you will. Beginning about your thirteenth year, you'll give me no peace. It's almost impossible for people, not just young girls, to resist what others do *en masse*. They all want to beautify themselves, yet the outcome is often dubious." Just then, Mathilde majestically flew in through the massive double glass doors. They were held open so wide by two fawning liveried doormen that three Inspector Maigrets could have walked in side by side.

As it had happened in the Vostok bar of the National in Moscow, father and daughter were astounded by the sight of a stunning woman walking quickly toward them. She was not twenty-two, like Dinara then, but thirty-six, like Célestin. Her natural beauty was complemented by French charm and elegance. And although the Mathilde he had known before was not a calculated person, he noticed that immediately after their brief hug and kisses on the cheeks, she addressed Odile in the most refined French manner—clearly intending to take the puzzled girl under her wing: "Odile! So pretty... you take so much after your lovely mother!" She did not lift the child, for it would not have been feminine. Nor did she bend—not an attractive stance for a woman. Instead, she sweetly squatted with youthful ease, tightly embraced Odile and confided: "I knew back then that a child of parents so much in love, would be wonderful."

Thus began their stay in Mathilde's Paris. From the start, she behaved as a family member. "At a hotel? *Mais non!* You'll stay with me. I live alone, and the apartment is spacious—here in the vicinity." Uninvited, she climbed with them to their room and helped the amazed girl pack. From a table, she picked up Simenon's book. "Who's reading *L'écluse № 1*? *J'adore Maigret. Si gros!*

And *la pauvre madame Maigret* enduring his stinking pipe in the house!" Odile timidly raised two fingers as if facing a teacher: "I also like the fat..." She could not keep a straight face and said through laughter, "I also like the plump *monsieur* Maigret, Inspector Maigret. And I think his old stinking pipe is funny. He's always chewing it, especially when he's hungry—which he often is."

Mathilde also laughed gaily, drew Odile to herself, and took her to one of the windows that looked on the right bank of the Seine. She pointed: "Exactly there, things are happening in your book. The clochards with whom Maigret is drinking sour wine, trying to ingratiate himself, live there. We're here on the islet Saint-Louis, and they are under those two bridges. The one on the right is Pont Marie, and the other, down the river, is Pont Louis-Philippe. Isn't it great your papa has brought you to this hotel from which you can look—through the window of *your* room—at what's happening in a book?!"

Odile thus learned a new and interesting way of connecting stories in books to reality. "But listen, *chérie*," continued her teacher, "Simenon wrote the book thirty years ago. Many things have changed. Our world and the people in it have changed and so have the clochards. Most of them have become very rough. They aren't anymore Maigret's make-believe *sympathique copains*! Of course, you can walk in daylight on that embankment of the Seine—but only with your papa or me. I'll gladly take you for *une jolie promenade*."

Without asking Célestin, who was busy settling the bill, Mathilde imperiously instructed the doormen to send a taxi with the luggage in an hour, not a minute earlier, to her address, № 12, rue de Buci, in the Sixième arrondissement. She gave them a sizable though not excessive *pourboire*, by the strict standards of the affluent arrondissements of Paris. By the small bridge De la Tournelle, they crossed to the Rive Gauche and strolled downstream. First, they passed Notre-Dame, which stood on the Île de la Cité, directly across from them. Soon after, continuing down the embankment, Mathilde put her arm on Odile's shoulder and showed her a massive building located, like the cathedral, on the other side of that branch of the Seine: "Préfecture de Paris, and there, in the Judiciary Police Department, sits our Maigret, ha, ha!"

The girl had never before felt as much like being in the center of the world as at that moment—even when she had stood with mouth agape in front of the Moscow Kremlin and the Peking Temple of Heaven. Mathilde continued: "And the imposing building a little farther, next to the Préfecture, is the Palais de la Justice. Maigret often went there to quarrel about his cases. And here, look, was Maigret's customary bar, his headquarters, where he drank lots of beer and who knows what else—absinthe, marc, Cognac. In the bar, he did many things unbecoming of a police inspector: blackmailed criminals, threatened witnesses, lied and pretended—all in service of justice?!" They stood in front of the bar that had changed its name from Simenon's times, directly across from the Palace of Justice.

Célestin observed the quickly developing camaraderie between Mathilde and his daughter. "Hmm," he thought. Then, to take the initiative, he asked Mathilde to lead them to her apartment because their precious luggage, with all the films and notes, would soon arrive from the hotel. Mathilde looked at him in a friendly way, but it was obvious she did not appreciate her courting of Odile being interrupted. "Fine, you're right, but tomorrow we'll go to Pont Neuf, over there," she nodded in the direction of the "new" bridge from 1607. So they turned from the embankment into rue Dauphine toward her apartment.

4.

Late in the evening, Odile read Maigret or explored her room walking barefoot on the soft carpet. She thought about Olya, Mathilde, her papa, and herself. What should she feel? And what did she really feel?

Earlier, when Mathilde had brought her to the room, she said: "I hope you'll like it here. This toilet is just for you. Put everything wherever you wish in the cupboard and drawers. The mirror is of a good size: Even little girls like to look at themselves, don't they?"

Both laughed. She wished to ask if her papa had his room or... but did not dare.

Mathilde had drawn the curtains open. "When you want to sleep, close them, it'll be quieter. Drunk tourists are noisy. Oh, another thing. See that window? Now it's winter, so it's shut most of the time, although... In the summer, a man often paces there—always the same guy, completely naked! And awfully ugly." They laughed again, but Odile was certain Papa would be wearing a wry smile if he were present. He would not have found an ugly naked man funny. Mathilde had then kissed her good night and left. She stretched catlike and opened the window wide. Night had fallen, streets were full of life. On the window across, the curtains stayed drawn. The weather was dry, and there was a cold winter wind. It blew yellow leaves up, all the way to her on the second floor. She managed to catch one, looked at it for a moment, and kissed it, suddenly thinking of Siberia and Olya. She would give the leaf to Papa so he could also kiss it—and Olya.

She returned to Maigret. If they were still in the hotel room, one could watch the cunning policeman with the clochards under Pont Louis-Philippe. He would be making inquiries about Ducrau, the shady owner of river barges. A new character, by the name of Aline, appeared in the book. She was a blonde girl, only nineteen years old, yet the mother of a two-year-old child. The girl lived with the child on one of Ducrau's barges. Feeble-minded, she thought and behaved like a ten-year-old. "How horrible," Odile exclaimed inwardly, "she's only a little older than I am." Nevertheless, she continued to read.

5.

The next morning, Mathilde took them for a walk. Her street, de Buci, was old and odd—narrow, lively, noisy, and a magnet for the residents of the Sixième. There were elegant five-story buildings, in one of which was Mathilde's apartment. At the street level, there were expensive stores, upscale restaurants, bars, and pâtisseries. However, a famous market, with its clamor and hurly-burly, sat across the street. The sellers arrived from all parts of Île-de-France and the more distant regions, each man and woman equipped with an idiosyncratic set of colorful incitements, entreaties, repetitive loud exclamations, brief expletives, and more complex oaths.

"Before I take you to breakfast," said Mathilde, after exchanging greetings with the concierge, "I'd like to show you № 18 in this street, just a few steps away." When they stood across the street from that house, she pointed to its top and went on: "High up there, in the attic, lived in the nineteenth century the poet Arthur Rimbaud, who was then only eighteen years old. As you probably know, Célestin, he often got drunk and took drugs with other poets. Paul Verlaine was a frequent guest. A talented scatterbrain, future nomad and vagabond, Rimbaud quarreled with merchants at the market to whom he owed money. And so, he would from his attic occasionally urinate—sorry, Odile—onto these people and their counters, calling them 'loathsome bourgeois.' They fought back by throwing eggs and rotten tomatoes at him. Because their missiles couldn't quite reach the attic, they changed tactics and targeted him when he would be leaving the building. But he managed, by using backyards and climbing over fences, to reach the exits of buildings down the street, including mine, № 12. There he would certainly have had a hard time with the then-ruling concierge. Anyway, that's the legend the market people and my concierge tell tourists. Regrettably, it's my only connection with poets!" All three laughed and went to Mathilde's favorite café, around the corner in rue André Mazet.

Odile thought of what she had heard from Mathilde and suddenly during breakfast asked: "*Cher Papa*, I know we are from the old noble family De Quernevelle, which acquired a large estate many centuries ago. We inherited it from your great-grandfather, grandfather, and parents. *Alors, Papa,* would the poet call us 'bourgeois répugnant'?"

Mathilde raised eyebrows, but Célestin first laughed and then answered seriously: "That, *ma princesse*, is an excellent question. You see, the market vendors were throwing rotten tomatoes at the *très vulgaire* young Rimbaud who owed them money, and he didn't know by which *nom dérogatoire* to call those mostly poor people who dared not to admire, imagine that, his *talent divine—* as he and Verlaine vainly thought. The real bourgeois are wealthier, city people, which is the origin of the word, who sell far more expensive goods—usually the products of others' poorly paid work—and then buy, and sell again, and so on. Everything they do, they do for profit. Such people would never bother with Rimbaud, nor would our family members—in the sense of throwing rotten eggs at him. The fact is, your great-grandfather Olivier had long ago bought and read Rimbaud's book of poems, one I've myself read several times in our library. You, *mon chou*, will have to wait a little to understand it—three or four years."

Odile and Mathilde nodded as all of them—chuckled Célestin privately—relished eating marvelous bourgeois croissants, brioches, and madeleines. "In addition," he resumed the monologue, "we're not city people but live in the country, which, by itself, is not significant for our social position. We pay workers on our estate more than any other landowner in the environs of Metz. Unlike the *grand bourgeois,* we neither buy nor sell nor rent out houses and apartments. We inherited a part of the bank in Metz to which I often took you; there we have money earning money. Nothing to gloat about, but it's the economic system in our country. And France is all we have.

"Don't forget my degrees from Universität Göttingen and the unremunerated lectures at universities in both countries and to the students at the Metz Lycée. I did it the best I could, out of love and responsibility. Also, I've written numerous scientific articles on comparative linguistics. Income from the estate and the bank leaves me time for study but more importantly, for taking care of you, day and night, for more than eight years."

Odile jumped up, embraced her father, and remained for a while in that position. Mathilde kept quiet, as Célestin concluded: "Keep in mind, *mon ange,* we're not buying a new car every year and don't have an unnecessary apartment in Paris in the luxurious Huitième. Instead, we use our money to see the world, which is an incredible privilege. Otherwise, we would've never seen Peking, Baikal, Moscow, Leningrad... Nor met our Olya!"

And that was how Mathilde first heard of Olya. She wisely refrained from inquiring, for she could always milk Odile. So she changed the subject and asked Célestin who had raised him. Back in Koblenz, Patrizia told her that his parents had died in the Nazi bombing near Metz in 1945 when he was a baby.

"I was raised by my father Joseph's parents, *grand-maman* Charlotte and *grand-papa* Olivier—truly wonderful, well-educated, intelligent people," he answered. "I had two wet nurses from the vicinity of our manor and afterward several governesses. I loved one of them, Frau Else from Alsace. She was like a mother to me, though sometimes a strict governess. They all died before I was twenty-five when I met Patrizia. For an orphan—which sounds strange—I had a very happy childhood, with a lot of love from my granny, grandpa, and those other women. And from many horses and cows, and even two bulls."

Mathilde was sitting a little away from the café table, creating space for her slender legs to be gracefully crossed. She sipped coffee and observed her guests. "*Mon Dieu*, how close they are, how gentle with each other—yet without unctuous solicitousness. The woman who tries to insinuate herself between them will not fare well," she thought. Aloud she said: "My parents are, *grâce à bon Dieu*, alive and healthy, living in Cadillac in a nice old house among their beloved vineyards. They are in their sixties but ride bicycles everywhere. Papa is often in the vineyards with the workers, and *Maman* supervises everything. And they swim in the river! There is a small sandy beach on the Garonne by the vineyards. Bordeaux is only half an hour by car... All right, enough about them, and we can talk about me another time. Now we'll go to Pont Neuf to visit King Henri IV and Inspector Maigret."

6.

One can claim Pont Neuf is the very heart of Paris—more than the Louvre or the Opéra or La Madeleine or the Concorde. Even its postal address, Paris 75001, proves it. At the center of the bridge is a grand equestrian bronze statue of King Henri IV, the first King of France from the House of Bourbon; he ruled for about twenty years during the transition from the sixteenth to the seventeenth century. The statue was placed on that spot in 1618, eight years after the assassination of Henri by a Catholic fanatic.

Walking on rue Dauphine with Mathilde, father and daughter needed only ten minutes to reach the bridge. As soon as they approached the statue, Odile borrowed the camera, exclaiming, "Papa, this king and his horse aren't as good-looking as Pyotr the Great and his stallion, but I still wish to take a photo."

Mathilde told them: "He was raised a Protestant but converted to Catholicism to rule more peacefully, or so he thought. He mounted the throne in 1589, only seventeen years after the massacre of Saint-Barthélemy when the Catholics killed many thousands of Protestants-Huguenots." Célestin responded: "I read a lot about the bloody event: The conversion to Catholicism didn't help Henri. The Protestants despised him as a traitor, and the Catholics distrusted him as a fraud, which tends to happen to converts. You know he survived a dozen assassination attempts before the fatal one."

He turned to Odile: "Do you remember the beautiful church in Leningrad with the strange name Savior on Spilled Blood—strange until one knows that Russian Tsar Aleksandr II was killed there by assassins?" She answered right away: "Yes, I remember it. The church stood on the embankment of a canal. But I didn't take a photo, it was too sad. Our dear Olya showed us the church."

Although politesse may have dictated that Mathilde should inquire about "dear Olya," she surprised herself and again refrained from doing it. As before, she changed the topic: "You've learned more than enough about bloody events and King Henri. Let's return to our Maigret because he is also nearby. What d'you say?"

Odile agreed, remembering what she had read the previous evening: "You say Maigret is close by. Yes, he would be in the little tobacconist shop over there, Bar Tabac Henri IV. It's in the novel I'm reading, the one you saw when you came to our hotel. Maigret walked into it with Ducrau, the moneyed owner of barges who was bigger and stronger even than Maigret!" Some thirty meters from Henri's statue, there was an inconspicuous bar about which Simenon wrote. It was known only to the owners of barges and the Seine boatmen. "But let's please not go there," requested Odile plaintively, "not because it's an ugly, small place full of smoke but because it's sad."

Célestin did not have a clue what all that was about, but Mathilde knew the novel and felt sorry for the girl: "I can guess why you find the place sad; let's not depress your papa by going on about it." Odile, however, was used to talking about everything with her father, so she resisted anyone telling her, even the pleasant lady, what she should and should not divulge. "I'll tell him, anyway. You see, while Maigret and Ducrau were drinking in the bar, one of the boatmen arrived dismayed but somehow managed—even though terrified of Ducrau's temper—to tell him his only son Jean was dead, he'd hanged himself."

He hugged his daughter: "*Oui, c'est très triste, mon enfant*, horrible for anyone to hear, most of all the young man's father. But *mon trésor*, it's only a novel." Célestin knew his words lacked conviction and decided he would in the future be less indulgent about his daughter's choice of reading. Simenon's novels were not, as he had imagined, just superficial police buffooneries. He was embarrassed in front of Mathilde, although they were both at fault.

Mathilde thought the same so yet again changed the topic: "I suppose we've all had enough of real-life murders from the distant past and suicides in novels. So, let's look at my secret place through this passage. There'll be things to photograph, delightful trees even in wintertime." She led them some fifty meters toward the Palace of Justice, to a hidden Parisian jewel, the triangular Place Dauphine. Its shape and dimensions were almost identical to those of the elegant garden that spread from Pont Neuf, cutting the Seine, to the western, downstream cape of Île de la Cité. The cape was like a dagger or the nose of a swordfish. The whole area was architecturally and aesthetically perfect, something more characteristic of Paris than of any other metropolis on the planet.

7.

Odile was gushing about Place Dauphine, so Mathilde concluded the girl had a cultivated taste and a keen eye for photographic details. However, afraid to appear insincere, she did not praise her, not yet. Mathilde was aware she was not behaving naturally and wondered about the cause. Soon she admitted that Célestin had become too attractive as a man for her to risk his daughter's disapproval.

At Place Dauphine, they entered a bistro of Mathilde's choice: "It's the most classic and stylish and the least smoky." Neither adult smoked, but she mentioned the tobacco fumes because of the child. Again she reprimanded herself: Is she being overly attentive? Is he conscious of her insecurity? Is he comparing her to...

Unaware of Mathilde's feelings, father and daughter enjoyed the bistro's decor and the old, masterfully framed photographs of Pont Neuf and Place Dauphine from the nineteenth century. Célestin ordered freshly squeezed orange juice for Odile and Kir Royale for Mathilde and himself. That was a dark-red cocktail consisting of first-class, authentic, *très sec* Champagne and *crème de cassis*—the black currants grown in the environs of the rich old city of Dijon in Burgundy. When the Kir arrived in the customary flute glasses, the trio celebrated their meeting in Paris by raising them. A vague question crossed Odile's precociously astute mind: "Did madame Mathilde and Papa look at each other too long when clinking their glasses?"

Mathilde resumed her attempts to befriend the girl by mentioning something amusing. "There's another famous nosy man: This one is a private detective by the name of Hercule Poirot. Have you ever read a novel with him in the main role?" "No, I haven't. Is he as stout and strong as Inspector Maigret?" "Oh, no, he's quite different, although he's also sly and likes to eat, including some strange specialties. Usually, he wears a white suit and carries a fashionable walking stick. This bizarre personage was created by the English writer Agatha Christie and appears in some forty novels of hers. He's a Walloon Belgian and makes mistakes in English typical of us French speakers. They are funny to English ears. I won't say anything about how droll English people sound when trying to speak French.

"*Ma chère fille*, I'm telling you all this because maybe even your papa doesn't know that monsieur Poirot's favorite drink is the one he and I are drinking right now. Very likely, Mrs. Agatha liked to imbibe it herself!" Célestin guffawed and thus signaled to Odile she could be all smiles. Encouraged, Mathilde went on: "Georges Simenon is still alive, he must be around eighty, and Agatha Christie lived into her eighty-fifth year—she passed away recently. Together, they filled our entire century with their novels, Georges with almost five hundred, and Agatha with close to seventy. They made the lives of countless readers around the world a little happier with their descriptions of cops and robbers."

"You said it well, Mathilde. I've never looked down on those novels—neither as a reader nor as a person. And in Odile's education, I've tried to open her eyes to the most diverse books, paintings, sculptures, and music," said Célestin dreamily, and then, rousing himself, continued: "*Alors, ma mignonne*, thanks to Mathilde's little Hercule, we've forgotten all about Maigret and Ducrau in Bar Tabac on Pont Neuf." Odile had indeed forgotten the sad bar, and although her father reminded her, she realized she could by that time view the fictitious suicide from a greater distance: She felt less and understood more. "Perhaps his reminder wasn't accidental," thought Mathilde. "How well he knows his little girl... he also praised me a little."

Meanwhile, Célestin's attention was drawn to an excellent painting hanging prominently in the bistro. In a sophisticated impressionist manner, it represented Pont Neuf glimmering in a winter sunset, like one they might witness. The painting was done from a spot on the right bank of the Seine, upstream from the Louvre. He got up, apologized to Mathilde, and walked with Odile to the painting. They studied it for some time. The signature was a barely legible "H.G." He explained where the painter must have stood with his easel and palette. A waiter approached, delighted to become involved: "That was painted before my time by an artist from this area—and I've worked here for thirty-five years. Our old *patron,* who recently passed away, told me the painter—his name was Hervé—had been a talented and well-educated artist but became a clochard and 'lodged' nearby under Pont Neuf. The *vieux patron* admitted he'd paid Hervé only a handful of *sou* for the painting and had not allowed him to sit in the bistro—he... he stank. *Excusez-moi Madame et Monsieur, excusez-moi jeune Mademoiselle.*" He bowed to all of them.

"On one occasion only a few days before his death, while staring long at the painting, the patron said to me: '*Mon vieux Gaston,* I treated Hervé badly! That's one of the many dishonorable things I've done in my life. *Par exemple...*' The rest isn't of interest to you—people confess when death is near, mostly to waiters, bartenders, and barbers."

Gaston tried to leave—he remembered his old boss and became dispirited, but Mathilde stopped him: "*Attendez, Monsieur* Gaston. I sometimes come here in the morning when the weather is sunny to read the newspapers. I always sit on the terrace and never order Kir Royale. So I know you, but you don't know me," she smiled, "because I'm usually without makeup to be imperceptible. But please listen to what I'll say to my friends about Hervé. You may want to know it, and your patron probably did."

Mathilde turned to Célestin: "This picture was painted by Hervé Gautier. He was a scion of an old family from the deepest south of France, under the Pyrenees. His great-great-grandfather was our distinguished writer Théophile Gautier. He studied art in Limoges. Before he died, Hervé had paintings hanging in reputable Paris galleries, all quickly bought up after his disappearance... without a trace. Not a single sou went to his family, nor did anyone try to find them. So what happened? Killed himself, and the clochards threw him in the river so they wouldn't be accused? Jumped into the river, sober or drunk, some dark night—or on a beautiful Paris spring morning? Our revered Seine absorbed him."

Odile, Célestin, and Gaston gaped at her with a mixture of horror and admiration. Mathilde said to the girl: "Well, *chérie,* again you are hearing about terrible things, but life is often sad and has always been, including in the heart of Paris. You were born, my dear, in Koblenz, but France is your country through your papa, and Paris is your city—one that has often, very often, been bloody. Unfortunately, it will always be." Mathilde did not restrain herself anymore: She lifted Odile and while hugging her felt the girl's tears on her cheek.

8.

Gaston hospitably brought more drinks and the *gâteau Opéra* for Odile as a *cadeau de la maison*. Mathilde opened up and spoke to Célestin in faultless German: "When I met Patrizia and you in Koblenz, I was on my way to Hamburg. There I spent several years intensively studying German language and literature. Afterward, I spent three more years in Germany—at the Munich Academy of Fine Arts. My parents supported me generously, sending me more money than I needed. For additional pocket money, I was translating German texts about art into French, including a book about the Munich painters' circle *Der Blaue Reiter* for the French publisher Gallimard."

Célestin responded, also in German: "Wonderful. We'll buy that book today. I'm fond of those painters from the beginning of the century. I love Kandinskiy's *Blue Rider*—on a white horse!—and even more Franz Marc's *Blue Horse*. You'll see, *Schatz*, how pretty is the little horsie."

"A blue horsie? Really? Blue, blue?" she asked, eyes shining with excitement. Mathilde told her: "The horse is young, just a foal. And the color? Well, his flanks are dark blue, kind of in a shade, and his chest is pale blue, in full sunshine. You'll like it." She added: "Gallimard has a store on Boulevard Raspail, but I'll gladly give one of the copies I still have to Odile so she can look at the blue horsie before she goes to sleep." The girl often thought of her loyal Pasha before falling asleep and sometimes dreamed of her but did not think she should mention it.

Languages, art, horses—Célestin and Odile found much in

common with Mathilde. She went on: "Back in France, I spent five or six months with my parents. I regularly painted *en plein air* using watercolors, tempera, even oils. The gorgeous landscapes along the Garonne were my motifs. Then I moved to Paris to my present address. My parents owned the place, but I bought new furniture and modernized the kitchen and bathrooms."

After they returned to the apartment, Odile, curious, asked Mathilde to show them her paintings, and Célestin joined the request: "Are they on the walls here? I saw only some rooms." In truth, he had seen the entire apartment, not noticing any work that could be Mathilde's. She hesitated and finally responded with a touch of melancholy: "I have to disappoint you. I don't show my paintings to anyone—no one! I'm still searching for... I'm not sure what. To be original in painting now is more difficult even than attaining originality in contemporary serious music. After the genius painters of this century, what new is there to say? Maybe I lack talent and am condemned to tinkering forever with boring art theories and criticism.

"There's not a single painting of mine in the apartment. I don't want to look at them and feel despair. Most are locked in the attic. So when there's a storm, the roof will leak and they'll be destroyed, ha, ha. But I'll share a secret with you. Some of my paintings are exhibited in one of the small galleries off Boulevard Saint-Germain. The signature and date are in my hand, but there's no name and the surname is fake. The gallerist knows my real name and surname, but he's not allowed, by a formal contract, to reveal them to potential buyers. He says: 'From Paris, around thirty-five years old.' The rascal admits that when he senses a client's particular proclivity, he says instead: 'A young pretty lady painter, *Parisienne*.' Well... Yes, the paintings are for sale and do get sold. Occasionally, the price is surprisingly high. I receive forty percent of the amount the buyer pays. I don't know if the gallerist is cheating and don't care."

Pondering it all, Célestin asked: "Have you ever revealed to the gallerist the reasons for hiding your identity from buyers?" Mathilde smiled drily: "No, I haven't—and he's not snoopy.

Perhaps he imagines I have a conceited, self-important, *grand bourgeois* person for a husband." She continued the self-ridicule: "And monsieur LeClercq doesn't appreciate that his precious *épouse*, madame LeClercq—for whom he buys everything desired by her frivolous, pampered mind—sells trite little pictures in second-rate galleries."

9.

The wind of the previous evening had calmed down, but the weather was bleak and chilly as they strolled to Pont Neuf again the following day. Nothing could, however, spoil the extraordinary view from the enchanting bridge downriver—to the Louvre, the pedestrian Pont des Arts, and the Eiffel Tower. As they were slowly crossing, Célestin remembered the article he had read at their hotel on Île Saint-Louis about the bizarre Bulgarian artist Christo Javacheff, who succeeded in wrapping diverse objects. He recalled that while reading, he felt certain the bureaucrats running Metz would never permit Christo to wrap an elegant Moselle bridge, let alone the magnificent cathedral. Inhabitants of his native city would first be bewildered and then horrified, while the media would begin by mocking and sneering, and end with ugly insults. Besides, the impertinent pseudo-artist was from the Balkans, a Bulgarian, who outrageously dared to call himself Christo!

"All right, but what would happen here in Paris," Célestin conjured up a wild hypothesis, "in this global sovereign of cosmopolitanism and openness to the craziest novelties, if the selfsame Christo were to seek permission to wrap up pillars and arches of this glorious bridge on which we are walking? After all, impressionism and cubism were not accepted without resistance, although in the end, they became dominant. But this? This is the most famous bridge in Paris. To allow the wild foreigner to swathe it like a parcel?"

He went on musing: "Yes, there was the Eiffel Tower, somewhat comparable in the initial outrageousness and obvious uselessness—and, moreover, planned to be permanent! But such an idea could curry favor with both the bourgeoisie and the ordinary people living in that epoch because of their common desire for 'progress.' Yeah, it was going to be monstrous, but certainly a great engineering achievement—a tall, nay colossal, structured pile of iron. Besides, Gustave Eiffel, despite his German surname, was a homegrown engineer from Dijon, who had been building graceful bridges and viaducts around France. And the grotesque tower of his might have been reasonably expected to astonish the whole world at the Universal Exposition in Paris in 1889.

"And Christo? What would he accomplish by wrapping the bridge or parts of it?" Célestin generated an internal grin, remembering that after thinking about the magazine article, he had reached a possible explanation for Christo's fearless artistic act: Make something very familiar new! By the seemingly meaningless wrapping of something well-known and long existing, without changing its bona fide shape, one could renew the unabashed admiration many Parisians had once felt—but which the passage of time had gradually changed into a *blasé* tolerance if not boredom.

Beyond the far end of Pont Neuf, on the Rive Droite, he told Mathilde what he had read about Christo. "You're asking me if I've heard of Christo Javacheff? You're really puzzling," she cried out. Well, he thought, at least I am not a crude fellow who is traipsing with a young daughter through China, Mongolia, and Siberia rather than being busy with the fashionable novelties in European capitals. Mathilde went on: "*Tout-Paris* has been buzzing about Christo for the last five years. The Las Vegas bookies, I mean it, have posted betting odds on whether or not Jacques Chirac, the Mayor of Paris, would allow Christo to wrap up this bridge, you understand, this very bridge—and all of it." Gesticulating, he responded excitedly to Mathilde: "*Vraiment incroyable!* Is that possible? You won't believe me, but I've been wondering just now: What would happen if Christo wished to wrap no less than Pont Neuf?"

Mathilde exclaimed: "Now you've truly amazed me! Instead of being a provincial conservative from Lorraine, you've succeeded not only in rejecting the notion that Christo is an ordinary charlatan and the people who might give him permission senile old goats but in miraculously divining that he would want to wrap this particular bridge." Célestin retorted: "Even while praising, you underrate me. Let me tell you why I think Christo may be doing what he's doing and why this bridge is his target."

Having listened carefully to the detailed explanation, Mathilde apologized, saying his conjecture about Christo's artistic intentions was the most inventive she had heard and that it also accounted rationally for ordinary people's attraction to the previous wrappings. Christo himself, she added, talked about his works in abstruse terms—sheer arcane esoterica that no one objective and informed, not even she, after her comprehensive study of theory, could understand, let alone accept.

Célestin took his daughter's neglected hand: "No big deal, she knows she's deeply loved." When they returned frozen to the apartment, Mathilde led the girl to the kitchen to prepare hot chocolate. At the ellipsoid dining table, an equilateral triangle was formed. Célestin, attuned to details others missed, and Odile, who shared many of his traits, realized they were not sitting as they habitually would, close together and facing the third person. Even so, the atmosphere was relaxed.

After Odile went to her room, he pointed at the ceiling: "So, that's where your canvases are, in the attic." Mathilde looked at him seriously: "Yes, and we won't talk about it anymore. I have enough money to live well and don't care about becoming famous. I don't want any sponsor. And I don't want a husband, either rich or poor. One of these days, I'll retire from the Paris neuroses to the peace of my parents' vineyards. I've known all about grapevine since childhood. Sometimes the stress here gets to me."

"She is an intelligent woman and beautiful," thought Célestin, looking at her dispassionately. "Physically, Olya and Mathilde both have lovely, delicate facial features, hair of almost identical chestnut color, slender bodies, fine hands, and... yes, high breasts. Mentally, however, the contrast between them is stark. Mathilde is bitter and unfulfilled despite, or because of, a comfortable life, whereas Olya has been imprisoned for her idealistic beliefs and for courageously loving me. How dare I compare them so coldly?"

He sighed, then requested: "Tell me about Christo's project." Mathilde had much to say: "I think his wrapping of our breathtaking bridge, including the precious old lanterns, will indeed happen in three or four years—after Chirac has gained courage by winning the next election for Mayor of Paris. Christo is convincing when he appears in front of the city and state committees, his nebulousness and phantasms notwithstanding. That level of decision-making has already been passed successfully. Incidentally, his wife is much more persuasive, even irresistible, to the local bureaucrats. She is *une madame française, noble et très charmante*, with a father who is a general in the army. Still, in art terms, she's a complete ignoramus—but one who knows how to bluff. Christo wants to wrap both wings of the bridge and all of its twelve arches—five to Rive Gauche and seven to Droite. Every Paris pupil knows it before the age of ten. Maybe you also knew it as an *écolier* in Metz."

"I did, as a young child, thanks to Grandpa, whereas you, in Cadillac? Metz is a metropolis compared to your village!" came the repartee. He said it teasingly and then asked: "But what will happen with those magical lanterns on the bridge?" "Christo was repeatedly questioned in the committee meetings," she answered, "and promised he would personally supervise that each of the forty-four lanterns was individually wrapped. Such devotion to Paris brought many aestheticians to his side: The Bulgarian visionary, or brave lunatic, would not wrap the lanterns carelessly together with the bridge."

"What an uncanny joke, this whole project. But it could end up being interesting, aesthetically gorgeous, and amusing," thought Célestin. "Mathilde, one basic question is the color of the wrapping material, and the other, how will it feel to the touch— the bridge from afar and the bridge intimately close." Mathilde replied: "This will not satisfy you, but the brochures I have received from the City of Paris and the Sixième say literally this:

'The wrapping material will be the color of golden sandstone and silky in appearance.' Tomorrow, I'll show you the color of chalk on a canvas and how it looks when a small layer of gold paint is delicately added. And the touch? That'll be yours to imagine."

The next day, the Paris sky acquired the blue of early winter. Mathilde sent Odile to the bakery at № 10 to buy croissants and brioches. In Paris bakeries, the salespeople were accustomed to the children of lazy neighbors, some as young as five or six, doing the morning shopping. Odile was pleased with her purchase and cheerfully helped Mathilde set the table. She saw herself as a responsible girl in whom *Tante* Mathilde had confidence.

During breakfast, the conversation continued about Christo's project's political aspects. "It's typical," Mathilde said, "that the demagogue Chirac insists in the newspapers Christo must negotiate with the clochards who live under Pont Neuf on Rive Gauche, while not allowing any clochards under the bridge on Rive Droite, which is close to the Louvre and the silk-stocking rue de Rivoli."

They talked more about clochards, and Odile was long-winded about the topic—her information drawn from Maigret. Mathilde and Célestin exchanged looks: Will you or should I? He began patiently: "*Mon ange, écoute.* Maigret doesn't extol the clochards, so you shouldn't either. Many are good people, but some are far from it. Each is defending his nest under a bridge at all costs, often violently. *Tu comprends?* Many are drunkards, which makes it impossible for them to be kind to their families, or turns them into dangerous criminals. It would be better, *ma chère fille*, if you insist on having a hero in the world of crime, to develop an affection for Hercule Poirot, Mathilde's funny Belgian. Or to return to books we read together in China and Russia—some will appear in your exams in Metz in the coming years."

10.

Later, Odile had the chance to be alone with Mathilde, who guided her to a sofa: "What's the problem, *chérie?* I see something is troubling you." "Well, you know I've never seen *Maman* except in photos. And everything I know about her, Papa has told me. He adored *Maman*, and I love him incredibly much. You don't know how good he is—always just and kind to everyone... Dear Tante Mathilde, you knew *Maman* in Koblenz before I was born, so I wanted to ask you to tell me—something, anything, about her. Maybe things *mon cher Papa* doesn't know or doesn't remember or doesn't wish to tell me. Excuse me, please, for bothering you." She broke down.

"*Mon Dieu*, what a sensitive child. I'd give a lot for her to be mine," thought Mathilde. She did not know what to say but had to say something. "Odile, *chérie*, I understand you but can't help you. I knew Patrizia for only about a week in Koblenz. We were in some ways similar—in age, appearance, even our eyes were similar. And in our views on many things in life. Two or three times we walked arm in arm along the Moselle. I think we were sincere with each other. I can tell you one thing: Your mother was a happy woman. She adored your papa! He is a wonderful man and you'll never be alone or unhappy while he's alive. Very few little girls are so lucky."

11.

After an hour of effort, Célestin reached Olya's mother in Kazan on the phone. They spoke Russian, and both were in tears. It was clear Mrs. Olga did not blame him or hate him. An enormous weight was lifted from his heart, yet guilt and self-contempt remained. In a frayed voice, she said: "Olya is in prison. They refuse to tell me where. I don't know if there was a court hearing, what she has been accused of, or whether she has been sentenced. I heard other people were arrested in the same *chistka*, the same purge. I spoke to her only once on the phone, briefly. She told me that if Tino succeeds in calling, to tell him she loves him very much..." The line was broken.

In the late morning, the pair went by taxi to the Soviet Consulate on Boulevard Lannes, near Bois de Boulogne. To the morose official, Célestin submitted a written request that Dinara

Alimova Naratovna be released from prison and given an exit visa for travel to Metz in France for the purpose of marriage. "With whom?" asked the man curtly. "With me," the petitioner answered icily.

They returned by metro to the area near Mathilde's apartment, getting off at Saint-Germain-des-Prés, next to the famous church. The café-restaurant Les Deux Magots was across the street, and they went in. Odile noticed her papa was in a rare dour mood and quietly studied the sophisticated café. Célestin was indeed sullen, but nevertheless explained: "The church over there is old and well worth visiting. As for this café, it's often called 'mythical' or given some other over-the-top appellation by snobs—out of worship of the resident intellectuals. A few deserve high regard, but many are wannabes, shallow, intellectualizing men. Women too."

He calmed down with the help of tea. "About the consulate, please, *ma douce*, don't ask me anything. We did what we could to release our Olya from prison. But I did a terrible job, I was too arrogant... because I've become more and more furious about them putting an innocent woman in a horrendous prison. And while I was filling out the forms, I made important decisions on the spot. If they release Olya and let her come to France, and if she wishes, I'll marry her. You'll have a young mother. Please don't ask me anything now. I'm too much on edge. I know you love Olya, and she loves you. Otherwise, I wouldn't have signed those papers."

Odile was sorry Papa was tense and depressed, refusing to explain anything. Confused about what to think and feel, she mumbled inwardly: "Yes, I love Olya deeply. But that she should, all of a sudden, become my mother? Just like that? And what happened with Auntie Mathilde?"

Mathilde was shocked even more by the news of Célestin's plan to marry. While the girl napped after their late lunch—her sleep agitated, not a child's—the adults talked in the sitting room. "During the last few days we got to know each other a little, so I'm taking the liberty of asking whether you really want to marry some Russian woman, this Olya? Of course, I'm uncomfortable questioning it. I'm not your sister nor your guardian; in fact, I'm almost nothing to you. But I'm a mature woman who wishes you well."

Célestin seldom got angry, but it happened. He almost jumped from the armchair: "So, that's how things stand! My daughter has become *une bavarde*, a chatterbox, which she has never been. Mathilde, I'm not accusing you, but listen: Olya is not 'some Russian woman' but a stunning, educated, young person. We love each other very much. She loves Odile dearly and is loved by her in return. But I wonder why only until today? For the first time, I'm ashamed of my daughter."

He nervously paced. Mathilde comprehended she had hurt something vulnerable in him. A crucial *faux pas* had been made, but she was not yet able to admit the dreadful miscalculation. "We were... just chatting." Then, going on a counteroffensive, she asked: "Is it true what I sensed that you're again planning to travel far with Odile?" Célestin sat down. It was not in his nature to remain upset for long, especially with his daughter: "Yes, it's true. We'll travel to Israel."

Mathilde thus got another shock, albeit a mixed one. The Russian woman could not be part of the plan! They were quiet before Mathilde's cannonade: "To Israel? With your little daughter? Are you conscious of where you're going and what you're doing? You must know what happened in Munich during those Olympic Games. Before only—only eight years! Many Israeli sportsmen were killed by Arab terrorists. And then, more recently, only three or four years ago, when the Air France plane full of Jews was hijacked by Arabs and taken somewhere in Africa. You want to take a little child to Israel, to that horribly dangerous country? You've recently had China, Russia, and our Paris, *Ville-Lumière*. And you'll soon have your manor by the gorgeous Moselle. But nothing is enough for you! You must risk two lives. Don't do it, I'm speaking as a friend." She stopped short of calling him an irresponsible father: Even in her anger, she knew the accusation would be laughable.

Her alleged worry failed to stir him. Beneath each chastisement, he recognized a selfish motive, one she would never acknowledge. So he replied calmly: "Much of what you said is only partially correct. Unlike you, I am aware of the details of those events. The horrid ones are not relevant to us. What you don't understand is that Paris, for example, is on a per-event and per-capita basis more dangerous than Tel Aviv and Jerusalem. But even if it weren't so, I would choose to go to Israel, naturally with Odile. I took everything into account. We certainly won't fly with Air France but with Israeli El Al, a much safer option. Israelis and their Mossad know who they are dealing with. And we'll fly from Munich airport, the safest in Europe with regard to Arab terrorism."

She did not know what to say, so he went on: "Odile has only one parent. You shouldn't find it odd that I wish, with all my heart, to develop in her some views and emotions seated deep in me. To see and feel the world! It's been many years since I've wanted to visit Israel, the Holy Land for the three monotheistic religions. A unique country. The magnificent city of Jerusalem: City of the human race. I'd give a lot that my parents weren't killed and could take me to Jerusalem when I was Odile's age. I'd know how to appreciate it. And I'm sure so will my daughter. She still doesn't know about our trip. Please don't mention it to her. I'd like to do it myself all at once or by the spoonful—as I'll one day do with her listening to Wagner's operas."

Making it clear the topics of Olya and Israel were exhausted, Célestin switched to a conciliatory tone: "Let's calm down and speak about the past. You know a great deal about me, whereas I know almost nothing about you. Tell me about your years in Hamburg and Munich."

12.

He moved to an armchair while Mathilde slowly walked around the room. Sometimes she would stand looking out the window and speak in a monotonous drone. "In Hamburg, I was married to someone for a year and a half. Christophe was a Frenchman from Nantes, the same age as I, from a wealthy, conservative family. He was ambitious, studied ship construction and economics, and wanted to acquire an heir as soon as possible. His father was probably behind it. Christophe was a decent man, everybody liked him, but I found him, well... boring. We parted without quarrels. His family still sends me Christmas cards.

"When I moved to Munich, the first year was difficult. I couldn't understand why I was accepted at the Academy of Fine Art, an eminent school: Why me, with my modest body of work? I doubted my talent, as I do still. I was lonely, didn't know anyone. The students at the Academy were conceited, full of themselves. As for the city—the Bavarian mentality is different from mine. I didn't like the local food, and *Bayerisch* differs a lot from the *Plattdeutsch* dialect of Hamburg. But after some six or seven months, I got to know a group of young painters of both sexes. They gathered every evening in an old inn, which had been, at the beginning of the century, the favorite meeting place of Kandinskiy and others from the 'Blue Rider' circle—you and I talked about it. A fabulous expressionist painting by Aleksey von Yavlyenskiy from that group was hanging on the wall. Oh, I must remember to give a copy of my book to Odile." Mathilde walked to the bookshelves and took one out. From afar, she showed him the front cover, and he recognized Kandinskiy's *Blue Rider*.

"Because you love Kandinskiy, maybe you know he was buried in 1944 here in Paris, in the exquisite Russian Cathedral of Saint Aleksandr Nevskiy in the Eighth arrondissement." "I didn't know," he answered, "but Odile and I learned in Moscow that Tsar Aleksandr II endowed the cathedral and that Shalyapin was buried there." Mathilde exclaimed: "And I wasn't aware of that! But I'm going to shock you: In the cathedral in 1918, Picasso married Olga Hohlova, and the witnesses were Cocteau and Apollinaire. One deep believer next to another, ha, ha."

She placed the book on the table. "I'll write a few words and give it to Odile when she wakes up... Where did I stop? Yes, painters at the inn were not stuck-up and haughty. Every single one had either been refused admission or thrown out. So they claimed to despise the Academy and called themselves avant-garde. They found me acceptable, perhaps because I was French but more likely—let's be honest—because of my appearance. All these men and women were talented to some extent, but I was convinced a new Kandinskiy or Gabriele Münter would not be found among them. Did you know she was an informal student of Kandinskiy? And his lover, they lived together.

"There also appeared people who had nothing to do with art but were flattered to be the painters' bohemian buddies. Every evening, there was drinking, smoking, and cocaine. One stayed late, and there was sex. If you expect me to say I had nothing to do with any such thing, that I was unsullied, pure as a lily—you won't hear it. I participated in all the promiscuity as much as other women who came there. I didn't have a steady boyfriend: The custom was to be passed from bed to bed. I needed a year to extricate myself from this scene and was saved by a middle-aged lady professor of sculpture at the Academy to whom I confided before an imminent collapse. So I did earn the diploma, though not with high marks. Such are the highlights of my years in Germany about which you should know."

They were silent for a long time. The winter day was ending. Not a sound could be heard from Odile. Mathilde walked around the room lighting a few lamps while Célestin looked through her collection of records. He took one out, the first album of the Canadian songwriter Leonard Cohen from 1967. "I hope you have nothing against listening to Cohen's 'Suzanne.' When I heard it the first time, Patrizia and I were sitting in a small bar in Cologne, it would've been 1971. A young American woman with long hair sang it with feeling, her guitar barely audible." Mathilde thought a moment: "Yes, that sad song is dear to me also, please play it." He placed the needle on the record, and they heard Cohen's strange, dark voice:

Suzanne takes you down to her place near the river
You can hear the boats go by, you can spend the night forever

*And you know that she's half-crazy but that's why you
want to be there
And she feeds you tea and oranges that come all the way
from China
And just when you mean to tell her that you have no love
to give her...*

Célestin returned to his armchair and appraised what he had heard from Mathilde while listening to the music. "Yes," he thought, "she slept with who knows how many men—drunk, on drugs, out of habit, certainly lovelessly. Why should that be better or more acceptable than what Olya—feeling guilty and disgusted—did to feed her loved ones?" True, he did not like the idea of judging anyone's morality. "At least not openly and publicly," he castigated himself, "for I'm certainly doing it privately!"

Later that evening, they looked through the book Mathilde had translated from German. The girl loved the gift and the warm words "M" had written for her in French and German. He could not find the heart to mention Olya and admonish Odile for her talkativeness—her telling Mathilde about the Soviet Consulate and his possible marriage to Olya. It will have to wait for another day.

In contrast, he was expeditious in taking irrevocable action about something he had long contemplated. A single glance at Odile's room vouched that she could pack up swiftly. "*Mon ange,* we'll leave on a long trip the day after tomorrow. We'll travel to Munich by train and from there fly to Israel. Believe me, you'll enjoy it enormously! I'm going to let Mathilde know. And you, *ma petite sirène,* get ready for bed, I'll come back for a goodnight kiss." He left before she had time to open her mouth.

Mathilde tried to receive the news calmly, as he added: "I realize you and Odile have grown on each other, but please don't sadden her before our departure." The icy response was: "I'll behave as you wish." When he returned to Odile's room, she ran out of the toilet in her long pink nightgown and jumped into bed, pulling the cover to her chin. Her silky hair spilled out on the tiny pillow. Célestin sat on the edge of the bed, waiting. She did not cry, but her lips trembled. In a little voice pitched higher than usual, she said softly: "*Cher Papounet*, can we please, please, first go home to Metz so we can greet Pasha and walk a little in our fields and by the Moselle? And then we can continue our trip." How could he refuse?

During the trio's next morning stroll, Mathilde unveiled: "If Christo manages to wrap this bridge, it'll stay open during the exhibition but only for pedestrians. Macho Paris joggers, who have eagerly embraced the American craze, can't wait to run on the 'silky material the color of gilt sandstone.' Female joggers are still rare here; true *Parisiennes* don't like to wear ugly sneakers and be sweaty in front of onlookers!"

* * *

Early the following day, at № 12, rue de Buci, there were tears in the eyes of Odile and Mathilde, while Célestin held back. He hugged their hostess half-formally and thanked her for the generous hospitality, but requested that she not see them off at Gare de l'Est. It was hard for Mathilde to accept...

Alone in a comfortable train compartment, they talked casually about the events in Paris, but he then addressed a serious topic. "*Mon coeur*, you're growing and maturing fast, a wonderful sight! But maybe it's all happening too quickly for you to understand that your behavior affects lives other than yours, including mine and our Olya's. Regardless of my enormous love, you can't always be the only person in my life. You disclosed my private affairs to Mathilde, after which she nastily denigrated Olya. I know Mathilde was kind to you, and I'm certain you didn't think you were doing anything wrong, but still... You should've talked to me first and remembered how much you loved Olya."

Her eyes became huge and filled with tears. "I do love her very much!" she wept. He let her cry. After several minutes, she snuggled next to him, mumbling: "Papa, *cher Papa*, are you annoyed with me?" He reassured her: "I'm not, *ma douce*, far from it, but you're not a tiny child anymore, and I had to tell you. You see, it's normal for children to take more responsibility on their shoulders year by year and care not just for their own but also their parents' well-being."

They were sitting embraced when he spoke again: "I want to stress something else in your 'chat' with Mathilde, as she called it: Loyalty. You understand? Faithfulness, fidelity, loyalty—devotion! For example, we're now traveling to Metz because of your devotion to Pasha: I didn't want us to return home at this time. I wished for us to travel to Israel, but understood your need. So I ask you: Where is your loyalty to Olya? Where's the love you showed her so often? Where's the sorrow she's languishing in prison? And where's the respect for my love for Olya that I loudly announced even at the Soviet Consulate?"

He sensed the scolding was going too far and would be onerous for her to endure, but believed that essential things needed to be said, even to a child. "Mathilde won you over, and then misused the acquired trust and your innocent years to find out private things about me. It happened because—I don't know how to say it—because she seems to have unreciprocated, unwelcome feelings for me: I love only Olya! That's faithfulness."

Odile thought and thought, sometimes tightly grabbing her father and occasionally sobbing and whimpering. In the end, she spluttered: "I was very naughty! I love, love our Olya!" They made peace. It was the first of the unpleasant lectures Célestin would give his daughter in the coming years—lessons plentiful in every human being's life.

Three hours later, when they found themselves ensconced at their manor near Metz, it seemed Mathilde had been left far in space and time.

PART FOUR

Odile's First Flirt

1.

After dinner, father and daughter sat peacefully in their spacious drawing room, the huge fireplace ablaze. Célestin was listening with closed eyes to Schubert's sonatas for piano: *"Mon Dieu,* how this Svyatoslav Richter plays!" Odile sat reading on the thick Persian carpet, leaning against her father's legs.

He sighed before speaking. The voice was calm but too serious, it seemed to her: *"Alors, ma chère fille,* we've arrived home. You've hugged and groomed your Pasha. How pleased she must have been to feel your old brush on her flanks. I had a firm plan for us to leave again in about a week. That would've been for my soul—and yours. Also, we might travel not straight to Israel but first to Berlin, West Berlin. You see, while we were away, some letters arrived from my friends who live there. A few were born there, while others moved to West Berlin as young men to avoid the compulsory military service in West Germany. Berlin would be—and, by Jove, it will be—yet another magical city for you. For me, it would renew memories from 1967 when I was only twenty-three, five years before you were born." He sighed again, and she sensed more news was coming.

"However, some important things have changed. Most of the missives I received have to do with tasks for me on the estate and in the city, but some are about you. The school says you need the annual medical checkup with Dr. Adele Beaufort—you've always liked her. After the New Year, they'll give you new study materials, and on the tenth of February, you are scheduled to take oral and written exams. The school Principal Gaubert is a fine, experienced man. *Mon ange,* you're privileged, mostly because you have top marks. The school has always been considerate toward us, but it's held responsible for each pupil. The principal's performance is overseen by the bureaucrats at the Ministry of Education in Paris. Please don't look sad. We'll be here longer, so you'll spend more time with Pasha and your classmates. And after you've successfully passed all the exams, you and I will leave in mid-February for Berlin and Israel."

Before she was able to say anything, Papa lifted her from the floor and sat her in his lap, hugging her. She felt so content she could purr. The news was, after all, not bad. Examinations were always easy. She would ride Pasha and play with her girlfriends. After a snowfall, the fields, hillocks, and woods would be majestically white. Finally, she thought: "Berlin and Papa's friends will wait for us, and the trip will make *mon cher Papounet* happy again!"

He readily admitted it was fortunate they returned to Metz. School duties were important, but so was Odile's love for Pasha. That early afternoon, as soon as they had arrived from the Metz train station, she went straight to the stable. Pasha greeted her by neighing, whinnying, nickering, and gentle tail-swishing. The girl loved her mare more than the fields and woods of her childhood. During their travels, she often remembered Pasha and would think of her whenever she saw a horse—living ones from trains and in bronze on equestrian statues.

Célestin was pulled from Metz by the entire magical world—a true dreamer. Suddenly remembering the poignant words Herman Melville had put in the mouth of Ishmael, he ascended the stairs to his study in twos. Near the end of Chapter 1 entitled "Loomings" of *Moby-Dick*, he found: "*But as for me, I am tormented with an everlasting itch for things remote. I love to sail forbidden seas, and land on barbarous coasts.*" Célestin knew Melville had written those words in the middle of the nineteenth century, but the writer's age at the time—thirty-two—was close to his.

A quite different reason for Célestin's wishing to travel far and wide was his mental exhaustion, a weariness growing over many years, which had its root in the painful memories of intimacy with Patrizia in Metz. The pain grew during the winter holidays when memories of their playing in the snow overwhelmed him. Still, he was pleased to make his daughter happy by returning before Christmas.

Winter ruled again in Lorraine but was much milder than the previous year. There was hardly any snow in December. The Moselle was free of ice and flowed violently, swollen almost to the arches of its splendid bridges. Father and daughter organized their life in the old way. The people who worked and lived on the estate—from the governess Frau Gerda, a German from Koblenz who had been brought by Patrizia, to the head maid and housekeeper Françoise, the cook Marie and her husband Gilles, the estate manager—were all entirely trustworthy, having spent decades with the family De Quernevelle. While her father took care of obligations in the city, the girl diligently studied and spent time in the stable and around the house. When Célestin would return home with a headache acquired in meetings with bankers and city bureaucrats, he would busy himself with gymnastics, showing some exercises to Odile. She had grown in height and strength during the previous year of travel and was able to mount Pasha without her father's help. He also did not need any longer to lead the horse with her on it. They rode bareback together almost every day through the winter fields and woods to the Moselle. Odile held Pasha by the mane more for pleasure than out of need.

Often they drove to Metz in their dark-blue Renault from Patrizia's time. Some details in the cabin were still hers, so he was reluctant to sell the car. "Papa, when will you teach me to be a *chauffeur*? I'll be careful," she entreated. "I'll buy a new car and teach you," monotonously responded Célestin, "when your feet reach the pedals." They swam in Metz's fifty-meter covered pool and sat in cafés with friends and their kids. Even when older than Odile, children faced with her serious, intelligent comportment sometimes behaved timidly. Her sincere eyes and open smile, however, invariably won them over.

Metz was an ancient, renowned, and affluent city but provincial in certain ways. True, an ostensibly Chinese restaurant was opened on a side street, but there was no trace of a Russian one.

Nevertheless, many citizens had heard gossip about the extraordinary travels of Célestin and Odile through the mysteries of distant Asia.

Whenever the weather permitted, they walked around the magnificent Cathedral Saint Étienne de Metz from the twelfth century, always admiring it as if they had never seen it before. On entering the superb edifice, they would be dazzled each time anew by an ocean of extraordinary *vitraux*, stained-glass windows—more of them than in any other cathedral in the world. Inconceivably high, perhaps forty-five meters far, the rib vaulting of the nave was magically suspended. On some occasions, the solemn, mysterious, crystal-pure, male voices resounded through the vast space: That was the monophonic, unaccompanied plainchant in Latin. Both Célestin and Odile, before she was seven, knew the Cathedral of Saint Stephen was the cradle of Gregorian chant.

And sometimes, regardless of all the differences, father and daughter thought of the churches in Russia: Those massive, forcibly shut in Moscow and Leningrad but also the touchingly modest, Siberian ones. She would whisper: "Why is Olya not here with us? We would show her all this and..." The girl would interrupt herself because she had matured enough to know it would be infantile to add "my Pasha." Her father would help: "And our friendly, tame Lorraine, our ancient city, and our Moselle—even when she's wild, like right now!"

Two days before Christmas, Odile hosted her girlfriends from school and the nearby estates. In her favorite pretty dress, she greeted them at the door while her father exchanged niceties with the parents who had driven their daughters. The young guests were nicely attired, perfumed, and coiffed. Gerda and Françoise, in their Sunday clothes and smart aprons, served juices and various tasty foods to the children. The little girls asked their hostess about her trip and entertained themselves with decorous games and music performances on the clarinet and flute; one girl even played a miniature violin. Since no boys had been invited, there was no unruly behavior, just a dainty party.

As they had been absent for so long, Célestin thought it politic to attend the traditional Christmas Midnight Mass in the cathedral. Metz was too small to be immune to gossip. They were already attracting unwanted attention because Odile, a motherless child, was not going to school regularly. In any case, they found the Mass moving and their beloved cathedral resplendent at night.

From time to time, he had friends over for first-class wine and cheese. They played chess and listened to Renaissance music. Couples were seldom among the guests because, when reciprocating the invitation, they typically tried to introduce to Célestin a marriage candidate of their choice.

Odile's ninth birthday, the 18th of January 1981, fell on a Sunday, so she invited a dozen girls and boys to come at eleven and stay for an elaborate lunch. Célestin hired several women to help Gerda, Marie, and Françoise in the kitchen and around the long dining table at which the guests were seated. The notion of the so-called "Swedish" self-service table did not exist in France at that time, nor would something so uncivilized be tolerated in the country of gourmands, even nine-year-olds. The lunch party was a success; Odile shone. She received many gifts, and it was obvious which were independently chosen by the guests and which by their parents.

Her father gave her presents dearest to her heart—a beautiful saddle and new riding boots. He said: "You'll never forget to ride a horse bareback—nor your bicycle—but the time has come to teach you to ride elegantly, which is misleadingly called the 'English' riding style. I can begin to teach you, but there are reliable instructors not far from us and..." She butted in, "I don't want any instructors other than you, *cher Papa!*"

On the 11th and 12th of February, Odile took the written and oral examinations for the fourth grade, passing them with flying colors. Her brilliant marks attracted attention even in town. Some fellow students envied her. For the girl and her father, it called for celebration, which in their case meant being able to travel again. On the eve of their departure for West Berlin, the 20th of February 1981, spring arrived—early and maybe deceptively. Célestin said: "Let's enjoy the sunshine, *ma tigresse*. I doubt it'll shine so brightly in Berlin. But what our Olya wouldn't give to see these green shoots and smell the first spring flowers?"

2.

In West Berlin, the pair had enviable accommodation in an apartment on Niedstrasse, near Breslauer Platz, in the Friedenau Quarter. They were guests of an old friend of Célestin's, Uwe Benz—an anti-Freudian clinical psychologist—and his wife Sigrid Klein who was an astrophysicist at the Max Planck Institute. They had twins of Odile's age, Sophia and Emil. The flat had to be sizable, as both Uwe and Sigrid needed a private study, and there was also a library. Emil joined Sophia in her bedroom, while Célestin and his daughter shared the boy's—in which a sofa bed from the library was also placed. The guests were received very warmly. Odile gave some typically French gifts to the twins, and Sophia did her best to help her feel at home.

Sigrid and Uwe prepared a lavish dinner for six. Unlike Célestin's domestic situation—with the child's governess, a cook, and maids—the Klein-Benz couple had no help. Three children in the kitchen only hindered the proceedings, but much more important to the adults was that the young ones got along well: There was a lot of gaiety. After dinner, the children went to bed without complaints, probably because they were uncertain about the reactions of the adults unfamiliar with their caprices. In their bed, Sophia and Emil benignly chattered about Odile. The adults remained for a long time at the dining table, discussing Peking, Mongolia, Baikal, and the beauties of Moscow and Leningrad— but also the gulags in the USSR.

Their attention was devoted to two specific problems, one major, the other minor. The big problem was the Berlin Wall and the possible unification of Germany. The solution to the small problem was equally unforeseeable: Would Sophia and Odile join forces against Emil, or would genes cause Sophia to help her twin brother resist another female factor in the house? They all laughed, but Célestin—as the most versatile prophet—realized the merriment should be uncomfortable, for in these two issues one faced the perhaps most significant problems of world politics and future relations between the sexes.

3.

The Wall, *die Berliner Mauer,* was certainly the most powerful symbol of Berlin of that epoch. For tourists from all over the world and Germans from distant parts of West Germany, it was a unique attraction, a sort of crazy horror show. For West Berliners, especially the numerous ones who had relatives on the east side, the Wall inflicted pain and caused hate and contempt. For East-Berliners, it summarized their daily confrontation with a monster with multiple tentacles. Therefore, already in the mid-morning of their second day in Berlin, Célestin took Odile to see the Wall and witness the terrifying essence of German dividedness—a violent, bloody rupture. For those tireless walkers, several kilometers from Friedenau to Kreuzberg were a trifle. What they reached was not the opulent Berlin but the menial workers' part of town by Templehof Airport.

The edge of Kreuzberg bordering East Berlin contained observation towers. Most sat at the end of neglected streets in which poor people lived, the majority of them Turks with lots of small children. Few women wore a head covering.

Suddenly, the Wall stood in front of them, and touching it, a simple wooden tower. There was no one else, an overwhelming quietude ruled: The Wall was a silent evil spirit. Célestin took his daughter by the hand, and they climbed the two short flights of stairs. From the top, an incredible view to the east opened. Right next to the Wall, numerous clumps of barbed wire were amassed. These were not haphazardly thrown about, he thought sourly, but assembled in an orderly "Germanic" manner. Behind that, one could see at least seventy meters of open space, a death strip emptied of even the tiniest bush and rock. Next came more clumps of barbed wire. And then, there was a row of ordinary houses where people had once lived, but soldiers with machine guns occupied them. Célestin knew that whoever entered the empty space would be shot to death by the law of the DDR, Deutsche Demokratische Republik.

Furious, he grasped Odile's little hand tightly: His feelings were similar to those he had experienced near Vyborg at the Soviet-Finnish border. However, at the Wall, his anger was mixed with *Weltschmerz*. He asked himself: "How is this possible?" Because of Patrizia, because of the proximity of Metz and Koblenz, and their link by the Moselle, he had always felt half-German— despite the awful war in which he had become an orphan. Even the death strip was his country! And those poor souls, who had been ruthlessly kicked out of their homes, were also his people. Tears ran down his face. He felt sick, ready to vomit, and clung to Odile to steady himself, while she, as if mesmerized, continued to stare at the unreal sight, the horror of which was evident even to a young child.

Breaking the silence, he murmured: "This monstrosity has been standing here since the 13th of August 1961. It prevents people who wish to come here from doing so—even for a brief visit to relatives. I first saw the Wall in 1967, a few years before I met Patrizia. A young woman from West Berlin by the name of Annerose—I had met her the year before during a ski holiday in Sinaia in Romania—brought me to an observation tower like this one. On that occasion too, I became almost physically ill when I saw the horrible spectacle. Now I feel even worse. Then, we all thought the Wall couldn't last much longer, it had been standing for six years. But another thirteen long years have passed since, and nothing has changed. For nineteen years, babies have been born and people have died behind this despicable wall standing in front of our noses."

He clumsily tried to reassure the girl: "Even though we stand fully exposed, there's no reason to fear those soldiers with guns. It's never happened that they took shots at the people standing atop observation towers—even, I've read, at those who had escaped from East Berlin. It would be contrary to international law and the laws of the GDR, the German Democratic Republic. What they do to people on their side... They do it because they can with impunity."

An hour later, when they were close to the historic Zoological Garden, she asked: "So what happened with your girlfriend, that Annerose?" He laughed because Odile sounded like Mathilde: "What a jealous busybody you've become! Don't worry, *mon chou*. At the time, your mother didn't exist in my life, nor did you and Olya. Annerose certainly won't jump out from some doorway to embrace me. It's an old tale." She pretended to sulk but then made a joke at herself.

4.

He wished to take his hosts, their children, and Odile to dinner at some interesting restaurant, but Sigrid told him she had made preparations for a meal, and it would be more convenient to eat at home. Before dinner, he called Walter Schönflug, his long-time friend, to propose a rendezvous for the following day. Walter was excited but said he was flying to Tokyo the next morning for a congress of linguists, specialists in Chinese, Japanese, and Korean. Could he come to collect Célestin that evening at ten so they would have a little time to chat at a cozy bar? He agreed without hesitation knowing his hosts would not object. "It's fine," said Sigrid. "We'll finish dinner long before ten, and the children are getting along splendidly." The girls were busy with an important project of theirs, so Odile had nothing against her papa's departure with a friend. "Hmm, the permission was rather casual," he chuckled.

Precisely at ten, in front of the house at Niedstrasse, Célestin and Walter firmly hugged each other, as they had done since their teenage years when Walter would come with his parents to Paris and Metz and Célestin to Berlin. Horses, linguistics, art, and a healthy curiosity about the entire world had kept them close.

Walter ushered his friend into a metallic-gray convertible and drove to a wine bar called Beiz, located just off the boulevard Kurfürstendamm—West-Berliners' cherished Kudamm. They talked until two in the morning. Walter had known Odile since she was in nappies and asked Célestin to stay in Berlin long enough, some ten days, until he returned from Tokyo and could see the girl again. The proud father happily agreed.

The German came from a wealthy conservative family and was half-right on the political spectrum. Still, he was an objective and just man. He spoke to Célestin about the "champagne left-wingers" at his Freie Universität in the Dahlem district of Berlin, notably in the department of "critical studies of anthropology." The professor who presided over the department was a neighbor of Walter's in the opulent residential quarter of Dahlem. He lived in an expensive house with a large garden, not inferior to the one Walter had inherited from his industrialist parents. "He compensates," laughed Walter, "by allowing some strange people to live in his cellar."

Their conversation was taking place only three years after the "German Autumn," the peak period of terrorist activities by the *Rote Armee Fraktion*. The RAF consisted of the Baader-Meinhof and other groups of communists, Maoists, and anarchists—"criminal bands" as the German and other Western newspapers called them. Although Walter and Célestin were strongly opposed to the methods of these groups, they agreed with the RAF about one thing: Numerous ex-Nazis occupied high posts in important sectors of West German politics, industry, and banking. Moreover, that was permitted by countries victorious on the Western Front— the USA and Britain.

After a while, the two friends had had enough of the discussion about German preoccupation with the hostile intentions of the Soviet Union, yet Célestin did not feel sufficiently strong mentally to address a private matter and speak to Walter calmly about Olya. Instead, they switched to their favorite subjects, music and theatre. "In Moscow, Odile and I heard some superbly played classical music, not only orchestral at the Bolyshoy and the Chaikovskiy Conservatory but also solo recitals in smaller halls. And imagine this—even in the heart of Siberia, in Irkutsk, on Lake Baikal, we heard brilliantly performed Bach's Suites for solo cello. Who played them but a lady called Olga Schiller, her surname written in the program in Russian Cyrillic, of course. Where do you think she was from? Well, from the Siberian city of Tomsk, of which you've probably never heard. And in Leningrad: magnificent concerts at the Rimskiy-Korsakov Conservatory." He abruptly stopped because he had painfully stung his heart by the sudden thought of Olya. He so much wished to speak about her to his bosom buddy but was not able to. About the prison, yes, he could; but about her past? No. Not yet.

"It's splendid," said Walter, "that you gave Odile the opportunity for such experiences already in her tender years. Now you have also encouraged me to visit at least Moscow, Leningrad, Kiev, Riga, and Tallinn in that stunning country." Célestin thought for a while and continued: "Yes, during our long trip, my daughter passed with honors several tests of maturity. One example is how she behaved when we went to the famous Novodevichiy Cemetery in Moscow; maybe you've heard of it—it's their Père-Lachaise. I'd wondered if she was old enough to be taken to a cemetery, worried she might become despondent or simply bored. Well, she did become very serious but was learning, visibly learning. She was amazed at how many composers, pianists, and violinists whose music she had heard in our home had been buried there: Shostakovich, Prokofiev, Skryabin, Kabalevskiy... And Nikolay Rubinshteyn, Leonid Kogan, David Oystrah. Hey, prima ballerina *assoluta* Galina Ulanova! Also, the people who, for now, don't mean much to her but are dear to you and me: I spoke about them as well—the painter Vladimir Tatlin and the extraordinary writers Gogol', Chehov, and Bulgakov. She listened carefully and joined me in visiting their tombstones."

Walter repeatedly nodded, excited by the list—if one can decently say that about the people no longer living and their graves. Then he asked: "We both value the theatre, yet you haven't mentioned any of the celebrated Russian directors like Stanislavskiy and Nemirovich-Danchenko. Are they also there?" "Yes, yes, I forgot, we did see their tombs and also Zhenya Vahtangov's—that's how Chehov and others called him as a young man, it's a diminutive of 'Evgeniy'."

Noticing Walter's smirk, Célestin laughed: "I didn't mean to be smug! I learned tons in one of the well-preserved rooms where Chehov lived in Moscow. However, I am proud of something: I've become comfortable with the Russian script and have acquired a command of both the literary and spoken language, even some slang—far more than is necessary for communication with doormen, waiters, and cabbies. For example, I'll have you know, the word for your smirk a moment ago is *uhmilka*." Despite that bit of humor, Célestin again felt a deep longing for Olya and shame that he was unable to talk about her.

"It's good you mentioned Zhenya and these other theatre greats," smiled Walter, "because otherwise, I would've perhaps forgotten to suggest that you attend with Odile a play at the Schaubühne—you know the theater not far from here on Kudamm at Lehniner Platz. I've not been there since they recently installed some completely new stage equipment. One hears it's technically the most advanced in Europe. Just now, they are doing a play by a Russian, Aleksandr Ostrovskiy, in German, of course. I'm not sure which play it is—he wrote more than fifty."

"*Vielen Dank, liebe* Walter for the recommendation. Tomorrow I'll return to Kudamm with Odile, for we need to find a hotel. No matter what Sigrid and Uwe say, it's out of the question to stay another ten days with these hospitable people. We'll also check the Schaubühne and buy tickets. Is Peter Stein still the chieftain there?"

Walter cried out: "But of course! He's been the boss for some ten years already, ruling with an iron fist. Some believe he's a genius director, but I'm not qualified to judge: Everybody is a genius or a legend these days. In any case, I bet a visiting director did the Ostrovskiy play. It's probably a comedy, which is not Stein's forte. Speaking of comedy, or farce, do you remember the scandal in Munich several years ago when Stein directed the play *Viet Nam*

Diskurs by Peter Weiss?" Célestin knew nothing about it, so Walter continued: "Stein aggressively insisted that all audience members contribute as much *Geld* as possible for the Viet Cong!"

They both laughed, but Célestin said: "To tell you the truth, I'm neither surprised nor shocked. That's child's play compared with the behavior of the Dada people sixty years ago. It would surprise me if Stein didn't do something like it. He needed first to build and then maintain the reputation of a righteous rebel. In our times, as you well know, it's far more courageous in many professions in the West to be against the Viet Cong and the RAF than to wholeheartedly support them. But listen, let's leave, it's almost two o'clock, and you're flying to Tokyo in a few hours. I'm grateful you devoted this precious time to me. We'll see each other in about ten days, and I'll tell Odile we'll stay longer in Berlin because you wish to meet her as an old girl! When you return, call Uwe, he'll know the name of our hotel."

In front of Beiz, they again hugged, kissing both cheeks. Walter had long ago learned to behave like a Frenchman with his friend. Célestin took a cab to Niedstrasse, not allowing Walter, who needed some winks of sleep, to drive him.

5.

The following morning, he asked Odile to have breakfast with Sophia and Emil, letting him sleep. An old friend, many emotions and memories, excellent wine—and Olya, so loved yet unmentioned. Or worse, unmentionable. When he finally roused himself, still with a hangover, he encountered a scene from a stage play in the dining room: A nine-year-old girl was giving a lecture on Baikal and Pyotr the Great to two attentively listening adults, Sigrid and Uwe. The children were at school, and they stayed home—obviously because of him, an idler, thought Célestin guiltily. He had a plan and told his friends and daughter about it: "Odile and I will spend the afternoon around Kudamm, but at half past seven, you, our dear hosts, together with Sophia and Emil, will meet us at a restaurant called Milanese on Schlütterstrasse—I noticed it last night, it's across from Beiz. The six of us will have a fun evening and an Italian dinner." Sigrid and Uwe readily agreed.

Declining lunch, Célestin took Odile for a long walk. He conveyed Walter's greetings and his wish to see her—therefore, their stay in Berlin would be extended, and they needed a hotel. After a pleasant stroll of some three kilometers to the north, they reached the Kaiser Wilhelm Memorial Church. When her father asked her what she thought of the half-ruined building, she took little steps left and right, inclined her head, reflected, and finally said: "I don't like it at all. They certainly have the money to repair it or knock it down. Why are they leaving it like this?"

He found the girl's logic intriguing and explained that the church stood in the middle of the entire city of Berlin, East and West, having been heavily damaged in the bombing of November 1943. "Why didn't they either repair it or destroy it? Well, I think their idea is this: The church stands for German sorrow and guilt. But I suspect that instead of an admission of guilt, it's a reflection of German regret that they lost the war. The war in which—let's make it painfully relevant for us—they murdered in a senseless, vindictive bombing my parents and your grandma and grandpa in 1945. I know it's hard for you to answer me, it's an adult question and you're only nine, but what do you think?" The child amazed him again: "About guilt: I know what 'guilt' means, but this, this is insincere! Look what nice buildings and shiny shops they put around their 'guilt'!"

He lifted Odile from the ground in the way he had not done since she was very small, and she embraced him with all her strength. She felt she had said something from the heart that was smart. They stood like that, with her in the air.

On arriving at Kudamm, they had sandwiches in a café and Célestin asked: *"Dis-moi, mon bijou,* when you spoke to Sigrid and Uwe about Russia, did you mention Olya?" He was worried he might perturb her with a reminder of the unpleasant situation with Mathilde but needed to know. She responded without hesitation: "I mentioned many good people we met—Olya, Lenka,

Oksana... even Pyotr, who wasn't nice but drove us well." He was relieved to receive an honest answer as Odile added: "I also mentioned the nice Chinese man with whom we visited the Forbidden City in Peking."

"I'm glad you remembered him! We're naughty not to have sent him a postcard from Moscow. I'm sure I have the address. His name is Deng Yang-zhou; you remember that in China the surname goes first, so you called him 'Yang' and I 'Yang-zhou.' He had names for us: You were 'Odi,' and I was 'Sel'! He was indeed a likable man—friendly, polite, intelligent, a linguist like me but a specialist in Japanese. He told us he wasn't from Peking, but from somewhere far in the south of China, I think from the city of Wuhan, which lies on the mighty Yangtze River, where it's very hot. So we were discovering the Forbidden City of Peking with a genuine Chinese man for whom the place was just as new, magnificent, and fantastic as it was for us."

At Kudamm 47, on the corner of Bleibtreustrasse, they saw the elegant hotel Mondial, which had numerous stars. It was a five-story building, like most in that part of Kudamm. Célestin immediately placed a deposit on a suite with two bedrooms and a sitting room, and told the receptionist they would return the next day with luggage. Even so, they were taken by elevator to the fifth floor to take a look. All rooms were comfortable and spacious, and there were two well-appointed bathrooms. Odile performed quasi-pirouettes in the sitting room: "Why do we need all this space?"

Célestin explained: "*Mon ange*, you are growing up. When it's possible to manage it easily, I prefer both of us to have some private space, but that also means you are responsible for your room and bathroom: You don't leave them in disarray before the hotel maid comes. I'll help you on the first day. But when in the future it's not simple to get so much space, we'll switch back to a single room with two beds, such as we had in Peking, Irkutsk, and Moscow. All right?" She nodded, saying to herself: "But what if I'm cold at night or have a scary nightmare? May I crawl into Papa's bed? Of course, I may!"

Kudamm was in Charlottenburg, one of the prettiest and wealthiest parts of West Berlin. The beautiful square Savigny-platz and Schloss Charlottenburg were both in the vicinity of the Mondial. Célestin intended to show his girl everything in the world-famous palace—paintings, sculptures, the porcelain collection, and gardens.

From the hotel, the pair continued on Kudamm and soon saw the Schaubühne on the opposite side of the street. They entered the unremarkable foyer and examined the programs of various plays. He was inwardly ironic: "Were these fancy, glossy brochures approved by the austere left-winger Peter Stein? They hardly fit the image of support for the RAF and the Viet Cong." Still smirking, he asked himself: "Because the full name of the theater is the 'Schaubühne am Lehniner Platz,' how many Soviets and Americans imagine the square in front of the theater is named for Lenin and not for the town of Lehnin near Berlin?!"

The play that was running was indeed by Aleksandr Ostrovskiy, the most influential figure in the Russian nineteenth-century realist theatre. The German title was *Ein heisses Herz*, A Hot Heart, but only when they bought a thick book in German about Ostrovskiy, did they discover the original Russian title was *Горячее сердце*—so the title had not been changed for the Berlin production. Célestin read aloud: "The premiere took place in 1868 at the Maly Theater in Moscow," and added, "as Walter supposed, it's a comedy—in five acts."

Privately, on Odile's behalf, he muttered "Ouch!" Late, after a busy day, how can a nine-year-old endure anything in five acts, with probably only two intermissions, even with superb actors and interesting scenography? Also, many of the characters had funny Gogolian surnames—not translated, nor perhaps could they be! So, the German audience and Odile would not be amused by that aspect of character shaping. Reading further, he found the director to be Swiss, Luc Bondy, not Peter Stein; Walter was right again.

No matter, it was worth trying, so they bought tickets for the following evening. Having heard from Walter about Schaubühne's excellent acoustics, Célestin wanted seats at the top of the steeply ascending auditorium, with a view of the entire stage but close to an exit. He smiled when asking at the box office, and the cashier responded in kind, guessing the reason for the request. "Excuse me, but are you German?" he questioned the young woman. "Of course not," she answered with a Slavic accent, possibly Slovak or Serbian. They laughed together ambiguously.

After exploring the chic neighborhood, they went to the Milanese to meet the Benz family. The dinner was first-rate, with outstanding dishes from Lombardy based on authentic Milano and Bergamo recipes. The wines were the Franciacorta sparkling and the Valtellina red. Despite the pleasant atmosphere, it was unavoidable for Célestin to announce that he and Odile would move to a hotel the following day. It was simply unacceptable that the couple frequently missed work for two more weeks due to guests. "There will be opportunities to meet and organize something for the children," he concluded.

Sigrid and Uwe were visibly disappointed but could not refute the friendly reasoning, while the children quietened for a while, looking downcast. Still, the girls soon began to make plans. And the perceptive father noticed that Odile and Emil were exchanging poorly concealed glances. "Hmm," he thought, "this may be my daughter's first flirt. And look at the naughty little Emil!"

6.

Sophia and Emil set out early to the nearby school. Their mother had explained they would see Odile in a few days and that she and her father needed sleep before moving to the hotel. So the three adults and the girl had a leisurely meal—a typical Berlin breakfast incomparably richer than the typical French one. Afterward, Sigrid and Uwe drove their friends to the Mondial.

The French duo spent the day around Savigny Square sampling delicious pastry in a *Konditorei* and buying thank-you gifts for their hosts. It drizzled the entire time. He was pleased that the weather was unsuitable for lengthy walks: Odile would be less tired for the theater. Regarding gifts, they would buy an item for the Niedstrasse home and something for each child.

As soon as he had noticed a *Teppichgeschäft* off Savignyplatz, it occurred to Célestin that a perfect present would be a carpet for the entryway in their friends' apartment. The salesmen hovered near him obsequiously while she ran around tirelessly pitching ideas. Soon, a seemingly ideal rug caught his eye. He visualized the hallway and decided to buy a marvelous small carpet from Iran, two and a half meters by one and a half in size. It was a top-class rug from neither Isfahan nor Shiraz but from a little town in the northwest of old Persia. The basic color was ivory and the design asymmetrical, with subtle flower and animal details in indigo, sea-blue, green, rose-madder (*Rubia tinctorum*), chestnut, and pistachio colors. When Odile saw what he had chosen, she was at first speechless and then gushed: "How gorgeous this one is! Let's buy it, Papa!"

Célestin laughed and said to the enthusiastic boss of the establishment: "Congratulations, I see you are a first-rate salesman. You observe that the customer's child, especially a daughter, covets something and conclude that her daddy will go along, no questions asked. I'll indeed buy this one, but only at the right price. We are in Berlin, but a carpet store is still an oriental store. Here, please take this money—or we'll leave without more talk." He gave the boss a fraction less than half of the posted Deutsche Mark price in cash and requested a corner of the rug be turned over for him to write the name of the new owner on the backing.

The man looked like a stereotype of a carpet store owner: plump, smiling, greedy, persistent, hardened by experience, smart. Intelligence outweighed greed, for he estimated that an attempt at bargaining with the decisive, refined man might backfire; besides, the amount was satisfactory. So he bowed deeply with a beaming face and produced a felt pen. Célestin wrote "Sigrid und Uwe" and gave the owner a handsome amount for the expedient delivery of the carpet to Niedstrasse. The boss followed them to the sidewalk, bowing again. The entire transaction lasted less than fifteen minutes.

Odile's purchase of gifts lasted incomparably longer. They went to four or five stores, Célestin persisting in letting the girl make the choice. Finally, in a bookstore, they bought for Sophia an exquisite book about "Swan Lake," where from each page leaped out graceful ballerinas in various poses, with and without strong, but slender, partners. Choosing a gift for Emil took Odile even longer. In the end, she turned to him pleadingly: "Please help me, I can't make up my mind!" At first, he did not wish to interfere. Then he made comical suggestions that exasperated her: "Well, you can buy him thick red socks, it's winter, or maybe a pipe like the one Maigret had." Her final decision was to buy a large chessboard with the tastefully carved Staunton pieces: She had noticed a heavily scratched board and two chess books in his room.

It was still drizzling when they returned to Mondial and changed clothes for the theater. Their seats were very good. Célestin looked around and explained some details. The walls and a section of the hall's ceiling were meticulously integrated with the slightly tilted stage. The sliding curtain consisted, it seemed, of genuine logs, stumps, and one or two small tree trunks. The back of the stage was pale blue, and the total effect was one of great depth, which made possible several interesting relations among the various perspectives. Célestin decided that his eventual description to Walter would be that the stage was surrealist, with some mock rustic-Russian naturalistic details. The first few scenes were striking, visually and acoustically. Afterward, there was cuteness and repetition, but the numerous changes were ineffective. Much was done to demonstrate the new technical capabilities. Fireworks were more important to the visiting director than dramatic needs.

Act I lasted one hour and forty minutes, and even so, the curtain slid shut only for a major change of scenery, not for the spectators to stretch their legs. Célestin admitted that many aspects of the scenic design, choreography, and the "blocking" of groups of actors were superb, but the text was too weak to bear such an unwieldy aesthetic superstructure.

The first intermission took place after Act III, by which time Odile was drowsy, so they decided to leave. Célestin was glad Walter was not with them, for then it would have been polite to stay. The same woman—the one with whom he had spoken when buying tickets—worked in the cloakroom. He jested: "Better now and here than later through the row at the top of the hall!" "*Ja, mein Herr, viel besser,*" she also laughed, "the audience wouldn't like it, they are stuck-up and disdainful!" Célestin chuckled and could not resist asking: "I noticed you speak with a foreign accent, yet use a word like 'disdainful', which is quite rare in German." The girl was pleased: "Ha, ha! You see, we immigrant newcomers quickly learn such words because we need them *wenn wir klatschen* about our uptight employers." They all chortled, for the wide-awake Odile had understood the dialogue.

7.

Almost the entire next day, chilly but sunny, they spent in the magnificent Schloss Charlottenburg, located about two kilometers north of their hotel. Most of the time was spent in the old wing of the palace, dating from the end of the seventeenth century and all of the eighteenth, so its grand halls and other superb rooms were in the styles of both Baroque and Rococo. Odile was attracted to the exceptional porcelain collection like a humming-bird to a blooming flower. Célestin noticed that the colors of objects she liked best were subtle rather than ostentatious. "As were the colors of the Persian carpet we bought," it occurred to him.

During lunch at the Orangerie, he narrated the long and complex history of the almost mythical *Bernsteinzimmer,* the Amber Room—about which he had read in a book in Niedstrasse. Consulting his notes, he told her: "At the beginning of the eighteenth century, the best German and Danish stone carvers, masons, and sculptors built the room out of the most ravishing pieces of amber from the Baltic Sea. Gold leaves and mirrors were placed on the walls under the amber. The original intention was to install the room in this very palace when Friedrich Wilhelm I, King of

Prussia, lived here, but that never happened. At first, it sat in another palace in Berlin. However, in 1716, if you can believe it, Friedrich Wilhelm gave the entire room as a present to our old friend from Leningrad, or more correctly Sankt-Peterburg, Tsar Pyotr the Great. The one on the stallion.

"The Russian Tsar came here for a visit that year and admired the Amber Room. So the Prussian King got the idea to seal their friendship or alliance—he had joined Pyotr's victorious war against Sweden the previous year—with an extraordinary gift. You see how it went among kings and tsars. Pyotr the Great installed the room in a palace at Tsarskoye Selo, 'Tsar's Village,' near Sankt-Peterburg—I've had enough of Leningrad, in particular when speaking of the eighteenth century. But that's not the end of the story."

"So, what happened then?" Odile asked in the eager voice of a child engrossed in a fairy tale. "Then," continued her father, "there was an enormous quantity of amber, perhaps six tons, in the Amber Room at Tsarskoye Selo. Unimaginable! But after two centuries, during the Second World War, Nazi Germany plundered Tsarskoye Selo and stole the Amber Room. It's known that this was done by officers of the Army Group North. The bewitching room was disassembled and taken in pieces to the old Prussian city of Königsberg—which is now Soviet Kaliningrad—and it has not been seen since. It's thought that when the Red Army was destroying Nazi Germany from the east in 1945, the Amber Room, in pieces, of course, was hidden somewhere and then destroyed in the bombings. Or placed on a boat that sank. There are many stories, but nothing has been found."

They were quiet for a while, finishing a scrumptious walnut *Torte mit Schlagsahne*. "Who knows, maybe we'll see it one day—with Olya. I say it because an educated waiter at the Pribaltiskaya told me that after many years of gathering amber pieces, the Russians have begun the construction of a new Amber Room at Tsarskoye Selo."

"How wonderful it would be to see such a room—with our Olya! Even if it takes them ten years to build it," exclaimed Odile.

"She is growing and can now plan in decades," thought her father while they were walking toward the new wing of the palace, where the Rococo apartments of Friedrich the Great, the son of Friedrich Wilhelm I, were located.

Before they left Schloss Charlottenburg, Célestin did not need to suggest to his daughter to take a photo of another bronze sovereign. The instant Odile saw a massive equestrian statue in front of the palace, she grabbed the Nikon: The monument honored the generous King Friedrich Wilhelm I.

On the way back, the girl heard an interesting story from her omniscient father: "The design of that statue, your third bronze horseman, was created by the sculptor Andreas Schlüter, the same one who worked on the Amber Room. He has a street in Berlin, and we were in it together; it's the one in which the restaurant Milanese is located, remember? And the statue: From the early eighteenth century, it stood on some bridge in Berlin, just like the statue of Henri IV does on Pont Neuf. In the Second World War, it was removed to a shelter somewhere. After the war, when they were moving it back to the city on a barge, probably similar to Ducrau's on the Seine, the poor barge, too feeble to carry the overweight metal king, sank in the river. They managed to lift it years later from the bottom of the Spree—as you know, bronze doesn't rust—and since then it's been in Schloss Charlottenburg so you could take a picture today. How about that, *ma douce*?"

8.

A sealed envelope awaited at the Mondial front desk. "A gentleman left it for you a short time ago, *mein Herr*," said the man on duty. Célestin opened it and found Uwe's greetings: A letter from France had arrived at Niedstrasse. The postal stamp of Metz was on the enclosed thick envelope, and the handwriting undoubtedly belonged to old Gilles. In the elevator, he muttered: "Something from our Gilles, most likely a headache for me."

In their suite, Célestin took a juice and Gerolsteiner mineral water from the fridge. He drew apart the curtains and contemplated Kudamm through bare branches of trees reaching their floor. Leaning back in an armchair, he switched on the tall, elegant lamp and rested his feet on a tabouret. Finally, he opened the envelope in which, in addition to a note from Gilles and other mail, there was an airmail letter of the characteristic Soviet appearance. His Metz address revealed the recognizable handwriting of Russians when using the Latin script. "This was a registered letter that arrived today. You permitted me to sign for such letters. I am sending it immediately to the address in Berlin you gave me." Gilles was a responsible, devoted person, though a little boring and thus unfairly neglected in Odile's thoughts during their travels—in favor of Pasha and the governess Gerda.

"The postal mark is Kazan! And the handwriting seems feminine, but it's not Olya's—the letter must be from her mother. *Mon Dieu*, please give me good news," Célestin, deeply in love, mumbled while forcefully tearing the envelope open. "Dear Tino," wrote Olya's mother in Russian, "today I received a note from Olya. She's in prison in Kuybyshev, a city on the Volga, far to the south. She didn't mention she was well, which worries me because I have heard that prisoners regularly do it to please the authorities. But she wrote that she loves her Tino very much and underlined it! And she stressed that nothing is your fault—underlined. That's all I know. Thank you for calling from Paris. I was happy to hear your concerned voice. God willing, you'll receive this letter. Olya sent me your address in France the day before she went to Finland Station to see you and your daughter off... I am incredibly anxious, although Olya is very strong mentally: It's the Tatar-Russian mixture, invincible! Even if they cut her beautiful hair... Because Olya loves you, I also love you, Olga, mother."

He knocked on Odile's door and yelled for her to come out. She answered immediately: "Come in, Papa!" Célestin saw her curled up and sat next to her, the Kazan letter in hand. Noticing it, she exclaimed: "From Olya?" "Unfortunately not, *mon ange*, but it is from her mother." Embracing him around the waist, the girl heard the letter's content. To Célestin it seemed she was as sad as he. Odile did not understand what the "Tatar-Russian mixture" meant and why it was invincible but did not ask and held him until it became dark.

Célestin decided to submit another request regarding Olya to the Soviet authorities. He mentally prepared for days and gathered information about how to cross into East Berlin and reach the Soviet Embassy. A few times they walked from the Mondial—or took the U-Bahn from Uhlandstrasse station for two stops—to the well-known rail and metro station *Zoologischer Garten*. Once, they spent time at the Zoo itself. Odile seldom approached the enclosures where animals lived and preferred to observe from afar. He was not surprised by the scorn with which she regarded brash children of her age who tried intrusively to feed the animals or teased and mocked them. "How sad the animals are. And these kids—how cruel. Let's go, Papa."

Another time, they took a long walk in Tiergarten, the splendid park in which the Zoo was located. They came across small lakes, simple wooden bridges, and numerous flower beds wearing their gray, brown, and frosty-beige winter coats. Narrow, half-hidden paths led through dense woods. Guided by Célestin's infallible mental compass—which Odile did not inherit—they arrived at the northeast corner of the park, *Brandenburger Tor*.

As they looked through the fabled Gate to "the other side," he hugged her shoulders for reassurance and said quietly: "There, *ma chère fille*, begins East Berlin, East Germany. You've already seen an ugly part of that country when we looked over *die Mauer*. The Gate was built by a descendant of your Horseman № 3 at the end of the eighteenth century. It survived the spring of 1945, albeit with much damage, and was the only structure still standing in this part of the city at the end of the war. Destroyed buildings smoldered around it, and survivors searched through ruins for relatives who might still be alive..."

Odile felt miserable listening to Célestin because by being there, she saw herself as a part of the horrible history. She wanted to tell her father to stop. After all, she was only a little, very little, girl. But that time, still looking through the Gate, he acted as if he did not wish to hear her, as if he was oblivious—and went on:

"The broad street over there used to be the most famous avenue in all of Germany. It begins here at the Gate and Pariser Platz and runs east. It's called *Unter den Linden*, 'Under the Linden Trees,' but there are no lindens on it now. And the pathetic, half-repaired building on the right is the once fabulous hotel Adlon. For the two of us to have lunch in that hotel as it once was would be memorable." He had saddened her with the painful information, but about what? About *her* country. She needed to know the truth.

"On 'Under the Linden Trees,' also on the right-hand side but farther on," he changed the subject, "is the Soviet Embassy. We'll go there because of Olya." The girl looked at him with an odd mixture of trepidation and joy. "When?" she asked. "Tomorrow, *mon coeur*, although we won't be able to do it directly, through Brandenburg Gate, but in a roundabout way; we're in Berlin, and that's how things are done here."

9.

They took a cab to the corner of Friedrich and Zimmer streets, the location of Checkpoint Charlie—the only place where one could enter East Berlin on foot or by car from the western part of the city. The Soviet name for the border crossing was "KP Friedrichstrasse." On the East side, they obtained a one-day visa valid until 10 p.m. It cost five marks for Célestin and two for Odile, as a child younger than twelve. They also had to change twenty-five West-German marks into East-German ones at the rate of one-to-one, unrelated to the street rate.

The address of the Soviet Embassy was Unter den Linden № 55-65. It was only a kilometer north of Charlie, so they went on foot. Célestin knew the Soviets did not like hippies nor other foreign paupers; therefore, he wore a white shirt and an elegant navy-blue suit with a deep-red tie. Over his arm, he carried a raincoat while an expensive briefcase and black umbrella completed the formal mien. Odile, with carefully combed hair to her shoulders, and in a new green dress and short coat of burgundy color, looked like a genuine *jeune mademoiselle de Paris*. She skillfully handled her leather purse and a small white umbrella. When they arrived at the boulevard, they saw that the USSR Embassy—monumental and architecturally perfect—was only about a hundred and fifty meters away from Brandenburg Gate.

At 11:05, they entered the consular office, which was in № 63. There was no queue. Célestin introduced himself and Odile to the official and showed their French passport. Speaking German, but using Russian words when necessary, he explained that for a long time during the previous year, he had traveled with his daughter as a tourist in the Soviet Union. In Moscow, he had met a Soviet citizen, Dinara Alimova Naratovna. They had decided to get married—in Russia—but on the day of his temporary departure from Leningrad for Helsinki, she was arrested at Finland Station. "In front of my own eyes, and my little daughter's, on the station platform," he whispered, looking significantly into the official's eyes. The man looked astonished and confused, so Célestin pursued his slight advantage as in a chess game: "I've no idea why she was arrested. Since then, I've not been able to contact her. Is she in jail?" Prior to entering the office, he had decided not to mention either Olya's mother in Kazan or the prison in Kuybyshev.

"I've been at the Soviet Consulate in Paris, where I submitted a request that Dinara Naratovna be freed—so we could marry. Here's the confirmation." While the official was examining the receipt, Célestin explained in a steady voice: "I'm now in your office because I wish to submit the same request another time. My daughter and I are on a private visit to friends in West Berlin, so I decided to come here. I'm a serious man, as is Dinara—our intentions are sincere. My goal is not to enable her to leave your—and her—country. You must believe us!" That speech was entirely different from the one he had given to the dour consular official in Paris. In the meantime, he had resolved to change his tactics—to be moderate and conciliatory. The most important thing was to pluck Olya out of the horrible gaol. Everything else would then fall into place; if necessary, they would get married in Kazan.

The official examined the supplicant's appearance without saying a word—face, posture, hands. Then he made notes and sought permission to copy the passport and the receipt from Paris. He made two phone calls. A woman arrived and took the documents. The second call, from a distant corner of the office, lasted a long time. At one point, the official put the receiver down and approached Célestin. He thoughtfully looked at Odile and asked: "And the mother of your daughter? Are you divorced? Are you officially the girl's guardian?" Looking again into the man's eyes, he answered in a low voice: "My wife, Odile's mother, tragically died giving birth at the hospital in Koblenz, West Germany." The official winced again. "This man appears to be a human being; all the same, he won't be the one making the decisions— but he may at least properly convey my request." The employee left to finish the call with his supervisor.

Again Célestin wrote the request and filled out forms. Again he gave the address in Metz for further communication. The woman returned with their passport and the Paris receipt and gave him a similar one from the Berlin office. The official explained he couldn't make any promises. The case was exceptional, as it did not involve only the marriage and exit visa of a Soviet citizen. That was all. The man came out of his office and courteously opened the front door. On the sidewalk, they inhaled the crisp air. It was 12:15. Above them, the sky was gray, and drops fell from bare branches. It had rained.

Célestin draped his raincoat around their shoulders. Odile took her father's hand and walked even closer to him, sensing his mood matched the weather. They strolled westward to Pariser Platz and studied the Gate silently, that time from the east. Then they walked back, passing by the Soviet Embassy but on the opposite side of the avenue. The imposing building stood there— sumptuous, mute, forbidding.

After crossing the Spree at a narrow point, it took half an hour to arrive at Alexanderplatz, once the center of all of Berlin. The *Fernsehturm* stood there, but it was closed for repairs. The TV Tower, completed in 1969 after only four years of construction, was the symbol of the DDR, the communist East Germany: Three hundred and sixty-eight meters tall, with a revolving restaurant and an observation terrace. Odile was disappointed and so was Célestin—because of the girl's unfulfilled wish, but also because it would be fascinating to see from a great height how the Wall meandered through the city. "The aesthetics of cruel division," he reflected.

For lunch, they entered the first restaurant they saw. The food was abundant, heavy, and tasteless, with prices far below those in West Berlin. During the meal, Célestin explained that Alexanderplatz was named after Alexander I, Tsar of Russia: "You see, Russia and Germany have for centuries had close relations in both war and peace."

As it was not possible to say anything positive, he refrained from discussing their visit to the Consulate. And while refusing to lie, he would also not resign himself to defeat with words akin to: "Well, now we've done all we could." Any sign of her father's resignation might discourage the girl—and unnecessarily so because there was certainty in his soul he would continue to fight for Olya wherever he was in the world. He would not forget her. He was not a superficial, fickle man.

They wandered through the eastern part of the city. The cakes were disappointing, factory-made. In a bookstore, they bought small volumes about East German cities—Dresden, Leipzig, Jena, and Weimar. They purchased a gramophone record with classical selections performed by the famed Gewandhaus Orchestra from Leipzig. In terms of style and quality of clothes, most passersby were dressed not unlike those in Irkutsk and on Vasilyevskiy Island in Leningrad. Grays and browns were dominant on East German Wartburg and Trabant cars. They encountered small groups of tourists from communist countries: Poland, Czechoslovakia, Bulgaria, and Yugoslavia. Those people seemed surprised by the sight of the dressed-up, unusual couple in East Berlin.

At five in the afternoon, they took a taxi to Checkpoint Charlie, showed their purchases to a customs man, and walked into West Berlin. Only a dozen meters from the border on the west side, there was the notorious café Adler. They ordered hot chocolate, a *bierkrug* with a lid, and cakes. From their table, there was an unobstructed view of East Berlin. Near them, Westerners—Germans, Americans, and many others—prattled in an ostentatiously carefree manner.

10.

Sigrid and Uwe invited father and daughter to dinner to thank them for the marvelous Persian rug. The small carpet greeted the pair in the hallway of the Niedstrasse apartment in precisely the way Célestin had envisaged. Before they tasted the delicious dishes, Odile gave presents to Sophia and Emil. Everyone admired the ballerinas from "Swan Lake" while Emil moved a small table from the living room to his bedroom for the new chessboard. When Célestin went to look, he saw Emil had played the first five or six moves from the Najdorf variation of the Sicilian Defense. "As Black, you like sharp positions, don't you?" he asked the boy shrewdly. Emil scrutinized him with a twinkle in his eye: "You certainly play much better than my *papi*. When you two come to Berlin again, we'll play some games, if you agree. By then, I hope to be better at endgames too." The guests stayed until late. Emil gave a piano recital, and Odile clapped frequently. For him, she was not sleepy.

Days passed quickly, taken by long walks and museum visits. They went to Schloss Charlottenburg another time. The gorgeous gardens, maintained with love, shone. From the Belvedere, the view of the grounds was stunning. They circled the pond with fat, glittering carp and rested in the Pavilion.

Having bought plane tickets for the 18th of March, they prepared for the trip to Israel. Célestin talked to his daughter at length about that unique country. From West Germany, El Al flew to Tel Aviv only from Munich, and it was more interesting to take the train than to fly—one could see at least a tiny part of East Germany. Of course, while the Leipzig train station would be on view, they would certainly not be able to catch a glimpse of Thomaskirche, the church in which Johann Sebastian Bach was the *Kapellmeister* during the second quarter of the eighteenth century.

On the day he returned in the early hours from Tokyo, Walter Schönflug called Uwe Benz and learned where the pair was staying. As soon as he heard Walter's voice on the phone, Célestin invited him to the Mondial. He arrived at their suite in the late afternoon, still tired from the long flight but delighted to see his old friend and his daughter. He ran to Odile and hugged her: "*Bien, bien, jolie Mademoiselle,* don't you be shy with me! You and I've known each other since the first years of your life, although we haven't seen each other for at least four years. You were a cute and healthy baby, then a small, pretty child, and now you are a beautiful little girl." These words melted Odile, especially when she saw her father smiling happily.

Soon, a pot of Japanese *sencha* arrived from the hotel restaurant, accompanied by a first-class, medium-dry, sparkling *Sekt*—from the Moselle region, naturally. With a touch of ceremony, Walter opened his bag and gave Odile an elegant pink-purple fan wrapped in pale silk. Not only little girls and young women would have been won by such a gift. Then he presented father and daughter with tastefully boxed ivory chopsticks. "And for you, I have something I know interests you most," Walter said to Célestin, giving him detailed maps of Tokyo and Kyoto. They both laughed, but she said seriously: "*Mon Papa* wishes to know everything and go everywhere."

After a while, she retired to her room to look at the gifts and read about Israel. Without switching the lights on, the friends continued their conversation, sipping the wine and occasionally raising glasses for a toast. At Célestin's request, Walter began to talk about his time in Japan. "Everything was exceptionally interesting, strange, different. I'd need days to describe my impressions of life in Tokyo—that is, in the tiny section of the megalopolis with which I became acquainted. We'll have to await another opportunity: When you return to Metz from Israel, I'll come and visit. But listen, I'm dying to tell you something mischievous and a little naughty. I didn't want to do it in front of Odile—who knows, maybe she'd guess what I'm talking about, she seems awfully bright. So, I spent two days in Kyoto and can tell you the geishas—

they call them *geiko* there—are fabulous. They represent the ideal form of at least one sort of woman. Believe me, I fell in love more than once." Célestin avoided asking Walter questions and sharply stopped the rise in his mind of any thought that might lead to Olya. Instead, he let his friend talk uninterrupted.

Walter switched to the congress he had attended in Tokyo: "This may interest you more than my geishas. I met a youngish Chinese linguist from the city of Wuhan whose family name is Deng, Dr. Deng. During one of our meetings, he told me that in Peking last year he'd met a pleasant and super-smart French linguist who'd been traveling with a daughter of about ten. He couldn't remember the name and surname of the Frenchman, but said that he, Deng, had called the gentleman 'Sel,' and the girl 'Odi.' He'd even visited the Forbidden City in the company of the two. So, I immediately connected it all with you and must've been right. Wasn't I? I told him I'd see you in Berlin. Do you remember him?"

Célestin exclaimed: "Yang-zhou! Dr. Deng Yang-zhou is an intelligent and capable young man. Only about a week ago, we spoke of him. I have his address and will write from Munich. No wonder he couldn't remember my name and surname—Célestin de Quernevelle is for the Chinese totally unpronounceable and unmemorizable."

It was Walter's turn: "So I guessed correctly! *En passant*, I found it funny that when 'Odi' and 'Sel' are joined, one gets 'Odisel'—similar to the classical Greek 'Odysseus,' a name fitting adventurers perfectly—which is what you two are! Naturally, I didn't try to explain it to... what did you say? Yang... Dr. Deng. There's a continuation of the story. He invited me to be a guest at the University of Wuhan, 'the city on three rivers,' as he put it: Yangtze, Han—and another one. When I explained that the man he'd met in Peking and I are good friends, he asked me to invite you too. He said he'd organize a wonderful boat trip for us up the Yangtze through its western gorges all the way to—I forgot the name. Some gigantic city." "Probably Chongqing. That would be fantastic. How happy Odi would be and so would Sel!"

During the following two weeks, they went to museums, attended concerts, and visited Sigrid and Uwe, in whose apartment Odile felt at home. Sophia became very dear to her, and Emil even more. Célestin met Walter several times, both men enjoying badinage about art.

To take the flight to Tel Aviv on the 18th of March, the pair boarded the train for Munich the day before. It left precisely at 9:02 from Zoologischer Garten, arrived at 9:15 in Wannsee—the last station in West Berlin—and left again three minutes later. In the southwestern region of Berlin, there were calm, rich villages surrounded by lakes and stands of trees. However, already at 9:21, the train entered the somber station Griebnitzsee: Walls on both sides with watchtowers, barbed wire, DDR. Border officials with blank faces mutely examined their passport and the document of an elderly lady from West Berlin who shared their compartment. There was no customs check because no one had the DDR visa and could not get off anywhere in that country but only pass through its territory.

Their co-passenger breathed a sigh of relief as the train departed, quickly returning to the book she had been reading, with *Artur Rubinstein—Moje młode Lata* on the front cover. After a while, Célestin cordially addressed the lady in German: "Madam, I am sorry to disturb you, but permit me to ask you: Is the book you are reading about the famous Polish pianist?" She answered right away: "Yes, kind Sir, the book is his autobiography in Polish, which is his mother tongue. I am of Polish descent, although I have lived in West Berlin for a long time."

He nodded: "You see, I admire Rubinstein's emotional depth and pianistic technique and think he is one of the best interpreters of Chopin ever. Unfortunately, I don't speak Polish and am unsure what your book's title means. Years ago, I read his autobiography in German and its title was *Die frühen Jahre* (*My Early Years*). Is it the same work you are reading?"

"Yes. It's only slightly different in Polish, *My Young Years*. A fine book, by a great man. I'm delighted you have a lofty opinion of him. Let me boast a little. I was born in the city of Lodz in Poland, which is also Rubinstein's birthplace! Recently, I heard on the radio he is still alive, over ninety years old... born in 1887, lives in Geneva."

The train passed Potsdam without stopping and entered a hilly countryside. While Odile gazed through the window or read, Célestin and the Polish lady talked, avoiding politics. She opened a box of Swiss pralines and offered them to the girl with a grandmotherly smile. The station in Leipzig was unremarkable and Bach's Thomaskirche not visible. At 2:00 p.m., they arrived at the border crossing Gutenfürst, where they saw the last traces of barbed wire. There was no control—they had left East Germany behind.

The Polish lady got off in Hof, the first West-German town, located fifteen kilometers south of the border. She said her relatives, who were waiting at the station, lived there safely. Célestin took her suitcases to the platform but noticed the box of chocolates on returning to the compartment. He opened the window, but the lady smiled and indicated Odile. "What can you do, *mon bijou*? Everyone finds you adorable."

They traveled south through the misty landscape of eastern Bavaria: hillocks, woods, villages, and churches with steep spires. "About forty kilometers from here," he pointed to the right of the train's direction of travel, "is Bayreuth, an old city. When I was nineteen, I visited it with my grandparents Charlotte and Olivier. The town is known for its operas of Richard Wagner, which are performed at Bayreuther Festspielhaus—a playhouse of the composer's design. Performances take place only for a month and a half in the often very hot summer, so we didn't see any—we visited during a lovely Bavarian spring. Despite the heat, the Festspielhaus has no air conditioners because Wagner certainly wouldn't have tolerated any humming. I agree. Why can't ladies stop wearing furs and use fans like the one you got from Walter?

"As for his operas... Some people admire them above all other operas if not above all music. But many music lovers can't stand them. And those in the third group of *cognoscenti*—people who supposedly know a lot regarding what's relevant—enjoy some parts while finding the rest boring and pretentious. The fourth bunch is probably the most numerous nowadays: These people care about politics, not music. So they find Wagner's racial views too controversial to consider the musical qualities of his operas and his revolutionary approach to musical theatre. One thing I find noteworthy is that I've never heard of a nine-year-old child who loves Wagner's operas—even one who is musically gifted, has absolute pitch, and has been studying violin since the fourth year of life."

Célestin correctly anticipated what Odile would say: "And you, Papa, do you like this Wagner? Do you love his operas?" His answer was ready: "Don't ask me about him as a man. That's not essential for him as a genius musician, composer, and creator. And the operas? In Metz, we have excellent recordings of all of them. I wasn't planning to play them for you—not yet, but we can do it if you wish, or spoonful by spoonful."

While they were approaching Regensburg, the mist was turning to fog, a great river was close. At 4:15 p.m., the train crossed the Danube and soon reached the station. He remembered the joke about the Danube as the *Weisswurst Äquator*—white sausages ruled south of the Danube.

After eleven minutes at platform 8a in Regensburg, the train left in dense fog but still arrived on time in Munich at 6:13 p.m. They found a hotel near the main train station and dined in a simple restaurant—the goulash was tasty, unlike the Swabian baked *Spätzle*, a type of noodles. Célestin put Odile to bed early because a difficult day of travel awaited them. He, however, took time to write to Deng Yang-zhou, recounting what he had heard from Walter and thanking his Chinese colleague for the gracious invitation to visit Wuhan and make the splendid voyage up the Yangtze with his daughter. He signed: "Odi + Sel, looking forward to the future Chinese Odyssey!"

12

They boarded the airport bus at the train station the next morning at 8:15. The weather was perfect for takeoff, with no trace of fog from the previous day. The bus drove in meager sunshine through the orderly and clean streets of Munich, a grand city adorned by stately buildings, lush parks, museums, and fountains. Trees were scattered on the islets of the Isar River. At the airport, they pulled their suitcases fifty meters to the entrance of Halle C, from which El Al flew. In front of the hall, an armored scarecrow was parked—a military transport monster. "POLIZEI" was written on it in large letters, and it was indeed full of cops.

Halle C was not an ordinary hall for passengers waiting to board their plane. First came a narrow passage through a sturdy fence topped by barbed wire, controlled by two massive armed policemen who checked passports and tickets. Then one entered a shed, seemingly cobbled together not long before, where officials in civilian clothes checked the same documents. Passengers stood for a long time in that uncomfortable area, overheated by infrared lamps; Célestin and Odile waited an hour. Many people were elderly and looked weak, yet there was nowhere to sit: No one complained, even though they certainly would anywhere else. He repeated what he had said in the hotel, that the flight was not ordinary because Israelis were frequently the target of terrorists. "From now on, *ma chère fille*, we'll share their fate regarding safety even though we aren't Jews—it's our choice." He asked her to refrain from chatter and remarks about other passengers and officials.

Célestin remembered many details of the events in Munich in 1972 about which he had not wished to remind Mathilde: How the members of the Palestinian terrorist group "Black September" broke into the Olympic Village and kidnapped eleven Israeli sportsmen; how they killed them all; how they did it because their demands had not been met—namely, for Israel to release hundreds of Palestinian prisoners, and for West Germany to free

Andreas Baader and Ulrike Meinhof; and how "Black September" was allegedly acting in the name of the inhabitants of two Christian Palestinian villages who had been brutally expelled from their homes in 1948 by Israel.

Naturally, he also remembered the year 1976. At the end of June, an Air France plane took off from Tel Aviv for Paris with two hundred fifty passengers, mostly Jews. In Athens, it took on another fifty passengers, among whom were the four terrorists, two Palestinian men and two Germans, a man and a woman. The hijacking occurred soon after takeoff, and the plane arrived in Entebbe, Uganda, to a welcome from Idi Amin. The terrorists demanded that fifty Palestinians be released from prison in Israel and other countries. At the Entebbe airport, Jews were separated from other passengers. It was hard for Célestin to imagine the horror felt by the hundred or so Jewish hostages when they saw non-Jews being freed on subsequent days. However, a week after the air piracy, a miraculously successful intervention by about thirty Israeli commandos liberated all but three hostages. The hijackers were all killed, as was the leader of the Israeli operation, which lasted less than an hour.

He could not speak to Odile about such matters. Even though he disliked hiding things from her, exceptions had to exist. The appalling information could frighten the child to such a degree that she might not behave naturally in Israel. Perhaps she would not enjoy travel, history, and architecture. Or she might prematurely aggrandize some people and abhor others. He wished to let Israel and the different people living there teach her why that land was sacred to so many.

Finally, they reached Israeli security officials who asked each passenger numerous questions: Who they were; where they were from; where they had been before Munich; and why they were going to Israel. They spent over thirty minutes talking to two separate examiners, first a woman, then a man. Both were youngish, amiable, and smart. There was talk about their stay in China, the USSR, and Finland: names of hotels had to be provided. He gave not only the address and phone number in Metz but also the addresses of friends with whom they had stayed in Paris and Berlin. They inspected the bills from the Mondial in Berlin and the hotel where they had slept the previous night.

Then the examiners switched to the people they intended to visit in Israel. He gave the names of colleagues-linguists and other Israelis with whom he had been in contact in Europe over the years. Throughout, the Mossadniks kept apologizing, but as if imitating the employee of the Soviet Consulate in East Berlin, they inquired about Odile's mother. He gave them a brief explanation, preparing to become furious if they were to ask for some proof of Patrizia's fate nine years earlier. It seemed the female examiner was about to do so, but refrained when she noticed his sharp look of warning.

The parting of father and daughter from the two examiners was cordial, with handshakes. Nevertheless, he could not resist the temptation to tell them, in a slightly mocking tone, that the only time he had experienced something similar had been on the Soviet-Finnish border. They smiled sourly and cheered up only when assured that his behavior was quite different with the Soviets.

The next stop was the efficient German passport check. What was interesting to Célestin, however, was the behavior of passengers in the queue. It was his first chance to estimate what awaited them on the streets of Tel Aviv. Most were relatively young people who spoke Hebrew, which meant they were Jews born in Israel, the so-called *Sabras*. They behaved assertively, in an almost rude manner. "Well, before complaining about their lack of polish, one must keep in mind that all these people have been soldiers in the Israeli Army—men for three years and women for two," he thought, "but I expect them to have good hearts despite the roughness."

In the line could also be seen many elderly, and even very old, women and men who spoke German, Yiddish, or a mix of the two. Célestin asked himself: "How many of these people survived Nazi concentration camps, stayed in Germany after the war, and are now finally traveling to Israel to remain there, to 'climb toward Jerusalem,' making the Jewish *Aliyah*? And how many others have lived for a long time in Israel but dared come to Germany to see one more time a city of their childhood, early youth, first love?" He was not yet prepared to speak to Odile in detail about the Jewish painful twentieth century; among other considerations, her mother was German.

The following event in the long departure program was an incredibly conscientious manual inspection of the contents of their suitcases and carry-on bags by a team of exclusively Israeli officials. During the stay in Metz, they left behind most of the stuff accumulated on their long trip, simplifying the luggage for Israel. The Nikon and the Berlin films were immediately taken to "an X-ray machine and for dogs to smell," officials explained. The assurance, "nothing bad will happen to the films," reminded Célestin of comrades Solyony and Nataliya Ivanovna. At least five dogs of two different breeds roamed Halle C: "They probably have canine specialists for bombs, drugs, and who knows what else," he speculated.

Their suitcases and bags were first passed through a metal detector and then searched in front of them. He had to prove the battery-operated calculator functioned, the tape in the dictaphone moved, the flashlight could be switched on, and the alarm clock showed the correct time. She had to do the same with the little flashlight always in her bag. Unasked, officials returned each item where it belonged. Because of the nature of their job, these snoops could not be as smooth as the two previous investigators, but they were decent.

Body searches were the final stage. A young Israeli woman first talked to Odile in German for a couple of minutes and then lightly passed a hand-held metal detector over the girl's dress and shoes. He again thought of Solyony, remembering how the man had smugly pointed out that Odile's shoes were generously not checked. "Well," he concluded, "Soviets and Israelis search for different things in different places." He underwent a search analogous to hers but conducted by a chubby, smiling Sabra with a manly, no-nonsense technique. "Mossad has excellent employees, both male and female," reflected Célestin.

And so, at 12:20, they found themselves in an ugly waiting room, the departure time delayed by an hour and a half. At a newsstand, he bought a booklet about Israel in German, with the Star of David and a menorah on the cover. Finally, passengers boarded two buses surrounded by police cars. The buses drove past planes from various countries, among which was Aeroflot *CCCP* 85472, and stopped next to their El Al plane. They boarded and took seats in the seventh row; she naturally got the window seat. At 1:12 p.m., they took off for Tel Aviv; the flight was expected to last three hours and fifteen minutes. The pilot occasionally announced the names of cities over which the plane flew. The first of these, at 2:35, was Sarajevo in Yugoslavia. The pilot mentioned snowy mountains close to it and added that the next Winter Olympics, in 1984, would take place there. Thessaloniki came next, followed by the dazzling Greek islands. "Homer's sea-faring Odysseus came from an isle just like these," smiled Célestin. The Mediterranean was resplendent. Odile was not drowsy and read about Jerusalem in her booklet.

Meanwhile, he was skimming the previous day's *Jerusalem Post*. One news item was that two Arab men were arrested in Jerusalem, accused of having slain a sixteen-year-old yeshiva student near the Wailing Wall. Another item described the plight of a woman, a Soviet citizen, who had finally arrived in Israel after waiting for many months for the Soviet exit visa—yet the purpose of her coming was to donate bone marrow for her gravely ill brother. "*Mon Dieu!* Olya..."

At 4:15 p.m. Munich time, the pilot announced that the coast of Israel would be visible in a few minutes from the left side of the plane; his voice was immediately replaced by a patriotic song. To Célestin's surprise, only a few passengers joined. Soon they saw the lights of Tel Aviv. Above the city, toward Jerusalem, sailed clouds tinted a deep red by the setting sun. The plane landed at 4:30 p.m. Munich time, 5:30 Israel time. "Here we are, *mon trésor*, in the Holy Land. From here, all the way to China and Japan lies Asia—an unimaginable vastness in which very different people live. You remember the Chinese, Mongolians, Buryats, and Russians. But now, here, we'll look at the Jews and the Arabs with fresh eyes and open hearts. *D'accord?*" She sighed and hugged her papa firmly.

PART FIVE

Yerusháláyim...

1.

On a gray afternoon in late March of 1981, Odile and Célestin were walking next to the Mediterranean Sea, which wore a slight frown. The girl photographed the empty horizon and unattractive beaches, her father seldom interfering. The stronger her fingers and arm muscles became during their travels, the more readily the Nikon obeyed her. They had already been in Israel for a week and intended to walk that day over three kilometers from the center of Tel Aviv to the port of Jaffa, some four thousand years old.

Strategically important from ancient times, the town was built on a steep stony hill overlooking the sea. It knew the pharaohs, King Solomon, and Saint Peter. It experienced Egyptian and Assyrian swords and survived the Roman attempt to erase it sixty-eight years after Christ. In the seventh century, the Arabs arrived, with the Crusaders following in the twelfth. The latter primarily wanted to liberate Jerusalem and Christ's Tomb from the Muslims, or so they claimed. The Mamluks came in the thirteenth century and then the Turks. Napoleon conquered it in 1799 during his unsuccessful military undertaking in Ottoman Syria and Egypt: He primarily wished to deny the British access to India, or so he claimed. Jaffa was nevertheless under British rule after 1917—until it became part of the newborn State of Israel in 1948. The year before, India also finally rid itself of the British Crown. However, the British could not restrain themselves from arranging a parting act of malice toward it: They manipulated the proceedings so that two enormous territories, Western and Eastern Pakistan—later Pakistan and Bangladesh—seceded from it. Mahatma Gandhi was bitterly opposed.

On the other side of the road sat two luxurious American hotels, along with deserted houses and cranes. There were no trees. "It's not nice here," complained Odile, but her father responded: "When we return in ten or fifteen years, it'll be incomparably nicer. Israelis need time without war. Still, I'm sure this coast will never look like our Côte d'Azur or the Amalfi coast south of Naples." When she wondered why, he continued: "Because, *ma princesse*, nature has been close-fisted here. There are no high green hills above these beaches, nor charming islands in front of them. One day we'll go to the island of Capri, across from the volcano Vesuvius. I promise!"

In the oldest part of Jaffa, near the Mahmoudia Mosque and Franciscan Saint Peter's Church, Odile and Célestin admired the effort to restore every stone. However, restaurants with international names such as Chez Michel and Taj Mahal, and expensive shops selling kitsch artworks, were opened in many of the renovated houses, giving them a disneylandish look.

At sunset, she took a photo of the silhouette of Saint Peter's against dark-red clouds and sand dunes on the coast below the ancient town. They walked into a small park where five couples posed for different wedding photographers: All the brides wore white dresses, while the grooms wore white tuxedos, black trousers, and white kippahs. Odile photographed them collectively from afar. "I didn't want to bother them by coming closer. Do you think, Papa, they all got married together?" After a moment's reflection, he answered: "I'm not sure, but I doubt it. They accidentally came here at the same time—the place is fashionable. And only you have them all in a single photo! These people will probably never meet again." Odile refused to accept it: "Maybe they will. Didn't your colleague tell us, during our lunch at the university, that Israel is a village in which everybody knows everybody?" He was pleased: "You remember everything..."

They had dinner in one of the Palestinian restaurants surrounding Mahmoudia. By chance, at the moment when they were entering the place, calls to prayer began to emanate from the mosque's loudspeaker. However, no one reacted. Perhaps the guests were Jews? Staff members certainly were not. Célestin did not inquire—he was glad the mosque could loudly call to prayer in the middle of Israel.

Their dinner was vegetarian, abundant, and tasty: two kinds of hummus, succulent pickled peppers, roasted peppers in oil, eggplant stuffed with spicy rice, crunchy Arabic pita bread, fresh Jaffa juice for Odile, a cold Maccabee beer for Célestin, followed by a piece of baklava for the daughter and two for the father. Due to their German marks, food and transportation in Israel were cheap, but all luxuries were expensive.

After dinner, they boarded bus № 46, which brought them from Jaffa to the main bus station in a drab quarter of Tel Aviv. From there, № 5 took them to Dizengoff Square, the noisily pulsating heart of the city. A large fountain stood in the middle of the square. Not only multicolored jets of water but also music kept erupting from it. When they arrived, it was Sunday evening, and Maurice Ravel's *Boléro* was thundering. People chattered, flirted, kissed, and munched street food. From the square, Dizengoff Street ran to the north, full of shops, restaurants, and bars. They loved walking on it, mingling with the bubbling crowd. Tel Aviv was, for the most part, a modern, commercial, and secular city, with a whiff of Mediterranean spirit and inhabitants in ordinary clothes. When a man passed by in a long black coat with a black hat, he stuck out as if he belonged in a Jewish Orthodox quarter of Antwerp or Brooklyn. "It will be different, you'll see, in the old parts of Jerusalem," he said before they stepped into their hotel at Dizengoff Square.

2.

The lunch Odile mentioned had taken place in the cafeteria of the University of Tel Aviv in the northern part of the city, and the colleague was Jakob Shmotkin, Professor of Hebrew, whom Célestin had gotten to know through correspondence. Earlier that day, father and daughter spent hours exploring the outstanding collection of archaeological and anthropological objects at the museum Eretz Israel, "Land of Israel." Then they walked to the entrance of the university campus. A fence ran around it, but the young guards at the gate airily beckoned the pair to come in, exclaiming "shalom!"

Although it was the beginning of March, there was a lot of cultivated greenery, with gardens in small squares. Most of these carried the surnames of wealthy American donors, but the most striking plaza was named after Albert Einstein. All signs were in Hebrew, but Célestin easily communicated with students in English. Some told him they were from the USA, spending one, six, or twelve months in Israel. A few added that they would spend some time at a kibbutz. American student fashion in clothing ruled the campus.

They found Jakob Shmotkin's office; "shalom!" he smiled warmly. Knowing his colleague would come with a daughter, Shmotkin was ready to be kind and attentive to her from the start. He spoke both German and English, so the conversation flowed smoothly. Célestin told him he would visit Jaffa soon with Odile. "Jaffa is a special city, you'll like it. Some people here claim it's the oldest port in the whole world, but who knows what existed in China and India four thousand years ago? We Ashkenazim, immigrants from Europe, perhaps more than other Jews, find it difficult to admit anybody existing anywhere on the planet is 'older' than us!" Shmotkin laughed heartily, and Célestin joined him.

"At the beginning of this century, Jaffa was encircled by fortified walls and extremely densely populated. In 1906, most of the Jews left the city and settled in the area that's now Tel Aviv. But in 1948, when Ben-Gurion proclaimed the independence of our land on the 14th of May, Arab countries attacked Israel together the next day—and then lost the war. One of the many consequences was the escape of seventy thousand Palestinians from Jaffa to Jordan and Gaza. All that's Jaffa."

During the short monologue, Shmotkin's voice trembled with feeling several times, more sad than victorious. Célestin understood him; to change the topic, he said: "I read this recently and wrote it down." He took out the trusty notebook: "The proclamation by David Ben-Gurion took place near the center of Tel Aviv, in the hall of a museum at Sderot—Boulevard—Rothschild № 16. I saw on the map where that is, about a kilometer south of Dizengoff Square." Shmotkin smiled: "I see you're a great traveler and teaching your little daughter to become the same—or are you one already, Odile?"

She did not become confused or shy: "I like to travel with Papa and take pictures of different places. May I please look through your window and take a few photos?" Shmotkin readily opened the window wide. "Our campus is pretty, and there's no rain, so you can take good pictures."

To Célestin, Shmotkin said: "Please call me Jakob. Israel is not a country of formality and false politeness. People are direct, sometimes too much so; they can be uncouth and coarse. Let's not forget this is, after all, the Near East. But at least to me, it seems they are less fake than people in Europe and America." Without hesitation, Célestin agreed: "That was also our impression—already at the airport in Munich. My daughter and I adapt quickly. And Jakob, please call me Célestin. I can't help you with a nickname because I don't have one. It doesn't exist in French, which my parents had in mind when they named me. But you can call us 'Sel' and 'Odi,' invented by a Chinese friend." Jakob shook his head: "Oh no! Both of you have such nice names."

They went to a cafeteria for lunch. Odile liked Israeli staple food—fresh vegetables, yogurt, white cheese, and superb bread and fruit—so she chose that; the men opted for fish and rice. They sat at a table by the window. Jakob said: "Ben-Gurion, as you know, was an ardent Zionist, more fervent even than his predecessor Theodor Herzl. All his co-workers and confidants were Zionists. They dedicated their energy, their entire lives, to the fulfillment of the centuries-old dream of the return of European Jews to Eretz Israel. However, many also had socialist roots—ideas of equality and solidarity. These ideas are strongly represented in Israel in the enduring nature and daily functioning of our kibbutzim and moshavim.

"Such is the source of our resistance to phony formality, the cause of directness and lack of polish, which I've acknowledged. That's why this cafeteria exists on our campus, and we are in it. I had the opportunity to visit American, English, and recently German universities. Everywhere, my hosts took me to an elegant faculty restaurant near the Rector's office, into which students couldn't even peek. Well, there's none of that in Israel. At all our universities, it's like here: Students and professors, the old and the young, often at the same table." Jakob then tapped Odile's hand and added with a laugh: "But now we have another welcome novelty—an oldster professor and a nine-year-old girl at the same table in the university cafeteria." Jakob Shmotkin was only two years older than Odile's father.

Célestin posed a perceptive question: "Jakob, I expected this to be a modern city but was still struck by the relative absence of overt religiosity in the dress of women and men. A socialist influence, too?" He quickly added: "This is curious because I read that Tel Aviv was the first city in the world where Hebrew became the chief means of communication, both spoken and written, across all levels of education."

Jakob agreed: "The first high school, named for Herzl, in which all subjects were taught in Hebrew, was opened in Tel Aviv. Besides, the city had long been the meeting place of poets, artists, and actors who wanted to communicate in Hebrew: There were literary cafés, small galleries, and improvised stages. Yes, the majority of Israelis are proud of their ancient script and language, but that's one thing, and religiosity is another, maybe not quite another, but still..."

They left the cafeteria and ambled through the campus. Jakob exchanged greetings with students and explained the sights. The conversation touched on the extent to which it was possible to bring Hebrew into modern times, especially in technical terminology. "You see, I have been thinking about that problem almost since I learned to speak. Both my paternal grandfather Shlomo, Solomon, and my father Baruch, Benedict, were serious students of Hebrew. Everything else they did to support their families was secondary. So, I learned Hebrew at a very young age and spoke it with my father; with my mother, I spoke Yiddish. And they spoke both to each other, just as you and Odile speak French and German."

Jakob confided: "Because I live and work in Israel, sooner or later a visitor from America or Western Europe asks me—whether or not he's Jewish—where I grew up and what happened to my family. Usually, I choose not to discuss it. The questions are often ignorant and tendentious as if they hope to get first-hand gory information about Auschwitz or else receive words of gratitude for the alleged help they, Americans and Britons, gave to Israelis. It's very unpleasant. You are different, Célestin. I don't want to be patronizing, but I hear and sense you're not only knowledge-able—as if you were sixty-five—but have feelings of sympathy, nay, genuine compassion, for us."

Célestin was touched to his core and exchanged a look with Odile. To Jakob, he did not say "thank you," which would be, he felt, utterly ill-suited. "A minute or two ago," Jakob went on, "when I was speaking about my family, you were probably curious how I had spent my childhood and youth. You didn't ask me, and I am grateful. But let's go into the University Library and find something interesting for Odile to read; we can continue our talk there." In the lobby of the splendid building, Professor Shmotkin spoke to a librarian, asking her to find books about Israel in French or German for older children. The lady led them to a huge table: "The girl can find here what you requested. There are arm-chairs for all of you nearby."

"This seemed best," Jakob said, "because some of the things I'll tell you are not for a child's ears, no matter how intelligent and mature." He continued: "Members of five generations of my fam-ily were born in Poland, in a part of Warsaw that had been a Jew-ish ghetto for a long time. Grandfather Shlomo was born there in 1901, Baruch, my father, in 1921, and I was also a ghetto baby, born in April 1942. In the middle of July of that year, the Nazi SS General Jürgen Stroop organized the *Grossaktion Warschau* and supervised the deportation of a quarter of a million of us Jews from the ghetto to the concentration camps Treblinka and

Majdanek for cold-blooded extermination. Already at the end of July, the Jewish Fighting Organization (*Żydowska Organizacja Bojowa, ŻOB*) arose in the ghetto. Most of the founders were Zionists and socialists. My grandpa Shlomo joined because of family ties with the founders, whereas my father Baruch—although his first and only child had just been born—joined because he was a brave, unbridled youngster of twenty who admired the six years older Yitzhak Zuckerman, perhaps the most courageous of the resistance leaders."

Célestin did not know what to do: To remain silent or to ask, "what happened then," in Odile's manner. He knew everything that followed was horrific, and it seemed indecent not to say something. So he mumbled: "The year after, an uprising took place in the ghetto, I think in April of 1943."

Jakob long absently gazed at Odile, who was engrossed in reading. Leaning back in the armchair, legs crossed, she did not resemble the poorly brought-up students from Western countries who nonchalantly placed their feet on furniture. "You have a wonderful daughter," said Jakob and remained sitting quietly. Célestin worried that he had somehow caused offense but did not wish to break the silence.

Finally, Jakob spoke: "Yes, after the *Grossaktion*, men, women, and children began to build hidden bunkers in the ghetto. Not to shoot from them, you understand, but to survive the German patrols and raids for as long as possible. My father never described to me the horrendous living conditions in those bunkers. ŻOB members sometimes managed to smuggle weapons and explosives into the ghetto. No one was more skilled than Yitzhak Zuckerman, my father's idol. Yitzhak knew how to get out of the ghetto, make contact with Jewish and Polish saboteurs outside, and return to the ghetto. He sometimes brought my father along. And in the ghetto, the people prepared in every possible way for the rebellion, crazily believing they might succeed. Maybe they noticed the first signs of dread in the eyes of the Nazis when, at the end of February 1943, the news of the catastrophic defeat of Hitler's armies at Stalingrad penetrated those monsters' minds."

Another long silence, although Célestin felt its cause was the pain of recollection rather than Jakob's reluctance to open up even deeper. "The uprising in the ghetto began on the 19th of April 1943. Grandpa was killed on the first day, an hour or two after the tragicomic celebration in the bunker of my first birthday. My mother Leah committed suicide at the beginning of May. That was quite rare among the ghetto Jews, although it apparently isn't rare among Jews in the West when they feel existential angst... Oh, please excuse me: I apologize to my mother, to those people, and to you for saying it. And to myself."

Silence again and irremediable sadness in Jakob's eyes. Then: "On the 16th of May 1943, the uprising was crushed, everything in flames, destroyed. The night before, my father was able to pull me out of the burning ghetto through the sewage pipes—garbage and shit. It was Yitzhak who made it possible for Baruch to do this. Later, my father carried me through Europe with incredible resourcefulness. He fed me and took care of me like a most loving mother. Somehow, after several years of hiding and occasionally benefiting from human kindness toward a small child in many countries through which we passed, we managed to board a ship in Piraeus. It brought us to Haifa, where we arrived on the 12th of May 1948, two days before Ben-Gurion proclaimed Israel's independence. I was six years old and remember that everybody cried at the pier, those on the ship and those waiting. That's how it was."

There were dark clouds on Célestin's face, but Jakob went on: "I regret I saddened you. Even though we are of similar age, I'll take the liberty of telling you in a fatherly way that you are a good man. Perhaps I needed to relieve my bosom of these weighty stones. It's been a long time since I confided in anyone. And there's a follow-up. My father Baruch passed away in 1954, so I became an orphan at twelve. Pneumonia got him in a kibbutz by the sea, near our northern border with Lebanon. I grew up on that kibbutz, it was my home. Something else: Yitzhak Zuckerman also survived the horrors and reached Israel. In 1961, he testified at the trial of the executioner Adolf Eichmann in Jerusalem. He lives in a kibbutz by the Sea of Galilee, we call it 'Kinneret.'

I heard from friends that he is seriously ill. Very soon, I'll go to say goodbye to him. If he were healthy, I would take you with me to meet him. An extraordinary man."

3.

They were fascinated by the streets of Tel Aviv: Full of life, with shops and counters on every corner where one could drink freshly squeezed juice and eat tasty falafel. Gravel of various colors was embedded in many sidewalks, and the designs looked even prettier when wet. Célestin mentioned he had seen photos of similar sidewalks at the Copacabana Beach in Rio de Janeiro, and Odile quipped: "I know, Papa, that's in Brazil and you'll tell me we'll travel there." Laughing, he threatened: "You're a naughty urchin and deserve a little cuff on the ear!"

Fear of a new war did not seem to linger in the atmosphere of Tel Aviv, nor did trepidation that a terrorist bomb might explode at any moment. After many talks with colleagues, students, and other people, Célestin concluded that Israelis had unlimited confidence in their army—and the Mossad. No one said it word for word, but he sensed it. As for the army, virtually all Israelis were in it. Even after their long initial period of military service, both men and women continued to spend a month and a half each year participating in exercises. Depending on profession, occupation, marital status, and health, exercises could be more or less frequent and intense until the fiftieth year of life. Two categories of citizens had a special military status: Palestinians of either Muslim or Christian faith did not have to serve in the army, although they could do so voluntarily; ultraorthodox Jews also did not have to serve, but the law responsible was frequently challenged in the Knesset, the Israeli parliament.

What impressed Célestin was that he rarely heard any criticism of policies regarding military service, even from recruits with whom he had many opportunities to talk as they were everywhere. Numerous young men and women in uniform who were off-duty could be seen in cities and villages, in front of shops, and at bus stops. Rare was the young woman soldier, with a rifle over her shoulder, who did not smile at Odile. Israel did have a powerful protector, the USA, but it was small and surrounded by hostile countries and regimes. About the U.S., he more than once heard ambivalent comments: "Yes, Americans support us, but in exchange, we carry out various military and intelligence tasks for them, including spying and testing new weapons. Some jobs are dirty."

4.

From the hotel in the northern part of the city near Tel Aviv University, the two moved to the center, settling into the hotel Dizengoff. Their room on the third floor was spacious and airy. The music from the fountain was sometimes loud but did not bother them, nor did the buzz created by laughing strollers and excited children. The city's vibrant mood suited them, so all the windows were usually wide open.

On a small cassette player, they listened mostly to tapes brought from Metz, but a mildly provocative "pirate" station, broadcasting from a boat located just beyond Israel's twenty-two kilometers of coastal waters, could also be clearly heard. The music from that station accompanied the strains emanating from the fountain. The disc jockeys spoke Hebrew and English and had an amazingly eclectic taste. One evening, a particularly bizarre sequence could be heard: Sibelius's *Finlandia*, followed by a famous song of the Volga boatmen, "*Ey, uhnyem!*" (*Yo, heave-ho!*); next came "Brown Sugar" by the Rolling Stones; after the mysterious Grace Jones, came the Steve Miller Band, The Doors, and Elvis Costello. The station then emitted "Yo Ya" by the Israeli rock group Kaveret. In an emotional tone, the announcer introduced the song as the most popular in Israel—of all time! He said it was "full of Jewish humor." Célestin and Odile laughed, admiring their patience and recognizing that the cacophony was one of the fascinating components of travel.

One of the places they liked was a grassy area between the left bank of the Yarkon River and Bnei Dan and Ussishkin Streets. Not far, the river flowed into the Mediterranean Sea, creating Metzitzim Beach, deserted and with enough sand for walks. No one came there even when the weather was sunny, so they happily strode through small waves. Those were the first barefoot steps next to a huge body of water since Baikal. Suddenly, she said: "Papa, do you remember how we dipped without clothes in the freezing water of Baikal?"

Célestin was touched, although he was uncertain by what—his daughter's brightness? Or their memories of Russia, of Siberia? Of Olya, so immeasurably far? *"Oui, ma petite sirène, je me souviens,* and I'm glad you reminded me," he said nostalgically. "But here we're in the city, so we can't just remove clothes and plunge in, although the water is for sure five or six degrees warmer than in Baikal. What we can do is pour water over each other's heads. This seawater can't be sacred to the Buryats—you surely remember their mystical beliefs? But it was certainly sacred to some of the many peoples who have been on this very spot over thousands of years, so let it be sacred to us too!" Their ritual began with the girl pouring a handful of water over her father's bowed head.

Half an hour later, when they entered the nearby restaurant Little Old Tel Aviv on Ha-Yarkon Street, Odile's blouse and her father's shirt were still slightly wet and salty. The staff greeted them gaily because they had eaten several times there. It had been recommended for its authentic food by Shalom Yinon, a gourmet and well-known orientalist at Bar-Ilan University in east Tel Aviv. The owner brought tasty dishes in abundance.

Occasionally, Odile took a siesta, and he went out to stretch his legs on Dizengoff. Sometimes a person, including soldiers, addressed him in Hebrew, and when he answered in English, laughed and said in English they needed directions. Célestin, being Célestin, would then ask what they wanted to know. To their surprise, the foreigner gave precise information about the post office or a nearby street. If their English was weak, he would point and indicate, with a meandering hand, left, right, and left, as needed. The chance meeting often grew into a ten-minute chat. For him, it was another minute part of the tireless attempt to communicate with Israel.

That sort of thing happened in other countries, probably due to his trustworthy looks. However, it never occurred when Odile was present. Those who wanted free service seemingly thought it impolite to disturb a man taking care of a young child. In Israel, the situation was interesting: Célestin wondered whether a Roman Catholic from France looked to the locals like them. He naturally took into account that people asked because everyone in earshot spoke Hebrew. Therefore, the only thing his analysis confirmed beyond doubt was that he did not look non-Jewish, Gentile, *Goy*.

"More analytical nonsense," he thought. Keeping in mind the usually pale faces of Ashkenazim from Europe, the milk coffee to the dark bronze color spectrum of faces belonging to the Sephardim Jews from Morocco and Ethiopia, and the Sabras with their extremely diverse skin and eye colors—not forgetting every possible facial type—the conclusion was that just about every person could look like a Jew and an Israeli, and therefore he too. What he found interesting and even pleasant was this: For the first time in his life, he was in a microscopically small minority, and the Jews were members of an overwhelming majority.

Precisely when that chain of thought ended on Dizengoff Street, fate brought two blue-eyed blondes to his undivided attention. The young women chattered vivaciously in Hebrew at a window displaying the spring collection of ladies' shoes. "Alas," he thought, "this is fate only in the sense of proving my conclusion correct, not any other: These attractive women have already found, without asking me, what they were looking for."

5.

It was the beginning of April when they finally traveled to Jerusalem. After storing over half of their luggage at the hotel Dizengoff, they took the № 20 bus to the Tel Aviv train station. A light rain was falling. Having become accustomed to life in the noisy, young, optimistic city, where they had formed many friendships, they were sad to leave, although not reluctant—after all, Jerusalem beckoned.

The bus needed half an hour to travel from the city center through Ramat Gan, pass the Maccabee Football Club stadium, and arrive at the small station Bnei Brak in a dilapidated part of town. At 8:20 a.m., they boarded the train that had arrived from Haifa and was continuing to Jerusalem. The beginning of the journey was not promising. The tickets were dirt cheap, but the train was old, slow, not too clean, and stopped by each lamp post. It would take more than two hours to reach Jerusalem. Friends had told Célestin that no one took the train but traveled by bus, which arrived in an hour; in addition, the location of the bus station was more convenient in both cities. However, unlike the bus, the train was said to pass through stunning countryside, which carried more weight in his choice.

Outside the city, there were garbage dumps and cannibalized cars, followed by poor villages, probably Palestinian. Amidst them, one saw uncultivated, unappealing land, looking worse for the drizzle. But after about seventy minutes of travel, the train began to climb, the rain suddenly stopped, and the morning sun shone on a biblical landscape. Dusty green olive groves appeared on terraces carved into rocks, replaced after a while by steep hills of subtle colors—pink, mauve, pale violet. The old train hiccupped and coughed but kept climbing next to a brimming stream. By the time it ascended to Jerusalem's elevation of eight hundred meters, the vegetation had become a deep green. They arrived at 10:30.

Jerusalem! On the platform, in front of the modest station building, Célestin embraced Odile and told her in an excited voice: "I should've come here long ago, way back when Patrizia and I met and fell in love." As so many times before, when Papa mentioned *Maman*, she felt a sad unease and mumbled, "So, why didn't you come?" He explained it would have been difficult to do because the Six-Day War between Israel and the Arab countries had ended only a short time earlier. "The war took place in 1967, five years before you were born. In any case, now is a good time for both of us to come to this ancient, sacred city for the first time in our lives: For you, because I think nine years of age is perfect for the first visit, and for me, because I am here with you." Tears in her beautiful eyes.

There was no cab, so they boarded bus № 5 to get to the main bus station. Even though he was operating a bus that was falling apart, the driver entered each of the numerous curves like a madman and braked as if taking a herd of sheep to the slaughterhouse. In the bus, on the streets during the drive, and at the terminal when they somehow arrived without injury, far more Palestinians and religious Jews were evident than in Tel Aviv.

Oriental chaos prevailed at the station square: Dense crowds; people yelling in Hebrew and Arabic; idling buses shuddering, rattling, and rumbling; donkeys braying. Believers from all three religions ran here and there, carrying hefty books. Many uniformed young soldiers, with rifles over their shoulders, looked for transportation. Even in that ruckus, people were attentive to Odile, so father and daughter managed to get near the long row of public phones. Standing side by side, an incredible variety of men fought bitterly with the apparatuses: They yelled at them, hit them with open palms, forcefully banged the handsets, and probably cursed them. All were united in their loathing for the evil instruments, in part because the phones appeared to be programmed to steal money, like the Las Vegas "one-armed bandits." In Jerusalem, it was not an alleged theft of shekel coins, but of the precious "asimons," telephone tokens. Célestin always had a pocketful in Tel Aviv and even gave some to Odile to keep in her pockets.

While skillfully rejecting other candidates' onslaught, a black-hatted, long-bearded, orthodox Jew with thick glasses kindly let Célestin use the phone. Acting quickly, he first called the hotel where he had reserved a room the previous day from Tel Aviv: No reservation, no free rooms. No luck at another hotel. Then he called his close friend Mordekhai-Morkel Schwartz, a professor at the Hebrew University of Jerusalem. Morkel was very happy to hear from Célestin, greeted him with a loud, joyful "shalom," and said they could stay with his friends, who live near the university and have a suitable guest room. Forced to ignore the resigned sighs behind him, Célestin called Mrs. Dobrin and after a polite exchange obtained the address.

The sun shone more brightly. No longer nervous because of the commotion, they again realized they were in Jerusalem. Not far from the station square, they miraculously found a cab not more than seven or eight years old. The driver squeezed their luggage between two old tires. After about twenty minutes of calm driving—sensible either because of Odile or the steep uphill road—they arrived at Ha-Hagana № 26. The Dobrins' apartment was on the third floor of a modern five-story building with an elevator. From her balcony, Mrs. Dobrin heartily greeted them as they exited the car. Shalom!

6.

Rachel Dobrin was a slim, casually dressed woman in her early fifties. She had a regular, pale face and graying hair tied into a ponytail. Squatting in front of Odile, she lightly stroked her head and asked in American English: "Are you tired, honey?" Then she showed them a sunny room: "The view from here is to the east—all the way to the Dead Sea!" They were delighted, and he asked if the room was usually rented. "Oh, no, we've never done it," said Mrs. Rachel. "Our son and his wife live in Haifa and use this room when they visit. The cupboard and drawers are half-empty; feel free to use them instead of living out of suitcases. They have a three-year-old daughter, and so there are two beds. I hope Odile will like the small one. Sit on it, darling, try it out, I think it's good for healthy sleep."

She liked the lady with smiling eyes and knew Mrs. Dobrin would do everything to make their stay pleasant. Célestin shared these sentiments and profusely thanked the hostess. "You don't need to thank me. Professor Schwartz—Morkel—is a great friend of ours. Fortunately, I had a day off, so I was home when you called from the bedlam at the bus station. I work as a laboratory technician at Hebrew University. My husband Daniel also works there; his specialty is analytical chemistry. I'll call him now; if he's free, he could come to meet you. The university is only fifteen minutes on foot, so when Danny arrives, we'll all drink something refreshing." She showed them the bathroom and gave them towels.

While crossing the threshold of the apartment, Professor Dobrin loudly exclaimed the greeting. Wearing a broad smile, he approached his guest with quick, loping steps and used both hands to grasp Célestin's firmly. "I've heard so many good things about you from Morky. I hope you'll feel at home with us." Then he made a playful hop toward Odile and sang out, "Welcome, pretty girl!"

Danny was a tall, bony man with completely gray hair. On his otherwise handsome face, there were nasty scars, which gave him the serious mien of someone who had experienced pain. But when he smiled or made a joke, the entire room became more cheerful.

A new friendship thus began, its sincerity and openness owing much to Morkel Schwartz. After a light meal prepared by Rachel, Odile went to take a shower, unpack, and rest for a while. The three adults began an intimate conversation. "Danny and I were born in the same year, 1928, in similarly poor Jewish families in America, Danny in Minneapolis and I in Cleveland. As chance would have it, both of our families emigrated to America at the beginning of the century from the westernmost part of the then-Russian Empire, the city of Minsk."

Danny took over: "One trait common to our families was that they were feverishly saving money, driven by the all-consuming desire for their children to obtain a high education—so typical of us Jews, isn't it?" He roared with laughter, and Rachel joined him, whereas Célestin smiled uneasily. "We fell in love as students at Ohio State University in my native city. It has a good reputation, maybe you've heard of it," Rachel concluded.

"Yes, I have. But those degrees guaranteed fine careers in

America, yet you came to Israel. May I ask how it transpired?" Célestin spoke cautiously, hoping he was not inconsiderate. Rachel and Danny looked at each other and were briefly silent as if deciding who should answer. Stammering slightly, which was peculiar for a man so intelligent and physically strong, Daniel explained: "It was a very hard decision because we made it despite the fierce opposition of both sets of parents. You see, even though they were not ultra-orthodox, they were certainly *Masortim*, traditional Jews. So to us, it seemed illogical that to such strong believers, our social—and, one has to admit, financial—success in America was far more important than the return to Eretz Israel, our *Aliyah*!"

As if taking part again in the ancient family quarrels in Minneapolis and Cleveland, Rachel added in an agitated voice: "Our parents could not grasp why to the two of us, *Hilonim*, secular Jews— which we both had been even before we met—the return to Israel was so important. They did not understand how coming here meant above all—well above any biblical obligation—our participation in the construction of a new, young, Jewish country.

"We arrived in 1954, six years after the war of 1948 and Israel's independence. We were so happy! A year later, our son Noah, our only child, was born. A genuine Sabra!" Danny added thoughtfully: "He is now almost twenty-six, an Israeli first and only then a Jew."

They moved to Célestin's origin and family. He talked freely, as his hosts had done. The Second World War, Germany and France, the deaths of his parents, Metz and Koblenz, Patrizia's and Patrice's tragic demise, the birth of Odile, and her childhood years. Rachel and Danny were intensely curious about his travels with a daughter so young, and he described her reactions to people and sights in China, Mongolia, and Russia. He did not wish to hide Olya's existence and disclosed intimate information about her. His hosts listened with compassion. Danny said: "Here it's known the Soviets are not letting anybody leave—primarily because they are ashamed—but, believe it or not, they seem to be letting out Jews more often than they do ethnic Russians. Your

Olya would perhaps more easily get the exit visa if she were a hundred percent Tatar woman than one with a Russian mother. Outrageous doings."

Inevitably, they switched back to Israel and its wars, past and future, with Arab countries. Although Célestin refrained from probing, Danny offered information close to his and Rachel's hearts: "We came here idealistically to help build Israel but soon realized waging wars was part of it. In the war of June 1967, I participated actively, and even though it lasted only six days, I succeeded in getting seriously wounded." He pointed to the scars on his face, and Rachel said softly: "He was in the hospital for a long time." Danny went on: "Let me put things in perspective: I was then thirty-nine, and Noah was twelve. But already in October of 1973, there was a new war, the Yom Kippur War, when we were suddenly attacked on the holiest day in the Jewish year. Our son was then barely eighteen, and I was forty-five, so we both participated in the rearguard. Rachel was also active behind the lines— and fearing every minute for her husband and son."

"Horrible! I understand, I understand," Célestin whispered. At that moment, Odile, who had woken up, called her father from the door of their room.

7.

The following mid-morning, he took his daughter on foot to the Hebrew University of Jerusalem, the main of several campuses of Hebrew University and the best in Israel. They indeed needed only fifteen minutes to get there from the apartment of the Dobrin family, their convenient new abode. At the end of the previous evening, Célestin did all he could to persuade Rachel and Danny to specify a rental amount. "I don't know how long we'll stay in Jerusalem—and besides, we'd like to travel for short periods to the south and north of Israel, and then return here. Therefore, please be so kind as to come up with an amount I would pay in advance each week." They kept declining to grant the request and finally shyly mentioned a symbolic amount, which Célestin had to accept. He sighed inaudibly, preferring the amount to be realistic. The way things stood, he would have to remember frequently to buy a gift for Rachel or a food item for the household. He solved the problem by explaining it to Odile and assigning her the task of reminding him. She cheerfully accepted her new job.

The campus, erected in the seventies to replace the demolished one, was strikingly modern. There was a long, uneven row of structures, each consisting of three- and four-story "modules." Lecture halls, laboratories, offices, cafeterias, and cozy corners for talk and rest—all of these existed in each module. Wherever possible, natural light was allowed in, and there were many plants, sculptures, and small fountains.

They rushed to enter the library, which was in an imposing building. As soon as Célestin said "shalom" and gave his name to the lady manning the front desk, she vivaciously reciprocated and gave someone instructions. "Professor Mordekhai Schwartz told us you would be arriving with a little daughter, so we selected a few children's books in French and German." She greeted Odile, giving her the books. "I already notified the director of our library. Dr. Hila Bellin will presently come down to take you to her office.

It turned out Dr. Bellin was a tall, elegant French lady with short black hair and alabaster skin. She had penetrating greenish eyes and a regular nose similar to Célestin's. The conversation, naturally in French, took place in her office overflowing with books. From no less than five windows, one could see almost every corner of the campus. With Odile, Dr. Bellin was more genteel than warm: She shook hands with the girl and did not coddle her as many women did. Having been offered an armchair by one of the windows, Odile began to look through the books, paying no attention to the adults. Célestin thought: "This lady is a hundred percent *Parisienne* from a wealthy family. Very intelligent and ambitious. She probably doesn't have children, or at least is not used to having a child in her office. However, I bet Odilichka will soon win her over with her sharp mind and natural sweetness."

"Please call me Hila, and I'll call you Célestin, if you'll allow me. We are in Israel, an informal place, and I am, after all, older than you," she grinned. This was accompanied by a hint of discreet flirtation, meaning next to nothing to Parisians. She must have been only four or five years older than him. Instead of sitting at her desk, Dr. Bellin leaned back in an armchair directly across from her guest. Clad in a silk blouse, close-fitting jacket, and a knee-length, burgundy-colored skirt, she kept her long legs at an angle and close together. Her elbows were on the armrests, and long, fine fingers supported her chin as in prayer. "What an elegant, accomplished pose," admired Célestin but purposefully refrained—in a quite un-Parisian manner—from giving Hila any compliments, particularly about her youthful looks.

But they got along splendidly, talking spontaneously and with mutual respect. Hila asked her secretary to bring three glasses of fresh orange juice and tell callers she was out. They made sure Odile did not lack anything.

"The compliments Morkel Schwartz gave you! He's a close friend of mine. We met in Paris when I was completing my dissertation at the Sorbonne in the Department of Near-Eastern Literature, and he was Visiting Professor of Anthropology. Already then, he was working on projects regarded as inflammatory. For example, he carried out quantitative studies of cultural and other differences between Jews and Arabs, but also similarities! As you certainly know much better than I do, he has continued such work to this day. You see, I was born in a Jewish Parisian family, but neither to my parents, both of whom are still active as lawyers, nor to me and Morkel, has Jewishness been important in professional work. We do our best to be objective. Sometimes it's hard but can be done. Nor is Jewishness important, let alone essential, in my friendship with Morky."

Célestin listened to her attentively, discovering something new about his friend of many years. As for Hila, it turned out she had successfully defended, at the age of twenty-seven, a dissertation comparing the literature of Israel to writings in Arab countries around it. She had a command of several ancient languages, in addition to Hebrew and Arabic. "Had I not met Morkel, I don't know if I would've ever come to Israel, even to visit. After all, I'm not an anthropologist, and I certainly wouldn't have come right after the Six-Day War—as I did, twelve years ago. 'Do you seriously want to go there now, so soon after your doctorate and the war?' was all my parents said in lieu of criticism. That's the way they are, always trusting my judgment. But they were proud when I was named Deputy Director of Hebrew University Library six months after arriving in Jerusalem." Célestin said: "They had every reason to be proud." He did think: "Perhaps there was a little help from my naughty Morky!" There was no cynicism or mockery in the thought, just a bit of private fun.

Hila then recounted the history of that part of Jerusalem and Hebrew University, much of which was new and interesting to him: "The University was founded in 1918, thirty years before Israel's independence. Albert Einstein and Sigmund Freud were members of the first Board of Directors, can you imagine? This locality, Mount Scopus—it's a high mountain for this area, although the elevation is only 826 meters—was an Israeli enclave in Jordanian territory protected by the United Nations during the period from 1948 to 1967. In the Six-Day War, Israel acquired it and then confiscated some adjoining land in the Palestinian village of Al-Issawiya. That's the ground under this new campus. Construction began in 1968, and it'll be finished this year."

While Célestin reflected on what he had heard, Hila calmly continued: "Morkel mentioned you are staying with Rachel and Daniel Dobrin. I know their flat is on Ha-Hagana. Even though close to here, it officially belongs to French Hill. Every inch of land is precious to Israelis—but also to Palestinians. And from their point of view, the story of French Hill is even more sad than the one of Mt. Scopus. The name 'French Hill' comes from French Catholic monks who founded the monastery of Saint Anne in that area. The monks were said to be 'public benefactors' because they donated a small portion of 'their' land so a reservoir could be built for the water pumped in Ein Farah. The spring is located between Jerusalem and Jericho. Later, Jordan had a military outpost on French Hill.

"But the next point is important: Soon after Israel gained possession of the area in the Six-Day War, the construction of the residential quarter where you live was begun—already in 1969. Furthermore, just last year, 1980, Israel unilaterally annexed it based on the so-called Jerusalem Law. I'm sure you know about it. One rarely hears any discussion at the University that the annexation was and is illegal by the principles of international law. And the people who own apartments there—for which they paid a lot of money—don't want to even think about it, regardless of how secular and 'liberal' they consider themselves. Anyway, you can speak with Morkel about this; he is well-informed and open-minded."

Hila and Célestin looked at each other thoughtfully, and he said: "I'll tell you honestly, Hila, I admire you. You are a courageous woman, especially when your university position of responsibility is kept in mind. Yes, I'll speak to Morkel. But it seems you gave me the advice, in a roundabout way, not to mention this topic to Rachel and Danny. I wouldn't have done it even if you hadn't advised me.

"Well, you see, yesterday I had a long and frank talk with the Dobrins, and they didn't utter a single word on the Jerusalem Law, the annexation, and the shaky international status of French Hill as Israeli territory. And I—not just because I'm a foreigner, a guest here—I'm simply not able to enter someone's house and throw into the hosts' faces what they would certainly hate to hear."

"I completely understand. And thank you for calling me courageous. Your opinion is valuable to me, but I don't consider myself brave. There is freedom of speech in Israel. Besides, this University has many friends in the Knesset, as does Morkel. Even I do." She got up, wrote something on a piece of paper, and gave it to Célestin: "Here is my private number. This door is always open for you—with or without your beautiful, serious daughter."

Father and daughter walked to Level 2, Module 5, in the Social Sciences building to greet Dr. Mordekhai Schwartz in his office. Morkel was due to lecture shortly, so there was only time for him and Célestin to clutch each other in a prolonged bear hug, and for the esteemed professor to compliment Odile and kiss her loudly on both cheeks. He received thanks from the visitors for arranging their comfortable accommodation with the Dobrins.

After Morkel left, his secretary gave Célestin a pile of mail and took him and Odile to a smallish, well-equipped office they could use while in Jerusalem—№ 2516: Level 2, Modul 5, Room 16. They pensively looked through the window at the steeply descending desert landscape and then turned to the relief map of Israel hanging on the wall. He studied it for a while and explained to his daughter—one finger on the map and another pointing through the window: "The view from here is to the northeast, and there, way down in the hole, is the ancient town of Jericho. Using the scale here on the map, I'd say it's thirty kilometers away. Near Jericho is the border of Israel—here, you see—with Jordan. It's a country about which you and I know little. And fifty kilometers farther from Jericho, in the same northeastern direction, lies Amman, the capital of that country.

He sat down at the desk, and she returned to the window. "Because you always want to know everything and remind me when I forget: We'll hire a car and visit Jericho, the bottom of the desert—two hundred sixty meters below sea level. Imagine that! But we won't visit the city of Amman and the country of Jordan. Not now. It's too dangerous. There was a war thirteen years ago in this area and another only seven years ago. Even now, there's no peace. It's a great pity. Above all, of course, for the people living here but also for us. I'd very much like us to see the fabulous ancient Petra in southern Jordan. It'll have to wait."

While her father conducted phone calls with acquaintances in Tel Aviv, Haifa, and Jerusalem, Odile opened the mail from her school. In bulging envelopes, there were materials she would have to master. Then she made notes in her diary about the events important to her. Just as Célestin had done, she started the Israel diary on the day they arrived.

Hunger pangs made them descend to the module's street level. Next to a bank and a post office, they found a student cafeteria. During lunch, they overheard two young men's loud chatter in American English. The students were sitting at a nearby table and spoke as if they were alone. One of them said: "I don't like Sue... She's too snobbish and jappish!"

When father and daughter finished their meal, the students were still gossiping. Célestin, inquisitive and communicative, did not hesitate to go to their table: "I'm sorry to disturb you. We're from France, and our English leaves much to be desired. I had no intention to eavesdrop, but I overheard you describe some girl called Sue as 'jappish.' I'm curious, what does it mean?"

Far from being upset, the guys saw humor in the question and guffawed boisterously. One said: "I'll explain it, Sir. You see, in American cities where there are many Jews, there's a comical term 'Jewish American Princess,' or JAP; and 'jappish' is an expression used for conceited girls from rich Jewish families. Even Englishmen wouldn't understand, let alone Frenchmen. It's not really an insulting term; some of the gaudily dressed geese with excessive jewelry very much enjoy being called a JAP. After all, both of us are Jews, just as you and your daughter are."

Célestin laughed and thanked the student. The young man who had said nothing until then, added: "Just so you know, my friend here doesn't want to admit it, but he's head over heels in love with Sue, the pretty little JAP. His chances to capture her are nil, for he's no Jewish Prince!"

After the amusing lecture on Jewish-American slang, he recalled needing information from a book on Hebrew linguistics in French, which he had seen in Morkel's office. He had been given the key by Morkel and permission to use his library. Leaving the door open, he began to make notes from the book when Morkel returned and warmly greeted the pair: "I came back for a minute to take files for the next meeting. You can stay here or take the book home. It's good we ran into each other. My Deborah insisted I invite you and Odile to dinner as she very much wishes to meet you. If you agree, I'll pick you up by car at the Dobrins tomorrow evening around seven-thirty. Would that suit you?"

He readily agreed. Morkel and Deborah were married two years earlier. She was from New York City, and the marriage to Morkel was her second, whereas for him it was the first—at the age of fifty. As he was leaving the office in a hurry, Morkel smiled: "I spoke to Hila a few minutes ago. She finds you *très sympathique* and Odile even more so."

After making notes, Célestin said to the girl: "It's too late to go to the Old City. We'll do it tomorrow when we are fresh and energetic: Our first impressions will be more striking and memorable. So let's walk home." But his diligent daughter remembered her task: "Where are we going to find a gift for Mrs. Rachel?" The problem was easily solved because there were shops selling foodstuffs, flowers, and souvenirs near the post office. Rachel Dobrin would receive a fine box of rosewater *rahat-lokum*, a delight imported from Turkey.

9.

The weather was dry and crisp the next morning. Célestin and Odile spent time in front of the western wall of the Old City of Jerusalem studying the magnificent Jaffa Gate, where travelers arrived from the port ages ago. Once through, they reached, turning left, the Christian Quarter and then the Muslim. Turning right, first came the Armenian and then the Jewish Quarter. Walking to the east, more or less without turns, one arrived at Temple Mount, holy for all three monotheistic religions. However, he suggested: "Let's first walk next to the wall on the outside and see how the people live; afterward, we'll enter the Old City through one of the northern gates and begin to visit the holy sites."

They strolled along Jaffa Street by the small Palestinian shops and sidewalk vendors, then turned into a labyrinth of lanes and alleyways, until they suddenly ran into the Ethiopian Orthodox

Christian Church Kidane Mehret, "Covenant of Mercy." It was a quiet place, with a cultivated garden surrounded by tall cypress trees, where they found themselves alone after the city bustle. The church was a dignified round structure with tall windows and a massive green-gray dome. In the corner of the garden, an old man with very dark skin sat serenely. Astutely estimating his photogenic appeal, she took out the camera and respectfully sought permission to take a picture. He declined but did so in an old-fashioned, noble manner. She was astonished: That was the first failure in her short career as a photographic portraitist.

Soon they encountered a younger man in the garden, who wore a brown cassock and green fez. He was cleaning the paths with a broom and not paying attention to the visitors. But when courteously asked about the interior of the church, the sexton wordlessly unlocked a side door and entered. Following his example, father and daughter took their shoes off at the entrance. Célestin reminded Odile of what he had taught her at the small Saint Nicholas Church on Lake Baikal, and so, after a prayer, they crossed themselves in the Orthodox way. The man also prayed but in what seemed a mixture of Christian and Muslim rituals: He crossed himself as they had learned in Russia—not as Catholics do—but did it while kneeling and touching the ground with his forehead. They scrupulously looked at the icons on the walls and the frescoes inside the dome. Odile knew better than to try to take photos. At the end of the visit, Célestin pushed a note into the discreetly located donations box and thanked the sexton, who bowed deeply and let them leave through the front door. Their respectful behavior, perhaps unusual for Westerners, had won the Ethiopian.

Continuing farther north along narrow lanes, they soon found themselves in the heart of the ultraorthodox Mea Shearim, "Hundred Gates," one of the oldest Jewish quarters in Jerusalem. Célestin had read a lot about that neighborhood of Haredi Jews. German architect Konrad Schick, who was a Christian, created the original plan for the settlement. When founded thirty years later, in 1846, it was intentionally developed outside the Old City so better sanitary conditions could be secured. In the past, the Quarter was surrounded by a wall with gates locked at night. The progressive Herr Schick wanted trees and greenery in each of the numerous family courtyards, but failed—cowsheds were built. Still, Mea Shearim was the first quarter in Jerusalem with street-lights: Residents paid for the installation.

The Quarter never ceased being an island with its own rules. Many had to do with attire and were listed on large boards at each entrance as "Modesty Regulations." Some boards addressed specifically "Jewish Daughters" with an exclamation mark, whereas others spoke to all women and girls. The text was in Hebrew and English—Arabic did not exist in the settlement. Standing in front of one board, Célestin looked at what the two of them were wearing and decided they could enter. Odile's skirt was to her knees, and the blouse had long sleeves. Actually, he was uncertain at what age, in Haredi opinion, little girls become older girls. The board stated shorts and short skirts were forbidden, as well as low necklines, bare shoulders, and navels.

It was evident these ultraconservative men were well in-formed about the clothes appealing to Western female tourists—secular Israeli women probably found themselves in Mea Shearim rarely. As for his appearance, it also seemed acceptable, as he did not wear either shorts or a bodybuilder sleeveless rag. Additional rules were in force for visitors during Shabbat—from sunset on Friday to sunset on Saturday—regarding smoking, photography, and driving automobiles.

They walked along cobblestoned streetlets holding hands and observing people and houses. Every man had a beard and wore black clothes: a hat, a long coat, and polished shoes. Many had long *payot*, curly sidelocks, obviously very different from the *Backenbart* of Prussian officers. Sallow skin and glasses predomi-nated. The few women around were dressed in long dark skirts and homemade woolen sweaters and socks. On their heads were equally dark kerchiefs and hairnets. Now and then, they saw an unmarried girl or woman with braids.

There were specialized grocers, fish shops, and barbershops.

Through the window of one, Célestin and Odile watched a man's scalp being denuded to bare skin, with his payot lovingly coddled. "This would be an interesting photo, but please, *ma chère fille*, don't even dream of taking pictures of people, even children, in this quarter." That was an unnecessary prohibition because she was in culture shock the entire time. "I don't like it here," she muttered. "These people are too weird. Do they look as ugly to you as they do to me?" Célestin said nothing, which was a rarity.

To see the reaction of these allegedly weird people, he wanted to exchange at least a few words with someone—male, of course—even at the cost of posing a banal question. So, he asked in English a middle-aged gentleman wearing a full Haredi "uniform" for directions to the Ethiopian Kidane Mehret Church. The man stopped without hesitation and kindly, without rushing, explained in formal English how to reach the desired destination. In parting, he politely touched the brim of his hat.

"You see how gentlemanly this person was, no different from somebody in Metz or Koblenz whom I would ask for information. At one point, it even seemed he was going to offer to take us to that church! Such is the embarrassing fate of liars. I was so relieved he didn't do it. Perhaps he would have if I were alone, but it may be too odd in this quarter to see a resident walking around with a foreigner and his daughter who's without braids. So you saved me from shame." Odile laughed heartily, for the first time in Mea Shearim.

The pleasant encounter with a "typical" man from the Quarter encouraged Célestin to stop another victim of similar physical appearance and in almost identical clothes. He fervently hoped the first gentleman would not see him. In the second case, it quickly emerged that the man had grown up and married in the Jewish Orthodox Quarter of Antwerp in Belgium—the world-renowned center for diamond-cutting—before he arrived in Mea Shearim with his family. Naturally, he spoke Flemish and Belgian French. The dialogue with him flowed effortlessly and might have lasted even longer if not for the discomfort the men felt as Odile idly shifted from foot to foot. The man was unexpectedly open, "maybe because we're speaking French," thought Célestin, "or because he knows we'll never see each other again." He even said something that sounded to the Frenchman like a criticism of the Quarter: "Someone from Europe or America can come to live in Mea Shearim only if he has close relatives who are residents—I had them. To an incredible degree, the Quarter is traditional, inward-looking, and functions based on 'dynasties' and sects."

Before their friendly parting, Célestin was emboldened to say: "May I impose on you with a question? Only yesterday, I read something surprising—that members of certain groups in Mea Shearim speak Yiddish in their families and when conducting daily business in the quarter, whereas Hebrew, as the holy language, is reserved for prayer and study of the Torah. Is it true?" The man responded without hesitation: "It's true for some families. You find it surprising because you think it makes no sense for some Jews, especially the ultraorthodox—who finally, after thousands of years, regained their land and their ancient Hebrew language—not to use it in intimate settings with their loved ones. Isn't that so? Well, yes, you're right, it's not logical. Much is not logical on this islet, but also in the world outside. Some residents would rebuke me for revealing our alleged secrets to a Goy, a Gentile, but I'll tell you my wife and I speak a mixture of Flemish and Yiddish in our most intimate moments."

10.

It was two in the afternoon. Célestin and Odile had to admit that the visit to Mea Shearim, even though it was a valuable experience, mentally exhausted them. At the counter of a young Arab, near the long and broad King George Street, they bought their favorite street food—hummus, falafel, fresh salad, and crunchy pita—and ate it with gusto, sitting on a stone bench on Heleni Ha-Malka Street. The street was the northern edge of one of the first quarters developed outside the Old City at the end of the nineteenth century: The walled Russian Compound. For that reason, Mea Shearim was built farther north, about a kilometer from Jaffa Gate.

The walls of the Compound had disappeared, but the magnificent white building of the Russian Orthodox Cathedral of Holy Trinity, erected in 1872, remained—and was admired for a long time by father and daughter. Walking around it, they counted eight bell towers with the Russian cross atop each. They tried to enter, but all the doors were locked. Like the walls, hostels for pilgrims from Russia disappeared long ago. "Nothing surprising: all the doors shut and no notice when one can enter; typical Soviet business," he thought bitterly about it—and Olya. He knew that until 1948, under the British Mandate, the cathedral belonged to the "Russian Orthodox Church Outside of Russia," but when the USSR recognized Israel, the new State promptly "returned" all of the emigrated church's possessions to the USSR—to the Moscow Patriarchate.

Célestin reminded Odile of their walks with Olya and the locked churches in Leningrad and Moscow. He remembered reading a strange detail about the ex-Russian Compound and told the girl. In 1964, Israel bought from the USSR the entire Compound as it was in the nineteenth century, except the cathedral, for three and a half million dollars—and paid entirely in Jaffa oranges! "How greedily the communist apparatchiks must have indulged in the sweet fruit," sourly commented Célestin.

South of the cathedral toward the Old City walls, there were Israeli government buildings, but nestled among them, one could see a few small restaurants and even a nightclub. One of the restaurants was called Kamchatka and the club Saint Vladimir—all that remained of the Russian Empire, except for the padlocked white cathedral.

New Gate, one of the three entrances into the Old City from the north, was only a hundred meters farther. Unlike the majority of Jerusalem gates, built in the sixteenth century under Sultan Suleiman the Magnificent, New Gate was opened in 1887 to enable direct access to the Christian Quarter. It was a comparatively simple gate, but situated at the highest point of the entire wall, so after they had passed through, a spectacular view of the ancient city opened. The girl forgot being tired, took her father by the hand, and exclaimed: "Let's go, Papa!" Célestin kept her back: "*Non, ma douce*, let's not do it now. It's four o'clock. We've seen much, our minds are full of thoughts and images. Besides, Morky is picking us up at seven-thirty. We need to buy some presents. Being tired and pressed for time is not the right way to enter the holy city for the first time. Let's be patient until tomorrow."

They visited shops in the Ben Yehuda pedestrian zone and purchased a French silk scarf for Deborah and a Danish compass for Morkel—Célestin had an identical one. For Odile, he bought a spiral-bound drawing block with good paper, as well as color and charcoal pencils and wax crayons. "At school, you loved to draw, and during our travels, you took many photos, so now you can do both." She was surprised and happy.

Morkel arrived promptly. "Our drive will be short—Deborah and I also live on French Hill. We moved here two months after our wedding because Debbie didn't feel safe in my Old City flat, or so she claimed. I'd lived there happily for many years. Of course, there were Palestinians in the neighborhood, but never any problems." Célestin was surprised because he was familiar with Morkel's delicate emotional and mental balance regarding both Israeli and Palestinian aspirations: He remembered what Hila had told him about the history of French Hill. Although she had mentioned he could openly talk to Morkel, Célestin was reluctant to do so. After all, his friend had said nothing about French Hill's dubious past in connection with either the Dobrins' address or his own.

Odile charmingly gave Deborah the wrapped scarf, but Morkel's wife expressed thanks looking only at Célestin. After a while, she did praise Odile's amber bracelet from Gdansk. The girl said hesitatingly: "This bracelet belonged to my *maman*. I like it very much but rarely wear it. I'm afraid to lose it." Her father was not pleased with the turn the conversation took because Deborah was not likable. He preferred they did not confide in the garishly dressed middle-aged woman with too much jewelry about Patrizia—and as for Morkel, he already knew everything.

Sensing his guests' unease, he jumped in and extolled the gift he had received. Célestin was gratified: "I've owned the same model for a while and didn't know what to buy. This is probably a silly gift because you may have a better one from the army. But look at the back. In the shop, at my request, they immediately engraved your initials in Hebrew." Morky examined the back of the compass and was enthusiastic: "The engraver is a true artist! Yes, I have a compass from my army days, but this one is a jewel— an instrument made in Denmark yet looking like a smart Swiss watch. Thank you, my dear friend!"

From appetizer to dessert, the dinner Deborah served was her version of American fast food. It seemed that most of it was bought in a shop specializing in students' food preferences and reheated. During the meal, Deborah did most of the talking, addressing only Célestin. She did it in a loud voice as if he would otherwise not understand. Her English was corrupted by a grating version of the New York-accented slang, with a few mumbled Hebrew words thrown in. Morkel did not react and mostly stared at his plate, as Odile did at hers. He wished to speak to the girl, but could not because she sat too far away for him to break through the sound barrier his spouse had erected. For Célestin, it was difficult to watch how rudely Deborah ignored Odile. "Twenty years ago," he speculated vengefully, "this New York shrew was probably a perfect example of a conceited 'Jewish American Princess.' What a pity those *sympathique* American students are not here, especially the poor enamored soul, to see what will happen if he marries his jappish darling Sue." The mystery was how it happened to his exceptionally bright, good, and level-headed Morky.

Before coffee, Célestin arranged for Odile to move to the living room and drink her tea in peace, reading the book he had advised her to bring. Adults remained at the dining table, sipping an overly sharp Israeli brandy. He talked about travel through the Asian part of the USSR and the churches long shut in Moscow and Leningrad—which led him to mention the Russian Holy Trinity Cathedral in Jerusalem that they had also failed to enter. He did not want to mention Olya in front of Deborah and would do it when alone with Morky.

They spoke about Mea Shearim and unsurprisingly moved to the compulsory army service of all Israelis except for the ultraorthodox. "All men are in the reserve corps until they are fifty-five, and that's good," said Morkel calmly. Some three months earlier, Célestin's fifty-two-year-old friend had returned from a month-long spell in a military science center. He was a member of a team of experts that included Professor Shalom Yinon, whom Célestin had met in Tel Aviv. Their task was to advise the Israeli Defense Forces, IDF, about the need to prepare and possibly start an information campaign in which the public would be warned that the next war, perhaps with Syria or Egypt, could lead to incomparably more civilian casualties and greater destruction than all the previous wars combined. Was such a campaign desirable? "Military analysts have noticed," Morkel explained, "that Israel's enemies are fast learning our skills—unconventional actions, extreme mobility, and surprising preventive strikes—with the help of advisers from the USSR and other Warsaw Pact countries, notably East Germany."

Naturally, neither did Célestin ask, nor did Morkel volunteer, what the advisory team's recommendation ended up being. Instead, the Frenchman said: "There's no doubt Israeli and American generals are closely watching the war between Iraq and Iran that's been going on for almost seven months—including the morale and psychological preparedness of the soldiers and populace in both countries." Morkel immediately responded: "Ha, ha, indeed that's so! My team obviously considered it. But the war was then only in its third month: At the time, both countries could've still aborted all operations."

During their long discussion about Israeli and Near-Eastern politics, Célestin demonstrated a great deal of knowledge. Morkel was not surprised because he had long been aware of his friend's erudition and curiosity. Things, however, stood differently with

Deborah. Crudely and suspiciously, she asked the guest: "How and why do you know all this?" He only smiled and shrugged, but Morkel's temper boiled over. Because of the insultingly phrased question, or the unkind treatment of Odile, or even the embarrassingly mediocre meal, he spat out furiously: "Deborah, what's the matter with you? Célestin is a superbly educated man—something about which your New Yorkers would be green with envy. And now you impertinently address him as if he were a spy! Because he reads, sees, and understands. You are the first to cackle and chortle behind the backs of our foreign visitors when they display comical ignorance, but when you meet someone who knows about the world, including our Israel, much more than you do, then he must have suspect motives."

He threw it all into Deborah's face and leaned back. Many unpleasant past events must have burst into his mind. She blanched and stammered, trying to be ironic: "You are exaggerating, Professor Schwartz. I only thought..." Because she did not apologize to Célestin, Morkel mercilessly continued: "Oh, you 'only thought.' You did not—you're hypocritical! Here's an example about which I hesitated to speak to you before. When foreign visitors are here, including Jews, you pretend to be a big Jewess and never stop praising the religious depth and wisdom of the ultraorthodox types. As if you were trying to become one yourself! But when El Al, which is nonstop losing people's money, cannot fly on Shabbat, and it interferes with your plans, ah well, then you denounce the ultraorthodox. And when you hear they are planning to build a synagogue here on French Hill, you pelt them with verbal stones. Why? Because on Shabbat you won't be able to go shopping in our quarter, nor drive the car—they'll break your windshield with real stones."

Deborah's face changed all colors, but it seemed certain the feeling of guilt did not cause any of them. Morkel went on: "Hila Bellin told Célestin about our country's illegitimate usurpation of French Hill. I'm ashamed she had to do it. I had opportunities to tell him, but I failed because I was mortified. And you know well why we moved precisely here from the Old City."

Morkel did not receive a response from his spouse. After a minute or so, he took two cigarettes out of Deborah's pack and lit them both; he gave the first to her and drew two or three puffs from the second, even though he rarely smoked. Célestin used the opportunity to lead Odile to their coats; then he briefly thanked the hostess and hugged Morky: "We'll walk home to stretch our legs, it's not far."

11.

It so happened that exactly at 8:15 a.m., on Tuesday, the 7th of April 1981, Odile and Célestin de Quernevelle entered the Old City of Jerusalem through New Gate. They both experienced an incomparable and unforgettable feeling, as they wrote in their diaries. Each described the emotion in words atypical for the age of the diarist.

That northwestern corner of the ancient town was the Christian Quarter. Streets and houses were conserved lovingly, and the cobblestones sparkled in the spring sun. Father and daughter first passed by Saint Savior, a Franciscan monastery. In the sixteenth century, the building belonged to the Gruziyan-Georgian Orthodox Church but was later sold to the much better-off Franciscan monks—who were officially one of the Catholic almsseeking orders! When Franz Josef, Emperor of Austria and King of Hungary, came to Jerusalem in 1869, he donated ample funds for a new building.

Célestin said: "One day we'll talk about the power of the Vatican and its support for the monastic orders. Of course, we're Catholics, although... I think we won't be doing anything religious for Easter. This year it falls on the 19th of April, in less than two weeks, and there'll be huge crowds. Well, we did attend the Christmas Midnight Mass, but it was in our Saint Étienne de Metz with our fellow citizens."

There were few visitors to the Old City, so father and daughter ambled uphill to the east through the narrow streets of the Greek Patriarchate. The Church of the Holy Sepulchre, also known by its original Greek name, Church of the Anastasis, of the Resurrection, soon appeared in front of them. "One can say," whispered Célestin when they walked in, "that we are now in the center of the entire Christian world. By a long tradition, the last four Stations of the Cross, the last stages on *Via Dolorosa*, the Sorrowful Way, are located within this church: The places where Jesus was crucified, *Golgotha*; where he died; was entombed; and resurrected. The original church was consecrated in the year 336 under a very important Roman Emperor, Constantine the Great, one year before he died. At the time, it was called Constantine's Basilica."

They spent a long time in the edifice. The church was a large structure under a massive circular dome. In the center, there was a chapel that contained—according to traditional teaching—the remains of the cave where the body of the dead Christ had been laid, the *Aedicule*. Despite its size, the church did not, in any way, resemble a grandiose Gothic cathedral. On many levels within it, there were numerous chapels, galleries, and crypts created at different times and in diverse styles. During their wandering, Célestin and Odile came across small chambers, often half-hidden, intimate, and touching. Although the basic structure was built at the time of the Crusaders, much of it preceded that period or was added later, with the lowest levels bearing a resemblance to catacombs. There, tiny chapels were carved into sheer rock. Odile looked around carefully, but to Célestin it seemed she was sometimes overawed; he would then take her hand or hug her shoulders.

In the semi-darkness, he read from a book, explaining what he could to the girl. The church was the seat of the Greek Orthodox Patriarch of Jerusalem, but its various levels, chapels, and altars were under the jurisdiction of the Greek Orthodox, Roman Catholic, Coptic, and Armenian Orthodox Churches. Back in 1757, a so-called *Status Quo* was reached among them—a set of rigorous rules to which all Christian communities adhered. Célestin and Odile encountered custodians from all of them: Some cleaned the floor and dusted various objects lackadaisically; others snored, more or less loudly; and still others watched the visitors' every step suspiciously, making sure they departed in an orderly manner.

Father and daughter emerged into fresh air and sunshine that belonged to some other epoch, on another planet. However, they were both, although in different ways, enriched and at least temporarily transformed into better people. "Whether or not we are true believers—perhaps we are sometimes when our souls have a deep reason to hurt—this place, *mon coeur*, is the cradle of our civilization," he said seriously, and she closely listened.

In a nearby shop, they bought postcards to send. The owner was an Italian whom Célestin liked: He was kind to Odile, praised her choice, and charged half the price. "You must know a lot about the church," the traveler said politely, "whereas this is our first visit. But we'll certainly return. Do you have some advice?" The man was a talkative polyglot. He mentioned the existence of interesting chapels and cellars, which were kept under lock and key by the custodians.

"To be a guardian or custodian in this church is considered an honor, but those people are poor. Ask them civilly, give them a couple of shekels, and you'll hear 'open sesame!' Some will even refuse to take the money. I've run this little shop for many years and know many of the watchmen personally. They are mostly good people, jealously guarding their often minute part of the church, and keeping an eye on each other. Maybe your book mentions that two families from an old Jerusalem clan are in charge of the keys to the main gate of the church. One family unlocks the gate every morning at five, and the other locks it at nine in the evening. As it happens, the clan is Muslim, by the name of Nuseibeh, and all the Christian denominations have confidence in the families' impartiality. The tradition goes back to Sultan Saladin in the twelfth century."

They strolled downhill past several Stations on Via Dolorosa, having planned to walk along all fourteen in the near future but in the opposite direction, beginning with the First Station, where Jesus had been sentenced to death. On the wider street El Wad, they turned to the south and soon arrived at one of the entrances to the Western Wall. It was situated a little more than three hundred meters from the Holy Sepulchre. Nothing was far in the Old City, with its area smaller than a square kilometer. Odile had heard from her father many historical facts and Old Testament legends about the kings David, Solomon, and Herod. She also knew that the Second Temple in Jerusalem was looted and destroyed in the year 70 after Christ by Roman legions under Titus, son of Emperor Vespasian, as punishment for the Jewish revolt. Only the temple's western wall remained.

In front of the entrance to the Wailing Wall section of the western wall, some soldiers and policemen observed everyone. Two young men in street clothes sat at a table inspecting bags, reminiscent of the Mossad employees at Munich airport. After the visitors had placed their small rucksacks on the table, one of the men first exclaimed the greeting and then addressed the girl. Looking straight at her eyes and speaking in a jovial tone, he said: "How are you today, pretty Miss? Do you have a toy for us?"

He obviously saw through Mossad's little trick but did not interfere as the experienced Odile calmly opened her rucksack and took out the Nikon, speaking half English, half French: "It's not a toy and not a present, but I know from the airport it interests you." Those two laughed and let them pass, but Célestin remained at the table: "I read in the *Jerusalem Post* that a sixteen-year-old yeshiva student was knifed to death near the Wall. It must have happened around here."

The men laughed no longer. One of them stood next to Célestin and said in a serious, soft voice, as if to make sure Odile could not overhear him: "Yes, Sir, it happened over there," he pointed to a spot twenty meters away. "I was on duty at this table and saw the murder of the innocent young man—they attacked him from behind. I probably don't need to mention the killers were... I'm saying this because visitors to our country should know what's happening here." They shook hands, and Célestin led Odile through a passage, a small tunnel, by which they reached a stone square with a gentle slope toward the Wailing Wall. Military jeeps were parked behind them at the top of the slope.

That was their first view of the Western Wall, "the most significant holy site for Jews and the place of their pilgrimage through history," he quoted the guide. It looked incredibly ancient, being the retaining wall at the western edge of Temple Mount—the steep hill where, according to Jewish tradition, God had gathered dust to create Adam. They learned that the height of the above-ground, visible part of the "wailing" section of the Western Wall was nineteen meters, and its width fifty-seven. It consisted of blocks of limestone of various sizes, which weighed between two and seven tons. She counted seventeen rows of blocks.

At a distance of seven or eight meters from the Wall, a movable waist-high metal fence had been placed, but Célestin was convinced non-Jews would not be prohibited from approaching and touching the ancient limestone. He told Odile they would nevertheless remain behind the fence out of respect. Even from there, one could see details on the blocks' faces. They were rough, but the edges were smoothed by chisel. In some of the cracks between blocks, which could be reached from the ground, there were prayer notes; higher up, there were tiny green plants and blades of grass.

Two gaudily dressed middle-aged women were chatting nearby. One placed a note she had prepared in a crack at eye level while the other watched her, laughing loudly. When they were walking away, the woman who had left the note said to the other in American English: "The concierge at our hotel told me the notes were removed twice a year and—listen to this—buried at some Jewish cemetery! Doesn't matter; as you know, what I wrote was a joke."

Without comment, Célestin took the girl's hand and led her to the top of the slope: "From here we can see the entire Wailing Wall and you can take pictures without bothering anybody. I don't wish to lack piety, but this is just like the Schaubühne, the theater in Berlin, when we sat near the top of the sloping auditorium: One can see everything without moving one's head." At that moment, there were some thirty men on the left side of the Wall and no more than ten women on the right. The sight was more diverse among the men. Some stood with faces inches from the Wall, deep in thought. Others more or less sat on the folding chairs they had brought and placed two or three meters from the Wall: They assumed every conceivable pose. Still others stood at the randomly positioned lecterns and read aloud from the Torah or declaimed passionately without consulting any text. All these people prayed while making strange gestures and moving their heads and bodies as if they were alone in the world. They bowed to the Wall with raised hands, palms turned to it; or bent their bodies a little to the left, then to the right, as if they were performing a gymnastic exercise.

The sight was incredible, and the depth of religious feeling inconceivable, frighteningly strong. It emerged from the bosom of another culture, from a different world: For Célestin, all that was extremely foreign, alien. Just then, Odile took his arm and forced him to look at her: "Papa, in Berlin we wanted the exit to be near, don't you remember? Let's go, *cher Papounet...*"

At the exit, as they did at the Schaubühne, they exchanged goodbyes—on this occasion, it was with the two Mossad men sitting at the bag inspection table.

12.

The next morning, they sat in the kitchen drinking tea with Rachel; Danny had gone to the university. On the table, there was a copy of *The Jerusalem Post*, where a front-page article described the house-to-house search in East Jerusalem for the accomplices of the yeshiva student's Palestinian killers.

Father and daughter had truly enjoyed staying with the Dobrins, but it was time to let Rachel know they would soon leave for Eilat, a port and summer resort at the southernmost corner of Israel. They would then continue to the Sinai Peninsula and visit Saint Catherine's Monastery and Mount Sinai, also named Mount Moses. Célestin requested permission to leave some of their luggage behind and asked if they could stay at the apartment again upon their return. Rachel readily agreed, saying she was certain Danny would be glad.

Odile talked at length about their days in the Old City. Rachel listened attentively and disclosed that she and Danny went to Mea Shearim and the Wailing Wall only when escorting guests from abroad. She added: "For us, it's the same as when our American friends from California and Florida take their guests to the local Disneyland." Célestin mentioned the possibility of a new synagogue on French Hill, to which Rachel said: "Morkel must have told you about it. But the problem isn't a new synagogue nor the strict observance of Shabbat. The ultraorthodox will create a whole new quarter on French Hill and force themselves on the rest of us in various other ways. Life for secular Jews like us, for Morkel and Deborah, and many Hebrew University professors, technicians, and students, will change in major ways. We are very upset."

Alone in their room, Odile and Célestin talked for a long time about their experiences during the previous afternoon and evening. Leaving the Wailing Wall area, they had turned from El Wad to the east, deeper into the Muslim Quarter, and walked along narrow streets packed with people and artisan shops. The atmosphere was that of any Arab souk. Men sat in small coffee places talking loudly, gesticulating elaborately, playing cards, drinking liters of coffee and tea, and smoking single- and multi-stemmed hookahs. The occasional pulling of his sleeve into a shop was companionable rather than brash, as was the discreet waving of a necklace in front of the girl's face.

All types of jewelry were on offer. Célestin remembered Odile's comment to Deborah about the amber bracelet she had inherited from her mother, so when she looked a little longer at the jewelry on one counter, he took advantage of the opportunity. From the merchant, an old Arab, he bought a silver bracelet and necklace, bargaining only for the sake of the ancient ritual. She was delighted and joined her papa in drinking sweet tea with the gratified salesman.

In the early evening, at the approximate center of the Old City's north wall, they came upon the majestic, brilliantly illuminated Damascus Gate. It was built in 1537 and named for the glamorous city, over two hundred kilometers to the north, from which the then Ottoman rulers of Jerusalem used to arrive. Back in Metz, he read that archaeologists had found below the gate a part of the far older door to the city built by the ubiquitous Roman Emperor Hadrian in the second century after Christ. "He defies belief," exclaimed Célestin, "traveling and building both gates and walls from here to Britain!" They passed through the prodigious gate and turned left, to the west, on Sultan Suleiman Street.

Outside the walls, Palestinian men seemed younger than the ones within the Old City. They sat in modern cafés chatting and watching television. Without trepidation, father and daughter entered a large café. They were the only non-Palestinians. Even non-Jewish students from Western countries were not to be seen. "This is strange," thought Célestin. "Young Western travelers are usually adventurous, but maybe places like Marrakesh, Kathmandu, or Cuzco, where hashish is easily available, are more attractive." The father-daughter pair caused a surprise, accompanied by friendly smiles. The program on television in the café was then unknown in France, Germany, and the USSR: Its star was a giant bronzed in a tanning salon, with a thick white mustache hanging next to his powerful, jutting jaw. He was called Hulk Hogan and was a champion in choreographed melodrama wrestling.

By the end of their long conversation, it was almost noon. In the kitchen, they found sandwiches, salad, fruit, and halvah covered by a freshly ironed cloth. The Hebrew word for *bon appétit*—*be'te-avon*—was written on a note.

After lunch, Célestin called Hila from the Dobrins' living room: "I'm glad to hear from you, dear friend," she said pleasantly. "I made a nice little plan that concerns Odile. Can you both come to my office today to find out if she likes it? Around four-thirty? I'll be free of obligations." Next, he arranged with Morkel to have the midday meal with him the following day. Morky deeply apologized for Deborah's behavior and promised he would try to explain, though not excuse, her actions.

When Célestin returned to their room, Odile was standing in front of the mirror in one of her prettiest spring dresses of a pale lilac color. She was wearing the new silver necklace, while her right wrist was graced by the finely crafted bracelet. As soon as she heard her father, she turned toward him. With arms spread wide and an irresistible smile, she sang: "*La ... LA!*"

They walked to the campus and in one corner found a fenced-off playground for professors' and graduate students' children. The lady in charge gladly allowed them to spend time there whenever they wished. They first teased each other using the seesaw, and then Odile chose the highest of the three swings. Her father gradually pushed her more and more strongly, and the pink-cheeked girl flew higher and higher. Célestin studied his daughter as objectively as possible. She was a lovely, healthy, intelligent, Franco-German, nine-year-old girl, at that moment delighted to be on a swing in the sacred city of Jerusalem. The lilac dress was a tad too short for Mea Shearim, and the jewelry came from a Palestinian shop. Her gold-brown hair was blown by the flight. Although born without a mother, she was blissful. "We need Olya pushing the swing with me," thought Célestin wistfully.

Hila greeted them as if they were old friends. After kissing Odile on the forehead, she praised the jewelry: "From the Arab Quarter, right? Very pretty—and feminine. They do it better than we do. From ancient times, they have been skillful in artisanry, genuine artists. And here, now, they have to eat, don't they? Poor people." Hila then described the plan for the following day. "I have a girlfriend, she's about fifty and has a married daughter, who, in turn, has a daughter, Leora, ten years old. After thinking about what I could do for Odile, it occurred to me to introduce her to Leora. The girl's been decently brought up and speaks good enough English. When I talked to my friend about it, she not only agreed, but the two of them later called me to propose a ladies' day at an outdoor pool. I'll give myself a day off. Do you like swimming, honey?"

She had learned to swim already as a young child, but her only recent whole-body encounter with some big water was being submerged for one second in Baikal. Enthusiastically accepting the invitation, she said it would be wonderful to acquire an Israeli girlfriend. "Perfect," said Hila: "So, there will be five of us, three adult women and two girls. Sometimes, lifeguards organize games. One is called 'fun water polo.' Children play in two teams. They paddle in car tires and pass a ball to each other. The purpose is to score by throwing the ball between two floating goalposts guarded by the opposing team's goalie. The idea of floating appeals even to me because I'm a poor swimmer! Please don't forget to bring a bathing suit, both parts. You and Leora are already grown-up little girls."

Once the plan was finalized, Odile went to the ground floor. The lady librarian smiled in recognition, took the borrowed books, and brought a new set. Meanwhile, Célestin thanked Hila for making the arrangements, and during the hour at their disposal, described Patrizia and their surviving daughter's childhood in quick strokes. He felt Hila had earned his trust.

At ten the next day, the pair returned to the library. Hila looked forward to the day at the pool as much as Odile did. After escorting the two to Hila's car, Célestin realized that for the first time in a long while, he would be without his daughter's company for many hours. Before meeting Morkel for lunch, he read about Hebrew literature in his office and stared at the desert toward Jericho, concerned vaguely about safety in Odile's water polo debut.

The lunch lasted two and a half too-short hours. Morky spoke about meeting Deborah and falling in love with her in New York City while she was still unhappily married. He described how much she had suffered because of the loss of her daughter Michal in ugly divorce proceedings; the girl was only seven at the time. Explaining, he said: "Abraham, Deborah's ex-husband, an American Jew, did all he could to prevent Debbie from taking

Michal across the ocean to Israel. According to Debbie, a bizarre moment occurred in the courtroom when Abraham told the judge, 'I hope, your Honor, you won't let her take our child all the way to Israel, somewhere behind God's back?!' I could understand the man's feelings, but Deborah... It's clear, even based on her account, that she behaved arrogantly in the courtroom. And then, like a boomerang, a judgment unheard of in American divorce cases was pronounced: The judge, *a woman*, gave the father full, hundred percent, custody of the seven-year-old child—a *female* child!"

Célestin let his friend go on: "The judgment hurt Debbie, and it had, for some reason, an adverse effect on our relationship. Nevertheless, we got married soon after, too soon. I'm unable to go into details... even with you. As for Deborah's nasty behavior—again, please accept my humble apology. And tell Odile she's dear to me. Debbie's heart isn't bad, but she often conceals it. Maybe she learned something from what I threw at her that evening."

They were quiet. "She's not content in Israel. Nor is she happy with me as husband, at least while we're here, and I don't want to live anywhere else. Sometimes she's conceited, American-style, and it's not easy for her to adjust to life here—hard-working or plain hard. This happens to many American Jews when they move here, and they leave after a few years. It's thought the reason is the relative poverty of our country, but I think the adjustment problem has deeper roots."

PART SIX

"*The Man with the Child in His Eyes*"

1.

It was very hot early. The half-empty air-conditioned bus with darkened windows left the main station in Jerusalem at ten-thirty and stopped at French Hill on its way to Eilat. The bus then drove steeply downhill to the east, toward the Dead Sea. Soon, before eleven, they saw a board next to the road on which the elevation of zero meters was announced. Célestin knew they were still some four hundred thirty meters above the Dead Sea.

While he talked to Odile about the below-sea "elevation" of the California Death Valley and the Dead Sea, they had plunged into a brutally dry, whitish, stony desert. Rare human silhouettes could be seen on cruel hills long ago exhausted by the sun, and an occasional camel would be barely moving among the rocks drained of strength. Yet, amidst the wasteland, there were giant beat-up advertisements for Coca-Cola in Hebrew and Arabic. When the Dead Sea came into view, the bus stopped for several minutes. Célestin and Odile were the only passengers curious or crazy enough to exchange the coolness of the bus for the scorching air. They looked at the unique sea in the distance. Instead of taking a picture, Odile exclaimed: "But it's bluish and doesn't look dead!"

She was right from that distance, but her father spoke without romanticizing: "Nevertheless, it's dead or almost dead. It's ten times saltier than any ocean, and nothing can live in it except microorganisms. Do you see how the coast is sharply drawn, as if by a ruler, how it's not eaten up unevenly by wave erosion? That's because the water has a huge density and weight, so the winds have a hard time creating waves. I told you one can float on the

Dead Sea, but not swim in it—as you did in Baikal and the other day in the pool with Hila."

The bus descended to the sea and traveled south along the coast. On the right-hand side, there was the desperately dry, knobbly desert, reminiscent of the Moon's surface on television. On the left side, however, the Dead Sea glittered vivaciously. Some fifteen kilometers to the east, across the sea, the gray-blue mountains of Jordan twinkled, reflected in the water. Everything surrounding them represented a new experience in the Holy Land—a savage desert and a super-salty sea at the bottom of their planet's crust.

Now and then, Odile spoke of her day with Hila and Leora: How sweet was her new girlfriend; how kind was Auntie Hila; how much she enjoyed swimming; and how she once succeeded in throwing the ball between goalposts—and how the girl defending the goal fell out of the tire...

The bus stopped long enough in the oasis Ein Gedi to drink a glass of juice in the garden of a small hotel managed by kibbutzniks. "On our way back from the Sinai, we'll spend a night here and float," promised Célestin. Farther down the coast, there were modern hotels but also military installations. Near the southern end of the sea, the bus arrived at the entrance of a snake farm where one could buy harmless lizards as house pets. Father and daughter came out of the bus and found a meager shade rather than go to the farm. From there, they gazed at the scary hill steeply rising to the west, quivering in the heat. Célestin knew that at the top of the hill, there was a rocky plateau where once stood the ancient Jewish fortress Masada. They returned to the bus and purchased a brochure from the driver. Masada's ruins were less than two kilometers away, high up, overlooking the Dead Sea.

When the bus departed, he read aloud: "'It is known that the Roman Tenth Legion, under the command of the Governor of Iudaea Lucius Flavius Silva, besieged Masada for two months, and that finally, in April of the year 73 of the New Era, the legionaries managed to climb—using a siege-assault ramp 114 meters high— to the edge of the western side of the plateau.' No, we couldn't see it from the snake farm, *ma chère fille*. 'And from there, the Romans broke through the wall of the fortress with a battering ram on April 16'."

He did not wish to continue, but Odile, who had been listening intently, said in a determined voice: "Certainly something terrible happened then. But please, Papa, tell me everything. I'm not a little child anymore." Célestin obliged her: "All right if you insist. When the Romans penetrated the fortress, they didn't need to kill anyone; there was complete silence. A thousand defenders were dead. Some had committed suicide by jumping from the east wall into the abyss, whereas others had killed each other. No surrender, no matter what. The legionaries found only two women and five children alive."

Odile sadly looked at her father and asked who the defenders were. "They were one group of Jews who called themselves Zealots. Please don't ask me what I think. It happened almost two thousand years ago."

Célestin did not reveal to his daughter what was on his mind—that far worse atrocities had happened in their own twentieth century. She, for her part, did not ask if they would visit Masada on the way back from the Sinai.

2.

It was early afternoon when they arrived in Eilat and found a room in a simple hostel fifty meters from the bus station. All rooms had bunk beds for six occupants, but Célestin rented a whole room, paying for all the beds. The hostel owner was pleased with the arrangement, also because breakfast was included in the price, and those two guests would probably eat only one and a half meals.

Eilat was not to their liking. It was a dry little town dominated by unfinished houses and unattractive bars and restaurants. Young men and women with backpacks and sleeping bags were wandering about. They were from Western Europe, America, and Australia, many in a dubious hygienic state. The girls attracted attention with semi-nude torsos, torn jeans, and the shortest shorts. Because the beach was empty and unclean, Célestin expected most of the young backpackers to travel to the enormous and mysterious Sinai Peninsula, as the two of them did.

The locals were less civil than in Israeli cities to the north. The town was a sort of "wild South" of Israel, where a border atmosphere prevailed. No less than three Arab countries were nearby. When they sat down on the terrace of a café close to the sea, he oriented the girl: "Over there, directly to the east, across the bay and only three kilometers from here, is the town of Aqaba in Jordan, with those gray-brown hills above it. It too is ancient, like Jaffa, inhabited for six thousand years."

He unfolded a detailed map bought half an hour earlier. Odile could see Eilat, Aqaba, the Sinai, and the border between Jordan and Saudi Arabia. "That border is roughly over there," he pointed. "Those mountains to the southeast, across the sea, are only about twenty kilometers from here. There begins Saudi Arabia, with its huge red-hot desert. And this sea is not a proper sea but the Gulf of Aqaba. It's narrow and long, bordering the entire length of the Sinai, and extends to the Red Sea. Israel's third Arab neighbor is Egypt, of course. Here on the map is Cairo, and here, near the Egyptian capital, is Giza with its three giant pyramids about which you learned in school."

While alternately gazing at the mountains on the opposite side of the gulf and studying the map, Odile directed questions at Célestin: about the endless Arabian desert, the mirages and the horrifying quicksand traps, and the ancient pharaohs and pyramids. As it happened, the resumption of the Egyptian part of the story soon took place. After riding in the № 15 bus from Eilat for nine kilometers, next to nondescript small hotels and camping grounds, they reached Taba on the Egyptian border. They walked past Israeli guards and reached the "no man's land" between the two countries. It was a mediocre beach of two hundred meters on which stood the grand modern hotel Sonesta. Célestin had learned from Morkel that it would be impossible to stay in the hotel, but the restaurant was open for business. They entered the agreeable, empty dining room and chose a table with a view of the sea and Saudi Arabia. Egypt's Sinai began only fifty meters to the southwest. The manager was overjoyed to see guests and quickly brought a cup of hot chocolate with vanilla ice cream for Odile and a top-class German beer for her father.

Before the trip to Israel, Célestin read extensively about the exceptionally important peace treaty between Israel and Egypt, which had been signed at Camp David two years earlier, in March of 1979, by the Israeli Prime Minister Menachem Begin and President Anwar Sadat of Egypt; U.S. President Jimmy Carter was the sponsor. The two most significant points of the Treaty were: Mutual recognition of the two countries, with Egypt becoming the first Arab country to recognize Israel; and the complete withdrawal of Israeli armed forces and civilians from all of the Sinai, thus returning to Egypt the territory captured in the Six-Day War in 1967. During the two years after the signing, Israel had mostly retreated, and Egypt had positioned its border guards in Taba.

Morkel provided important information: "Begin and Sadat accomplished something of historic importance; they are very brave men," Morky had said. "However," he had anxiously continued, "I don't know how long those two will survive and can only hope, with all my heart, the Treaty will outlive them... Both men have unforgiving, sworn enemies in their own countries, hard-core groups that will stop at nothing—these are, one could say, the Jewish and Arab zealots of our time. On both sides, they hate their own man, thus supposedly serving God. In my country, one assassination attempt—on Begin's life, fortunately unsuccessful—has already happened and been hushed up. Please remember he is an extreme right-winger and has a flawless Zionist biography. I happen to know there was an attempt to murder Sadat in Cairo, also unsuccessful, luckily, and covered up. Regrettably, I think this is a disease that time does not cure."

Without being asked, the manager brought another cup of hot chocolate for Odile, prepared that time in Viennese style with whipped cream. Célestin invited him to sit with them, and the man gladly did. He was certainly an Israeli because the hotel's border location was a sensitive one. However, he had worked for a long time in Vienna and Montreal and therefore missed conversing in German and French.

The guest's first question was about the strip of no man's land. "Well, things stand as follows," the manager began: "The Sinai Peninsula was Israeli for over ten years, since 1967. For many countries, that's a very short period, but not for us. We're so small that we always try to become bigger. We build quickly, we're not lazy like, for example… well, like some of our neighbors. In the Sinai, we made ourselves at home—we figured there would never be peace, it would be ours forever. They don't need it anyway. All Arab countries, Egypt included, possess vast unpopulated territories.

"And so, we did a lot in the Sinai wilderness during those years. There were new settlements, among which the biggest had two and a half thousand inhabitants. The town was called Yamit and was located on the coast of the Mediterranean Sea between Gaza and the Sinai. The plan, Sir, was for Yamit to grow into a city of two hundred thousand people! I guess the idea was to encircle Gaza from all sides."

Célestin took out the map and, finding Yamit, showed it to Odile. He asked the manager: "I notice you're using the past tense when speaking about Yamit. Do you mean this town is no more?" "Precisely," said the man, "during the past spring, my country—in the course of returning the Sinai to Egypt—evacuated Yamit's entire population and destroyed by bulldozers all the existing houses and other structures that had been built."

The traveler was surprised but not overly so: "Do you mean Israel didn't give Egypt the opportunity to buy the houses at low cost for its own people? Actually, sorry, that's a silly question. Egypt would not need Yamit: Cairo is more than three hundred kilometers from Gaza, and between them, there's just a handful of Bedouins, as elsewhere in the Sinai. Besides, from what I've read, the Bedouins prefer the open desert to living in constraining towns."

The shrewd but amiable hotel manager smiled ironically: "Egypt's lack of need for the Yamit housing was a distant secondary reason for which Begin did not offer the houses for sale. The main, or rather the only, reason was that if he had made such a move, the fury of the ultraorthodox and other right-wingers would have boiled over. Begin would not have survived—and I don't mean politically."

"I understand what you're saying. I heard similar dark premonitions from a friend in Jerusalem. So what's the story with the hotel Sonesta?" The manager answered promptly: "The hotel is new but was built before the Treaty. Ownership is Israeli, yet it's not clear on whose territory it sits and how big the no man's land is. Two hundred meters? Three hundred? The Treaty specifies the issues of Taba, whereas the hotel will be subject to arbitration—it may take five years! That's why you and your sweet, serious daughter are in this restaurant and not in a fabulous apartment upstairs with a view of the Gulf of Aqaba."

They returned to Eilat by bus and spent the evening reading in the garden of their hostel. When several young men began to play chess at a nearby table, Célestin pretended to stretch his legs but in truth to kibitz. He was reluctant to participate, not wishing to leave Odile. But his psychic daughter had already begun to move their chairs, and one of the young men quickly helped her. He was an Israeli from Haifa, and the other two players were Swiss Jews from Lausanne. Communication was easy.

By the universal protocol, members of the foursome exchanged basic information before play began. There were no clocks, but the *piece touché, piece joué* rule was enforced. The victor of a game stayed at the board, while the others, one by one, faced him as rivals. After Célestin won the first game, he did not get up but nonchalantly dismissed the aspiring greenhorns' attempts. "We'll see each other at breakfast," he teased, but one of the Swiss had a repartee: "If we play in the morning, it will be against Odile—hoping she hasn't learned much from you!"

While walking to their room, she said: "Papa, you won all six games. These fellows didn't manage a single *remis*. The Russians in our Siberian train succeeded at least that much—I have it in my notebook." He answered simply: "I'm glad you remember Vasiliy and Pavel, they are good people... It doesn't mean much, but I haven't lost a game for years. I'm mostly playing against patzers—casual players. I did tell you that Grandpa Olivier had taught me to play when I was half your age. Later, I faced strong players in my chess club in Metz."

Two past events flashed through his mind. In Moscow, he had promised Odile he would buy a pocket chess set for her and instruct her regularly. In Berlin, they bought a chessboard for Emil, and even that did not prompt him to keep his promise. So he apologetically shared those thoughts. She smiled: "*Merci, cher Papounet*, for remembering it all. But I had forgotten your promise and wasn't envious when we gave the chessboard to Emil. Besides, I liked the book we gave Sophia more, with the graceful ballerinas from Swan Lake! Papa, you teach me so many things, we travel so much. A pocket chess set? For some future birthday?"

3.

They had breakfast under tall cypresses, staring at the hills above Aqaba. In the morning light, the hills were softly gray, not nearly as brutish as usual. From time to time, they exchanged friendly words with a group of Israeli women sitting nearby. One of them, by the name of Osnat, came with her coffee to their table, wishing to talk to Odile and Célestin in English. She was a third-year law student at the Hebrew University of Jerusalem, and it emerged that her mother was from Armenia and her father from Yemen, both Sephardi Jews. The young woman was exceptionally beautiful. The skin on her face was like dark silk; her nose was small, atypical for Armenians; her black hair was long and naturally curly; and her eyes—well, those eyes were the color of the highest-quality anthracite coal.

When Célestin revealed that Odile and he would soon take the bus to Sharm El Sheikh, a small resort at the extreme southern end of the Sinai, Osnat exclaimed that she and her four girlfriends also planned to travel to Sheikh. Coming up with an idea, she swiftly ran to the girls' table, and after a brief discussion, returned pleased: "We unanimously agreed to invite you two to travel with us! It'll be tight in our small Honda, but it doesn't matter. By bus, you'll travel four and a half hours, while we'll get there in three. Sheikh is two hundred thirty kilometers from here."

Célestin weighed the girls' kind offer only briefly before amiably declining it. There was no need to inconvenience them, as there were buses. Osnat seemed disappointed: "All right, I understand. If you and Odile catch a bus soon, you'll arrive in Sheikh before us. We'll leave only in the afternoon because of the heat. When you arrive, I recommend going to a hostel called Sea Cliff. Although climbing a small hill is required, it's worth the trouble; the place is impeccably clean. We'll also stay there, all in one room. I hope we'll see each other this evening—in Egypt! This is the first trip to a foreign country by any of us. When we went to Sheikh before, it was Israel. A newly built village called Ofira then existed nearby, but was bulldozed out of existence a month or two ago."

While riding in the № 15 bus to Taba, Odile expressed disappointment that her father had declined the girls' offer—she liked them, particularly Osnat. He listed the reasons: "It would be unbearably tight in their Honda: Four and a half people on the rear seats, and you are already bigger than a half! Then, the heat. Even if their air conditioning is first-rate, which I doubt, it would work poorly with those numerous bodies. And finally, the luggage, who knows how much they have?

"But the most important reason is that their car has Israeli license plates, whereas the Sinai is now Egypt. According to the Treaty, Israelis are allowed to travel in private cars to the Sinai without a visa—although not in rented cars—along the entire coast of the Gulf of Aqaba from Taba to Sheikh and also to Mount Sinai. However, the whole situation is so new and fragile that one doesn't know how smoothly it will go. We shouldn't have problems either on the border or elsewhere on the peninsula, but I didn't wish to speak to those girls about it, for they might be offended." Odile was first silent and then said: "It seemed Osnat felt a little snubbed anyway."

After showing their passport on the Israeli side of the border and paying the modest exit fee as foreigners, they were transported in a minibus past the Sonesta to the frontier of Egypt. The driver for those two hundred meters was an armed Israeli soldier, and they were the only passengers. Along the way, Célestin showed Odile the receipt specifying that the exit fee for her was only half-price. They smirked and arrived in high spirits in Egypt, the ancient land of *Misr*.

On the Egyptian side of the border, the procedure lasted twenty-five minutes, although there were no other arrivals. Four officials checked their passport. They were polite but worked at a snail's pace. Célestin changed not shekels but American dollars into Egyptian pounds.

About a hundred meters from the border stood a mirage-café where they drank lukewarm mineral water and spoke to some Danes from Aarhus. Finally, at 11:30 a.m., they boarded the bus for Sharm El Sheikh; four and a half hours of travel awaited them, in a bus in which the air conditioning barely worked.

They traveled south down the coast, with splendid views of hills and mountains to the east, across the Gulf of Aqaba—first in Jordan, then in Saudi Arabia. In a village called Nabq, two blond young women from Stuttgart boarded the bus. They described themselves as "explorers of Arabic culture" and proudly wore on their heads pristine, incorrectly folded keffiyeh.

At Nuweiba, the biggest village since leaving Taba, they climbed out of the bus for a few minutes. The temperature was thirty-two. In front of a tiny shop stood a lonely palm. Two Bedouins were sitting under the tree—not on camels but on chairs.

Moving away from the sea, the bus entered a monotonous desert landscape. About half an hour from Nuweiba, on the right-hand side, a smaller uphill road parted from the main highway. A sign in English stated: "Monastery of Saint Catherine 82 km." He explained: "On that road to the interior, through a very rugged desert, we'll travel in a few days to the monastery at the foot of Mount Moses. It's the only possible way to the heart of the peninsula from the east coast." The girl was hot, waved brochures, and obediently gulped water from a liter bottle whenever he put it in her hands.

The bus kept driving south. Near the dusty townlet of Dahab, the road touched the sea and again turned inland. They reached Sharm El Sheikh on time, at four p.m. The place was not attractive, but the desert heat had let up, and the air smelled of lush vegetation and the Red Sea. At the hostel Sea Cliff, Célestin grabbed what was available—two bunk beds in a room where the other two were taken by young men from Ulm, a fine city on the Danube River in southern Germany, who readily promised they would be discreet in their speech and behavior. He was pleased they did not need to be asked. "Don't worry, we'll manage, these guys are OK," he said to Odile in German to be overheard.

Célestin then talked to their roommates about Ulm and the incredibly steep spire of its Minster, the tallest church in the world. He remembered climbing its innumerable steps with Patrizia—"exactly 768," one of the young men exclaimed proudly. Closer to the top, each step was so narrow that even Patrizia, with her small feet, barely managed.

Odile naturally chose the top bunk bed. As they went out, leaving their roomies alone, they heard from below the ringing voices of young women chitchatting in Hebrew. Osnat gaily greeted them: "Ah, there you are, that's good! We left Eilat at two, and here we are. Is your room alright? I inquired if you were here—there aren't many men in the Sinai traveling with a young daughter—and was told you're in a room with two Germans. We reserved our room long ago."

"Hello, Osnat!" exclaimed the girl. "Was it hot on the way?" Osnat, scantily clad, sighed: "Oh, yes! Honda's pitiable conditioner breathed its last near the solitary palm in Nuweiba. Our whole car was like a giant ember." He joined in: "Thanks for the recommendation. Everything here is indeed clean, and the German guys in our room are decent." Osnat said: "Am I ever glad that's so! I'm going upstairs to wash up, but will need only ten minutes. If you don't mind waiting, we can take a walk—it's much cooler now." Before Célestin could have half opened his mouth, Odile burst out happily, "we'll wait!"

Breathing the fragrant air of early evening and gazing at the Red Sea, an exciting new sea for father and daughter, the three-some took a stroll. Osnat and Odile were busy getting to know each other, which suited Célestin because it gave him time to plot his plan for the next day, which did not include either of them. They bought lemonade and sat down by a basketball court. Men of a variety of ages, in street clothes, were playing. Some wore sneakers, some shoes, and some ran around barefoot. They seemed to take the game seriously, so there were frequent dis-putes. Disagreements were understandable because the light was fading and the baskets were missing nets.

Osnat said to Célestin: "I didn't tell you this right away be-cause I thought it might appear bold; besides, I wanted to get to know your daughter. But when my girlfriends and I arrived in our room, the girl closest to me proposed that we invite her to sleep in the sixth bed. You did say those two guys in your room were well-behaved, but still..."

Odile was delighted and entreated her father to let her move in with the Israeli girls. Célestin was quick to decide: "This is an exceptionally thoughtful gesture on the part of you and your friends. I am touched. As for my darling daughter, she rarely de-mands anything or beseeches me like this, so if you both want it, I'll go along." For her part, Odile thought: "Even though those two German guys are all right, they'd still be in the way. And how super-nice Osnat is, good and young... like Olya!" Moreover, it seemed to the girl that with her gentle demeanor and slender body, Osnat resembled Olya—and was as striking with dark skin. Yet neither then nor later did she convey any of it to her papa, as she was afraid such a comparison would sadden him.

Célestin agreed to the proposal because he was glad Odile would spend time with women much younger than, for instance, Hila. Also, he liked the idea because his plan for the next day would be facilitated.

"Perfect! Thank you for trusting us," said Osnat. "As for the bed, Odile, the one above mine is empty, but I'll gladly give you my bed if you don't wish to sleep so high." However, even before she got a response, Osnat backed out: "No, on second thought, I'm withdrawing the offer... because I'll be responsible for you. It could happen, God forbid, that in deep sleep you fall. How would I face your father? So, you'll take the lower bed, and I'll clamber up the ladder." He was again moved.

4.

He went to the breakfast room early, not wishing to disturb the girls by knocking on their door, even though he overheard chatter. But Odile soon came down with the young women, and her radiant face instantly dispelled any concern he may have had. They all sat down, and Osnat reported that the night had passed uneventfully.

The five women were the same age—twenty-three. They had spent two years in the army and then began to study at various universities in Israel. Like Osnat, her best friend Avigail attended the third year at Hebrew University, but studied Arabic language and literature. She shyly revealed her name meant "father's joy." Osnat then explained that her name originated in ancient Egypt and meant "belongs to God." Avigail quipped, smiling teasingly: "So, she's untouchable by noxious pests, though not by good people!"

Osnat took over: "Last night we spoke about your names. For us, both are very unusual; we've never heard them, even though there are many foreign students, Jewish and non-Jewish, at universities in Israel, and some are from France." She took out notes. "Our committee came to the unanimous decision that the name 'Odile' is written אודיל in Hebrew and yours סלסטין. Avigail, who has an enviable command of Arabic, contributed with أوديل for Odile's name, and سيليستين for yours. Do you like it?"

He was thrilled by the girls' kindness and the scripts' aesthetics: "How fantastic this is! You see, Osnat, you belong to God, but

'Célestin' in French means 'celestial, heavenly.' What do you say, O God's Daughter?" Thus ambushed, Osnat said nothing; she blushed—as far as it could be perceived—and chuckled.

During breakfast, the women decided to spend the day on the beach. When Odile asked him what the two of them would do, Célestin could no longer delay presenting his plan. Still, he first asked the girls: "Has any of you ever been to Ras Muhammad?" They looked at each other, exchanged a few words, and shook their heads. Osnat said: "We know Ras Muhammad is the southernmost point of the Sinai Peninsula. It's far, and only a scorching desert exists between here and that area. It's not possible to go there."

Célestin shrugged: "It's possible and I'm going today—alone!" He turned to Odile and spoke to her in English so the girls would understand: "Darling, you heard Osnat. Everything is exactly as she said. It's far, it'll be hot, it'll be hard, but I must, must go. And I can't take you along. Please don't cajole me into consenting. You're an intelligent girl." He looked into her eyes, squeezed her hands, and embraced her tightly.

As Osnat had begun to fidget, he spoke to her: "Nor do I dare to take anyone with me. Here's what I'll do. At 9:30, the bus from Dahab will arrive in Sheikh and continue along the western edge of the Sinai all the way to Cairo. However, from here it first goes south for about thirty kilometers and only then turns westward and later goes north. I'll get off the bus at the southernmost point of the road. From there, I'll walk to Ras Muhammad—about twenty-five kilometers. I know from reading that there are no tall dunes in that part of the desert. And Odile, there are no quicksand traps! I can manage it in four hours.

"At the Cape, 'Muhammad's Head,' I'll spend an hour. I want to taste the sea and swim. I'll come back the same way. Don't expect me before nine in the evening. From Ras Muhammad, a man with God's eyes would see two thousand kilometers down the Red Sea to the 'Gate of Tears.' That's the name of a strait between Yemen on the Arabian Peninsula—the birthplace of your father,

Osnat, you told us in Eilat—and Djibouti and Eritrea in the Horn of Africa. Girls, imagine what I'm saying!"

Odile was barely able to hold back tears, but managed because her father firmly held her hand. The five young women looked at him with astonishment. "But my whole plan," continued Célestin, "because Odile seems, hmm, to have agreed, depends on you, dear girls. May I ask you to be my daughter's guardians today?" Osnat responded readily: "Monsieur Celestial, excuse me, but you're a little crazy—although I understand you. I'd love to do the same and must return here when I'm in a better physical condition, after some training in our Negev Desert. As for Odile, we'll gladly take care of her, she's so sweet and smart." Upon asking her girlfriends in Hebrew, Osnat received nods from all.

When swimming skill came up, the powerfully built Shoshana—in Hebrew 'lily' or 'rose'—mentioned she was a member of the swim team at the University of Haifa and promised she would be Odile's "sea buddy." He then thanked them, embraced his daughter again, and hurried to the bus stop—his backpack slyly prepared in advance. Six pairs of female eyes saw him off.

He was the only person who got off at the southernmost point on the Taba-Cairo route—and the amazed bus driver stopped only at Célestin's timely request. It was a few minutes before ten o'clock. He was greeted by absolute silence, except for the buzzing of one fly. The sound would disappear and reappear, revealing a big black insect, and he wondered how it could be so fat in the desert. In the hot air, purplish, pale-blue mountains winked in the western washed-out sky; the Red Sea waters glinted to the east; and the way directly south, toward Ras Muhammad, was faintly marked by shallow tire tracks in the sand. There had not been much wind to erase the tracks. All around, the desert was empty, as if humankind had never existed there.

Célestin marched in a fast, disciplined tempo for almost two and a half hours and believed he had covered between fifteen and eighteen kilometers. He carried a rough stick and wore a white cap with a long shield; around his head and neck, a white towel was wrapped Bedouin style. The old Vuarnet sunglasses had been tested when skiing with Patrizia in the Alps. He had an excellent compass, a twin brother of the one he bought for Morky in Jerusalem. Besides, unless there was a sandstorm, it would be fairly hard to get lost: At several places, the sea was visible on the left or right side. In his backpack, perhaps senselessly, he had a reliable flashlight lent to him by Danny Dobrin and a Swiss knife, a screwdriver, and Odile's pocket camera. The Nikon stayed at the hostel.

That, plus the sunscreen and bags with walnuts and raisins, was all. He was aware of being comically under-equipped—not tragicomically, he hoped. But once they had arrived in Sheikh, he could not resist the powerful impulse to carry out the solitary desert trek to Ras Muhammad, something he had not foreseen in Eilat. There were facts in his favor. The first was his outstanding physical condition. The second, and more to the point, was mountaineering experience, often also solitary, which had taught him how to look for and smartly use signals from all parts of his body when exposed to stress. And water? Célestin thought he had enough, but suspected one never knew anything for certain in the desert.

Those two and a half hours were uneventful. Exactly two cars passed by, both irreversibly disappearing in the direction opposite to his. At one point in the wasteland, he came across a shack from which two dogs flew out, ribs showing. Neither his stick nor a stone was necessary—the gesture of throwing sufficed. Later, he saw a structure looking from afar like a crazily pointless military blockhouse. Three men were in front of it. Célestin was not sure whether or not to feel fear. On coming closer, he realized the three were either soldiers or common bandits: Using oil from a bucket at their feet, they were cleaning machine guns and bayonets. "They must be soldiers or renegades because I doubt bandits use bayonets and could survive in this desolate terrain," he thought, trying to be calm.

There was nothing he could do but approach them as if everything was normal and peachy. One of the men wore military fatigues that were not Israeli, Célestin knew. Still, to be on the safe side, he greeted them in English, not Arabic. The trio, however, responded in one friendly voice with *"As-salamu alaykum!"* (*Peace be upon you!*). Before father and daughter left for the Sinai, they had learned some Arabic greetings, so he used the first opportunity that arose to exclaim the traditional response *"Wa 'alaykumu s-salam!"* (*And may peace also be upon you!*). Encouraged by the Arabs' genial disposition, he asked for drinking water, and one of the soldiers brought a large unopened bottle. Célestin put it in his backpack as a reserve and offered two pounds, about three dollars, for the water, but the men declined to take the money with a shy smile. The parting was cordial.

The noon heat in the southernmost part of the Sinai was becoming horrendous, yet he walked persistently and stubbornly, with no rest. It seemed he was in a lucid trance, which allowed him to be fully alert about everything while performing the basic activity automatically—walking at a steady tempo. He felt healthy and never considered going back. But was he a good father? What would happen to Odile if he perished? She would become an orphan, albeit a rich one, like he was. At the bank in Metz, he had long ago deposited a will securing an excellent education and a comfortable life for his daughter.

Precisely during one such period of self-examination, he heard a sound not belonging to the desert—the hum of an automobile engine. Soon a dusty passenger car stopped next to him without being waved down. But there was no reason for alarm; it turned out the vehicle's occupants were three smiling Egyptians from Cairo, traveling to Ras Muhammad as tourists. After a brief exchange in English, they invited Célestin to jump in, and he gladly accepted. He had done enough laborious trekking—thus proving himself. Proving himself? If that was it, it was not very smart.

All three men were in their late thirties. Khaled was a banker, and Magdi and Muhammad engineers. They spoke English and some French. Célestin introduced himself as "Tino" to facilitate communication. Even by driving slowly, it took them only seven to eight minutes to reach the Cape, which meant he had been less than five kilometers from Ras Muhammad when he climbed into the car.

"We have arrived!" yelled all four happily, in two different languages, with raised fists. They were at the extreme southern point of the Sinai Peninsula. Behind them was only the desert, and in front were the dark coral rocks on the reef and the Red Sea beyond. Above them, there was only a flaming star in its zenith.

Magdi said to the Frenchman: "Tino, I understand what coming here—to the end of the world, after an arduous, perilous, solitary trek through the desert—means to you. It's the achievement of something exceptional and exotic, and the proof you're still young and strong. But for the three of us, something else is far more important: To come here from Cairo, without crossing any border, means this land is again ours, Egyptian. The sand, the rocks, the sea, and this deserted Head of Prophet Muhammad—all this is again Egypt!" Célestin patted Magdi on the shoulder, saying he understood. Suddenly, he thought of his treasured Russian patriot Olya, a million miles away in prison: "Patriotism, pride, love of one's native country: In one way or another, they touch everyone." His thoughts proceeded: "Yes, everyone, including this serious engineer, who has traveled all the way from Cairo to stand here."

Given the friendly atmosphere, it was not odd that Célestin suggested a swim. They took off their clothes to underwear—at their age, being stark naked required a longer familiarity. A place among the rocks where one could enter the water was found, and the sea sent only soothing waves. He left the Egyptians in the shallows and swam away by himself. A new sea! He hoped Odile was at the same moment enjoying a swim in the same sea and was safe with Osnat and Shoshana. Then Célestin tasted the water and thought of Baikal and the Buryats. He remembered how Odile and he submerged their heads in the Mediterranean in Tel Aviv.

Khaled brought a player from the car and inserted a cassette with Egyptian music. Célestin would have preferred the lapping of the sea, but these people were so kind. They invited him to visit Cairo with Odile. All of them had children under the age of ten—Magdi and Muhammad daughters. Suddenly, a song in Arabic was heard, a plaintive female voice, and the Egyptians fell silent, he with them. When it ended, he asked Khaled to play it again and then another time; he felt he was listening to something extraordinary.

They explained the singer was Umm Kulthum, the "Star of the East," the "Fourth Pyramid of Egypt," and the most beloved singer in Egypt and the Arab world for half a century beginning in 1920. The ballad they heard was recorded in 1968 and called *Al-Atlal*, which meant "ruins, wrecks, scars," the debris of a once boundless love. Many people, Khaled said, considered it the crowning jewel of the Arab song.

Having dried themselves and talked some more, they started the return trip. It was half past two and far too hot to remain at the Cape. The Egyptians drove Célestin to the same spot where he had descended from the bus. Addresses were exchanged, and during the parting, Khaled presented the *Al-Atlal* cassette to their new friend, who loved the gift and therefore objected weakly.

Because he had no idea when the bus for Sheikh might appear from the west, Célestin started walking, again wearing the improvised headgear. After about forty minutes, a cab stopped. The sole passenger, an Egyptian, politely offered a ride to Sheikh, turning down the offered money but sharing the remaining walnuts and raisins with the Frenchman.

The gentleman, another Muhammad, was a well-educated wholesale merchant from Cairo, articulate in English. Célestin first asked him some apolitical questions about Egypt, and from there the conversation flowed easily. "I'm not certain," Mr. Muhammad said, "but it seems the majority of people in my country feel above all Egyptian, then Muslim, and only then—maybe— Arab. But this man, our driver, is a Bedouin. They don't consider themselves either Egyptians or Arabs but a different sort. Very proud people. They've been living for hundreds of years in their own way, but they're adaptable. It's known they preferred life under the Israelis to life now under us. It's a question of money. When Israel was here, the Bedouins controlled the whole taxi business in the Sinai, whereas now it's infiltrated—albeit in an unorganized way—by people from the north of Egypt, from Suez and Cairo, who often work for less."

Célestin inquired: "So where are the Copts in the whole story?" Mr. Muhammad sighed: "Ah, the Copts. I think nothing but the best of them. As you probably know, they're Christians—from ancient times. They represent at least ten percent, perhaps fifteen, of Egypt's population. They speak a language and use a script derived from the old demotic Egyptian. Most importantly, they have their own ethnic identity and refuse to adopt the Arab one; however, they accept Egypt as their nation. Physically, you can't distinguish them from Egyptians who are Muslims. Moreover, their everyday customs are similar to ours. Nevertheless, they're different, and as Christians, they suffered terribly under Gamal Abdel Nasser's pan-Arabism. And now again, they're always threatened and mistreated by the Muslim extremists."

When approaching Sheikh, Mr. Muhammad told Célestin he could drop him off at the foot of the hillock below the hostel or take him to the marina six kilometers farther where he was going. Célestin wished to see the marina and invited his host for a juice or a beer. Mr. Muhammad had to decline because his wife, whom he had not seen for a week, was at a marina hotel. "By the way," he said in parting, "I am a Muslim, but I occasionally drink beer. It would be a pleasure to have a glass with a polite Frenchman. In my experience, many are not. Sorry..."

As a result, Célestin sat alone on the terrace of a small restaurant. While looking at sailing boats and thinking about Mr. Muhammad, he consumed an excellent pita sandwich and drank a cold Egyptian beer. Around a quarter to seven, he decided to go back to Sea Cliff and find his daughter. He did not feel guilty about not returning earlier because he wanted a whole day to himself. Besides, he did not know where Odile and the Israeli girls would be, as he was not expected before nine. On the road from the marina to Sheikh, no bus appeared, but a pickup truck stopped. He exchanged salams with the young driver, who was, it seemed, an agricultural worker. Without thinking it over for a second, he accepted the offer. The pickup was small, and there were three men in the cabin, so he clambered into the roofless cargo area and sat on bundles of grass.

An evening sea breeze cooled him while the pickup drove. Célestin reflected: "How wonderful were all the Egyptians I met today. If one behaves with them kindly—which, after all, should not be in the least hard for anyone decent—they reciprocate doubly. I must convey this to my daughter and those dear young Israelis."

As soon as she saw her father, the little girl ran to embrace him. "How dark you've become, *mon cher Papa!*" she exclaimed, equally bronzed. Five smiling suntanned women observed them from their table in front of the hostel.

5.

On the Sheikh beach the next morning, Odile and Célestin walked from one end to the other and swam in the calm sea. When he wished to swim far, Osnat and Shoshana looked after the girl. While she later built castles and moats with other children, Célestin and Osnat lay very close, face to face, under a sun umbrella. In Osnat's long and silky black hair, there were grains of sand, and she smelled invitingly of the sea. One could say it was a poorly concealed flirtation, which they both considered a little risky and the result of which was unpredictable. Still, they regarded the liaison as appealing enough to commit to a meeting at Hebrew University. Effortlessly, almost without intention, they achieved a remarkable closeness. Both were delighted that not one of five possible candidates interrupted their tête-à-tête.

Around three in the afternoon, father and daughter took time to part from the girls who would stay several more days in Sheikh. They packed quickly and went down the hill to the bus stop. To their surprise, Osnat was there. Over her bikini, she wore a half-transparent, pastel-colored beach dress and looked stunning: "I wanted to see you both off by myself." When the bus from Cairo arrived, Odile firmly hugged Osnat, who in turn embraced Célestin even more closely.

The bus traveled north toward Dahab, Nuweiba, and Taba-Eilat. They planned to get off at Nuweiba, spend the night there, and begin the "pilgrimage" to Saint Catherine's Monastery on the following day. During the three-hour trip, she mostly dozed, tired from the sunshine and swimming. In Célestin's case, for some reason, the images of different women he had met during their long travels danced in his mind's eye: Oksana, Olya, then Mathilde and Hila, and finally Osnat. He did not compare them. Only Olya was and firmly remained truly essential to him—the only woman since Patrizia. Eight long years.

He thanked fate that all of them were gentle with Odile. Of course, if one were not, he would not have looked at her twice. His daughter was a bright and endearing child whom it was easy to love, but he would have quickly recognized sham warmth and fake kindness. Luckily, that never happened, with the possible exception of Mathilde. He leaned over and tenderly stroked the girl's head. She smiled sweetly but did not wake up.

In Nuweiba, they found a small bungalow. The evening was balmy and fragrant. They went for a short walk before dinner at the restaurant Oriental Tent. They wrote in their diaries as dusk became night. Many people, Egyptians and foreigners, smoked hookahs. Traditional Egyptian music could be heard. Célestin mentioned Umm Kulthum to a man at a nearby table who said: "Yes, she was cherished and respected her whole life. She passed only five or six years ago."

* * *

From the threshold of their bungalow, they watched the sun inching up behind the mountains of Arabia, on the opposite side of the Gulf of Aqaba. Odile was unusually quiet. While Célestin shaved, she finally divulged what bothered her: "Papa, I had a terrible nightmare." He immediately put the razor down, took her hand, and with his face still soapy, intently listened: "Well, it was like this. You and I were climbing a hill during a big snow-storm. I'm sure it was you, and it was near our home in Metz. We climbed and climbed, kept falling in the snow, and continued to climb. Finally, we arrived at the edge of a horribly deep abyss. The snow was falling into it but couldn't fill it up. You firmly gripped my hand—like this—because we were next to a chasm, and it was slippery. You didn't allow me to stumble and fall...

"Then I saw on the opposite side of this deep hole a small group of women and children. One woman screamed, and you put your hand over my eyes so I couldn't look. But I was naughty and wanted to see everything. With my free hand, I removed yours exactly when the woman screamed again, and with a child in her arms, leaped into the abyss. That was dreadful! Then an-other woman picked up a child and jumped. I heard the child cry out... and woke up."

"Aah, my poor Odile." He hugged her and kissed her nose, leaving some shaving soap. Stroking her head, he thought the nightmare was not a silly, weird, and completely unprovoked one, and so he said: "A strange dream, but perhaps not so strange—except for the snow. Do you remember when we were standing outside the snake farm by the Dead Sea? Not far from us, the ancient Jewish Masada lay in ruins. The Romans had be-sieged the fortress, and when they broke in, only a few women and children were alive."

Odile responded: "Yes, I remember. You were reading to me about it when we left the farm." They were both silent for a while, and she surmised: "So, the defenders jumping into the abyss to escape the Romans got into my nightmare. And I turned those Jewish women and children who were found alive into the ones who were jumping?" Célestin agreed and went on: "Yes, some-thing like that. But another thing is instructive for naughty little girls. On the bus, I read to you the whole story only after being pestered; I didn't wish to read it, but you won. Remember? And in your nightmare, I put my hand in front of your eyes so you wouldn't see the horror of women jumping into the abyss, but you removed my hand, right? So..."

She had to laugh: "Papa, you were right! It's not pleasant to hear about such terrible things. But where did all the snow come from?" Célestin pondered a few moments: "Well, I'm not a psychoanalyst nor a fortune-teller who interprets dreams, but as a layman, I would say that in dreams, important things are sometimes turned upside down. In your nightmare, you turned the women and children who had, in reality, been found alive into those who had leaped, so maybe the blizzard appeared in your dream because it was the opposite of the hot desert by the Dead Sea. A nice tale, don't you think? Usually, it's laymen like me, not neurologists, who tell the best stories!

"But let me ask you something else, and then we'll forget your scary nightmare. When you woke up because of the awful scene, was it in the middle of the night, after which you went back to sleep, or this morning, just before you got out of bed?" Odile readily answered: "It was this morning, and I got up immediately. At first, I didn't want to describe the nightmare to you, but I changed my mind when we were looking at those reddish mountains across the sea."

Célestin hugged her again: "I'm glad you told me everything so we could calmly talk about it—you even laughed at one point. But I want to teach you something from current science about the nature of dreams and sleep—not the interpretation of dreams, only their time course. So, when someone wakes from a dream, it's reliably known that it occurred right before the waking, not in the middle of the night, hours earlier. Also, even though it seems to the sleeper that the dream or nightmare lasted a long time, it occurs very rapidly. Such things are known because brain waves can be measured... All right, enough, your turn to wash. We certainly deserve a good breakfast."

Their meal in the garden of a nearby restaurant consisted of an omelet, fresh tomatoes, green peppers, and pieces of hot

Arabic pita. They drank canned orange juice because the fruit from Jaffa was not available in Egypt. The French bottled water Vittel was in Egypt called Baraka, meaning "blessing." Célestin said with a smile: "During the race 'Tour de France,' each cyclist drinks numerous liters of this Vittel water, but close to the end of each stage, to reduce weight and increase speed when sprinting, they throw away many bottles filled with blessing!"

Bedouins passed by the garden, keeping themselves apart from other Egyptians. In their long white djellabas without collars and buttons, with either red-white *shemagh mhadab*, or Palestinian black-white keffiyeh, on their heads and necks, they looked proud, almost vain. Their camels stood next to the restaurant fence, with their heads often over it, which led Célestin to say: "Who knows, maybe their instinct is pulling them across the sea to the sands of Arabia? Or they're just attracted by our fresh green peppers?" For four pounds a day, one could hire a Bedouin with his camel and ramble in the desert. Unlike the majority of local Egyptians who did not consume alcohol, the Bedouins did; allegedly, they drank copiously in their settlements in the desert.

Most Bedouin women were tall, with backs straight as an arrow. They were clad in black djellabas, a few in white. Every woman had wrapped the keffiyeh such that only her brilliant eyes could be seen. Their habit was to return the salam looking into Célestin's eyes, paying little attention to Odile. It was not so with male Bedouins—most directed greetings to both foreigners.

They sat down to drink tea in the lobby of the hotel to which their bungalow belonged. He observed the staff at work in the hall, and as expected, there were no Bedouins, male or female, to be seen. The workers wore gray or brown djellabas and performed their duties at a slow pace. On their feet, which they dragged, one saw multi-colored plastic flip-flops instead of the traditional *balgha* leather slippers. A question of price or an effect of Western fashion?

At eleven o'clock, they boarded a special bus for the monastery, the ride costing three Egyptian pounds even for children. For about thirty kilometers, it traveled south on the main road and then turned west into the desert and mountains. "You remember, *chérie*," Célestin brought up, "when we were traveling from Taba to Sheikh, I showed you the turning toward Saint Catherine's Monastery and Mount Moses. Ahead of us now is the real Sinai, not the tame and meek one, embraced by the seashore, with beaches and bungalows we have so far enjoyed. What comes now will sometimes be strenuous. Also, we'll probably need to share our room with others. But everything will be fine, you'll love it." Odile was in thought and then asked: "But, Papa, are we going to be able to enter the monastery?" "We'll succeed, *ma princesse*, you'll see."

The bus kept climbing on the narrow road and was soon surrounded by a serious, stony, hermits' desert. The hills were dry and tortured, as if God himself, when in an angry mood, had torn them apart and crushed them. They saw a few Sinai acacias that somehow survived in the brutal environment, and three or four camels, lonely and dispersed in the hills. To their amazement and delight, one was a pure albino.

Bedouin settlements were nestled on rocky hillsides. These mountain dwellers belonged to the tribe Jebeliya and were reputed to be descendants of the people whom Byzantine Emperor Justinian had used in the sixth century as guards of Saint Catherine's. They lived in ghostly stone huts, low and with flat roofs. The walls consisted of pieces of rock of different sizes that had been stacked up with mind-boggling patience and effort.

The road became even steeper. Jabal el Gunna, a mountain plateau, rose on the travelers' right, to the north. It ran about thirty kilometers in the direction of the monastery, parallel to the road. Narrow canyons descended steeply from the plateau. "The Bedouins," said Célestin, "must know how to avoid torrents plummeting from hillsides when it rains and yet obtain drinking water."

At two in the afternoon, they arrived at the modest Bedouin village of Saint Catherine—in Arabic it sounded like "Sanketrn"—about a hundred twenty kilometers from Nuweiba, at an elevation of 1,586 meters: A small mosque; two tiny shops; Bedouins drinking tea and watching belly dancing on television in a dark penurious cafe; and heaps of garbage in the desert. A settlement forgotten by gods, yet only two kilometers away from the ancient, magnificent Monastery of Saint Catherine—Catherine of Alexandria…

To assuage their hunger, Célestin bought feta cheese for one Egyptian pound. The enticing smell of hot pita, wafting from around the corner, helped them find the shop—its name was written in Latin letters, "Bokry." They joined the line of five or six male Bedouins. The bakery was located in a small stone house. In its front wall, a sizable, irregularly shaped hole gaped, probably opened long after the house had been built. Two men and a boy of Odile's age worked in the dark interior behind the big hole. One baker was expertly kneading, tearing, and shaping the dough; another used a wooden peel—at least two meters long—to place round lumps in the oven; and the precocious boy was responsible for taking the money from customers, three piasters for a piece of delicious pita. Father and daughter bought five pieces. Célestin gave the cash to Odile, and she paid "fitn" piasters, as her Bedouin agemate had stated the price. The two children carried out the transaction seriously, unsmilingly. She was the only person of female gender in sight.

Sitting on some rocks, they savored the simple repast of hot pita and salty feta. The bottled water was insipid, but so what? After a while, two Dutch women arrived from somewhere and described the situation in the village and the surrounding area. Following the advice, father and daughter walked to the basic tourist camp where they secured a room with four beds in one of the Lilliputian stone houses. They spent the afternoon making plans for the three days that followed. The fourth day was a Friday, when the monastery would be closed to visitors out of respect for the local Muslims' religious customs.

6.

They got up before dawn and left the camp. The Bedouin hired by Célestin had come with his young donkey, bringing a blanket for Odile. She liked the animal at first sight: It was tame, cute, and albino, just like the camel they had seen on the slope of Jabal el Gunna. The girl immediately invented a name for him, *Zucker*, explaining that "sugar" was nicer for a sweet animal than *Esel*—donkey in German. Célestin agreed, and the Bedouin's opinion was never discovered.

For a while, they walked through the pitch-black night next to Zucker, who seemed to radiate light. The Bedouin obviously knew every pothole, but Célestin sometimes took Odile's hand and switched on the flashlight. After half an hour, the massive silhouette of Saint Catherine's Monastery appeared. "We'll visit it tomorrow, *ma douce*." She was content, not the least bit sleepy; the night adventure had been exciting. For the first time in her life, she was climbing a sacred mountain, and doing it in the company of not just her beloved papa but also a biblically white donkey!

The path turned uphill, so Célestin placed Odile on Zucker and covered her back with the blanket. For a girl who could ride Pasha bareback, sitting on the donkey was child's play. She thought: "What's Pasha doing now? Is she hungry? Does she miss me?"

And so, at a pace chosen by Zucker, began their ascent of Mount Moses, Jebel Musa, Mount Sinai, Har Sinai. There were two paths leading to the summit with an elevation of 2,285 meters. One was easier, but longer and slower; it was called Camel Trail and could be used by camels and donkeys almost to the top. The second path was shorter and far more demanding, requiring skill and stamina. Its name was Moses Trail or Seven Thousand Three Hundred Steps of Penitence. It was very steep in some places. In others, hefty rocks needed to be negotiated, which would be impossible for Odile even with help. However, the idea of reaching the peak by that path too, already existed in his mind.

In the half-darkness, walking next to Zucker, he spoke to the girl about the holiness of Moses, refreshing her familiarity with legendary beliefs. According to the Bible, after the Israelites' exodus from slavery in Egypt and their crossing of the Red Sea, Moses received God's Ten Commandments on the mountain, with the directive to convey them to his people.

They patiently continued to climb for several hours and into the first hints of pink light. On arrival at the spot from which there were supposedly seven hundred fifty steps to the top, the Bedouin insisted that neither donkeys nor camels could go farther uphill through the rocks. Odile dismounted and fondly patted Zucker's neck. The Bedouin promised to wait, so Célestin carried his daughter up the harsh, steep slope to the summit—at times on his back, at others in his arms.

As luck would have it, they arrived at six o'clock, minutes before the rim of the sun rose above the mountain peaks in the east. The entire gray-brown Sinai was suddenly aflame. What a stunning red wilderness presented itself! They stood speechless, with arms around each other, intoxicated by the unique desert beauty that the newborn sun illuminated. Whether or not they were standing precisely on the spot where Moses had received the two tablets of blue sapphire with God's Commandments three thousand five hundred years earlier, and whether or not he existed to receive them, was not essential.

There was a locked chapel on the summit and two stone shelters with open sides in which some twenty people continued to sleep past sunrise. Only five or six drowsy, shivering creatures crawled out, draped by sleeping bags they were dragging. The rest missed the moment for which they had climbed for hours and endured the freezing temperature. Unlike them, Célestin and Odile were awake, vigorous, and happy.

On the way down, she succeeded—carefully using her hands and with her father's occasional help—in making those seven hundred fifty treacherous steps and safely reaching her Zucker. Still, during the remaining descent, she spent more time walking than sitting on the donkey, even though the animal was stepping downhill gingerly.

From a spot far below, a splendid view of the entire magnificent Saint Catherine's monastery opened up. Célestin told the girl he had somewhere seen a black-and-white photograph of the monastery, taken from about the same spot in 1852! "So, let's take a color photo ourselves. Look how beautiful the monastery is in the morning sun," exclaimed Odile. They captured the scene with two cameras. Naturally, she also wanted a photo with Zucker but not sitting on the animal: She stood next to the pretty donkey and lovingly hugged his neck.

Starved on their return to Sanketrn, they immediately went to the small cafe they knew. Lentil soup, scrambled eggs, feta cheese, pita—all delicious. Then they walked to their room in the stone house and slept for hours. In the early evening, they again ran into the Dutch girls and went with them to the same cafe. The women were from Den Helder, north of Amsterdam, whose fathers were officers in the Navy. One of them, Liv, was small and wiry, while Nora was chubby, with a sonorous laugh. The two had explored the surrounding desert for a few days under the scorching sun, and while Liv experienced nothing untoward, Nora developed blisters and was barely able to walk. She was lucky her feet were aptly bandaged by a monk in the monastery's infirmary. Full of praise for the unexpected care, she said there were also two Bedouin patients in the infirmary, which was apparently a common occurrence.

Another bunch of young people soon joined them: Two Australian guys from Adelaide; a New Zealander from Hamilton on the North Island; and two sisters from Vancouver in Canada. As curious travelers would, they shared impressions of the Sinai, Cairo, and Jerusalem, while drinking countless cups of tea. Nora was dispirited because of her painful feet, but still summoned the energy to talk with Odile in English and German. She did it naturally, never patronizing the girl. Célestin noticed that Odile enjoyed Nora's company and was asking many questions about Holland—tulips, chocolates, and wooden shoes; the famed canals in Amsterdam; and the story of the boy who had saved his village by plugging a hole in the dam with his finger.

At the end of the long chatting session, the travelers decided to meet again the following evening. While Odile gently tried to cheer the invalid up, Nora managed to hobble back to the camp with her arms wrapped around Liv and Célestin.

* * *

While father and daughter were approaching Saint Catherine's Monastery the next morning, they saw two monks whose small flock of sheep grazed on scant grass amidst rocks and bushes. They wore black cassocks—monastic black signifies not only sorrow but repentance—and on their heads a black *kalimavkion* from which a black veil hung onto their shoulders and upper back, fluttering in the wind. "Take a photo, Odile, this same scene could have happened one thousand five hundred years ago."

In the spacious courtyard of the monastery, they were met by solemn silence. There were no other visitors. As they saw from high ground when descending the previous day from the mountain, the monastery was encircled by a wall of reddish Sinai granite. It belonged to the Greek Orthodox Church, and its formal name was the "Sacred Monastery of Mount Sinai on which the Lord God had trodden." A monk's silhouette flitted by near the entrance to the main church, dedicated to the Transfiguration of Christ. They silently walked around the courtyard. Célestin requested: "Try, *mon trésor*, to absorb everything around here into your soul instead of taking photos."

Within the monastery walls, there were twelve chapels. Adjacent to the church, seeming to grow out of it, was a large blackberry bush, the legendary bush once in front of Moses's eyes. According to the biblical narrative, God spoke to the prophet through an angel within the burning bush, yet the flames never turned it into blackened branches and ashes. In the year 330, Empress Saint Helena built on that spot a chapel dedicated to the Burning Bush and the Mother of God. As he explained to the girl, Helena's son was Constantine the Great, born in Niš in Serbia— then Naissus in Moesia Superior.

From the courtyard, they climbed a steep flight of stairs to a broad balcony, entered the monastery's renowned museum, and studied the exhibited wondrous paintings, photographs, and diverse old documents and maps. In the initial centuries of Christianity, there had been many monastic communities and solitary desert hermits at inaccessible locations. The most influential of the Desert Fathers, as they were called, was Antonios the Great, who had found refuge from the year 270 in the Skete Desert—thirty-eight meters below the level of the Nile in northern Egypt. Meanwhile, in the Burning Bush area and closer to the summit of Mount Moses, other groups of monks lived at the end of the third century. In the year 530, two and a half centuries later, Emperor Justinian and his wife, Empress Theodora—forty-eight and thirty years old at the time—were able to complete a three-nave basilica of red Sinai granite, which enclosed the Chapel of the Burning Bush. "During the following years, a high wall was erected," whispered Célestin, "but I doubt that's the main reason why it has never been destroyed. In any case, it's one of the oldest monasteries in the world still active. We are incredibly privileged to be here."

Odile listened to every word: "You already spoke about Saint Catherine, but please, Papa, tell me more." They sat on hard wooden chairs in a secluded corner of the museum when Célestin began the Catherine story, often consulting notes. "All right. Dorotea-Dora was born in the year 287 after Christ in Alexandria, a city in Egypt on the coast of the Mediterranean Sea. So, Alexandria was the name she had received in her educated and affluent polytheistic family—meaning they worshipped many gods. At a young age, she acquired wide knowledge and learned several languages, but also showed great goodness of heart toward almsseekers. Her early youth was the period of intense persecution of Christians by Emperor Maximian in Egypt, which was then ruled by Rome. But the young girl's love of Christ could not be extinguished by terror, and—if the old annals can be believed—she was baptized as Catherine at age fourteen, only five years older than you are now.

"However, since there's almost no risk of your becoming conceited, let me tell you I believe there is no nine-year-old girl who is more mature and knows more than you do. I'm your father and can't be trusted to be objective, still... And Catherine? God only knows the truth. According to ancient records, she was brilliant and dedicated. And exceptionally courageous: Despite being horribly tortured by scourging—don't ask me to describe it—she 'fervently testified the Christian faith.' In various sources, she is always described as being prepared to die in unbearable pain rather than renounce her beliefs. Tortured in different ways, including the monstrous wheel on which her bones were broken, she died at eighteen. That was in November of the year 305 after Christ, for whom she had sacrificed her young life."

Odile thoughtfully looked at her father: "*Un grand merci, mon cher Papounet*, for those kind words about me. But please tell me: Do *you* admire Catherine?" Célestin was silent for a long time, knowing the question implied another: Does he expect his daughter to admire Catherine? Her unswerving gaze forced him to go on: "Based on what is claimed by tradition about Catherine, she is venerated by the church fathers as a saint and great holy martyr, or 'megalomartyr.' This has been true for over a thousand years.

"And then. You know that Jeanne d'Arc, a saint, martyr, and virgin like Catherine, who was burned at the stake in 1431 at the age of nineteen, is considered a French national heroine and presented as such to all the children in our schools, including you and me! According to old writings, Jeanne regarded Saint Catherine as her ideal, claiming she had regularly appeared in visions to provide advice. What connects the biographies of these two young women is not just unmatched courage—which is admirable, although maybe not to be emulated—but also *visions*: And visions are sometimes signs of mental disease, as is fanaticism. So my answer to your question is this: Yes, I admire Catherine, yet don't want to be a fanatic—in anything. Moreover, from the depths of my heart, and in all sincerity, I advise you never to be one!"

Odile thought and thought, then asked: "What were the visions Saint Catherine had?" Célestin had a response ready: "Well, again according to Church tradition, in one of Catherine's visions—while awake or dreaming—Christ gave her a ring, which was a sign to devote her life to God."

"Hmm. I want to ask you something about which you've just now advised me, that I should never become—how did you put it?—should never become a fanatic. It crossed my mind... Do you remember my nightmare about those women who were jumping with babies in their arms from Masada into the abyss? At the time, you told me the defenders were jumping from the fortress or killing each other because they didn't want to surrender. What did you call them?" "The Zealots," he replied. "Yes... So, were Saint Catherine and Saint Jeanne Zealots?" Célestin was pleased: "Bravo, well done! The two saints were not Jewish, but in an important sense, they were like the Zealots."

The girl had another question: "Papa, why is this monastery named for Catherine when she was from Alexandria, far from here, on the Mediterranean?" He smiled: "Congratulations again. We are dealing with legends and visions another time. After Catherine's passing, angels transported her body to the top of a mountain, here in the Sinai, now called Mount Catherine. That's not the one we climbed yesterday, but it's only four kilometers away as the crow flies. It's the highest mountain in Egypt."

Célestin went on: "Five hundred years after Saint Catherine, a ninth-century monk from this very monastery had a dream in which angels enlightened him about the location of her 'holy remains,' or relics. He, together with others from the fraternity, found them and brought them here to the monastery, where they have been kept ever since in a sarcophagus, a marble coffin. Since then, this has been Saint Catherine's Monastery. I confess feeling no urge to inquire about it and contemplate the possible contents of an ancient sarcophagus." He did not enjoy disclosing such skepticism and, worse, expressing it in an ironic tone, but had to be truthful.

After the long visit to the dark, silent, mysterious, extraordinary museum, they were blinded by the desert sun. Not far from the bell tower, there was a mosque of modest dimensions, and they saw Bedouins entering or leaving. Célestin knew Muslims were welcome in the monastery; some worked in the monks' bakery to earn money sorely needed by their families. Each Bedouin they encountered greeted them with a polite salam and received a like response.

In the shade of the bell tower, Célestin said: "You see, during its long history, the monastery was often the only haven open to members of the Christian communities in jeopardy throughout the Sinai and was itself repeatedly attacked by brigands. But the greatest threat was undoubtedly the rise of Islam in the seventh century and the arrival in this region of the merciless warriors of the bellicose new religion. Byzantium largely disappeared from the Sinai. The monastery passed through a difficult period, for it had become a small, rich, almost undefended Christian island in the Muslim sea. This mosque is the consequence of the monks' adjustment to the new powerholders.

"According to some, the monks did what they had been ordered to do by the new rulers and so built a mosque, leaving the monastery doors open to Muslims. Other historians state the monks built the mosque preventively, without compulsion. And still others maintain the monks at times claimed Prophet Muhammad himself had issued a dispensation to the monastery. Be as it may, they somehow managed to survive, together with all their relics, books, and icons—managed to save their bare lives and not become Muslims by force. So, *ma chère fille*, while the monks are indeed deeply devoted to their God and faith, they are not Zealots." Odile nodded, hoping it was the last of those fanatics.

On entering the ancient church, Jesus Christ blessed them, his image in the dome. They approached the altar. On its right side, a massive, yet exquisitely shaped sarcophagus of white marble stood. Célestin squeezed his daughter's hand: "We spoke about this." On its left side, the sacred blackberry bush grew, and it appeared its intricate branches were not only touching but penetrating the wall of the church. "Do you recall we saw a bramble bush growing outside, precisely next to this wall? I'm at a loss for what to think," he admitted. Pondering the sight with eyes wide open, Odile at first hesitated to speak but finally protested: "Papa, I can't understand how this dry bush can be three thousand years old. And the green one outside—which, you said, never yields blackberry fruit—can grow out of this one..." Célestin laughed louder than he wished: "That, *ma mignonne*, the church fathers call 'Divine Miracle'!"

Holding hands, they spent a long time studying the superb old icons illuminated only by candles: Saint Peter, Saint Catherine, Mother of God in the Burning Bush with Jesus in her arms, Saint Mary with Saints Theodore and George, and other jewels. Célestin reminded Odile of the superlative icons by Andrey Rublyov they had seen in Moscow, and the girl remembered her father's tears. Next, they stood in front of an icon on which the visage of Christ was unusual and mysterious. While they talked about it, an old monk introduced himself in French: "Excuse me for disturbing you, Sir—and your pensive daughter. I overheard you speaking French. You see, my mother was French, but here I rarely have the opportunity to converse in that mellifluous tongue. My monastic name is Paisios; I've almost forgotten my baptismal name, Achille, Ahilleys...

"I noticed you were gazing at this outstanding icon: It represents Christ as Pantocrator, the Almighty. The work is from the sixth century, the most valuable in the monastery—we don't say 'our monastery' because it's not the property of us monks, but God's. This icon is especially dear to me. Ages ago, I completed my novitiate and then gained the monastic habit in a monastery of that name, Christ Pantocrator, on *Agion Oros*, Holy Mountain, Mount Athos, in Greece. My father was Greek. Like my mother, he's no longer in this world; he was a priest and... excuse me for talking so much, you probably think I am too loquacious for a monk, but we also are human... To return to the icon: You may have noticed Jesus's face is somehow odd and asymmetrical, as if two men are represented, two Sons of God. Am I right?"

They were delighted to have met the old monk with a kindly face who spoke a perfect, if old-fashioned, French. "Monsieur

Paisios—excuse me, I'm not sure how to address a monk, Brother Paisios?—we are overjoyed you approached us. This is my daughter Odile, and I'm Célestin. And you are correct: To us, Jesus's face on the icon seemed peculiar, eccentric. How do the monks explain it?"

"Monsieur Célestin—yes, 'Brother Paisios' would be welcome—there are several explanations, one of which is that the icon-painter was mediocre or outright bad!" The monk laughed merrily. "Quite silly. The majority of monks and visitors who are intimately familiar with Christian iconography think the left side reveals goodness, love, tenderness, soulfulness, and compassion, whereas the right side portrays righteousness, decisiveness, courage, consistency, asceticism, pain—even the premonition of Crucifixion. That's also my opinion: Pantocrator, the Almighty, is not just the Son of God but a man like you and me."

Brother Paisios devoted attention to Odile: "I'm sorry I can't take you and your father to the library. Fabulous ancient manuscripts with sublime pictures are to be found there, and I'm certain they'd astonish and dazzle you. Unfortunately, we've been forced by untoward circumstances to disallow library access for all visitors, not just children." Célestin had spoken to Odile about the famous library: It was the oldest in the world that had never stopped functioning; it possessed the only copies of many priceless books and manuscripts; and the Vatican alone owned a greater number of manuscripts. So he was shocked and disappointed that visitors were no longer welcome.

The monk read his thoughts: "Unspeakable thefts and vandal destruction of books and manuscripts have occurred in this divine library, which we, the monks, have been guarding for hundreds of years with love and our very lives. The most painful was the treacherous theft of the Codex Sinaiticus, one of the most important manuscripts in the world, the oldest Christian Bible with the entire New Testament. It's in Greek, dating from the fourth century. Around the middle of the nineteenth century, the manuscript was 'borrowed' by the then highly respected German scholar Constantin von Tischendorf at the end of his last visit here—and never returned! We still have the signed promissory note. It's a long, sordid story of scientific dishonesty, fraudulently acquired fame, and money.

"After that time, the manuscript passed through the hands of many powerful people and institutions in Europe. Somehow it ended up—surprise, surprise—at the British Library in London, where it's nowadays proudly exhibited. Since our loss of the Codex, we have accumulated many bitter experiences. Scholars from many countries have visited us on seemingly irreproachable educational missions, only for us to discover later they had cut out precious pictures and tables from illuminated manuscripts or even broken off entire sections. Therefore, we have this new rule."

Ahilleys-Paisios, the friendly Franco-Greek monk, accompanied father and daughter to the door of the church, saying: "Nevertheless, all travelers are God's children. Our doors are open except for a few hours on a few days. As I said, the monastery is God's property."

Before they departed, Célestin and Odile thanked the good monk from the heart. After a short pause, Paisios reflected: "Not long after I became a monk on the Holy Mountain, a much older Brother at the monastery there, a man whom I loved and esteemed more than all the other Brothers—I repeat monks are human and like and respect some people more than others—that Brother had advised me to go to the Sinai. I've always remembered what he had said: 'We know where the worldly capitals are, but the Sinai is God's capital on Earth: That's where he announced the Decalogue, the Ten Commandments, to us.' So I came here and never regretted it, but am distraught because we now have only nineteen monks in Saint Catherine's...

"Thank you, Odile, dear child, for coming to visit us in this cruel desert. I'm certain you are grateful to your father for bringing you here. He is a rare man. And I congratulate you, Brother Célestin, if you permit me, for helping your daughter learn about God and the world at such a young age."

7.

Lila—who at twenty-three was the younger of the Canadian sisters—made a bold proposal at the desert cafe: "Why don't we all together, tonight before dawn, climb to the summit of Mount Sinai by the steep Moses trail? None of us has done it!" The level-headed among them thought of the nine-year-old girl and of Nora, whose feet were still bandaged. Even before admitting that her limp remained bothersome, the young Dutch woman mentioned Odile. He asked his daughter whether she would mind staying with Nora, and she whispered: "I know how much you'd like to climb the mountain on the difficult trail and that it's not for me and Nora to do. And she is super-kind."

"You'll need to get up very early, Célestin. So if you both agree," Nora offered helpfully, "I'll sleep in one of the empty beds in your room, and when you leave, Odile and I'll sleep on. I'm not bashful. All of us here are friends and traveling rough. All right?"

At half past two, seven of them took off from the camp, passed the silent monastery, and reached Moses Trail. Almost by itself, it transpired that Célestin headed the column, alternately lighting the ground in front and behind. Lila climbed after him, then her sister, the two Australians, and Liv; Rick, the New Zealander, clambered last, sending up a beam of light.

After introducing a moderate tempo to allow his companions to adjust to the rough terrain, he gradually increased it while ensuring no one needed rest. There were steep sections and others with dangerously positioned rocks. One was not likely to fall off the mountain, but being careless or inept could easily result in breaking an ankle or wrist. At many places, Célestin was helping Lila, one of the Australian guys her sister, and Rick earnestly supported Liv. After an hour's climb, they rested for five minutes and then proceeded to the summit. It took them less than two hours, faster than the guidebook estimate.

Everyone gushed about the climb and the ghostly silhouettes of the Sinai mountains before dawn. At the summit, the sight was similar to the one Odile and Célestin had encountered two days earlier: A dozen people stood and shivered in small groups, while others were appearing from the stone shelters, some coughing but smoking.

Half an hour after they had arrived, several members of their small company hailed the newborn sun in booming voices, whereas he silently stared at the wild, otherworldly beauty. Rick and Liv were also mute, clutching each other. "What a touching moment for new love," reflected Célestin; to him, the moment brought a painful memory of Olya's cherished face.

The group broke up for the descent. To reach Odile sooner, he wished to return by the steep trail and was joined by Lila and Jim, one of the Aussies. The others opted for Camel Trail. When Saint Catherine's came into view, the sight was incomparably more dramatic than what he and Odile had seen from Camel Trail, and it was exciting to photograph the monastery again. Early-morning sunshine created astoundingly sharp shadows in the pure desert air. Instead of waiting for the end of the photography session, Jim decided to continue downhill by himself, but Lila did not part from Célestin.

When they had almost reached the bottom of the trail, there was Jim massaging his ankle: "My foot got stuck between the stones! I was careless for a second, gaping at the monastery over the wall. Hopefully, it's only sprained. Célestin squatted, removed the sock, and tentatively moved Jim's injured foot. "I'm certain it's only twisted, but keep your weight off it. I'll help you to the flat ground, it's not far. There'll be a donkey or a camel in front of the monastery to take you to our camp—slowly, like a big-city cab in a traffic jam!"

A Bedouin brought the invalid to the camp on his dwarf camel for "peanuts," in Jim's words. He and Lila sat on rocks to wait for others while Célestin ran off to his room. Odile threw herself at him, bombarded with questions about Moses Trail, and reported she and Nora had slept like babies. Nora's feet felt better, but after hearing of Jim's mishap, she wryly joked that Moses must have cursed Westerners' presumptions.

At breakfast, Liv and Rick played the part of new lovers, feeding each other, whereas Jim and Nora, jesting about jinxed feet, perceived more in each other than before. As the grand parting approached, Liv, Nora, and Rick embraced oriental adventure, hopping on a bus to Cairo, the guys from Adelaide stayed put, waiting for Jim's ankle to recover, and the Vancouver sisters set their sights on Nuweiba. Because Célestin and Odile were heading back to Taba-Eilat, passing Nuweiba, a foursome materialized.

Their successful negotiation with the driver of an available station wagon—three pounds to Nuweiba, six to Taba—was disrupted by the fuming Bedouin cabbies who claimed the price was lower than bus fare. Tension lingered, but no physical interference ensued. "Maybe they backed off because of Odile," Lila speculated. On the road, the driver, an Egyptian from Suez and a registered taxi man, explained that the Sanketrn Bedouins wanted to control the fares illegally, whereas he legitimately charged the foursome less because he had a return customer from Taba lined up. "Good for everyone—except those Bedouins," he chuckled, but a moment later muttered he would pass through Sanketrn quickly.

In Nuweiba, Célestin and Odile bid farewell to the sisters. Lila underlined her name on the slip of paper with their address: "You'll remember I was the one who came down Mount Moses with you!" The girl, unimpressed, later remarked, "I forgot to tell Lila I came down with you too!" He laughed: "Don't be jealous. Perhaps she's a philatelist who needs French stamps."

About fifteen kilometers north of Nuweiba, in a small settlement of four stone houses, the driver and his passengers picked up two young hitchhikers from Germany. They were bound for Taba, eager to explore a miniature nearby island adorned by an ancient Crusader fortress and renowned for scuba diving. When Célestin inquired, he learned: The island lies seven kilometers south of Taba, just 250 meters from the mainland, but dunes hide it from the road. From Taba, the guys would find the island, whereas Célestin and Odile crossed back to Israel.

To their only moderate surprise, the Israeli border officials again asked them numerous questions, even though there were no planes around and their baggage was modest in size and full of dirty laundry. From the border, they took the familiar № 15 bus to the center of Eilat and obtained a room in the hotel Red Sea. They wished to swim and rest for a few days before returning to their hectic life in Jerusalem.

In the evening, they sampled Israeli and Arab dishes in a simple restaurant and then walked to the marina, called "Lagoona." Many sailing boats were moored in front of expensive hotels. Before going to sleep, they stopped at the bar in their hotel, which was a bad idea. The place was filled to the gills with smoke, noise, and heavily inebriated English and Australian men and women staggering about. Célestin's and Odile's acoustic nerves vibrated unhappily under the onslaught of loud Cockney and Yorkshire accents.

Soon a fight broke out between two groups of young drunkards. One consisted of Australians, whom the Englishmen in the other group called "Aussie convicts." The name that Aussies used for the English was arguably more insulting, "Pommy bastards." As soon as the melee began, Célestin threw money on the table, grabbed Odile's hand, and took her out with amazing speed. Even in their room, they had no peace till dawn—women and men were shrieking, squealing, screeching, and crying piteously in rooms near and far and on the street.

After breakfast, they moved to the much better King Solomon hotel at the Lagoona, and soon they were contentedly swimming in the pool. Nearby was the Gulf of Aqaba beach with manageable waves, so in the afternoon they swam again. While Odile was developing a correct backstroke style, she admired the view of red hills above Aqaba. She swam a little and floated a little, Célestin's hand supporting her back: "On our way to Jerusalem, we'll stop again by the Dead Sea—I promised, remember?" As the girl nodded, she swallowed some water without becoming scared. "You'll be able to float without my support, as if you are somehow hovering. Well, that's how I imagine we'll feel. But if you swallow water, it'll be by far your saltiest gulp ever!"

They spent the following day similarly, except for Célestin making inquiries at the hotel desk about Crusader Island mentioned by the Black Forest scuba guys. The helpful clerk said: "Yes, a small island with ruins of a Crusader citadel indeed exists, although I've never been there nor have I seen it with my own eyes, even when the Sinai was ours, Israeli. But I know it's located about where those divers told you—seven or eight kilometers south of Taba, next to the road to Nuweiba. It can't be seen from the road because it's hidden by dunes. I also remember that an old Egyptian couple had a guest house on the beach directly across from the island. I think it was called 'Saladin.' Maybe they have a rowboat. You can get to the vicinity of the place by taxi or bus from the Egyptian side of the border."

While Célestin was discreetly leaving a tip, the clerk exclaimed: "Wait, Sir, there used to exist a good brochure, but I haven't seen it recently. Let me look in the back, I hope it's not just in Hebrew." After a few minutes, he returned pleased. "Eureka! I found it, the text is in Hebrew, English, French—and Arabic."

The brochure was informative. The name of the island was Pharaoh's and of the fortress Saladin's. So, thought Célestin, it was Salah ad-Din, the renowned and feared twelfth-century Sunni Muslim Kurd, the most successful anti-Crusader warrior and the first Sultan of Egypt and Syria, who built the citadel. That was not entirely correct, for Saladin only extended the original fortress erected in 1116 by Baldwin I, King of Jerusalem, the most ferocious and able "Western" military leader in the First Crusade. The fortress, Crusaders had hoped, would help them defend the southern part of the Kingdom of Jerusalem from their hostile Muslim neighbors and ensure pilgrims could travel safely between Jerusalem and Saint Catherine's Monastery.

Through laughter, Célestin said: "Listen to what else this anonymous sly author wrote: 'The Crusaders extorted exorbitant sums from Muslims to allow them passage to Mecca for their

Hajj, but it is probable Christian pilgrims also had to pay a lot for protection.' Hmm. This must've been written by someone from a third interested party!"

The brochure stated the sea around the island was ideal for swimming and snorkeling, but boats from Eilat and Taba traveled there irregularly, and there were no structures for accommodation. "Doesn't matter. Tomorrow, *ma chère fille*, we'll take a look at this island and its ancient citadel. *D'accord?*" Odile agreed, and not only because she knew nothing would change her father's mind. He may even have a secret plan, she thought—and was right.

The next day, Célestin obtained a safe deposit box at the front desk and placed cash, checks, and Odile's jewelry into it. He packed a small bag and took along their passport. On the way to the bus, they bought water, cheese, nuts, and fruit. By ten o'clock, they reached the Israeli border and crossed into Egypt, following the familiar procedure. As a bus for Nuweiba was about to depart, they jumped into it without bothering to hire a cab. To the genial bus driver, he showed the number seven with his fingers and added, "hotel Saladin, please." After paying double the fare, he stood directly behind the driver and noted the starting mileage—86620 kilometers. The man drove expertly, and when the bus reached 86627, he stopped in the open road, literally in the middle of nothing, and pointed to the left, toward the sea.

Célestin gave the bus driver a tip and helped Odile come down the high steps. He instinctively trusted the driver and thought few people would want to be cruel to his little girl. After the bus took off, they crossed the road and found a path that seemed to lead in the right direction. Indeed, as soon as they passed a dune, they saw the citadel on its island: The sight was from a fairy tale.

From below the dune, a house on the beach came into view. It was a dilapidated building with peeling faded-yellow walls. On arriving in front of it, they saw an elderly woman who sat sideways on a ramshackle deck chair, deftly paring roasted peppers. They exclaimed salam, and she smiled at Odile, greeting them in a hoarse voice. After standing up with difficulty, she conveyed in

Arabic and with hand gestures that the hotel was closed. An even older man appeared at the door of the house and repeated, in barely understandable English, that the hotel was permanently shut. Like the woman's, his toothless smile seemed good-natured. Looking around the beach, Célestin realized that not even a small rowboat was available. The islet, spread in the sea in front of their noses, was unreachable: "At least for Odile," he concluded.

The island lay in a north-south direction, parallel with the mainland. It was not directly across from the old hotel but slightly to the north. They stood quietly and admired the impressive ancient fortress. Its most formidable fortifications were in the south of the island, while the wall was much lower in the northern part. In the middle, facing the mainland, there was a narrow shingly beach, about a hundred and fifty meters long. From the hotel, the closest point on the island was no more than a third of a kilometer away but rocky. However, if they were to take a walk to the north, they would find themselves directly across the little beach. The distance would then be about two hundred and fifty meters, just as the German divers had said.

Finally, Célestin revealed to Odile his quasi-secret backup plan, which did not overly surprise her. "As you see, there are no boats. And the island is so close! For me, the distance is nothing to worry about. I can easily swim over there in less than fifteen minutes. There may be a current: When I'm a third of the way across, I'll find out.

"On the island, I'll come out at the little beach so we can wave! You can take a photo of me, although I'll be tiny. The fortress is magnificent. Then I'll swim back. I'm not crazy to step around barefoot because the rocks may be snake-friendly. Now you'll ask me, 'Why, then, Papa, do you want to go there?' But you know why. For me, being right under the citadel, eight hundred sixty-five years old, is an honor. You'd feel the same if you were ten years older. We'd then swim together—that's in our future."

Odile understood everything. She knew the swim to the island was an adventure like the desert trek to Ras Muhammad and the climb on Moses Trail—something her father could not resist.

Even so, she was worried. He was an excellent swimmer, but she would not be able even to call for help if there was trouble. She decided to keep mum and instead asked: "And where will I be?" He was ready: "*Ma petite sirène*, I thought this through carefully. These old people seem decent, but I don't trust leaving you in their care. So, without saying anything to them, we'll walk down the beach to that rock: I'll swim across from there. But first, we'll take a short swim together, so you can experience the sea across from the old citadel."

The water was magical—warm, blue-green, transparent. As Easter fell the day before, Célestin improvised that the swim was a belated celebration. After a while in the water, he said: "All right, *ma douce*, please go out and wait for me. I'll be back in a jiffy."

After Odile ran out of the sea, he blew her a kiss and swam toward Pharaoh's Island. There were no waves nor a noticeable current, so the swim was easy and enjoyable. While he was still in the water, the ancient fortress loomed over him. The small beach was covered by sharp shingle, with a rock here and there. As soon as he emerged from the sea, he turned around and saw the girl waving excitedly. He sent her kisses and posed for a photo. Then he explored the beach, stepping gingerly. The flag on top of the fortress billowed: It was still Israeli! "If my new friend Magdi were here," Célestin recalled the patriotic fervor of one of the three amiable Egyptians whom he had met at Ras Muhammad, "he would find a way to climb up there and replace it."

He again waved and plunged into the sea. When, after a swim of ten minutes, he arrived at her feet, she ran into the water and embraced him. He exclaimed: "Our next stop is the Dead Sea!"

8.

Their bus for Jerusalem left Eilat at nine. "It'll be fun to compare the water of the Gulf of Aqaba, which is part of the Red Sea, to the Dead Sea," spoke Célestin merrily. They arrived at the oasis Ein Gedi around eleven-thirty and obtained a room with two beds in the small hotel where they had rested in the subtropical garden on the way to Eilat. It belonged to the nearby kibbutz that had existed since 1956. The room was modestly appointed but included an impeccable private bathroom. They put on bathing suits and strolled through the garden to the small beach. The shoreline was straight as if drawn by a ruler. Célestin advised the girl: "Take a step or two and lie on your back on the water. Submerge your head once, quickly, to feel the dense, salty liquid, but don't swallow. All right, let's go in together."

For about ten minutes, they were lying next to each other on the surface of the Dead Sea, which was at first an exciting novelty but soon became boring. "So what do you think?" he asked Odile while they were returning to their room. "I'm glad we came here," she answered, "and I'll always remember it. What a strange feeling on the skin. And the body is somehow without weight. But the Gulf of Aqaba is much livelier than the Dead Sea—and prettier!" Later, a kibbutz van drove them to a small waterfall and lush botanical gardens. It took generations of kibbutzniks years of hard work and patient, loving cultivation to coax beautiful gardens out of the desert.

The next morning, their Jerusalem bus first climbed four hundred thirty meters to elevation zero and then another eight hundred thirty to the French Hill stop. When they reached Morky's office, he was delighted to hear their impressions of the Sinai. Célestin agreed to give a talk in French on books dealing with Hebrew linguistics and literature published during the previous fifteen years in France, Quebec, Swiss Romandy, and Belgian Wallonia. He had gladly promised to do that soon after arriving in Israel. An evening reception in his honor would be held after the lecture at the University Club. Morky added: "I'll invite many colleagues who wish to meet you; Hila will also be there." He also mentioned Deborah had left for a month in New York to be with Michal, her ten-year-old daughter. Although Morky tried to sound casual, Célestin detected a hint of resignation in his eyes.

When he called Osnat from his office, Odile ran to stand by. The women had returned from Eilat, and she inquired about their trip into the Sinai mountains. Célestin invited her to the lecture, adding his daughter would be present and suggesting she ask Avigail, the student of Arabic, to accompany her. "Avigail and I speak only elementary French, but Odile can translate for us! We'll enjoy seeing you in action that has nothing to do with trekking in the desert, swimming at Ras Muhammad, and chatting with some Israeli girl under a sun umbrella," said Osnat mischievously. "Perhaps it does?" he grinned.

They visited Hila, who said to Odile in French, "Your girlfriend Leora keeps asking me about you. We'll have to organize something soon." He mentioned the lecture, adding: "Morky has probably done it, but this is a personal invitation from the speaker."

Returning to his office, Célestin found a pile of mail, including letters via the estate manager Gilles. An envelope in the Soviet airmail format, with the Kazan postmark, fell out of the heap. The handwriting was not Olya's but her mother's.

It was another unabashed letter from an exceedingly disconsolate mother. Odile noticed her father's trepidation and ran to him. "It's from Olga," he murmured, quickly reading the handwritten letter in Russian. Olya was still in prison in Kuybyshev. She and other members of her "anti-Soviet gang" had received prison sentences of two to eight years. Olya's, among the shortest, was two and a half years, which would be reduced by the six months she had spent in prison since October 28, 1980, when she was arrested in Leningrad. Prison conditions were somewhat better, so Olga was allowed to send her daughter 1.5 kilograms of food twice a month. Finally, underlined: "Olya loves you more than ever, begs you not to forget her, and embraces darling Odile." Célestin hugged the girl firmly and translated the letter word for word. Both wept.

A quite different-looking envelope also arrived in Metz from the USSR. It contained a formal letter in Soviet legalese from a government office in Moscow confirming that "monsieur Célestin de Quernevelle submitted certain requests, in the USSR Consulates in Paris and Berlin, in connection with comrade Dinara Alimova Naratovna, who is serving a thirty-month prison sentence." Those requests, the letter stated, "were forwarded to the appropriate judicial bodies for their opinion and consideration."

"Well, it's at least something," he muttered to Odile. "They state my requests to free Olya are being looked at. And they inform me, which they were not obliged to do, of the duration of Olya's prison sentence—the same dreadful duration Olga had mentioned. Their authorities may think that being confronted with the length of the prison term would discourage me and make me forget Olya. But it will not happen! Let's, *mon coeur*, rejoice a little, hoping the first step toward Olya's freedom has been made." They embraced each other.

* * *

Célestin woke up early but stayed in bed without speaking to his daughter, who was sitting still in pajamas at a table drawing. He thought about Olya's suffering and the news he had received the previous day. With a father's love and pride, he observed Odile's profile. What a wonderful child. As she drew with a graphite pencil on a large sketch block, her posture and movements displayed utter dedication. From time to time, she looked at a vase with spring flowers in the corner of the room. Has the petals' daintiness inspired her? On occasion, it seemed she was adding shadows to some detail of the drawing with tiny strokes, whereas at other moments, she would stop and reflect, looking at the ceiling, and erase something. Then she would blow away the rubber particles and remove the ones remaining with her knuckles or the edge of her hand. She would study the drawing, her head bent to the left, a pout indicating dissatisfaction.

"*Bonjour chérie,* did you sleep well?" Célestin exclaimed, jumping out of bed and kissing the girl on the cheek. "Not so well. I woke up long before you and was thinking about Olya in prison. How terrible it must be for her... Then I got up and combed my hair, trying not to wake you. Before tackling these white flowers we bought yesterday—they're pretty but a little boring—I was drawing something from my head, different and fantastic. With colored pencils, I did a gorgeous bird of paradise. Can you believe it? The lovely bird is sitting alone but free on a branch in a lush green forest. Free as only a bird can be...

"I don't want to show you the drawing, it's not finished." She got up and put on her pink peignoir, saying she would prepare tea. "I hope I won't be in madame Rachel's way in the kitchen." Célestin put two and two together and was moved by his daughter's sadness. He stroked her cheek and walked to the window: "I'd love to see it when it's ready."

Then he sprang into action: "Listen, let's forget the tea, there's a lot to do. First, we'll book the hotel we looked at before going to the Sinai. Now that we are more familiar with Jerusalem, it'll be interesting to stay in the city center, where there are all kinds of different people, both Israelis and Arabs; around here, everyone is a professor or student. I'll let Rachel and Danny know today, but we'll move after my lecture." Odile understood her father's never-ending desire to learn something new and therefore did not object to the move—although she had become accustomed to their cozy room with a view of the Dead Sea, the kind Dobrin couple, and the familiar French Hill.

He continued: "But this afternoon, we'll make the most essential visit in Jerusalem and all of Israel: We'll go to Yad Vashem. I've spoken to you about that memorial museum to the victims of the Holocaust, the destruction of six million Jews during the Second World War. The museum's role is not only to document the perishing of the innocents but also to celebrate the heroes. Maybe you remember I spoke to you in Tel Aviv about Yitzhak Zuckerman, the courageous leader of the uprising in the Warsaw Ghetto. Professor Jakob Shmotkin told us a great deal. I recall you were taking photos of the university campus from the window of his office." Yes, Odile remembered but with difficulty—she was learning so many things. Célestin added: "I must call Jakob while it's still April because I know he was born in this month in 1942, just two and a half years before me. He'll be surprised, I hope pleasantly. What a man he is—so sincere and open with us."

While they were walking toward the № 27 bus stop, it began to rain. The gloomy sky spoke of late fall rather than spring. By the time they got off the bus at the intersection of Jaffa and King George, the very center of the city, the rain had intensified, but the hotel Palatin on Agripas Street was only about a hundred meters away. They reserved a well-appointed room for the 28th of April and beyond. After a few more errands, they took a bus to the western part of Jerusalem. There, on Har HaZikaron, Hill of Remembrance, was Yad Vashem.

The bus took only fifteen minutes. Near the museum, the rain became heavy. There were some curious sights: Many of the ultraorthodox passersby had draped transparent plastic bags over their black hats for protection, but the wind blew the bags into huge bubbles. Others had placed Sony Walkmans over their soaked kippahs.

* * *

The strong emotions experienced by Odile and Célestin at Yad Vashem are difficult to describe. Although long familiar with the essential information—even Odile, by her only ninth year of life—the two were profoundly moved. Sometimes one, and sometimes both at the same time, helplessly sobbed or choked soundlessly. Célestin had not been able to predict how he would feel. The power of horrifying facts and monochrome photographs on a black background, accompanied by a few carefully chosen words: Words of sufferers and cries of their tortured souls engraved in black granite. Eternal sorrow.

Célestin was incapable of imagining how an old Jew would feel in that place, especially an old Ashkenazi Jew, and above all a Jew who had survived an extermination *Lager* and was living in Israel. Perhaps the man would feel appallingly, pitifully guilty remembering those who had not survived.

Without an umbrella in the unceasing rain, they strode back to Jaffa Street and took a bus to French Hill. For the rest of the day, they talked softly and were able only to write in their diaries.

Two hills in Jerusalem, Remembrance and French, what a difference.

9.

They went to the Old City again the next day. Near the Wailing Wall and in the Arab section, east of El Wad, soldiers and policemen were studying each passerby. Since the murder of the yeshiva student, unpleasant events had occurred daily. Students of the yeshiva set Palestinian homes on fire, threw furniture out of others, and beat people randomly. The Mayor of Jerusalem condemned these actions and provoked many ultraorthodox Jews by saying that "the existence of the yeshiva in that part of the Old City is a thorn in the eye of Israeli-Arab relations." Right-wing members of the Knesset clamored: "The Arabs cannot be trusted; they are hiding the killers and deserve to be given a harsh lesson."

Despite the palpable tension on the streets, Célestin and Odile braved half-empty souks, occasionally making a wrong turn and arriving in a deserted, desolate cul-de-sac in which he caught a whiff of danger—or thought he did—but nothing untoward happened. They entered a small Palestinian coffee place and were served decently, almost obsequiously.

The respect they felt did not permit them to avoid visiting the Wailing Wall a second time. About forty men were again facing the left three-fifths of the Wall. A greater number of women than during their previous visit, including young girls with traditional braids, were on the right side. The women and girls, unlike the men, stood immobile while ardently praying. Perhaps they were less feverish in prayer, Célestin thought, or less argumentative with God than the ultraorthodox men?

From the Wall, they walked to the affluent, scrupulously maintained Armenian Quarter, which occupied the southwestern part of the Old City. The Armenian Patriarchate was housed within the ancient Cathedral of Saint James. They took time to examine the finely carved twelfth-century stone crosses in the splendid courtyard. In a peaceful corner of the quarter, where the southern and western walls met, was a garden in which they ambled listening to songbirds. Célestin told Odile that Armenian Christianity was very old, with its origin in the fourth century, and that those people's presence in Jerusalem dated from early times.

Not far from the garden, next to the imposing Zion Gate—the only passage through the southern wall—they found an Armenian restaurant where they had lunch. Afterward, they patiently traversed the entire Old City, proceeding in a complicated zig-zag manner through various quarters, until they emerged in front of the formidable Lions' Gate, interestingly also called Sheep Gate. They passed through the eastern wall and climbed a hill on which the Muslim cemetery of Yeusefiya was spread. Nothing was too strenuous for Odile when she was with her father.

A deep silence ruled among the tombs, each adorned by exquisite Arab calligraphy. From time to time, the cacophony common before Shabbat reached them from the major street on the east side of the hill, Derekh Jericho. However, it was the view southeast, toward Mount of Olives, which took their breath away—a sight so ancient as to be otherworldly. On the sacred Mount with an elevation of eight hundred thirty meters, at different distances from the Yeusefiya, stood fabulous historic structures. Looking from north to south, these were: the Tomb of the Virgin Mary; the Russian Orthodox Church of Mary Magdalene, blue-white, with five golden onion domes; the Chapel of Christ's Ascension; Carmelite Monastery Pater Noster; a small Catholic church, only a quarter of a century old, near the ancient Byzantine tombs, with the name *Dominus Flevit*, the Lord Wept (over Jerusalem); and southernmost, the catacombs of Haggai, Zechariah, and Malachi, the last three prophets in the Hebrew Bible.

Célestin explained as much as he could, and she was immersed in his vivid storytelling during the two magical hours they spent at the extraordinary place. For them, it was a watch tower of history, not a tourist lookout. In the opposite direction, toward the north, Hebrew University was visible, comfortably spread atop Mt. Scopus. The university had become very dear to them. However, from where they stood, it appeared to be a mono-lithic, cold, granite bastion.

* * *

It was almost time. Every Friday at four in the afternoon, the Franciscans led a procession along the entire Via Dolorosa, a route comprising all fourteen Stations of Christ's suffering. They returned to the Old City through Lions' Gate and, after walking some three hundred meters toward the beginning of the Sorrow-ful Way, arrived at the Churches of Condemnation, Flagellation, and Imposition of the Cross. By a long tradition, those were the places where Jesus was sentenced, whipped, and burdened with the cross. Behind the altar, they saw a representation in stained glass of Pontius Pilate, the Roman *praefectus*, governor of Judaea, washing his hands after passing the sentence of crucifixion. Other panes of stained glass showed Jesus receiving lashes and Barabbas relieved that his death sentence had been commuted.

He resumed the narration: "It's not known where Pontius Pi-late's chamber, the *praetorium*, was located, just as much else about the Stations is shrouded by time and mystical beliefs. The first Good Friday processions were held in the fourth century, and all sorts of claims have been put forward since then." Nearby, they saw a spacious courtyard in which innumerable Franciscan monks and nuns from Jerusalem and the whole world were gath-ered. Many others who intended to walk along the Sorrowful Way to the Fourteenth Station within the Church of the Holy Sepul-chre joined the monks.

The courtyard belonging to the Umariya School was in an-cient times occupied by the Antonia Fortress, erected by Herod the Great. "First Station" was written on a prominently placed plaque. Célestin looked around and said a tad sarcastically: "I read there are other candidates for the location of the First Sta-tion. It doesn't surprise me they chose Antonia because the court-yard is suitably vast!"

At the head of the procession, four men carried a massive wooden cross on their bare backs, which alluded to the pain Jesus would have felt when carrying the cross alone. The procession slowly moved along Sorrowful Way, halting at each Station where a Franciscan priest recited a description of the event that had occurred—according to traditional teaching—two thousand years earlier, first in Latin, then in English. The Second Station, *Lithostrotos*, was the place where a "crown" of thorns was derisively placed on Jesus's head, and Pontius Pilate pronounced the fateful words *Ecce homo!* (*Behold the man!*), thus placing Jesus's life in the unmerciful hands of the people of Judaea.

At that spot, Via Dolorosa was five or six meters wide. Father and daughter looked at the famous arch looming above them. Célestin said: "The arch is called *Ecce homo!* But it did not exist at the time of Christ. It was erected later, in the second century, by whom else than Emperor Hadrian." Odile was intrigued by something else: "Papa, does someone live inside the arch? Look, there's a small window with open shutters!" He laughed heartily: "I'm glad we've discovered together I'm neither an all-knowing man nor a liar! If I were an official guide, I'd probably invent a story about an imprisoned Arabian princess who's permitted to open the shutters only on Tuesdays to see her prince, ha, ha!" Odile first frowned and then also laughed, "Oh, you, Papa!"

When the procession entered El Wad, the pair decided to leave it. They had walked the entire length of the Way on previous occasions and spent much time inside the Church of the Holy Sepulchre. Besides, being part of a throng was not the individualistic duo's cup of tea. Célestin felt hemmed in, if not experiencing claustrophobia in a clinical sense, while Odile's little feet were stepped on frequently. There was a lot of pushing and elbowing by the crowd, many of whose members were hardly the meek, serene believers participating symbolically in the Passion of Christ. Sometimes an entire section of the Way was completely blocked, which caused difficulties for the Palestinians who tried to pass in the opposite direction.

While they were climbing other narrow streets to reach the final Stations, passing the medieval Mosque of Omar, he remarked: "You see how poorly it sometimes goes for Arabs here.

The Franciscans, Catholics like us, lead a procession each Friday at four in the afternoon. That day and time were evidently chosen on purpose: Friday, because of Good Friday, while starting at four guarantees that the procession would reach the Holy Sepulchre before sunset and the beginning of Shabbat. But where in the scheduling are Muslims, for whom, according to their Quran, Friday is a sacred day of worship? They can't pass along many streets without hindrance—even men, let alone women." Odile nodded solemnly.

Near a souk, they reemerged on Via Dolorosa at the Eighth Station, where Jesus had spoken to "daughters of Jerusalem," consoling them. On the wall of an Orthodox monastery, a Latin cross was engraved, and around it was a Christogram, Christ's monogram, composed of the Greek letters "chi" and "rho". As the Friday procession approached, they again escaped—up a steep staircase toward the impressive mass of granite that was the Coptic Orthodox Patriarchate and its church. In front of it, they managed to elude the persistent pursuit of a man, undoubtedly profit-motivated, and entered the church.

Unfamiliar with Coptic customs, they took off their shoes and crossed themselves in the Russian manner. The church was empty and exuded authentic Christian simplicity, particularly in its altar, reliquaries, and ornaments—with some Eastern additions that were difficult to pinpoint and interpret. Wherever they saw text, it was written in Greek letters, but Célestin knew the language was based on ancient Egyptian. He said: "When Islamicized Arabs conquered Egypt before the middle of the seventh century, they immediately outlawed the ancient Egyptian language used by Copts and imposed Arabic. Sabre-waving conquerors behave likewise to this day. Even now, radical Muslims make life difficult for Copts in Egypt, so I've been told by a fair-minded Egyptian in Sheikh."

Coming out of the church, they encountered two photogenic Coptic monks in long cassocks at the door of the adjacent monastery. Odile asked in French for permission to photograph them. They did not understand, but a young woman who spoke Coptic appeared and helped out. The monks smiled benevolently while the woman explained she was a Copt born in Jerusalem, whereas the men were from Alexandria.

The promising interaction was interrupted by the man with sinister looks who had bothered them earlier—the polite young woman's elder brother! While Odile was taking a picture of the monks, the man shoved a worn-out "Bethlehem" postcard and some dry "Flors Holi land" petals in plastic in front of Célestin's nose, aggressively demanding two shekels. The woman apologized—sincerely for her brother's impudence but not for the family business.

* * *

Soon they arrived in a cul-de-sac located immediately to the east of the main dome of the Church of the Holy Sepulchre—a hushed courtyard with a luxuriant tree in the middle. A priest in a dark cassock was resting on a bench, a green fez on his head. The corner was blessed by a profound peace, yet it was the priest who began the conversation, cordially greeting the pair. His English was fluent as he had spent many of his younger years at the Ethiopian Church in London. Célestin mentioned they had visited Kidane Mehret on their first day in Jerusalem. "I am pleased to hear it," said the man, "because I love that church and often pray in it. In the Old City, there is always clamor, and the noise enters our Ethiopian Orthodox Patriarchate, which is just across this wall—look, it's the dark gray dome."

They liked the priest. He had attractive features and skin of a chocolate color. Despite its dignified Apollonian beauty, his face was full of life. On the bench beside him, a book lay open, so Célestin asked whether the language was Amharic. "Yes, Sir," he agreed in a throaty voice, "you are well informed. This Bible is in Amharic, and our script is called 'Fidäl'."

He waited for the Ethiopian to continue, but after a brief silence posed a question: "I understand, but is this Bible, which seems to be a newly published book, written in 'Fidäl' or perhaps even in 'Geëz,' the classical Ethiopian?" The priest looked at

Célestin with a beatific expression: "It's impressive, Sir, what you know! No one knew it in London. People came to our church because we were exotic." The Frenchman privately speculated: "Yes, some came because of exoticism but many Englishwomen because of you!"

Unable or unwilling to read Célestin's indelicate thoughts, the priest went on: "Exotic, ancient, and half-dead Ethiopians and also Copts and Armenians... yet we are all in Jerusalem next to each other. But to continue about the script in this book. As you certainly know, Fidäl is based on the much older Geëz, which is one of the oldest scripts in the world and considered extinct like a prehistoric animal. We are trying to revive it and bring it into the world of the living. This recently published book, printed in Addis Ababa—a name which in Amharic, maybe you know, means 'the new flower'—is the first fruit of our efforts. Eh, my good Sir, I'm not an envious man, but if we Ethiopians had just one-twentieth of the funds our Jewish neighbors possess—and even the Palestinians do, admittedly only sometimes, when the Saudi sheiks find it opportune..."

Célestin asked if he could take a look at the book. After examining it, he said: "At home in France, I have only a few books in Amharic, all of them with the Fidäl script." The priest looked at him kindly, took the book, and using a pencil the girl had quickly taken out of her purse, wrote a dedication in Amharic and British English at the beginning of the volume. The recipients read it together: "Dear Sir, I am honoured to present to you the first book with the revived Geëz script. Thank you for being a friend of Ethiopia and the Amharic language. Humbly yours, Father Nahome." When Célestin politely objected, the Ethiopian reassured him: "We have enough copies at the monastery and can always get more from Addis. Many of our priests are only beginning to learn Geëz."

Father and daughter were grateful. Shyly, he placed twenty dollars on the bench for the monastery. Then he opened the book, chose a place at random, and said: "Respected Father Nahome, you would make us happy by reading aloud a part of this page. My daughter and I truly wish to hear the sound of Amharic." The priest smiled, got up, cleared his throat, and solemnly began to read in a velvety voice. When he raised his eyes after perhaps ten minutes, they thanked him warmly and reluctantly said goodbye.

While walking away, Father Nahome's words continued to ring in their ears. Firmly grasping the book he was given, Célestin said to his daughter that those words must have sounded at least a little like they did two thousand years earlier when some priest in Ethiopia had spoken them.

Outside the Coptic Patriarchate, they noticed a Roman pillar on which a sign was affixed marking the Ninth Station where Jesus had fallen the third time. Nearby, at the entrance of the Church of the Holy Sepulchre, stood a densely packed group of people, the remnant of the procession. Using side streets, they walked westward to Jaffa Gate and boarded a bus for French Hill.

10.

Saturday morning was spent quietly but not lazily. Célestin got up early and spent a long time preparing the lecture scheduled for the next day. As it was Shabbat, there were few cars on the streets, although some people dared to drive, at least on French Hill. After his fourth cup of tea, he went to the kitchen and chatted with Rachel and Danny while preparing Odile's breakfast. He carried the tray to the bedroom and pulled open the curtains. For a while, he enjoyed the spectacular view to the east and then tenderly woke his girl: "Please get up, *ma mignonne,* and take a look through the window. The Dead Sea is still a sunny ribbon, but the rain is advancing toward us from Jericho. At the end of breakfast, she remembered: "Papa, yesterday we left our laundry on the roof to dry, so I'll go up to collect it." But he suggested: "Let's go together to breathe fresh air and exercise before the rain arrives."

Spring rain stopped at lunchtime. At three, buses were still not running, so they eagerly walked for half an hour, mostly downhill, to El Wad in the Old City. Soon they discovered Chain Gate was open, one of twelve through which one could reach Temple Mount. After climbing some twenty steps, they found themselves at the western edge of an immense rectangle. Below that side of the Mount—its support, in fact—was the Wailing Wall. It was what remained of the Second Temple, itself erected by Herod the Great on the foundations of a far older temple of King Solomon.

Temple Mount was a fantastic sacred space. Célestin and Odile took a dozen steps and stopped, speechless and amazed. Along the edges of the Mount were dark-green pines, cypresses, and other lush vegetation, but the entire area was dominated from its approximate center by the Dome of the Rock. It was a surreal structure looking like a mirage that had emerged from the Arabian desert. He thoughtfully said: "By taking a single glance at this extraordinary, breathtaking structure from the end of the seventh century, one has in truth witnessed the incomparable upsurge of Islamic beliefs and the implacable might of the Mohammedan scimitars at the time." She whispered only: "The golden dome is so beautiful."

"It is indeed, although it shouldn't be forgotten that the Dome of the Rock was in many ways—including its octagonal plan and the mosaics—modeled after the Byzantine churches and palaces in Jerusalem built much earlier... Incidentally, it was gold-plated only in 1960."

Twice they circled the structure on ancient paths. He estimated the diameter of the Dome was about twenty meters. The mosaics, carved windows, and tiny pillars were superb. "And where, Papa, is the Rock above which sits the Dome?" Odile asked logically. "I understand why you're puzzled. As it happens, ancient beliefs, traditions, and myths of the three religions are connected with that. Under the Dome, they believe, is the Foundation Stone, and near it is the dust from which God created the world and Adam, the first human being.

"Muslims believe their prophet Muhammad began his Night Journey to heaven from the same Rock. A *surah*, a chapter in the Quran, is written about it—look at those Arabic letters running around the whole structure. If I'm not mistaken, it's Surah 17."

They walked southward toward the dark, austere, enormous Al-Aqsa Mosque, built at the beginning of the eighth century and the third-holiest site in the Muslim world. With its brown walls and black dome, it was unabashedly devoid of beauty. But between the Dome of the Rock and Al-Aqsa, the pair admired the ablution fountain Al-Kas, "the bowl." Muslim believers ritually cleansed their fingers, feet, legs, and faces there before entering the mosque.

"And now the conclusion about Muhammad's night journey in the year 621. During the same night, the prophet physically and spiritually flew twice. The first time, he rode on a little winged horse named Buraq—neither an adult horse, nor a mare, nor a donkey, nor a camel—and traveled from the Great Mosque in 'Mecca the noble' in Saudi Arabia, to this very mosque in front of us. After praying here with other prophets, he flew to heaven. So now you know everything, *mon trésor*," Célestin said in a tired voice. "Wow!" exclaimed Odile in English and added, "Pasha certainly couldn't do it, even if we bought her wings!"

* * *

Father and daughter descended from Temple Mount and ambled through the prosperous Jewish Quarter in the southern part of the Old City. Like the Armenian Quarter, it was lovingly renovated and kept immaculately clean. Instead of clashing with the old and even ancient styles, modern architecture was skillfully adapted to complement them. Stone houses were connected by complicated mini-tunnels, arches, and gates with gorgeous wrought-iron railings. There was street life after Shabbat, but the Quarter did not cater to tourists. On miniature stone squares, children played merrily, and some boys, of all the games, chose American football.

In a cul-de-sac at the border of the Jewish and Armenian Quarters, they met two young Englishwomen—in fact, it was Odile who, by some words, gestures, or picture-taking, had inadvertently initiated the acquaintanceship. The foursome came out from the Old City through the nearby Zion Gate and sat down in a modern café located directly across the Jewish cemetery and King David's Tomb.

Both women were from Chester, in the west of England, but were taking a four-year nursing course at the Westminster Hospital in London. They were well-mannered, good-looking girls, especially Sophie—with her deep-set eyes, slender build, high forehead, fair complexion, and naturally blond long hair: Célestin knew that in her home country, she would be described as an "English rose." Karen was a tall, strong brunette who often laughed; a touch of plumpness suited her well. Because they were intelligent women who had attended excellent schools, he asked them why they did not opt for medical studies. "Yes, our fathers, both doctors, paid for our expensive middle schooling, but we didn't manage to obtain a sufficient number of high grades in the most important subjects, only three A-levels each," Sophie reported. They came to Israel for two weeks before working in the geriatric ward for the conclusion of their second year of studies.

He let Odile talk, starting with her impressions of Temple Mount and Wailing Wall, while the girls offered witty remarks. They described the inexpensive accommodation they had obtained at a Lutheran hostel for women in the heart of the Old City—only five shekels per night—but with cots in a rowdy dormitory for thirty women. "The hostel is carved into rock and clean, but when we return in the evening, some alleys are scary. Luckily, there are usually Israeli soldiers around," Sophie told them.

The safety talk led the young women to a sensitive issue in the Old City, Bethlehem, Jericho, and Hebron. "Our parents are worried, not because of the ugly street encounters between Jews and Arabs, but something else about which they had repeatedly warned us before we left," Sophie explained. "It turned out they were right, and so we don't dare broach the topic on the phone," Karen added. "Mind you, from the start," Sophie went on with a wry smile, "we have been dressing modestly, as you see us now, nothing provocative: loose jeans, long sleeves, high neckline, no jewelry, never in shorts."

Karen took over: "And still... I'd like to be candid, but please interrupt me if you think what I'm saying is not for Odile's pretty ears," she smiled. "From our first day, and wherever we found ourselves, particularly near the sites for which we came, but also at bus stops and in stores, we've been the target of disgusting remarks and proposals of a sexual nature. Countless times a day, we've heard 'Do you want to f...' and such. Already the first afternoon, we stopped bargaining about prices in souks, which most tourists enjoy doing, because of what we heard from sellers, even some at least seventy-five years old—'offers' that we could get a bracelet free if we agreed to 'spen nit togeter.' Not to mention men trying to rub against us in buses and souks."

After listening to Karen's words, Sophie ventured: "I think you guessed this always comes from Arabs, but rest assured we're not racially prejudiced. Maybe all racists say that, but I have relatives—aunts, uncles, and their children—in Kenya. Since I was twelve, I've been there for long visits. I learned to speak Swahili fluently, acquired black girlfriends, and remain close to them."

Célestin looked at Odile and was almost certain she had understood the girls' complaints but was more puzzled than shocked; fine, he would speak to her. Also, he decided to ask Osnat and Hila if Israeli women were subjected to similar insolent behavior from Arabs or if that was a foreign female visitors' preserve. He would also request that they tell him if young Israeli men were different regarding such shameless targeting of women tourists. To Karen and Sophie, he said: "I understand you and am sorry scoundrels are making your life in this fascinating country miserable. I don't believe racism on your part lies at the root of what you've been experiencing. But I must remind you that such indecent behavior happens all over Europe. I hope no local Arab has— excuse me—pinched your behinds, but in France and Germany that's considered a Roman specialty, and the targets are by no means only foreign women. These things also frequently happen in Paris, the bullies claiming they are complimenting women who appreciate it!"

The Englishwomen were listening with serious expressions, as Célestin continued: "Nevertheless, I think the local situation is different and we must face another reason for such behavior, although it too may be inextricably connected to sex. Remember that white male Westerners have for centuries been impertinently stomping all over the pride and honor of Arab men, with English and French men undoubtedly the main culprits. What's happening to you may be Arab revenge on the white Western man by means of intimately touching the white woman against her will. That's an old idea, not mine. Some would call it a racist thought—with what logic? After all, I'm not saying it's something inborn, transmitted by genes, but rather passed orally across generations from father to son."

"Yes," Sophie exclaimed, "my father said something similar to us, although he's not as rational as you are. He related it to Kenya and the many rapes of Englishwomen by black men during the Mau Mau rebellion in the fifties. Because of those guerrillas, my parents escaped to England in 1957, two years before I was born, although my dad's sister and brother remained there, without anything dire happening to them. You see, sometimes I feel guilty because of what the English have done in Kenya for a hundred years, and the guilt is written on my forehead. So I'm toadying, kowtowing, too much to the local Arabs."

Karen jumped in: "Nonsense! You see, even though Sophie's blond, which in women's opinion attracts men, especially dark men, the world over like bears to honey, and she's much prettier than I am—yes, Sophie, you are!—I'm the one who is more often assaulted. And I am both taller and stronger than she is. To the scoundrels, as you called them, Sophie probably seems distant and cold as a statue on a pedestal, utterly unattainable. And as for guilt, I also have those feelings to some degree."

Then they talked about medicine, politics, and even philosophy but addressed Odile from time to time. At one point, he asked the girls: "I'm not asking this because of your future profession, which demands a modicum of humanism, but because of the impression I've formed during our talk: Is it the case that you both possess a goodly dose of idealism, an irresistible desire to help the weak and the poor?" "Of course!" exclaimed Karen, "we're both hoping to help in the 'Third World' while we're young, for instance, through the Peace Corps. Sophie wishes to return to Israel and work without pay as a nurse in a kibbutz in the hinterland. Israel is the only place to which her stern parents would let her go without disowning her! And we're not Jewish. But I'd like to help the poverty-stricken people wherever they are in the world."

Sophie looked at her with a touch of mockery: "Karen and I are very close, but sometimes I don't understand her. She can be awfully stubborn, as if she's got the Mother Teresa complex. And she doesn't learn from examples even when they're in front of her nose. You see, Karen has another girlfriend but similar to her in that regard—or at least, she used to be. As soon as she had obtained the nursing diploma, the ultra-idealistic girl went to Peru to work at a colony for lepers. In the jungle, of course. It turned out the colony was a front from which drugs were smuggled, and no one, except a few old people, had leprosy! She had an incredibly hard time surfacing from there alive—by escaping at night and walking alone for a couple of days. Sorry, Karen, but I had to tell our new friend about this."

Before they parted, having agreed to meet again, Célestin said: "Karen, I hope you'll take it seriously. I've heard from trustworthy people that the CIA, among others, often uses the Peace Corps and similar organizations—with their recruits' youthful humanism, altruistic instincts, and naive do-goodism—as a front for all sorts of things. Last year, on the train from Leningrad to Helsinki, we met a young, utopia-seeking Finnish girl who was the Secretary General of the Finnish Youth Peace League, financed by the USSR."

* * *

The following morning, Célestin called Osnat: "My lecture at the Department of Linguistics is today at five and will last two hours. Please warn Avigail. Afterward, around seven-thirty, there'll be a reception at the University Club. Because I'm not the host, I can't invite either of you. And I have a request. Odile will be at the lecture, but she's too young for the reception. I propose that after the lecture we take her to the Dobrins' apartment and you kindly stay with her until I return. She'd love to spend time with you. I'll tell Rachel and Danny. What d'you say?" Osnat agreed and promised to bring photos of Netanya, her native town by the sea north of Tel Aviv.

For obvious reasons, the Department of Linguistics held a position of importance at Hebrew University and was affiliated with the Departments of Anthropology, Sociology, History, and Psychology, as well as with the study centers of Hebrew, Arabic, and other Semitic languages. About a hundred scientists, doctoral students, and top administrators attended Célestin's lecture. He and Odile might have been the only non-Jews in the auditorium. "This is an honor for me, as has been the entire treatment we've received here," he thought gratefully and modestly. Near the top of the auditorium, Odile sat with Osnat, Avigail, Hila, and Morky: The little girl must have carried out the introductions! Many of the people present were certainly not fluent in French. However, Célestin used many explanatory slides; in addition, a competent interpreter, at a sign from the speaker, conveyed in Hebrew the gist of what had been said during the previous ten or so minutes.

At the end of the lecture, he answered a dozen questions with ease and charm. Then he accompanied Odile and Osnat to the Dobrins' apartment and introduced the "babysitter" to Rachel and Danny. She congratulated the speaker: "The lecture was fabulous and what applause! I saw several of my law professors clapping energetically. Thank you for inviting me. By the way, in Sharm El Sheikh, on occasions when we spoke French, we switched to 'tu'; but now, when I see you so highly regarded, perhaps I should address you formally with 'vous'?!"

"Of course not, Osnat, please don't offend me. We're sticking to tutoyer. And thank you so much for spending time with Odile." He reminded his daughter of the sandwiches they had prepared together. "Bring them from the kitchen, please, and offer Osnat juice." He kissed both on their cheeks, promised to return as soon as possible, and strode to the University Club.

During the reception, Morky and Hila introduced Célestin to

various people, with one of whom, Dr. Simha Grenstein, Professor of International Law, he made an appointment to meet the following afternoon. When he returned home, Osnat and Odile told him their time together had passed pleasantly, talking of Netanya, Baikal, and Metz, and photographing each other "artistically," as the clever child put it.

Before he accompanied Osnat to her students' residence on French Hill, she and Odile said goodbye as if they were the closest relatives. He was glad to witness the warm parting, although in a corner of his mind, there arose the question of whether it was wise for his daughter to become so attached to a woman who was not Olya. Despite that doubt, he hoped to see Osnat again the next day and had to admit sometimes missing adult company, especially female.

While slowly walking along the street, close to each other but not touching, he said: "Osnat, would it be interesting for you to see something Christian in the Old City together with us, something, I've been told, most tourists never see? The place in question is a cave or catacomb in the Church of the Holy Sepulchre. So, if you are willing and don't have other obligations tomorrow..." She studied his expression and answered: "Mondays at nine, I have a lecture on Contracts but find the material the most boring in all of the law. I planned to skip it and prepare for a student court-case simulation in which I'll participate next week. But that can wait. Listen, I really like being with you—and with Odile, naturally. So, when tomorrow, and where should I come?"

When they met the next morning in front of the Holy Sepulchre, Célestin took Osnat and Odile to the small shop down the street. The elderly Italian owner again stood on the shop's threshold and jovially greeted the French pair: "You're still with us in Jerusalem, how nice! And you brought a lovely friend!" He smiled at Osnat in the fake-seductive style with which he had grown up in Rome. Célestin responded: "Yes, when we were here about three weeks ago, you informed us of some locked subterranean parts of the church."

The man nodded: "Yes, it's possible to see some catacombs

that are under lock and key. Just go to the entrance of the church and discreetly ask the old Arab who's now standing there to introduce you to Hannah, the Armenian priest and keeper of the underground caves. Money isn't always necessary; decide for yourself." Célestin thanked the shopkeeper while Osnat and Odile bought postcards.

As they strolled to the church, he asked Osnat whether it would be uncomfortable for her as a Jewess to enter a Christian sanctuary. "Oh, no," she said immediately, "I always like to see and learn something new. Besides, my mom and I are secular Jewesses, my dad less so. And didn't you notice I'm dressed suitably for a holy place?" Only then did Célestin realize he had not warned Osnat about the dress code. "Yesterday evening, my womanizer," he thought mockingly, "you were absorbed by other thoughts regarding Osnat!"

The tall, stern Arab at the entrance of the Holy Sepulchre sized up the visitors and helped them find the Armenian priest. Hannah was a serious man with a Modigliani face, long gray beard, and hooked nose. "It will be my pleasure to show you our ancient domain," he said in formal English. "Our Patriarch Vargarsh and I are the only people who have the key." He took them behind the altar in the Armenian part of the church, where numerous mosaics decorated the walls, and unlocked a narrow metal door. A steep staircase led to the underground, where there was a pond.

As in a fairy tale, they arrived at another locked door. Another key, even more massive. They stepped cautiously into tomblike darkness. When Hannah threw light on a wall with his lantern, they saw a pale drawing: "Noah's Ark," Hannah said softly. "Or something," Célestin thought, "that bears resemblance to hundreds of depictions done through the ages." They stood motionless, deep below the ancient church. Odile took her father's hand, learning what absolute silence meant. "No one knows," Hannah whispered after a minute, "not even our omniscient Patriarch Vargarsh, who and when was here to draw the Ark built by the tenth, the last, biblical Patriarch before the Flood."

They climbed back to the surface and thanked Hannah. Célestin put a few coins in the contributions box, and Osnat followed suit; he also gave a coin to the Arab at the entrance. As they were leaving the Old City through New Gate, he quipped: "Regardless of what that drawing represents and who did it, we saw something new, at a unique place. But please, you two, tell me honestly: Has my sense of smell completely given out? I'm worried because the pond…" Both girls laughed, but the little one was faster: "*Non, cher Papounet,* everything is all right with your nose, the pond didn't stink at all!"

* * *

Célestin treated his young guests to lunch in a fine restaurant he had noticed on Ben Yehuda. During the meal, Osnat talked about her childhood, which she described as a happy one, in spite of not having siblings. Odile listened, some of her queries guided by Osnat's Netanya photos. "When you begin to tour Israel and arrive in my town," Osnat said, "I'll show you everything I like there. Just let me know, I'll drop everything here and come right away. Netanya is only thirty kilometers north of Tel Aviv and less than a hundred from Jerusalem."

In a measured manner, mindful of the presence of Odile and Osnat's sentiments as an Israeli, Célestin described the indignities experienced by Karen and Sophie. He explained the two were well-educated young women who neither dressed nor behaved provocatively. Osnat was quiet, tapping on the table with two or three thin fingers. "Unfortunately, I'm not surprised by what's been happening to these decent girls, our welcome guests. Jewish girls, students from various countries, have revealed similar things to me, despite being embarrassed. This means if you're female and a foreigner, you're a target whether you're Jewish or not. And if you're from Israel? Well, our local Arab girls, I'm convinced, are also victims in many situations, but they conceal it, they won't tell me because they're ashamed and think there's already more than enough rejection of Arabs, even contempt. I sense that because I have Palestinian girlfriends—of course, they don't study at my university, you can figure out why. And young Israeli women as Arabs' targets? That's rare. Girls here are taught how to defend themselves, starting with classes practically in kindergarten and ending with army combat training. For an Arab bully to do something impertinent in public to an Israeli woman would be close to fatal: The girl would need to exclaim only two words."

Célestin remained silent, respecting the young woman and believing her words. Odile was attentive as Osnat continued: "Everything I said so far relates to Arab hoodlums. I think the English women correctly identified their ethnicity. Of course, there are scoundrels among our boys too, but because of the circumstances of life here, they are less in contact with young female foreigners, Jewish and non-Jewish, than are Arabs whose undisputed domain is the souk." Looking into the distance, she concluded: "When one adds it all up, the only clear thing is that from the sexual angle, sadly, it isn't easy for young foreign women in Israel; and it won't change, I think, for a while. As for street thefts, women, regardless of age, are an obvious target—with their capacious bags and flashy jewelry, faux or not!" Osnat laughed, pointing at her necklace and sizable bag. "What a melodious ringing laugh this girl has," Célestin admired her secretly.

"Thank you, Osnat, for being objective, but please tell me something else. It interests me, in part because my child is a girl who I hope will return to Israel when she's older: Would you use the word *shiksa* for Karen and Sophie?" Osnat answered vehemently: "Certainly not! I never use that term for non-Jewish women, regardless of how they look and behave. Some people claim the word is harmless, just a waggish expression with no bad intention, but my parents and I, and my girlfriends, we all know that's a lie. It's an ugly word. If I had a sister or a brother and they'd say it, I might slap them—it's scornful and disrespectful.

"Sometimes I hear from Jewish-American women students that the word is often used in New York, and they don't disapprove of it—while at the same time, they lecture us on how we're prejudiced against Palestinians. So it goes. Here, the term is used mostly by the ultraorthodox, but they also have nasty words for us, secular Sabras. Of course, we certainly have choice words for them." Célestin laughed weakly and so did Odile, without quite knowing why.

When they finished lunch, he said: "Girls, may I ask you to spend the next few hours without me? In less than fifteen minutes, I'll have a meeting with a professor whom I met at the reception. He's an impressive man who teaches comparative law at Hebrew University. He proposed we meet in Café Atara, which is nearby. It's supposed to be a place with a distinguished ancestry. Stay here as long as you wish, then have an ice cream somewhere, and let's meet again here around five o'clock. Osnat, can you please do this for me?"

The girls readily agreed, but Osnat asked: "Is that law professor Dr. Simha Grenstein?" "He's the one, how did you guess?" "I haven't yet taken his course, it'll come in my final year, but I know how he looks. I saw him applauding after your lecture. He's known to be one of the top experts on international law in Israel, although he's so young." Célestin was pleased that Osnat thought highly of Professor Grenstein and would not feel he was leaving for a trivial reason. He placed some banknotes in Odile's purse and assigned her the task of paying for what might come up later. Then he kissed them both and paid for lunch at the exit.

11.

Simha Grenstein was waiting for Célestin at the entrance of Atara and took him to a table in the far corner of the smoke-filled café, which had an interesting shape. Black-and-white photographs and framed caricatures of historical significance were hanging on its walls. As soon as they were seated and ordered from a waitress, Grenstein said: "Dear colleague, I really liked your lecture. Much of what you said about comparative linguistics and the problems of translation and oral interpretation should and must find an application in international legal and diplomatic relations, in which, even at the United Nations, the show is now run by pretentious amateurs. That's why I'm glad you found the time to talk to me." Célestin thanked him sincerely, thinking a genuine friendship might be on the horizon.

"I invited you here because Atara has existed a long time and is full of Jerusalem legends, in addition to smoke," said Simha. "Before 1948, under the British Mandate for Palestine, their officers often came here while the leaders of the Zionist paramilitary organizations Haganah and Irgun might have been sitting at the same time in another corner. Later, and to this day, the place has been taken over by politicians, journalists, artists, and film people with pet starlets. The boss of the café is that large blond man, Uri Landau, who resembles a healthy peasant from Swabia more than a hunchbacked Jew with a hooked nose and pince-nez. He has good connections in every important office in Tel Aviv. Because of some strange principle, he never employs young women but always waitresses like ours: middle-aged, married, in stained white blouses and long boring skirts."

They moved to a discussion of comparative linguistics, international law, ultraorthodox Jews, and the inferior position of Palestinians not only in Israel but also in Syria, Jordan, and Lebanon. Their fear of a nuclear confrontation between the military superpowers hovered above all aspects of the conversation. They also spoke of many private matters, including Patrizia and Patrice. Simha was the sort of person to whom Célestin was able to speak—without hesitation and in some detail—about Olya. For his part, Simha disclosed how he had survived *K. L.* Auschwitz as a baby. "In Auschwitz, they stopped liquidating the remaining Jews in November of 1944, while I was born in December in the women's camp there. No, they didn't incise a number in my arm—if that crossed your mind. At the time, they were already preoccupied with destroying as much evidence as possible of their horrible crimes and making escape plans. Sorry, I find it difficult to talk about my parents at Auschwitz."

Even though Célestin told Simha about the ample lunch he had consumed, he could not prevent his host from ordering Atara's delicious chestnut puree with whipped cream, as well as some mignon cakes and fruit. Before he began to eat, Simha took a kippah from the inside pocket of his jacket and placed it on his head, explaining: "Perhaps you find my kippah a little surprising, but I am a rabbi, I have finished the entire schooling necessary for the calling. In fact, my rabbinical college will soon promote me to their *Doctor honoris causa*." Célestin wholeheartedly congratulated Simha, smiling inwardly that there remained nothing in Israel which could surprise him: After all, across the table sat a man who thirty-seven years after surviving Auschwitz as a newborn had become a rabbi in Jerusalem!

As soon as their repast was over, Simha took off the kippah and put it in his jacket carefully folded. Célestin was impressed by the depth his host repeatedly demonstrated in questions of international law, ethics, and rabbinical studies and by his unblemished objectivity regarding numerous issues that came up, some of them rather ticklish for a prominent Israeli Jew. They parted as new friends who respected each other, agreeing to have lunch with Morkel at the Maiersdorf Faculty Club at Hebrew University.

Across the street, he met the girls who looked cheerful and content. They rode the bus to French Hill together, but before parting, Osnat learned that he and Odile were moving the next day to the hotel Palatin in the city. "I'm not sure how long we'll stay in Jerusalem. We want to rent a car and travel to the east and north of Israel. Then we'll stop in Netanya, hoping to see you... We wish you success in the court case simulation. But listen," he confided, "I mentioned your name to Simha Grenstein and related many positive things about you, hoping you wouldn't mind. I wasn't able to ignore your existence while talking to that fine person." Ignoring her purple color, he continued: "You can call us at the hotel whenever you feel like it or stop by when you're in the city." Osnat hugged them both exceptionally firmly—him frontally, like an uninhibited lover.

The following morning, Célestin and Odile thanked their hosts again and took a cab to the Palatin, where an airy corner room on the third floor, with an en-suite bathroom and telephone, awaited them: They were in the hub of the modern part of Jerusalem. While having lunch on Jaffa Street, they studied through the windows the amazing diversity of physiognomies, clothes, and behavior of men and women who walked and jostled on the sidewalk. The Near East—facial features of some passersby must have been Phoenician...

The restaurant owner, Mr. Otman, introduced himself, eager to talk. He was a dark-haired, light-skinned, forthright man of Célestin's age. Speaking acceptable English, he revealed being a Muslim, a Palestinian with an Israeli passport. He had all the rights of a Jewish citizen except to serve in the army and could do that too if he switched from the Muhammadan religion to any other, including Christianity—which he refused to do, although he did not pray to Allah. There was no sickly sweetness in the man, but it was unclear why he was confiding to a stranger.

"Maybe he's lonely?" the precocious girl suggested during their promenade. "We may never find out, but we'll go back there, the food is excellent," he replied. On the busy Jaffa Street, Odile was surprised to see how many school children of no more than seven or eight boarded buses alone. "Yes, *ma chère*, it's clear they are brought up to be independent early. Also, these streets and buses are probably safe for children, as adults who are around habitually watch over them. Israel is a small country with few people, so every child is precious," he said.

Despite it being almost May, they saw on young women's hands what must have been the latest fashion: Woolen gloves without fingers. Even more amusing were such gloves on the hands of two exceptionally pretty women in army uniforms, who were loudly arguing, rifles slung over their shoulders, about delicate silk dresses in a shop window. "Let's buy those gloves for Osnat!" proposed Odile. "But why only for Osnat? I'm sure they have the right size for your little paws," gaily responded her father. Instead of fuming, the girl counterattacked: "Papa, you said we'd now go to see Sophie and Karen, and your shoes are dirty. The shoeshine man over there seems nice." In front of Jaffa Gate, the wrinkled old Arab diligently cleaned Célestin's shoes for two shekels, often making funny faces at Odile.

They went to meet the Englishwomen at the Lutheran hostel. Sophie and Karen were waiting at the bottom of the curved marble staircase framed by rough rock faces. Together they walked to Moonlight, a new music café inside Jaffa Gate. The music and decor were tolerable, and the conversation flowed spontaneously. It was a goodbye evening, for the young women were returning to England shortly.

Célestin briefly recounted his talk with Osnat, and the future nurses were sorry they had not been lucky enough to meet such an Israeli girl—only foreigners like themselves. When he went to the counter to order more drinks, Célestin met Rafi Kamar, the owner of Moonlight, and exchanged a few words with him. On the spur of the moment, he invited the interesting man to their table. Rafi arrived with juices and beers: "This is on the house. We're new, I hope you'll recommend us."

Lively banter ensued. Rafi was familiar with various European countries, but his heart was "pure Mediterranean," as he put it. In reality, he was a Lebanese Maronite and thus an Eastern Catholic. "We, whose origin is in the foothills of Mount Lebanon, have always been Christian and never accepted Islam—which the ultraorthodox types in Israel refuse to acknowledge, claiming we're Arabs in disguise. How offensive and ridiculous. But we are few, so they do whatever they want."

They listened to him quietly. The man had endured a lot: He looked fifty but was ten years younger. Karen asked him if he had problems during the disturbances in the city. "Of course! After the cowardly murder of the youngster Amedi, I was forced by the threats from the ultraorthodox to close my heavy metal shutters at midday on several occasions." Then he took out a bunch of keys, separated the six most massive, and said with a wry laugh: "These keys are for the locks at the bottom of the shutters, which cost me an arm and a leg."

At the parting, they promised Rafi to return—Célestin and Odile in a few days and the women in a year or two. The soon-to-be gerontology nurses wished to breathe Jerusalem's early-evening spring air, so they walked their French friends to the Palatin. *Bon voyage,* promises, and a single, almost passionate, embrace among the merely amicable.

Father and daughter spent the beginning of May discovering fascinating corners of the Old City and revisiting the loved ones. One early afternoon, Osnat and Avigail took Odile to a matinee showing a Disney film while Célestin had lunch with Morky and Simha at the Maiersdorf Faculty Club. From the terrace, there was a spectacular view of Mount of Olives and the eastern part of the city. The club was elegant and out of students' reach—not just because of the prices. He mentioned how Jakob Shmotkin had told him all restaurants and cafeterias at universities in Israel were open to students. Morky and Simha knew Jakob well, so they looked at each other and laughed. Morky said: "For patriotic reasons, Jakob tries to paint Israel as more egalitarian than it is. Besides, colleagues at other universities are sometimes envious of our Hebrew University because it receives bigger donations from American Jews—such as Mr. Leon Maiersdorf, whose gift we're presently enjoying. When Jakob comes here to visit us, he loves this terrace and being away from students' eyes and ears."

Célestin thought of Osnat and said nothing, but added he regarded Jakob highly and was looking forward to seeing him soon in Tel Aviv. "Odile will also be glad, he was very kind to her. I wonder if he had been able to see Yitzhak Zuckerman." Simha shook his head: "Yes, Jakob told me he intended to go to Yitzhak's kibbutz, but I informed him I'd heard from a nurse he had ceased to recognize even the people closest to him."

Being an atypical pair, Odile and Célestin attracted diverse people and sometimes made startling acquaintanceships in cafés on Ben Yehuda. Once, at their table could be seen: A young officer from Israeli Defense Forces; a belligerent Moroccan female communist of Franco-Jewish-Berber-Arabic background; a chuckling middle-aged Jewess from Egypt, bound for marriage in Marseille ("I barely know him, I'm gambling"); and an elderly man from Johannesburg who had arrived in Israel three months earlier for the first time but forever—he was making his *Aliyah* not knowing anybody in Israel.

Jerusalem's air and light were magical that spring. One mid-morning, Hila came to the Palatin. They walked together through the entire Old City, came out of the walls through Lions' Gate, and ended in the Gethsemane olive grove. Odile knew Jesus was arrested at the foot of Mount of Olives after the treachery by his disciple Judas Iscariot—according to traditional Christian teaching.

Father and daughter climbed several times to that ridge, from where the views of Jerusalem, the Dead Sea, and Jordan's mountains were magnificent. One time, when Osnat was with them, an unpleasant incident occurred. They had carelessly come off the main path when a group of Palestinian boys, not older than twelve, jumped out of bushes and threatened them with stones, screaming insults—in English! Without signs of anger or fear, Célestin approached them and apologized in a peaceable voice. The boys did not run away but lowered their arms, so the trio completed the climb unmolested. He noticed Osnat and Odile had blanched, so he casually brought up the stunning view. When they returned to the Old City, he intentionally maneuvered the young Israeli woman and his little girl to a busy souk where they enjoyed kofte, falafel, tahini, and humus with hot pita.

After several days, when it was time to leave for Tel Aviv, they did it comfortably. On Jaffa Street, they secured two seats in a Mercedes taxi for eight passengers. That was fast and cheap transportation, taking less than an hour and costing twelve shekels for two. The car was the color of desert sand, "like Jerusalem," said Célestin. While descending toward the sea through the pale green, terraced olive groves bordered by brown rocks of every imaginable nuance, Tel Aviv came into view—all of it aquiver. Odile whispered: "Do you remember, Papa, the day when we first came from Tel Aviv to Jerusalem? Somewhere around here, our old train was gasping for air, climbing next to that brook…" They remembered everything about the first day in Yerushaláyim.

Meanwhile, they had discovered, explored, and adopted as their own the most magical city in the world.

With his passengers' permission, the driver switched on the radio. Soon they heard Kate Bush softly singing about "the man with the child in his eyes."

12.

In Tel Aviv, they stayed again at the hotel Dizengoff, in the same room with a view of the music fountain. The staff quickly brought up the luggage they had stored a month earlier when leaving for Jerusalem, Eilat, and the Sinai. The fountain, for its welcome, again played the "Bolero" for a quarter of an hour.

Standing a long time by the window, they observed the goings-on in the pulsating center of Tel Aviv. It looked as if the entire city and all of Israel were introducing themselves. What an incredible, exciting, and chaotic street performance, perhaps more interesting—because of a greater diversity of men, women, and their behavior—than anything one could see in a bigger and more important European city. Stroking Odile's hair, Célestin thought: "I'm glad we came back. Although Jerusalem is a beautiful, extraordinary city, it slowly grinds a man down. Too much pain and too many tears; too much senseless craziness and too many ancient structures that steal fresh air; endless suffering and destruction; too much unutterably deep love and devotion—all of it too long, far too long..." He did not wish to share such thoughts with his daughter, which was a rarity—he wanted to but did not know how.

They had an early dinner at the restaurant Hungarian Blini, where the small buckwheat pancakes with spinach and sour cream were served Russian-style with spoonfuls of red caviar. Following the tasty meal, while Célestin was looking through his notebooks, Odile showed him phrases about Tel Aviv, which she had written on a paper napkin. "We can use them on postcards for Olya and Osnat," she mumbled. He was taken aback and gave her a look, but the little rascal, with a naughty smile, avoided his eyes and thus prevented any questions. "*Mon Dieu*, how fast my child's growing."

After a few days, he gave an exceptionally well-received lecture at Bar-Ilan University in Ramat Gan, a populous eastern suburb of Tel Aviv. His talk was organized by Professor Joel Kozlofski, a renowned comparative linguist, and attended by some fifty scholars. At the intimate lunch, Kozlofski revealed his parents had managed to emigrate in 1935 from a small town near Kiev in the Ukrainian Soviet Socialist Republic, but he was born in Palestine under the British Mandate. Joel was a kind, soft-spoken man who looked sixty rather than forty-five.

During Célestin's colloquium, Odile sat in the last row of the hall, listening a little but mostly reading. After the lecture had begun, a lady with a wizened face and a mass of disheveled gray hair arrived and sat next to the girl. It appeared she had given herself the task of entertaining her. However, that expert in biblical Hebrew, as she turned out to be, did not know with whom she was dealing: Odile evaded her well-meant advances. Afterward, she complained: "*Cher Papa*, the lady was leaning too close to me and didn't... smell nice. Awful odor of tobacco. Do you think the smell was in her huge hair?"

The next afternoon, Jakob Shmotkin came to their hotel, and they went for a stroll. It was a warmhearted repeat meeting of new, yet proven, friends. Jakob apologized that he could not attend Célestin's talk at Bar-Ilan the previous day. Then he succeeded, with effort and entreaties, to convince his French colleague to give the same lecture at Tel Aviv University. "We'll organize something special, I think over a hundred people will attend." He mentioned a high honorarium, which Célestin politely turned down, as he had done for two previous colloquia he had given in Israel—but he did not have the heart to decline Jakob's request.

After the walk, during which the poor health of Yitzhak Zuckerman was mentioned, Shmotkin took father and daughter to the popular café Sleeping Beauty, where fanciful illustrations from Grimm's fairy tales were hanging on the walls. Later, as they were all leaving, Jakob was called by a couple sitting nearby. He was pleased and took Célestin and Odile to the table, saying on the way: "These people are good friends of mine, and I think you'll enjoy meeting them." So they sat down again, that time across Lidya and Shaike Ophir. Having made a witty introduction, Jakob hurried home.

Shaike Ophir was a theater and film actor, comedian, and mime artist. As Célestin found out, he was an important person in Israeli cultural life. His wife Lidya, a refined woman, was a librarian who knew Hila Bellin. All four at the table sometimes talked at once, or there were two parallel conversations, one of which included Odile, while Shaike took part in both. The topics changed with lightning speed: Chehov, Kierkegaard, the Bible and the Torah, water temperature in Baikal, Christo Javacheff's possible wrapping of Pont Neuf, Moselle wines, and finally the impressive fact of Shaike's family living for eight generations at the place where the new Israel was eventually born.

Because it seemed to Lidya the whole café was listening, the Ophirs invited the French pair to their home. "You'll meet our daughter Karin. She's fourteen and, thank God, doesn't yet talk about becoming an actress," Shaike said laughing. A cab ride of ten minutes brought them to the peaceful Be'eri Street. During the drive, Lidya mentioned her early childhood in Poland, in the ghetto of the old cathedral city of Częstochowa.

Having witnessed Shaike's effervescence at Sleeping Beauty, Célestin was surprised by the peacefulness prevailing in the Ophirs' apartment. Like Lidya, it was unpretentiously elegant. As for Karin, she was a cute, well-proportioned teenager: Intelligently bubbly like her father and sweet, endearing, and utterly natural like her mother. She was delighted to have guests. Time passed in high spirits on everyone's part. Paying no sanctimonious attention to the children present, Shaike tirelessly told sharp and self-critical Jewish jokes in Yiddish and English, one after the other. However, the most entertaining was his uproarious demonstration of the three ways in which Israelis walk: Ambling, one foot in front of the other, "the Jerusalem shuffle";

dragging their feet noisily, "the Tel Aviv shuffle"; and skipping and cavorting, "the Haifa shuffle, when people walk downhill from Mount Carmel." To father and daughter, that was adorable: They had witnessed the first two kinds many times, and Mount Carmel, Haifa, and Osnat's Netanya still lay ahead.

Karin translated the jokes to Odile and offered her to eat and drink everything she liked herself. Sometimes Célestin caught her looking at him with a girly fascination. When Lidya and Karin returned from the kitchen toward the end of the evening, the mother said to him: "You must excuse her, but Karin fell in love with your ascot necktie. Could you show her how it's tied?" He immediately removed his blue-gray silk necktie and gave it to Odile, saying: "*Je t'en pris, ma chère,* tie it around the neck of our young hostess as it should be done." Having watched her father knot ties and ascots for years, she indeed knew how to do it. She squatted in front of Karin, who was sitting in a small armchair, and tied the ascot properly around the girl's delicate neck. Then she stood up and slid it inside her blouse without ceremony. Karin thanked her and ran to the bathroom to look in the mirror. He called after her: "If you like it, don't take it off! It's a gift from us."

The Ophir family saw their guests off affectionately, which included their dog with long hair in several dark colors. Célestin called him "Coptic-Ethiopian" because the dog's disconsolate eyes reminded him of the slightly odd priests they had encountered in Jerusalem. Shaike proclaimed the nameless dog a messenger from the unknown.

There were other cozy cafés on Dizengoff Street. In one of them, called Zula, they saw ingenious posters on Bauhaus themes, including *Pianola* by the Slovak artist Yuri Dojc. On one occasion, while drinking tea there—and wishing to say a few words to Odile about the Bauhaus phenomenon—he reminded her of the gift she had received in Paris, Mathilde's translation from German to French of the book *The Blue Rider*. He said, "After we returned home from Paris, you often studied paintings and illustrations in that excellent work. You see, a handful of artists from the circle in Munich subsequently participated in Goethe's

Weimar in the work of a new, influential group of architects, painters, art theorists, and innovative designers called Bauhaus. The most talented of them, in my opinion—an unfeigned genius—was the Russian Vasiliy Kandinskiy. Among other accomplishments, he was the main creator of 'abstract art'—about which we'll talk in a few years. The group's academy, with Kandinskiy as a member, existed until the Nazis abolished it in 1933. Posters you see here in Zula were undoubtedly inspired by ideas of those extraordinary Bauhaus men."

With apologies to other guests, he took Odile from poster to poster, answering the girl's questions. They were approached by Mr. Haim Rosen, Zula's owner: "Excuse me, Sir, I only wanted to tell you how glad I am when I witness a parent teaching his child about art from a young age. I did the same with my daughter when she was less than ten years old." These words were a prelude to a longish dialogue during which Célestin asked Haim for permission to photograph the posters and the café's interior when there were no guests. The art-loving proprietor immediately agreed, and they made a date for ten the next day. "I'll ask my Orit to come and meet you two."

In the midmorning of the next day, Odile was sitting with Haim and Orit Rosen in Zula drinking her favorite green tea. They spoke English and watched Célestin photographing the posters from various angles, sometimes changing the lighting. To reinterpret the images, he often placed next to a poster an object he borrowed from behind the bar. Also, he brought in Orit's bicycle, which had been innocently standing in the hallway near the entrance, to complement one of the posters. After taking photos for an hour, Célestin joined the others. "Orit and I observed you while you worked. Seeing how you studied an object and composed images, we concluded you were a professional," said Haim with a smile.

"Actually," he went on, "I have a business proposition for you. I own three other cafés in Tel Aviv: Two of them are by the sea, and the third is in Ramat Gan. Each one is different. I paid a lot of money to the best designers in town to create interesting decor, unique to each place. Different color schemes, furnishings, lighting. Some embellishments and a bit of finery without frippery. And now I was hoping Orit and I could create a classy brochure about the Rosen Cafés without ostentation. Would you be interested in helping us by doing the photography? For a decent compensation, of course. Orit would take you to all the places and ensure you have every convenience while working."

Célestin was more surprised than flattered, but Odile was neither. She knew her father had many skills and understood his personality. Therefore, she anticipated correctly what would happen next—he would reject the offer: "Thank you for the compliment, but no. I'm not a professional photographer. What I was doing here in the café was for the modest artsy side of our being in Israel." Orit jumped in, disappointment in her voice: "But that's precisely what father and I wanted! An artistic, personal impression, not a brochure with glitzy, saccharine imagery printed on glossy paper. Sorry, this didn't come out right, though I'm sure you know what I mean. You see, I'm studying applied arts at the university but have limited experience in photography." Célestin promised to give them copies of his slides without compensation. Orit still felt let down but smiled and went to make a cappuccino for him.

Orit was twenty-five, had completed military service, and was a fourth-year student at Tel Aviv University. Only weeks earlier, she had returned from a study trip to Amsterdam and Delft. Célestin suspected—flippantly, he was aware—that Orit had a strong will and was very smart, possibly an only child who had grown up without a mother. "In other words," he reflected wryly, "as far as such traits and life circumstances are concerned, perhaps I'm looking at Odile in fifteen years." So it did not surprise him when he discovered a coolness in his daughter's attitude toward Orit.

When the young woman returned with the coffee, she said: "I'm glad you added the rear wheel of my bicycle to the poster by Dojc. Was it a joke or hommage to Marcel Duchamp?" He answered: "The latter. And intentionally the rear wheel, without the handlebar. For Dadaists, a handlebar would be a symbol of nauseating social control." Orit added: "Yes, control and discipline." Haim looked at his daughter with pride, whereas Odile did it with pouting lips. Orit continued: "Still, I think no other Dadaist had Duchamp's painterly and even filmic talent, as in *Nude Descending a Staircase*; let alone his sense of humor. To some, it seems rough or pointless, but to me, it's subtle. Anyway, my heroes in the twentieth century are Kandinskiy and Piet Mondrian."

He thought well of the young woman's taste, which seemed her own, not learned by rote for exams: "So because of Kandinskiy, you chose those posters related to Bauhaus?" "That's right. It wasn't easy, but I managed to convince my dear daddy," she responded, smiling at Haim. "And because of Mondrian—by the way, I prefer the original Dutch spelling of his name, with two 'a', don't you?—because of Mondriaan, I recently spent two incredible weeks in Holland thanks to my father." Célestin and Odile glanced at each other: Orit knew how to endear herself and usually got what she wanted. Aloud, he stuck to the painter: "I also prefer Mondriaan, as it's the authentic spelling for a person from Amersfoort. But he changed it himself to please Parisian critics or buyers. He was thirty-nine when he did it, not a kid."

Célestin went on: "Have you found something notable about our 'double a' painter when you were in the Netherlands?" Orit responded immediately: "Yes, at least to me, his 'rasters' are mysterious, particularly the geometric relations among the differently colored rectangles in paintings from that period. One Dutch professor suggested to me to explore the role of the 'golden section' in those relations, so I tirelessly measured and computed." She looked at him with raised eyebrows. Célestin knew well that the proportion called golden section, or golden ratio, had since antiquity attracted famous minds and was studied intensively not only in painting and architecture but also in poetry and music—although he had serious doubts about the research in the last two. "Yes, Orit, I know what the golden section is. As a layman, I think what interests you in the rasters is well worth exploring. Of course, one must keep in mind that the golden section can be found all over the place, all around us, but it takes an educated eye to recognize it."

While looking, deep in thought, through the window of the café, Célestin's eyes were drawn to a white van parked in front of Zula on which there was a large blue Star of David. He pointed to it and said: "For example, I recently read that the hexagon within which the star on Israel's beautiful flag is located contains three implied rectangles whose sides are in the ratio you've been studying." Orit and Haim watched him intently, and then she suddenly tore a piece of paper from a notebook, drew the two interlocking triangles of the Star of David accurately, and after about fifteen seconds, sketched in the three previously "invisible" rectangles containing golden sections. "Marvelous!" Orit exclaimed gleefully. "Yes, the golden section is ubiquitous," he said, "but one must find answers to three questions: Has the artist used it intentionally? Is it visible to those looking at the painting? And, most importantly, does its presence contribute to the aesthetic appeal of the painting?"

Orit thought for a while, agreed, and thanked Célestin, saying she would write to the Dutch professor and ask whether or not it was known that the painter had intentionally used the golden section in his raster works. Haim was happy as a clam at high water to have organized such a delightful art matinee for his daughter's pleasure and growth, whereas Odile inwardly smirked at the thought that in the knowledge contest, her papa had convincingly defeated the hoity-toity Orit—which was how the young woman quite unfairly appeared to the girl.

Célestin delivered his last lecture in Israel in an auditorium of Tel Aviv University. Almost two hundred scholars and guests attended. Jakob Shmotkin, Chairman of the Department of Hebrew Language and Literature, presided. He placed Odile on a seat next to him in the first row and took care of her throughout. It was, in a sense, the girl's first entrance into the academy, and she and her father were grateful to Jakob for being considerate. Célestin's colleagues from Jerusalem who were in Tel Aviv were also present. He noticed Lidya, Shaike, and Karin Ophir, whom he had notified of the lecture, but did not expect to come. "These people are so kind," he thought. Jakob told him the lecture had been publicized in various newspapers, and many people who played important parts in the cultural life of Israel's capital came despite not having much to do with linguistics. "Shaike and Lidya certainly did not come to be seen," Célestin was confident. At the end of the lecture, while surrounded by men and women wishing to shake his hand, he saw Haim and Orit Rosen waving amiably from the exit, not wanting to impose.

As he was leaving the auditorium with Odile and Jakob, an elderly couple who had been patiently standing to the side approached him. Jakob exclaimed: "Oh, Shulamith, Hans, I'm so glad you came! Please meet our lecturer, our dear friend!" Based on those first names, Célestin guessed he was being introduced to the illustrious Kreitlers, whose book on the psychology of art had impressed him years earlier. They were outstanding scientists, top-echelon scholars. After exchanging greetings, Hans Kreitler said: "Shulamith and I would really enjoy talking to you and meeting your daughter. Are you free tomorrow, at any hour, to meet with us? We're both retired and have plenty of time." He was exhilarated by the unexpected meeting with these eminent psychologists and aestheticians. They agreed to meet the following afternoon at the Sleeping Beauty on Dizengoff.

While driving father and daughter to their hotel, Jakob said: "Your lecture was magisterial. Everyone I talked to said so, even those usually cynical and cutting. And the Kreitlers—you saw how impressed they were. One can say without exaggeration that they are legends of empirical psychology here. In fact, the two of them founded the psychology department. Shulamith got her doctorate in Bern, and Hans in Vienna, where his mentors had been Karl Bühler, the highly respected psychologist and linguist, and Egon Brunswik von Korompa, the even more influential functionalist and methodologist. In addition to psychology, Hans studied musicology, and Shulamith painting. Truly remarkable people but warm and modest. And they'll fall in love with Odile, for they don't have children."

At the "Beauty" the next day, the French pair got the best table because the manager remembered them from the lively meeting with Lidya and Shaike. When the Kreitlers arrived, excellent rapport was soon established based on similar views on many issues, especially the need for a high degree of methodological rigor and objectivity in scientific investigations. Shulamith behaved toward Odile like a Viennese-Jewish grandma—tenderly plying her favorite granddaughter with sweets. Admittedly, the café's *Reform Torte*, a nine-layer elaborate cake, was popular for good reasons. Without reluctance, they spoke of intimate matters. Hans was worried about the speed of his mental aging, and Célestin spoke of their travel in the USSR and about Olya in the Kuybyshev prison. Odile confided that "pretty Osnat and Leora" were her best Israeli girlfriends, which prompted Shulamith to ask whether those two girls attended the third or fourth grade.

Commenting on daily life and customs in Tel Aviv, Célestin brought up an oddity. "I have often noticed a situation like this: Two people are chatting in a café, or on a bus, or waiting in a queue, but the so-called dialogue consists of one person talking non-stop, without pausing to take a breath, words just flowing, and this lasts and lasts—whereas the other doesn't attempt to say a thing, although he or she doesn't seem bored, or absent, or angry, or sleepy. It could be two women, two men, or a couple. Quite unbelievable. Are Israelis such breathtaking storytellers? Elsewhere, in my experience, even skilled but overly talkative raconteurs get interrupted more or less rudely."

Shulamith and Hans looked at each other and burst into laughter. She said: "An accurate observation! Hans and I have also often chuckled about such behavior. And it's a Tel Aviv specialty. Right now, in this café, we could easily find a pair like that. Tel-Avivians, particularly those originally from *Mitteleuropa*, Ashkenazim like the two of us, simply adore hearing themselves talk, even more than the New York Jews do. And the most voluble among us are always looking for a less garrulous person who's willing—without feeling like a victim or blockhead—to listen without interrupting the flow!"

Their rendezvous lasted for almost two hours, and the parting was touching in a way that could have hardly been expected after such a brief acquaintanceship. When they were leaving the café, the waiters bowed deeply, which was not customary. Shulamith walked first, holding Odile's hand. Four or five steps behind, Hans put his arm under Célestin's and spoke softly: "My friend, you're very dear to me, and I'd like to tell you something. I beg you not to take it the wrong way. On the contrary, please accept my words as the biggest compliment an elderly European Ashkenazi Jew can give you… You're a man who is the closest to Jews a non-Jew can ever be." Hans almost teared, and Célestin remembered Yad Vashem, shivers running down his spine.

13.

Several days later, father and daughter left Tel Aviv for the northeast of Israel. They traveled by bus to Tiberias, an ancient city on the western shore of the Sea of Galilee. The trip lasted two and a half hours, during which Odile read brochures and enjoyed the changing landscape while Célestin spoke to an intelligent eighteen-year-old. Before joining the IDF the following February, the youngster was living at one of the big kibbutzim with over fifteen hundred residents. He was not formally a member, but the kibbutz let him earn pocket money by working in the lemon and grapefruit orchards. Occasionally, he received a special favor, such as a two-week trip to Greece with twenty-five other kibbutzniks. His mother was Danish, his father Iranian, both Jews. In a young person's innocent way, he was honored by Célestin's attention and gladly described many aspects of communal life: the kibbutzniks' age, in terms of range and average; general atmosphere; politics; facilities and equipment; medical services; and the enforcement of rules regarding drug use and sexual behavior. His interlocutor listened carefully, thinking that someday Odile might get the idealistic idea of joining a kibbutz. He was unsure what advice he would give her, but certain he would not initiate such an action.

Having left much of their luggage in Tel Aviv, they easily climbed up all five levels of Tiberias to a hotel at the top from which there was a splendid view of the famous sea or lake—both terms were used. From that height, the shape of the Sea of Galilee indeed resembled a harp, *Kinnor* in Hebrew, from which the name "Kinneret" was derived. Actually, they agreed with a chuckle, it resembled a double bass more than a harp.

As they were returning downhill to the ancient, coastal part of town, Odile hopped and skipped strangely. When asked, she reminded her father: "Well, Mr. Shaike showed us how Israelis walk downhill!" He grinned: "He had in mind citizens of Haifa descending from Mount Carmel—which we'll visit—but your shuffle is useful for Tiberias too."

While strolling along the embankment, she wished to taste the water and find out if it was salty. Her dad stopped her: "Don't, *ma princesse*, can't you see the oil from the motorboats?" He then explained: "Galilee is a freshwater lake, the lowest such on our planet. It lies two hundred meters below the Mediterranean Sea, yet it's almost as much above the level of the Dead Sea. Its water is supplied by the Jordan River, which, there to the north," Célestin pointed, "flows into the lake, runs through it—yes, rivers can 'run' through lakes, you recall Angara at Lake Baikal—and then flows out, somewhere over there at the southern end. Afterward, it flows into the Dead Sea."

In the sunshine of the late afternoon, they sat on a terrace from which Galilee's eastern shoreline could be seen, about ten kilometers from Tiberias. To the northeast, the Golan Heights were discernible through haze. By coming to the Galilee area, the pair had significantly approached the zones conquered by Israel in the Six-Day War.

A man of Célestin's age, who was reading a newspaper at a nearby table, addressed them in English: "I don't speak French, Sir, but I overheard you mention the Golan to your daughter, so I wished to ask if that region interested you." He readily responded: "Yes, we arrived today by bus from Tel Aviv, wishing to stay a day or two in Tiberias and rent a car. Then, we planned to drive to the east side of the lake and climb to the Golan Heights to see how the famed area looks." The man smiled, but there was melancholy in his voice: "Yes, now you can safely drive up. Fourteen years ago, during the Six-Day War, I was there for the first time. A greenhorn recruit. Twenty-three years old. The view of Galilee is fabulous. However, at that time, my buddies and I looked only eastward toward Damascus…"

Célestin learned much about Israel from Ira, a thoughtful and sensitive man whose left arm was crippled on the Golan in 1967. He had nevertheless advanced through the ranks to captain in the IDF and simultaneously become a member of a moshav near Tiberias—a very dissatisfied member, as it turned out. Such settlements were not communes like the kibbutzim but rather agricultural cooperatives consisting of individual homesteads, each with a farm and a house owned by a single family. Ira, with his wife and children, managed well until the time of Israel's runaway inflation, when the moshav began to demand shocking taxes from homestead owners and thus cheated him—as Ira claimed—of a huge amount of money.

That was the first time in Israel Célestin heard a complaint against something communal and cooperative, which was a surprise, notably coming from a patriotic army officer. On the other hand, Ira's criticisms of the ultraorthodox were no sharper than what the visitor had heard from friends in Jerusalem. "They are incredibly single-minded and obsessed, in the way the ultraorthodox Jews have always been, but unlike those in the previous two thousand years, who were—at least I think so—sincere believers, these people now use religion to exploit us other Israelis in various ways. I'm not speaking just of their avoidance of army service and that a handful of their delegates blackmails our entire country in the Knesset but also of the purely financial advantages they receive on religious grounds. No one dares to point the finger at such outrage."

Ira paused and grinned, having reached a tentative conclusion: "So, as you can see, I'm neither a leftist nor a right-winger but only a true Israeli who loves to talk!" As soon as Célestin also laughed and was about to speak to his somewhat neglected daughter, Ira resumed his monologue: "Please excuse me, dear little girl, I have a daughter your age: I want to tell your daddy another thing. You must have heard, Sir, of the Sephardi rabbi Maimonides, Moses ben Maimon, from the twelfth century. He was a celebrated theologian, mathematician, and physician. We call him Rambam, an acronym by which he has been known through the ages in the Jewish and Arab worlds. Well, he died in Egypt and was buried there. However, the followers of one tradition in Judaism have persistently claimed his earthly remains had been brought here to Tiberias, so his white tomb, not far from the coast and the town center, has long been a place of zealous pilgrimage.

"All right, such things happen in all religions, but here the ultraorthodox have also violently interfered with the legitimate archaeological work near the tomb. Besides, they get a sizable percentage of the funds the town obtains from tourism—because Rambam is allegedly only theirs—while Arabs aren't allowed even a peek at the tomb. They say rich Arabs should spend money at the expensive hot springs spa two kilometers south of Tiberias, which just happens to be the place where the ultraorthodox have invested tons of shekels. In the brochure your daughter has been reading, it undoubtedly states the hot mineral springs are of therapeutic value for skin diseases and have existed for two thousand years, from before the Romans arrived."

At those words, the officer abruptly stood up, explaining: "Maybe I went too far with my criticisms. It's hard to know if I'm entirely objective, but I do think the truth is close to what I've told you." Before their friendly parting, Ira gave Célestin his phone number and promised he would arrange a discount on a reliable rental car at a service in town.

During their two slow-paced days in Tiberias, the ancient town bathed in fine weather. There were almost a dozen synagogues. A Greek monastery, a Catholic church, a mosque, and the ruins of a Crusader fortress were all situated in the oldest quarter near the lake, in a circle of about two hundred meters in diameter. They splashed at a mediocre beach but did not find the shallow lake attractive for swimming.

The spa and its clientele were of no interest. The tomb of Maimonides was close to the Crusader bastion, but when Célestin and Odile went there, staggering crowds and the deranged appearance of some of the believers with unhinged wild eyes discouraged them from approaching.

* * *

Early on their final day in Tiberias—with the help of IDF captain and moshavnik Ira—they rented a modest Japanese car at a low weekly price for an indefinite period. The Suzuki was in good condition, even with 54634 kilometers on the odometer. After a goodbye to Ira, they left Tiberias. Instead of driving south and east around the lake to reach the Golan Heights, they first took a road in the southwesterly direction to Nazareth, the town where, according to the New Testament, Jesus Christ had spent his boyhood.

The road went mostly uphill, passing through poor Arab villages in which everyone wore traditional attire, men with sparkling white keffiyeh around their heads and necks. Nazareth was on top of a hill, from which one could see, toward the southeast, the green Megiddo Valley, renowned from ancient times for fertility. Beyond it, one could espy Mount Tabor, its 588 meters making it about two hundred meters higher than the top of Nazareth. Tabor stood thoughtfully alone and separate. It was sweetly rounded—like a gigantic cake.

Célestin and Odile tirelessly climbed the steep streets of Nazareth. At the noisy market, they bought oranges and consumed them in the shade offered by the stupendous Catholic Basilica of the Annunciation, the largest Christian object in the Near East. It had a pyramidal dome covered with copper and two stories connected by massive marble staircases. The lower story was supposed to represent the Grotto of the Annunciation in which the Virgin Mary had lived when Archangel Gabriel announced she would become pregnant and bear Jesus, the Son of God. Célestin spoke to Odile in a calm voice, often repeating "according to Christian tradition," but striving that ridicule not appear either in his voice or on his face. Odile was confused.

He was more openly critical when speaking about the fabulous sums spent on the pompous edifice. "Much of the money must have come from the Vatican, which is not unimportant for us as Catholics, regardless of whether we're fervent ones or not. You could see how poor those Arab villages were and also their quarter here. I read that most of the Arabs who live in this ancient town are full-fledged citizens of Israel, and almost half are Christian. But what's their benefit?"

While walking eastward to the Greek Quarter, Célestin continued: "In the church we have just visited there's nothing ancient—it was completed only ten years ago. But its past, or rather the history of the location on which it was erected, resembles that of the Church of the Holy Sepulchre in Jerusalem, which we were fortunate to get to know well. In the fourth century, Emperor Constantine ordered a church to be built; it was destroyed during the Arab conquest in the seventh century; Crusaders rebuilt it in the twelfth, but Mamluks knocked it down in the thirteenth. The church to which we're now going had a similar history of construction and destruction, accompanied by numerous innocent victims. I think it's the elegant one over there, with a slender bell tower." The Greek Orthodox Church of Saint Gabriel was indeed very handsome. It had subtle proportions and walls of light-gray stone. Built in the eighteenth century, the church had time to acquire a patina.

"In this book it says," read Célestin, "that according to the beliefs of the Greek Orthodox Christians, Archangel Gabriel didn't make the announcement to the Virgin Mary in her cave but instead at a nearby spring where she was filling her earthen pitcher, and that the present church, like the original fourth-century one, was built on top of the same well." The dark, serene interior of the church was at first pleasantly cool, but soon its ancient, taciturn repose brought goosebumps to their arms. A state of irredeemable loneliness prevailed. They descended a dozen steps to a subterranean chapel with a small altar. Below it, there was supposed to be a spring or at least some water channeled from a distant source. Yet no gurgling could be heard, no water existed. Father and daughter looked at each other in the gloom. Neither revealed any thoughts or feelings. Silently they walked to the car and left Nazareth in the southeasterly direction toward Mount Tabor.

Landscapes in Israel changed quickly and dramatically—in colors, shapes, vegetation, and inhabitants. Leaving behind the steep, wild hills south of Nazareth, the road entered the gorgeous fertile valley of Megiddo, with its dispersed villages. About ten kilometers farther, they passed through an abandoned settlement and found a little-used, narrow road leading to the heavily wooded Mount Tabor from the west. Theirs was the only car. The road was full of gaping potholes, but much scarier was the absence of guardrails as protection from chasms. "If we drove off here," thought Célestin, sensibly slowing down, "our corpses wouldn't be found for ages. No one knows we're here; Ira the captain thinks we went to the Golan Heights. It's something I should consider more often."

He had somehow suppressed morbid thoughts by the time they passed through a splendid ancient stone gate and drove along an *allée* bordered by tall cypresses. Thus they reached a spacious plateau, the top of Mount Tabor.

They immediately noticed a Greek Orthodox monastery. Like the Greek Saint Gabriel's Church in Nazareth, the monastery's proportions were exquisite. Nearby stood the far grander, or at least much bigger, Catholic church; in Célestin's opinion, it was too imposing for the summit of such a modest mountain, no matter how revered it was in Christian teachings. Both the church and the monastery were dedicated to the Transfiguration of Jesus Christ. They came out of the car and closed the doors respectfully, soundlessly. Not a soul anywhere. The silence on the lonely mountain was complete.

After a walk, enjoying the extraordinary view northeast toward Galilee, Célestin took a small book about Tabor from his jacket and said: "This place, precisely where we're standing, is sacred to Christians because of the alleged saintly event that occurred during Jesus's visit with several disciples. In the book, they cite the New Testament, listen: 'According to Matthew, in the third year of his preaching, Jesus Christ took his apostles Jacob, Peter, and John to Mount Tabor. In the course of the following night, Jesus transfigured himself in front of their eyes and became like *light*.' It also says: 'Mount Tabor is often given as an example of the sublime and the magnificent.' Well, that's something with which I wouldn't necessarily agree! Tabor is pretty, but only someone who is a profoundly believing Christian would, *ma chère fille*, think of it as sublime and magnificent. About the Muslims, I'm not sure, but I know the Buddhists would call 'sublime and magnificent' countless other places before they would *notre minuscule Mont Thabor*."

Odile did not need much time: "Alright, Papa, you told me long ago I was christened, and you often say we're Catholics, which means I'm a Christian. But am I a 'deeply believing' one? I don't know, it seems I'm not—nor are you! Each time you're doubting something, I also have doubts. Are we both naughty, *cher Papounet?*" Célestin felt pride in his daughter's reasoning and courage. He stayed quiet for a minute, then smiled and finally said with all seriousness: "I think we're not naughty. And who would pass judgment on us? I certainly wouldn't accept the Pope in Rome as arbiter—even if the claim he's the direct descendant of Saint Peter were not just Vatican politics. Neither was Saint Peter God, far from it. Have I bored you to tears, *mon ange?*" Odile said only "well..." and fell silent, smiling.

After they had returned to the car, he said: "I just remembered something funny. Your *maman* and I traveled several times to Czechoslovakia. We loved Prague, the stunning old capital of the country but also ventured into other parts of the fertile Czech Lands. On one occasion, we spotted a round hill cozily sitting utterly alone in the middle of the plains of central Czechia. It resembled Tabor, although it was lower and with a flatter top. We even thought the Czechs called it Mount Tabor after this biblical one. But they didn't. In a roadside beer inn, the friendly keeper, a round personage himself, told us the hill was called *Řip* (pronounced Rzyp), which meant a mushroom with an adorable cap—and listen to this, poisonous!"

They both laughed. While driving on a much better road down the eastern slope of Tabor, he added: "Czechs have a good sense of humor. That big hill Rzyp, with its modest 459 meters— an attractive but deadly mushroom—is on the list of Czech national monuments because the area, by their legends, was the first where they had settled. We, the French and Germans, would never do it. We're too stuffy and strait-laced about our national symbols. Not to say pompous."

In the early evening, after driving about twenty kilometers to the east, they arrived back at the Sea of Galilee. There was a small hotel near the southern shore. Their day was exhausting, but after dinner, they walked in a beautiful oasis with numerous palm trees over twenty meters tall, with rich clusters of dates hanging just below the fronds at the trees' crowns. The night air smelled of tropics.

* * *

The fragrant night was quickly turning into a scorching day when Célestin and Odile left for the Golan Heights. They hoped Ira's friends had given them a car able to tackle the hot dry hills. Soon they crossed the bridge over the River Jordan flowing out of Galilee and looking quite unremarkable. The road left behind lush greenery and sharply climbed into wild hills, bare except for rocks thrown about the slopes, as if by a malevolent giant's hand. The lake disappeared from even an occasional view, and the road took them to the blocked frontier of Jordan established in 1967; had the main road been open, it would have taken them to the Jordanian city of Irbid. Beyond the fenced-off border, far down in the valley, there was a narrow river. The bridge over it was halved by bombs or explosives. "River Yarmuk," he whispered as in church, "it flows into the Jordan south of the lake."

Rows of dense barbed wire sat next to the ninety-degree turn of the road to the north—the three-country border point. They drove on, Syria on the right instead of Jordan. No one anywhere in sight. Afterward, there were steep inclines through the stony desert, with barbed wire and dire minefield warnings next to the road. The wire disappeared after driving north for another fifteen kilometers, and an unbroken, astonishing panorama of Syria opened up: the Golan Heights! It was immediately obvious Israel had already made itself at home in the region. Only a little farther, highway № 98 led deeper to the east and meandered through green, conscientiously tilled fields. On a road sign, next to which Célestin stopped the car and took a photo, it said in three languages that they had arrived at the "new kibbutz named 'Afik,' founded in 1972, as the first Jewish settlement on the Golan Heights." He muttered: "How quickly the Israelis moved in!" There was surprise and admiration in his voice, although complicated by a certain rancor, of which he was not proud. The bitterness was justified because close by, on the other side of the road, the wreckage of many small houses was visible. The map showed that the Syrian village of Fiq once stood there.

Soon they reached an intersection at which a narrower road, № 789, led west from highway № 98, whereas a tertiary road, after snaking through the Golan, would bring them back to the Sea of Galilee. Even though there was no one at the crossroads, they hardly passed fifty meters before a young man got up from the ground and lifted his thumb. Célestin stopped without hesitation. The youngster was a soldier with an IDF-issue rucksack and a rifle slung over his back. He addressed Célestin in Hebrew, but the answer he received in English did not induce him to give up on his request for transportation to Ramot, a sizable settlement by the lake below the Golan. Célestin agreed immediately but calculated with lightning speed while getting out of the car: "One needs to be smart. I'm not going to allow someone we don't know to sit behind us—and with a rifle in his lap!" He opened the passenger door, asked Odile to move to the back seats, and then helped the soldier put his backpack and rifle in the trunk. The young Israeli was not in the least worried that the unknown stranger had disarmed him and calmly took the passenger seat in front. Father and daughter introduced themselves to the conscript Samuel-Sam, who then pointed to Ramot on the map. Driving off, when the chauffeur exclaimed "seatbelts, all," Odile and the soldier cheerfully obeyed.

Sam was a gay, handsome, twenty-year-old. He had learned some words of French, which he was studying from *French in 100 Lessons,* as he desired to spend a year in Paris with his girlfriend. From a breast pocket of his army shirt, he took out the book, wrapped in a cover fashioned from a newspaper. He turned and gave it to Odile, correctly pronouncing the French words: "*Regardez, Mademoiselle.*" Célestin was certain she was as delighted by the gesture as he was. The girl thanked Sam and immediately plunged into the French and Hebrew of "Lesson № 1."

The conscript was on a two-week leave and had spent the first visiting his girl who was a member of the kibbutz Afik. "Leah is two years older than me and has done her military duty," Sam said proudly. The driver smiled to himself: "The friendly neophyte is pleased that unlike his fellow recruits, he has an experienced girlfriend!"

Sam was going to spend the second week with his parents in Ramot and help in the family orchard. He had been in the army for two and a half years but eighteen months remained. "I'm serving four years rather than three because I chose to be in an elite unit," Sam declared, again with youthful pride but of a different sort; it seemed he was expecting a question. However, Célestin was too clever to pose it. He was not particularly interested and besides, did not wish to place the young man in an awkward position. "Of course, perhaps he slyly wants me to inquire about his elite unit, so he can haughtily refuse to answer, saying it's a military secret," privately chuckled the Frenchman again.

It turned out Ramot was a moshav, and Sam had joined it with his parents when he was only eight. They arrived from Tel Aviv in

1969, in the first year of Ramot's existence, and invested all the money they had saved into a fruit orchard; other founders generously helped them. "And now the orchard is ours, thriving and blooming!" happily exclaimed Sam, in a sing-song voice. "I'm glad to hear it," said Célestin, sharing with Sam a bar of chocolate Odile had passed, "because recently I heard a different story from a dissatisfied moshavnik from the other side of the lake." He hesitated briefly, then spoke on: "But something else about Ramot is mysterious. I've read the entire eastern shore of Lake Galilee is formally a part of the Golan Heights, and even the full annexation of the region by Israel—an action many countries and institutions consider illegal—has not yet occurred. The formal annexation is supposed to happen in December of this year. How, then, was your moshav Ramot founded in 1969?"

Sam's young, honest face instantly darkened, seemingly not in anger but more likely due to a guilty conscience. He responded softly: "I'll tell you about the beginnings of our moshav. I was a little kid like Odile is now, but my *eema*, my mom, has told me. After the Six-Day War, there were calls by the government to the young people throughout Israel to join in the foundation of kibbutzim and moshavim on the newly conquered territories. Although no one was forced, it was evident that such behavior was considered patriotic. My *abba*, my good-hearted father... The government promised him every possible help, including military protection, because many Syrians and Palestinians—more than a hundred thousand, as you probably know—had been forced to leave their villages. That didn't always go smoothly...

"So a moshav was founded in the present Ramot area already in 1969 under the watchful eye of the military command. During the first two years, we lived in abandoned Arab houses in the nearby village then called Skopye. Only in 1973, we moved to the location where the moshav is now, the two hills area, which is what Ramot means. What can I tell you? Sad for the Arabs but happy for us. I can't do a thing about it." Célestin failed to find in himself the strength to cry over the fate of Syrians, irreconcilable haters of Jews, nor to rejoice over the success of Israel on the Golan. And he was reluctant to condemn Sam and his parents, even though they eagerly took over others' hearths.

While negotiating the curves on the narrow macadam road that gradually descended to the lake, he watched the soldier's serious face out of the corner of his eye and could not resist asking: "Up there, near Afik, the kibbutz where your girlfriend lives, we saw on the other side of the main road many destroyed houses without windows. Is that the abandoned Syrian village of Fiq?" Sam agreed almost inaudibly: "Yes. It seems the kibbutzim didn't need the ruins as building material, which is odd, while the Arabs had left in haste. Perhaps they didn't completely destroy their homes because they were hoping to return soon, believing the lies of their government in Damascus. Or they feared further reprisals if they put to the torch what we needed... maybe our zealots threatened them."

Incredibly, the entire Sea of Galilee came into view. "Papa, please stop! I'd like to take a photo." While she was busy, Célestin said: "I'm grateful to you for being candid. In France, we say a passenger confides to a total stranger during a flight because they would never see each other again." Sam responded irrelevantly: "My girl and I have never been on a plane. But we'll be—flying to Paris!" Célestin's words improved Sam's mood: "As opposed to what you said, we Israelis claim we'll meet every stranger again because our country is only a big village."

They arrived at the lake sparkling in the sunshine and turned north on 92. Almost exactly an hour after leaving Afik, they stopped in front of a large "Shalom" sign at the entrance of the moshav Ramot. From there, one could indeed see two hillocks. Odile returned the book to Sam, who shyly mumbled *"Au revoir."* Célestin opened the trunk and, with a wink, gave him the rifle. Then they exchanged *"A bientôt à Paris!"*

14.

After Ramot, № 92 first moved away from the lake and then, as № 87, turned sharply west and passed through the romantic Bethsaida Valley. It crossed the River Jordan about three kilometers north of where the river flowed into the northeastern corner of Galilee. Soon the road returned to the lake, gleaming brightly in the torrid air. Célestin and Odile continued to drive westward along the northern shore until they stopped for the day in the ancient village of Tabgha. At a small pebbly beach with crystal clear water, stood a simple hotel. How delighted they were at the prospect of swimming!

In the afternoon, although it was already Shabbat, a tiny shop was open, so they bought necessities. Outside, they ran into two middle-aged Germans with tropical hats. One was an archaeologist and the other an archaeologist-cum-Benedictine monk. The men explained they were working on new digs involving a church from the fourth century. "Our old friend, Constantine the Great again," chortled Célestin. A benevolent expression on his sunburnt face, the monk explained in formal German: "The church walls and mosaics were discovered here in Tabgha by German archaeologists back in 1932, and since then this place has been of much interest to us Germans, archaeologists and religious people alike. The mosaics on the church floor are of rare beauty. They are dedicated to the miracle when Jesus fed five thousand people with five loaves of bread and two fish. You are, of course, familiar with the legend." He smiled half-guiltily and added: "If you were to return here in a few years, the little church, with its precious mosaics, will be open to visitors. Now, unfortunately, we can't show you the digs; we don't have permission from the *Deutscher Verein vom Heiligen Lande*, which is financing our work (*The German Association of the Holy Land*)."

Father and daughter returned to the beach and had their simple dinner in solitude. Long into the night, they remained sitting on pebbles, observing the changing colors of the lake and talking about the Golan Heights, Fiq, Sam, Afik, Ramot, and Galilee the ancient. Wistfully, Célestin spoke about people's need to believe—to believe that someone, *someone*, will give them sustenance when they are starving, be it only a bread crumb and a fish eye.

The morning was peaceful. Through the open window flowed the sweet air of Galilee—the breath of the biblical Holy Land. Célestin inhaled deeply, pensively, leaving Odile to her cozy snooze. When she got up, they swam in the lake, ate a light breakfast, and left Tabgha for the north. From Galilee, highway № 90 climbed sharply through stony hills, providing an astonishing vista of the southern shore at least twenty kilometers away. After reaching an area with gorgeous conifers, the road climbed again, arriving finally, through numerous curves, in ancient Safed.

Although only twenty-five kilometers from the Sea of Galilee, Safed was the town at the highest elevation in Israel. Célestin parked the car on the main street and bought cakes and a booklet. The mountain air was cool. Munching the delicious pastry, they tolerated a vapid pop song on the car radio. He read aloud: "'During the pre-Christian epoch of the Second Temple in Jerusalem, according to the Talmud, the area now Safed was one of the five high places in Israel on which fires would be regularly lit to mark the first day of a new month'—called Rosh Hodesh. This makes me wonder about the different uses to which high places, both natural and man-made, are put in various countries. When we visited the Great Wall in China, we learned soldiers used to light fires on top of the wall when they noticed the approach of an enemy—which would alert troops in the interior." Odile said astutely: "Yes, but here they did it at only five places in the whole country. How can it be? Everyone tells us Israel is just a big village, but it isn't that small!" "It's not," agreed her father, "but it's mostly flat and sometimes below sea level."

Driving on from Safed, they passed through a forested area below Mount Meron and emerged in a small valley where cows were peacefully grazing. The early-morning gluttons were already lying down chewing cud. While Odile observed the docile animals and Célestin stretched next to the car, he caught sight of an enormous mountain in the northeast and stared in amazement. The mountain was under glittering snow, grander and much higher than everything else. He rushed to a map and compass to ensure he was not seeing a strange cloud formation. But no, it was Mount Hermon.

When he showed the wondrous apparition to the girl, she merrily exclaimed: "*Mon Dieu! Quelle beauté!*" Her father added contentedly: "You see what traveling brings: cows ruminating on one side of the road and a snow giant on the other." He was delighted to see his girl so enchanted by natural beauty: "On the map, I see Mount Hermon is only about forty kilometers from here, and it's even closer to Damascus, the capital of Syria. It also seems—look here, *ma belle*—that the mountain forms the three-country border between Lebanon, Syria, and Israel. And because its elevation above sea level is 2,814 meters, it's the highest mountain in each of the three countries. No wonder all three fervently claim it's their peak—and only theirs."

In the townlet of Gush Halav, highway № 89 turned sharply westward, and four kilometers farther, near the kibbutz Sasa, they found themselves only a kilometer from the border of Lebanon. Even before, numerous patrols and military vehicles had been appearing. But being curious and having confidence in the behavior of the Israeli Army, Célestin turned onto № 899, an even tinier road, thus reaching the border. Driving westward on № 8933, he got to a stone's throw from Lebanon and warned Odile not to take the camera out of her purse. Being exhilarated and mildly apprehensive, he tried to make jokes, mostly lame; the best was that the moment was not ideal for going to the toilet behind a tree. She coolly responded: "For such things, there's never a good time."

On narrow roads hugging the border, they crawled through many checkpoints. At each stood a group of armed soldiers who closely studied the car and its passengers. No doubt they informed subsequent checkpoints and a local command center, as there were no other private cars in evidence. Laughing, he told Odile her age and gender were responsible for their easy progress. But she had matured in Israel and learned a lot from the search at Munich airport and multiple Sinai crossings, so her response was skeptical: "It's not because of me, Papa. They're far too smart to trust little girls!" He grinned: "You're probably right. Maybe our humble Suzuki functions as 'open sesame!' at the checkpoints—or it's you and the decrepit-looking car combined."

Driving westward from the moshav Zar'it, located at the Lebanon border, with a variety of military equipment on its territory, they sometimes encountered soldiers-hitchhikers who evidently did not care about Shabbat. "War is war, and a little time off does wonders for the spirit of a soldier," observed Célestin. Although feeling sorry for them, he had decided not to take aboard anyone with a raised thumb in the border area: He was afraid it might complicate their passage through checkpoints. The decision needed to be justified to Odile, who not only had a kind heart but enjoyed the French-Hebrew lessons in the likable Ramot Sam's book.

From the high ground on № 899 near Ya'ara, another moshav, they saw the Mediterranean Sea. "What a beautiful and touching sight," they thought. It was not far, about five kilometers. The road descended to sea level, passed by a shady oasis with palm trees, and arrived at one of the most famous kibbutzim—Rosh HaNikra, "top of the cave" in Hebrew. It was established in January of 1949 on a location previously occupied by the Arab village Al-Bassa—which, as explained in the forthright brochure, "had been depopulated in the Arab-Israeli war of 1948." The founders were Holocaust survivors and members of the Zionist Youth Movement. Célestin remembered and gently reminded Odile that two of the survivors who had found refuge in the kibbutz were Baruch Shmotkin and his young son Jakob, their good friend.

They parked the car above the caverns that the sea had been mercilessly carving into the white limestone for an eternity. In the kibbutz hostel, the pair obtained a room. The staff worked in the small restaurant, disregarding Shabbat. Nearby, through huge piles of barbed wire, there was a passage to the north, to the border area and Lebanon. In front of the narrow roadway, the heavily armed Israeli soldiers were letting through only the United Nations "blue helmets" in their jeeps. Next to the passage and entrance to the caves, a massive control tower stood atop the cliff. Despite all that, the setting—at least on the Israeli side—resembled a seaside vacation spot much more than the border between two Germanys or two Koreas.

At the hostel, they tried to find out how to explore the sea caves. A muscular, deeply tanned kibbutznik of Célestin's age set down his bucket and mop. He advised them patiently: "It's best to use the cable car, but now it's only three o'clock, still an hour before the end of Shabbat. People who work on the cable car aren't from our kibbutz and often don't open on Saturday afternoons at all. You would only waste time waiting. Because you'll spend the night here, you'd do much better to be the first in line at the cable car tomorrow at nine. And today, since you're here by car, my advice is to drive a kilometer south. Then, strolling along the beach, you can return to the base of the chalk cliff with the caverns. Can the little girl walk that far?" As her father had expected, Odile told the kibbutznik huffily that she certainly could. The man chuckled affectionately: "Sorry, sorry, kiddo! But be aware it's not possible to enter the grottoes from the beach except with scuba gear. You'll see them much better tomorrow when you descend in two minutes by cable car."

Following the advice, they ambled along the deserted beach. It was the end of May, too early for Israelis to swim in the sea. The weather was delightful, free of the heat in the interior. They arrived at the foot of the white limestone cliff at least thirty meters high. Much of the entrance to the grottoes was below sea level, but the waves were small, and Célestin was certain he could swim into the caves without difficulty. But once inside, what then? How to find his way around in the semi-darkness? And what would Odile do alone on the beach? He decided swimming and free diving into the caverns would be an act of irresponsible stupidity rather than proof of courage and skill.

From the beach, they saw the lower cable car station at the hip of the cliff, about ten meters above the sea. He could easily clamber up the rocks and walk into the caves. But again: What about Odile? How would she see the renowned emerald blue of the waters within? The girl understood what her father was calculating and was sorry she was a burden—but just then she received a hug of reassurance: "Let's go swimming!"

They swam out to where the view of the white cliffs was superb, and because the bottom, seven or eight meters down, was shingly, sea life could be inspected with eyes open underwater. While playing in the waves, Célestin exclaimed: "Here we are! We've swum in three seas of Israel: The Mediterranean, Galilee, and Red; and in the fourth, we at least floated—you know which one." Odile thought for a while, making small arm movements, and said: "Yes, but you swam without me at that... Ras on the edge of the desert." "No matter," he retorted, "it also counts as the Red, and you swam at Sheikh."

The next morning, Célestin called Netanya. He was relieved Osnat answered, unsure in more ways than one how he would have communicated with her parents. She seemed delighted and a little nervous. "How young she still is, even if in the fourth year of law school," he marveled. While they talked, two powerful detonations were heard from the Lebanon border area. Osnat worriedly asked what was going on. "I've no idea," he responded, "someone's been playing with explosives again. Frankly, I'm not worried. It must be an everyday thing around here. I only hope the sea grottoes did not cave in, as Odile and I are about to go there!"

With only a young Canadian couple, they soon entered the small, brightly painted cable car. "Don't worry," Célestin comforted Odile, "this was probably constructed by Swiss or Austrian engineers; of necessity, they are the best at this type of job." They descended fifty meters to the lower station in only two minutes, just as the kibbutznik had told them. The incline was an incredible sixty degrees, "the greatest in the world," as the brochure proudly stated.

The entrance to the labyrinth of caves was at the place they saw from the beach, but inside they were greeted by surprises. In addition to the naturally linked cavernous spaces created by wave erosion, there was a tunnel of the railway line Haifa-Beirut dug during the British Mandate for Palestine, as well as a tourist tunnel connecting the grottoes, pushed through in 1968. The cable car was built only in the seventies.

A walkway, protected by a railing, snaked about two hundred meters through caves and tunnels. Not far below it, the waves that had penetrated the caves assumed—under the fantastically dancing sunrays—a unique emerald-green color. From time to time, a wave splashed the visitors, accompanied by the music of Odile's joy. The sea rumbled, gurgled, and murmured announcing its everlasting arrivals and departures. The pair returned to the surface in a daze, not from the steep ascent but from the otherworldly beauty.

Around noon, after a walk in the kibbutz park, they departed on the coastal № 4 to spend a day in the port city of Akko, twenty kilometers to the south. A small hotel near Old Town was easy to secure and then venture on foot through the walls into a maze of passages and alleyways. Arabic was the sovereign ruler, spoken by many people who were not Muslims—Maronites, Druze, and Catholic Arabs. The town was as ancient as Jerusalem and Jaffa. Although it had been destroyed in countless appalling sieges and attacks, desperate periods of resistance, and merciless conquests, its great age was palpable to all senses. In the main souk and covered bazaars, there were noisy throngs and much jostling of residents—tourists seemed nonexistent. Of the edifices they saw, el-Jazzar Mosque, from the end of the eighteenth century, was the most imposing. Known as the White, it stood by the main souk and could be seen, it was said, from far out at sea.

Old squares with stone arches and run-down houses that had escaped destruction seemed more authentic than anything in Jerusalem because incomparably less money had been spent on renovation. Urchins, boys and girls together, probably all related, created a happy clamor in the passages. No child begged. The girls studied Odile, and she appraised them. During their long walk, they encountered several small churches: Greek Orthodox, Maronite, Roman Catholic, and Greek Catholic.

They devoted most of their time to the Crusader fortress and the old port beside it, even though only fishing and tourist boats were there. Everything of importance sailing into and out of Israel would be in the modern port of Haifa, twenty kilometers away, at the southern end of the bay. But in the previous fifteen centuries, Akko's fortified port was essential for many Near Eastern and even European armies and fleets. For two hundred years, Akko was also vital to the Crusader Kingdom of Jerusalem. The Germanic military Teutonic Order, later very powerful for centuries in Europe itself, was founded in Akko in 1192. In 1799, with an army significantly weakened by the defeats in Syria, Napoleon long besieged Akko, but the defenders, Ottoman Turks, with the aid of an English fleet, resisted all the onslaughts—allegedly there were eight of them.

While they sat on the terrace of a small restaurant in the port, Célestin shared his troubled thoughts: "When I read about our countrymen—Germans and French—I feel both anger and sorrow. The Teutonic so-called knights rampaged through the Holy Land, the Baltics, and elsewhere in Europe, pillaging, plundering, and laying to waste—all allegedly in the defense of the Holy Land and Catholicism. And Napoleon's entire disastrous undertaking in Syria and Egypt was a sick expression of his megalomania—that's when a person has a crazily inflated opinion of himself. Those dependent on him were often 'yes men' who cosseted him. And so, Napoleon's Near Eastern adventure ended not gloriously but as a tragedy for France. When we travel to Haifa tomorrow—look, one can make the city out from here, you see, down there on the coast—I'll tell you what happened to French soldiers while they were retreating from Akko to Egypt."

"*Mais cher Papa, si cette histoire est très triste,*" Odile asked her father plaintively, "do you really have to tell me?" He thought a while: "The child is posing a good question, but she should—she must—know." So he went on: "The story about the violent Germanic Teutons and the debacle and suffering of French soldiers just here where we're traveling is not about the Japan and China of old but about *our* ancestors! Who knows what the teachers at your school have to say about it—if anything. They may have the best, yet deluded, intentions or are submissively following the program dictated by the Ministry of Education. In either case, they may too lightly pass over the horrors and defeats in our history. We'll look into it on our return, if for no other reason than to find out about your exams at the end of June."

When approaching Haifa from Akko the next morning, a structure of gigantic size on the biblical Mount Carmel was visible from afar. Consulting a map, Célestin concluded it must be near the Haifa University campus and surmised the edifice may be a bizarre monument. However, as they turned off the main road and began to climb toward the university, they realized it was a building of twenty stories in the shape of the United Nations headquarters in New York. In the lobby, they discovered that the entire institution, with all the academic departments, lecture halls, and administration, was located in the building. It was imposing not because of the number of stories but because of its unique position on a hill above the city, with a view west to the horizon and Akko in the northerly direction.

While scanning the list of departments, he said: "You remember swimming with Osnat's girlfriend Shoshana at Sheikh? Well, she's studying here, but we won't be able to find her. Also, the son of Rachel and Danny works in Chemistry, but since we've never met him, it's better not to disturb him. However, I talked from Jerusalem with a colleague in Linguistics, so let's try to say hello."

They took the elevator to the fourth floor and found Dr. Noam Kantor's office. Although he had never met Célestin, the linguist was delighted to see the visitor and warmly greeted Odile. A lively chat ensued, and Noam proposed to show his guests the University Club on the twenty-fifth floor. In the high-speed elevator, Noam complained: "As you noticed, I'm on a low floor—or a lowly one—I can't see the sea!"

As it was only eleven o'clock, there were few people in the Club, so they sat by the window with a fabulous view of an expanse of the Mediterranean. The city bathed in sunshine. As expected, Noam knew most of Célestin's colleagues in Israel. They spoke for an hour, during which Odile, with Noam's smiling approval, took *The Jerusalem Post* in English and *Haaretz* in Hebrew from the wall on which newspapers were hanging. Around noon, Noam apologized, saying he needed to attend a seminar but would be pleased if they had lunch as his guests. The offer was kind, yet Célestin could not accept it, so they said goodbye to Noam in the lobby.

The edge of the National Park of Mount Carmel was close to the University, so the pair spent several hours walking under conifers and resting in sunny glades bordered by cypresses and eucalyptuses. Amid the soothing beauty of nature, one quickly became aware of why people had been fascinated, nay, bewitched, by Mount Carmel and considered it the abode of their prophets and deities for thousands of years.

15.

From the University, they needed only twenty minutes by car to traverse the ten kilometers of the entire Haifa peninsula and reach the hillock by the sea on which stood the Discalced Carmelite Monastery of Our Lady of Mount Carmel, Stella Maris. While strolling in the vicinity of the well-proportioned edifice, massive yet mollifying, they breathed in the fragrant smells and splendid colors of that quarter of Haifa—with tall cypresses, multicolored oleander bushes, bougainvillea, and numerous flowers. The monastery, built in the nineteenth century, was situated about three hundred meters from the sea. However, the Carmelites, sometimes known as Whitefriars, had been associated with Mount Carmel since the twelfth century, from the time of the Crusaders, albeit in different locations. Over time, many of their dwellings and sanctuaries were destroyed by Muslims.

The conventions and even the name of the monks in the area of Mount Carmel and Cape Haifa changed from time to time, depending on the political situation in the Holy Land and France. Célestin explained that for already a hundred and seventy years, the monastery in front of them belonged to the Order of Discalced Carmelites, "monks without footwear," which was supposed to indicate their spiritual ties with barefoot hermits, notably those who lived in caves. "In fact," he said sardonically, "it ought to be 'monks without shoes,' which is the meaning in Latin—because in this book it states sandals are permitted! After all, sandals are durable and protective footwear, as proven by our own."

They entered the beautiful monastery and talked in its church with two courteous, quite barefoot, monks, originally from France, who flew and glided, more than walked, on the highly polished stones. The friars showed them paintings from the end of the nineteenth century and then led them to the altar. There, all four of them stood within the eight-pointed Star of the Sea on the marble floor, the Stella Maris. Below the altar was a softly illuminated space representing the cave in which Prophet Elijah had allegedly dwelled nine centuries before Christ and almost three thousand years before the nine-year-old's moment in the monastery.

The monks were educated Frenchmen who quickly deduced with whom they were dealing. They did not refer to Elijah's cave in a dogmatic or God-fearing manner. After all, like Célestin and even Odile—who had been thoroughly prepared—the friars knew there were six other spots on Cape Haifa and Mount Carmel about which passionate claims had been made since the twelfth century of being the prophet's cave. Still, both the monks and Célestin knew the Carmelites had closely linked themselves with Elijah and his cave in part because the legend brought them identity, recognizability, high repute, and occasional French and Vatican funds.

The conversation turned to Napoleon, about whom all four had been taught in school. Célestin said: "While unsuccessfully warring in Syria, at the same time, in August of 1798, he lost all the ships in the battle of the Nile. Therefore, he did his utmost to take Akko and ascertain the English didn't enter the port. But the desperate attempt failed—on top of which the plague beset his army."

A friar agreed: "Precisely what happened! In March of 1799, after Napoleon's Akko fiasco, our monastery was turned into a hospital for French soldiers—the wounded and those infected by the plague. The building at the time had been erected during the three decades at the end of the eighteenth century but was heavily damaged in 1799—from the sea by the English and from the land by the Akko Ottoman Turks. As soon as Napoleon's army left Haifa, retreating south to Jaffa and Egypt, the Turks massacred the wounded and destroyed the building. Few brothers escaped. Twenty years later, the Turks flattened what had remained, first having stolen the stones for the palace of the Pasha of Akko. The present monastery was built only in 1836, and the small monument for French soldiers, in the shape of a pyramid topped by a cross, dates from that time. You must have seen it."

Célestin took Odile's hand and was about to take leave of the friars but changed his mind and addressed them again: "I've read serious books describing Napoleon's tragic retreat from Akko, Haifa, and Jaffa to Egypt. The soldiers were starving and exhausted, many were carrying the plague sufferers. It's known that Napoleon often walked beside the sick and the wounded, but also that his troops were leaving a wasteland behind like locusts; his stubbornness was undoubtedly responsible. Don't you think?"

The second monk spoke up: "True and awful. And there's more. It's thought Napoleon proposed euthanasia for about fifty soldiers who were at death's door. They would be given an overdose of opium and cease to suffer. The retreat would be faster, there would be less chance of additional infections, and the dying soldiers wouldn't be tortured by Ottomans if they were found abandoned. However, the army doctors refused to comply: Unlike Napoleon, they didn't dare to act like God in this sacred land..."

Holding hands, father and daughter departed in deep thought from yet another place in Israel. There would be no convenient answers to Odile's probing questions. He had learned it was impossible to tell the sensitive child the full truth about human suffering and evil without her sometimes waking up in nightmarish sweat, as had happened in Nuweiba after Masada.

They drove to the Bat Galim quarter and found a hotel by the beach. He called Osnat and told her they would arrive the next day. Their words were intimate and gay, although nervousness again crept into it, palpable that time in his voice as well.

During dinner on the terrace of an Italian restaurant, he noticed in Odile's eyes that she had sensed the faltering of his confidence regarding Netanya but chose not to ask. Be that as it may, they both admired the Mediterranean purple-red sunset over the placid sea and calmly talked about Pasha until a moonless, fragrant night fell on Haifa.

Although they arose early, feeling joy about seeing Osnat—and the weather could not have been gentler—it was eleven before they drove south toward Netanya, sixty kilometers away. Célestin stopped often, allowing the girl to take pictures. It took them an hour to cover forty kilometers to Caesarea, where they entered a cafe deserted like the beach in front of it.

Having ordered their customary beverages, he leaned back and assumed an educational tone: "Town names in Israel are fascinating. For example, this smallish town of Caesarea got its name from the port that existed in antiquity. It was constructed under Herod the Great from the 22nd to the 10th year and called Caesarea Maritima. The years before Christ, or 'before our era,' are designated as decreasing toward a zero point, which many consider the year of Christ's birth, whereas in our time..." She was impatient: "*Oui, oui, Papa*, you explained it twice before! But this Herod, is he the one you mentioned about the Wailing Wall?" He grinned benignly: "Don't get annoyed with me, *ma princesse*, when I repeat myself. As for Herod, your memory has also served you well, although there are things you don't yet know—because only in two years will they teach you the history of ancient Rome and the basic elements of the Latin language. It was different in my school days...

"So Herod, although King of Judea, was a faithful vassal of Rome. Caesarea was named to glorify the first Roman Emperor, that is, *Caesar*, Octavianus Augustus, who was crowned in the 27th year before Christ, only five years before Caesarea Maritima was built—right here! Incidentally, the month of August got its name from this emperor. And something else: Emperor-Caesar Augustus was the adopted son and heir of Julius Caesar, the great

Roman military leader and officially the 'Dictator.' In his case, the word 'Caesar' was only a nickname, but from Augustus on, it became transformed into a title, the supreme title—from the Czars of Russia to our Napoleon."

Odile's face darkened: "*Aïe!* I'm not afraid of Latin, Papa, you've been teaching me. But the history of Rome, with all those names and years to remember!"After mulling it over, she laughed in a childishly malicious way: "But what you've just explained will be useful. My fellow pupils will certainly mix up Caesar Julius and Caesar Octavianus!" Célestin laughed: "I bet they will. However, *chérie*, you too have already mixed them up: Julius was Caesar, but Dictator rather than Emperor, while Octavianus was Emperor, that is, Caesar, but his name was not Caesar. We'll need to work some more." "*Aïe,*" sighed Odile again.

"And let me add," he proceeded mercilessly: "The Roman Senate named the month of July to glorify Julius Caesar, who was born in that month—which had previously been called *Quintilis*, the fifth month. You see, in the old Roman calendar, there were only ten months, and the year began in the spring with March. The month of August, before Augustus, was called *Sextilis*, the sixth month. *Bien*, it's all clear to you now; if not, there's plenty of time to learn. Let's go."

Once he resumed driving, Célestin spoke: "I mentioned how diverse the town names are here. There was Caesarea, tiny despite its ancient history. And now, in about twenty kilometers, we'll reach Netanya, with a fifty times bigger population and a totally different origin and city name. In their brochure, it said the town had been founded fifty years ago, and the name in Hebrew means something like 'God-given.' However, there's the Jewish man's name Nathan meaning the same. The truth is the town didn't get its name because God gifted it to the inhabitants but in honor of the American Jew Nathan Strauss, a wealthy entrepreneur and co-owner of Macy's, the biggest department store in New York City. Funny, no?"

To her father's surprise, Odile objected: "I don't get what's funny. Let's ask Osnat. She was born in Netanya and knows more than us." These words were a revelation to Célestin: His daughter had accepted the idea that one could buy everything with money, including the name of a new town—and while the buyer was still alive! But he was also proud of her because she did not think her father was an unchallengeable authority even on what was funny.

He had promised Osnat to call for advice when they arrived, yet his nose led him straight to acceptable lodgings. Hotel Gal Yam was comfortable, had private parking, and was situated only two hundred meters from Sironit Beach. Their room was on the fifth floor with a sensational sea view westward, all the way to where the curved horizon might have persuaded even medieval Popes and contemporary flat-earthers. Above their floor, there was a spacious sunbathing terrace with a pool and showers.

Almost all the time in Osnat's company, they spent the day and the following two in Netanya. Father and daughter woke up early, swam briefly in the pool on the roof, and after breakfast greeted Osnat. With her, they went for long walks in town, visited a few shops on Herzl Street, and drove for hours through fertile fields east of Netanya. Sironit Beach was friendly, even with water much colder than at Sheikh. Each day, Odile took a siesta after lunch and studied for school for an hour or two afterward. It was impossible to divine whether or not her conscious intention was to leave her father alone with Osnat. The two were developing a new physical intimacy even in Odile's presence and much more so when they were alone on the beach and in the sea.

On the very first day in Netanya, Célestin had found an opportunity to convey to Osnat essential facts. He understood, he said, it would be best not to introduce him to her strict father, which automatically excluded her mother. Although Osnat did her best not to reveal it, he was certain she was relieved. After all, what to say, how to explain the intimacy?

He also disclosed that shortly, probably in less than two weeks, Odile and he would depart from Israel. They had to be in Metz by the end of June for her exams, and he wished to arrange a surprise. As she adored animals, they would fly from Tel Aviv to Nairobi in Kenya for ten days and visit a wildlife park. He would thus thank his girl for being a wonderful companion during their long, complex, and demanding trip.

Osnat was saddened and remained silent for several minutes. Then, "I thought you'd stay longer... Soon, I'm returning to Jerusalem, to the university, and hoped..." Tears welled in her eyes at the precise moment when they heard Odile's voice from the bathroom, requesting something trivial. He yelled "Coming!" while Osnat flew to him, passionately embraced him, and tremulously whispered: "I understand, my dearest. I won't wreck Odile's surprise with a single word." She went to the window and looked at the sea to calm down.

Nonetheless, all three enjoyed the time spent together afterward. The last evening was especially merry. They went to a Hungarian restaurant on Herzl Street where a small orchestra was playing. Before dinner, Ishtvan, the restaurant owner who was a Hungarian Jew, personally served *barrack palinka*, the renowned apricot brandy, to Osnat and Célestin in old tulip-shaped glasses. Then they tried various dishes, all extra spicy, while Ishtvan opened a bottle of his best *Egri Bikaver*, "Bull's Blood of Eger," a full-bodied dry wine. Later, the trio even danced with other guests something that was supposed to be *csardas*. Despite all the previous dishes, no one could refuse a slice of *Dobos*, a homemade cake composed of numerous layers of chocolate buttercream with a crunchy caramel top. And Ishtvan, pleasantly tipsy with teary eyes, bent over his guest and nostalgically sighed: "Oh, Sir, if only I could now be in my old Buda by the Danube..."

Back at Gal Yam, Osnat and Célestin tucked in the sleepy child. Yet without saying a word, father and daughter guiltily remembered Olya doing the same—seemingly so long ago—at the Pribaltiskaya in Leningrad. While he busied himself shutting the windows, Osnat and the girl were saying protracted goodbyes, accompanied by promises and tears. He hugged his daughter, saying: "Because of the wine this evening, I'll take Osnat home by taxi. *Dors bien, mon trésor, je reviens bientôt!*"

However, instead of a cab, the hotel roof called. There was no one there. Everything was silent except for the soft gurgling of the pool. They leaned on the metal railing and looked for a long time at the barely visible horizon. Then they mumbled, whispered, and murmured sweet nothings, while passionately kissing and embracing. Somehow, they reached a deck chair. And then... Even though they refrained from pursuing the matter to the very end, they undoubtedly went far too far to allow Osnat to say to some future lover she had been an innocent lamb, whereas Célestin could not assure Olya, once freed from prison, he had been faithful.

16.

The pair quickly covered the thirty kilometers between Netanya and Tel Aviv, although the traffic was heavy on the approaches to the capital city, as always before Shabbat. During the drive, they talked about Osnat, but Odile found a way to mention Olya as well. She understood that both women were important to her father, not for a moment feeling she had lost something because of them: She loved and missed them both.

Cheerily greeted by the Dizengoff staff, they were escorted to their old room. Before arrival in Israel, Célestin had not expected they would so quickly feel at home in the magical land, but almost three months had, after all, passed since the afternoon when they first saw its coastline.

They drove to Tel Aviv University because the secretary of the Department of Linguistics had left a message saying she was holding a "hillock of mail." "*Todah*! You've come on time," Mediva exclaimed when they arrived. "I must get home by four as I live in a quarter where the ultraorthodox are super strict about Shabbat." Odile smilingly presented a box of chocolates to her.

Next, they went to a coffee house on Dizengoff open despite Shabbat like many on that cosmopolitan street. Father and daughter made a beeline to a table in the corner, but on the way, he briefly responded to a hello from a fiftyish man whose face was familiar: He sat at the bar with an elegant lady of his age and a young woman in uniform. At his table, Célestin quickly looked through the pile of mail. Some letters had arrived in Tel Aviv from France and Germany, while others were forwarded from Hebrew University. Odile received letters from Mathilde and Oksana in response to her postcards from Jerusalem. However, the mail he sought had not arrived—nothing from Olya's mother in Kazan nor the authorities in Moscow.

Soon the man sitting at the bar came to their table: "You don't remember me, but I recognized your little daughter right away! I'm *maître d'hôtel* at Sonesta, the hotel at no man's land in Eilat-Taba, and we spoke for a long time just before your trip to the Sinai." Célestin symbolically tapped his forehead, saying: "Of course, how rude of me. You seemed familiar, but I didn't connect Taba and Tel Aviv. I don't seem to learn what everyone tells me: Israel is just a big village. But now I remember you told me you had worked in Vienna and Montreal. So please, sit down with us, bar stools are still too high for Odile!"

The man, Yehuda Shechter, agreed: "I'd be glad to and will bring my wife and daughter." Additional chairs were pulled. "These are my Daphne and our Dina, who, as you can see, is in the Army during the day," laughed Yehuda and courteously requested to be the host when a waiter appeared.

Father and daughter described where they had been in Israel and learned much in return. Daphne and Yehuda lived in Eilat but often drove to Tel Aviv to see Dina. They had met in Montreal many years earlier after Yehuda had optimistically emigrated to Canada from Austria. "In Vienna, even though I was young, I was the manager of a restaurant, which meant nothing in Montreal. It wasn't antisemitism, the city is full of wealthy Jews, but I had to start as a dishwasher. And Daphne," he looked at her lovingly, "she was born in Nairobi, in Kenya, where her parents became well-off merchants despite the discrimination at the hands of the conceited English colonials. Couldn't join the golf club, couldn't be treated at the Anglo hospital, and so on. When they'd had enough, they moved to Montreal, where they prospered. Because I was dirt poor, our liaison shook up not just Daphne's parents but the entire rich Montreal. Even when our child was born, our lovely Dina, nothing changed for the better. So we turned our backs on them and came to Israel."

The waiter placed the juice in front of Odile and distributed glasses of draft beer. Saying she would return presently, Dina went somewhere with her bag. Daphne explained: "Dina's serving her last six months in a unit near Tel Aviv. She's busy with training during the day and sleeps in the barracks. But in the evening, she can make a little money by working in town. For the last three weeks, she's been working in this café where Yehuda knows the owner. Today she'll start at six even though it's Shabbat. It doesn't bother her, nor us. She went to the restroom to change clothes—for her waitressing job and to have a beer with us. It's not permitted in military uniform."

Célestin suggested they wait for Dina's return before toasting, which pleased her parents. Soon the girl, in a pretty, navy-blue dress, joined them at the table and laughing youthfully explained: "I'll put on the white apron later. As for makeup, I don't use more than is permitted in uniform!" She looked different, even though the uniform suited her well.

All, including Odile, clinked glasses in a new-friendship toast. He asked Dina if she planned to study after army service, and she talked about developmental psychology. "But I'd like to see a bit of the world first," a wish similar to Oksana's in Siberia. Dina went on: "If my parents agree," she threw them a timid look, "I'd enjoy spending a couple of months in Kenya. As you've heard, Mama was born there. And Lina, her first cousin, lives in Nairobi with her husband Saul and their children. They are twins, the girl is Daniella and the boy Daniel. So nice! They are a year older than I am." But Daphne declared in a voice that reflected her overbearing maternal worry: "First get the army service out of the way, and then we'll see. And you, Célestin, you've traveled so much, have you been to Kenya?"

Wanting Kenya to be a surprise for Odile, not a shock in front of strangers, even if very kind people, he was astonished by the coincidence and responded diplomatically: "Unfortunately, we haven't been anywhere in Africa but hope in the future to visit the fascinating continent." Daphne thoughtfully advised: "Well, Kenya is complicated but gorgeous; it would be a perfect starting point for you and Odile. If you ever decide to travel there, I'll gladly give you the address of my Lina, it's always good to know someone." Célestin agreed and sincerely thanked her.

Then they spoke of Eilat, Taba, Pharaoh's Island, and Saladin's fortress while Yehuda was raring to announce news from his adopted orphan, the hotel Sonesta. "Odile, do you remember the restaurant with windows facing the beach where you sat with your dad? You were sipping hot Viennese chocolate with whipped cream, which I'd prepared specially for you." The girl cheerfully replied: "I remember *Schokolade mit Schlagsahne,* you made two cups for me! But when Papa mentioned Pharaoh's Island, he forgot to say he swam there from the beach and also returned swimming! I waited for him on the shore and saw it all." The Shechters were surprised by Célestin's behavior, odd in their eyes, but were pleased to hear the child praising her father. Dina said she sometimes swam in the outdoor pool near the barracks but would never dare to swim to Pharaoh's Island—certainly not alone and without fins.

Yehuda continued about Sonesta: "We've renovated several rooms and suites and are charging an arm and a leg. The guests are mostly businessmen. Recently, a strange thing happened. Around nine in the morning, two policemen and a secretive fellow in civilian clothes suddenly appeared. They entered the restaurant and without saying a word approached a guest who was munching his breakfast in peace. Before you could count to ten, they had him in the car, driving away. Alright, I thought, some scoundrel, nothing strange. But around three in the afternoon, one of those cops returned to the hotel with the man who calmly went to his room!

"This cop I know well, he's worked in Eilat for a long time, an okay guy. He sits down, I bring him coffee, and he tells me what happened. Mossad interrogated the man for many hours about his role in organizing a secret meeting in Bucharest, Romania, between extreme left-wingers in the Knesset and the PLO people.

You know, Palestine Liberation Organization. But then they let him go and told the policeman to return him to the hotel!"

Yehuda went on: "Nothing makes any sense! Was it a foolish game of Mossad's or a ruse on many levels? Why did they say anything to an ordinary cop? Why didn't they forbid him to talk? Why did he tell *me* anything? Why am I telling *you* anything? I'm saying all this because it must be comical to you as a friend of Israel, considering the high reputation Mossad has everywhere. The incident is obviously of minor importance. The man left the hotel yesterday, having paid in cash. With a sizable tip, I must admit."

Daphne chuckled: "Well, you bored your guests to tears with this story. And me, for it's not the first time I hear it. Admit, dear Yehuda, you are proud that your hotel has become a lair of international spies!" Everything ended with laughter and with Yehuda's pleased blushing. The story was interesting to Célestin, for it seemed that ordinary Israelis admirably did not always think of Mossad as a sacrosanct institution.

When Odile needed the toilet, Dina got up to show her the way. As soon as they left, Célestin spoke of his daughter's love of animals and revealed to the Shechters that he had planned a big surprise for Odile by taking her to Nairobi—no less! He had barely finished before Daphne took out a notebook and began to scribble the address of her relatives, exclaiming: "Wonderful, I'm glad! You'll both fall in love with Kenya. And tomorrow from Eilat, I'll call Lina in Nairobi to tell her." On learning they did not have a visa, she added another name: "This gentleman is a friend of ours. He works at the Consulate of Kenya in Ramat Gan, it's not far. He'll help with the visa. I'll call him on Monday after the office opens. It's better not to land at the Nairobi airport without a visa, no matter which passport you have. They have strict rules to which they stick."

Thus, when Odile returned chattering with Dina, preparations were already ongoing for her travel to the country of mighty and gracious wild animals. While goodbyes were taking place, the girl did not notice that Daphne and Yehuda, unlike Dina, were looking at her benevolently, full of unspoken best wishes.

"We've slept well," said Célestin the next morning, "so I suggest we don't laze in Tel Aviv but travel to new places. New for us
but ancient. I've told you a lot about some, but we've never managed to visit them. Since they're fairly close, we'll return tonight.
Please put on light clothes, it'll be hot. But also bring long pants
and a blouse with sleeves because we'll visit an extraordinary
church. Ça va?"

They spoke excitedly to the receptionist in the Dizengoff
foyer: "We're going to Be'er Sheva. Will it be hot?" "Thirty-four
today, the radio says, quite mild for the queen of the Negev Desert at this time of year," she responded laughing.

After a few kilometers on the main highway to Jerusalem,
they switched to № 6 which led to Be'er Sheva, a hundred kilometers to the south. The fine two-way road through the flat desert
made it possible for Célestin to drive constantly at hundred and
twenty kilometers an hour. A dull person might but would be
wrong saying there was nothing to see. They were repeatedly
amazed by the miracles Israelis had created: Intelligent irrigation and patient hard work injected fertility into the barren desert. Among the cultivated fields, one occasionally saw small circular groups of trees, serving little purpose than aesthetic appeal
and providing a modicum of shade to toilers. Still, these trees
grew from seeds lovingly inserted in the ground by human hands.

In Be'er Sheva, the heat was desert-dry, so they bore it easily.
Despite its recorded existence of six thousand years and vivid
presence in biblical accounts, the place had for many centuries
been a small oasis inhabited by Negev Bedouins. Even in 1948,
when Israelis defeated Egyptian units at Be'er Sheva, there were
only three thousand inhabitants. However, Célestin and Odile encountered a city of some size—another miracle—where people
strolled in the shade of palms. Everywhere there were Bedouins
and Palestinians, as well as Mizrahi Jews who had migrated to the
Negev after 1948 from Arab countries.

Cafés and restaurants were packed despite Shabbat. It seemed
Arabs and Jews were more tolerant toward their neighbors than
elsewhere in Israel. Odile was fascinated by the picturesque

street life: "Only men are sitting on the café terraces, and every single one is smoking. Perhaps they wouldn't allow you to sit with them?! As for shops, only women are going there, lugging oversized bags, with little girls in tow. Hmm, I see there are boys of my age at some tables. I guess they're sitting with their fathers—not to bother their mothers who're shopping!"

He laughed at the analysis: "Few adults are as observant as you! I also watched those men in clouds of smoke. Maybe they wouldn't want me to sit with them also because I don't add countless sugar cubes to the tea. What's heartwarming is how these people are joking, laughing, and teasing each other—they're happy. They're full of *joie de vivre,* behaving like Mediterraneans with kippahs on their heads. And everyone knows everyone... All right, let's go. First, a cold Jaffa lemonade and ice cream; then, we'll be off to Bethlehem!"

Bethlehem—"house of bread" in Hebrew, "house of meat" in Arabic—was situated seventy kilometers north of Be'er Sheva and ten kilometers south of Jerusalem. Odile knew many people believed Bethlehem to be the birthplace of Jesus Christ, but her father had explained they were probably mistaken. The Gospel of Mark, he said, the oldest Gospel, does not mention Bethlehem and simply states Jesus was from Nazareth. Only in the later Gospel of Matthew, which uses Mark as the main source, does Bethlehem suddenly appear as the birthplace. Célestin concluded: "It's useful you're aware of such matters, but not essential."

In the car, Odile was puzzled when her papa said out of the blue: "Only on Monday will you find out what my gift to you for the next Christmas is, although you'll actually receive it long before Christmas—but not on Monday!" None of it made sense, and he stubbornly resisted answering her questions. "Enjoy the true desert," he said enigmatically.

And indeed, as soon as they left Be'er Sheva on highway № 60, they encountered the serious face of the Negev, the uncultivated, unsubjugated, primeval desert. In it, men and women were very different from those in the nearby city. Next to the road, Bedouins of various ages rode fast on good-looking horses: They looked wild, with white keffiyeh flying and features as if carved into facial flesh by dry wind. Women, all in black djellabas to the ground, walked erect, usually carrying a heavy load. There were no hostile gestures from anyone toward their car with Israeli plates, even though they had entered the southern part of the West Bank under the Palestinian National Authority.

Israeli friends had warned Célestin not to drive anywhere on the West Bank and to avoid № 60 in particular. The roundabout route, back to Tel Aviv and then to Jerusalem and on to Bethlehem, would have added forty kilometers, but that was not why he declined to heed the warning. He knew the advice was well-meant but felt it was important for him and his daughter to see and feel at least a little of Palestinian land. Besides, he believed their attitude toward Arabs was humane—by being objective—which would help them remain unharmed on the West Bank. Maybe even their non-Jewishness would help, although it was not written on their foreheads: Or was it to Arabs?

He drove carefully through the mysterious low hills with odd-shaped rocks. Having found a radio station playing exclusively Arabic music, he was enamored of the strange rhythms, unfamiliar instruments, and hoarse voices that sounded as if spurring on belly dancers in a raw and hungry male manner. The music sounded sexual and age-old like the surrounding hills. Even though he noticed Odile pouting, Célestin increased the volume, calmly saying: "Sorry, but this music is for adults, for my soul... You'll grow up and understand."

By the time they reached an area halfway to Hebron, cars and trucks had trickled down to few. At one point, they stepped out of the Suzuki to take pictures of an intriguingly desolate area above which clouds had gathered—clouds of a black so dark as to be rarely seen in nature. They paid no attention to a small solitary house, cube-like and ugly, stuck among the rocks thirty meters uphill from the road. "It must be deserted because there's no laundry hanging in front," he decided.

But in truth, the house was packed. The carelessly parked Israeli car and the harmless-looking couple in front of it had been covertly observed by many curious pairs of eyes. Suddenly, the front door opened, and seven or eight children from about five to thirteen burst out. They ran noisily down the slope but on the stern command issued by their elder sister of about seventeen, who was descending behind them, all stopped as one some ten meters from the car. What a fabulous scene, thought Célestin. The children were serious, but as soon as he had made a few steps toward them, with a broad smile and calling out salam, the little faces melted and joyfully exclaimed the same magical greeting of peace among people. The teenager, a tall shapely beauty in a spotless white blouse and blue jeans, without any head covering, added in a friendly voice the two-syllable greeting in English.

He lifted the camera slightly, thus requesting a photo. The girl nodded and swiftly lined up the children in the traditional style of family photos worldwide—by their height. Then she took a teacher's position behind the row. During the previous minutes, Odile had been standing stiffly next to her father, so he murmured that everything was fine. He took her by the hand, led her up the stony path to the Palestinian children, and gestured his intention to the teenage mother hen. The girl estimated Odile's height and placed her in the right spot. She relaxed and smiled weakly at the girl beside her. Then the sister returned behind the line, and he took several photos. On the first, everyone was solemn, but by the fifth, they were all, including Odile, waving, laughing, shouting, and squealing. The teenager already knew how to pose in a feminine way.

Quite at ease, Odile insisted on taking a picture of her papa with the children. He gladly relinquished the Nikon and courteously, by gestures, asked the girl whether he could stand next to her. She agreed and mumbled her name was Nahla. Célestin whispered he was Tino and extended his hand. With hesitation, she took it, and Odile, the little *paparazza*, pressed the shutter. The children admired her skill.

Had he not felt drops of rain on his forehead, they would have stayed longer with Nahla and her siblings. The goodbyes were quick and warm. In the moving car, he exclaimed: "How dear and handsome are those black-eyed children! I feel they accepted and trusted us." She responded softly, while looking through the grubby windshield: "Yes, they are very nice. And Nahla—she's beautiful, looks a little like Osnat."

Célestin threw her a glance: "You're right, there's a resemblance. You probably remember that 'Osnat' means 'belongs to God' in Hebrew. While Nahla... she's close to the soil, to this dry land. She speaks a few words of English and told me her name in Arabic means 'a drink of water.' Incredibly appropriate because she's kind and takes care of the children. For any desert-dweller, a drink of water is cherished as a life-saving gift from Allah."

Worried by the deluge, he slowed down until the car crawled, headlights useless and wipers dealing poorly with the intense rain. He mused aloud: "I hope those children's parents are living and were working somewhere while Nahla watched the young ones. She can do it until she gets married. All the children seemed healthy and well-nourished. And clean, not one face was grimy. She must be a hard worker. When we shook hands, her palm was rough for a girl so young—maybe from doing all the laundry. As there wasn't any in front of the hut, it must have been hanging in the back, and all eight are busy right now moving it indoors."

The rain let up only briefly when they entered Hebron, the largest city on the West Bank. Along treeless, flooded streets, one could barely make out the unattractive square houses with flat roofs. Soon after they noticed the sign for the Caves of the Patriarchs—an important sanctuary for all three religions—the rain intensified mightily and was turning the streets into swamps. He told Odile: "*Chérie,* we must leave Hebron and the ancient Patriarchs, Abraham and the rest, for our next visit to Israel. Now we'd almost need Noah's Ark to negotiate the streets."

Because he could not find any sign showing the direction to the Bethlehem highway, Célestin stopped near the only vehicle in sight—a parked medical emergency van with a Red Crescent on its side—and ran to the driver's window. Although the man was contentedly chewing a massive American-style hamburger, he took pity on the foreigner and invited him to follow. After driving behind the emergency vehicle through a labyrinth of streets and huge puddles, Célestin finally saw the sign for № 60 at one intersection. He gratefully honked and smiled at Odile: "I hope the good man's lunch didn't get cold." Then he added: "Twenty kilometers to Bethlehem. You can now jump to the back seats and change your clothes for the church. Also, the weather will be much cooler than in Be'er Sheva."

17.

It was around four in the afternoon, and only a few agitated but harmless clouds remained in the sky when they arrived in the town claimed by many churches and countless believers to be the birthplace of Jesus Christ. After parking near the Church of the Nativity, he admitted: "Whatever the truth is about Jesus and his birthplace, being in Bethlehem is a unique experience for me. I leave it to you to decide how you feel." Bemused, the girl looked at her papa thoughtfully and chose not to respond.

Bethlehem was a dirty-white town, its slopes consisting of time-worn layers. In one direction, the cross of a dilapidated church stuck out from the rubble, whereas in another, an elegant minaret was visible but with the muezzin's balcony missing. Unwelcoming brown hills lay north toward Jerusalem and east toward the Dead Sea, while the foothills greeted the visitor's eye with piles of garbage. Father and daughter walked around for an hour and then returned to Manger Square. As they stood amidst the crowd in front of the Church of the Nativity, he said: "The whole point, according to Christian tradition, is this: One of the altars in the church, the Greek Orthodox one, is above the cave in which Jesus was born and where Mother of God placed him in the cradle. Like any normal mother would do, one thinks, with her newborn. Called Mary or something else." She nodded, her eyes grave.

In a matter of milliseconds, the pang in his chest made Célestin comprehend that a nurse, not the dying Patrizia, had placed the newborn baby in a medical "cradle." He prayed Odile did not hear the careless words. She said nothing, but painful thoughts might have crossed her mind. A sensitive and kind child, she would not want to hurt him... If he were fortunate, the matter would not come up.

Priests, monks, nuns, and other jostling visitors from the world over noisily roamed Manger Square, sometimes inconsiderately. He begged her: "*Ma douce fille aie de la patience*. Imagine how it must be at Christmastime. I hope we'll somehow manage to enter the church. There used to be three entrances, but two have been walled up, and the third one—look how low and narrow it is." For Odile to see, Célestin had to grab her by the waist and lift her high above the crowd. "The Crusaders did it to prevent Muslims from riding into the church on horses, as they had allegedly done.

"One more thing. The Church of the Nativity is one of the oldest in the world and dates to the fourth century. The story is similar to other places we've been lucky to visit, including Jerusalem. Roman Emperor Constantine the Great and his Empress Mother, sanctified as Saint Helena, built it. That was followed by demolition at the hands of the newly Islamicized Arabs, then the rebuilding by the Crusaders, followed by more destruction, and so on. The important difference, according to the historians of ecclesiastical architecture, is this: The present shape of the church is exactly the one it acquired already in the sixth century under Justinian, Emperor of Byzantium... All right, you're shifting from foot to foot, so let's try to enter the church. After all, we're here in Bethlehem. Besides, it'd be a pity if you put on churchy clothes in vain!"

Pulling Odile by the hand, Célestin squeezed into the church. A bullet-proof cage was a few meters away. It was packed with Palestinian policemen and Mossad types in civilian clothes who monitored the shoving visitors. As father and daughter moved on in tiny steps, it became impossible to ignore the heaving crowd. With its odors, pushing, and Babylon babble, the area near the Greek altar felt like a world market where food and air were scarce. Despite the press, they were taken with ancient mosaics partially preserved on the wall by the altar.

Once outdoors, they walked to the side of the church. Surprisingly unmolested by throngs, three photogenic sisterly monasteries stood there mutely in awe of the ancient Church of the Nativity—Greek Orthodox, Armenian, and Catholic.

"It's only six o'clock, and we might enjoy a cold lemonade at the terrace we saw earlier," proposed Célestin. It belonged to the hotel Al Andalus, located at the southwestern corner of Manger Square. All the tables were occupied, but a gray-haired elderly gentleman who sat alone courteously invited them in French to join him. The man was elegantly dressed and said he was a Canadian from Montreal who came to the Holy Land twice a year. "When I was here last Christmas, the size and density of crowds in Manger Square were incredible. And the police and the army—Israeli, of course. They were everywhere with machine guns, even on roofs."

Monsieur Guillaume and Célestin were mutually fascinated and engaged in a lengthy exchange of confidences. At one point, the man described how he had managed to enter the Church of the Nativity the previous Christmas. "That's an amusing story; I had, as Americans aptly say, preferential treatment. Not because I'm an important Catholic donor or fund-raiser—excuse me, another Yankeeism gobbled up in French Canada—but because... well, for a different reason. I'm acquainted with the Cardinal of Montreal, and he formally recommended me to Giacomo Beltritti at the time when Monsignor Beltritti had just been named by the Vatican as the Latin Patriarch of Jerusalem. And he was the celebrant of the Holy Mass on the 25th of December last year. So I entered through a secret door and had an excellent seat."

Célestin then asked Guillaume to permit him two private questions: "First, why do you visit the Holy Land so often? And second, are you religious, even though, as you said, you were not a big Catholic?" The Canadian looked long into the Frenchman's eyes, then threw his tie over his shoulder and started to unbutton the shirt below the knot. But thinking it over, he stopped after two buttons, returned the tie to its place, and explained to his baffled interlocutor: "I changed my mind because of Odile—I didn't want to frighten the girl. You see, I first thought the sight of violent scars on my chest would be the most succinct response to both of your questions. Three years ago, thanks to my God, I managed to survive a quintuple coronary bypass, the most complicated and dangerous bypass surgery. Since then, I don't consider myself either a Catholic or a religious man in the sense of an institutional religion or church but simply a man who profoundly believes in God. In truth, I believe more deeply when I am here in the Holy Land."

After their cordial parting, Célestin praised the inspiringly sincere man: "What a survivor, I admire him! And how delicate he was with you." As they walked to the car, bells on numerous churches suddenly rang in unison. They stood still as everything in Bethlehem seemed to do. Various bells complemented each other in their invitation to prayer. "How sad this sound is," whispered Odile and heard her father murmur: "Yes, and moving. I'm so glad we came to Bethlehem."

Bypassing Jerusalem, they drove to their hotel in Tel Aviv. It was the evening of a long day when he said: "The people in Israel are open. The healthy attitude seems to infect even foreigners and non-Jews, as with our poignant monsieur Guillaume. Maybe you were partly responsible for his frankness. People don't think the father of an angel can be a bad man who would harm them."

The first thing he did the next day was to call Morkel. There was no answer at either of his numbers, even though it was Sunday, a working day. However, he got Hila at her office: "We recently made wonderful short trips, and soon we'll leave your amazing country. Odile and I naturally want to say adieu to you. Also, she hopes to see Leora again. Can we come on Tuesday? Any time you wish."

Hila called him back half an hour later, saying she had arranged everything with Leora's mother. "Please meet me with Odile on Tuesday around noon at the library. Leora's mother will take the girls from there to the same swimming pool. But I would like to invite you to a goodbye tête-à-tête lunch at the Maiersdorf."

He thanked her: "I can't wait to see you. What about Morky? I couldn't find him this morning. Is he in Jerusalem?" Hila took time to answer: "Unfortunately, since you're leaving soon, Morky and you won't see each other. Several days ago, he suddenly flew to New York. He's got serious problems with Deborah. That's all he wished to tell me on the phone. Oh, he also said he was unable to find you at the hotel and didn't want to leave a message worrying you." "My good, bighearted Morky," thought Célestin when the phone call was over.

* * *

To reach Jericho by car from Tel Aviv, one had to drive through Jerusalem and then continue on a road that plunged from Mount Scopus to the River Jordan. On its west bank stood Jericho—perhaps the oldest inhabited place on earth, with as much as twelve thousand years of documented existence. While he slowly drove downhill, the Dead Sea appeared in the southeast—a shimmering mirage.

"According to Christian teachings, which we both encountered in school, the key event in Jesus's parable of the Good Samaritan took place on this very road from Jerusalem to Jericho. I'm reminding you because an eager pupil like you might enjoy being in an ancient exotic setting her teachers had talked about without truly knowing it."

Odile responded after a minute's reflection: "I remember the parable and want to thank you, *cher Papounet*, for bringing me to Israel—I love it here!" Célestin smiled, keeping his hands on the wheel and his eyes on another sharp curve. Later he said: "In Metz, I'll show you a reproduction of the painting *The Good Samaritan* by the Flemish artist Jacob Jordaens. He did it at the beginning of the seventeenth century. You should know old Jacob was a great painter but had no idea how this dangerous road looked. Nor did he care, I think"

It was still intensely hot when they arrived in Jericho at three in the afternoon. They parked on the main street, drank all the water they had brought, and purchased cheap straw hats. Nearby, there were three ugly signboards. On the biggest, it was written in many languages that Jericho, situated two hundred fifty-eight meters below sea level, was the lowest town in the world. The second stated the Dead Sea was fifteen kilometers southward. The smallest signboard was for Christian tourists and quite ornate: It claimed Jesus of Nazareth had healed blind beggars there.

Jericho was a small and poor Palestinian town. Freshwater springs attracting people to Jericho in ancient times could not be seen. "It's hard to believe," thought Célestin, "that Marcus Antonius—not Shakespeare's but the historical one—gave this town to Cleopatra as a gift. What would a woman, accustomed to the extremes of luxury, think if she came here today? And maybe even then, around the year 34 BC?" He related none of it, feeling Odile needed a rest from history.

In a camp teeming with refugees, they spoke to several Palestinians who knew some English: Sad faces; angry faces and bitter words; eyes without the tiniest glimmer of hope. Not far, Israeli soldiers lounged in jeeps parked under canvas canopies. They seemed glad to talk to unexpected foreign visitors. Odile soon made friends with girls who served their army terms in Jericho. All of them were dressed in impeccable uniforms, as if ready for a fashion catwalk on Dizengoff or Ben Yehuda. They spoke English better than the male soldiers, sometimes even managing to pronounce words without the throaty Hebrew "r." With pretty eyes and charming smiles, they posed for Odile's pocket camera.

At sunset, the pair turned back. From the deepest bottom of the desert, already in shadows, the car climbed through rocks resembling the surface of the Moon to heavens adorned by an embroidery of colors the like of which they had never seen. They stopped at a small gravel clearing next to a precipice and stared silently. While the sky slowly darkened—bright reds becoming purple and lilac, and yellows ochre—they were entranced by the silhouettes of churches, fortresses, and mosques atop ancient hills. *Yerushaláyim!*

18.

To give Odile a fair chance of restful sleep without the intrusion of wild animals, even if friendly and handsome, Célestin described his "Christmas" present—the trip to Kenya—only the next morning. His heart gladdened when he saw the delight on her face. She jumped around the room, attempted a handstand, and repeatedly ran to her father to hug him.

They arrived at the Consulate of Kenya in Ramat Gan at ten o'clock and twenty past had the visa. Namely, when he mentioned at the entrance the name jotted down by Daphne Shechter, a suave dark-skinned gentleman appeared and arranged the issuance in no time. Preferential treatment due to a convenient "connection" overpowered the endemic bureaucratic dilly-dallying at a consular office far from its home in the heart of Africa, as it did, for monsieur Guillaume, at the Church of the Nativity, far from the Vatican. In the car, he explained the quick Kenyan visa was, in a way, Daphne Shechter's gift while Odile was with Dina in the restroom. "*Cher Papa,* it wasn't me who was a 'little rascal' this time!" grinned the girl. "All's well that ends well," said Célestin philosophically.

At the El Al office in the center of Tel Aviv, they bought tickets for a flight to Nairobi on June 10, in only two days, as well as from Nairobi to Paris on June 22. "When we return home, two strenuous weeks of studying for exams await you," said Odile's father. But her laughing, self-assured response was rapid-fire: "That will also end very well!" On the way back to the hotel, they bought boxes of Belgian pralines to give as gifts before leaving Israel.

When they were minutes away from leaving for Jerusalem the next day, she remembered to grab the bikini. When Patrizia and he were Odile's age, Célestin reflected, nine- and ten-year-old girls wore only bottoms on the beach, which remained the Côte d'Azur custom. But the New Puritans demanded tops. However, to the rational Frenchman, it seemed bizarre that the puritanical sheriffs had not dared to protest vociferously when their seventeen-year-old daughters succeeded in reducing both tops and bottoms of their bikinis to pathetic scraps of cloth no bigger than twenty square centimeters.

After reaching Jerusalem, they circumnavigated the entire Old City along the walls and made their way through other parts with which they had fallen in love—forever? Then they drove to French Hill. Rachel and Danny were not at home, so they left a goodbye-for-now note and chocolates with a neighbor. At Linguistics, the secretary who had taken such good care of them was not around, so they left the tastefully wrapped pralines on her desk with thanks. He visited colleagues with whom he had discussed esoteric questions of comparative linguistics.

In front of the Library, while Odile and Leora were hugging, Hila presented Leora's mother. The girls were impatient, so Hila and Célestin were soon left alone. "I'm delighted Israel has been to Odile's and your taste—both are suntanned and in top physical condition. Let's go to lunch, dear friend!"

Hila was elegantly dressed and looked more feminine than when he had first met her. The hair was longer, *décolleté* deeper, skirt shorter. Her skin shone, and her greenish eyes seemed warmer. "This would be the right woman for my Morky," thought Célestin.

Once seated at a corner table on the Maiersdorf terrace, Hila ordered the extra-dry *Tio Pepe* from Jerez de la Frontera as their apéritif. Without further ado, he asked her about Morky and Deborah. Hila responded thoughtfully: "You must've noticed they are not quite compatible, and the marriage survives because Morky gives in on everything. About six weeks ago, after Deborah had flown to New York by herself, supposedly for only a month to be with her daughter Michal, Morky told me he was afraid she wouldn't come back. 'I am convinced,' he said, 'she didn't leave because of Michal. Israel and I are not for her, we're irritating her. She doesn't have the soul for either me or this land.' Maybe you heard something similar from him. Recently, Deborah told him on the phone she didn't want to return and wouldn't sue for divorce only if he went to live in New York—something he won't do. To his core, Morkel is attached to this country and this university. So, what do you think as his friend and as a man?"

"The only sensible outcome for Morky is to get a divorce as soon as possible," said Célestin calmly, "and then to fall on his knees and ask you to marry him. Don't squirm and frown. I know you two have been close for a long time and you must be aware of his desire to become a father. And I hope you'd like a child. Please don't think me crude, but your biological clock, as they say, is ticking. If the two of you don't do what I'm suggesting and what I'll also tell Morky, then you're both—well, I don't know with which dumb animal to compare you. Besides, I am fond of even the stupidest animals."

They both laughed, clumsily chasing away the moment's seriousness. But then, after staring at him, Hila said softly, with emotion: "Your kindness has helped me a lot. Let's have another sherry to celebrate your words—fateful, indeed momentous, for Morky and me. There's no other way of describing them." Hila smiled and got the waiter's attention.

Simha Grenstein was the next topic. Célestin was aware that Hila had known Simha since her arrival in Israel and remembered she was the one who had introduced him, together with Morky, to that wise and complicated man. Therefore, he did not hesitate to describe in detail the long meeting with Simha in café Atara. "It surprised me he was a rabbi, but not overly, and I was happy for him," Célestin recounted, "and because we're in Israel, it certainly didn't shock me his parents had been prisoners in *K. L.* Auschwitz. But when he said he had survived the horrific extermination camp as a baby and added that his birth had taken place in the women's section... Naturally, I did my utmost not to reveal the astonishment and confusion I felt as a result of a quick, almost unwilling—please believe me, Hila—calculation, but... Simha told me he was born in December of 1944—two months after me, as it happens—and that in Auschwitz they'd stopped killing babies only a little earlier, in November. In the end, he just stared at the tablecloth, muttering it was too hard for him to speak of his parents."

They were silent for several minutes before he continued: "I don't wish to poke around anyone's past, to be jabbing into extremely painful experiences. It was important to Simha to talk to me about Auschwitz. Perhaps he wished to show how much confidence he had in me. But two questions are puzzling: How could Simha's mother's lawful husband be his biological father? How is it she wasn't killed in 1944 when the prison guards realized she was with child?"

Hila, when she spoke again, uttered each word slowly: "I understand your dilemmas. I had them myself after the first similar conversation with Simha. Only in the third, he disclosed everything. It happened during three successive evenings—and the two of you won't have such an opportunity. Therefore, I'll tell you the truth. I'll do it because I know he values you a great deal. I'm certain he won't hold it against me, on the contrary! I'll take a burden off his soul. Maybe it was easier for him to share everything with a woman, a Jewess. I don't know. But I'm sure he would've confided in you himself sooner or later." Célestin interrupted her: "Are you certain, Hila? Please don't if..."

She started in a plaintive, monotonous voice: "The last name of Simha's father, only in the sense he was the legitimate husband of his mother, was Grenstein. The Nazis killed him near the end of 1943 in the Warsaw ghetto and transported his mother to Auschwitz. At the beginning of 1944, working as a secretary or interpreter, she more or less willingly engaged in a sexual liaison with a German officer. Raped? No. In March, she told him she was pregnant. The officer, with a rank of major, hated the war and the K. L. He had a wife and children in Dresden. In any case, he did everything he could to keep Simha's mother alive, providing her with better food and other forms of protection.

"Simha was born on the 10th of December 1944. On January 18th, 1945, as a five-week-old baby, he was sent with his mother and fifty-six thousand other prisoners on a death march to Wodzislaw, fifty kilometers from Auschwitz. The officer could not prevent it. He stayed at the camp. The Soviet Army entered Auschwitz on the 27th of January, 1945, and he was executed.

"The mother and baby Simha somehow survived the march resulting in the slow, terrible death of fifteen thousand others. Later they were helped by various international agencies. Later still, Jewish organizations transported them to Israel. Simha learned all these brutal details from his mother who lived until his thirteenth year. Even at her death hour, she was adamant in claiming Simha had not been the result of rape—and so forceful was her assertion he sometimes thinks she was almost proud of it, that being the product of rape was a more despicable possibility."

Hila was staring at the tablecloth, just as Simha had done in Atara at the end of his disclosures, while Célestin was first looking very far, all the way to the Dead Sea, and then long peered at Hila's serious, beautiful face. Israel. The Jews. God! What unthinkable suffering had those people torn from their souls and offered to his eyes and mind... And thus forever trustingly planted into his conscience.

"Thank you, Hila. Yours was an unfathomable service to both Simha and me."

* * *

Wednesday, June 10, 1981. In less than half an hour from the hotel Dizengoff, Odile and Célestin arrived around seven p.m. at Ben-Gurion, Israel's main airport. After filling the tank, they returned the Suzuki undamaged to the company. The final odometer reading was 55778, so they had traveled 1,144 kilometers. Their flight, El Al 511, was scheduled to leave at ten p.m. for Nairobi, so they chatted with the airport security people. He had to list the people with whom they were in contact in Israel and rattled off an incredible multitude from memory. The Mossadniks were impressed by many of the names but most of all when they heard: "Shaike, Lidya, and Karin Ophir."

Father and daughter arrived in Nairobi before sunrise, at four a.m. local time, and plunged into their first African dawn filled with strange and magical sounds.

PART SEVEN

Pink Flamingoes and Necking Giraffes

1.

In the main hall of the Nairobi airport, a massive bronze plaque awaited them. In Swahili and English, it literally stated: "Airport was opened on 14 March 1978 by Father of Our Nation, first President of Republic of Kenya, Mr. Jomo Kenyatta. Five months later, after his death on 22 August 1978, airport received a new name in his honour." Reading the plaque at four in the morning, tired from the flight, was not hard for travelers eager to learn about Kenya.

In Heron Court, a "colonial" hotel with the pretense of luxury, they obtained a fine room on the fourth floor with a modern bathroom for a hundred-thirty Kenyan shillings, about twelve dollars per day. They took out of their luggage only what was needed for a semi-tropical stay of ten days and went to the restaurant to have breakfast. It was simple and tasty: Tea, scrambled eggs with French toast, papaya, pineapple. Afterward, to relax from night travel, they swam in the pool and sat in the shade.

At the airport, they had received lots of maps and information from an agency and immediately booked a three-day safari in Amboseli National Park—with the departure set for four days later. They were delighted by the choice they had made. According to the courteous employees, that wild-animal park was one of the most interesting in Kenya, although—with an area of four hundred square kilometers—certainly far from the biggest. It was situated on the border with Tanzania, about two hundred kilometers south of Nairobi. Getting there required four hours of travel, first on the highway leading to the ancient and rich port city of Mombasa and then on unpaved minor roads. Amboseli was known for its vast herds of elephants, as well as numerous lions, cheetahs, giraffes, zebras, impalas, hyenas, jackals, and many other animals.

Agency employees showed on a map that from the park, they would have an incredible, unparalleled view of the majestic Kilimanjaro. The mountain, with its 5,895-meter-high Uhuru Peak, was in Tanzania, only fifty kilometers southeast of Amboseli. With its three volcanic cones, Kilimanjaro was the highest mountain in Africa, the transcendent "Mount of Whiteness." In the opposite direction, a hundred and thirty kilometers northeast of Nairobi, stood Mount Kenya, after which the country was named; at 5,199 meters, its Peak Batian was only seven hundred meters lower than Uhuru. African employees presented these facts with pride, not blasé in the least. Even though Célestin had known much of it, he was excited to hear about the mountains from Kenyans.

"*Cher Papa*, isn't this a tropical country? We're sitting in the shade, but still, I'm not at all hot. How's that?" He explained: "A sensible question. You see, Nairobi is only two hundred kilometers south of the equator, closer than Metz is from Koblenz, but it's in the highlands, at an elevation of almost 1,800 meters. When we arrived at the hotel, I wanted to carry the luggage to our room, but the porter reasonably grabbed it to get a tip. My idea was to check whether I'd get short of breath. After he took the elevator, I asked you to climb the stairs with me and noticed we got a little winded by the fourth floor. Did you feel it?" Odile said she did but thought they were tired from traveling.

"The altitude will affect us, *ma chérie*, but only for a couple of days until we get acclimatized. It's now almost the middle of June, and the months from June to August are here the coldest ones— the opposite of Metz in our northern hemisphere. Luckily, it turns out that rains are infrequent in June. That's important because when it does rain, it may rain tropical cats and dogs, and the tiny unpaved roads in Amboseli become impassable quagmires. So, we came in the best season, but you'll need a sweater in the evening. Even now, at noon, it can't be more than about eighteen degrees."

"I understand, Papa. But at the airport, I heard you talking about renting a car. So why didn't you when it's now dry season?" Her father grinned: "I'm glad you enjoyed having a car in Israel and wish to drive in Kenya. But it wasn't possible. They didn't want us to have an ordinary car for our safari in Amboseli or the much bigger Park Tsavo—which is also close to Kilimanjaro, but the view isn't as fabulous—because we could get stuck in a morass after a rare June rainstorm. Since I neglected to book in advance, they'll have a car with four-wheel drive only on the last day before our departure: It's too risky. But I managed to reserve two seats in an all-terrain vehicle driven by an experienced local man in the agency's employ. He'll drive us and six other people to Amboseli and during the three days there. Accommodation will be provided. Having co-passengers will be a new experience for independent people like us. It might be pleasant or unpleasant, depending on… who knows what?

"It's to our advantage to have a local driver," decided Célestin. "Listen to what it says about driving in Kenya in this brochure we got, keeping in mind it's a document from the official Tourist Board: 'The rule in Kenya is to drive on the left, but don't rely on that. The driving standard is shocking. Many people, especially those who drive the *matatu* (a communal mini-bus) and *tuk-tuk* (a three-wheel motorized ricksha), don't acknowledge any traffic rules. Also, to say only that those and numerous other vehicles on our streets and roads are defective would be lenient and polite toward their irresponsible drivers.'"

Odile laughed merrily: "Those who wrote the brochure were really honest!" But her father answered cynically: "Maybe. But it's also possible the Tourist Board scribes were bribed by agencies who want visitors to hire their drivers. Anyway, what's important for you to remember is that here they drive on the left. You've never been to a country like India, England, or Japan with such a traffic rule. So, to cross a street, you first look to the right and only then to the left. We'll do it together, at least during the first few days."

While they talked, children of Odile's age played in the pool. They were handsome, healthy, well-behaved kids, monitored by parents sunning themselves on balconies above the pool. All were Africans with very dark skin—as was the case with the airport and hotel staff. When riding in a taxi that morning, the only white people the pair saw were middle-aged men with reddish faces and swollen cheeks: "Most likely of British colonial origin—or inclinations, or manners," thought the Frenchman in Célestin derisively.

Heron Court was in a quiet part of the city. To reach the central area, about a kilometer away, they first had to walk through Uhuru, an old park with tall trees, luxuriant vegetation, and deep shadows. It was frequented by mothers with shiny-eyed children and teenage girls who held hands while they walked chatting and giggling. Men stood or squatted on the edge of paths, some jovial, some serious. Whatever their age, they smoked and unabashedly ogled the girls.

There was not a single person who did not study the pair: They were an unusual sight. For instance, no other white child was in view, even in the care of an African governess. To Célestin, the majority of looks he caught seemed friendly, and he responded to smiles with smiles without fawning. For her part, Odile clutched her father's hand almost feverishly, focusing her gaze on the path. Only rarely, her eyes wandered off to a pretty girl. The two did not talk, as if they had tacitly decided not to reveal their origin.

In truth, there was something unnatural in the situation. In Israel, Célestin and Odile could easily pass as Israelis or at least as Jews from somewhere. In China, they were often the only white people in most settings, but no one paid attention, at least not visibly. Still, he remembered how Odile, then a year younger, resolutely told him in Peking why she did not like that amazing city: "It's full of black-haired children who're always watching me." He, however, was not at all bothered by unwanted attention in China; weeks would pass without him noticing, let alone pondering, the issue. Yet in Uhuru, a park near the center of the cosmopolitan, ex-colonial Nairobi, the impact was immediate—felt by both of them.

Finding himself a member of a tiny minority was a new and almost unique experience for Célestin. He could not resist the impression that the stark difference in skin color—far more pronounced than in China—was by itself responsible for the uniqueness. It was necessary to habituate quickly to external differences so as to feel and behave naturally, to enjoy Africa and Africans.

Reaching the park's eastern edge, they walked on through the city center. A lot of greenery was bordering the streets and the narrow channel of the Nairobi River. The appearance of the filthy body of water certainly did not evoke the origin of its, and the city's, name—"fresh water" in the Maa language of the famous tribe of warriors and hunters, the Maasai. Hardly any building or other object in the city center appealed to the visitors, but they felt no aggressiveness or tension on the crowded streets. Instead, they were immersed in energy and vivacity. Women wore colorful dresses or white blouses with yellow and red skirts, bright like the heat of the tropical noon. Even many young women were overweight. "It must be the local proof of wealth and health, relevant for marriageability," thought Célestin. The men were often slender, wearing light jackets.

They entered a huge covered market that bespoke Nairobi's cosmopolitan, capital-city status. In addition to exotic fruits and vegetables, an amazing variety of meats, fish, and other comestibles was available. On busy stands, there were carved figurines of brave chiefs and ample-bosomed matriarchs, as well as decorative items made of animal skin and ivory. "We won't buy anything made of ivory, *ma princesse*. As you know, elephants are magnificent, highly intelligent animals." Odile, frowning, pulled her father from those counters in a childishly persistent way.

Walking for hours around the city, they saw numerous churchy buildings. Kenya and other parts of central Africa were flooded with missionaries displaying various degrees of fanaticism. Most churches were Catholic, but the Methodist, Baptist, and Pentecostal ones were also present. Minor sects occupied barracks, often with bombastic exhortations on their roofs.

There were also mosques at every step, although the majority of Muslims in Kenya lived near the Indian Ocean, along the Swahili Coast, mostly in Mombasa. Those Muslims, called *Shirazi* and *Shihiri*, had arrived centuries earlier from Yemen and spoke Swahili, not Arabic. Most of them were traders, as were many inhabitants of Mombasa and Nairobi who were originally from Bombay and Kerala in India, and for whom Swahili had also become mother tongue.

In front of the train station, they encountered clamor and a mass of flamboyant vendors but managed to enter the building. In response to Célestin's question, the smartly dressed, smiling lady at the marble ticket counter said the train, traveling at night to evade the heat, took thirteen hours to reach Mombasa, five hundred kilometers away. Outdoors again, he said: "I wanted to inquire because the thousand-year-old city, once the capital, is probably astounding: colorful architecture, Arabs speaking Swahili, tropical climate by the Indian Ocean. Pity, but this time we won't go there. Far too far, and one doesn't see anything in the countryside at night." Odile complained: "*Quel dommage!*"

Walking back to the city center, he conveyed several facts: "The train to Mombasa is an ancient one. It's called the Uganda Railway, although the line never reached that neighboring country but stopped at Kenya's western border, the vast Lake Victoria. The track was constructed at the beginning of the century with a narrow gauge, only a meter wide"—he demonstrated—"between the rails; such a track is easier to build when the terrain is rugged and the climate tropical."

In the hotel Excelsior's café, they found a corner table and ordered a papaya juice and a Tusker Lager, noticing there were no other white people around. Well-dressed, mostly male patrons spoke Swahili and English. Odile reminded her father that he was going to tell her more about the Uganda Railway. Célestin waited for the drinks to arrive: "*Bien,* the railroad was *not* built by the local Kenyans, Africans, but by people from what was then British India, yet now consists of no less than three separate countries—more about it another time. As for Kenya, it was part of British East Africa. So, believe it or not, the British—*Europeans*—transported in ships some forty thousand laborers from one of their enormous colonies in Asia to another one in Africa. Those people were called coolies and paid a pittance." Ten percent did not survive even the initial sea voyage and land transport."

Odile stared at her father. Mombasa did not seem attractive anymore. He carried on: "*Oui, ma chère fille, la vie était certainement terrible pour les travailleurs.* In addition to the daily toil under harsh conditions, this is what happened. One year, I read it was 1898, while a bridge over the Tsavo River was being built, laborers were for several months the targets—you'll be aghast—of two man-eating lions. They were the kind of male lions without a mane. The pair would sneak into the camps at night, kill a couple of men, and pull their bodies into the bush to devour them. You can imagine how the victims' screams affected the others. What panic must have ensued! The laborers began to escape from the work site en masse. In the end, the British railroad owners somehow managed to kill both man-eaters. The company admitted to twenty-eight victims, but other sources reported as many as one hundred thirty-five." After a long silence, Célestin apologized: "*Je suis desolé, mon trésor,* but I had to tell you about this awful and strange event in Kenya's history. I wanted you to understand how those people lived, how they suffered, and what the European colonial powers did for the sake of profit. Please remember our France did similarly terrible things in its colonies in Africa and Asia..."

After mulling things over, Odile said: "Children think *all* lions are terrifying and eat people. Yet from this story, alright, it's not just a story but history, it seems those two lions were exceptions. Is it because they didn't have manes?" He responded cautiously: "*Non, mon enfant,* there are many maneless lions. It's a sort living mostly in Africa. Those two man-eaters were exceptions among such lions. There was at the time a so-called theory, I've read, which went as follows: The victims were Indians, often vegetarians, and their body odor was maybe particularly tempting to the lions. Most likely utter colonial nonsense, but who knows? Anyway, please don't forget why I talked to you about such horror in the first place."

"I won't, Papa, but I have a question. While we're sitting here, many people talk among themselves a little and look at us a little. Why?" Célestin was not surprised because he was aware of his own thoughts about being in a minuscule minority. He said: "They're looking at us in part because you're the only child, and perhaps there's no local custom of fathers coming to a café with a young child. But surely the most important reason is we're the only white people. You noticed everyone looking at us in Park Uhuru—I know because you were clutching my hand and looking straight ahead. Wasn't it so?"

Odile agreed, so Célestin continued: "No one is looking at us in a hostile way. They're just curious, as we are about them. We came to Kenya desiring to discover something new. Almost everyone around us here has black skin. To you, it seems they're very different from us and in many ways they are, but it doesn't mean we should be uneasy. Also, keep in mind that during your childhood in Metz and Koblenz, you hardly ever saw a black person. However, there were some, and think about how they felt surrounded by white people. A black man would have been not only in a minority but often completely alone. All kinds of different people occupy our planet, so one ought to enjoy the diversity. I agree it's not always possible, not entirely. But we'll adapt and by being ourselves have a good time. Isn't that right, *ma douce fille?*"

Precisely at the moment when Odile was responding affirmatively, a large Kenyan man abruptly sat down at their table, and the girl recoiled in alarm. He did it without asking for permission, having pulled a chair from a nearby empty table with a grating sound. Célestin nevertheless tried to welcome the man but asked himself: "Am I sincere, or am I not objecting only because he's black? Or because I imagine his harsh manner is a local custom? Or because I'm as curious as he likely is? Or because he's a decently dressed, middle-aged man, with a broad smile? Who knows? But here we go!"

The man's face was deep black but not blue-black—if such a description made sense. "I'm greeting you in English, although I'm sure you're not a pompous Englishman; also, it's unlikely you speak my native language, as I'm of the Kikuyu people," said the gentleman in an animated voice. "I should add I'm a respected employee of Kenya Post, very busy on a boring job!"

As if he had been waiting the whole day for the chance, he explained: "Because I am the firstborn son of my father's wife number one, I was given the important name 'Matenge,' which means 'buck.' You see, long ago, before the arrival of the bandits from England, our clan owned many herds of goats on the land near our stupendous Mount Kenya. And for goats, the buck is the boss!"

Célestin took a moment to tell Odile he would later explain many things of which Matenge spoke. "Polygamy still exists all over Kenya, including in my immediate family. The political situation is stable because our President, Daniel Toroitich arap Moi (*arap* means *son of*), is popular and capable. He became president after the death of Jomo Kenyatta in 1978 and won the election two years ago as the only candidate. As for the one-party system—well, we're still too undeveloped to play at politics. Moreover, in comparison to the newly independent countries nearby, we're doing better than any of them except Nigeria, which had the chance in the seventies to leap high above the rest of Black Africa but failed because of corruption and the high living of their chiefs. Since you're probably wondering about crime, I'll tell you. Last year, the Organization of African Unity held a congress in Nairobi, due to which surveillance increased threefold. Personally, I've never had problems with criminals, although there are lots of them, including very young ones. The police leave alone citizens like you and me, but they've shot to death many street thugs caught breaking into shops and cars."

Matenge's curiosity about France was assuaged. Is *La Poste* functioning well? Are citizens satisfied with the service? Do the police open people's mail? Father and daughter cordially declined the hospitable Kenyan's offer of a drink and warmly parted from him.

* * *

Since Kenya is an equatorial country, sunrise occurs around six in the morning and sunset at six in the evening throughout the year. But because it was their first day in Nairobi, Célestin and Odile were surprised they encountered a dark sky at eight o'clock when they emerged from the Excelsior café. Streetlight was minimal, and cabs and tuk-tuks were nowhere in sight, but the air was delightful. Besides, he realized they would need only about twenty minutes on foot to the hotel. After a casual walk taking about half of that time, they arrived at the entrance to Park Uhuru. The beginning of the path was lit. On the left, a few men were smoking silently, watched by two policemen who stood in deep shadows across the path.

But soon the park lights disappeared, and the stars must have been covered by clouds: Uhuru became almost pitch dark. Odile walked close to her father, grasping his hand with both of hers. Small, silent groups of people could be glimpsed but no policemen. Célestin suddenly felt that the two of them were vulnerable, defenseless. Lights from the cars occasionally passing on the nearby street illuminated his shirt and Odile's skirt, both white, as chance or fate would have it, and "our white faces, of course," he thought wryly. He mercilessly castigated himself: "I've committed a stupid error by stubbornly not looking for a taxi longer, as any normal person with a child would've done when finding himself at night in a strange city." He whispered a few words of encouragement to Odile and extended his stride: "We won't run, but we'll step lively; please canter without breaking into a gallop. *Allons-y, ma fille!*"

They arrived in front of Heron Court out of breath. Célestin hugged his daughter tightly and said he was proud of her courage. "I'm sorry for having done something dumb, *mon trésor*. I was overconfident, smug. It's true that no one threatened us or tried to rob us. Still, the fact is that we were completely alone. And those people who stood around in the dark shadows…" Odile mutely embraced her father.

The two went to their room to change before dinner. While the girl was washing up and polishing her shoes, he phoned Mrs. Lina, Daphne Shechter's cousin. She was delighted and immediately recounted that Daphne had called from Eilat and told her all about him and his sweet daughter. She would phone again the next day with a plan for an outing, as her husband Saul was out for a walk.

The hotel bar-restaurant was incongruously called Buffalo Bill's and the customers wishing to drink at the bar counter, including women, had no choice but to straddle cowboy saddles. The food, however, was Kenyan, nourishing, and tasty. They ate an excellent beefsteak with green beans, spinach, and the local vegetable specialty *irio*, which consisted of mashed sweet potatoes, peas, and corn.

During dinner, Odile suddenly asked: "Those people in the park: If they thought we were rich, they'd be right, wouldn't they? When we were having breakfast with Mathilde in that Paris café you told me so. Remember?" He smiled broadly calling to mind his daughter's amusing "bourgeois" query: "Your memory is amazing! Let's admit those people would be right. But they wouldn't profit much by accosting us and demanding money, or, in the worst case, by roughly robbing us. My pockets contained only about seventy shillings, and there were another three hundred inside my sneakers. Trifling. In your mini backpack, there was nothing valuable except the single-use, pocket Kodak, with which we took photos all day. Well, we'd lose those photos, but being hard-headed, tomorrow we'd visit the same places and take similar ones. As for our passport, money, checks, my watch, your jewelry, the Nikon—it's all in our safe at the hotel manager's office. You know I do this in hotels, always including your jewelry. We're experienced travelers, *ma fille*, and don't easily surrender to muggers and petty criminals."

2.

Their morning meal was neither Kenyan nor cowboy-style but a comical "English" breakfast consisting of sunny-side-up eggs swimming in oil, burnt beans, and triangular pieces of thin toast covered with slightly rancid butter. "This seems to poke fun clumsily at English colonials' taste in food, or last night's competent chef overslept," grumbled the Frenchman. They were too polite to reject what the young waiter Mukami brought, but left the milk meant for their tea untouched. After the meal, Célestin skimmed *The Kenya Times* and read aloud the news snippet that caught his eye—an understated "hmm" being his only comment: "A young man, fifteen years old, who had worked for a hauler in the town of El Wak, in Mandera County, was yesterday sentenced to one month in jail because he had stolen merchandise from the lorry belonging to his boss. The court also ordered he be caned six times."

Odile remained mum, but her father consulted the waiter who spoke without hesitation: "The sentence is nothing unusual. The boy will be struck six times with a thin cane on his bare bottom. It depends on the court-appointed executor or 'hangman,' as we say, how much force will be used. Which depends on how much money the hangman will get from the boy's dad. And on the hangman's relationship with the lorry's owner. Also..." The voluble Mukami needed ten minutes to explain the effect of the complex web of human relations in a typical small town on the way court sentences were carried out. The town was located in a mostly Muslim region in the distant northeast of Kenya near the border of Somalia.

Back in their room, Lina called: "Saul sends his greetings. We thought it would be nice for the four of us to spend a day at Lake Nakuru, a world-famous National Park with literally over a million pink flamingoes. Our children adored the sight when they were Odile's age, and she'll certainly also love it. There are many other animals around Nakuru. The park is a hundred and seventy kilometers northwest of Nairobi, and it'll take three hours to get there. We could pick you up in our jeep tomorrow morning at seven. All right, Célestin?"

He looked quickly at Odile and smiled, telling Lina: "Thank you, what a fabulous plan! We'll be ready. But listen, Daphne and Dina told us you and Saul have twins, a boy and a girl, only a little older than Dina. Are they busy tomorrow, or is there not enough space in the jeep?" "No, there would be space for six; thank you for thinking of our twins. But as of just a few weeks ago, Daniel and Daniella are together in the USA! They have been accepted for postgraduate studies in geology at the University of Colorado in Boulder. So Saul and I are alone in the house after twenty-two years. Our niece Dina, of whom we're very fond, wrote to us saying she would like to visit for several months after she's done with the army, but her parents were reluctant to let her. It doesn't surprise me now that I've experienced how empty our house feels. Oh, excuse me for boring you like a typical Jewish mother." Célestin's chuckle was good-natured as they said goodbye. But then, after explaining the Lake Nakuru plan to Odile, he suddenly embraced her firmly, as if she had just turned twenty-two and was about to travel somewhere far.

Before heading to the city center, they decided not to avoid Park Uhuru because of the unpleasant event, or non-event, the previous evening. The plan was to behave as if they belonged. Indeed, while strolling along the same path, she recognized some of the girls and exchanged shy smiles with them.

Through a maze of streets near the University of Nairobi, the pair walked north and after half an hour reached the National Museum of Kenya. Their visit began in the main building, where they were awed by the extraordinary display of various geological formations, particularly rocks and fossils from the Great Rift Valley—which was, in fact, a gigantic crack in Earth's crust. And they were delighted to spot Lake Nakuru on a wall map of the valley.

An entire wing of the building was devoted to the exceptionally important paleoanthropological discoveries by Richard Leakey: *Australopithecus africanus*, *Homo habilis*, *Homo erectus*. Leakey was born in Kenya in December 1944, two months after

Célestin, and still lived there. Odile was happy to read he had a pony as a child. While they were examining the anthropological exhibits, it was hard to convince the girl, and even himself, that the findings were 1.5 to 3.7 million years old.

A separate small building was devoted to reptiles—crocodiles, turtles, and incredible snakes—but he left for the end what she would find the most appealing: the unusual decorations for head and body the natives had produced, as well as their tools, pottery, food utensils, weapons, and jewelry.

Filled with impressions and munching salted corn on the cob sold to them by a charming street vendor four or five years older than Odile, they cheerfully talked on the way back. After a light lunch at the New Stanley on Kimathi Street, they returned to their hotel in a noisy, snug tuk-tuk. Célestin swam in the pool for a long time while she played nearby with visiting Ugandan girls who had a multicolored beach ball. From a balcony, their parents watched benevolently. However, his behavior may have lifted eyebrows: Adults, foreign or domestic, should have more important things to do—like gossiping—than waste time swimming. That evening, they went to sleep early, for the exciting trip to pink flamingoes awaited.

* * *

Lina and Saul were pleasant people in their forties, somewhat on the heavy side and content with life. They brought little gifts for Odile and devoted attention to her. Célestin apologized: "I realized today is your Shabbat." Lina smiled: "It's kind of you to remember. But like most Jews here, we don't practice the custom: We work on Fridays and don't work on weekends. There are synagogues... and antisemitism. So, in our family and with friends, Saul is Saul, but with the English, he is Paul, like Saint Paul!"

During the drive, Célestin sat next to Saul, with Lina and Odile in the back seats. "Both of us and also Daphne were born in Kenya," began Saul, "and although we've visited Israel several times, we've never wished to live there. Nor anywhere else, for that matter—for example, in England, where we could've gone in

1963 when Kenya gained independence. There have been difficult times, notably in the fifties during the Mau Mau violent rebellion against the British colonial authorities. At the time, we'd been married for only a few years and managed a tiny coffee plantation when the rebels one night set our house on fire. Luckily, we were spending the night with my parents in Nairobi, but the arsonists, the killers, seeing our jeep in front of the house—they stole it—probably thought we were inside being burned alive. We then abandoned the farm and moved to Nairobi, where our twins were born in 1958. The Mau Mau rebellion was crushed in 1959, with lots of blood spilled. Nevertheless, one of the chief guerrilla leaders, Jomo Kenyatta, became the first president of the Republic of Kenya four years later, as you know."

Célestin was captivated by the subtle nuances of African colors he had seen nowhere else but still managed to listen carefully to Saul. Remembering Sophie, the English girl in Jerusalem, whose parents had escaped from Kenya in 1957, he asked Saul to tell him more about the Mau Mau. "That uprising—well, one can assuredly say it was a just rebellion by the Kikuyu tribe... Kenyatta was a Kikuyu, born in Ngenda, a village between Nairobi and Mount Kenya. They are the biggest tribe in the country, although even they are no more than a quarter of the native population. According to legends and tradition, the most important thing for the Kikuyu was ownership of land, and before the arrival of the English, they possessed far more of it than any other tribe. However, the invaders brutally grabbed much of the most fertile land of volcanic origin on the southern and western slopes of Mount Kenya. Vast coffee and tea plantations were developed on the Kikuyu land by the British colonists and other arrivals from Europe, including many Germans. Fortunes were made at the expense of the Kikuyu people by those robbers."

Lina, who was chatting with Odile, added to Saul's narration: "Kenya is rich, and the English did not hesitate to use force to keep it as their colony. Churchill himself was very involved. You wouldn't believe how much of everything imaginable they sucked out of Kenya during the Second World War. It's often mentioned how they built the railway from Mombasa to Lake Victoria, but that was primarily for their selfish benefit. They brought thousands upon thousands of workers from India by sea for the project, and after the railway was finished, they settled the coolies here as a demographic counterweight to the Kikuyu. Divide and rule. The Mau Mau consisted mostly of the Kikuyu, so it's not surprising they called themselves the *Land* and Freedom Army; they did horrific things but so did the British to the natives. The counter-insurgency measures included the sequestration of eighty thousand Kikuyu in abysmal camps under inhuman conditions, and almost half of the rebels, close to five thousand, were killed."

Célestin listened with great interest, though making sure his daughter did not feel neglected. In truth, it was not necessary because Odile was not only becoming fond of Lina but also enjoyed the wonderful landscape. So it happened she was the first to see, on the right side, the immense, lonely, snow-covered Mount Kenya. The girl exclaimed loudly, with delight and wonder. Lina said: "Yes, my golden child, that's the beautiful Lady Kenya! It has three peaks, all over five thousand meters high. The one we see is the highest, Mr. Batian."

After they had passed through the village of Naivasha, Saul found a safe place to stop. From there, the giant mountain was even more breathtaking. Standing by the jeep, Saul explained: "We're halfway to Lake Nakuru. Batian is about a hundred and ten kilometers from here. From Nairobi, the mountain is farther by some twenty kilometers but even if it were closer, it wouldn't be visible because of pollution. No wonder Kirinyaga is a sacred mountain for the Kikuyu and Maasai tribes."

"And what do your English acquaintances say about the nasty history?" Célestin asked when they resumed the journey. Saul responded readily: "You said that correctly, 'acquaintances'; among them, we don't have friends. Without a single exception, they have an entirely different attitude toward everything Lina and I've told you—even though it wasn't their house burnt down but ours! Already ten years earlier, after Israel had gained independence in 1948—I was still a teenager—the English advised my parents and many other Jews to leave Kenya and move to Israel. The motive behind the advice wasn't a friendly one. Apart from wanting to take over our businesses cheaply, they were offended that Israel, by its independence, had finally got rid of the lordly British Mandate. Yet we, and other Jews, were born in Kenya and regarded ourselves as Kenyans. As for the English, many escaped with their money to England after Kenyan independence in 1963, displeased to see their unlimited power gone. Many escaped to South Africa. The Boers, the Afrikaners, don't like them but have to tolerate them: Old colonial money rules."

For a while, they devoted themselves to the gorgeous views in silence, and then it was Lina's turn again: "For you to know us better, we should reveal our family's strategy. One fact Saul and I had to consider was that our children didn't want to serve in the army in Israel. What regularly happened was this: One day they admired Dina for doing it, and the next they felt sorry for her because of the two 'lost' years. Besides, all four of us are convinced Israelis are clever and practical people, so if the twins wish one day to live in Israel, they'll be able to manage it smoothly, thanks to their high academic degrees from America."

Saul jumped in: "Yes, particularly if they end up getting doctorates in geology, as is their current hope. You are aware that the Great Rift, over five thousand kilometers long, begins in Israel. From the Sea of Galilee, it runs below the River Jordan and the Dead Sea—where you two were recently—and stretches all the way to Lake Turkana in the northwest of Kenya. Then it continues southward to..." Here Célestin interrupted him with a smile and said, winking at Odile: "Yes, southward to Lake Nakuru, as we saw on a wall map at the Museum of Kenya!"

He went on: "You're undoubtedly right about top geologists being in demand in Israel. And thanks for sharing your family plans." He added he had read a lot about the Great Rift and turned to Odile: "Isn't it special that we swam in Galilee, crossed the River Jordan several times, and floated in the Dead Sea? At Lake Nakuru, we'll arrive close to the southern end of that gigantic geological crack in our planet. You heard how long it is: Five thousand kilometers—like from Moscow to the middle of Mongolia! And we did that too, by train! How fortunate we are, *mon bijou*. In some places, the width of the Rift is as much as eighty kilometers. Right, Saul?" His words confirmed, she was remembering their fantastic travels, glad her father mentioned them.

Looking fondly at Odile, Lina felt the need to speak of the twins: "We took our children often to Lake Nakuru from a young age. One can't swim there, but they fell in love with flamingoes. Later, they outgrew the birds and became enamored of the chain of volcanoes stretching to the north along the Rift Valley toward Lake Turkana. Some of those volcanoes are still active. And now, both will become geologists! Daniel plans to specialize in plate tectonics, whereas Daniella adores vulcanology. Hmm. As you know, there are no volcanoes in Israel, at least for now, and certainly none are needed!"

Célestin responded seriously: "For Kenya's sake, I hope they'll choose to live and work here. Africa needs scientists born on this land, people of all races who are familiar with local culture and tribal customs and languages of Kenya." Lina and Saul wholeheartedly agreed. Célestin then showed Odile some details on a map of southeast Africa: "The huge deep rift, a humongous fracture, continues from Lake Nakuru to the south. Here, you see, at the border of Kenya and Tanzania, the mighty crack is located under the extraordinary Lake Natron and then turns westward. It reaches Lake Tanganyika, which lies in the north-south direction. That super-elongated lake is also connected, in a way, with our travels because it's the second deepest in the world. And what do you think, which is the deepest?" She immediately responded: "Our Lake Baikal! And Lake Tanga... I didn't grasp the name properly, but you told me in Siberia it was the second deepest. Don't you remember, Papa?" Everyone laughed, and the father relished the moment.

Saul resumed his account, feeling love for Africa: "The Great Rift extends beyond Lake Tanganyika to the south and ends only on the border of Zambia and Zimbabwe, in the lower reaches of the Zambezi River, not far east of the renowned waterfalls classi-fied as the largest in the world. Their name in the Chitonga-Zambezi language is *Shungu Namutitma*, Boiling Water, whereas the colo-nial British name was Victoria Falls. What stunning beauties and unimaginable riches this magnificent continent possesses! Céles-tin, you probably know that Zimbabwe only last year gained inde-pendence from the British Crown and its colonial, racist heir called Rhodesia—unlike Zambia, which became independent soon after Kenya, in 1964." He had indeed learned about Zim-babwe's independence in France before leaving with Odile for China at the beginning of July of the previous year: "People in France were delighted, but if you probed for their true motives, you found it was just another aspect of the historical Anglo-French rivalry and mutual antipathy."

"I'm aware of those sour feelings," Saul snickered. He kept driving prudently and elucidated more facts: "You mentioned Lake Natron, Célestin, and rightly called it extraordinary. It's one of the so-called 'soda' lakes, which Lake Nakuru is too, but Natron is far more extreme. The alkalinity in Lake Natron—bicarbon-ates, sodium carbonates, hydroxides—can reach the level of am-monia. Also, it's exceptionally salty, so caustic it can burn the skin and eyes of birds. When there isn't much rain, and the ther-mal springs at the bottom are active, Natron's temperature may reach sixty degrees. You see, the lake's greatest depth is less than two meters; Nakuru is even shallower, with an average depth of only thirty centimeters."

Having listened with amazement, Odile timidly asked: "So there can't be flamingoes at the weird lake, right?" Lina hugged her: "You got it almost right. Natron is an extremely inhospitable place for the majority of birds and animals, but that includes predators which elsewhere destroy baby flamingoes. Therefore, small islands in Lake Natron are like safe cribs for them! Also, flamingoes' bodies and organs have adapted to conditions pre-vailing at lakes like Natron. They have hard skin on their bodies, scales that preclude burns on their feet, and can drink boiling water. Mother Nature, darling."

When they arrived at the village of Gilgil, Mount Kenya looked even more magnificent. Parking in front of an eatery on a hillock, Saul suggested: "We left early and still have forty kilometers to Lake Nakuru, so it might be wise to stretch our legs and have a bite. Here we're even closer to the mountain than when Odile first saw it from Naivasha—the elevation must be about one thousand eight hundred meters, same as Nakuru." Lina added: "We've known the owners of this modest place, a husband-and-wife team, for twenty years. She's Maasai and he Kikuyu. Such marriages are not rare when both parties own land. And even though they don't have children, he didn't acquire another wife, which he could've done by both tradition and prosperity. Now, *that's* a rarity. The couple cooks together, another rarity, and skillfully prepares typical local dishes, such as *mutura* and *ukuru*. You'll see."

Greetings boomed from the small restaurant's entrance: "*Karibu! Karibu!*" The smiling hosts, both in their early sixties, yelled their welcome in Swahili, and Lina and Saul responded with "*Asante!*" Then Lina asked: "*Habari?*" (*How is it going with you?*) and received "*Yambo sana!*" (*Very well, good health!*) from the hostess. It turned out that Lina and Saul had a respectable command of three tongues, Swahili, Kikuyu, and Maasai, while the hosts knew some words of English.

The planned light meal became a substantial lunch. Célestin was a typical Frenchman as far as food was concerned—a connoisseur but also an adventurer willing to try anything once; he had attempted to teach his daughter the same approach. At Gilgil, they ate with pleasure everything served, only later inquiring what the dishes contained. *Mutura* consisted of sausages filled with intensely spiced goat blood and entrails, with peas and spinach, whereas *ukuru* was roasted goat meat with a puree of fermented corn, millet, and another high-altitude African cereal. For unknown reasons, the strange puree was very tasty. Dishes with entrails existed in many regions of France and Germany, so *mutura* was not too odd. However, father and daughter agreed to think twice before ordering adult goat meat in the future.

They drove through Lanet Gate of the Lake Nakuru National Park, three kilometers from the northeast corner of the lake, and continued southward along the eastern shore. Célestin showed Odile the map they had obtained at the entrance. The lake was an irregular ellipse with a north-south longer axis of about twelve kilometers and a shorter axis of no more than six and a half. By its shape and orientation of the longer axis, Nakuru irresistibly reminded him of Galilee—so distant, sitting at the northern end of the Great Rift. Although the similarity between the two lakes ended there, he mentioned it casually to his co-passengers. Saul agreed while Lina and Odile could not recall Galilee's shape. Célestin was not surprised that the girl's eyes acquired a thin veil of gloom because of her memory lapse, but the mild sulks were immediately transformed into a bright smile when he reminded her of harp and double bass. Besides, that was thrown into insignificance a few moments later when the child in Odile was astonished by the unforgettable sight of innumerable pink flamingoes densely lined up along the lakeshore. Behind them, one could see numerous pelicans and cormorants—but they were not pink!

At a place where it was permitted, they came out of the jeep, spellbound by the dreamlike pink fantasy. Odile was so impressed by the lake and the birds that she neglected her camera until much later. They were visiting Lake Nakuru in July, the best month for avoiding the heavy rains and the onslaught of tourists. And because of the high elevation, the temperature was ideal, in the low twenties. Under the crystal-blue sky, in the clean, unpolluted air, the steep slopes of the Great Rift Valley arose near the lake, with cliffs at several levels. On shelves covered by the savanna grass stood the picturesque Kenyan *Euphorbia* trees: They looked like chandeliers turned upside down. Visitors also spotted many perfect specimens of the fully grown Fever trees.

The lake's size was sixty-five square kilometers, Célestin read to Odile, but the park covered a three times bigger area. On the map, one could see a passable road around the entire lake, always not farther than three kilometers from the water.

While crawling along the rim, the birds continued collectively to enact the role of a pink curtain in front of the lake. "In
Kenya, and elsewhere in Africa south of the Sahara, the dominant species of the flamingo is less tall—though still measuring a
meter—than are other species," said Saul. They could see that all
the birds were frequently bending their long necks to grab something below the water's surface. "What is it flamingoes are hunting?" asked the girl. Saul grinned: "Well, not really hunting but
certainly ingesting non-stop. The birds swallow an astonishing
quantity of small pieces they tear with their beaks off the countless clusters of blue-green algae growing in the warm alkaline
water of this and other lakes in the Great Rift Valley—grow, believe it or not, thanks to the flamingoes' excrement. Interestingly,
this sort of algae is poisonous as food for almost all other birds
and animals: The algae create chemical substances that destroy
the liver of the unadapted species."

After a while, Odile said: "So the people around here can't steal
the food from flamingoes by taking those poisonous algae from
the lake, and the algae would disappear if there were no flamingoes and their excrement." Saul praised her: "Perfect! You, dear
Odile, are on the way to becoming an expert in African ecology."

Lina smiled: "Perhaps you've already asked yourself why the
flamingo is so prettily pink. Well, that's because of those same
blue-green algae and the pigment they contain. And you'd probably also like to know what the birds do when Lake Nakuru freezes.
Simple: It never does, despite the high altitude. Here too, there
are thermal springs at the lake's bottom, although not as many
nor as hot as in Lake Natron. You'll see even hot geysers when we
get to the western shore."

The sharp girl had another question: "The Dead Sea and Lake
Nakuru are both very strange, and I know few creatures can survive in them, but they still must somehow be different from each
other. How?" Saul and Lina exchanged a glance, nostalgically recalling the questions their twins had posed as children. He let
Lina answer: "Yes, both of those water kingdoms are strange, and
both are in the Great Rift. How remarkably rare you've been to

both so early in life! I'll tell you what Saul and I know about the similarities and differences. The Dead Sea is super-salty, ten times more so than an ordinary sea. Its alkalinity is average, so it isn't a soda lake. Nor is it quite dead because various microorganisms live in it. Lake Nakuru, in contrast, is super-alkaline, an out-and-out soda lake; however, it's also rather salty, although nowhere near the Dead Sea level. The percent of ordinary cooking salt in Nakuru depends on rain and evaporation: I'm not sure, but I think it's between thirty and fifty percent."

Odile felt privileged to have the hosts' binoculars at her disposal. At one place, they watched ostriches. The mature males were almost two-and-a-half meters tall, with the females shorter by a third; the shaggy chicks were playful. Then, they were astounded by a group of giraffes, called the Maasai or Kilimanjaro giraffes. The animals, the tallest on Earth, were browsing in the crowns of acacias. As Saul explained, the bulls of these ruminant ungulates grow to five and a half meters in height and well over a ton in weight. The cows are smaller and have only two bony protrusions on their heads, whereas most bulls have a third *ossicone* between their eyes.

Utterly fascinated, they scrutinized them for a long time. Odile suddenly noticed the strange behavior of two specimens: The giraffes stood in front of each other swinging their long necks and hitting each other exclusively across the necks. "What are they doing?" shouted Odile. Lina laughed: "They're fighting! But don't be afraid, they won't kill each other. Those are adult males using only their muscular, powerful necks to fight. The victor— one with a stronger neck and a harder skull—will gain access to females. Their mating is governed by the harem principle: Your dad will explain it better than I can. This male symbolic fight using necks as weapons is predictably called 'necking' by zoologists, but it's amusing that the same term in slang refers to the intimate actions of young women and men."

"Ah, Lina, Lina, thank you! It'll take me an hour tonight to explain it to my inquisitive daughter," Célestin pretended to be irritated. "I'm lucky you didn't discuss the mating of hippos in a muddy pond." They all tittered except Odile—who did not long remain in a quandary and began to prepare hippo queries.

The girl adored zebras—so much like horses yet so different! She could not imagine her Pasha having stripes, and Saul told her something interesting: "You may not know that each animal has a different pattern of stripes, so no two zebras are identical. The same holds for the spots on the coat of giraffes: Each individual has a unique distribution of spots. And as everyone knows, no two people have identical fingerprints. The incredible, mysterious geometry of nature."

In a savanna with bushes and acacias, they saw several Southern White rhinos grazing as peacefully as cows in Holland. "Ooh, how big and fat they are! Each must weigh a ton," exclaimed Odile. "And they're not white as is written in the Nakuru brochure, but gray. Are they just dusty?" Saul expected such a reasonable question: "All right, dear girl, first, regarding weight. The giant over there, the one on the right, is certainly an adult male, and it wouldn't surprise me if he weighed over *two* tons. And his huge front horn—it must be a meter and a half. But for a mammal of that size, he has a tiny brain weighing only about half a kilo. Incidentally, when you see a rhino with two horns, like the Southern Whites here, you know it's African; Indian ones have a single horn. And look how the one over there is tearing grass from its roots? It's because rhinos don't have front teeth, so they use their thick, hard lips to grab the greenery."

Odile's eyes sparkled: "How amazing it all is! But what about the color?" "Yes, the color, that's complicated," admitted Saul. "In Africa, there are two species of rhinoceros, both with two horns, called the Southern White and the Southern Black. However, even though they certainly differ in anatomical details, they're both of a color ranging from grayish to yellowish-brownish. In short, they don't differ in color. So, the two-ton White is not dusty but of a genuine gray color and White only by name. Also, the Southern Black ones got the name only to be distinguished from the allegedly White ones. For a while, it was thought the White rhinos were called white because of an error in translation from

Dutch-Afrikaans into English, but this idea was later nixed. The conclusion is that the reason for the incorrect color naming is not known! And it doesn't matter because the genetic differences between the two species have been correctly described. Now it's all clear, right?"

Mirth ruled the car. "So, Odile," Saul went on, "if you ever get a difficult homework and wish to put your dad in a like predicament, ask him: 'Why do African rhinos and those from the Indonesian island of Sumatra have two horns, whereas those from India and Java, which is also an island in Indonesia, have only one?'" Everyone laughed, including Célestin, while the rhinos kept grazing peacefully, their enormous heads lowered to the ground. Saul pointed at them: "They are Whites grazing; if they were Blacks, they'd be browsing leaves from the bushes."

The mood changed when Lina said: "What's not funny but horrible is that poachers are mercilessly killing rhinos wherever they live. It's because of the horns. In Southeast Asia, rhino horns are in high demand as ornaments and even more for use in traditional medicine, ground into powder. On the black market, they cost as much as gold, yet horns consist of keratin, the same protein found in hair and nails."

The small group was having a fun day. At a distance of less than fifty meters from the jeep, they saw several cheetahs. One of them ran at full speed, incredibly fast, as if hunting something—or was "just exercising his sprint," Saul joked about the speediest animal on the planet. "From zero to a hundred and ten kilometers an hour, the cheetah manages in three seconds flat and would put to shame a Ferrari," gloated Saul, proud of African animals.

A couple of lions were lying in the shade. Odile could not believe her eyes when they encountered these beautiful animals so close to the jeep—free in the savanna and not behind bars. "When you go to Amboseli," Lina said, "you'll see many big cats. That park abounds in extraordinary animals."

At the end of the visit, they went to the baboon cliff. Members of baboon families played their customary roles: The self-important old patriarch, infants who rode on the back of their mother or hung from her belly, and immature, quick delinquents who tried to steal a sandwich or apple from unwary tourists. Odile was not a victim, for she did not eat when walking.

In Heron Court, while falling asleep at the end of a marvelous African day, she already saw her papounet and herself among the lovely animals of Amboseli.

3.

They rose early and went for a swim. Breakfast consisted of pineapple, yellow melon, cereals with milk, a five-minute egg, and freshly baked buns with butter. The three-day safari in Amboseli was scheduled for the next day, so they took time for errands. The afternoon and evening were reserved for a performance of tribal dance and music at the Cultural Center of Kenya in south Nairobi. The official name of the Center, in existence for almost ten years, was *Bomas* of Kenya, meaning "native households, settlements, and customs."

Reaching Bomas at two, they had several hours to visit the reverently prepared ethnographic exhibition. Young curators enthusiastically gave them information about the displays. As it happened at the National Museum, Odile was delighted by the fantastic diversity of body ornaments, personal garb, and masks of the tribes inhabiting the length and breadth of Kenya. Meanwhile, her father assiduously studied the exhibits depicting the architecture of the permanent native villages and temporary nomad settlements. He also asked curators numerous questions about traditional methods of hunting, fishing, farming, and livestock breeding.

But Bomas was best known for tribal dance and music. The performance was held in a spacious area surrounded by lush trees. Father and daughter took their seats near the vast stage. There was a wildly enthusiastic welcome for the Center's resident ensemble, *Bomas Harambee Dancers*, consisting of thirty musicians and dancers from all over Kenya. The goal was to present the beauty of ancestral tribal music and dance in all their diversity.

About twenty dance numbers ensued. Some were tediously alike, yet incorporated technically difficult and cleverly provocative dance movements and gestures that Odile found exciting. Players on simple string and wind instruments provided musical accompaniment, but it was the percussion-driven rhythmic complexities that received the wildest yells, clapping, and cheers. Beating, striking, and banging drums and many other objects by hands, fists, mallets, sticks, and metal rods were abundant. Most of the instruments looked brand-new and mass-produced, but one, a strange-looking drum, seemed old and authentic; it was created from a hollowed tree trunk and had rough, slash-like slits.

Odile liked very much what was just a tourist show; Célestin tolerated it for her sake. Analogous shows could be seen wherever there was tourist money—from Bali, all over India, Africa, and South America, and as far as Hawaii and Norway. Besides, he lacked sufficient knowledge of Kenya to judge authenticity. His goal was for Odile to see something new and enjoy it. And she, like any child, was fascinated by the energy and colors of the spectacle.

With a similar purpose and suppressing skepticism, he took his daughter for dinner at Utamaduni after the show. The restaurant was also run by the Center and advertised itself as offering "wonderful traditional dishes, as diverse as the native cultures of Kenya, including *nyamachoma, muthokoi,* and *mukimo.*" He said: "Here, you see, they're not offering either mutura or ukuru we consumed yesterday with Lina and Saul at Gilgil. Are those dishes too cheap and folksy, or too good for this luxe restaurant?! No matter, let's eat." In Odile's mind's eye, the girls still danced, and she kept hearing a distant echo of wooden sticks rhythmically hitting a hollow trunk. But she was ravenously hungry and grabbed her father's hand, pulling him toward the entrance. "Karibu!" Two doormen in Maasai festive garb greeted them loudly in unison.

They ordered all three dishes mentioned on the board. Nyamachoma consisted of barbecued goat meat or beef ribs, with a thick gruel of potatoes and peas. Remembering Gilgil, they chose beef; ribs were eaten, according to the restaurant etiquette, using the fingers of the right hand only. Both muthokoi and mukimo were vegetarian stews—one a kind of hominy, strongly spiced corn with shells removed, and the other a puree of carrots and wild greenery. The meat was bloody but tasty, so they thought everything was correctly prepared. For dessert, she chose a tall cup of yogurt made from goat milk, topped with lots of honey and a scoop of ice cream. Her father drank a glass of red wine imported from Bulgaria. The wine had fermented, but Odile liked the ice cream and drank the sweet mixture of yogurt and honey to the last drop.

Returning to the hotel around ten, they immediately went to sleep. The jeep with a driver and guide was scheduled for the next morning at nine. But at two after midnight, Célestin heard worrisome sounds from the bathroom. The door was wide open, and she was vomiting. When he ran to the bathroom, he saw the girl on her knees, bent over the toilet bowl. The best he could do was hold her hair and stroke her upper back. When she had stopped groaning and retching, he wiped her mouth with a wet towel and helped her get up. She whimpered from the effort and was barely able to mumble, clutching her stomach: "My tummy hurts, Papa, I feel queasy..."

4.

Odile was always a healthy child, so Célestin did not have much experience with her being sick. She had also been in robust health during the whole year of their sometimes trying journey from China to Kenya. Nonetheless, that night in Nairobi it was necessary for him to act as a parent-doctor, quickly and without panic.

Only a few minutes after she had returned to bed, Odile needed to hurry to the bathroom again. He left the door ajar: "If you have to vomit, call me to help you, but if you get diarrhea, I need to know it too." He found the first-aid box they had carried and began to study the booklet. While quickly finding the relevant section, he castigated himself: "I should've learned this long ago, but thank God there wasn't any need." Odile came back ghostly white, saying she was thirsty. He poured bottled water into a clean glass but stopped before handing it: "Wait a few moments until I finish this page. It seems you shouldn't drink right now when your tummy is in shock—you'd vomit again. Yet because of the runs, you'll need to drink a lot of water. And it'd be better if you lie on your side, in case the puke comes to your throat."

Reading on, he thought: "Bellyache, vomiting, diarrhea. A stomach virus or food poisoning? It probably isn't norovirus because the incubation is at least twenty-four hours; moreover, it's highly infectious, so I'd get it too. This means food poisoning in the restaurant, involving bacteria. Usually, Salmonella is the culprit, and the symptoms appear about four hours after the meal—so that's possible. The main candidates, says here, are meat and milk products. But I have no symptoms, and we ate the same food, even the bloody meat. Ah, not the same: While I was struggling with the fermented wine, Odile drank goat yogurt with ice cream. Yogurt must be it!"

He felt her forehead, relieved it was warm but not hot. "*Ecoute, ma petite princesse,* you've got a little sick, likely because of what we ate. But it's nothing serious. Here's the water, please take only a few sips. We'll wait an hour, and then you might be able to hold it without puking. Please sit up, I need to measure your temperature." She weakly raised herself, eyes cloudy. "My poor sick lamb," thought Célestin tenderly, placing the thermometer into her mouth. "You have a fever, but it's not too high, thirty-seven point nine. Now please lie on your side again while I get ice and more water. Be careful, *mon bijou,* if you must go to the toilet."

When he reached the door, Odile stopped him in a worried little voice: "I'll be much better in the morning, Papa, won't I? We'll go to Amboseli, won't we?" He expected it: "Let's hope this will last only one night and you'll wake up healthy. In any case, animals will wait for us."

Instead of taking the elevator, he descended to the foyer three steps at a time and woke up Mukami, the night porter and namesake of their favorite waiter. *"Upesi! Upesi! (Quickly!)* My daughter is sick! Where does the kitchen boss sleep?" Mukami responded the main cook rarely sleeps in the hotel because... He intended to wink but changed his mind seeing the look on Célestin's face and hearing his stern demand that the hotel manager be woken up. So the man ran up the stairs, followed closely by the worried father, and knocked timidly on a door in the mezzanine. When there was no response, Célestin did it much more decisively. Sleep-heavy and displeased, the manager abruptly opened the door, but his face softened when he saw the guest.

"Samahani (Excuse me), my daughter has food poisoning!" Célestin exclaimed apprehensively. The face of the manager, a short, stout man, fell visibly. He was fearful of any sickness appearing in the hotel, especially food poisoning—and worst of all, affecting a European child. Célestin went on politely but energetically: *"Tafadhali lete hapa sasa"* (*Please give me right away*) "three bottles of water and a bucketful of ice." The manager reacted with lightning speed. Without closing the door, he put on pants over his pajama bottoms and while already running down the stairs barefoot, yelled over his shoulder: "We'll bring everything immediately. Please go to your daughter!"

He flew into the room, found Odile retching, and helped her to bed. Soon the manager and Mukami arrived carrying what Célestin had asked for but also a small pile of towels and a washbowl. After hearing about the events of the evening, the manager agreed with the food poisoning diagnosis. He admitted being hugely relieved they had eaten at Utamaduni and not at Buffalo Bill's. The good-hearted man approached Odile's bed on his toes, and receiving permission, gently placed his large hand on the girl's forehead: "It's not too high."

He dismissed Mukami and said softly: "I'm also a father, so I understand your worry. Unfortunately, food poisoning happens often in Nairobi. Poor hygiene, many newcomers. That's why I sent Mukami away—although, believe it or not, food poisoning occurs less often in tribal settlements like the one he's from than in cities. About your safari, don't be surprised if your girl recov-

---

ers only in a couple of days. But tonight, all night, I'm ready to help. Tomorrow morning, if you wish, I can call a trustworthy doctor. *Usiku mvema,* good night." "*Usiku mvema, asante,*" answered Célestin.

Half an hour later, the anxious father gave Odile ice cubes to suck, but only at five the child could hold the water she sipped. He alternated between placing a cold handkerchief on her forehead and helping her in the bathroom. She fell asleep when daylight crept in, but he remained sitting by her pillow.

At half past seven, speaking quietly, he canceled their Amboseli safari, not asking for the portion of the money to which he was entitled. From the booklet, he learned that in cases of runs caused by bacteria, it was wiser not to use anti-diarrhea medication but to allow the organism to destroy the pathogens in the stomach. At nine, he phoned the manager and asked for ginger tea, also requesting that the chief cook be instructed to send items Célestin would order. He decided not to inform Lina and Saul about Odile's illness because it would unsettle them unnecessarily and take his attention away from the care only he could provide for his daughter.

Weak and drowsy, the girl woke up realizing there would be no Amboseli. She hugged her father who had the thermometer in hand. Teary-eyed, she murmured: "*Alors, cher Papa,* we won't go..." "*Non, ma douce,* not this time," he responded. The temperature was thirty-eight. He gave her water and tucked her in: "I'll order our breakfast and then you must sleep."

He called the cook and asked for sickroom items. Soon Mukami the waiter appeared, wearing a worried expression and carrying a tray with minimalistic food. To his patient, the pediatric apprentice prescribed a third of a banana and a piece of toasted white bread with honey. He let the girl drink water and was glad a trip to the bathroom did not ensue. Once he darkened the windows, the child fell asleep. On hearing the maid in the hallway, he asked her not to use the vacuum near their room.

Sitting by the phone, Célestin debated how and whether to find a doctor. There were several options: a physician recommended by the hotel manager, someone Lina and Saul would recommend, or a pediatrician working for the French Embassy. Finally, he decided to take care of Odile himself. Her sickness was not serious enough to justify inviting a stranger who might disquiet the girl. So he phoned the cook and requested the acceptable food items: chicken broth, rice without spices except for salt, peanut butter, white bread, ginger tea, bananas, and dry cereal.

They defeated the sickness together. He cared for, encouraged, and read aloud when asked, eating the same tasteless food and never leaving the room. Thus, another precious experience was acquired.

5.

After two critical days, Odile was recovering quickly. The nausea disappeared, and a good appetite returned, blessing the girl with her customary sunny mood. From the manager to cooks, waiters, and maids, the entire staff did their best to please her. She went for short walks with her father, and already on the fourth day, received his permission to swim. Lina called, thinking they had returned from Amboseli, but understood why Célestin had kept mum about the sickness. She then invited herself and Saul to come to Heron Court the next day, explaining there was no other time to say goodbye: They were scheduled to undergo medical examinations lasting several days. These were routine but detailed, a regimen they followed every two years.

Célestin was trying to think of something special he could do for Odile before their return to France. There was a National Park near Nairobi, but he knew nothing about it. After breakfast, having asked Mukami to be at hand, he left his girl in the restaurant and went to the manager's office. The good man's opinion was favorable: "The park is beautiful and has existed for over thirty years. You'd be able to see many animals during a single day's safari. Of course, it can't be compared with Amboseli or Maasai Mara as a game park, but it's close to here. It's hard to believe, but the main entrance is only ten kilometers south of the city. I know it has an area of about a hundred and twenty square kilometers—which means it's about three times smaller than Amboseli. There's a fence on three sides, but the fourth, to the south, is open, which makes possible the migration of animals from the savanna plains of Kitengela. I'm convinced Odile will be delighted! If I were you, I'd call the same agency with which you planned to go to Amboseli. They have reliable drivers and jeeps."

Naturally, Célestin asked himself if he was incautiously pushing matters given Odile's still fragile health, but his optimistic nature assured him the girl's joy outweighed the risk. So, he called the agency. The director sounded pleased by the unexpected call. "For Saturday, Park Nairobi... You and your little daughter who is, thank God, much better... I'm glad! You're calling late, but I understand you're flying home to France. Let me see what I can do." After a few minutes, he was back: "Yes, we can manage it in one of the oversize jeeps! And we'll give it at half price since you so generously turned down the refund for the canceled Amboseli. All the best wishes to your girl, have a great time, Park Nairobi is awesome."

When he returned to the dining room, Odile was gaily chatting with Mukami and two young waitresses, Maasai teenagers newly arrived in Nairobi from the village of Kisumu at the Kenyan end of Lake Victoria. He interrupted joyfully: "The day after tomorrow, *mon bijou*, we'll visit the Nairobi National Park. You'll end up seeing many gorgeous wild animals after all!" The girl jumped up and, hugging her father, exclaimed in French: "Marvelous! How did it happen?"Stroking her hair, he said: "I managed somehow. It's a magnificent park. We're going in a jeep with other people and will spend the whole Saturday at it. But that means you need to rest and sleep today and tomorrow!" Switching to English, he thanked Mukami and the Maasai girls for keeping Odile company.

The next morning, Lina and Saul came to Heron Court bringing little gifts: a leather tribal bracelet and a finely carved wooden rhino about twelve centimeters tall. "First we planned to buy you a small glass sculpture of a pink flamingo," said Lina, "but the legs were sooo long and thin they would break for sure during your trip to France." Odile was happy to see these warm people again and loved the presents, immediately placing the bracelet on her wrist. They all sat by the pool for an hour, engaged in a friendly conversation and drinking ice-cold lemonade. Lina praised Odile's healthy appearance while Saul answered the girl's questions about the National Park. Studying his guests, Célestin was relieved they were genuinely gay and carefree: their forthcoming medical tests were indeed only routine. They parted like old friends, and thus the strong link of father and daughter with Israel was indirectly further reinforced.

* * *

As the jeep left the final passenger-pickup hotel, the portly, fortyish guide and driver introduced himself as "Michael, a Nairobi Kikuyu" and then began his lecture in fluent English: "People who aren't familiar with our National Park often think it's just another city safari circus. What else could it be, so close to a major capital city, spread in the shadows of the concrete jungle? They are badly mistaken. After all, what is it exactly that's lying in the shadows? Well, ladies, gentlemen, and the young Miss I notice back there: Near this polluted, heaving city, you'll find primeval intact savanna. And it's home to all sorts of our African animals. Very diverse animals, mind you. They are all here except the elephants. It's true that in the part of the park close to the main gate, you'll perhaps be able to photograph a giraffe whose head seems to tower over a skyscraper behind her! So what? Interesting, isn't it? To have an area equal to a third of the world-famous Amboseli, for which you need at least three days, is certainly not something to snigger at. Our park has the Mbagathi River and wild cliffs in the southeastern section near the Athi, a bigger river into which the Mbagathi flows. You'll see some incredible wilderness."

Michael was forced to interrupt his impassioned monologue that never sounded blasé because they had already reached the entrance gate of the park. It took them only about twenty minutes to arrive from Heron Court, despite the morning traffic. In addition to Odile and Célestin, there were eight other passengers, travelers from America, France, and England. She was the only child, as Michael had announced. "In the park, there are many places where one can spend a long time," he said while negotiating the red dirt road. "From here, for example, a long path leads through a virgin forest. Sometimes I come here with my wife and son, he is now ten. There's no danger a visitor would be assaulted by an animal—or a hoodlum!"

Thus began their safari, which lasted until seven in the evening. "You're lucky, dear passengers, you came to Kenya in June. The weather is dry, and the avalanche of tourists will happen only in the next two months. Even though it's the weekend, I don't think we'll see too many other jeeps. However, if you come next month, you'd be likely to witness the unforgettable sight of the migration of zebras and gazelles into the park from the south. In the southeast, the Mbagathi River is the border, but there's a section completely open, without the electric fence, to make the natural seasonal migrations possible. But even now, we'll see large herds of antelopes, gnus, and other ungulates."

Father and daughter were delighted that Michael's prediction was correct: They saw gracious Thomson's gazelles, various other kinds of antelopes, and many gnus—but also giraffes, ostriches, warthogs, and *secretarybirds* of prey. All those animals roamed free in the eternal vast setting of open savanna, with its tall grasses and giant acacias. Michael expertly found the places where hyenas and cheetahs could be seen from the road, close enough to take Odile's breath away. "There are many leopards in the park, but even I see them rarely—they are extremely wary and alert. But if you want lions, I assure you we'll get them!"

That promise of Michael's was also fulfilled, for Célestin and Odile suddenly heard several passengers' exclamations on seeing a pride of lions in tall grass. "These are lionesses and their cubs," said Michael, "as for the big boss... yes, there he is, standing under the acacia, look how handsome!" By gaping admiringly at the huge tomcat with a luxuriant mane, Michael made it evident he had not become indifferent to the beauty of the animals he saw every day. The lion stood stock still about twenty meters from the motionless jeep. Gazing at him, nose pressed to the window-pane, she whispered: "Papa, Papa, the lion is staring at me." Only after a minute or so, the girl dared to take a photo through the glass. When the jeep moved on, she mumbled, smiling shyly: "He didn't get scared... nor did I!"

During the break for lunch, they sat at a table by themselves, eating the tasty—and, above all, trustworthy—sandwiches prepared in the Heron Court kitchen. Michael inquired if everything was all right. Célestin courteously asked him to join them and explained they were eating their own sandwiches as a precaution: "My daughter has just recovered from food poisoning, and we're due to fly to Paris in two days."

The guide nodded: "Of course, I understand, I'd do the same if it were my son. But may I ask: Where did this happen? In your hotel?" He shook his head: "No, not at Heron Court. It almost certainly happened close to this park's entrance at the restaurant Utamaduni." Michael was astonished: "Wow, I'm so sorry! That's terrible. I must look into it. What's more, this little restaurant where we're now, where I've brought my passengers, belongs to Utamaduni! I must convey this to the director of my agency. Food poisoning of any of our passengers would be disastrous. By the way, the director respects you—I've no idea how he managed to get you seats in this fully booked jeep."

Célestin thought that by revealing the likely location of the poisoning, he had done a favor to Michael, the agency for which he worked, and their future passengers. In the jeep, Odile said she had understood the purpose of the talk with Michael. Out of the blue, she added: "His son is my age, isn't he?"

Soon after lunch, they saw rhinos grazing in the savanna. Michael explained: "There are about seventy rhinos in the park, scientifically classified as Black and White, although both species are actually gray. From this distance, I can't see the small anatomical differences existing between them. But because the White kind is far more numerous, that's what those you see probably are." The passengers were surprised and laughed, except for Célestin and Odile, who exchanged a look. Recalling Saul's extensive lecture, the girl asked: "Should we tell Michael those rhinos are certainly White because they are all grazing and not browsing?" Only then did he chuckle: "No, let's not. It might embarrass him. Anyway, he probably knows it and didn't want to go into details."

In the late afternoon, Michael let passengers climb out of the jeep and took them for a stroll to several murky ponds that were home to hippos. The massive animals were perfectly camouflaged and visible only when they loudly fooled around, splashing in the water. Beside one of the ponds, the visitors saw attractively dressed, very erect Maasai women who exchanged greetings with Michael. "There's a small Maasai village a little way off, but these women have to lug water for their livestock all the way from here because hippos have taken over the pond by the village," explained Michael.

As the jeep approached the park exit, a young American sitting next to Célestin addressed him: "Excuse me, Sir, I didn't want to disturb you earlier, but now we've almost arrived. I speak French a little and am frankly amazed by the maturity of your daughter." Odile blushed while her father thanked the man for the compliment and asked him the usual travelers' questions.

Jonathan grew up in Upstate New York and finished college in Albany, the State capital. He joined the Peace Corps and spent three years at the extreme western end of Kenya near Lake Victoria, adding that his contract had expired only a week earlier. It occurred to Célestin that he could learn a lot about Kenya from the amiable man, so he invited him to Heron Court. "We'll sit by the pool, have a beer, and talk about Kenya; Odile can read a book." Jonathan happily agreed and gave instructions to Michael in seemingly fluent Kikuyu about his new drop-off location.

On arrival at the hotel, they thanked Michael and gave him generous tips. Odile went to wash up, while her father and Jonathan sat by the pool. One of the new waitresses came running and humbly greeted Célestin in poor English. He ordered *bia mbili* in Swahili, stopped the waitress from leaving, and said to his guest: "This young woman is Maasai, new to Nairobi, and has just started at the hotel. I remember that her girlfriend, another new waitress, said they were from around Kisumu at Lake Victoria, which may be close to where you worked all those years. You probably speak Maasai, as well as Swahili and Kikuyu. I'm sure she'd be happy to hear words in her native tongue."

Jonathan gladly obliged, and the girl's face lit up. She merrily twittered and chirruped with Jonathan for a few minutes. When Odile arrived, Célestin ordered *maji ya limau* lemonade for her, and the waitress ran off to bring the drinks. Jonathan, who had a solid command of Maa, explained: "African languages are fairly easy because they tend to be phonetic, unlike English or even French." The Frenchman agreed and added: "I'm a linguist, and Odile is a bilingual Franco-German; we're always glad when we meet people who speak several languages fluently." Now Jonathan's face reddened in a young way. For a short time, they were silent, each man nursing his beer.

Before his conversation with Jonathan began, Célestin said to Odile, wishing to engage her a little longer: "I'm sure you remember those nursing students from England who wished to help in the 'Third World' after college. They planned to join the Peace Corps and work in some country plagued by poverty or plague itself." "Of course, I remember Sophie and Karen, they were such nice girls."

He spoke bluntly with the young American: "Please don't take what I'm going to say to heart. You see, when I talked to those enthusiastic women, I usurped the role of an elder brother and preached to them in an attempt to change their minds. I said young people's idealism in 'Western' countries—like mine, theirs, and yours—is routinely misused by certain agencies whose modus operandi I find odious. The supposedly humanitarian work is all too often used as a screen for much that's revolting. Have I, Jonathan, badly erred, at least in your case?"

The young man gave Célestin a serious look and responded: "You have not! Absolutely haven't. Neither in mine nor in the case of many other people in the Corps whom I got to know. We all began as idealists—you put it well—just like those English nurses. To join, we often defied the well-intentioned advice of family members, level-headed friends, and people like you. But later... Well, troublesome things happened to many volunteers in various countries, not to speak of endemic diseases and epidemics. And I mustn't forget literal starvation because sometimes there simply was no food for anyone in a village or even region.

"As for agencies misusing volunteers: I know whom you have in mind. That too is true. Also, and not only in the U.S., every piece of unfavorable news about the Corps is instantly hushed up. As for me personally, I was in such boondocks I couldn't have been of use to any spy agency, and in any case, I wouldn't have collaborated. Fortunately, I was in a fairly well-off part of Kenya and had no real problems. In addition, I've always been willing to learn new languages and am fluent in four tribal ones plus Swahili. Ordinary people in Kenya, where there are over seventy tongues and dialects, appreciate this skill and think of people who have it as well-disposed—as did the Maasai waitress just now." Jonathan and Célestin talked for a long time, while Odile studied French. The hard-working, ambitious girl already imagined herself taking exams in Metz.

"I'm grateful to you," said Célestin, "for everything you've told me. I would regret being unjust or scarily dogmatic with you and those nursing students. Please tell me a little about your life here."

"I'd be glad to—a bit about me and a bit about Kenya. I received a hundred thirty-five dollars a month from the Peace Corps, out of which I was able to save a little because I had a room free of charge at the elementary school where I taught English and basic math. But believe it or not, even with money it was impossible to maintain a healthy diet. I put on lots of undesirable fat. However, I had plenty of time to talk to people and to study. I made tons of notes for a possible book.

"As for Kenyan customs, okay, I'll tell you a few things. Some of them you may already know, others not. For example, polygamy is a Kenyan tradition, and there's hardly a politician who dares to fight it. To have two or three wives is common: It's a sign a man is well-fixed, if not exactly rich. The accepted signs of wealth are women, children, and livestock. Regarding white people, it's assumed every white man is moneyed—even I! Promiscuity is also a Kenyan tradition, except for a few tribes. Among the Maasai, there are small groups in which adultery is punished.

"The Maasai and the Samburu are the most warlike of the tribes but not against each other: Their languages are similar, and territories don't touch. The Maasai to this day attack other tribes, using spears and even rifles smuggled from Tanzania. They have the predatory habit of stealing livestock and do it self-righteously due to a convenient belief they hold—God long ago gifted them all the cattle in the world!

"Well, I've certainly exhausted you," concluded Jonathan, "and Odile's almost fallen asleep after our exciting safari. Or she's gotten bored by French grammar. If I've correctly read the title from here, it's for higher grades, and she's only nine and a half, as you said." Odile heard it and gave him a sweet smile.

After they exchanged addresses, Jonathan said goodbye: "It's late, so I'll take a tuk-tuk to my hostel. You're probably aware that Park Uhuru is sometimes dangerous for whites. I don't want something weird to happen to me just now before my imminent departure for New York—after managing to be safe in Kenya for three years."

As the night fell, father and daughter talked on. When almost asleep, she said softly: "It was a wonderful, wonderful day, Papa. The only thing missing was for us to spend a whole night in the savanna, surrounded by the mysterious sounds of night birds and wild animals."

PART EIGHT

Festival of the Plow

1.

Their Lorraine, medieval Lotharingia, greeted Célestin and Odile joyfully with her gentle, pale green, cultivated smile as the morning train from Paris carried them home. It was the beginning of summer, the 23rd of June 1981. The previous day, they arrived from Nairobi to the fairly new Charles de Gaulle Airport near Paris, after flying for nine untroubled hours. It was too late to catch the train to Metz, so they stayed at a hotel near Gare de l'Est.

During the journey of almost three hundred kilometers, Odile talked to her father expectantly about returning home and seeing everyone and her Pasha again. Or she looked through the window at the verdant, welcoming land in which she had grown up— so different from austere Israel and lush Kenya. When she became drowsy, she laid her head on her father's shoulder and dreamed. In one scene, there were pinkish creatures on long thin legs whose names she could not remember; in another, a big and powerful, yet friendly animal stood under an acacia, gazing at her, and she knew his name was Lion.

However, the memory of an unpleasant event suddenly rushed into her mind. It took place before Christmas the previous year, after their stay in Paris. They were returning to Metz sitting in a similar train compartment when her father scolded her for babbling to Auntie Mathilde about their private matters without remembering Olya. Her papa chided her, as he said, for being disloyal to Olyechka. How could she err so much that her father, always so understanding, would become angry with her? She recalled crying, being sorry, and his forgiveness. How relieved she had been ever since because Papa never brought it up again.

The train stopped in Rheims, the capital of Champagne, so he talked to his daughter about the famed cathedral in the city. Later, while they were rushing through the tranquil green fields where the bloody Battle of Verdun had taken place in 1916, Célestin noticed Odile had dozed off. He ruminated: "I'm glad she's asleep, this isn't for a child. Precisely here, there were eleven months of horrific butchery and bloody fighting for each trench. In poison gas! A quarter of a million killed and half a million wounded young men. Yet without any personal consequences for the arrogant, bloodthirsty Wilhelm Hohenzollern, Hindenburg, and Ludendorff. Wilhelm was permitted, after his abdication, to live peacefully for over twenty years, to the end of his natural life, in Castle Doorn in Holland. The other two criminals even sent their ex-Kaiser twenty freight cars filled to the gills with automobiles, furniture from Schloss Sanssouci in Potsdam, and a yacht in parts. In the Weimar Republic, those cruel old villains again obtained important positions. Yet they pretended to be unable to prevent Hitler from coming to power. What a gang of criminals fit for the gallows."

Those thoughts led to another: In his mind's eye flashed the sight of the dark gray Sverdlovsk train station and Odile with him, sorrowful, standing in the drizzle on the deserted platform. In that city, which was on the fateful 17th of July 1918 still called Yekaterinburg, another Kaiser, Russian Tsar Nikolay II Romanov and his entire family were mercilessly executed by the new Soviet regime. A German Kaiser and a Russian Tsar with very different destinies. Thinking of the killing fields of Verdun, Célestin concluded that if there existed a just God, Wilhelm Hohenzollern would have suffered an infinitely worse end than being shot in a cellar as Nikolay Romanov was.

He refused to spoil his daughter's elation about coming home with such appalling thoughts. Besides, for her age, Odile knew more than enough about Verdun and the Germanic warlike readiness to attack neighbors and grab their land and possessions.

"Hmm, just what Jonathan said about the Maasai predators!" thought Célestin. If Patrizia were alive, he was certain their daughter would hear from her mother, a pure German, the same opinions.

When the girl opened her eyes and stretched like a cat, the train was entering the station of their good old Metz.

2.

Their good old Gilles, the estate manager, was waiting on the platform and helped them put the luggage in the trunk of their good old dark-blue Renault. "We've arrived home in the perfect weather of early summer. So much in our lives is good and old here," Célestin thought contentedly. Odile thought the same about her middle-aged mare Pasha, who was healthy and expecting her mistress impatiently—thus announced Gilles on the platform as soon as he had put the girl down on the ground, having kissed her loudly on both cheeks.

Gerda, Françoise, and Marie, Gilles's wife, were waiting at the threshold of the manor house. Having exchanged hugs and kisses with those dear women, Odile ran off to the stable where Pasha neighed happily like a filly. Right after lunch, she lovingly combed and groomed the mare and put on her new riding boots for the first time since January. Those boots and a fine saddle were presents from her father for her most recent birthday, the ninth. Together, they put the saddle on the horse, and he adjusted the buckles on the girth. With the help of a step stool, she got on and grabbed the reins. Célestin set the stirrups and, leading the horse out, said in a serious voice: "*Mon trésor*, please remember what you had solemnly promised when I gave you the saddle. You have far more experience riding bareback. Last January, you rode only once or twice on the saddle, always with me present. For now, when you're riding alone, do it only near the house and never faster than a trot. Obey Pasha, and she'll obey you. I'll now inform her what you're not allowed to do." Hugging the horse's neck, he whispered. The ride was a joyous occasion for the girl and horse.

Already that evening, after she unpacked her suitcase and displayed the gifts, including the sweet little rhino from Lina and Saul, the girl turned to textbooks and math exercises. During the following week, only Pasha was able to separate her occasionally from books. Célestin never needed to urge her, and everyone in the house ensured she could study undisturbed. Gerda, her old governess, who kept using endearments in the Franconian dialect of Koblenz and Metz, regularly brought water and fruit tea to the cozy room serving as her playroom and workroom. Françoise did not permit the younger housemaids to bother the girl with chatter in the hallways. And Marie added something special to every meal. At school, everyone who knew Odile was glad to see her again, from Principal Michel Gaubert and her homeroom teacher Philippe Marceau to the elderly female custodians. Her girlfriends hugged and kissed her, marveling at the African suntan.

Examinations took place at the beginning of July, and she did very well. True, unlike previous years, her grades were not the highest in class—two other students were at the top. She was disappointed but not envious, especially since the "competitors" were girlfriends with whom she had corresponded. On the contrary, those two harmlessly envied her travels to distant, fantastic lands.

When Célestin spoke to Marceau and Gaubert, not one of the three men was concerned. He argued his daughter's grades were lower than before in geography because the exam covered mostly France and her colonies, and also in history because no exam questions dealt with Napoleon's defeats in Russia, Egypt, and the Holy Land. He mentioned she had learned a great deal about the Second World War, which was not taught in French and German schools, and reminded them the inadequate coverage of various wars was one of the main reasons he had originally taken his girl out for homeschooling. Finally, he admitted Odile's knowledge of French grammar was not on par with what was expected from a top student, but explained that during their travel, they spoke mostly colloquial French and German. As a *coup de grâce*, he added she had been surrounded by Russian, Hebrew, Arabic, and Swahili languages and used many words and phrases in them.

"She even knows some words in Maasai and Kikuyu!" Célestin mischievously concluded.

"I know you're joking a little Monsieur De Quernevelle," said Gaubert in a friendly tone, "but I wholeheartedly agree with much of what you said. You probably remember I was strongly in favor of homeschooling. I don't think it's important for an intelligent and hard-working pupil to be top of the class on all the exams. I had a longish talk with your daughter. During the past year, she has seen and learned much that's new, important, and interesting. Many such matters are unfortunately not represented on our old-fashioned exams. You gave her an extraordinary, most enviable opportunity to grow in a variety of ways, although it couldn't have always been easy to travel with a child. Odile is taller, stronger, more mature. She's acquired a degree of self-confidence rare for her age—but not to excess. She's as kind and well-mannered as she has always been. Congratulations, if you permit me to say so."

3.

Célestin—a highly individualistic, rather unconventional, and occasionally adventure-prone father of a female motherless child—was certainly very pleased to hear Gaubert's words. It was important that the serious, professional educator of children and young people was supportive of the goal to include a great deal of travel as part of schooling. As he saw it, the plan was simple: To open Odile's horizons early in life.

The morning was gorgeous. Célestin walked along the bank of the Moselle, which he had not done for a long time without his daughter, but he needed solitude. Decisively doing away with the feeling of self-satisfaction that had arisen while listening to Gaubert, he asked himself: "Still, how long will you be dragging the child around the world? You really mustn't take it too far. Every child, even if smart and independent, needs daily interactions with other children." On Quai Félix Maréchal, near the Metz cathedral, he temporarily turned his back to the magnificent edifice and by a nameless little bridge crossed to the small Île du Saulcy in the middle of the Moselle. From a tiny green area, he faced the cathedral: Saint Étienne de Metz! The view had taken his breath away innumerable times in his life. At sunset, it would have been even more dramatic, for the heavenly stained-glass windows reflected pink-purple rays at that time.

As he ambled through the islet near Metz Opera, one of the oldest in France, he asked himself: "So, what should I do? It seems the first step ought to be staying at home for a few years. I could always go alone on a short trip somewhere when the urge strikes me because reliable people who adore Odile live with us... The second step would be far more difficult."

Célestin reached the western edge of Petit-Saulcy, along which flowed another branch of the Moselle. He long stared at the water. "I need to find a woman whom I'd deeply love as spouse but who's also likely to be a good mother. And help Odile when physiological changes hit in three or four years. The child deserves it.

"This is all blah-blah. Let's look at the facts. After Patrizia, the only woman I've been able to imagine as my wife is Olya. And that's it! Also, I don't think I'm deceiving myself when I feel certain that Olya and Odile genuinely love each other. I hope with all of my heart Olya will soon, somehow, be free. I have to try harder."

He slowly crossed Pont Saint-Marcel and sat down in the elegant foyer of Hôtel du Théâtre intending to have a beer. But even before the waiter, young and swift-footed, reached the table, Célestin had firmly decided: "Under no circumstances will I marry Olya if I discover even a smidgen of selfishness in me, if I realize I'm marrying her because she would be useful—first as a child's nanny and later as a teenager's confidante. That wouldn't be good for anyone."

Having taken the order, the waiter had barely gone a few meters away when the serious, distracted guest was already talking to himself: "Hmm, all these plans are well-intentioned but confused and unrealistic. First and foremost, I must get Olya out of prison." The next morning, he would phone her mother and the Soviet Consulate.

4.

Olga did not respond to phone calls for four days, but he would persist. As for the Consulate in Paris, Célestin was certain the forbidding voice belonged to the same sulky man with whom he had spoken face to face seven months earlier, in the middle of December, when he visited the office with Odile. The KGB man probably remembered the demanding Frenchman, his young daughter, and his Tatar lover in the Kuybyshev prison. The official repeated bluntly that he was not authorized to disclose anything. In a bad-tempered manner, he emphasized that coming to Paris would be of no avail: The information he sought could come only from Moscow. How long did he need to wait? No idea. Why wasn't he as amenable as employees at the Soviet Consulate in Berlin? So? Berlin is Berlin, Paris Paris.

Finally, one evening a week later, when it was almost midnight in Kazan, Olga answered the phone. Her voice was tired and trembled on the verge of tears but happy: "Dear, dear Tino! How glad I am to hear from you! How are you, how's Odile? She's healthy and growing fast?" It was the first time she addressed him using the familiar version of "you," and so he did too. He was glad they were becoming closer and managing it even in Russian. Then he heard what he was hoping for: "Olya loves you, deeply loves you. Each of her letters is filled with love for you, asking me to tell you when I can. And she always sends love and greetings to *malyshka*." But to Célestin's detailed questions, Olga responded briefly, obviously hesitating to speak openly about Olya's condition in prison because of the likely eavesdropping: "She writes she's well, she's healthy, but you know prison is prison."

She choked and continued with effort, ignoring the possible listeners: "You couldn't get me on the phone... Well, I work three jobs, almost day and night. I'm not complaining, it's just the veins in my legs. But I must earn money to send Olya better food. Also, I need to save for when she's released. It'll be hard for her to get any job. Since the thirty-month sentence was decreased by the six she had spent beforehand—and on condition that no time is added for some transgression—she'd be released at the end of April next year, 1983. But if they conclude she didn't comport herself well..."

He had calculated the likely release date many times before, but his sorrow was doubled while listening to the bitter sobbing of the grieving mother. As he waited patiently for Olga to speak again, he heard his daughter's barefoot steps on the old-fashioned parquet. Having heard Russian words, the girl guessed with whom her father was speaking and ran in her nightie down the corridor to his study. She hugged him as he stood by the desk.

"Olya's mother," he said. Olga's voice had recovered: "Thank you again for calling, dear Tino. Please kiss your sweet malyshka for Olya and me." Célestin exclaimed: "Wait, please, here's malyshka!" Giving her the handset, he whispered she could say anything she wanted, at which Odile spoke a dozen gentle words in French and Russian. Olga's voice had then become almost cheerful. She praised the little one and ended the call with the optimistic words, "I hope you'll hear from us very soon!"

In the huge house, the silence was complete. Célestin sat at his desk facing Odile who had settled in her favorite deep armchair. Next to it stood an old floor lamp with a tall, spiral, gold-leaf painted body and a shade of amber silk with copper birds and a crimson fringe. The lamp was throwing a soft shadow on the serious face of the girl. Having listened attentively to what her father had conveyed about his talk with Olga, she silently studied him. Meanwhile, he thought: "How beautiful and tender is my child... And how thankful I should be I've heard at least something about Olya." For her part, Odile was delighted that Olya had not forgotten her and loved Papa so much. There was goodness in Olga's voice, but he looked somber, so she ran behind the desk to hug him: "All will be well, you'll see cher Papa, Olya will come to us."

He tucked her in and paced long into the night. The very end of the conversation with Olga suddenly grabbed him and sent a shiver down his spine. She had said: "I hope you'll hear from us very soon!" Maybe those words had no significance beyond being kind. But perhaps, just perhaps, he would soon receive something concrete from Olya herself. After all, Olga's voice while uttering those words was unexpectedly lighthearted.

5.

Awaiting news from Olya, he threw himself into solving various minor but long-neglected problems together with Gilles. With Odile, he went riding every day farther. She spent a lot of time with her friends, also a little neglected. On hot days, they played games or read to each other in the shady groves by the manor house. Sometimes Célestin or one of the other parents chaperoned the children for a whole afternoon at the open swimming pool in Metz. The lifeguards were trustworthy and there were trees around the pool, even a small restaurant.

From time to time, he went to the City of Metz chess club of which he had been a longtime member and financial supporter. Despite being an expert player, his visits gradually became less frequent. He loved chess gossip but generally avoided smoke-filled rooms. His nonsmoking friends who were solid players were occasionally invited to his home for games using chess clocks but nevertheless accompanied by jokes, teasing, and choice wines and cheeses. Club play, however, presented true challenges. There he played deadly serious rapid chess with half-hour, five-minute, and even one-minute time limits per player for an entire game. The rivals' alternate pressing of buttons on the small box containing two adjacent clocks—especially near the end of a game when time was running out for one or both players—was so fast and forceful that the clock-box would sometimes be in danger of falling off the table.

Many players at the club were heavy smokers, and it seemed to Célestin that a rapid game was the only time when they did not smoke—for fear of losing precious seconds. The chess was serious, by the rules, so noisemaking, chattering, and taking back one's moves were absolute no-nos. Yet such behavior is a key feature of patzers' play in parks—and on long-distance trains, as was the case with his games against Vasiliy and Pavel in Siberia. Silent kibitzing was allowed, but for suggesting a move to a player one flew from the club. The role of enforcer was played by the elderly, diffident monsieur Herbert, the club's nominal janitor. In actuality, he was an educated pensioner of modest means who was the archivist of tournament results as well as an outstanding coffee maker. At the park across the street from the club, Herbert was a chess god to the aging patzers with whom he conversed in the archaic Franconian dialect like Odile's Frau Gerda.

There were female members too. Years earlier, they claimed the most comfortable corner of the club. The ladies played against each other and had a separate ranking table with which they did not entrust even monsieur Herbert. Male kibitzers were not welcome. The majority played without a chess clock or with a much longer time limit per game. That certainly suited the heavy smokers among them, identifiable by fingers and teeth yellowed from tobacco.

At the club, there were also youngsters—eighteen-, fifteen-, and even twelve-year-old boys, some very talented. From both the purely chess and amusing emotional angles, Célestin found it fascinating to observe the behavior of the strongest players in their twenties toward these boys. One saw who wished to teach them and who avoided playing, fearing a single loss. He helped the youngsters, recognizing his immature youth. He remembered being a twelve-year-old sapling in games against players twice his age: Controlling stage fright, relying on natural talent for endgames, and trying hard not to gloat after a win against a strong player.

* * *

It was already the end of July when Mathilde, uninvited and unannounced, arrived in Metz from Paris, saying she stopped by on her way to Hamburg. Only a day later, the ardently hoped-for letter from Olya arrived—under odd circumstances.

6.

As soon as he came home one afternoon, Célestin caught a whiff of a perfume he knew belonged to another time and place. In the high-ceilinged drawing room, an unexpected sight greeted him. Mathilde LeClercq sat in the middle of a long sofa, where she had assumed a formal pose, with her back as straight as a Prussian officer's and legs set at an angle befitting a well-brought-up society lady. She wore a superbly tailored light-blue traveling suit with a matching tiny hat. Entering, he first encountered the guest's refined profile and then heard the self-assured voice. In exquisite French, Mathilde was speaking to Gerda, who sat on the edge of a chair, her big hands awkwardly clasped on her knees. Odile, who until then was sitting in a distant armchair, ran joyfully to embrace her father. Over her head, Célestin saw two elegant suitcases and a round hat box.

He was somewhat ashamed about not being more gracious when they exchanged greetings—she was a generous hostess in Paris—but refused to be phony and also noticed Odile's discomfort, for which he was partly responsible. Mathilde's story about being on her way to Hamburg and spontaneously deciding to get off the train in Metz and take a cab to the estate did not sound convincing. He sensed the motive for the visit and felt like a mouse in a cat's trap that lacked even cheese. Still, elementary hospitality could not be neglected. "You'll spend the night with us, of course," he said and asked Françoise and Marie to make the necessary arrangements.

The next day, he got up before six and quickly left the house into the musical chirping of birds. It was a gloriously fresh yet already fragrant summer morning by the Moselle. For over two hours, he walked in dewy meadows, over hillocks, and through dark-green groves. Upon returning, he greeted the likable young mailman who was putting letters and journals into the mailbox:

"Now, Lucien, if you will, go through the back door to the kitchen and have a coffee with Marie and Gilles. It's a quarter past eight, so Gilles has probably finished his apéritif—he makes it himself from mirabelle plums grown here. But now you've safely delivered our mail, Gilles can let you try a glass of his potion!"

Célestin climbed the stairs of polished dark wood to his study and closed the door. Not a sound could be heard from either Odile or Mathilde. In the pile of mail, one letter caught his attention. It was an ordinary envelope for internal use in France, but the handwriting, unfortunately not Olya's, seemed to belong to a Russian person. Also, it was addressed to *Tino* de Quernevelle! Feeling a mixture of hope and trepidation, he frantically tore open the envelope. Inside, there was a single folded sheet. His heart beat faster because the handwriting was undoubtedly Olya's! The whole letter, dated the 19th of June, was in Russian and began with "*Moya dorogaya mamochka!*" (*My dear mommy!*) The content was banal, but here and there, he noticed words that did not belong in a letter to Olga. And near the end, out of the blue, there were two sentences about music, one of which was "concer*Tino*."

Slowly he connected the disparate details and realized Olya's letter was meant for him but camouflaged as one for her mother. She probably sent Olga an envelope containing two pieces of paper with different dates, for instance, the 18th and 19th of June. And in the letter meant for Olga, there must have been a hidden message that the second sheet was for him. Putting together words and phrases from several places, Célestin concluded Olya had sent him disguised sighs of love and longing.

He strode in circles for a minute and then sat down in Odile's armchair. Despite the letter in his lap, he was depressed. Unfortunately, although the dear piece of paper had reached him, it did not bring Olya a single step closer to his embrace. He got up and long looked through one of the windows, whispering: "Will she ever see this beauty while standing here next to me?" He sat down again and shut his eyes. Despair had replaced initial joy.

Only after a period filled with troubled thoughts did he ask himself how the letter had managed to arrive in Metz. How did Olga forward it? And whose handwriting, seemingly feminine, was on the envelope? Then he remembered Olga's cheerful words at the end of their phone call. When she uttered them, she must have already received Olya's letter and maybe had an idea of how to send it to him safely.

He heard his daughter's knock and begged her to come in. They had just hugged each other for good morning when the phone rang. "Monsieur Tino, my name is Ilysiya..." The voice belonged to a young woman who spoke English with a strong Russian accent: "I'm your Olya's best friend and have a message for you! I'm calling from Paris but must be quick. Did you receive the letter I sent you yesterday from here?" Célestin froze with astonishment and mumbled he had just gotten it. "Super," exclaimed the girl with glee, "it's for you from Olya! She loves you so very much. She put that piece of paper in the letter to her mother, and the censors were fooled. Olga gave it to me, as well as your address and phone number, when she learned I was coming to Paris."

"Dear Ilysiya, I'm immensely grateful to you! Listen, I'll come to Paris right away. I'll drive like a maniac! I need to speak to you about Olya and..." "Oh, no," she interrupted him, "I'm sorry, Tino, but unfortunately that's impossible. You see, I'm here for only a few days as a dancer in a Tatar folklore troupe from Kazan. But six people with us are supposedly our tour leaders. You understand their role? They watch us all the time, like... what's the English word for the ugly bird of prey? Yesterday, I was barely able to sneak out of our hotel to mail the letter and now to get to a phone booth. I must hurry back. I've known Olya for a long time, we grew up together. She's a wonderful person and loves you very much—and hopes you still have the same feelings. Oh, I almost forgot, Olga asked me to give greetings to your daughter on her and Olya's behalf." He only had time to assure Ilysiya of his undying love for Olya before she had to run off.

After explaining to Odile what he had heard, Célestin nervously paced around the room, speaking a little to her and more to himself: "This Ilysiya, a real angel of a young woman, can't see me in Paris without creating huge difficulties for herself and her family in Kazan. Besides, if Olga has not yet been able to visit Olya in prison, then neither has Ilysiya. She doesn't know any more about Olya's state than Olga does. Also, I wanted to give some money to Ilysiya for Olga but that's a terrible idea. It would be dangerous for the girl to arrive in Moscow with foreign money. So, even if I were to rush to Paris to see her... *Ma douce*, we have not made any progress!"

Odile's caring eyes followed her father as he despondently wandered from desk to chair to window and finally said: "It's not quite so, *cher Papa*. Please don't be so sad. We've received the first letter written by Olya's hand. Isn't that grand? And how much she must have worked to compose it so cleverly! We've also found Olga isn't the only person who cares about Olya: She has a girlfriend who loves and cherishes her." These were mature words that almost brought tears to his eyes. Ashamed, all he could do was hug his daughter and thank God, yet again, for the child. "You're right. I mustn't lose faith and become disheartened. Instead, I should be thinking, we both should, of the Tatar young woman, Ilysiya: She not only cares for Olya but has done something dangerous to help her."

Later in the morning, as he was absentmindedly turning the pages of the Paris daily *Le Figaro* for that 31st of July 1981, an announcement caught his eye:

Come celebrate Tatarstan's traditional summer "Festival of the Plow," Sabantuy, *together with outstanding dancers and musicians from the City of Kazan in the USSR! At Concert Hall Olympia, 28 Boulevard des Capucines, 75009 Paris. At 20:00h. Tickets at the box office and in the best hotels, 175-700 Fr.*

"Yes," thought Célestin, "it really wouldn't have made any sense if I went to Paris. I'm no Rambo in an American thriller to

look for Ilysiya, I don't even know how she looks. And to tell her...
what? I told her everything important in as heartfelt a way as I
could. Ilysiya and Olga have certainly estimated what degree of
risk was not insane."

He went behind the main building to the vegetable garden
where Odile was helping Marie. The girl had escaped from keeping company with Mathilde. Célestin showed her the announcement for the Tatar performance at the famous Olympia. "It seems
they're very popular," he said, "because the capacity of the hall is
two thousand spectators. Tonight must be their last show, as tomorrow is the first of August, and the mass exodus from Paris to
the country, seaside, and mountains will begin."

The entire day, they were correct but lukewarm with Mathilde.
Already after breakfast, she showed signs of wishing to delay her
departure. He, however, was not disposed to chat interminably or
take a walk with someone with whom he could not talk about
Olya. So he informed her that the next morning at 10:24, an express train from Paris to Hamburg would arrive in Metz and leave
eight minutes later. He added he knew the train station chief and
could ask the gentleman to secure a seat in first class at the last
moment.

Mathilde had no choice but to accept the situation, expertly
hiding the disappointment even from herself. Being aware of the
panicky demand for tickets on the first of August, she managed to
interpret Célestin's offer as a considerate gesture. "Life is long,"
she philosophized, "he'll come around." They parted cordially at
the station. Odile had said goodbye to Mathilde already the previous evening.

7.

In mid-August, a letter arrived from their Baikal guide, and it
delighted them. Oksana wrote she had gotten married to Alyosha
at the Irkutsk cathedral, and they had previously been baptized.
"As I confided to you, we had long felt Orthodox Christians, so the
baptism was a moving event for us. We couldn't imagine life

afterward without it and feel privileged, dear Célestin, to have received your guidance. When we conveyed the facts to our parents, they had no choice. To our surprise, they attended not just the wedding but even the baptism. Curiosity may have played a part, but maybe, as years pass, their blind belief in the communist doctrine is fading.

"My husband and I must confess something: We didn't tell our parents about your well-meaning advice. They'd immediately start about the 'anti-Soviet activity of hostile foreign factors,' and we didn't have the strength for quarrels. They are our parents who have given us all they could. We love and respect them. What we did was not a real lie, we thought, but something called an 'innocent lie' in Russian. Is it called 'white lie' in English? While on the subject, how's your Russian going? You and Odile were making fantastic progress." She concluded the letter with numerous questions about life in Metz.

"It's you who's responsible for this letter: Oksana enjoyed the postcards you sent her." Odile answered: "She was so good to us! I like her a lot, with the sweet round face, pretty blond hair, and a little chubby." They talked about the gift they would send to the newlyweds—something the couple would like but not so valuable to disappear in transit.

Before the 1st of September, when the new school year would start, an oversized postcard arrived from Osnat, Avigail, and Shoshana. To Odile's delight, the picture showed the familiar friendly beach at Sharm El Sheikh. Osnat wrote they had rented, for a modest sum, a dilapidated terrain vehicle rescued by a shrewd operator from the Egyptian Army junkyard. They managed to drive to Ras Muhammad and back in the monster. "True," she admitted, "several times we almost got stuck in the sand. And the heat was unbearable. We were even more in awe of your walking there alone. But swimming in the open Red Sea was fabulous! We missed you two..."

A few days later, a thick letter arrived from Osnat, who was by then at her parents' home in Netanya. Unlike the previous warm but short letters, the new one was long and detailed. Although much of what she wrote had to do with the imminent beginning of her fourth year of law studies at Hebrew University and with events in her family circle, the tone was more intimate than ever. Even so, there were no unrestrained declarations of love nor sentimental reminiscences of their nocturnal intimacy on the hotel terrace in Netanya. But there also was no mention of a boyfriend, whether a casual one or a devoted suitor. It seemed Osnat was maturely trying to measure the pulse of their feelings and discover the possible course of the relationship.

Célestin's conundrum was how to sever the close but hopeless emotional and sexual tie without hurting the kind and in many ways remarkable young woman. So in his lengthy response, he swam from the platonic to the romantic bank of the river and back to the platonic but always striving, albeit gently, to reach the main current leading out to sea—and Kuybyshev! He admitted that his meandering, evasive sentences were unworthy both of him and the two of them, but there was no other solution. He would not stoop to writing to a woman like Osnat: "What happened, happened—and now we are…" What, precisely? Quits?! If he could continue to have her as a friend, it would be invaluable but seemed unrealistic. Time supposedly heals everything, he sighed, and became conscious that his feelings, thoughts, and words, even more than before, were influenced by the absent Olya: She was bodily in prison, far away, but her heart and soul were not powerless. With Odile, she had become the most essential part of his life.

He regularly drove his little girl to school, after which various obligations in the city awaited him. Back at home, he did calisthenics or went riding one of the horses—never Pasha. Often, while walking in the fields, he would sit down under a tree and read; it could be a novel or a scientific article. Journals published in many countries on topics ranging from comparative linguistics and other sciences to history and the law regularly arrived. He also maintained an extensive correspondence with colleagues and friends. More often than Gilles, it was Célestin who picked Odile up after lessons and took her for walks in the city and along the river. They visited museums and art galleries. She sketched the cathedral's stained-glass windows or photographed them.

One of his frequent correspondents was Simha Grenstein. Sometimes they addressed an interesting language issue that had popped up in the then-current Israeli-Arab negotiations and concerned international law. As their relationship became more easy-going, there were jokes, usually self-directed. Recalling in one letter their first conversation in Atara, Simha wrote that on a visit to the café the previous day, he had nostalgically ordered three portions of chestnut puree with whipped cream—of which two were meant for Célestin and Odile. "Unfortunately, I was alone and had to eat all three—with the kippah on my head, of course." But in a serious, jubilant letter in mid-September, rabbi Simha invited Célestin to attend, as his honored guest, a formal ceremony on the 27th of October at which Professor Grenstein would be promoted to *Doctor honoris causa* by his rabbinical college.

Célestin would have gladly flown to Jerusalem to attend the ceremony. He would have done it for Simha, the high regard in which he held him, and their friendship. But also out of curiosity. And Osnat would be nearby, hmm... Still, he had to decline the invitation. "Dear Simha," he wrote, "I'm honored and touched by your invitation and normally would be delighted to attend—with a kippah on my head! The problem is not Odile's school, nor that my thirty-seventh birthday also falls on the 27th of October. What prevents me is this: I have invited two old friends of mine, a married couple, to come from Berlin for my birthday with their children, whom they'd take out of school for several days. The kids are twins of my daughter's age, a boy and a girl, and the three became 'bosom buddies' earlier this year when we stayed with this family. To her delight, these friends will be present at the party to which she's invited a group of her schoolmates who'll spend the day at our house. Their parents have approved the plan, although it's a weekday. I can't cancel all that." He concluded: "Naturally, I'm not asking that your promotion be postponed by a few days (!!) but am using this opportunity to tell you Odile and I would welcome you in our home on this or any other day."

She was studying diligently. Her hunger for knowledge was induced rather than sated by traveling. When there was information in a school text that she had acquired first-hand during their peripatetics, a pleased, naughty smile would grace her lips. Before his birthday, when Célestin visited the school, her homeroom teacher Philippe Marceau said the girl's grades in all subjects were again the highest in class, but her nose was never in the air.

Over time, she had accepted the notion of being partly responsible for their correspondence. Instead of considering it a boring obligation, she viewed it as a route to new knowledge. Once she acquired the habit and was flattered when a grownup from a foreign country responded to her letter or postcard kindly and seriously, her dad ceased to remind her to whom and when to write. Odile corresponded not only with Sophia and Emil Benz in Berlin but also with Lina and Saul in Nairobi, Daphne and Yehuda in Taba-Eilat, and even with their daughter Dina, the soldier in the barracks in Tel Aviv. In her notebook, it was pedantically written who was who and how different people and families were related. She never forgot to note when a person did something helpful or generous and which gift she received from whom. Rarely, she bore a grudge and described Morkel's wife Deborah as "a witch from a fairy tale." She chose postcards herself and often left barely enough space for her father's signature—he welcomed it. However, if she wrote a letter, she would show it to her papa, and he might add a page.

But with Morky and Hila, Célestin insisted he deal with them alone. He explained that the life situation of those dear people was delicate: "I think, *ma chère fille,* they're so preoccupied with their own decisions they can't pay attention to other people, even us."

In truth, Morkel had already sent news in a letter from Zurich. He had arrived there after a stay with Deborah in New York, during which the couple quarreled fiercely, with Michal adding oil to the fire in a childish, yet malicious, manner. Finally, they agreed to get a divorce in Jerusalem, where they had gotten married two and a half years earlier. Following the instructions of a local lawyer in whom they both had confidence, the necessary papers were promptly sent, and the divorce was obtained expeditiously, without the presence of the two parties being required: Their lawyer knew the judge. Morkel then flew to Switzerland to recover from the ordeal. He wrote: "I need mental rest from Deborah and the New York clamor and hubbub. I'll remain in Zurich til mid-November and then return to the ruckus and babel of my beloved Israel."

Shyly, at the end of his letter, Morky announced his truly important news: "I'm happy Hila will soon join me in this boring Zurich. As you undoubtedly noticed, she and I have for a long time felt a strong mutual affection. Still, it has always been from afar, platonic. When she comes, we'll see how it goes." Célestin responded the same day, wishing the couple love and happiness. He also invited them to Metz, writing: "Here it's quieter and less nervous than in New York or Israel, but sometimes more boring than even in Zurich." Of course, he remembered the lunch at the Maiersdorf in Jerusalem with Hila: He had at the time expressed hope she and Morky, then absent in New York and married, would one day have a child together.

Walter Schönflug had planned to come to Metz for his friend's birthday but called a week earlier to apologize. He had received a rare invitation to give a series of lectures in Japan and South Korea and could not miss such an opportunity. Although Célestin had pretended to be sorry, he felt relieved—both sad and glad, genuinely ambivalent. Being in a quandary about what to say, he failed to open up on several occasions in Berlin, so Walter knew nothing about Olya's existence! Being in prison was not a problem (!), for it was a consequence of resistance to Soviet repression, thus both factually correct and praiseworthy. But her past? Walter might willy-nilly connect such information to his experiences in the Gion Quarter of Kyoto. His fascination with the geiko certainly had a vulgar side. How could Célestin calmly talk about Olya as his future loving wife and Odile's stepmother? "I'd need several irksome days filled with mutual anger, hurt, and disappointment. All the toil, nay, hard *labor* to justify I love her and find her amply deserving of my feelings," he thought unhappily after Walter's call.

8.

The early morning of his birthday was clear, windless, and delightfully fresh. The giant oaks in front of the manor still displayed orange, crimson, and umber leaves: These two-hundred-year-old trees had the monarchist pedigree of *Ancien Régime*. Célestin took a solitary walk and calmly appraised the achievements of his thirty-seven years of life. He reckoned the gentle, good-natured, and wise Odile was his greatest success. Behind her came a certain inherent quality of his nature that nevertheless had to be consciously molded—the ability to overlook undesirable aspects of someone's past and discern what was good and even admirable. The bronze medal belonged to distant travels inspired by a love of the amazing diversity of the world's cultures and languages. After reciting the list in his mind, Célestin grinned, climbed several hillocks, and returned home.

Her pink alarm clock having rang at six, Odile quietly walked downstairs intending to ask Gerda and Françoise to remain quiet so Papa could sleep. Meanwhile, he had entered and was tiptoeing. At the foot of the stairs, she exclaimed and embraced him with all her strength, wishing her dad the most joyous day in the world.

"*Mon cher Papounet*, I have presents for you. Let's go to my room, that's where I hid them! I so much hope you'll like them." First, she gave him the birthday card she had written. Standing with an arm around her, he read it several times, deeply touched. Then she produced an object the size of a large notebook wrapped in soft light-blue paper. It was a professionally bound stack of some thirty charcoal and pencil drawings she had made in

Russia, Paris, Berlin, Israel, and Kenya. He looked at all the drawings and said something thoughtful or complimentary about each. That was a wonderful gift, but the next one—even though less personal—astonished him: A very old layout plan of their estate under glass, exquisitely framed. It was made for Louis Fernand de Quernevelle and had a seal with the date 11th of May 1760. From Louis Fernand to Célestin, there were nine generations in a direct line of the family De Quernevelle.

The birthday celebrant profusely thanked his daughter for the superb gifts and then asked how she accomplished it. "*Bien*, it was like this. Long ago, I decided to give you my best drawings because you chose all those marvelous places. And the layout plan of the estate... Last year, you showed it to me. Maybe you don't remember, it wasn't a special occasion. You were telling me about your grandpa Olivier and then about his father and grandfather. The old plan was beautiful, and by chance, I remembered into which drawer of the armoire in your study you'd put it away. The drawer caught my attention because it was hard for you to pull out, and it screeched awfully. *Bien sûr*, for me it was even harder, but I managed, twice! *Cher Papa*, please don't be upset that I took the plan from your study without permission, but I so much wanted to surprise you. And I'll never open the armoire again, I promise!"

"Everything is fine, *mon bijou*, please don't worry," Célestin reassured her, and Odile continued. "Three or four times, you couldn't come to pick me up after school, so I knew already in the morning it would be Gerda or Gilles. When Gerda came, we went together to a store where I bought your birthday card. Also, I asked Gilles to find a shop that could bind my drawings and frame the plan. He did it, so on one occasion when I knew he would be coming for me, I brought the plan and the drawings to school. After classes, he took me to a workshop on rue Georges Clémenceau; the entrance is from the courtyard behind other shops. It's a bookbindery and a framing shop in one. I chose the cover for the stack of drawings and the frame for the layout plan. Some weeks later, Gilles learned the job was finished, so we returned there. I made sure the stack and frame were properly done. The staff was gracious and lowered the price! *Tu vois*, for months, I was putting an amount aside from my weekly pocket money. I'd never borrow money from Gilles or Gerda."

For a long time, with a broad smile and immeasurable fatherly love and pride in his heart, Célestin gazed at his daughter. He embraced her, murmuring: "You're an absolute miracle of a little girl. Because of you, I'm having an unforgettable birthday!" While tears of joy were flowing down Odile's face, he kissed her and went on: "*Ne pleure pas, ma douce...* I'll take your precious drawings to my study, and we'll go down to the *salon* to find a nice spot for the layout plan."

Then he took her hand and led her out of the house. Standing under the grand, stately oaks, he whispered: "*Regarde ces chênes géants...* Imagine, they were just green saplings when the layout plan of our estate was drawn."

Around eleven, the Benz-Klein family arrived in their station wagon. They had covered seven hundred kilometers the previous day, spending the night with relatives in Mannheim and driving the remaining two hundred in less than two hours. No one minded the long journey because they wanted to see Célestin and Odile and wish him a happy birthday. In Berlin, Sophia and Emil often mentioned their French agemate, *liebe Odile*, which sounded musical to them in German. Father and daughter warmly greeted their friends. While they chatted in the drawing room drinking lemonade, the estate layout plan hanging on the wall attracted the guests' attention. She cocked an ear at Uwe's question and was pleased when her father proudly said: "A birthday present from my daughter."

Sigrid and Uwe gave Célestin a present for his study: A pair of metal chess knights made in Uruguay, each a fine beast over twelve centimeters tall. The twins, amusingly competing with each other, gave separate clever gifts to Odile.

Soon they went for a leisurely autumn walk to the Moselle. Leading Pasha and often stroking her neck, she spoke to Sophia and Emil in a gay, singing voice about the paths along which she usually rode her horse. Meanwhile, the children's parents discussed various events that had taken place since their time together in Berlin. At one point, Célestin said: "Believe it or not, if it weren't my birthday, Odile and I would right now be in Jerusalem attending the promotion at a rabbinical college of my friend, a professor of law and rabbi, into a Doctor of Divinity *honoris causa*." Then he talked at length about Simha Grenstein, a baby from Auschwitz, which his German friends, dedicated anti-Nazis, found amazing to the verge of disbelief.

Festivities were exuberant from early afternoon. Immediately after school, parents brought Odile's young guests and gave gifts to Célestin. He was pleased that despite being the recipient, the feel of the party was young, with his daughter the main celebrant. She exuded joy. After initial hesitation, children began their games, running around trees and through gardens. They would only stop for a moment to taste some of the many types of delicious finger food on offer—some of it exotic. Emil skillfully entertained everyone by playing the pianino, becoming popular with the girls—a veritable mysterious stranger. Sophia and Odile sang ditties in German and French and even danced an allegedly Israeli number. Children were tireless until half-past eight when their parents arrived to collect them. Célestin introduced them to Sigrid and Uwe and made sure they were all served a piece of cake and a glass of wine.

As the hostess and the twins did not want the party to end, they approached Sigrid. Odile gamely requested: "Tante Sigrid, I know you're an astronomer, no, excuse me, an astro...physicist. Physics for the stars! Well, the three of us have noticed many stars are already visible. Would you please tell us something about them?" What could Sigrid do but leave her glass of semisweet *Sauterne* almost untouched and gather a bunch of inquisitive boys and girls around her, some distance from the oaks? Not only did she identify the most luminous stars but also recounted anecdotes about those "enigmatic inhabitants of cosmos," as she called them affectionately.

9.

On the 9th of November, Hila and Morky would arrive from Zurich and Paris for a three-day visit. In the middle of December, Odile would have four days of exams, but it seemed certain her marks would be excellent. After pondering the matter, Célestin made an audacious plan for which he needed the girl's enthusiastic agreement and permission from *messieurs* Gaubert and Marceau.

After driving her to school one morning, he visited several shops. In a bookstore, the manager walked him to the shelf dominated by a massive volume about the famous Kruger National Park in South Africa. It was full of magnificent photos of wild animals living in stunning landscapes. Next, he went to a store selling photographic technical goods and bought a high-quality slide projector and screen with a solid stand. These items would replace the archaic equipment they had—and the wall.

At home, he selected eighty of the hundreds of slides they had taken at Lake Nakuru and the Nairobi National Park. He filled two projection carousels, opting for an aesthetic sequence at the expense of chronology. Having placed the projector and the screen appropriately in his study, he closed the heavy drapes on all the windows. As he pressed a button on the tiny hand-held device, brilliant African colors and fantastic sights of Kenyan animals materialized.

While driving home, Odile chattered about schoolmates who had thanked her for the "best party of the year." He let her eat in peace the snack Marie had lovingly prepared, but when she had finished, placed the Kruger book on the table: "Take a look at this volume about a world-renowned wild animal park in South Africa. I bought it today. When you finish, climb up to my study."

Célestin had temporarily opened the drapes, curious about her reaction. Odile appeared after an hour, carrying the book pressed to her chest and looking astonished. She walked around the desk and placed all of Kruger, it seemed, in front of her father: "How wondrous it all is, *cher Papa!*" Remembering some page numbers, she turned the leaves to show the pictures of animals they had encountered in Kenya—giraffes, cheetahs, lions, rhinos, hippos—and stayed even longer on pages with specimens she had never seen, even in a zoo. From time to time, she exclaimed with the delight expected from a younger child.

"You didn't see this when you entered, it must be too big," he laughed pointing to the large projection screen and closing the drapes again. "Today I bought a new slide projector and a good screen. Let's look at our photos from Nakuru and Nairobi. Sit in your armchair, and I'll project the slides. If you want to look at something longer, let me know; I can easily go back."

The photo editor was pleased that he heard Odile's joyful exclamation or amused comment in response to almost every slide. As with many other things in life, their taste in photography, nature, and animals coincided. It was obvious that the appetite of the budding adventurer had been thoroughly whetted.

After he had shown all eighty slides, Célestin opened the drapes. She blinked, sighed, and finally said: "Like an animal fairy tale! I'm certainly not a photographer like those in the book, but some of my photos are not that bad. Don't you think, Papa?" "I agree, they're not, and they'll be even better with more practice." He grabbed the moment: "As you remember, *mon trésor*, our trip to Kenya was my Christmas present for you. And even though our stay was fabulous, those three unfortunate sick days prevented us from going to Amboseli. So, how about traveling to South Africa and visiting not only Kruger but also other fantastic places, such as the gold mine museum in Johannesburg and the Kimberley Big Hole from which diamonds used to be excavated long ago? And being right at the Cape of Good Hope?!"

Odile's eyes grew wide, and her throat and mouth almost created a scream of joy, but he calmly interrupted: "You'll be done with exams in the middle of December and will get excellent grades. A day or two before Christmas, we'll fly from Paris to Johannesburg, the capital of that country. And in Kruger, with gorgeous wild animals, we'll celebrate your tenth birthday. Hey, the tenth! We'll be in South Africa for a month and a half, provided we're able to make arrangements with your school.

Her joy knew no bounds, but she added cautiously: "When we're in South Africa, at least for a week before we go to Kruger, there'll be no goat yogurt for me!"

10.

Around noon, as Odile was at school, Célestin awaited alone the arrival of the Paris train bringing Hila and Morkel to Metz. He came early to allow ample time to visit the station master Jacques Marceau, his longtime friend and chess partner. First, he thanked Jacques again for helpfully finding a seat for Mathilde LeClercq on the train bound for Hamburg. Monsieur Marceau smiled knowingly in a French way. Then he picked up the phone and ordered coffee and Mirabelle plum brandy from the station restaurant.

After briefly chatting about local news, Jacques took a conventional dual chess clock from a drawer and placed it on the table where they were sitting in a corner of his office. He wound up both clocks and began to adjust their hands, asking: "A five-minute game, *ça va?*" Then he ritually showed the clocks to prove that precisely five minutes before the fall of the red flag was set on both. They agreed to play a "blindfold," *sans voir*, game but without the board and pieces and thus without the need for blindfolds. The game began, their fifty-first. Being the guest, Célestin played as White: He immediately called out "pawn to e4" and quickly pressed the button on his clock, stopping it. Jacques responded with "pawn to c5" and stopped his clock as quickly. So they continued, alternately calling out the moves and stopping their respective clocks, only occasionally glancing at them. Except for the moves, neither uttered a single word. Jacques mostly stared at the empty table, sometimes shutting his eyes. Célestin's eyes were always open; he seemed to be disapprovingly studying the cobweb above the old ceramic stove in the opposite corner. There was a knock and Jacques yelled, "*Entrez!*" When the waiter opened the door, the station master wordlessly showed him where to place the tray. Seeing chess clocks and hearing the mysterious words, "bishop b5 takes on d7," the man understood the seriousness of the situation, soundlessly put down the tray, and tiptoed out.

Nine minutes and fifty-eight seconds into the stormy game, Marceau's flag fell, whereas Célestin's clock showed two seconds remaining. They both took a sip of brandy and wished good health. The winner said: "This game doesn't count, Jacques. Let's say you haven't lost it. You expended one or two seconds on the waiter, yet the tray's contents benefited me too. This doesn't mean I'll be merciful next time!" Jacques laughed heartily and wished 'long life' to Odile, well aware his older brother Philippe was her homeroom teacher. "Metz is far more of a village than Israel," chuckled Célestin inwardly. The station bell announced that the Paris train was entering the station.

11.

Hila and Morky had become more intimate during their stay in Zurich and could relax in the company of their hosts free of doubts about the future. Attired in resplendent colors of autumn, the manor grounds welcomed them with open arms. The weather was often sunny, but there were romantic mists above the Moselle. Célestin, Odile, and the entire staff did all they could to make the newlyweds comfortable—as they thought of the Israeli couple. Even so, instead of receiving gifts, Hila and Morky gave them to the hosts. Three tranquil days passed pleasantly.

As longtime friends of Simha, Hila and Morky had also received the invitation to the doctoral promotion and, like Célestin, were sorry not to be able to accept it. Late one evening, after Odile had gone to bed, the trio sat in front of the blazing fireplace sipping Cognac. They talked of Simha's incredible life and only then did Hila reveal to Morky she had told Célestin at their lunch at the Maiersdorf the truth about Simha's father, the German officer. He noticed Morky's frown and felt hurt, asking himself: "Is it possible that despite our great closeness of so many years, I remain for Morky a non-Jew to whom certain secrets mustn't be entrusted?"

He was relieved when the questioning grimace on his friend's face disappeared after a few seconds, and Morky said to Hila: "You did the right thing. I know how much Simha respects our friend. He told me he had disclosed to Célestin 'almost everything' about his life. I understood what he had left out, what had been desperately hard for him to utter, although he had sincerely wished to do it. And knowing Simha well, I'm certain it had nothing to do with Célestin not being a Jew. After all, ninety-eight percent of the Jews who know Simha have no idea about the German officer. Yes, Hila, you did Simha a favor."

They toasted each other. Morky went on: "Besides, Hila, let's proclaim our friend a Jew *honoris causa*—which he has anyway long been for me!" Célestin lifted his glass: "I gladly accept the honor. And declare you two French, if you permit me—which is comical in Hila's case, as she's a born Parisienne who grew up there and was educated at the Sorbonne."

"Merci profondément, cher Célestin, au nom de Morky et bien entendu de moi!" exclaimed Hila. She continued: "Regarding Paris, my parents still reside in their apartment in the Huitième. They love each other and are very active. Morky and I took a plane from Zurich to Paris intending to visit them, but we enjoyed the autumn season in the secluded corners of the city so much that we changed our minds and came straight here. Perhaps we got cold feet, Morky can be quite shy. But from here, we'll return to Paris and spend several days with my parents before flying to Israel. We have so much to tell them. As I told you the first time we spoke in my office, my parents have always respected my judgment. We'll have their support."

Another festive toast, one including Odile's health and happiness, ensued. Then Célestin poured a few more sips of Cognac into everyone's glass for a peaceful night.

After the departure of their guests, father and daughter fondly talked about them, but she once said: "As you know, they kindly gave me a cuckoo clock. Gerda and my girlfriends adore it, and it must be expensive, yet I don't like it at all—neither the wooden decorations nor the bird and its sound. Especially the sound. May I give the clock to Gerda? You told me a gift one receives shouldn't be given to someone else. But I don't want it in my bedroom, I'm sorry."

"Célestin Solomon Shlomo" needed only a minute to decide: "All right, let's not follow the etiquette to the letter in this case. Give the clock to Gerda, explaining it's not a gift but a loan—for ninety-nine years! To tell you the truth, I don't like such clocks either, they are too gaudy. I once told you what the word kitsch means. *Bien*, that's what these German, Swiss, and Austrian clocks are, in my opinion. Please don't say it to Gerda, she'd be hurt. You see, Hila and Morky love you, but they still don't know your taste well enough." He brought a ladder and took the clock off the wall.

Time passed quickly. She studied indefatigably, while her father managed to obtain the school's permission to take his daughter to South Africa for six weeks. It took all of Célestin's persuasive skills in three lengthy talks with Gaubert and Marceau, separately and together, before they went along with his plan. He then bought all the necessary gear and made arrangements for the vaccines with Dr. Beaufort. The Air France flight from Paris to Johannesburg, leaving on Wednesday, the 23rd of December at dawn, would return them to African soil. There would be a stop in Nairobi but no change of planes.

PART NINE

Dima and Kolya

1.

Barney's Inn, Johannesburg, the afternoon of the 1st of January 1982: Although Barney's certainly was neither the most appealing nor the healthiest spot in South Africa in which a girl of almost ten might spend several hours of New Year's Day with her father, Odile de Quernevelle felt enviably well and found everything around her remarkably interesting.

That morning, they had a good breakfast in their hotel Harrison Reef in Hillbrow, one of the city's central quarters. On the recommendation of Carl Goode—a specialist for East African languages at the University of Witwatersrand, known as Wits—they found a suite at the Harrison, with breakfast included and a spacious terrace, for only thirty-five rands a day. Muriel, the courteous front desk manager, addressed them on their way to the underground garage: "I hope you slept well. Your apartment 601 is the best and quietest in our hotel. What are your plans for today if I may ask?"

They looked at each other, and he winked at the girl to respond: "Well, Mrs. Muriel, we have a long list for Joburg. But today we planned to dig for diamonds." Muriel laughed: "Hmm, Miss Odile, that you'll need to do elsewhere in our rich country, for example, in the Big Hole in Kimberley—but it's a little far, about five hundred kilometers! However, not far from here, you can dig for gold already today." The girl blushed: "Yes, just what I meant. We'd like to visit Gold Reef City Theme Park."

Muriel exclaimed: "Good idea! You'll both have a splendid time in our golden disneyland, only about ten kilometers from here. Take the M1, Mr. De Quernevelle, and then switch to the

Oranje-Vrystaat highway south for Bloemfontein. From there, you'll arrive at Gold Reef Park after seven kilometers. By the way, I'm glad you took my advice and parked your Rover in the hotel garage. Even though our parking is ridiculously expensive—armed guards don't come cheap—it's a sound investment. Several cars parked on the street in this neighborhood were set on fire last night; others were turned onto their roofs like cockroaches. You see, they—you can guess who—were celebrating the New Year."

Their rented Land Rover awaited them intact in the garage. It was a pale-green diesel-powered 4WD vehicle with two doors, a light-brown canvas roof, and a fat spare tire lying on the hood. Tall, wide, and powerful, more like a grizzly bear than an African savanna animal, it greeted Célestin and Odile ready for distant travel and safaris. They arrived quickly at Gold Reef City and slowly oriented themselves; there was much to see.

The sun was hot, a lovely first day of January, suitable for celebrating the precious yellow metal and the origin of Johannesburg. There were many people in the park, mostly black. In the fantasy settlement with house façades, horse-drawn four-wheel fiacres, and artisan shops from 1890, one could buy tobacco, lace, and women's hats and dresses. All the salespeople wore sham late-nineteenth-century clothes. The theme of the park was the notorious "gold fever" that broke out there in 1886.

Odile and Célestin were fascinated by the remnants of the original mine with gold ore still visible and by a superb model of the entire mine with geological explanations. The extensive authentic machinery for the extraction and purification of the ore took their breath away. Amazing original furnaces were on view, as well as an exhibit of molten gold being poured into molds—a phase where ingots consisting of eighty percent gold, ten percent silver, and some copper, lead, and zinc were made.

Such ingots were then additionally purified by sulfuric acid to obtain gold bars used in international trade. Each bar weighed four hundred Troy ounces, which equaled 12.4414 kilograms of twenty-four-karat, 99.6 percent pure gold. The remaining 0.4 percent was copper, for it increased the hardness of the alloy, without affecting its gold color. Odile jotted down the information, so he commented: "It seems you're preparing a lecture about gold for your girlfriends—or the entire class together with monsieur Marceau!"

They learned the origin of their hotel's name. In 1886, a prospector by the name of George Harrison discovered gold in the Witwatersrand wilderness and promptly sold the rights for ten British pounds, which was the beginning of the widespread "gold fever," the biggest ever and anywhere. Would-be prospectors arrived from all over the world, each carrying a pickaxe, shovel, and gold pan. Three thousand astonishing photos in the museum documented the "disease." The gold mine functioned until 1971.

2.

In the late afternoon, hunger led them to a lower level and Barney's Inn. There were few guests. They ate sandwiches and then rested, talking quietly. Odile was drinking a lemonade and contentedly writing an entry in her diary. Célestin was sipping a beer and studying the behavior of men, women, and waitresses. At some tables sat white men and women, at others black men and women, and at still others, people of both races. The waitresses were both black and white, and they served all customers in the same manner. There was clearly no segregation in the restaurant, probably because—he guessed—the golden disneyland catered to many international tourists. At the entrance, there was neither a white cardboard circle hanging on the door, standing for "whites only," nor a black one, for "blacks only," as was the case everywhere else in Joburg. All customers seemed middle class, but that rarely excluded segregation.

His hypothesis of the absence of racial segregation in the restaurant was soon confirmed by a Mr. Douglas. The very black gentleman's behavior in Barney's was strikingly similar to the action of the postal functionary Mr. Matenge in Nairobi. Just as their Kenyan collocutor had done, Douglas unceremoniously sat down at the table occupied by father and daughter, even though it was in a distant corner. The visitor wore a broad smile and carried a one-liter jug of beer. "I think it's not his first, but it's New Year," Célestin thought good-naturedly.

"Good day to you, Sir! Happy New Year to you and your little one! My name is Douglas. From afar one can see you're a foreigner, so I thought we'd chat a little if you don't mind. How nice that you're traveling with a young daughter. My wife and I have two children, a few years older than your girl." Célestin responded by wishing Douglas and his family all the best. He introduced himself as Tino, and for Odile mumbled "Dilla," not knowing why—perhaps, naively, to protect her. She peered at her father and their uninvited guest, also remembering Matenge. The change of her name did not escape the girl's attention, but she smiled at Douglas and returned to the diary.

With a regular face, tall and slender like Célestin, the South African was in his late thirties. From the start, their dialogue was friendly and open. Douglas worked as a decently paid machinist, whereas his wife received a pittance for her back-breaking work at a shabby supermarket. Despite the two salaries, in part because of their children's incessant demands, they could not afford to live anywhere but in the South-Western Townships, the infamous Soweto. Having said that, Douglas raised his eyebrows questioningly and added: "If you planned to go there out of curiosity, ignoring the cautionary stories of the local whites, don't go; listen to them! There's nothing to see, it's dirty and dangerous. I wouldn't invite you even to my house." To Douglas's surprise, Célestin told him: "I fully understand the reasons for your warning, and I'm grateful. But Dilla and I've already been there—for a short time only, in a nondescript car. It belonged to an acquaintance of ours, a decent white woman born in Joburg. In any case, she wisely drove only on the rim of Soweto. What can I tell you? Everything looked exactly as you've described it." Douglas nodded and murmured: "Then you've seen where we have to live."

Soon they switched to politics. "Of course, I support the ANC (*African National Congress*); my leaders are Nelson (Mandela), (Oliver) Tambo, and (Allan) Boesak. But I must admit the current

Prime Minister P. W. Botha (Pieter Willem Botha), although he's from the hated National Party, has improved things." Célestin had known even before arriving in South Africa that Botha's nickname was Big Croc, meaning crocodile, so he asked Douglas about it. The answer surprised him: "Not quite fair! It was invented and put into circulation by local British swindlers who own the yellow press. They hate the Boers as competitors and always try to acquire more power. P. W. seems a well-intentioned man, given the enormous constraints placed on him. We know of his secret meetings with Nelson."

Douglas looked around carefully. "Listen, Tino: I know my family, even in Soweto, lives much better than do black people in Nigeria, the Congo, or Zimbabwe, and remember we are in power in those countries. Hey, Zimbabwe—ex-South Rhodesia—has been an independent country for only one or two years, yet already there's no doubt their so-called president Robert Mugabe will hold onto power for life! A terrible dictator who'll terrorize his helpless subjects… His face, as it happens, is much blacker than mine, ha, ha."

Célestin asked him: "I notice you've been looking around. Are there plainclothes police agents or amateur informers in a place like this?" Douglas responded quickly: "Undoubtedly there are, but we aren't of interest. They know you aren't a lying journalist from England or Holland. Also, a sabotage plan wouldn't be discussed here, would it?

"About what you've asked me—I look around out of habit. But if you must know, the really dangerous situation for me would be if some ANC 'children' were listening to what I've been saying. Maybe not here, but I'm always watchful. You must have heard of 'children,' 'comrades,' and 'necklacing': They place old car tires around the neck of men, only black men, mind you, who aren't in their opinion one hundred percent loyal to the ANC, and set them on fire—alive! You've heard of it, haven't you?" Douglas spoke the last ten or so words almost inaudibly because he had seen Odile was watching him aghast. Sadly, resignation lining his face, he muttered: "Excuse me, please, dear girl."

They had been given a similar account of ANC children and necklacing by Wim, a senior sergeant in the South African police, only three days earlier in Roodeplaat, northeast of Pretoria—but Célestin was not going to mention it to Douglas. Instead, he revealed he had indeed read about necklacing in the French and German press, and that communists, anarchists, Trotskyists, Maoists, red-brigadiers, and other cynical leftists openly approved such actions as necessary for revolutionary success. He watched Odile with one eye as he spoke, aware that her ears had pricked up the moment Douglas mentioned ANC children. The same horrific information twice in less than a week since arriving in South Africa! He needed to talk to her and point out that they had heard the same thing from two men, one black, one white.

Célestin's principle was not to be constantly shielding his daughter from the unpleasant truth. What was the purpose of travel if he had to cover her eyes and ears each time there was a chance of coming face to face with disagreeable facts—especially facts about children not much older than she was? In eighteen days, she would be ten, and many ANC children were precisely that age. In international coverage, ANC supporters and anti-apartheid activists uttered the word protectively and "parentally," whereas others abhorred the children for being so cruel so young.

He asked Douglas not to hold back because of Odile: "I'll explain everything to Dilla later. We're close and trust each other. And there's no stepmother or old aunt who intervenes in her upbringing in a mawkish way." Douglas wordlessly looked at Célestin and went on in a sad voice, playing thoughtfully with his sizable key ring: "Listen, I'll tell you something: My wife and I fear for our very lives. And we aren't the only parents in Soweto who feel this way. We have a son of thirteen and a daughter of twelve who fervently believe everything a certain no-good boy of sixteen tells them. He belongs to the Junior ANC, doesn't attend classes, and is always hanging around the schoolyard talking to pupils, mostly girls. Sweet-talks them and bullshits—sorry! And gives orders. It begins with minor criticisms of parents, but we know, my wife and I, that it ends with necklacing. We can't any longer hug them without being pushed away and questioned: 'Why are you doing this and not...?' We'd somehow find the money to enroll them in a school away from Soweto, but now it's too late. It would doubly mark us."

Douglas's eyes darkened with pain and fury. Clutching the bunch of keys in his fist, he suddenly slammed the table, growling: "Killers with good intentions! They've poisoned our children. What does Nelson know and think about *that*?" The bang was very loud, but the words were softly spoken. Odile and Célestin were taken aback, although only a few heads turned. Even if some eyes rested on them, it was probably not because of the noise but due to the racial and age composition of the trio. She was the only child in the restaurant.

Little he had learned in South Africa until then prepared Célestin for Douglas's misery. He felt deeply sorry not just for him and his wife but also for their children. To change the topic, though not entirely, he asked: "May I ask you, Douglas, what you think about the Sharpeville massacre? I've read three hundred fifty people were killed there." Douglas thought calmly but again became excited before answering: "The correct numbers are sixty killed and two hundred wounded. Quite a few were wounded by protesters who stomped on them. It happened twenty-two years ago, when I was twelve, as is my daughter now. The fact is this: The Sharpeville police station was surrounded by about six thousand people who were throwing rocks at the cops and began to break the fence. No matter how one looks at the whole event—the reasons for it and the rest—there's no doubt horrible bloodshed would have happened. Not one of us blacks can forget or forgive what happened, but..." The words that followed were spoken through teeth: "What's the number of white criminals' black victims compared to hundreds of thousands of black villains' black victims, when one considers our entire black-green continent?"

The Southern Cross was already visible in the sky as Douglas, Odile, and Célestin exchanged goodbyes in the parking lot. The men hugged powerfully, something the Lorrain did rarely on a first meeting. When they remained alone, father and daughter felt the old gold mine still rumbling under their feet, or so it seemed. They spoke about Douglas, liquid gold, and the different starry sky one saw from the planet's southern hemisphere. "If Sigrid were here, she'd probably know a tale about sailors who had lost their way until they saw the Southern Cross," Odile said wistfully. He agreed: "It undoubtedly happened countless God-beseeching and thanking times during storms."

"And Papa, did you tell Mr. Douglas my name was Dilla, or did I mishear?" "Your hearing and listening are perfect, better than necessary! I said it because many people here have never heard our rare names so I tried to help. Don't worry, *ma douce,* your name has always been beautiful and dear to me. And to your mother."

3.

At Jan Smuts Airport, when Célestin and Odile arrived from Paris to Joburg, they were met by his colleague Carl Goode who drove them straight to the Hillbrow quarter to find accommodation. The first hotel Carl showed them was Harrison Reef and they booked the sole suite on the top floor. Carl and the doorman joined them in the elevator to make sure everything was in order. When the doorman left, the two linguists found beer in the sizable fridge and talked on the terrace, whereas Odile took a shower after the long journey.

Carl was a South African of English descent who knew Paris and obviously Kenya because of his linguistic studies. He was the same age as Célestin, a professor at Wits, and married to a South African woman of Dutch descent—Afrikaner or Boer (*Boeren* means *farmers*). On the terrace, he said: "I thought the two of you, sophisticated world travelers, would prefer to stay during your first visit to Joburg in a historic quarter such as Hillbrow, rather than in a mammoth American hotel near corporations. Nor would you like, I thought, a hundred percent white suburb, pretty and safe but boring, such as Sandton—ten kilometers north of here—where Silvia and I live because of our three-year-old Peter."

While the visitor looked over the city, his mental compass feverishly active, Carl went on: "Yes, street life in Hillbrow is colorful, but... being out late presents problems for whites and middle-class blacks." They looked at each other calmly. Célestin smiled and thanked Carl for the choice of hotel: "No worries, we'll enjoy Joburg without wandering into Hillbrow's nightclubs!"

"Very well! Get some rest, but if it suits you, I'll come tomorrow noonish to drive you to the university and show you around," Carl said. "Even though it's the day before Christmas, everything will be open. Wits is in Braamfontein, just over the hillock west of here. You can walk there, it's only a kilometer away. I'll introduce you to Joanna, the secretary of the Linguistics Department; you'll collect your mail from her. Then we'll drive to Sandton for a simple lunch with Silvia at our house. Around three, my sister Mary and a few other guests will come, mostly colleagues eager to meet you."

After Carl left, Odile joined her father on the terrace. They stood with arms around each other, watching the sunset. Joburg's elevation was over a thousand seven hundred meters, similar to Nairobi's. Despite the city's millions of inhabitants, the light of the early evening was magically limpid, not unlike the Sinai desert. As always when they arrived at a completely unknown place, Célestin and Odile were excited in a way different from any other pleasant sensation. Their dear old Metz was very, very far.

* * *

The next morning, Mrs. Muriel, the front desk manager, wished them a merry Christmas in advance and helped the guest call car rental agencies. A Land Rover was quickly chosen; Avis would deliver the vehicle before the New Year.

Carl had every reason to be proud of Wits. It was an expansive campus in the Anglo-American style. Thought and money had been spent to ensure buildings and green areas existed in a harmonious ratio of the classical and the practical. Even some aggressively modern elements were permitted. At first sight, Wits was racially integrated. There were many non-white students whose favorite T-shirt was black with green letters "USA for

Africa." The colors were similar to those used by the ANC in its propaganda, but the three capital letters could not be seen together. The Linguistics secretary Joanna, as helpful as Carl had promised, made an effort to befriend Odile.

At the Goodes' handsome house, they were greeted by a domestic scene in which Silvia, red in the face, was energetically chasing the happily screaming little Peter around the swimming pool, presumably so he would not fall in?! The pool was surrounded by a fine garden, lush in the South African summer. Odile chuckled at the sight of Peter's escapade and tried, in a role new to her, to entertain the boy. Her father was pleased she was not put off by Peter's almost complete lack of speech at three years of age, despite the efforts of dedicated parents and therapists, as he was later told. It was clear to someone as observant as Célestin that the boy's mother—a good-natured lady in her early thirties, solidly built like the young village women in Holland—had already acquired a degree of parental guilt complex.

Guests began to arrive after lunch. The first was Mary Goode, Carl's affable only sister, ten years his junior. Odile was soon on warm terms with her. Later, when they were back in their hotel, Célestin learned more than he wished about Mary: Even though a pharmacy college graduate, or because of it, she disliked pharma companies, pharmacy stores, and almost all pills; she had a fiancé Paul who was of Carl's age and "professed," as Odile said, sociology at the University of Cape Town; and even though they got along, they could not agree about basic things, such as where to live and how to continue their six-year-long engagement; and also... she wished to continue but was wickedly interrupted by her father.

At the reception, there were many academics, Carl's colleagues from Linguistics and other departments. Célestin heard diverse and wisely expressed opinions about the status of science, politics, and race relations in South Africa. He also received useful practical advice. The new acquaintances told him about Kruger National Park and knowledgeably responded to his questions about the Kingdom of Swaziland, a semi-independent small country south of Kruger. Out of curiosity, Célestin had planned to visit it before traveling to Kruger for the celebration of Odile's birthday. Late in the evening, when Carl drove them back, they thanked him for a superb day.

Around two in the morning, a hailstorm with gigantic bolts of lightning and frightening claps of thunder woke them up. They stood holding hands in front of the glass doors and admired the tempest. Big pieces of hail were falling. When there was a brief lull, he ran swiftly onto the terrace and grabbed a few pieces larger than walnuts. Returning to the room, he gave them to Odile, exclaiming: *"Joyeux Noël en Afrique du Sud, ma princesse!"*

4.

At the downtown business center of Joburg, it was dangerous even at noon, especially on a nonworking day such as Christmas, when few whites milled about. They arrived by taxi because in public buses the racial segregation was total, and Célestin did not wish to take part. All around stood monumental modern buildings, international banks, and companies filled to the brim with money, diamonds, and gold. In their marble foyers, around fountains and abstract sculptures, one could see numerous heavily armed security types. Nevertheless, to enter a building and go to an office, it was sufficient to have white skin. Among these citadels of power and wealth, there were dangerous empty spaces, impossible for the police to defend. Images of no man's land in Taba and the death strip on the east side of the Berlin Wall flashed through Célestin's mind.

After the stormy night, it was a day without a cloudlet in the sky. At first, there seemed to be no one in the streets and squares. Not one café with outdoor tables and sun umbrellas was open. However, when he peered stealthily at the nooks around the megalomaniac edifices, he saw small groups of young black men loitering. They could be dangerous, he had been warned.

But after all, Johannesburg was the cosmopolitan major city of a rich, important country, so various institutions in the center were open on Christmas. Out of concern for Odile's safety, he did not allow shame to guide him but unabashedly copied the behavior of other white people he saw. To go from a bank in one building to a travel agency in another, a hundred meters away, father and daughter ran at full speed. When they barged into a luxurious foyer out of breath, the blank-faced security guards—some white, some black—let them in without questions. Célestin and Odile smiled weakly at each other: They both remembered their nighttime run through Park Uhuru in Nairobi.

In truth, the worry about her well-being was not the sole reason for his running like a hunted animal. Unlike the dangerous quarters of European cities, he was ignorant about the locals in Joburg: Their language, the meaning of their facial expressions, their intentions, and the degree of hostility. He could not predict their behavior. Carl Goode, who considered himself a progressive person and a strong opponent of apartheid—which he certainly was, at least in the academic milieu—had warned him not to naively imagine he could endear himself to the local people with criminal intentions by explaining he was a Frenchman, someone who commiserated with black people's plight. And so, to return to their hotel, they again took a taxi.

Carl phoned in the evening: "My hospitable sister Mary has offered to take you two for a spin around Joburg tomorrow. She'd come to the Harrison in her car around ten. I can assure you she knows the city perfectly and is a better driver than I am. What should I tell her?"

* * *

"I'll stick to the edge of the settlement, we won't go in deeper," Mary said in a calm voice, driving slowly, but not too slowly, along the narrow dirty streets of Soweto. "Even policemen rarely come here and then only black guys in unmarked cars," she added. Her own car was an inconspicuous Japanese model with darkened rear windows. Odile was in the back seats for safety.

And thus, after a long tour of many parts of Joburg, they had arrived in Soweto, to which Célestin did not object: He agreed with Mary they should not be visiting only the opulent quarters like Sandton and Braamfontein. "African workers in the gold-mining industry—they had the hardest and most dangerous jobs—were forced to settle in these so-called townships, on harsh land which was at the time outside the city," Mary explained while driving next to rickety shanties with tin roofs. Many of the shacks were jerry-built, using car parts and cardboard boxes. With fear and desperation in her eyes, Odile gazed at the children in rags in front of hovels. Being more visible, Célestin often caught the hostile look on young men's faces: Their eyes watched him unblinkingly from the shadows.

At his urgent request, they tiptoed out of Soweto. Mary spoke dejectedly: "Townships are crowded beyond measure, and everything here is interlaced with poverty, unemployment, and hatred. During our summer, beginning this month, the heat under tin roofs will be unbearable for the dwellers, whereas in the winter, rains will make their miserable household items soaking wet. Streams of mud and garbage will flow around the shanties. The settlement is often close to exploding. It's no wonder those young men looked at us the way they did. They hate us and they hate we're driving around Soweto as if it were a wild animal park."

"Yes, Mary, I couldn't agree with you more. For that reason, and not just Odile's frame of mind, I asked you to leave. I hope I didn't phrase it gruffly."

* * *

They got to know Mary even better during the subsequent days, so when she suggested escorting Odile to a children's park, they were pleased. As a lesson in politesse, he gave the girl money for all snacks and drinks.

Therefore, an entire afternoon opened for him to explore the local situation alone. His inquisitive nature demanded it be done regardless of the possible danger, but he prepared camouflage for the little exploit. It consisted of a dark T-shirt without pictures or lettering; old sneakers; well-worn jeans; a few rands; and a cheap single-use Kodak camera. He carried no bag, wore no sunglasses, and was thus less of a target for those who wanted to dispossess him of valuables. Yet he was aware that in South Africa, unlike Kenya, he remained a likely object of hatred as a white person.

Célestin walked all over Joburg and took numerous photos as covertly as possible. He came across various strange sights. One of them was at the corner of two ordinary streets where there was an ugly lawn with half-withered grass and low, gnarled trees nevertheless offering some shade. In that space, there was a jumble of as many as thirty bodies of black men. They were lying motionlessly. All one could hear in the heat was fat insects flying lazily above the men's heads. He photographed the scene and quickly walked away. Most likely, it was a desolate public lawn, the only one in the neighborhood on which manual workers and layabouts could rest. However, it crossed his mind that with minimal photomontage, supported by fake testimonies of the "surviving witnesses," the scene could be easily presented by tendentious media as a horrific police massacre of innocent people. Suddenly, he stopped in his tracks and walked back some fifty steps. To his relief, three or four "victims" were up, stretching and chasing flies. Naturally, he took another photo.

When he returned to their apartment at the Harrison, Odile was sitting at the desk writing. With her long hair wet, she jumped up and ran to Célestin to hug him. He heard a flood of words: "I've already taken a long shower! How are you, *cher Papa?* Did you have a nice walk? I had a wonderful time in the park, but it was hot. Mary pushed me on the swing, and I flew high, though not nearly as high as when you were doing it! Where was that? Oh, yes, in the playground at the university in Jerusalem. Here they had a giant slide, so I went down several times: It's good you told me to wear long pants. I like Mary a lot! She asked me to say hello to you." He was glad to hear it all and asked if she had played with other children. "Well, I chatted with some girls while we were waiting for our turn. They were nice to me." Since Odile had said nothing about the girls' appearance, he thought it best not to be curious.

When Célestin later called Mary to thank her, she chuckled: "You've admirably brought up Odile. I couldn't prevent her from buying me a lemonade." And when he inquired about segregation in the park, Mary responded: "By law, it exists even there, but children are, thank God, children—at least until... well, until about your daughter's age."

Then he called Carl and told him the Rover had been delivered by the agency. "During the next day or two, we'll drive north to Pretoria. It's only seventy kilometers, and it's the capital of South Africa, after all. In the New Year, we'll leave the Harrison and go on a longer trip, first to Swaziland and then to Kruger." Carl took time to offer suggestions and issue admonitions, while Célestin, like a naughty schoolboy, told the teacher nothing about the camouflaged photo adventure.

5.

Pretoria was affluent, with wide boulevards and tree-lined sunny streets. During their long walk, father and daughter stopped for ice cream and obtained a detailed map of Transvaal, a huge and historically important Boer province. No policeman could be seen anywhere. The city perfectly fitted Carl's description: Orderly and appealing in the best Boer manner, with a fine theatre and two solid universities—but a little boring.

After several hours in Pretoria, they opened the roof on the Rover and drove away in the northeastern direction, plunging into the fertile, rich, conservative Transvaal. Without a plan or goal, they covered some hundred and fifty kilometers in sunshine and amidst lush greenery. By a brook, they ate sandwiches and fruit the Harrison had prepared. Driving along a narrow road that followed the rim of an imperfect circle, they found themselves in a well-off, sleepy village by the name of Roodeplaat. The settlement was located at the edge of a nature reserve, with houses far from each other and surrounded by green fields and groves. When they spotted a small restaurant called Die Rooivlerkspreeu, it was about four o'clock in the afternoon.

The ambiance in the restaurant was different from what Célestin had expected—due to its charming name in Afrikaans, "The Red-Winged Starling." Because he thought it would be rude to turn around at the threshold, they entered and sat at a table farthest from the bar. The Starling had a high ceiling, solid furniture, and spotless tablecloths. What displeased him at first sight was the clientele. There were about a dozen middle-aged and older men, not one woman or child. With few exceptions, each man sat alone at a table, grasping his jug of beer. In every case, the motionless man, the jug, and the table seemed to form an indivisible sculptural whole. Their bloated faces were chalk-white, with touches of pink and purple. One customer sat at the counter and was speaking to the bartender. That man was the only one who had shown no interest in the newcomers. Everyone else, even the most befuddled, inebriated customers, turned toward the two strangers and did not take their eyes off them. These looks did not seem hostile but wondering.

Minutes passed without a waiter coming to their table. Perhaps the man behind the bar was the only employee and had to remain there, thought Célestin. By then, his stubbornness was triggered, so he decided they should stay and find out what was going on. "*Ecoute, ma chérie,*" he spoke to Odile, "it's not amicable here, but we'll stay anyway. Take out something to read, and don't look at those people staring at us. They're harmless."

He casually walked to the bar and stood next to the customer seated there, thus forcing the bartender to ask for his order. The bartender's look and voice were both decent, if not respectful. Célestin pointed at the beer the man was drinking: "Please give me a jug of the same kind and for my daughter a bottle of mineral water." The man at the counter addressed him: "I notice you speak English with an accent, as all of us do too. Ours is Afrikaans—and yours?" That was an acceptable question, so he answered peaceably: "We're from France and will stay in South Africa for at least a month, mostly because we want to spend some time in Kruger Park. Afterward, we'll drive to Cape Town and then all the way down to the Cape of Good Hope. We rented a car in Joburg and today visited Pretoria."

Ice was broken. Having overheard, the bartender said courteously: "You can sit down, Sir. I'll bring the drinks." A few moments after Célestin had returned to their table winking at Odile, the tray arrived. It was carried not by the bartender but by the customer at the counter. He muttered: "Our bartender Jakobus is spoilt. He gets tips for doing nothing." The man, in his early fifties, was neither tipsy nor did he look unhealthy. He was strong, suntanned, and readily accepted the invitation to join the French guests.

"My name is Wim. I have a day off, but normally I wear a uniform—I'm a police sergeant." Célestin forced himself not to express either surprise or discomfort. "I'm Tino, and my daughter is Odile. She'll be ten in Kruger." To show Wim he thinks of his profession as of any other, he went on: "On a working day, you're certainly armed. Do you carry at least a pistol?" Wim laughed merrily: "*Wel, natuurlik*—Austrian semiautomatic Glock pistol and their famous knife. And sometimes this and that extra. Of course, Roodeplaat is a quiet area. For now! I worked for a long time in Joburg, it's quite different there."

When Wim mentioned his pistol and knife, Odile glanced at him and then at her father, but he subtly asked her to return to the book. From Wim's superficial questions about Paris and Célestin's profession, they soon switched to the topic of police work in the circumstances prevailing in South Africa. Wim became increasingly sharp in his comments and barked on occasion: "We're in an impossible war with the blacks in which there can't be either rule of law or mercy. Their leaders are damn communists, all schooled in Moscow. And the English living here, in their usual perfidious style, are helping the blacks not out of blah-blah sense of justice but only to protect themselves and their profits."

Célestin was silently watching the sergeant whose face was serious and sad rather than cruel. Wim continued: "The blacks' children report their parents if they don't support the ANC. You must've heard about 'necklacing,' the horrific Soweto murders in which 'the children,' the so-called 'comrades' in the communist sense, place two or three old tires around the neck and body of their insufficiently revolutionary father—sometimes, rarely, mother—and create a public pyre. In Russia, at the time of Stalin, children were taught by the schoolteachers to report their parents who would then be taken to gulags. *Wel*, it's like that here in black townships, only worse. Tino, listen: It's a war we're bound to lose. The whole world has been turned against us by the false propaganda machinery. And the blacks are more numerous each day. They breed like... People like me will not survive, but we'll fight to the last man. As we did against the damn English in our two Boer Wars."

With a feeling of regret and resignation, Célestin realized he needed to speak to Odile gently, but at length, about much he had not anticipated before her birthday trip to the enchanting country of South Africa. The subjects were exceptionally sensitive: Children murdering their parents; abysmal racial relations; and Stalin, comrades, and gulags.

As for what to say to Wim, he was again at a loss. The police sergeant concluded his tirade: "I worked in Joburg for a long time. Soweto was my area. To punish me for my attitude, my superiors awarded me the rank of senior sergeant and sent me, despite all my decorations, to early retirement in these boondocks, albeit pretty. Even though you're probably an honest man, you've no idea what's happening in our beautiful country. Nor do you know what you'd think and how you'd behave if you lived here longer. But as things stand now, you probably regard me as a despicable racist, whereas I know I'm well-informed and realistic—and even have justice on my side. My wife Laura's opinions are similar."

Célestin wordlessly went to the counter to pay the bill but was told Wim had settled it. While returning to the table, he saw Odile showing Wim the cover of the book she was reading, Karl May's *Winnetou* in the German original. He heard Wim laughing and saying: "I also read that book as a boy, in Afrikaans, of course. In our games after school, I always chose to be the redskin Winnetou, chief of the Apache—never the paleface Old Shatterhand!"

Wim accompanied them to the car. After helping Odile into her seat, Célestin turned to Wim who was holding a piece of paper: "Here are my two phone numbers, at the police and home. Feel free to call me if you need anything in Joburg or anywhere else in this country. I have friends, or at least old colleagues, who can help you. And if you are again near Roodeplaat, please visit us at our home. I'd like you to meet my Laura. Our children have grown up and moved away. When you come, I'll show you— maybe while your daughter is elsewhere in the house with Laura—many authentic photos of necklacing with location, date, and so on. You'll see I wasn't just spinning ugly fairy tales."

After saying goodbye, Célestin was about to climb into the Rover when Wim spoke up: "Something else, for your own good. You said you'd go to Kruger. If you plan to enter the park at its top end, you must drive across north Transvaal, through Musina and Madimbo, all the way to Limpopo, the river that's the border with Zimbabwe. You'll even have to go through Venda. It'd be sheer craziness to travel there without a pistol in the car. I'll gladly lend you one. If, however, you intend to enter the park at the southern end, you'll probably first go to Swaziland to see how it looks there—in which case, you mustn't have a pistol because they'd confiscate it at the border of the Lilliputian make-believe kingdom."

Célestin was relieved he could truthfully tell Wim he had planned to visit Swaziland first and then use the southern Kruger entrance. He briefly thanked the sergeant, entered the car, and drove off with mixed feelings. He had never in his life been colder to someone who genuinely wished him well. A twilight surrounded them while they drove south toward Pretoria and Johannesburg.

6.

Around eleven in the morning, on Sunday, the 3rd of January 1982, Célestin and Odile began their drive from Joburg to Mbabane, the capital of Swaziland, about four hundred kilometers to the east. Since they would be away from Joburg for almost three weeks, they did not keep their suite at the Harrison but did leave several suitcases at the hotel. After a brief stop at the post office on Jeppe Street, they began their new adventure.

Sunny weather persisted, so they continued to drive with the roof open through the dazzlingly green, Dutch-Boer-cultivated, Joburg suburbs. Next, they took highway R122 toward Witbank, over a hundred twenty kilometers away: Beauty of fertile fields as far as the eye could see, with hillocks and low trees here and there. Farms shimmered in the sun, looking as if they had been made up by a cosmetician. What natural wealth was spread in front of their eyes, cultivated by hard work and love!

At Witbank, they joined № 4, a major highway from Pretoria, and headed east toward Middelburg. After about seventy kilometers, the highway lost two lanes but remained in top condition, with immaculate shoulders of bright red earth. At Belfast, forty kilometers farther east, the road climbed through a stunning, strange landscape. Some hills were bare with misshapen rocks except for low grass, whereas others were under a forest that was painted a lovely deep green. Among the knolls, far down, quaint farms could be seen, each with a house, cows, and sheep. Splendid views opened in various directions with buttes and ravines.

Near the next intersection, he stopped the car in a small clearing. There was not a soul around, so the two went in different directions to take care of private needs. Back at the car, he opened a water bottle, so they rinsed their hands and ate some fruit. After studying the map, he suggested: "We've arrived this far quickly, and there's no reason to hurry to Mbabane. Let's turn north and then, in a big arc and through several nature reserves, arrive at a different checkpoint on the Swaziland border. The sights are likely to be spectacular." She loved the plan and while still chewing an apple, her father was already on R540, driving toward Dullstroom thirty kilometers away.

Between that small village and Lydenburg, another sixty kilometers to the northeast, they passed through a gorgeous dense forest. Odile asked her father for the name of the trees. He responded shamelessly: "I've no idea, *ma belle*. You know African botany isn't my forte." Unlike Joburg, where during the previous days the temperature had been about twenty-five degrees, in the region through which they were driving—at a much lower elevation of about seven hundred meters—the thermometer in the Rover showed thirty-two. But they bore the heat well. After a long period of listening to birds, Odile switched on the radio and occasionally changed stations. From two with the best reception, one in Mbabane and the other in Maputo in Mozambique, they could hear engaging tribal music. ("Maputo" since 1976; "Lourenço Marques" for four hundred years as a Portuguese colony.)

At Lydenburg, Célestin made a turn of ninety degrees to R37 and drove twenty kilometers to the east on a narrow twisting road. It crossed the two natural reserves promised by the map. One of them, Sterkspruit, all of which was located within the other, the much bigger Makobulaan, was a breathtaking natural jewel—with quartzite gorges and wild streams running through miniature canyons that disappeared in abysses.

On a rare straight stretch of road, they saw an animal crossing some seventy meters ahead. Célestin crawled soundlessly, stopping seven or eight meters away from the strange creature. After a minute or two, he solved the enigma of the animal's identity: "It's a crested porcupine! It's moving slowly, perhaps it's sick or old. Together with its tail, it seems almost a meter long. I wonder why it came out of its den in daylight." The porcupine did not move any longer: It had either become terrified of the gigantic metal intruder whose hot front it could sense and smell or furious with it because it had raised its sturdy long quills with black and white alternate rings. "Do you hear those sounds, Papa? Like teeth chattering from the cold." Odile remarked. "The sounds aren't coming from its teeth, but from the special rattle quills at the end of its tail. Do you see how the back end of the animal is turned toward us? That's its defensive posture. But it's also ready to attack. It can seriously harm and even kill much bigger animals, such as hyenas, by attacking them with its long rear quills. Ha, ha, this time, *ma douce*, you didn't catch me being an ignoramus!"

"I didn't. But how is it you know so much about crested porcupines?" asked the girl. "It was supposed to be a secret. All right, I'll tell you. In our room at the Heron Court in Nairobi while you were sick, I read an article about this animal. It said they had multiplied a lot in Kenya and were doing damage to the crops. But they have also become a food item in high demand. Apparently, the taste is better than pork. However, in the restaurant Utamaduni, where we had the fateful dinner, I don't remember seeing on the menu the 'Kenyan délicatesse porcupine with short bristles or long quills as requested'." Odile giggled: "*Papa, tu es vraiment horrible!* Did you have to remind me?" When they looked at the road, the crested porcupine was gone.

Farther east, south of the village of Sabie, there were dark clouds, and everything in the glorious nature through which they were passing was thoroughly drenched—a heavy downpour must have ceased minutes earlier. The forest was evaporating, the water wildly rushed down gullies. Everything was steamy and dripping, but the Rover's roof remained open. Even though they were only about forty kilometers west of Kruger, they remained on R537 and traveled directly south. After thirty kilometers, they passed through the pleasant town of Nelspruit, which was even closer to the southwestern corner of the park. Continuing on R40, they drove through another alluring nature reserve and finally arrived in Barberton, an industrial town in a valley.

At that point, they were only thirty kilometers from the border of Swaziland; their journey was to become captivating indeed.

7.

From Barberton, they began a steep climb to the south through the dark, bare mountains. An extraordinary panorama opened to the west and northeast. Soon a dirt road replaced asphalt and they arrived at a South African Defence Force checkpoint. Three young soldiers, all Boers, came to the Rover. Célestin was cordially allowed to pass without being asked about weapons. Over the next forty-five kilometers, they drove through forests and among rounded hills of a magically pale-green color. Occasionally they saw malnourished cows and shacks where black families lived. The road was narrow, sometimes steep, and consisted of earth and stones—an easy job for their 4WD vehicle. They arrived at the subsidiary border crossing Havelock-Josefsdal at 4:45 p.m. There they were shocked to see a sign in Afrikaans on the shut metal gate: "*Oop van 8:00 tot 16:00*". They were forty-five minutes late!

The easygoing behavior of the soldiers at the previous checkpoint led Célestin to believe they might still be able to negotiate a crossing: Perhaps in the middle of nowhere not all formalities had to be observed. He honked once, came out of the car, and calmly stood in front of the gate. A middle-aged black man in a simple shirt and jeans emerged from the border house. Without any provocation, he waved the traveler off by arrogant gestures, as one might an annoying insect, and accompanied these actions gruffly by impertinent words in English. Hardly believing his eyes and ears, Célestin returned to the Rover and ignoring Odile's raised eyebrows, switched on the continual emergency honking that would be heard a kilometer away. Angrily he let the car do the noisy work for several minutes as he was certain someone more polite would be in the border house.

A young Boer in uniform soon appeared at the gate and began apologizing in good English. He was sorry for not coming out earlier—was watching television and did not hear the first honk. Despite personally being willing to open the gate, he was under strict orders not to do so: A commission of the South African Parliament had made firm rules about the opening hours of border crossings. He explained that even if he were to let them through, they would have serious problems on the Swazi side of the border, in the "backward, desperately poor village of Bulembu," as he put it. Almost certainly, they would have to pay a hefty fine: "A half would go into the pockets of the rapacious thieves there, and the rest would be their king's private booty."

Then the officer apologized that the soldiers at the checkpoint had not informed Célestin about the Havelock crossing closing early: Those three guys had been posted only a few weeks earlier and still did not know much they should. Finally, he profusely apologized for the "unforgivably rude behavior" of the watchman: "He likes to act in a bumptious manner but is not a bad man. And his wages feed a family of six." In sharp Afrikaans, the officer rebuked the man who abjectly stood to the side. Célestin said hardly a word, for he had quickly calmed down and felt sorry for the watchman.

The border officer explained how to drive to Oshoek, the much bigger border crossing open till midnight, an hour and a half to the south. Realizing they had plenty of time, Célestin asked the young man about the purpose of the high metal pillars that supported a thick cable from which hung numerous massive baskets. They had traveled many kilometers next to or below the strange construction traversing hills and valleys. The man readily gave a detailed answer. The entire system of pillars, cables, and baskets was constructed by the Germans in 1938 for the transport of gold ore from Havelock westward to a plant at Diepgezet in the valley. It had been, and probably still was, the longest such system in the world. However, it soon transpired there was not enough golden ore for profitable exploitation, but ample blue asbestos was discovered in the mines, so the ore-transport system kept on functioning: Baskets full of blue asbestos were gliding to Diepgezet.

* * *

They drove down the mountain to the southwest. The area was spectacular, illuminated by the setting sun. Some hills were adorned by subtly changing colors, whereas others were gradually enveloped by shadows, mist, and drizzle. In the valley bottom, as they stepped out of the car to breathe deeply, they were smitten by the intoxicating smell of flowers and plants.

It turned out Diepgezet was a quiet town of Dutch-colonial appearance. There were tree-lined streets, charming houses, abundant greenery, and even a country club with two red-clay tennis courts and a nine-hole golf course. Driving south through the valley in the damp twilight, the sun three-quarters below the horizon, they exchanged hand waves with black folk walking along the road. The Rover disturbed puddles that were pretty as a picture, reflecting an agitated sky. Our South Africa, they thought.

In the village of Lochiel, where the asphalted roadway reappeared, they turned east on highway 17. The drizzle had stopped, so they stood by the car admiring the last of the sunset: It weakly illuminated the green mountains from which they had come. Even the asbestos plant looked cuddly in a bizarre way, squatting plump in the valley.

A dark rainy night had fallen by the time they arrived in Oshoek. At the border crossing, they encountered chaos created by a multitude of people, mostly black, but also Indians and some probably British whites who lived in Swaziland. Formalities on the South African side were short. The Swazi border station Ngwenya was something else. One could say it summarized what was undesirable in the so-called Third World—from bureaucratic arrogance to incompetence and bribery. Célestin and Odile, harmless tourists, needed an hour to extricate themselves. Heading southeast to Mbabane, twenty-five kilometers away, he drove carefully in the rain. The pavement was badly damaged, and there were hardly any traffic signs. Local drivers were even more impervious to rules than the ones in Kenya.

Mbabane—pronounced "mmBaban"—was Swaziland's capital, but not its "throne city" in the literal sense. The country was a kingdom, an absolute monarchy, and the throne of the long-living King Sobhuza II was in Lobamba, eleven kilometers south. The King ruled Swaziland from the fourth month of his life in 1899 until the arrival of Célestin and Odile: Eighty-three years continuously and counting, longer than any king in history, anywhere!

The city was unattractive, if not outright ugly, and that initial impression was confirmed in the subsequent days when the weather improved. During the tediously unsuccessful search for a hotel room, the pair noticed many signs in Portuguese on shops and restaurants, which was not surprising given the ethnic ties between Swaziland and Mozambique. Still, the local franchise of Kentucky Fried Chicken was by far the most brightly illuminated establishment. Neither at the Holiday Inn nor in other hotels were they able to find a room at any price.

To ease hunger pangs, they entered a cozy Portuguese cafeteria and ordered tea and simple *sanduíches de queijo torrado*. The young black waitress cheered up the fatigued girl, and when Célestin asked about hotels, she brought the owner. Afonso was a squat Portuguese white man, surprised by the guest's fluency in his native tongue. He immediately recommended a hotel whose owners were Portuguese refugees from Mozambique. "The hotel is modest, but at least you'll have a clean room for tonight. They always keep one empty to meet requests from friends."

When the travelers were about to leave, Afonso waved off the payment. "But to acquaint you with prices in this town," he said, "your bill would be 2.5 emalangenis, about 2.5 South African rands. They're artificially keeping the currency on par with the rand, but the prices are much higher in Mbabane—typical for the Swazi-style swindlery. The money, both metal and paper, is 'Swazi,' but it's cast and printed in South Africa, like almost everything else of any value here."

At the small Hill Street Lodge, the owners Inácio and Mariana welcomed them cordially. *Senhor* Afonso had called minutes before, and the new guests got a spotless room with two double beds and a bathroom. The price was twenty-five emalangenis, much higher than it would have been in South Africa but still reasonable. Besides, if not in a royal, they were in a capital city—albeit one few people have heard of in Europe.

Before they went to sleep, Célestin said: "Do you see how important it is to speak many languages: You never know which one will help you... And when writing in your diary, you should know we traveled six hundred twenty-five kilometers today, mostly on demanding mountain roads, some earthen. Also, we saved one crested porcupine from a certain demise. *Bonne nuit, dors bien ma chérie.*" "*Bonne nuit, cher Papou...*" murmured the girl sweetly, falling into a deep sleep.

8.

Already before breakfast the next day, they decided to stay another night in Mbabane and then spend several days in Ezulwini Valley, ten kilometers south. That choice was made on the advice of their host while Mariana was singing in the kitchen preparing a Portuguese-Mozambican morning feast. Inácio said Ezulwini, with its canyons and waterfalls, was as stunning as the Diepgezet area and added that the Holiday Inn there was much better than the one in Mbabane. Célestin immediately called and reserved a suite for three nights.

After he had helped Mariana remove the dishes, Inácio spoke about Mbabane. "This ugly city is almost without history. In 1903, after the Second Boer War, when the English had forcibly grabbed the so-called 'Protectorate' of Swaziland—and kept it in their claws until 1968—they promoted a small desolate settlement into the capital: For their own needs, of course. In the thirties, the little town did get electricity and running water, but Africans were not allowed to live in it. They inhabited nearby villages where the living conditions were no better than in 1903. Each day, to earn a pittance in town, black people had to walk for hours and perform the hardest and dirtiest work for the English masters. In Mozambique, my Portuguese countrymen certainly were far from praiseworthy but, as far as I know, were nevertheless more decent than the English—in various ways, including racial integration. From what I've heard, your Frenchmen behaved in their colonies more similarly to us than to the English. But that's another story." Yes, Célestin thought, indeed another story, a long and sordid one.

Except for the air being clean and the temperature agreeable—Mbabane's elevation was a thousand two hundred meters—the two visitors had little favorable to say about the city, although they walked for hours. From the hotel, it took them only minutes to reach the Anglican All Saints Cathedral at the main square. Dating from the time of the British Protectorate, it was a dull, ungraceful building. About a kilometer south of there, they arrived at the Mbabane River. Like the Nairobi, it was confined to a narrow, unappealing channel. On the streets, they saw mostly young women and men. Inácio had told them life expectancy was short in Swaziland: People died early of tuberculosis and viral illnesses.

In the evening, to experience a bit of the local scene, they visited a bar called Lourenço Marques but left after several minutes because "Larry's" swarmed with prostitutes, pimps, and staggering Westerners. They returned to the hotel, chatted briefly with their hosts, and went to sleep.

9.

Leaving Mbabane at half past eight the next morning, the Rover quickly covered ten kilometers to the hotel at Ezulwini Valley. The windows of their apartment gave to the pool, distant hills, and dark ravines. Even while Odile was still unpacking, Célestin dove into the pool. The water was not heated, so he swam sixty lengths freestyle, delighted they had left Mbabane behind.

Around the pool, there were tall palms with healthy crowns, which Holiday Inn unfailingly obtained for its franchises. He bought a beach ball for a two-emalangeni coin and found a deck chair to read a book about King Sobhuza's Lobamba. Odile soon arrived, her attention drawn to the colorful ball. After thanking her father, she noticed it had lost air and disarmingly tweeted:

"*Cher Papa,* please blow air into it—at least for now, your chest is much bigger than mine!"

Later, she and two English girls played in the children's pool. To stretch his legs, he ambled over there. Odile introduced him and continued to play. Now and then, the children cried out delightedly. "How different girls are from boys," thought Célestin, "they are content to throw the ball straight into each other's arms or within easy reach; boys, even at that young age, would find a way to compete."

While returning to his deck chair, he noticed two men had taken the nearby ones and were talking softly. Even though he could make out only an occasional word, he was certain they were speaking Russian. When he had almost reached his chair, the older of the men said to him in solid English with a broad smile: "You're an excellent swimmer, Sir. We watched you earlier this morning and were envious of your style."

Célestin approached them laughing: "Thank you! If you wish, we can borrow the ball from my daughter and play a water polo match 'World against USSR.' But where to find goalposts?" With slightly raised eyebrows, the same man responded: "Since you've correctly guessed we're Russians, it must be you speak our language at least a little. But how did you guess we're from the Soviet Union and not Russian émigrés from... France?"

He answered right away, a smile playing on his lips: "You must be aware Russian princes and White Guard officers have long ago sold their last diamond and don't have money for trips to Swaziland: Now they're too old even to drive a taxi in Paris. By the way, you certainly know that Vladimir Vladimirovich Nabokov, a great writer from a noble Russian family and an émigré from 1919, died three years ago in Switzerland. But how did you guess I'm from France since I jokingly said 'World' for our fantasy water polo match?"

"Easy! Because two of the little girls in the small pool over there continued to play, we supposed the third one, who stopped and called to you in French, was your daughter." Célestin grinned amiably, after which the younger Russian took over: "You mentioned Nabokov. It's disappointing his novels weren't being translated and published in the Soviet Union during all those decades when he was writing them. I managed to get a hold of *Lolita* in the original, in English. An outstanding novel—and not only ironic but even comical in places. So many self-righteous busybody puritans in both America and our country were too narrow-minded or plain dumb to realize it. Later I read Nabokov's translation of *Lolita* into his native Russian. It's interesting that this translation, in my opinion, is language-wise substandard—and yet linguistic command and style are alleged to be the writer's forte. Living abroad for so long, Nabokov must have forgotten many Russian expressions and subtleties. Speaking Russian every day with someone intimate, as Nabokov presumably did with his wife Vera, is not enough."

Célestin was pleased that the younger Russian's contribution involved a literary theme. He asked: "So, what's the current situation with Nabokov's novels in the Soviet Union? Are things getting better?" The literary Russian responded readily: "Yes, they are, albeit slowly. You are certainly familiar with the novel *Pnin*, which Nabokov also wrote in English. I haven't read it, but Gennadiy Barabtarlo is translating it as we speak. Gennadios—that's how I call him, the name means generous and noble in ancient Greek—has assured me it's better than *Lolita*. He's a friend of mine, a first-rate translator from English, only thirty years old."

The three men thus got to know each other to their visible enjoyment. Since the Russians were well-educated people, father and daughter were not 'Tino' and 'Dilla' but retained their full names and surnames. The older Russian was Dimitriy Ivanovich Popov. Probably in his fifties, he was a suave man with striking features, warm intelligent eyes, and a receding hairline above his high forehead. Nikolay Yegorovich Zamyatin was about ten years younger. Despite being below average in height, he was an exemplar of Russian masculine good looks—with his elegantly sculpted nose, deep blue eyes, and poetically flowing blond hair.

Out of curiosity, when she saw her father talking to two strangers, Odile ran from the pool to the small group. The Russians politely got up and Dimitriy exclaimed: "So this, Monsieur Célestin, is your *charmante fille Odile... Bonjour, Mademoiselle de Quernevelle! Je suis Dima et ici nous avons Kolya.*"

A friendly relationship was established. The Russians had already stayed for four days at the hotel, but they worked several hours each day in Mbabane. They did not disclose the nature of the work. The suspicious Frenchman began to wonder whether the KGB function of one of them was to monitor the other. However, the fact they had separate hotel rooms did not support the hypothesis—all three room numbers were readily revealed as soon as the idea of playing chess had been aired. The crazy Russian love of chess became even more evident when Dima said: "Every afternoon when Kolya and I return from Mbabane, we swim in the pool and then play chess til midnight. Neither of us is interested in sunbathing or tourism in this country. Besides, each day there's a violent downpour or long-lasting rain or both. If you ask at the front desk, they'll lie and claim that in January it rains only on alternate days in Ezulwini!"

They agreed to play the royal game at seven o'clock in the apartment shared by Célestin and Odile. It was the most spacious in the hotel, with a sitting room and two bedrooms. Dima and Kolya would bring the wine and a chessboard. "Each of us has a small travel set," said Kolya, "but we secured a proper one from the front desk. A tip does wonders here—like everywhere." The Frenchman thought: "I'm ninety percent certain neither of these is a KGB guy. We'll see."

Because the family name Zamyatin seemed rare, it attracted Célestin's attention. He wished to ask Kolya whether his family was related to the writer Yevgeniy Zamyatin but gave up the idea during the very public meeting by the hotel pool. The matter was sensitive because Yevgeniy Zamyatin, even though a trusted old Bolyshevik, wrote the dystopian novel *We*—an extremely sharp satire on the Soviet regime and communist party. To boot, he smuggled the manuscript out to New York, where the English translation was brought out in the early twenties by a well-known publisher. Because of such a serious political transgression,

Zamyatin was mercilessly attacked and criticized. Nevertheless, he was allowed, allegedly by Stalin personally, to emigrate to Paris in the early nineteen-thirties.

"We'll see," repeated Célestin to himself.

10.

When precisely at seven the Russians arrived carrying a chessboard, a nicely wrapped 500-gram Lindt chocolate, and three bottles of red wine, they encountered a table with three chairs, as well as cheeses, crackers, juices, and mineral water. Odile was delighted by the chocolate and timidly thanked the guests in the correct Russian. Dima and Kolya were pleased but not overly so: The unusual pair did not shock any longer.

Meanwhile, Célestin was speechless, seeing the bottles were from Groot Constantia near Cape Town—because the wines from that celebrated estate were enjoyed by Napoleon and Bismarck in the nineteenth century. Before the trip to South Africa, a school friend of his, who had become a major dealer in wine and spirits in Bordeaux, suggested he visit Groot Constantia and meet the owner.

"Good heavens, how did you acquire this glamorous wine?" Célestin asked his guests. Dima and Kolya were gratified by their host's reaction. "Well, we spent the whole afternoon in the city. After work, we went to a store where we have an account: All sorts of wonderfully exotic items can be bought there—at a big discount. Coming to visit a Frenchman, we naturally didn't dare to bring plonk. Also, we didn't want to buy a French wine because we are here almost in South Africa," explained Dima. Célestin thanked them and did not inquire further. "These people," it occurred to him, "must be diplomats and have access to special government shops."

The chess tournament began. Odile watched and noted the outcomes. Regarding the games, the victor would stay at the board and the other two take turns as opponents. To Dima's and Kolya's chagrin, Célestin was not accustomed to getting up, so the rule was changed repeatedly. One was that he would rise if he failed to checkmate the rival by the thirtieth move, and she was recruited to count. Still, he sat as if nailed down—until finally needing to stretch his legs. The Russians, being good-natured losers, applauded and guffawed. So the games resumed with jokes in which she participated. Father and daughter liked the guests, and their affection was reciprocated. The superb red wine further brightened the ambiance. Odile nibbled cheese and served pieces of chocolate.

Après chess, the Russians and their host relaxed in armchairs. Hills seen through wide windows assumed rare colors as night fell quickly. Before retiring to her bedroom, she wished good night to Dima and Kolya, again in Russian. Célestin resolved it was high time to describe at least a portion of their three months' travel through the Soviet Union. "Fascinating—especially about Baikal, you know it better than we do!" Dima confessed and asked: "How old is your girl, eleven?" "Not yet. Let's see: Today is the fifth of January, so in a little less than two weeks, she'll be ten. The main reason for bringing Odile to South Africa at this time was my wish to celebrate her milestone birthday on the 18th of January near the wild animals she dearly loves." "Aha!" Kolya cried out, "perhaps you're planning to be in the fabulous Kruger on that day?" "Yes! Just today, I made all the necessary reservations by phone." "Really?" interjected Dima, "Kolya and I have been talking about a safari in Kruger. We have an all-terrain vehicle."

Listening to the Slavic melody in the Russians' English, Célestin heard Olya's unforgettable voice in his inner ear. All kinds of thoughts flew through his mind, and he decided to try to deepen the unexpected friendship: "Hmm. Well then, how about if we make our dates coincide? I hereby invite you to Kruger on the 18th of January for a celebration of my daughter's tenth birthday. I'm certain she wishes it too. What d'you say?"

Kolya and Dima gladly accepted and would spend five days in Kruger, including the 18th of January. "In Mbabane, we have a secretary whom we'll instruct to cancel our obligations for those days, starting from... what do you think, Kolya?" asked Dima.

Kolya quickly leafed through his planner and said: "January 18 is a Monday, which is convenient. Let's take a whole week from Thursday to Wednesday—the first and last day for travel there and back, and on Tuesday, the 19th, we'll be recovering from the celebration!" "That's a good plan," said Dima and went on: "We have a trip to Lesotho on the 23rd of January and to Maputo at the beginning of February. So you can tell Odile she'll have two friends from Moscow at her birthday party. Can you suggest a place to stay?"

After consulting his notes, Célestin said: "I'll tell you what I've reserved. We'll leave Swaziland on the 8th of January and spend two nights in Hazyview, a ritzy tourist village on the Sabie River, where I rented a bungalow. In case you'd like to stay there your first night, tired after the trip from Mbabane, I'll give you their phone number. About twenty kilometers farther is Numbi Gate through which you'll enter southwestern Kruger, and only eight kilometers east is Skukuza, a safari camp: I've reserved a *rondawel* from the 10th of January on. I'll write down the phone number and our name. Their desk will give us any message from you. So, Odile and I will expect you in Camp Skukuza on the 17th or 18th of January."

The Russians agreed and suggested a goodbye meeting before the French pair departed from Ezulwini. They would meet in the hotel restaurant at five in the afternoon two days later. By then, Dima and Kolya would have reserved their stay in Kruger. Looking at his planner, Célestin said with a blissful smile: "The date of our next meeting is the 7th of January, the Russian Orthodox Christmas, so I wish you *s Rozhdestvom*, a very merry Christmas, in advance!" Then he added quickly: "I hope I haven't offended you." But the Russians smiled without a trace of tartness and responded in unison: "Not at all, on the contrary, *spasibo!*"

11.

Father and daughter spent much of the next day driving in Ezulwini Valley. The nature was resplendent, similar to the Diepgezet area, as Inácio had said. From time to time, a rainstorm caught them, but their mood was not spoiled even when they walked through a downpour in their transparent capes with fragile hoods or when the Rover's mighty wipers haughtily chased jets of water away from the windshield. Near a waterfall, they left the car and spent an hour strenuously climbing up a poorly marked trail until they reached a spot from which a rivulet that had become a wild stream plunged noisily into a gorge. As fate would have it, the deluge hit precisely there, but they luckily discovered—faces joyful and heads drenched—a tiny shelter below an overhanging rock. They were excited to be the only souls in the magical wilderness. Even after the rain had stopped, thousands of drops escaped from the waterfall and interrupted their speech as they descended.

In Lobamba, they did not spend much time examining the various edifices devoted to the person and scepter of Sobhuza II—many Swazis superstitiously feared he was immortal—nor to the structures dedicated to the powerless parliament. During a long walk through town, the pair found refuge from yet another storm in a small eatery where they ordered their usual beverages. The lady manager had nothing against them consuming sandwiches they had brought from the hotel but was grateful for the generous tip. As the departure to Kruger was drawing close, Odile seldom forgot her food poisoning lesson.

During the evening, they wrote notes in their diaries, hoping the photos would be spectacular. They pored over a map of the park and became even more expectant. Kolya called at eight, saying Dima and he had made reservations in Camp Skukuza and confirmed the meeting for the next afternoon. Before ringing off, he said: "In case you're thinking about converting to Russian Orthodoxy and learning some of our church customs, Dima and I wish Odile and you a joyous and peaceful *Sochelynik!* Merry Christmas Eve!" As he was putting the receiver down, Célestin mumbled: "Some super strange Soviets..." Then he cheerfully imparted the Russians' Christmas wishes to his daughter.

After lunch the next day, he said: "It's better, *mon trésor*, for you not to be present at my meeting with the Russians. I must talk to them about something delicate, and you may inhibit them. I'll tell you everything afterward." Odile nodded seriously, and Célestin instructed her gently: "Come to the restaurant with me, say goodbye to Dima and Kolya, adding 'til my birthday,' and explain you have much to study for school. They'll understand. When you return here, please lock the door and wait for me. The meeting may take as much as two hours. That's why I prefer you to be in our room and not by the pool. Please don't worry."

At five o'clock, when father and daughter arrived, Dima and Kolya were drinking coffee at a table in the corner. Odile warmly thanked the Russians for planning to attend her birthday party and excused herself.

Kolya produced a piece of paper with his and Dima's last names, along with reservation dates for a rondawel in Skukuza. When the conversation began in earnest, Dima apologetically inquired about the girl's mother. Considering the question acceptable when well-intentioned, Célestin took time to speak about Patrizia, Patrice, Koblenz, and Metz. Then he was the one who hesitated before asking Kolya: "Your last name is rare, as far as I know. May I ask whether your family is related to the extraordinary writer Yevgeniy Zamyatin?" With smiling eyes, Kolya exchanged looks with Dima and answered: "You're right, my family name is rare. And it doesn't surprise me that you, as a cosmopolitan intellectual, have heard of Yevgeniy Zamyatin; incidentally, by everyone in the family and fellow writers, he was known as Zhenya or ZZ! Also, long before your stay in the USSR with Odile, it's likely you read, in an English or French translation, his famous critique of the Soviet system, the prescient and wise novel *We*: Maybe in the E. P. Dutton's 1924 New York edition or as *Nous autres* published by Gallimard in 1929 in Paris. Am I right?"

"Yes, I've read the novel in those two languages but also in Italian, *Noi*, and German, *Wir*, both put out, believe it or not, only in the late Fifties. I did it in all those tongues because I wanted to see how certain, hmm, ticklish notions were handled in different countries. Also, because I was then a novice in Russian, by comparing the various translations, I strove to tease out what Zamyatin must have meant."

They were all deep in thought for a while, and then Kolya went on: "In short, your question about the family relationship is logical and acceptable. Zhenya Zamyatin and my father Yegor were both born in Tambov, about four hundred kilometers southeast of Moscow, between Saratov and Voronezh—Zhenya in 1884 and Yegor in 1915. Yegor's father, my grandfather Pavel, was born in 1887: He and Zhenya were first cousins, two brothers' sons. But I think, and so probably does Dima, you're asking about kinship primarily because you are curious regarding two other things. First: If a family relation exists, did my family suffer from the new Soviet regime after the novel had been smuggled to New York and published there in 1924? The honest answer is: No. Zhenya Zamyatin was a loyal old Bolyshevik, and Maksim Gorkiy, a very influential writer and public figure, protected him in every possible way.

"Second: What do I personally, privately, think about the writer and his novel? The honest answer is that the writer is outstanding, top echelon, as you said yourself, and the novel is exceptionally courageous and important. It's a great pity Zhenya's voice was brutally suppressed in the Soviet State." Kolya Yegorovich fell silent for a moment and then added: "Of course, his fate under Stalin could've been much worse than emigration. If it were not for the graybeard Gorkiy... But as you probably know, Zhenya passed away in Paris in 1937 utterly destitute. So, it wasn't the case that only Russian princes died in penury in your country."

To interrupt the resulting silence, Dima said: "You certainly understand how painful this topic is for Kolya. Another thing might interest you: My own opinion about Yevgeniy Zamyatin and his novel is the same as his."

For Célestin and his secret "liberation of Olya" project, these were excellent news. He was touched and spoke in a voice reflecting it: "Dear Kolya, dear Nikolay Yegorovich, thank you very much for your sincerity. It's an offer of friendship. At least, that's how I dare to interpret your confession."

They ordered more coffee. Célestin decided the moment had arrived for a key question: "Since we've switched to intimate themes—I spoke about my late wife Patrizia and Odile's birth, and Kolya about his family—please allow me to inquire about your work: Are you Soviet diplomats?" Dima did not dither: "An understandable question, and there's nothing to hide. I'm a Cultural and Trade Attaché of the USSR Embassy in Maputo, Mozambique. The embassy has existed since 1975 when diplomatic relations were established. I have the title of Counsellor, which is fairly high. Kolya, who is almost exactly ten years younger, is my assistant and has a corresponding title. We have diplomatic passports.

"Our embassy in Maputo also has an official but non-residential diplomatic presence in the nearby independent Kingdom of Lesotho, a country twice the size of Swaziland, yet also landlocked. The capital, Maseru, is about six hundred kilometers southwest of here; Kolya and I have the same titles and jobs there as in Mozambique, although non-residential."

Célestin was delighted by such candor and spoke with gratitude: "I've been able to guess only a few details—from what you said about the Groot Constantia wine and your imminent trips to Mozambique and Lesotho." Dima carried on: "We weren't hiding any of it. To finish: In Swaziland, the situation is different because the USSR doesn't have official relations with this country. Several years ago, Swaziland was offered mutual recognition, but Sobhuza II, under South Africa's massive pressure, refused to give us accreditation. Yet permission was obtained to open an office in Mbabane so Kolya and I could conduct cultural and trade activities.

"Naturally, some of our colleagues are busy with other work. As for trade, it's minuscule. We present expensive furs to them as gifts, rather than sell them: Yes, even in this climate, the royal wives are crazy about full-length fur coats. No one knows their exact number, I mean of wives. And the Swazis, they present expensive diamonds to us, rather than sell them—they get them free from South Africa as aid. All that counts as trade, which Kolya and I supervise. South Africans know all about it but allow us to travel there with diplomatic passports."

Kolya apologized and went to the toilet, which was an opportunity Célestin needed. He bent across and spoke to Dima sotto voce: "Thank you very much, but I'd like to ask you something else. If I'm being impertinent, please tell me I've crossed the line. So, what's Kolya's job as your assistant?"

Dima did not get cross but grinned: "I expected this question the moment Kolya got up. You think, as would any Westerner who imagines being cognizant of the Soviet system of control and supervision, that Kolya was appointed to look over my shoulder and inform a gray KGB type. Surely there's plenty of such stuff. But you err significantly in our case, and I'm not a *naïf*, as you say in France. Kolya and I've been exceptionally close for many years: I love him more than my biological younger brother. Many years ago, I was Kolya's professor of economics at Leningrad State University. I entered the diplomatic service first, and he joined much later.

"In Moscow, they consider us an excellent team. You should be aware that things are changing there too. New winds are blowing. Ability and efficiency are being sought and rewarded. And there's something else... Kolya and I..." Kolya, returning to the table, was a dozen meters away when Dima quickly finished the sentence: "... are married to twin sisters. He got married first, and I followed when I saw how happy he was."

Kolya sat down and immediately spoke to Célestin: "The old tomcat's facial expression tells me he was talking about women, most likely our wives. I bet he told you his twin is prettier than mine!"

Célestin was disarmed. A ray of hope appeared in his mind that thanks to these good people—presumably well-connected Soviet diplomats—Olya may be granted an early release. He asked them: "Dear Dima and Kolya, something is not clear: How have I earned not only your confidence but your affection and friendship, if I may say so?"

The Russians smiled and Dima said: "Eh, my dear fellow! You're traveling far and wide with your sweet, intelligent daughter, so life brings something interesting and new each day. You've never been in the diplomatic service, locked up, figuratively, in an incredibly boring country at the end of the world. Around here, days are so monotonous that everyone becomes emptier and duller. We are hungry for the company of people like you, educated European men and women who are versed in languages, literature, history, philosophy, the arts... And who even know and like our native country! And, to top it all, you are an excellent chess player! We're honored Odile desires our presence at her party. So there's the explanation for our feelings and behavior: Affection for the little girl and friendship for you."

12.

Arriving around seven at the border-crossing Ngwenya, they kept only a dozen emalangeni coins that Odile wanted as souvenirs and to give to girlfriends for fun. They crossed to Oshoek and drove seventy kilometers in a northwesterly direction to Badplaas. From afar, they smelled sulfur, but that did not prevent them from having a tasty Boer breakfast in the spa.

Then they traveled north through areas they had previously visited and arrived in the small town of Sabie lying on the same-named river. Its color was a soft brown, slightly darker than the red of Transvaal's earth. Listening to birds, there was peace in their souls. They wished good morning to each other, finding themselves again in the country with which they had fallen in love.

From Sabie, they drove through gorgeous scenery east to Hazyview. The engineering quality of the broad-shouldered road was exceptional, with accurately tilted long curves. There were also sections straight as an arrow, with the road very steeply rising and falling. "When you drive downhill fast, my stomach feels as if I'm rushing downward from the top of a tall slide in a park."

Célestin smiled absently. He had been thinking intensively about Olya and feeling hopeful. Describing to Odile his time with the Russians the previous evening, he said Dima and Kolya were very good people, so he was glad they would come to the party. Even though her papa did not mention the poor prisoner, she privately linked the Russians' friendly behavior with Olya being freed.

At the Sabie River Bungalows in Hazyview, he had reserved a two-night stay, wanting Odile to have a day of sports and relaxation before meeting Elephants & Co. Their bungalow was spacious and well-equipped. The windows framed several greens on the golf course spread out in the sunshine. After a long swim, they moved to a red-clay tennis court. She struggled with a heavy Wilson wooden racket, which was then all the craze: When using the backhand, she frequently missed the balls he gently sent toward her. She declared not to like tennis because her shoes and socks had become unappealingly red.

Odile did much better with a golf putter. Occasionally she managed to hit the ball into the hole from two or three meters—a respectable distance even on a flat putting green. Despite her "short game" being good, she complained: "Holes could be a little bigger, Papa." The pair also played with other children and their parents something remotely resembling volleyball. Later, Odile commented: "All these sports—tennis, golf, volleyball—are nice, but I miss riding my Pasha." "She's a bit nostalgic, which is both good and not so good," he thought.

After lunch, they arrived at a badminton court where players were hitting a shuttlecock over the net. She was familiar with the game from her school in Metz, so they sat down to watch. Soon, a tall girl named Annette asked for a match. Seeing her eager to play, Célestin suggested: "Go to our bungalow and put your tennis shoes back on; I'll return the tennis rackets and rent one for badminton." Odile leaned toward him so Annette could not hear: "*Mais Papa,* my tennis shoes are dirty, scarlet red!" He laughed: "*Vas-y, ma douce*, don't whine. This way, everyone will know you're a tennis player!"

When he returned from the sports shop, Odile and Annette were on the court talking. He handed her the racket and whispered, "*Bonne chance!*" She looked sulky, maybe because Annette was taller and stronger, about two years older. Not dwelling on it, he sat down on a nearby chair and studied the dinner menu, not intending to root for his daughter noisily. He disliked it when pushy parents became overly involved in children's games and competitions.

The girls were about to begin when Célestin was approached by a casually dressed man his age. "Excuse me for disturbing you, Sir. My name is Steve McLaren, and I live in Swaziland. I'd like to check a possible funny coincidence. May I ask if you walked around Mbabane three or four days ago? Together with the girl who's now playing badminton in red tennis shoes?" He looked the man up and down and noticed nothing offensive. All right, Israel is a village, but South Africa? "Yes, we were recently in Mbabane. Still, I'm amazed the two of us looked and behaved so memorably that you recognized us here. Of course, you might be an MI6 or KGB man."

Célestin saw from the corner of his eye that Odile had lost a point after a long exchange. "No, no, nothing like that," laughed Steve. "I've no idea why I remembered you. Probably because tourists who are inquisitively strolling through Mbabane instead of getting drunk are rare and a foreign father with a little daughter virtually nonexistent."

Steve had stopped at Hazyview for two days' rest on his way to Pretoria. Célestin invited him to sit down and learned a great deal from the man, not only about Swaziland but also about other countries in the southeastern part of the African continent. McLaren was born in Lusaka, the capital of Zambia, in 1944, when it was the British Protectorate of Northern Rhodesia but has lived in Mbabane since 1979 as a journalist.

Regarding Swaziland, Steve had a very negative opinion: "Things stand as follows: Incredible corruption; a ruler, almost eighty-three years old with exactly hundred and thirteen wives, as is claimed by 'well-informed circles'; several dozen uneducated princelings who lead an extravagant, profligate lifestyle with secret funds the source of which nobody knows; many sons and stepsons of King Sobhuza are in jail, along with the fathers, uncles, and brothers of his wives, whereas others are licentiously wasting money in Monte Carlo; it's a parasite ministate, backward and poor, but vain—because it receives spending money from three or four powerful countries vying for influence in this part of Africa and because it's also important for Black Africa as a conduit for secret trade with evil South Africa."

Célestin noticed Odile had lost the set and challenged Annette to another. She sent him a petulant look, presumably because he had not closely watched her play: Her exasperating papa just blew her a kiss and turned again to McLaren. "Well, Mr. Steve, I've heard similar remarks from other 'well-informed circles,' but am at a loss to comprehend why you've been living in Swaziland for three years already, as you've told me." "Because I consider Swaziland the safest, even the only possible, refuge for me in this part of the world. Which I love dearly!"

"Really? Can't you live safely in Zambia where you were born?" asked Célestin, although he sensed it was an almost impertinently naive question. "Ha!" cried out Steve and then lowered his voice: "From the time of Zambia's independence in 1964, Kenneth Kaunda, that is, the 'First Son of the Zambian Nation,' has been foreordained to be 'President for Life'—and this status of his has been maintained by force. The same can be said about rulers like Kenyatta in Kenya, Nyerere in Tanzania, and Mugabe in Zimbabwe. And it's not restricted to Africa: The communist dictator Broz in Yugoslavia, whom his adoring subjects sweetly call 'Tito,' is another 'First Son and President for Life.' But to return to Kaunda. He's been imprisoning whomever he wishes, both black and white people he considers opponents. Most white journalists born in Zambia have a shooting target drawn on their backs.

"I was thrown in jail in Lusaka for a whole month because of an innocuous little article. Recently, a white New Zealander born in Zambia spent three weeks in jail until they set him free because of an international uproar. On top of the many indiscriminate arrests, prison conditions are medieval—I experienced the interior of the slammers personally. The man from New Zealand was arrested because of an honest piece about the bloody food riots in Lusaka. And so, my native Zambia will not see me in the foreseeable future, nor will Tanzania, Zimbabwe, or Mozambique. All those countries are similar—devious and brutal artifices."

"I understand, Steve, thank you. Nevertheless, one wonders if..." Just as Célestin was beginning a minor rebuttal, his daughter ran to him flushed with pride. Before he could speak or introduce her to Steve, the girl exclaimed: "Annette escaped from the *champ de bataille!*" It turned out Odile had convincingly won the second set and challenged Annette to a decider when her rival ran off crying to her mother. She grumbled: "The unfair lady had sat next to the court throughout and loudly cheered Annette in Afrikaans while no one supported me! Anyway, this means I won, doesn't it, Papa?" "Yes, you won, *mon bijou*, bravo!" He hugged her and wiped off beads of sweat from her forehead and neck.

After she was seated, Célestin said: "This is Mr. Steve McLaren. He saw us on the street in Mbabane and recognized us here!" Odile greeted Steve absentmindedly, for she was still thinking of her badminton rival. *"Tu sais, Papa,"* she said, *"cette fille Annette n'est pas sympathique.* She probably chose me to play with because I'm smaller than her. Well, I showed her! Before you brought my racket, she had snootily announced she was from some city 'Bloomfont,' the 'city of flowers' or 'roses,' I don't remember. And when I said I was from Metz in France, she pretended she'd never heard of our city, imagine! *Bien*, our beautiful Metz is not Paris, but Papa—should I've said we're from Paris?"

Unlike the smiling Steve, Célestin was serious: *"Non, ma chère fille,* you did well. Many Metz citizens, if they were in South Africa, might say they were Parisians, but you and I are proud of our city. As Annette is of hers. It's a pity you two didn't get to know each other. By the way, her home city is called Bloemfontein. The major highway from Joburg by which we reached the Gold Reef Park goes there; we saw the road signs."

Steve asked if they would like to join him in a game of croquet—he had noticed a grass area for that old sport. They readily agreed and rented three croquet mallets and three wooden balls of different colors. Célestin asked innocently: "Would you like to invite Annette to play? She and Steve against us." Odile's rejection was immediate: "I won't invite her. Even Annette's mother gave me a mean look. Why? And Annette... slobbering like a child." He privately sympathized with his daughter's feelings: "I think even an objective person would conclude she's fair rather than vengeful."

Six wire hoops positioned in an ellipsoid pattern were embedded in the grass court. Steve and Célestin skillfully used their mallets to strike their ball so it hit other players' balls. Then they tried, using an additional permitted stroke, to send the rival's ball as far away as possible—ideally off the court and down some stairs. As if by chance, they rarely hit Odile's ball. Therefore she was able, relying on her weak but precise lady-style strokes, to drive her ball untroubled through all the hoops and win the game. She knew what Steve and her father were doing but did not want, like some child, to spoil their pleasure of letting her win.

At the lavish dinner, the waiters, some white, some black, served appetizers, salads, soups, main courses, dessert, and fruit. Instead of political talk, Steve entertained with benign journalistic anecdotes. For no reason other than the dessert wine's excellence, he and Célestin raised their glasses in a toast to His Majesty Sobhuza II, wishing him and all his wives eternal life. The girl's smile oscillated between amusement and harmless mockery.

Addresses were exchanged. As a souvenir, the head waiter courteously presented Odile with an embossed copy of the fourteen-page restaurant menu in five languages.

13.

It was an hour before sunset. On a narrow, empty, red-earth track, Célestin drove very slowly, then in first gear, and finally switched off the engine. He made sure the roof was securely latched. With his daughter, he sat in the car motionlessly, giving the animals time to get used to the presence of the metal monster.

On the right side of the tiny road, high among the rocks, a group of baboons had frozen when the vehicle arrived but after a minute resumed ordinary pursuits and spirited communication. On the opposite side, there were several tall acacias. Beyond them, an open savanna stretched to the horizon. Many gnus and zebras were so close, less than fifty meters away, that Célestin and Odile could observe them without binoculars. One blue gnu or "wildebeest," which was watching the Rover attentively, went on grazing. It was a giant animal, at least a meter and a half tall at the shoulder and weighing maybe two hundred fifty kilos.

"You see gnus and zebras are together for mutual safety," he whispered. "With their unequally developed senses of sight, hearing, and smell, they complement each other in the ability to discover the presence of predators early. A sort of symbiosis, about which we've talked." "Yes, we did, Papa, but didn't we also learn baboons were the first to notice danger? They help other animals by raising a racket." "True, but don't imagine baboons do it out of a need to help other species."

They did not feel like leaving the lonely place where there were no people. Insects buzzed around the car while a heavenly chorus of birds sang to them from acacias. Yet his next remark defined the setting as far from idyllic: "Probably you remember there are one thousand two hundred lions in Kruger. This hour of the day when visibility decreases is their favorite time for hunting." Odile meekly protested: "You don't think, Papa, lions would arrive right here, just now, to hunt—so we'd admire them?!" Célestin smiled: "No, they won't come to do a show for us, but look how many young, carefree gnus and zebras are there! And how about those miniature antelopes not bigger than calves among the gnus? They're called duikers. One of them would seem to be the right size for a lion's evening meal. I know you'll now say I am horrible."

Had her father's clairvoyance not disarmed the girl and made her speechless, she would have probably said that. But suddenly they heard the indescribably loud uproar of the baboons' barks, screams, and "yaks." He grabbed the binoculars and looked at the herd of grazing animals. She did the same and was the one who spotted the lions: A pair of them rose from the grass through which they had previously been crawling and gave furious chase consisting of huge leaps. At the same time, the tremendous thud of countless panic-stricken animals' pounding hooves was heard. A truly frantic gallop.

The lions' hot pursuit could not last long—and did not have to because less than about eighty meters was enough for them to pull down three animals. The more experienced lion butchered a zebra with incredible speed and then managed to grab an immature gnu's rear leg. The other lion had no problem killing a small zebra. All three victims were young. A lioness appeared from the grass, and the three mighty cats pulled their kill into the thicket where they could eat in peace, free from the attentions of hyenas and vultures.

Everything was over in three minutes. By then, the herd would have gone far away; baboons behaved as if nothing had happened; and lions had probably begun to eat the entrails. Primeval peace descended on the savanna. Father and daughter looked at each other wordlessly. It was not the first time in Odile's life she had seen the death of a living creature. In Metz, Marie, their cook, never wrung chickens' necks in her presence, but the girl had witnessed animals butchered on the marketplaces in China.

Nevertheless, the violent deaths of large animals in the savanna were something else, and she was in shock. Célestin understood and began to drive back to Camp Skukuza without comment. Instead of prattling about the inexorable laws of nature, he let his girl muse and brood on her own. Evening air and a drive of twenty kilometers would help refresh her. Odile was aware that her desire to see wild animals in their natural habitat would be inextricably linked with seeing them in their daily merciless battle for survival. She pensively whispered: "Neither that... symbiosis nor the baboons' uproar helped those animals survive."

By the time they reached their rondawel, night had fallen. The girl immediately took a shower, enjoying the cool water after the hot day. Pulsating jets helped dampen the intense vividness of the lion kill. She consoled herself that the next day would bring new stunning landscapes and animals to her eyes.

* * *

The previous morning, after a swim and healthy breakfast at the Sabie River Bungalows, they had left Hazyview and entered Kruger through Numbi Gate, soon arriving at Camp Skukuza. Their luxurious rondawel was indeed perfectly round and had the traditional tall conical roof made of natural thatch. The interior was comfortable, with a modern bathroom, kitchen, and several rooms of unusual shape. "We'll have this airy, spacious living room for your birthday party; everything is as they promised when I called from Ezulwini," said Célestin gaily.

Upon studying the detailed map of the park, they made plans for the important first day. Kruger National Park was enormous. With an area of twenty thousand square kilometers, it was much bigger than all of Swaziland and almost twenty times the size of Amboseli. Its east side, four hundred kilometers long, was the frontier of South Africa with Mozambique, and in the north, the park and country bordered Zimbabwe. It was named in honor of the Afrikaner-Boer Stephanus Johannes Paulus Kruger, who had proclaimed the territory a protected natural reserve under the name of Government Wildlife Park in 1898. The proclamation was based on an Act of Parliament of the independent Republic of South Africa, of which Kruger was president. "How enlightened and far-sighted was that decision, especially at the time: Perhaps a country needs independence to accomplish great things," thought Célestin with admiration. (*The Republic became the* dependent *Transvaal under England after the three-year Second Boer War ended in 1902.*)

They decided to spend the first three days in the southern part of Kruger, using their rondawel as a base, subsequently driving north and staying at Camp Shingwedzi in the central part of the park. However, the same rondawel in Skukuza would be theirs from the 16th to the 20th of January—which included Odile's birthday and the arrival of Dima and Kolya.

During the whole morning, with the roof open, they drove southeast toward the Lower Sabie River. The animal and plant life was so delightful, plentiful, and extraordinary that even Célestin was unable to see and hear everything properly. On the open savanna and the treeless *veldt*, many hundreds of gazelles, impalas, gnus, elands, duikers, and zebras were peacefully grazing. Giraffes were browsing in the crowns of acacias. Birds of paradisiacal colors announced themselves and sang. Numerous unfamiliar trees were packed with screeching monkeys. And warthogs, chasing small prey, would noisily dart from the dense shrubbery. Often they saw surrealist piles of rocks, many with green and yellow mineral layers: Baboons rightly considered these jumbles as their unassailable fortresses. On a smooth flat stone in the sunshine, there was a giant lizard at least eighty centimeters long, so long its whole tail hung over the edge. Huge turtles could be seen within reach while a herd of buffalo grazed far in a vast field. Elephants were noisily drinking along small tributaries of the Sabie River. As if all that beauty was not enough, they saw in the distance the lofty, grayish mountain chains in Mozambique. Above the mountains, fantastically shaped clouds sailed across the azure sky.

It was January, a partly dry season. Even the biggest rivers— Sabie, Crocodile, Olifants, Shingwedzi, Limpopo—were reduced to narrow channels. Visitors could see much farther with grass shorter and bush thinner, but... Skukuza rangers convincingly claimed all seasons were spectacular in their way. "Is it true predators don't attack at watering holes?" Célestin asked one. The answer was quick and unequivocal: "That's sentimental Hollywood nonsense. Many set up ambushes there. Besides, photogenic watering holes are quite rare."

All those animals were genuinely wild, in the sense that they were not given food and water. The only exceptions, the rangers said, were large water tanks they would see as they drove around Kruger. The tanks were filled with water during the dry period and were so tall that only elephants and giraffes could drink out of them. After all, there were fences around Kruger. On two sides was the international border, whereas just beyond the other two, there were villages and farms. Because of the fencing, animals could not search for water outside the park—and elephants needed two hundred fifty liters per day, giraffes about fifty.

Although animals were sometimes near vehicles full of people, they were not in the least tame. Even the baboons were not domesticated like those at Lake Nakuru. From the start, Odile and Célestin witnessed many beasts frantically escaping the Rover. He found it touching, whereas she felt sad—as if animals were fleeing her. Dozens of timid gazelles and duikers suddenly took flight with high, long leaps; a mature giraffe meekly walked away; even one warthog cutely turned around and returned to the shrubs from which it came.

Around two in the afternoon, they arrived at the small Camp Lower Sabie located only seven kilometers from the border of Mozambique. No one was around except for the resident Afrikaner couple in their sixties. Joop was a retired ranger who guarded and cleaned the camp while Greet cooked and gardened. She served still-warm homemade fruit pie to the visitors. Those two lonely, amiable people proceeded to recount the history of the park, describing their experiences of many years. "We love Kruger so much we've never wished to live away from it," Greet said with a catch in her voice. "Hmm, maybe we've never wished," Joop corrected his wife gently, "because we wouldn't have known how..."

Responding to Célestin's request, Joop smiled: "If you'd like to see Mozambique firsthand, or at least a few trees in it, you can! A tiny dirt track begins behind the camp... over there. It runs seven kilometers to a spot where a stream flows into the Sabie, and the river, coursing directly east, leaves South Africa. On the opposite side of the stream, now shallow enough to ford on foot, is Mozambique. The track is very narrow, with lots of loose stones but won't be a problem for your Rover—and it hasn't rained for four days. Don't step out of the vehicle and don't open the roof."

They reached the spot Joop had described and stopped close

to the Sabie on its left bank. In front of them was a shallow stream, less than a quarter of a meter deep, flowing into the river. Across the stream: Mozambique! The forest over there was dark and dense and the shrubbery high and impenetrable. They sat in the vehicle and absorbed the ambiance. After the day's many hours of exhilaration and overexcited delight, they learned not to talk, to enjoy nature quietly, and to observe the subtle features of animals and even plants. "Apache Chief Winnetou would behave just like us," decided Odile. "A smart remark despite the wrong continent," was her father's humble witticism.

Their newly found patience was rewarded after ten minutes, for an adult cheetah had soundlessly emerged from the Mozambican thicket. It was a gorgeous, healthy specimen, golden with black spots. The splendid cat carefully looked around, and after noticing the Rover, only about forty meters away, studied it for a minute. Silence ruled. With its pale-green body and light-brown roof, the motionless vehicle's camouflage was solid, but it was nevertheless square, unnatural, and therefore potentially threatening. When Odile attempted to lift the binoculars, Célestin held her hand: "Not yet." Breathing fast, the girl murmured: "He's looking straight here, not just at the car, but at our eyes." After another minute of hushed two-way observation—or communication, mused the two peaceable, animal-loving humans—the cheetah hopped lightly down to the stream and began eagerly to slurp the water.

"Now lift the binoculars," he went on softly: "We read it was difficult to determine a cheetah's sex based on physical appearance, but I think this one is male. He has a large head and a weight of—I'd guess—sixty kilos. And he's both long, perhaps a meter and a half, and tall, certainly over eighty centimeters. Oh, what a beautiful animal!" The cheetah attentively looked around and resumed noisily quaffing.

"Look, Papa, at those black streaks on his face below the eyes, like tears. Does only ours have them, or do all cheetahs?" "All of them do. I read the black streaks reduce sharp sunrays and also, like the scope on a sniper, help them focus when they peer at prey—like us!" He recklessly laughed. Born with exceptional sight and hearing, the cheetah naturally heard it, threw one glance at the Rover, and by a single vigorous, elegant leap disappeared in the thicket. The long golden tail was the last they saw of their cheetah.

"*Désolé, ma douce, j'étais vraiment stupide,*" Célestin apologized, started the engine, and turned the Rover around. Odile was lost in thought and whispered: "The more I think the surer I am our cheetah was female: Elegantly dressed and graceful."

About two hours remained till sunset. Despite experiencing so much, they were insatiable, and instead of driving west toward Skukuza, they turned north. He brooded: "Our pretty cheetah—have it your way, let her be female, although it's strange such a lady would be slurping so loud... My point is this: She's much safer in the distant corner of Mozambique by the border than at many other places in that country. For five years, there's been a bloody civil war between the pro-communist FRELIMO and the anti-communist RENAMO. One could say the USA and the USSR have been waging a war against each other but using those unfortunate people as proxies. I'm certain our France is helping someone, probably RENAMO: She never minds her own business."

14.

During breakfast, Odile was tempted to mention the lions' bloodthirstiness they had witnessed in horrible proximity but restrained herself. She did not want to spoil his mood, conscious that it would tire him to explain, yet again, the inexorability of nature. Only in Africa did the girl understand that the young, the old, and the sick were the most frequent prey of the exalted King of the Beasts. She therefore acted more chipper than she felt, but the need for innocuous deception disappeared as soon as the Rover plunged into the park.

However, two hours later, Kruger proved afresh that it was not an entertaining theme park. This was shown by the immutable law governing lions and zebras, the lovable striped horses. They were driving near Lukimbi and the Crocodile River, about forty kilometers south of where they had been the previous evening, when he noticed a group of busy rangers. Soon he realized their task was gruesome: "I must stop here because it's dangerous on this narrow road to crawl past them, but you, if you don't want to see what they're doing, look at those trees over there. You're not a child any longer whose eyes I need to cover with my hand."

The rangers were using shovels and pitchforks to load the bloody remains of one or more animals onto a truck. "Lion kill, a recent one, Sir. Please don't step out of the vehicle near here, and because of the vultures keep the roof closed," said a ranger politely. On the pitchfork he was holding, they saw a bloody lump of flesh covered by striped skin.

Célestin thanked the rangers and drove off. Aloud he said nothing, but in his heart, he bitterly blamed himself: When the trip was planned in Metz, he had not forewarned his daughter that brutal events might happen in Kruger where wild animals behaved in accord with their inherent nature. But Odile sensitively undid her seat belt and scooted to her father, seizing him round the waist: "Please don't worry, *je t'en supplie, mon cher Papa.* Everything is all right. I'm so grateful we came here. The park is out of this world."

They reached the Crocodile River. It was not dry but shallow, flowing lazily. In the vicinity, there was a natural pool bordered by flat rocks on which five or six hippos were lying, lazy like the river. Others were submerged in the pool, with only their fat cheeks, small ears, massive nostrils, and bulging eyes visible. "We haven't seen them since the Nairobi National Park," he said. "I remember, Papa. Our Kenyan guide Michael let us walk near the hippos."

"Yes, he was a knowledgeable person; in Kruger, we aren't allowed to leave the car," Célestin added regretfully. Odile was observant: "Look, on the rock over there I see a strange drawing; please drive closer, Papa." An ancient reddish drawing of a giraffe and a gazelle buck was on the rock's flat face. He partially opened the roof so they could take a few photos but then quickly closed it. Suddenly, from behind the Rover, they heard the clatter of a bicycle painstakingly ridden over uneven stones. When the cyclist, a gray-haired man with a noble, very dark countenance, reached the car, he politely greeted the occupants. The man wore a faded ranger's uniform drenched in sweat; a rifle hung over his shoulder. Célestin worriedly asked if he had disregarded a park rule. "No, no," smiled the elderly man amiably, revealing two gold teeth in his upper jaw. "That question, dear Sir, shows you're a city person nervous about regulations!"

The ranger readily accepted the invitation to join them in the car. He propped the bicycle against a rock and dangled the rifle from the handlebars. Next to the driver's seat in the Rover, there were two separate seats but not wide enough for people unfamiliar with each other. So at her father's request, Odile moved to one of the jump seats in the back. While the man was climbing into the car, she asked her father to open the roof, claiming the air was stuffy.

"My name is Sam, I'm a Zulu man. I've been a ranger here for many years, a warden for the hippos in the pond and the crocodiles in the river. Of course, we don't feed them. On this spot, it's safe to open the roof, even though it's not an official *uitkykpunt*, a lookout point. Today it's hot, thirty-four degrees and muggy, so there'll be a downpour tonight for sure." Acting as a hostess, she took a couple of cans of juice from the icebox and handed them to Sam and Célestin along with granola bars.

Sam gratefully nodded to the girl: "I noticed you took photos of the drawing, so I'll tell you about it. Experts believe it's a finger painting created two and a half thousand years ago in the late Stone Age and that the artists were hunter-gatherers called San. Today, these people are usually called Bushmen, from the Afrikaans *Bosjesmans*, which means 'people from the bush.' But they continue to be known as San, Kung, Khwe, and many other names. It's an ancient race stubbornly striving not to die out, despite the persistent efforts of many others to make the struggle both backbreaking and hopeless. Nowadays, most of them live in the Kalahari Desert in Namibia. There it rains once every ten years so the vultures have not tried overly hard to grab their sand and stones. I can't quite claim they're my ancestors. The Zulu people arose much later, south of Kruger, between Swaziland and Lesotho, but still..." winked Sam.

Munching granola, the pair pondered Sam's words and moved from the car to a pile of stones with his permission. "I'm using this name because it doesn't give away whether I'm for the Boers or the English!" A playful chuckle. For his part, Célestin explained that his background was neither Dutch nor British. "Aha! So you've brought your little daughter here to learn about my country, and you both love it! Well, in that sense, you're much closer to the Boers-Afrikaners than to the English. We, the Zulu people, don't like the English. Not so much because they defeated us in war but because their victory—following ours, under the great Chief Cetshwayo kaMpande—was achieved by lies and deception." Sam bent his old gray head and fell silent. Célestin and Odile were touched to the core by his sorrowful voice, wrinkled face, and the strange tones of Anglo-Afrikaans-Zulu speech.

Confirming the proud and kindhearted Zulu ranger's prediction, an awesome thunderstorm hit southern Kruger that evening. In their rondavel, father and daughter softly spoke about animals not far away. Did they become habituated to the terrifying sounds, or were they shaking panic-stricken in the undergrowth? Maybe they immediately quenched their thirst at a watering hole? The learned zoological books rarely concerned themselves with animals' fears and other emotions: After all, they were only animals.

15.

They drove on roads of wet red earth bordered by acacias and dense shrubbery. Kruger was evaporating after the previous night's tumultuous downpour. The beauty of pink cloudlets and distant mountains' contours gave Célestin no choice but to stop the Rover. "How marvelous it all is, *mon trésor*! I propose that for once we break the rule, step out of the car, and inhale with all our might. The open roof is not enough. *Ça va?*" They did it, holding hands. No lion could do them harm and would not want to.

After breakfast at Camp Skukuza, they embarked on a drive of almost a hundred kilometers—via Tshokwane, Mzanzene, and Timbavati—to the Olifants River, one of the biggest in Kruger. They used only secondary roads S83, S36, and S39, encountering few cars. Those narrow roads mostly led north and were almost equidistant from the east border of Kruger with Mozambique, about forty kilometers away, and the west border with Transvaal, about thirty. Nevertheless, at the Olifants, they were still over two hundred kilometers south of Kruger's northern border with Zimbabwe. Driving along the river, they noticed more water than elsewhere. "Perhaps last night's rain was heavier in this part of Kruger than south near Skukuza. But even here, the water depth can't be more than a meter," he said.

Despite the intense heat of the early afternoon, the roof remained shut as a precaution. While chatting worry-free, something unforgettable happened. As they approached a bridge with two lanes over the Olifants—driving along a road that would climb onto the bridge and continue north—they heard a frightening uproar ahead. The source of the noise was located in the dense forest on their side of the river, a short distance beyond the bridge. Their blood froze. With the help of the name "Olifants," Célestin concluded elephants would be the cause, but it was improbable those giants would cross the bridge. So he pressed the accelerator, sharply turned onto the bridge, and stopped in its middle, some thirty meters farther on the legal left side. Bedlam was continuing, elephants were close. However, the bridge was six or seven meters above the water, which, together with metal guard rails on the opposite side, made it impossible for him to see what was happening.

Since no cars were around, he ignored the elementary traffic rule and made a U-turn from the legal lane in which he had stopped to the one running in the opposite direction—and then parked next to guard rails. Even from there, he saw poorly through the railing and thus broke a more important rule, one that regulated safety. He opened the door and squeezed through the gap of about forty centimeters between the car and the rails. Odile exclaimed: "But what should I do, Papa?" "Slide over to my seat quickly and wait a moment. Please give me the Nikon."

Finally, he had a clear view. Two massive mature elephants and behind them three smaller ones, together with two calves, exploded from the forest to the boggy area by the river. They broke everything in their way, tearing and eating branches of young trees. The slice of land through which they had crashed was a green wasteland. Seven animals were no more than fifty meters from the bridge. He took photos using the camera's burst mode and then noticed Odile was dejectedly trying, sitting low in the driver's seat, to see something through the rails. Judging the danger to be minimal and the opportunity unique, he allowed compassion and common sense to outweigh the rules.

"Elephants, *ma chère fille*, many! Pull yourself quickly out of the car and stand next to me. Leave your camera behind—we may need to drive away fast." Odile wriggled from the vehicle and clung to her father. She then saw a sight she would never, never forget: Elephants were rushing into the river unbelievably close to her, roaring and emitting many other sounds. There were grunts, trumpeting, barks, snorts. The giants were happy like children stepping into the sea on the first day of summer vacation.

Father and daughter were thrilled watching the sublime scene and almost stopped breathing—in equal parts from delight and an ill-defined apprehension of witnessing something incomprehensible. "Look how magnificent they are. Genuinely free..." he whispered. "But Papa, did you see how they were breaking young trees in the forest?" "Don't worry about the forest, *ma douce*. Elephants were only acting their role in nature's eternal cycles of birth, death, and rebirth."

All seven animals entered the river, the water barely reaching above the knees of the babies. After a heavy drinking session, showering began. The two sweet calves, behaving like joyful naughty children, did not hesitate to direct jets of water from their small trunks at adults, even though they received strong jets straight at their foreheads in return. The grown-ups happily romped around, roaring, rumbling, and trumpeting, while the young ones frolicked, making high-pitched snorting sounds. When the calves gamboled almost under the bridge, shivers ran down the spines of Célestin and Odile out of love for the animals. In contrast, elephants either did not notice human figures on the bridge or did not consider them worthy of attention.

After they had driven away, Odile breathlessly chirruped about the baby elephants. When he finally got the chance, Célestin the linguist commented: "During the showering, the calves were making strange little sounds for which our rich and allegedly sophisticated languages don't have names. Perhaps the Bushmen, about whom old Sam was telling us, do. I know one of their languages, *!Kung,* has numerous vowels and consonants, as well as the so-called 'clicks,' like 'tsk! tsk!,' which means 'I don't want' or 'no good' or 'I am annoyed.'" Odile listened carefully, and then the mischievous child quipped: "Very well, but what's the click for 'I am glad'—as in 'I am glad, Papa, I learned all that'?"

16.

Some days later, they were sitting on the camp terrace and writing even though the night was falling fast. High above them, branches of an old baobab were full of songbirds, their melodies accompanied by the muffled sounds of distant Zulu drums. Mystery and splendor. The pair would miss Skukuza when they temporarily moved the next morning to Camp Shingwedzi, far to the north.

Three Kruger rangers arrived and called out greetings from afar, so Célestin invited them. While the men sipped beer, Odile bravely asked questions about the park. Steyn, an amiable guy five or so years younger than Tino, was delighted when Dilla asked him whether elephants used the bridge to cross the Olifants River. "It'd be child's play for them to climb onto the road and cross the bridge," said Steyn, "but they seldom do. Wild elephants don't like or trust man-made structures. Can't blame them. Maybe if the Olifants went completely dry or in case of a forest fire… No, on the bridge you were safe out of the car from both elephants and other animals. Only rarely, at night, do we find lost young monkeys without parents on the bridge."

Pursuing the elephant theme, Casper, the eldest of the threesome, said ecologists objected to the dry-season water supply for elephants and giraffes by providing tall water tanks. "The population of elephants has grown too much even for Kruger, although three hundred die every year. It's also essential that their corpses be removed quickly to avoid the spread of disease and an inordinate increase of scavengers and vultures. We do it by helicopter. Unfortunately, in Zimbabwe and Mozambique, the care for animals in parks is poor. Botswana is more pragmatic: Instead of being busy with pride, they allow us to help them," concluded Casper with a wry smile.

He was a helicopter pilot and had begun to describe how an elephant's corpse was transported when Odile whispered to her father that she was tired and needed to pack for their departure. Célestin apologized to the rangers, saying he would accompany his daughter but return soon. In the rondawel, he told her: "I'm sorry, *ma princesse*. I understand why that saddened you, but those people are doing important and dangerous work, which they wouldn't do if they didn't love animals. I'll go back to them but won't stay long. Let's see: All the windows are shut, switch on the air conditioning if you wish." He kissed her and returned to the terrace: "Please continue, Casper."

"Tino, I must apologize," said the ranger. "Of the three of us, I'm the only one without children and forget how young ones react to the mention of dead elephants and gazelles ripped apart. As for where I stopped: Well, when the helicopter is flying with the corpse hanging below, the biggest vultures, like hellish giant wasps, attack the huge body with their beaks and claws. A truly horrible sight. I'm glad Dilla went to sleep."

"Do you have weapons in the helicopter?" asked Célestin. "Yes, we do, but we don't use them against vultures. Who knows on whom those birds of prey would fall? No, our weapons are for self-defense when we land in a remote corner of Kruger and encounter poachers or guerrillas. Those are often heavily armed."

When the rangers were leaving, he walked with them. Their vehicle was an American military Humvee, next to which the Rover looked like a toy. "We have Glock semiautomatic rifles that are nevertheless no match for some guerrillas," said Steyn while giving Célestin his phone number. "Who knows, you may need it," he added, which reminded the recipient of Senior Sergeant Wim in Roodeplaat. Casper not only gave his phone number but offered to take him along on the next mission: "Needless to say, without Dilla, both because of her feelings and those of our insurance guys."

Returning to the rondawel, he stood again under the baobab tree and somehow managed to find the grand Southern Cross through its branches. He was surrounded by the African night full of mystique and secret murmurings of animals.

He liked the rangers. Hard-working like their Dutch ancestors, these Afrikaners had an affinity for order, decency, and courtesy. They did not consider themselves newcomers but white native Africans who felt great devotion to the country and nation they thought theirs, though not exclusively theirs. Nor could one ignore their passionate attachment to the land, the earth, the very soil—a worship they shared with the original Boers.

During the extended goodbyes, it occurred to Célestin to invite the trio to Odile's birthday party. Hmm... no way! The problem did not lie in more talk about lions' kills, dead elephants, vultures, and orphan monkeys—but in Olya. He ardently hoped to get help from Dima and Kolya and did not know what the Soviet diplomats would think of the rangers and vice versa. He felt shame but...

17.

The modest Camp Shingwedzi was situated in a picturesque area, on a wooded hill above the dry bed of a river with the same name. In a few months, once it has revived, the river would flow southeast and after fifteen kilometers enter Mozambique. The hillock was part of the foothills of the low mountains Lebomboberge, Portuguese Montes Libombos, which rarely reached over five hundred meters. The chain ran for hundreds of kilometers along the eastern border, all the way south to Swaziland. In the rondawel father and daughter had rented for two nights, there was no air conditioning, but the fan worked. They did not mind, as heat remained an immutable component of Odile's enjoyment of Africa.

The pair adored Kruger. Bearing the heat and long hours in the Rover was easy when the wild natural park rewarded them every day with extraordinary vistas and an amazing diversity of animals, vegetation, rivers, streams, and watering holes—dry or not. Even the forms of the boulders, crags, and bluffs were uncanny, antediluvian. During their first outing from Camp Shingwedzi, they drove forty kilometers to the northwest on dirt roads and dusty minor highways S55 and S56, sometimes along the dry Mphongolo River, till they reached Babalala, a forested area with rough-hewn picnic tables and a shelter. The next day, they proceeded on the narrow S50 along the dry bed of the Shingwedzi and into the Lebomboberge. On dirt tracks with a never-ending series of curves, they finally reached Dipeni Buitepos, two hundred meters from Mozambique.

Odile learned map reading and orientation by compass in Siberia and was learning to drive in Kruger. Célestin knew that many ten-year-old farmers' sons and daughters in the American Midwest were taught to drive pickup trucks and small tractors. So why not his daughter? Her first lesson in practical driver education, impulsively improvised, took place on a deserted track without ditches. He controlled the pedals while she, sitting next to him and leaning over, held the steering wheel with both hands and kept the Rover moving straight. On another occasion, with the engine switched off in an empty rest area, Célestin moved the driver's seat as far forward as it would go: Odile's feet could then reach all three pedals, and he familiarized her with their purpose and resistance. After additional lessons, she drove the car in first gear, whereas he kept one hand on the steering wheel and the other on the ignition key.

They agreed her first real outing as *conducteur* would take place on the Metz estate, in the old Renault, which was easier to drive than the Rover, even though it also had a manual gear shift. She kept certain thoughts to herself: "How my classmates will envy me—the girls, but even more the boys! Maybe it's better not to tell them? Their parents might think Papa has become insane from an African fever when he's teaching me to drive at my age."

Not far from the camp, three small rivers flowed into the Shingwedzi: Bububu and Nkokodzi from the west and Mandzembo from the east—flowed, that is, in the rainy season. In the early evening of their first day, they drove on the unsigned dirt roads to the area between the dry riverbeds. Dozens of different animal voices could be heard. "Perhaps there's a watering hole somewhere nearby," he said.

Soon they reached a fair-sized grove where a large colony of baboons awaited them. The closest ones were only about thirty meters away, some in low trees, others on the ground. However, only by far the biggest and evidently the most experienced baboon paid attention to the Rover. They noticed him staring suspiciously.

Except for the adventure on the Olifants bridge, father and daughter adhered to the rule of not stepping out of the car. But seeing the numerous baboons, he could not restrain himself. The enthusiasm of a passionate photographer, almost an impulsive gut reaction, took over. He slipped out and placed his elbows on the roof of the Rover, the Nikon in his hands. In a hoarse voice, he instructed: "Please remain where you are. From your side of the car, you can even take pictures—but only through glass!" Feeling safe because the massive vehicle sat between him and the baboons, he raised the camera and adjusted the focus.

Célestin overlooked something elementary: By stepping out of the car, he became a new stimulus, possibly quite rare even for the baboon chief. The cunning elderly fellow reacted with surprising alacrity, nimbly running at full speed through the grove, down the slope, and to the dry riverbed. All the other baboons, at least fifty of them of all ages and sizes, followed him instinctively. It was an impressive mass flight.

Contrite, he sat in the car, baffled by the consequences of his reckless action. "What can I say? This foolish exploit was distasteful. I, a man of seventy-two kilos, have caused primal panic and distress in the brains and bodies of animals weighing, all together, maybe three tons! And these are baboons, *ma chérie*, not little gazelles—they have brains and emotions far more similar to ours. Contemptible." Odile commiserated and tried to change her father's mood: "At least, Papa, you took good photos. I managed to click only three times—through mucky glass." But Célestin responded sharply: "My photos? Oh, no. You took more photos than I did! I pressed the shutter only twice because the moment the big baboon jumped up to run, I grew furious with myself and stopped shooting. It was a fiasco. *Hein, ma douce*, it's not so funny."

The evening brought them another valuable acquaintance-ship—in the almost empty outdoor bar at Camp Shingwedzi. Odile was again sipping a chilled club soda and her father a Lion Beer. Even though their glasses were not empty, the young waiter, almost a boy, suddenly appeared carrying a new round. "From the one over there, a good one," explained the cheerful youngster who was from the Xhosa people. They looked at the man who sat smiling at a distant table. Wordlessly, Célestin consulted her and then got up, bowed formally, and yelled: "Please join us, good Sir!" As the man approached, the waiter put a hand to his mouth and was in stitches about the Western ceremony.

Hendrik amiably greeted the Frenchman who told him: "My daughter Odile and I are not accustomed to such chivalrous gestures harking back to Paris—in the nineteenth century!" Taking a seat, the man laughed: "Yes, I'd seen such rituals in old films about Paris and now, from my old table, I overheard French words. My offer of drinks was a friendly joke to make the introductions smoother. To be honest, I'm fed up sitting alone in this improvised bar for the third evening in a row and speaking only to our young waiter in his language—which I speak better than French."

A pleasant red-haired man in his thirties, Hendrik was an Afrikaner, an officer in the South African Air Force. He won Odile by first asking her innocuous questions about animals and then pulling from his wallet the photos of his two sons, sweet boys with reddish hair, five and six years old. After another quickly consumed beer, he divulged being a military pilot until eighteen months before. The admission was followed by another: His superiors had forbidden him to fly because of his "unsettled personal life." Having gone through a stormy divorce, he lost custody of his sons.

Noticing how much the topic had upset Hendrik, Célestin did his best to avoid pursuing it. He was also curious what the intelligent and educated officer would say about issues Sergeant Wim had so vehemently addressed—notably the future of racial relations in South Africa. However, he thought that before conveying Wim's opinions, it was decent to disclose to Hendrik something about himself and his daughter. So he talked about Metz, Patrizia, Odile's school, and their travel to South Africa via the USSR, Israel, and Kenya. Only then, explaining who and what Wim was, obviously without naming him, he summarized the sergeant's harangue.

Hendrik looked at Célestin for a long time, occasionally glancing at Odile: "Yes, there are such people among us, although there's truth in much of what he said and not only blind hate." Then the disgraced officer added bitterly: "Maybe his wife left him... But some policemen are beasts in the worst sense, just like those they're fighting every day—as is the case, after all, in Britain, France, and America."

They again fell silent. Célestin offered Odile the option of retiring to the rondawel, but she preferred to stay. So he continued: "No, his wife didn't leave him. In fact, he invited us to visit them. And while the wife would be smelling flowers in the garden with my daughter, the sergeant would show me authentic police photos of murders committed by ANC comrades, including by necklacing. We didn't have the chance to do it and didn't wish to. Then, absolutely not; now, I'm no longer certain."

He switched the subject: "May I consult you regarding our itinerary? When I told the sergeant we'd travel to Musina and Madimbo in northern Transvaal, then follow the Limpopo River all the way to Venda and enter Kruger through Pafuri Gate, he said I was crazy and immediately offered to lend me a pistol. I declined with the false explanation I didn't know how to shoot—at which he looked at me suspiciously. In the end, we entered Kruger from the south. However, in about a week, we'll go out of the park in the north and from Pafuri travel through Venda to Musina."

After considering the matter, Hendrik said: "Regarding Venda and the area around Musina toward the Zimbabwe border, the sergeant was right because guerrilla activity is frequent there. Still, I don't wish to change your mind about leaving through Pafuri Gate. That's where I entered Kruger three days ago, unarmed. I own a service pistol but never carry it—mostly out of silly pride: I'm a pilot and not an infantryman or policeman. However, be careful, Célestin, because..." By an almost imperceptible head movement, he indicated Odile.

"You've sincerely tried to get to know us, and I appreciate it," Hendrik continued. "I respect you as an educated, forthright man who learns by traveling and isn't a journalist for a lying Dutch, English, or American rag. During these difficult years, we haven't had many visitors of your caliber, courageous people who'd try to understand both sides—three, because the allegedly liberal hypocrites of British descent are something else. Your honesty and clear head will open the hearts of many Afrikaners to you, regardless of their age, gender, and political views."

It was late evening. All three sat still, listening to Kruger's subtle sounds. The Xhosa boy dozed behind the bar. Without making an effort to cheer up the visitors, Hendrik, his voice breaking several times, said: "I'm aware many things in this beautiful country I love dearly must often produce tension, even horror, in Odile and you—which is precisely how we, Afrikaners, Zulus, and Xhosas, feel. I believe no one should allow himself to become indifferent either to his own or others' cruelty—including that sergeant. I ask you to feel compassion for him and his wife, as I beg my God to have mercy on me."

Looking at the Southern Cross, hands folded behind his head, Célestin spoke, mostly to himself: "Kruger is a dream that helps one understand animals are better than people, white and black—which certainly isn't an original thought."

18.

Kissing Odile on her cheeks and forehead, he covered her with a light sheet: "Tomorrow is your, our, special day. *Fais de beaux rêves, ma douce.*" She whispered sleepily: "*Dors bien, mon cher Papa.*"

On returning from Shingwedzi to Skukuza, they reclaimed the old rondawel. It was thus easier to carry out birthday preparations, but even twenty-four hours later, much remained for Célestin to do. First, using a broad-tip pen, he wrote "Happy Birthday" on long, multicolored strips of paper in several languages—French, German, Afrikaans, English, and Russian. He also wrote "*Usuku olumnandi lokuzalwa*" in Zulu, and after giving it some thought in Xhosa: In the latter case, the words were identical but written in a different order. The two languages were similar—dialects of the same language—and used the Latin script. However, both the Zulu and the Xhosa people insisted their language was different and separate. As a linguist, Célestin knew there were many such cases around the world, while as a historian, he was aware that the insistence of two nations or peoples on the existence of minimal differences sometimes led to envy, hate, and war.

Using adhesive tape and tacks, he hung the strips around the rondawel's living room. Cards from Odile's girlfriends had arrived at their home in Metz, and Gilles sent them with his, Marie's, Gerda's, and Françoise's to Wits in Joburg. Hoping for birthday mail, Célestin had phoned Carl Goode's secretary from Swaziland and given her the Skukuza address. The package had miraculously arrived, so he placed the cards at various prominent places in the room. Then he wrote loving words on the card he had bought in Metz.

At the camp shop, he had purchased an ochre-colored T-shirt with a giraffe below Kruger's name, so he placed it, wrapped in tissue paper, on the dining table beside a cute children's safari hat. Already in the afternoon, Odile had tried a new dress and been delighted; it was of Zulu design, in vivid colors. He needed to give it to her ahead of time, hoping she would wear it at the party—and she wanted to! His darling daughter knew the main present for her birthday was their being among the wild animals in the mysterious and often incomprehensible Africa.

Tribal music played softly on the radio. "My little girl is ten years old... incredible," Célestin thought, switching off the light. He leaned back on the sofa and stared into the night through the open window. They had become accustomed to the night insects of Kruger, but animals' voices never repeated themselves. Only two or three hours earlier, a group of duikers ran through the camp. And the evening before, when tired and sweaty after the long trip from Shingwedzi they were parking the car, a tall *rooibok*—male impala—was seriously studying them from the bush. Animals sometimes ruled in Kruger, which was good, he smiled.

Earlier in the day, Dima and Kolya had arrived from Mbabane in their terrain vehicle and settled in a rondawel. Their meeting with father and daughter befitted old friends.

* * *

In the morning, after Célestin had appeared in the shop to buy divine-smelling bouquets, sunny young women and men who worked in the camp brought to the rondawel what was needed for Odile's party: Vases, a more powerful radio, a good-sized fridge, another table and chairs, bottles of South African sparkling and red wine, beer, juices, and various edibles. He told them the girl was still sleeping, so the young Zulus and Xhosas did everything without speaking or making other noise, even when arranging glassware; it was a touching sight. To a small extent, they worked for themselves because everyone was invited to the birthday party. The restaurant chef would bring the birthday cake.

After staff members had tiptoed away, he arranged everything in the living room so it would please the celebrant: Flowers in vases; gifts on the table topped by his card; and other cards spread around. Kruger's breeze sneaked in through the windows and caressed the balloons Célestin had blown to bursting. He had to tie them to the foot of a small table or they would have flown high into the rondawel cone.

He knocked on the door of Odile's bedroom and immediately heard her gleeful voice: "I've been awake for a long time!" She jumped out of bed and ran into his arms. Célestin hugged her firmly, kissed the crown of her head, and wished her boundless joy and fulfillment of all her dreams. "*Merci, Papa, merci pour tout,*" she whispered, and smelling the flowers exclaimed: "*Ça alors! Oh là là! Comme les fleurs sentent merveilleusement!*"

* * *

They had breakfast with Dima and Kolya. As soon as the Russians saw Odile, they cheered "*S dnem rozhdeniya!*" and gave her an attractively designed Russian picture book of Siberian animals. She slowly turned the pages and happily chirruped another "*ça alors!*" when encountering a huge Siberian tiger, surrounded by the whitest snow and the most elegant birches, staring at her. Odile had become so confident about Kruger that she advised Dima and Kolya where they could start exploring, and they promised to be back in time for the party. Two bottles of Moskovskaya and several of Sovetskoye Shampanskoye had already been placed on ice in the camp kitchen.

By the time the chef arrived with a large chocolate cake at five in the afternoon, tribal music had been playing for a while. In addition to the radiant Odile and her father, as well as Dima and Kolya, over a dozen jolly camp employees were present, including the camp manager, an Afrikaner. Célestin opened the proceedings by warmly welcoming guests, particularly those from distant countries. As miniature candles could not be obtained, he produced a thick one and lit it in the middle of the sumptuous cake. Using a sharp knife, he then wrote "10" and apologized: "I couldn't write 'Happy Birthday' because French and German, your hosts' native languages, like Afrikaans, the manager's, and Russian, our special guests', and also English—hmm, it seems it's not a native language of anyone here, although we're all speaking it—all these languages require too many words for the top of even this big cake. Bravo, *Mnumzane* Chef, and *Ngiyabonga!*"

Like a seasoned speech giver, Célestin courteously raised his hands both to acknowledge and to interrupt the hearty applause by the guests, among whom the chef's clapping was the loudest. "However," he continued, "on the little banners I wrote my heart-felt birthday wishes to Odile in all those languages. The longest expression is in Zulu and Xhosa. The words aren't only best wishes for my daughter but also reflect our gratitude to all of you for being here.

"Oh, yes, something else. You've probably all sung 'Happy Birthday to You' as an inevitable song, but it's American from Kentucky and thus foreign to all of us here. Odile and I never sing it, so I ask you not to do it either." The manager, Dima, and Kolya noisily applauded while the birthday girl smiled benevolently and clapped her slender hands. Others seemed mystified but laughed. "Hmm. They'll for sure remember this expression of my sincere anti-colonialist attitude—as if I'm not myself from an entrenched colonializing country," thought Célestin ambivalently.

It was Odile's turn to approach the table and be greeted by ear-splitting applause and exclamations of love and approval. She was wearing her new pink cotton dress, short and with narrow shoulder straps, which suited her perfectly. From above the chest to the middle of the stomach hung numerous—maybe twenty-five—strings of glass beads of various colors, sizes, and shapes. On each string, there were beads of only one of four colors: red, light blue, pale yellow, and dark green. That combination of colors was called *isisshunka* and signified "natural charm." He bought it in a shop, so despite being inspired by Zulu tradition regarding the choice of colors and patient handiwork with glass beads, it was a distant cousin of tribal grass skirts and bare breasts.

Odile was proud of her dress and looked festive and naturally charming. She leaned self-consciously over the cake, and with a quick smile at her dad, blew on the candle so forcefully it almost fell: It had not been thrust properly into the six layers. The guests rewarded her with exuberant laughter and applause. She was ten years old!

The celebration lasted until eleven and had to be halted because of noise regulations, although the manager, who had been fraternizing with Dima, Kolya, and Moskovskaya, certainly was not overinsistent. When Célestin was seeing his Russian friends off, he suggested they have breakfast the next morning and added he needed to ask them for a favor. They agreed with pleasure and exchanged what he thought was a quick but significant look. Even if they did, what would it mean—that he planned to offer spy services? Comical nonsense, too much *shampanskoye*.

"In my life, two things are essential," he thought. "One is that my daughter is a healthy, happy, intelligent ten-year-old child likely to grow into a genuinely good, well-rounded woman. The other is that Olya and I love each other passionately—even though she's in prison, till who knows when."

19.

They had woken up early and sat contentedly on the rondawel terrace in young sunshine. She prepared a coffee for her father and a fruit tea for herself, delighted that so many different people had enjoyed the party. Soon, a Xhosa woman arrived, exclaiming "*Usuku lokuzalwa olumnandi!*" She gave Odile fresh flowers and a necklace of blue beads on behalf of the party guests. After receiving appreciative thanks, she asked whether her coworkers could clean up the after-party mess. The pair gratefully left for a walk.

All four were in an upbeat mood at breakfast, the Russians showing no signs of a hangover. They, too, gave Odile flowers and thanked her again for inviting them. Kolya, the duo's driver, described plans for visiting more of the park: Kruger's animals charmed them, so the departure to Mbabane was abruptly postponed. At the end of breakfast, Célestin walked his girl to the rondawel, explaining he would speak to their friends about adult topics.

He addressed the Russians without beating around the bush: "Dear Dima and Kolya, I hope you have a little bit of time to listen to what I'll tell you about a wonderful young woman, a citizen of the USSR, whom Odile and I met in Moscow on the 22nd of September 1980. In part, I remember the date because my mother was born on the 21st of September, which is the feast day of Saint Matthew the Evangelist by the Catholic calendar. She's not alive— my parents were killed together near Metz during one of the last Nazi bombings in the spring of 1945; I was just a baby. So this young woman, with whom I've become exceptionally close..."

"... is called Dinara Alimova Naratovna, born on the 17th of May 1958 in Kazan," Dima interrupted Célestin and immediately added: "We weren't aware of all the details you've now mentioned, such as the date of your first meeting with Dinara—whom, we know, you usually call Olya, probably because of her mother Olga—or the fact you were a war orphan, but we've recently learned a great deal about you and Olya; all right, let's agree to call her that."

He was astonished and about to say something angrily, but Dima stopped him with a slight hand movement. "Wait, wait, dear Célestin! Kolya and I expected our sudden knowledge of your intimate relations with Olya would astound you and disappoint you—you would doubt our friendship—but only at first, we hoped: Because we are your friends, you must believe it. You see, although Kolya and I are trade and cultural attachés, so diplomats and not KGB operatives, we are Soviet functionaries and as such loyal to Moscow. Therefore, we neither can nor wish to deviate arbitrarily and substantially from the official line."

Again, Célestin attempted to speak, yet managed only "but

how..." before Kolya interrupted him: "Please be patient a little longer. You certainly remember our three conversations at the Holiday Inn in Ezulwini, the first two by the pool and in your suite playing chess, and the third in the restaurant two days later. From the beginning and throughout, we liked you and Odile. We told you so truthfully when you asked us. However, as an experienced traveler and someone familiar with international relations in Europe and the situation in the USSR, you realize that the two of us hold sensitive posts, and Moscow is very inquisitive about the behavior of its diplomats. So we had to, literally had to, investigate who you are. Please don't be upset, that's the way it had to be: Our friendly feelings toward you weren't in any way diminished."

Célestin decided not to interrupt the Russians anymore and even discovered a ray of hope in his heart. He leaned back and with arms crossed listened to Kolya: "You probably also remember we disclosed being married to twin sisters. What we didn't tell you at the time was that Lyudmila, Dima's wife, and my Anya both hold fairly important positions as analysts in two different ministries and can, in the course of their daily work, obtain confidential information. If they weren't our wives, and if all four of us didn't have unlimited mutual trust, Dima and I would've had to investigate you differently, and who knows what the outcome would've been," concluded Kolya.

"Yes, thanks to Lyuda," Dima took over, "we quickly learned the entire contents of your and Olya's files, including the info about your liaison that's been no secret to the 'agencies' from the beginning. We discovered all of it by phone, using a scrambled line from our office in Mbabane. Already between our first two meetings, we knew you were as blameless as a lily, and Olya had not done anything serious. Neither of you'd been 'blacklisted'. So when we saw you the third time, remember, it was the seventh of January, and you wished us a merry Russian Christmas..."

"No," jumped in Célestin, "already after the chess games, I wished you Merry Christmas in advance for the day of our third meeting, and neither of you, so it seemed, objected—on the contrary."

"Right," agreed Dima, "I see your memory is excellent, and you've been studying us, which is not surprising. Anyway, Kolya and I came to the third meeting convinced no one could blame us for being friends with you. A burden fell off our shoulders because we had become genuinely fond of Odile and you. Wasn't it so, Kolya? Therefore, we could gladly accept the invitation to her birthday party and tell you about our Kruger reservations."

Kolya spoke up energetically: "Please understand that during our third meeting in Ezulwini, we couldn't tell you anything about our 'verification research': We couldn't—until you began this conversation. But when you consider the strange circumstances, we hope you'll realize we're not bad people and you won't be upset. Your anger would sadden us."

"After this explanation," Célestin spoke softly, "I can assure you I'm not angry. I understand it all and enormously appreciate your sincerity and friendship. I wonder if you can tell me what's in my file?"

Dima calmly recited from memory: "Let's see. There was the encounter with Olya at the hotel National and later meetings in her apartment in Moscow; at the time, she was watched for political reasons and could've been arrested without delay. Then, her trip to Leningrad and visits to your room at the Pribaltiskaya. Plus, your allegedly rude behavior toward Soviet employees on the border with Finland and your accusatory description of Olya's arrest. Also, there were your visits to Soviet Consulates in Paris and East Berlin, and insistence that Olya be released. Finally, your numerous contacts in Israel and Kenya were noted." Dima concluded: "In short, the file's thick but of no significance to the security agencies."

The remarks about Olya hit Célestin in the chest, but he uttered only several words: "An amazing amount of attention's been devoted to me... And Olya's file?

"As it turned out," Kolya spoke, "her dossier is no thicker than yours and of equally little interest. Regarding Olya's visits to the National, you're well aware of what she'd been doing there before she met you: She herself told you the gist of it during your first meeting. We know because the agency's informant at the bar—a trained lip-reading bartender—reported it. I'll tell you something you may be glad to hear: Despite being repeatedly pressured, Olya refused to collaborate. Needless to say, the agency operatives have noted that you and Odile had visited Olya in her apartment and, by utilizing listening devices, are privy to, *heard*, every move and sound that occurred. In the opinion of our spouses, it was an unnecessary, wicked action. Someone's spiteful, vengeful move."

They were quiet before Kolya marched on: "Then, there's Olya's 'anti-State political activity'—more nonsense. Her 'illegal group' is indeed a group, but a smallish bunch of several dozen idealistic students. If the authorities insisted on punishing their behavior, wouldn't it be more reasonable to sentence them to two nights in jail and be done? Instead, these sacrificial lambs got long sentences in harsh prisons during a pointless display of toughness by someone in authority. Our wives sympathize with Olya."

"And are aware," added Dima, "Kuybyshev is a nasty prison. As you've heard from her mother—you guessed it, they're listening—Olya was sentenced to thirty months and will not be out until April 1983. Another fifteen months."

Célestin had collected himself while listening to the Russians and cautiously determined they were on Olya's and his side. He felt these men and their spouses were his friends—as much as it was possible considering their positions. A barely visible flicker of hope had become a flare.

Encouraged, he said: "I know what I'm going to say is a huge, maybe inappropriate or even impertinent request, but I must ask you: Can you do something, anything, for the authorities to pardon Olya, to annul her unjustly severe sentence, or at least allow an earlier release? And I'm asking this on Odile's behalf also! It's obvious you like my daughter, but perhaps you're not aware that she and Olya became very close when we were all together in

Russia. I intend to marry Olya if she wishes. My hope is for the three of us to live in peace in Metz and for Odile to have a living mother."

A long silence ensued, but he did not feel it signified the Russians' resistance to his request—they were pondering his words. After an exchange of looks with Kolya, Dima said: "So, your and Odile's fervent desire and most optimistic wish is for Olya to be granted a pardon and receive a passport with the Soviet exit visa for France. Well, I think I'm speaking in Kolya's name also when I promise we'll do all we can to achieve that outcome. Of course, neither we nor our spouses can make such decisions. However, the two of them have had official and even friendly relations over many years with people who occupy influential positions. In Lyuda's case, there's a friendship with the wife of a person with considerable power. And you know how women sometimes... That's all we can promise you."

He gasped and felt tears welling up. When he finally spoke, it was with an effort—he was repeatedly choking with emotion: "How can you imply what you'll do is somehow not enough?! It's incredibly, strikingly much! You are humane and compassionate. Olya, Odile, and I will never forget this promise of yours, this stunning gesture, regardless of the outcome."

The Russians received these words in a warm and gentlemanly manner. Dima addressed Célestin seriously: "We must agree about a few essential specifics while we're still face to face. First, Kolya and I request you don't come to Moscow or Kazan, alone or with Odile, under any circumstances. It would only complicate matters or destroy what's been achieved. Second, please don't again visit or even write to the Soviet Consulate in Paris. Third, don't enlist anyone at the French Ministry of Foreign Affairs to act on your behalf: It might look suspicious to someone who's not sympathetic to Olya and you, and perhaps alert the person that something's cooking. Fourth, write to Olya via her mother from time to time, and phone occasionally, as you've been doing, so the two of them know you still love Olya. But do not, with a single word or hint, reveal that Olya might be granted an early release. That would be disastrous—for all of us. We trust you to be unwaveringly self-disciplined."

Célestin gave his word, overcome with joy that the Russians had considered all the angles. However, the least expected instructions followed when Kolya took over: "Fifth, communication between us. Dima and I have discussed this at length, hoping," he smiled amiably, "the conversation with you would take the course it did. So please understand: Mail from you to us, and from us to you, is out of the question. The same goes for phone calls—from South Africa and France on your part, and from Mbabane, Lesotho, Maputo, and Moscow on ours. Telegrams are also out: You won't have our postal address, and for Dima, me, Lyuda, or Anya to send you a telegram from Moscow, we'd have to show ID at the post office. In short, no form of communication is safe. When are you returning to France?"

"They're truly singular people; I must never, never, betray their trust and put them in jeopardy," thought Célestin and responded: "We'll leave Skukuza tomorrow, come out of Kruger in the north, stop in Joburg for a day or two, and then drive to Cape Town. Our plan is to stay there for about two and a half weeks and then fly to Paris in time for Odile's school. So we'll be in Metz around the tenth of February."

"Let Olga know that date but nothing more. And now, one of the most important things. Have you ever been to Japan?" asked Dima. Célestin was nonplused but answered calmly: "No, I have not. Why do you ask?"

"Here's why. I wouldn't waste time telling you about this if I weren't convinced of three things: You deeply love Olya; you're a wealthy man; and you're in charge of your time in a way few people are. And so... The tenth anniversary of Lyuda's and my wedding falls on the fourteenth of March this year. It's a red-letter date for us! We wanted to do something memorable and decided to spend two weeks in Japan. Somehow, we managed to obtain permission not only for a private visit to the capitalist country but also for a two-week leave—from the ninth to the twenty-third of March.

"We read about Japan for months and decided where we'd be on our anniversary. Instead of Mount Fuji or an ancient Zen temple, we chose Hokkaido—the northernmost of the four islands of Japan. At *its northern end* is a small town by the name of Wakkanai, and only a few kilometers away lies Cape Soya. That's the northernmost point of Japan from which, in good weather, forty-three kilometers away, one can see the southernmost point of our Russian Sahalin, the biggest island in the USSR. Cape Soya seemed to my beloved Lyuda and me a very romantic spot, even though there would be snow, ice, high winds, and bitter cold. We don't care, we're Russians, northern people, used to long fur coats and our fabulous *ushankas*, fur hats with ear flaps. And perhaps when we're there and it's dreadfully cold, the sky'll be crystal blue and we may see a tiny piece of our homeland!

"So, here's what I'm proposing to you in the same crazy style: A Cape Soya rendezvous, exactly at noon, on Sunday, the 14th of March, on top of a hillock by the lighthouse! We've even examined a topographic map of the area—Lyudmila got it from colleagues who're in charge of such things."

"A superb, exciting plan, I'll be there!" almost shouted Célestin. After reflection, however, he added softly: "I hope when we're there face to face, including Lyudmila, you'll be able to tell me about Olya's release, even if not conclusively. And I've already decided to bring Odile with me. She's old enough to remain in Metz without me, for we have reliable people at home, but I'd like her to see Japan. As for it being a severe winter on Hokkaido, well, we'll buy Russian fur coats and ushankas in Paris. And sooner or later, we'll also use them when we travel to Leningrad again—with Olya, in the winter."

"Listen," responded Dima, "Lyuda and Anya will begin right away to work on this. Right, Kolya? Six weeks will probably be a long enough period to get a reliable yes or no answer—because if something's going to happen at all, it'll happen by the claws of the snail-like bureaucracy being bypassed. For you, the trip to Japan is risky only financially if the outcome is negative, but I think you'll gladly accept such a risk. Besides, Japan is interesting, and you two love to travel. That's why we didn't hesitate to make this bizarre plan."

"It's up to you, Célestin," pitched in Kolya, "but you can be certain Lyudmila and Dima will be standing by the lighthouse at the end of the world—to their waist in the snow if need be—precisely at noon on the fourteenth of March. They are that kind of people... Anya and I will be green with envy for not being there."

With a jot of brooding, Dima looked at Kolya and concluded: "All right. Keep your chin up, dear Tino, everything will turn out well. Take this note, I prepared it with the necessary Hokkaido, Wakkanai, and Cape Soya information." He threw a glance at the paper and read: "3 Sōyamisaki, Wakkanai-shi, Hokkaido 098-6758, Japan." Grinning inwardly, Célestin thought: "The lighthouse has a mailing address! Ah, those perfectionist Japanese..."

20.

Even though it was only ten, father and daughter had traveled over a hundred kilometers on Hi2 toward Pafuri Gate in the northeastern corner of Kruger. They had gotten up before six, had a quick breakfast, and thanked the Camp Skukuza manager and young staff for their kindness. The girls were still hugging Odile when the chef emerged, having instructed a young man to place sandwiches, water, and juice in the Rover. Finally, with much hand waving and loud Zulu and Xhosa exclamations, they drove off into Kruger's morning freshness.

The previous evening's goodbyes with the Russians were touching. Célestin could not find the words to thank them: He was conscious of the risk to which Dima, Kolya, and their spouses would be exposing themselves by trusting him and by unselfishly helping Olya, a prisoner they did not know personally. Unfortunately, he could inform Odile only superficially about it all.

For many hours, he kept driving through the great natural beauty of Kruger entirely unspoiled by man. On Hi3, Hi4, and Hi5 there were almost no automobiles. They passed Satara and Letaba, stopping for half an hour at a shady rest area between

Mooiplaas and Shingwedzi to have an early lunch. By four in the afternoon, they had left Babalala far behind and switched from Hi7 to the secondary S60. The track they took next, S611, was narrow, straight as an arrow, and of red earth seemingly baked in an oven. In a veldt, gnus, impalas, and zebras blissfully grazed. From afar, Célestin spotted a giraffe browsing in the crown of a tall acacia on the left side of the road. The rear legs of the animal were inches from the narrow track, so extreme caution was demanded when driving by.

The picture of the solitary giraffe almost as tall as the tree was idyllic, fit for a young child's gilt image of paradise. An idea crossed his mind. To share it with the girl, he stopped the car about fifty meters from the animal. "*Ecoute, ma princesse*, do you see that marvel of a giraffe? When we pass by her, she'll be very close to the car on your side. So let me ask you: Do you want to touch her?" Odile was amazed but immediately responded, her voice excited: "I do, I do! But how?"

"It'll be simple. Your window is open. Sit on the edge of the seat. You see how she's standing. Her rear left leg is on the road, and I'll stop right next to it. We'll keep mum and do nothing to frighten her, so she won't leave—or kick the car! You have nothing to fear. When I stop, reach out and touch her. If she doesn't react—and she won't because your touch will be softer than a breath of wind—you can caress her. Then I'll slowly drive away." They smiled at each other. He had confidence in his brave daughter.

The Rover crawled to the giraffe. Although the afternoon sun blazed, the car was in the shadow of the animal. The silence was disturbed only by the drone of insects and the purring of the engine. From up in the acacia, the contented munching was audible. Odile's window was no more than fifteen centimeters away from the giraffe's leg. The girl's heart stopped as she extended her hand and touched it. The animal sedately continued to chomp. Emboldened, Odile kept stroking the leg. "What velvety fur," she murmured, eyes closed.

They stayed like that for over five minutes without the giraffe moving at all—much longer than Célestin thought possible.

"Giraffes evidently have their own flow of time, free of nervous haste," he mused. The girl continued to caress the wild animal as if she were Pasha, admiring her beauty and gentleness. Her father pondered God, evolution, and the preternatural creature that had somehow survived on the mystical continent.

"*Bien, ma douce,* shall we go?" "*D'accord, Papa.* Imagine, *cher Papounet,* I caressed a giraffe in the wild, in Africa! How wonderful!" He engaged the first gear and soundlessly glided away from their girlfriend, who did not seem to care or miss them. "Thank you for the T-shirt you bought for my birthday with a Kruger giraffe," she whispered, "although I won't need to wear it to remember this magic." She showed him her left hand: "Only a minute ago, my fingertips were on a living, breathing, wild animal."

Back on Hi8, they resumed traveling north, and it was already twilight when they saw the silhouette of Baobab Hill. They drove around it on S64, a mere dirt track, and reached the dry bed of the Luvuvhu River. On its south bank, they found a camp. Leaving their luggage in the tiny room, they climbed a hillock and stood holding hands in the evening silence. "The camp will be fine for one night, we had a long trip today. Over there, less than ten kilometers away, is the Zimbabwe border on the Limpopo River," he pointed across the Luvuvhu to the north. "And there, to the west, is Pafuri Gate, through which we'll leave Kruger tomorrow—fifteen kilometers away."

As night fell, they watched an elephant on the opposite bank of the Luvuvhu, perhaps two hundred meters away. The animal was alone and walked at an extremely slow pace. Célestin had read legends about elephant graveyards and thought they were gazing at an old, lonely elephant seeking its final resting place. However, he also knew that many elephants, from as early as puberty, live alone or with other males after they leave the family group.

Anyhow, he did not wish to spoil his daughter's mood by talking about graveyards: "Look, *mon trésor,* what a beautiful elephant. The largest land mammal. You know elephants are similar to whales and dolphins in terms of high intelligence. Some zoologists claim healthy elephants display compassion for the injured and dying ones. I'm not sure. Maybe scientists feel empathy with elephants they've been studying for a long time: They 'adopt' them and imagine having discerned complex feelings, such as an absence of self-interest. After all, scientists are human and can't always remain objective. Sometimes this happened to anthropologists who 'adopted' a tribe in Melanesia or Papua New Guinea with honorable intentions but still condescendingly. Let's go to sleep."

The morning was rainy, the first water from the skies in a long time. Pafuri Gate had a makeshift appearance: Both the office and the toilets were in a trailer attached to a terrain vehicle. Among the chickens and cats behind it, an old tribal man was removing a ranger's uniform from the clothesline. The rooster was mute, detesting the drizzle. A shaggy red dog seemed to be dreaming about something agreeable. The ranger, a middle-aged Afrikaner, advised Célestin to be careful driving through Venda because "serious unpleasantries," as he put it, had been happening there. He apologized for not knowing the details. They thanked the ranger and, climbing into the Rover, sent a loving kiss to Kruger and its animals.

Pafuri was located only a few kilometers south of the Zimbabwe border. It occurred to Célestin that he had unconsciously chosen it precisely for being close to a perilous frontier. Did he not enjoy driving in Israel right next to the border of Lebanon? And also along the borders of Jordan and Syria—at the time less risky, but still… Is it desirable to impose his obsession with the smell of danger on his little daughter?

They traveled several kilometers through the low hills and lush vegetation of northeast Transvaal. A smiling black ranger waved to them from his bicycle. A little farther, at the entrance to Venda, which was a Bantustan, an autonomous homeland, there was a striped barrier but raised. Out of the rain, under the eaves of a small house, officials, all black, were idly standing. Célestin signed a shabby register before proceeding to Musina, first passing through another Venda checkpoint. There, the officers intended to inspect the Rover but changed their minds after being told the travelers were French.

The weather was different from Kruger's but also lovely. Once the drizzle had stopped, outlandish clouds scurried across the blue sky, whereas mysterious mists partially covered hills to the north. During their entire drive to Musina, Zimbabwe was a stone's throw away. At the Madimbo intersection, an asphalt road led south to Tshipise, but he decided to remain on the red-earth road to Musina. That road soon veered even closer to Zimbabwe and hugged the Limpopo River. They entered an unusual semi-desert area with splendid trees and flowers. He could drive very fast on the empty road, raising clouds of red dust. When the car ran into deep puddles at full speed, spraying huge jets of water all around, Odile found it exhilarating.

An indigent settlement of the Venda Bantu people was squeezed between a steep, stony hill and a plantation surrounded by a four-meter fence with barbed wire on top. "An overprotected plantation—raising what? Perhaps marijuana," smiled Célestin, not sharing the thought with Odile. At the edge of the destitute village, the half-naked children, who had been playing in the dust by the road, ran away swiftly as the slow-moving Rover appeared. However, when he stopped the car, and Odile waved, all the children did the same, smiling shyly. The villagers lived in small, dilapidated rondawels and other shacks somehow knocked together. Surprisingly, many were decorated with psychedelic multicolored drawings. As they drove off, father and daughter looked at each other: Poverty-stricken tribal people; smiling children in the red dust; psychedelic drawings; Zimbabwe over there...

Just before Musina, they arrived at a checkpoint manned by black and white South African policemen. He came out of the car to stretch his legs, and the two oldest men, both white, approached him. They were easygoing as far as the passport check but thorough when it came to their itinerary from Kruger. It turned out that only three days earlier in the vicinity of Musina—partly in Venda and partly out of it—an armed skirmish occurred between the police and an ANC group. Intruders had arrived from Zimbabwe by simply walking across the shallow Limpopo. Their goal was to place land mines on roads, which they succeeded in doing. Four were killed and one captured, while two were able to escape, having shot two policemen. Land mine removal teams worked for two days before the roads were reopened. Some stretches requiring meter-by-meter scrutiny had been precisely those along which they had traveled.

When he climbed into the Rover, Célestin was pale. Hiding the shaking of his hands, he reassured Odile telling her they would stop in Musina to eat. The small town had a mildly tropical air and spotlessly clean tree-lined streets. Searching for a restaurant, he yet again remembered the words of Sergeant Wim in Roodeplaat about the need to be armed: His warnings had directly addressed the dangers of travel in Musina, Madimbo, and Venda. Then he recalled talking with Steyn, the youthful park ranger in Skukuza, about that very region. His mind conjured up the likable, intelligent face of the suspended pilot Hendrik at Camp Shingwedzi, who thought the sergeant had been right to speak of the dangers arising from ANC activity in northern Transvaal. "Of course," he concluded morosely, "carrying a weapon wouldn't have saved Wim, Steyn, or Hendrik from a land mine explosion or a confrontation with half a dozen heavily armed guerrillas—and most certainly wouldn't have saved Odile and me." Still, he condemned himself as a naive idealistic person and an irresponsible father.

They parked in front of an eatery next to a newsstand. In a low voice, Célestin asked the seller to find him a newspaper that had most truthfully described the "recent skirmishes," as he put it. The young man thought for a moment and pulled one from below the counter: "This paper was published yesterday, but it contains the most detailed description of the events—you don't need to pay, Sir." Even so, he left two rands. The youngster helpfully added: "If you drive south from here, you'll see the biggest baobab in our vast country; we call it the 'Tree of Life.'"

While they were eating omelets, he said: "I apologize for

reading during our meal. You know I don't like doing it, but this is important. I'll tell you later why." Once he saw the dates of the skirmishes specified in the newspaper, he realized the conversation with Hendrik had taken place two or three days before the violent events. So he could not have warned them concretely—only generally. However, because he did enter Kruger through Pafuri Gate and perhaps planned to leave the same way, Célestin could only wholeheartedly hope the pilot remained unharmed. When he had finished his third cup of coffee, he finally told Odile the police had fought the ANC near Musina several days earlier, but they could safely continue their trip to Joburg.

The main road south led toward the city of Louis Trichardt, about a hundred kilometers away. After covering a third of that distance through the gorgeous hilly countryside, they saw a gigantic baobab with innumerable thick branches. "Just what the proud youngster claimed; look at the beauty, a true wonder of nature! Let's park and take photos. I know this type of tree is renowned for the thickness of its trunk, but this particular specimen must be extraordinary if it's indeed the biggest baobab in South Africa."

From early in the morning, Odile was in a buoyant mood, whereas in Célestin's case, it was so only until he heard about the land mines and the killings. But the Tree of Life restored his frame of mind. Thenceforth, they cheerfully drove four hundred and fifty kilometers to Joburg—via Pietersburg, Potgietersrus, and Pretoria. South African, Zimbabwean, and Botswanan music provided lively company. He drove straight to Harrison Reef, where Muriel naturally made sure they could have 601 for two nights.

21.

As soon as he woke up the next day, Célestin wrote a love letter to Olya and a solicitous one to Olga. Both contained as much encouragement as could be expressed in words. He mentioned they would be returning to Metz on the eleventh of February, and the girl added a touching message to Olya. At the Jeppe Street post office, as she processed the envelope to Kazan, the employee's eyes showed disbelief, if not shock, upon seeing the USSR address. Even though the man and his adorable daughter did not seem to the middle-aged Afrikaner lady like ANC sympathizers, one never knew with those communist scoundrels.

At Wits, Odile gave the secretary a bouquet, thanking her for promptly sending the mail to Skukuza, important because of the birthday cards it contained. By childishly revealing her fete, she forced Joanna to take a chocolate bar intended for another purpose out of a drawer—and present it with a smile and birthday wishes.

Both Silvia and Mary Goode were with Carl in his office when Célestin and Odile arrived; the two women were planning to visit an art exhibition. After a lively chat about Swaziland and Kruger, he announced they would visit Cape Town for two weeks. "How are you going?" asked Mary, and immediately went on: "I know the luxurious 'Blue train' traveling to Cape Town from Pretoria and Joburg several times a week is always booked for months in advance, and as for flying..." Célestin interrupted her: "Flying is out of the question. We want to experience the size and landscapes of this country. No, we'll drive. Our Rover performed superbly in Kruger."

Mary became very interested. "Driving? You certainly know Cape Town is one thousand four hundred kilometers away from Joburg. It takes at least eighteen hours to get there." Before he could say anything, Mary blurted out: "What would you say to me as co-driver?" They all looked at her surprised. "Maybe you remember that Paul, my fiancé, lives there; he's an associate professor at the university. We've been planning I come for a visit," Mary explained and continued: "From here to the 'mother city'— the traditional name of Cape Town, though many prefer just 'Caypee'—the trip is long, hot, and demanding. Paul and I did it twice in his car. For the most part, the road is absolutely straight and sleep-inducing. Having a co-driver would be safer for you. And I'm a competent driver, ask Silvia and Carl. Naturally, I'd pay for half the petrol. This would be really convenient for me. As for you, in addition to my taking over the wheel when your eyes are closing, Odile would be entertained by my knowledgeable and amusing narration about the areas we're passing through, ha, ha! What do you say to my plucky offer?"

Célestin looked at Odile, and they instantly agreed. "All right, Mary, we accept you as our co-driver! Everything you said was logical. But listen: We're leaving tomorrow morning at eight. Can you get ready by then?" "Of course, it's not a problem," Mary quickly responded and turned to Silvia: "Please excuse me, dear, I can't go with you to the exhibition." He went on: "Very well, but there's another thing. In our Rover, there are no comfortable back seats, only two lateral jump seats. However, in the front, next to the driver, there's a longish seat on which two slender persons can easily sit. Mary, if you'll permit my observation, both you and my daughter fit that description—although Odile's figure filled a little at her birthday party!" Mary and the girl laughed, and the arrangements for the long trip to Caypee were thus set.

He said: "You've offered to pay for half the petrol. Because our Rover uses diesel fuel, the cost will be lower. I'm joking, you'll be our guest. But if you want to do something nice, take us to lunch tomorrow in Kimberley." Mary was ready: "I'll take you to the renowned restaurant The Diggers; it's not in Kimberley but Wolmaransstad, also on our way. Their *Veau Cordon Bleu* is outstanding."

* * *

By four in the afternoon a day later, when they parked in front of New Grand, a hotel near the town hall in Kimberley, Mary had become a fully accepted member of the traveling team. Célestin drove most of the time, but when Mary took over, she did it skillfully. During the almost nine-hour drive—interrupted by an excellent lunch at The Diggers—they were traveling through the vast, monotonous plateau of Hoëveld, gradually descending from Joburg's elevation of thousand seven hundred fifty meters to Kimberley's of thousand two hundred.

There was not much to see on the way. The heat was sweltering. At many places along the edge of the road, black men, women, and children were sitting on the ground. They stared blankly at the Rover, not bothering to get up and raise a thumb, even though from afar it could not have been obvious that only white people were in the vehicle. Very few buses could be seen; they appeared and disappeared in the torrid haze like ghosts. "These people are waiting for some raggedy pickup, or a miserable moped barely able to pull a tiny, roofless, two-wheel trailer, to transport them for a small fee," explained Mary. She spoke flatly, without contempt or mawkishness, just like she did when driving Célestin and Odile in Soweto. After all, being born and raised in South Africa, she was accustomed to almost everything.

When they walked into the cool lobby of the New Grand and placed their documents on the counter, the receptionist, a polite Afrikaner, looked at them quickly and said: "We have a suitable room with a double bed and a small bed for your child; I think the girl is not too big for it. Would you like to see the room?" All three guests laughed merrily. To the man's surprise, they opted for three single rooms—247 and 249 facing the small square, and 248 with a view of the garden.

After leaving the luggage in their rooms, they drove through the handsome historic town. Unexpectedly, despite the still, dry air and the intense heat, the sky was a cobalt blue, not drained of color. Pretty houses glittered in the sleepy afternoon whiteness. Soon the travelers reached their goal, the abandoned diamond mine known around the world as the Kimberley Big Hole.

The sight was extraordinary and the gigantic hole—there is no poetic word for it—exceptionally photogenic. It did not have the shape of a volcanic crater, as Muriel at their hotel in Joburg had described it, but was simply an unimaginably large and deep hole created by the arduous individual work using pickaxes and baskets. Countless miners from the entire world worked there during the last two decades of the nineteenth century, with the qualification that the better-off ones hired black workers whom they insultingly called Kaffirs. Pieces of rock would be taken out of the hole in baskets and only then broken into smaller ones in the feverish search for diamonds. Being harder than steel, diamonds could not be damaged by picks. Such a method of extraction meant a hired man could not swallow a diamond before the basket was brought up from the hole—which was possible in the alluvial mines not far from Kimberley where diamonds were dug out of river silt.

Almost vertical walls of the hole consisted of numerous rock layers of diverse colors, whereas at the bottom was a magical green lake. The three visitors, completely alone, stood spellbound for a long time. It was almost six in the afternoon, sunset. Inside the hole, birds happily flew about, although the rocks were too smooth for nests to be built.

At the museum, they learned the hole was more than two hundred meters deep, with a circumference of a kilometer and a half. During less than half a century when the mine functioned— it was shut forever in 1914—twenty-two million tons of rocks were extracted from the hole, in which two thousand seven hundred kilograms of diamonds were found.

On the way back to the hotel, they saw groups of black men sitting under stunted trees. A gas station in twilight mimicked an illustration by Norman Rockwell. During dinner, Odile kept on about uncut diamonds.

* * *

Immediately after breakfast, they resumed driving to the southwest. From the Hoëveld plateau, the road entered the Karoo, a vast semi-desert area. Mary told them: "When I went to school, it was called the Groot Karoo. We were taught that the early explorers had described it as a frightening place of great heat, great droughts, great frosts, and great floods." At Hopetown, a hundred and fifty kilometers from Kimberley, they crossed the life-giving Oranjerivier, Orange River. It was wide and full of yellow-brown water, unlike the many rivers with dry beds they had previously crossed. Hour after hour, they drove through arid low hills on which thorny bushes resistant to heat and man's grabby hands were scattered. Time passed. Célestin and Mary often replaced each other at the wheel. The one not driving nevertheless remained awake to ensure the driver was not bewitched by the monotonous, hot desert. Odile dozed off and on. From time to time, like a mirage, a solitary cow would appear standing motionless near a water pump operated by the desert wind.

Just before Beaufort West, more than five hundred kilometers from Kimberley, a long and high mountain chain suddenly emerged from the bottom of the desert. It shimmered mysteriously in the pinkish haze to the south. "Look, Odile, aren't those mountains magnificent? Their peaks are over two thousand three hundred meters high!" exclaimed Mary: "They look rosy in this strange light, so you'd never guess their name: It's Groot Swartberg in Afrikaans, Big Black Mountain."

They kept driving through the desert and passed Laingsburg, noticing a sign for the Flood Museum. On Mary's advice, they stopped only at Matjiesfontein, seven hundred kilometers from Kimberley. It was an attractive town, with a train station and other buildings from the olden days, all of which had been lovingly renovated. As they ate a tasty lunch at Laird's Arms, Mary mentioned that the "Blue train," about which she had told them in Joburg, stopped at Matjiesfontein. "But our trip is much nicer," Odile declared confidently.

When they started again at half past three, Mary said: "Cape Town is still two hundred fifty kilometers away; however, our drive of four hours over two high passes will be unforgettable." Beginning with the first pass on Hexrivierberge (*Hex River Mountain*), the views became spectacular. From Du Toitskloof (*Du Toit's Rift*), they descended through stunning mountains with sharp peaks to the wine-growing area around the town of Paarl. And then, some forty-five minutes later, there was Cape Town spread below them—the magnificent city with its hills, crazy peaks, and the Atlantic Ocean. "Look, look, Table Mountain, Lion's Head, Devil's Peak," Mary recited breathlessly.

"You and I will climb all of them, *mon bijou*," Célestin promised Odile. Both fell in love instantly with the awe-inspiring city in the extreme south of Africa.

PART TEN

Cape of Good Hope

1.

When they arrived, Mary graciously helped Célestin and Odile find a hotel, and then they took her to the Mowbray Quarter where Paul lived. In front of the three-story apartment building, the parting was warm: "I'll introduce you to Paul another time, now we're all tired. Thanks again for accepting me as a travel companion. You've done me an invaluable service. Paul will also be grateful. I'll call Silvia and Carl and tell them we've safely conquered the Groot Karoo. I very much enjoyed our journey, thank you both!"

Father and daughter returned to their elegant hotel Helmsley on Hof Street. It was located in the wealthy central quarter of Gardens, but the price of their suite was only fifty rands. They were in high spirits despite the two-day trip. In the garden restaurant, they were served a light supper during which Célestin tried a fine white wine from Stellenbosch, an area close to Cape Town. Sitting alone among the fragrant plants, they gazed upward, carefree and content, at the massive, dark silhouette of Tafelberg. Table Mountain, with its thousand-meter-high steep slopes and its amazingly flat top, protectively overhung the city from the south. "Something so flat has never been so magical," he murmured.

The following morning, they drove to the university in the Rondebosch Quarter. Ivy-covered buildings, modern and classical fountains, and a natural stream shared the lovely sloping grounds of the campus. Célestin greeted colleagues in the Linguistics Department, explaining that he had arrived with Odile for only two weeks and would not need the office, which had been courteously offered. He conveyed regards from Carl and

Silvia Goode, adding Carl's sister Mary had arrived with them. Rose Jenkins, the administrator, a vivacious South African of English descent, nevertheless proudly took them to the superbly equipped office. "From here, you'd have had a splendid view of Devil's Peak!" She volunteered that should mail arrive from Wits or Europe, she would leave a message at the Helmsley.

The visitors then enjoyed iced tea with Cornelius Boshof. For several years, Célestin had maintained a lively correspondence with the linguist, a friend of Carl Goode. Nelius was an Afrikaner in his fifties, an expert in Hebrew, Dutch, and Afrikaans—a tall, large, ebullient man with a wild mustache and auburn hair. Despite such appearance, he was kind and joked with Odile: "Watch out, pretty Miss, that my wife Viola doesn't appropriate you, for you'll then rarely see your daddy!"

All three were sitting in the shade provided by a reed canopy. The terrace was on the opposite side of the Linguistics building from the unclaimed office. Nelius was not shy: "Viola and I have been married for over twenty years, yet despite our desire, we don't have children—and Viola adores them. I was joking, dear colleague, but if you have a meeting at the university that can't include Odile, feel free to leave the girl at our house with Viola. We have a big garden, three self-important cats, and many books and music records."

Before the visitors left, Nelius walked them to the railing and pointed east: "There you see the airport. A bit to the right and a little closer to us, on the flat treeless ground, you see the bunched-up shanties." After a moment, he went on: "That's the infamous settlement, the so-called township called Crossroads. It's less than ten kilometers from here and similar, unfortunately, to Soweto in Joburg. The settling began six or seven years ago; in 1977, eighteen thousand people lived there and now almost forty. The density is unimaginable and so are the heat, garbage, dust, and the rest. Horror!"

Father and daughter looked at each other and long stared at Crossroads. Then the girl bravely addressed Nelius: "We've been in Soweto by car and know a little bit how it must be there."

Nelius looked at Odile astounded, so Célestin explained: "Yes, by car with semi-darkened windows and only near the perimeter. But even that was sufficient to get a realistic impression. It was Mary, Carl's sister, who drove us in her car."

Professor Boshof concluded good-naturedly: "What a wise, smart girl you are! It's bewildering how much you know and what you've already seen in your life. As if you're twenty, not ten. It seems likely you can teach my Viola a few things."

2.

They were pleased to have their Rover at hand. From Rondebosch, they drove through the central business district of the city and quickly arrived at Green Point on the Atlantic coast. A small island was visible from there. They knew it lay in the ocean about ten kilometers north of the city and seven west of the beach suburb of Bloubergstrand, and also that it originally got its name from seals, *robben* in Afrikaans. Moreover, father and daughter were aware Robben Island was not a paradise with palms, swimming pools, casinos, and discotheques for rich tourists: It was a penitentiary exposed to the icy winds of the Atlantic. During the previous eighteen years, since 1964, Nelson Mandela was incarcerated there in harsh conditions. He slept, it was widely known, on a straw mattress in a damp cell measuring two by three meters.

Holding hands, the two talked for a long time, Mandela's suffering not the only subject. They were standing at the edge of an ocean Odile had never seen. She gazed at the horizon, having been told the next continent, infinitely far to the west, was South America—and bothered to estimate conscientiously on the map that the landing point of her ship would be Montevideo, the capital of Uruguay. Even her father had not seen that ocean since the time he spent holidays with Patrizia in Bretagne and Portugal on the North Atlantic.

Regarding Mandela, Célestin asked whether she remembered the sincere black man by the name of Douglas with whom they had talked in Joburg. It did not take long before she answered: "I remember him, it was on New Year's Day in Gold Reef City, wasn't it, Papa? Mr. Douglas lived with his family in Soweto, didn't he? The place Mary drove us to and Mr. Nelius mentioned just today?" Her father probed further: "That's right. Do you recall what we talked about?" "Well, it was you who talked to him, I was reading. But when saying something about his children, he spoke softly so I wouldn't hear—in vain, because I heard everything. Afterward, you told me about those horrible 'necklaces' made of old car tires they put around people's necks and set on fire!

"Poor Mr. Douglas seemed afraid," Odile went on, "his son and daughter would do it to him. And his wife, their mother, didn't dare any longer to hug the children." They were silent for a moment, Célestin sensing she had not finished. "You also reminded me we'd heard similar things from a white man, from—what was he? Yes, a policeman, like some sergeant, who was boring you for a long time in a village bar... but who had read, like me, *Winnetou* as a child."

"*Oui, ma chère fille,* you remembered everything. I can't say I'm delighted you did, but we both respect the truth, don't we? Mr. Douglas first said Nelson Mandela, the man who's suffering on the island," Célestin pointed toward Robben, "was 'his leader'; but at the end of our talk, with fury in his face, slammed his fist on the table. He held a bunch of keys in his hand, and we were both taken aback. Angrily, like a trapped cat hissing, Douglas spat out—I'll remember his bitter words forever—'those killers with good intentions have poisoned our children; what does Nelson think about *that*?'"

Odile squeezed her father's hand: "True, Papa, yet it's important we came here to see the island, isn't it?" He agreed but tried to change the topic: "Those friendly young people at Camp Skukuza who came to your party—they spoke Zulu and Xhosa. Well, Xhosa is Mandela's mother tongue."

They drove two kilometers down the coast to Sea Point and descended on foot to the charming Promenade. Below it, a chain of sharp black rocks protected a narrow sandy beach. Beyond them, there were swelling afternoon waves and surfers taking a chance close to the rocks. "We'll find more suitable beaches for you, but even this one is possible—the waves are small behind the rocks. Elsewhere, you'll step into the waves only next to me. Cape Town is not Sharm El Sheikh, *ma douce*. The ocean is mighty and majestic, with waves sometimes folding into themselves near a beach. The currents, with which I'm not familiar here, can pull anyone, even superb swimmers, far out from the beach—and fighting them and the waves can be exhausting. Still, we'll swim often. From now on, we'll always keep bathing suits in the Rover. It's our South Atlantic."

3.

After breakfast, Célestin and Odile were relaxing by the Helmsley pool. "This is a little boring," he suddenly said, looking at the map. "I have an idea for a sports day: In the morning we'll climb Lion's Head, and in the afternoon we'll swim at one of the four Clifton beaches; what d'you say?" She agreed, putting down a schoolbook. "And Lion's Head," her father pointed to it, "is that dark, stony marvel looking more like the crest of some bird of prey than the head of a lion." Odile thought for a minute and said with admirable wariness: "It seems very high. And its top is a bare, steep rock. Will I be able to climb up there, Papa?"

"No words about children of your age in what I'm reading. But I think you'll be able to do it, you're strong and brave. If I judge it's dangerous, we'll just turn around—no shame in it. Let's try! As for the elevation, it says here: six hundred sixty-nine meters. Table Mountain, our girlfriend from the first evening in Caypee, is almost a thousand one hundred meters. Doing two-thirds of her height today will be a preparation for climbing to the 'long dining table' on another day."

From their hotel in the Gardens Quarter, they drove a kilometer steeply uphill to an intersection with the curvy Kloof Nek Road. To the left, it led to the Table Mountain cable car; to the right, after about two hundred meters, the road brought the pair to a shady parking lot. Water, nuts, raisins, and binoculars were

the entire contents of Célestin's backpack. A path through conifers led them to Contour Trail. They followed it around the Head
until they reached a spot from which one looked down on the familiar Sea Point Promenade.

A steel ladder, with about fifteen steps, was fastened to the
rock face. By climbing it, they would eliminate an entire loop of
Contour Trail. "Instead of taking the long, circular way around,
let's do a bit of mountaineering here, *mon trésor*. This ladder will
be all right for you because your hands are free. You go first, and
I'll be behind you, supporting you if need be. Take your time. You
can't fall." That was easily accomplished, so when they encountered another ladder higher up, she strolled to it confidently as if
it were a schoolyard game. Still higher, the pair ran into several
young men who were waiting for their hang-gliding companions.
They praised Odile, which contributed to her already pink color.
Those were the first people father and daughter saw on the Head.

From there, a trail led uphill through trees and bushes. "That's
the greenery below the stony crest we glimpsed from our hotel
pool. It means we're not far!" she exclaimed optimistically. "It's
not far for a bird, but for us—we're now coming to the most difficult part," he informed her truthfully.

They were in front of a very steep section, which could not be
circumvented. One could proceed in two ways. The first was the
classical rockface ascent, with the climber's face and body hugging the rock. Célestin saw a sufficient number of hand and foot
holds, which would make his climb fairly easy, but not of use to
her. However, the second option was feasible. There were three
steel chains set into the rock, one below the other. Odile would
combine the hand-over-hand method with convenient footholds
and never be in danger of falling. She would again go first, with
him providing support. Having received reassurance, she calmly
found the footholds and mastered the chains. On top, she was
delighted and proud.

There was no one else on Lion's Head when they arrived. The
view was incomparable: A kilometer-long slope with serrated
rocks, small trees, and chasms all the way down to the beach and

the President, a hotel next to the Promenade. They were thrilled, absolutely elated. Far to the north, the sand at Bloubergstrand, of which they had caught a glimpse from Green Point the previous afternoon, glimmered through the mist. Identifying it for Odile, he added: "From there, the view must be fabulous of Lion's Head and Table Mountain." Neither the daughter nor the father wished to remind the other that the best view would be from Robben Island.

4.

By taking a headlong plunge down the western section of Kloof Nek Road, they proceeded to the ocean. The aromatic conifer forest, resembling the one on Mount Carmel near Haifa, half-concealed the numerous twists and turns. Odile shrieked and Célestin bellowed from excitement and delight. Every curve opened up unreal views. After reaching the ocean, they drove along all four Clifton beaches and wisely chose the southernmost. At one end guarded by rocks, she could swim in the tame waves. How happy the girl was: In one day, she had conquered both Lion's Head and the South Atlantic!

The thrill and achievement explained why the cold water did not bother her. Also, before stepping into the waves, she had learned that the water in that part of the Atlantic was always cold—only nineteen degrees even in January, the hottest summer month. A trivial matter to the girl.

Célestin came out of the water ahead of Odile, so he could quickly envelop her in a towel when she stepped onto the warm sand shivering and laughing. Another reason for choosing Clifton № 4 was that he had seen half a dozen local youngsters surfing. With her in tow, he walked to the corner of the beach completely open to the mighty waves and talked to a wetsuited youth who had emerged from the ocean with his board. They exchanged greetings, and the newcomer inquired about the treacherous "rip" currents. The surfer responded there were none at the time, but... He looked Célestin up and down, estimating his physical fitness and noting he had neither a surfboard nor a wetsuit. Nevertheless, perhaps out of respect for his age and foreign accent, the youngster made no remarks about the missing equipment and only added that the waves were dangerous.

"*Chérie, excuse-moi,*" he apologized to the girl, "but I must do the first swim in the South Atlantic in my way. After I've swum out, I'll wave to you as I did from Pharaoh's Island. Of course, the Gulf of Aqaba was as lukewarm as the pool at our hotel. This is something new, another welcome challenge for me. Please wait here and don't worry."

Although his French was elementary, the young surfer, a suntanned Afrikaner whose name was Luuk, understood the gist and asked for permission to stay with Odile and watch him swim. They had nothing against it. Laughing, the foreigner then told the youth to study how the proper "front crawl" is done in France.

With a long-repressed desire, Célestin threw himself into the waves. He swam fast through a group of surfers waiting for the right wave and continued over a hundred meters farther. Diving skillfully under the peaks of three lines of breakers, he reached the area where the ocean rose and fell as if it were a giant living creature breathing deeply. When on top of one huge wave, he turned toward the beach. Rising water-polo style out of the water to his waist, he waved to Odile and Luuk, who waved back. He then turned again to the horizon and thought of the ocean as a mighty wild dog who loved him and was wagging his tail and licking his face.

While swimming back, Célestin joked with the surfers who were still waiting for the ideal wave on their picturesque boards. He teased them that without those painted logs they would surely drown. Odile was waiting for him with a towel. After exchanging goodbyes with Luuk, she said while entering the car: "This Luuk—he's a student of something—told me you're a great swimmer. Now you know!"

In Ezulwini, Célestin was amazed when Dima and Kolya showed up for the chess evening with bottles of red wine from Groot Constantia in Cape Town. At the Helmsley, accidentally reminded of that occasion, he found the phone number of Petrus van Schilte, the owner of Groot Constantia: It had been sent to him by a mutual friend. On the phone, he heard a cultured, high-spirited voice: "*Bienvenue au Cap, Monsieur Célestin!* I hope your daughter—I know her lovely name, Odile—enjoyed the long trip. And how is our friend Marcel? He wrote to me about you and your brilliant little girl, adding you're a super-papa. And Marcel? What's he selling more of this year, Cognac or wine? I'm joking, I know the wine and liquor trade is not your thing. As you'll see, it's not mine either. Listen, my spouse Olivia and I would be delighted if you could come with Odile to dinner with us. How about already tomorrow? The day after, I'm flying to London to see our married daughters."

"We'd be happy to! Thank you and Mrs. Schilte. Marcel's in fine health, and his business is going well." Célestin's friendship with Marcel Sauveterre had begun early, back in primary school in Metz, and remained when Marcel moved to Bordeaux with his parents and later became a major wine and spirits merchant.

"Perfect! If you can, please come early, around three o'clock. That'll give us time to take a leisurely walk in the vineyards and inspect our new winery. And please plan to spend the night here. We'll be doing wine-tasting, so..."

Groot Constantia was a vast estate located twelve kilometers south of the center of Cape Town. In the early afternoon the following day, father and daughter were driving through the eastern foothills of Table Mountain. He explained they would be visiting the first wine-cultivation area in South Africa: Wealthy Dutch colonists were responsible for it at the end of the seventeenth century.

They drove through Constantia's massive iron gate, which was wide open and without a guard. After proceeding some two hundred meters down the elegant tree-bordered driveway, they arrived at a semicircular area covered by fine gravel where they parked. All around, there were fig and pomegranate trees. The seventeenth-century main building of the estate was in the classical Cape Dutch style, dazzlingly white in a resplendent contrast with the subtropical vegetation.

Olivia and Petrus van Schilte were gracious hosts who came down the broad staircase at the entrance to meet the guests. While Olivia was greeting Odile in a motherly manner and was leading her into the building, the men stayed outdoors chatting. The host was in his late fifties, with a personable smile on his sunburnt face. Casually dressed and free of the slightest traces of arrogance and affectation, Petrus was a lord of the manor of Dutch-English origin. To Célestin, he said: "Petrus is an old Dutch name and has nothing to do with the château in the Pomerol area near Bordeaux; their Château Pétrus manages to be more expensive than my best! And please call me 'Petry.' Let's go inside and find out what our ladies would like to do."

To begin their walk from the highest point on the estate, Petry drove them up the hill in a terrain vehicle for over twenty minutes. A splendid view to the south opened from the summit, all the way to Muizenberg, Strandfontein, and Valsbaai (*False Bay*)— that almost, but not quite, belonged to the Indian Ocean. Below, toward the main building, a hundred fifty hectares of vineyards, hillocks, groves, ponds, glades, springs, and reservoirs were spread. Birds flew about, and Olivia pointed out several harlequin quails. All the narrow roads were of red earth and the vineyards lined up like Roman legions. When they came across a young vineyard worker, Petry asked him to drive the jeep back, whereas they would walk down the hill. From time to time, they tasted white grapes that were close to ripe, and Olivia proudly announced: "Last year we got the First Prize in South Africa for our Sauvignon Blanc, which is the first award for our new winery, you'll see it."

Farther below, they first came to the old winery and then the brand-new one. The top of the building resembled the deck of a seafaring ship. To reach the "captain's bridge," one had to climb a steep metal staircase and lift the hatch cover. "Is that lid watertight or winetight?" Célestin jokingly asked Petry. Olivia showed Odile how to climb the sixty-degree staircase safely and then open and fasten the cover. The girl treated it as a game on a pirate ship and used the opportunity to tell her hosts about the steel ladders she had climbed on Lion's Head. The bridge was a still unfurnished, spacious room with sensational views in all directions. They spent time discussing how its qualities could be enhanced by furniture and other items. While Odile and Olivia were drinking juice, Petry poured for Célestin and himself a glass of the winning white wine for 1981 his wife had mentioned. The stateroom next to the bridge served as an office housing the impressive prize cup.

Then they visited the new winery, in which many rows of shiny metal mini-tanks stood. Petry explained how the modern cooling system for slowing down fermentation functioned. All four descended to the cellar with Gothic pointed arches of rough stone. Large wooden barrels and smaller casks would eventually be sitting in it. "Like the cellar of an ancient castle," thought Odile. Together with Petry, she verified its acoustics: A thirteen-second echo, as in a church. In the end, they all went to the labs where the acidity, sugar content, and other chemical characteristics of wine were tested. A heavy ornate door led to a gorgeous tasting room with wood-paneled walls.

They left the winery and continued downhill. Along the way, Olivia and Petry exchanged genial greetings with workers who were repairing the thatched roof of a building. Father and daughter saw modern barracks and a canteen for single workers, which bore no resemblance to a Potemkin village. Stables, two grass tennis courts, and a small swimming pool were situated farther down.

The main building contained exceptional specimens of Dutch and other European furniture. Hosts led their guests through the dining room with a high yellowwood ceiling, a French *salon,* and an English-style drawing room. There was also a chapel. Throughout one saw private studies, each differently furnished. But they were impressed the most by the endless park behind the manor house: flower beds, manicured shrubs, and countless trees. Beyond the park, one saw the southern foothills of Table Mountain.

During the time in the library and archive room, two hundred years old orders, receipts, accounts, and other amazing records of transactions with individual clients and shipping companies were on show. In the nineteenth century, the crowned heads and aristocrats of Europe were merrily drinking the superb Groot Constantia wines.

Finally, they sat down for a light dinner and were served lamb with asparagus, salads, cheeses, and many types of nuts and fruit. All the vegetables and fruit—including the perfectly ripe figs—came from farms and orchards at the estate. Various Constantia wines made an appearance, notably the famous Pinotage (Pinot Noir and Cinsaut), but also the jewel of that magnificent wine-growing *terroir, Grand Constance* (100% red and white Muscat de Frontignan). Olivia seldom sipped the wine and kept company with Odile, drinking mineral water. On the other hand, Petry and Célestin did much more than taste the wines—they savored them.

After dinner, Olivia talked about their two daughters and mentioned that Petry would see them the following day in London. Odile had become a skillful raconteur—specializing in the art of travel narration without the Baron-Münchhausen elements—and spoke vividly about Baikal, Moscow, Israel, and the Sinai as if she had been there the week before. Olivia and Petry were astonished when Célestin told them he had only three weeks earlier, in Swaziland, drunk *Grand Constance* in strange circumstances. Petry was surprised until he remembered the Swazi royal chancellery had ordered and received two hundred fifty bottles. Being a discreet person, he did not inquire about the strange circumstances, assuming them to be some ostentatious Swazi function, whereas Célestin preferred not to talk about Dima and Kolya. Odile wisely kept mum.

When they retired to their bedrooms, the guests were filled with positive impressions. After a goodnight kiss, he took time to think. During the seven hours with their hosts, it emerged that Petry and Olivia were one-quarter old aristocrats, one-quarter very wealthy people, and one-quarter folks who did not hesitate to roughen up their hands in a vineyard. To complete the picture, they were educated horticulturalists, as well as enologists, masters of wine. Quite evidently, but unobtrusively, they considered themselves white natives, no less genuine Africans than someone who was a Zulu, a Xhosa, or a *Kaapse Kleurling* (*Cape Coloured*) person from the apartheid-designated mixed-race group. Rightfully so?

At nine in the morning, Petry said goodbye, rushing to catch the London flight. Célestin remembered, but did not mention to Odile, that to reach the airport, Petry would drive along the edge of Crossroads, the shantytown. They had breakfast with Olivia, who had stayed in Cape Town for appointments. Perhaps surprisingly for a lady of her kind, she divulged badly missing their daughters but not the husbands! At parting, she produced a radiant smile on her beautiful fifty-year-old face with very few wrinkles, an open invitation to Constantia, and a bagful of divinely smelling figs. There was also a stylishly wrapped bottle of wine chosen by Petry.

6.

Just as he had begun to unwrap Petry's gift at the Helmsley, the phone rang. Rose Jenkins from Linguistics announced mail had arrived from Wits. After he promised to come after lunch, she added: "Half an hour ago, Dr. Glott asked me for your phone number. I hesitated a little. Have I done the right thing by giving it?" "But of course Rose, thank you, I'll be glad to hear from him." By then, he had managed to unwrap the bottle and was delighted to discover the kingly red Groot Constantia wine.

He showed Odile the bottle, thinking at the same time about John Glott. Célestin had become acquainted with the serious, knowledgeable man at a congress in Paris a few years earlier and maintained correspondence with him. John was an expert in Hindi, Urdu, and other languages from that family spoken in various regions of India and Pakistan. It would be nice to see him again, thought the Frenchman. In South Africa, there were many people of Indian descent, and he also remembered that John's grandmother was born in India.

While he was still studying the label on the bottle, John telephoned, and Célestin gladly accepted the invitation for lunch at the Glotts' home in Strandfontein on False Bay. John was delighted: "My wife Laurel loves to cook for guests, and we haven't had any for a long time. Please have only a light breakfast! I think you and Odile will find my family interesting. See you tomorrow."

At Linguistics, Rose cheered up when she saw the inseparable duo. But he said: "What's happened Rose? I noticed when we walked in you looked worried." She smiled: "How accurately you perceive people! Better than most women. Maybe because you've raised a wonderful girl all by yourself. And yes, you guessed correctly. Earlier today, I had to make a difficult, irrevocable decision. I hope to tell you about it while you're still with us, even though we barely know each other. You would be an objective listener." "Thank you, let's leave it at that," he replied.

The students' pub Pig & Whistle was a convenient place to open the mail. In the hefty bunch, only one piece mattered—from Kazan. Olga had received a letter from her daughter and conveyed the gist: Olya loves Tino passionately and does not wish to complain because she is healthy, thanks to her God; he should embrace Odilichka, kissing her ten times for her tenth birthday. Olga deeply regretted being unable to accompany her heartfelt birthday wishes with a gift. He leaned toward Odile and instructed her to count the kisses, as he kept kissing her on both cheeks. "Ten times... for my birthday! It must be from our Olya!" Odile squealed excitedly. "*Oui, ma princesse.*" The students drinking beer at the nearby tables cheered.

Then they took the familiar road to Constantia but beyond the turn for the estate, drove fifteen kilometers farther south to Muizenberg on False Bay. From the small beach hotel, Strandfontein would be an easy drive for lunch with the Glotts the following day.

The evening sky was somber as the pair walked the length of the deserted beach twice. The soothing waves and the smell were different from the Atlantic's at Clifton № 4, and on entering the water to their knees, they found False Bay much warmer. It was not yet the Indian Ocean, which began at "Cape of the Needles," officially the Portuguese Cabo das Agulhas, a hundred sixty kilometers southeast of False Bay. To geographers and hydrographers, Agulhas was the southernmost point of Africa, but that meant little to the staunch denizens of Caypee and its latest French admirers. To them, the Cape of Good Hope was the true end of the African continent, and the Indian Ocean began there. "Scientists are certainly correct," he mumbled, "but numerous molecules of this warmer water have undoubtedly arrived from the Indian."

A young moon appeared between two mighty clouds. Under its pale light, father and daughter held hands, peering into the black vastness. "I know you're aware, *ma douce*, that from here to the south, all the way to the Antarctic, incredibly far, there's nothing except salty water. Oh, all right, there's frozen freshwater—icebergs breaking off glaciers."

They slept with windows wide open. Silence prevailed. The endless, enormous, cold waves of the Atlantic could not be heard.

7.

In the morning, waves remained small, so Odile swam farther from the shore than usual, but Célestin floated watchfully nearby. Afterward, they went for a walk around Muizenberg. By half past nine, it was much hotter than during the previous days in Cape Town. Remembering John Glott's jocular warning, they had a minimalistic breakfast at a coffee house.

While they were sipping tea, she decided to add more details to her diary about the visit to Constantia. To kill time, he bought a copy of *The Cape Times* at the cafe counter. The tabloid resembled the London ones but was even more primitive. The real shock awaited him on the third page: There was a large color photo of two provocatively half-naked girls who were "wistfully remembering their late boyfriend." He was thirteen and the girls twelve. They spoke about him in the past tense because the boy had been found in a garbage can, butchered into pieces. His mother identified him from a deformity of one of his feet.

Aghast, Célestin went back to the counter and showed the page to the cafe owner, a middle-aged black man. It was obvious from the man's reaction that he had seen the photo and read the "interview" with the pre-teen girls. He looked sadly for a few moments at Odile writing peacefully in the corner. Then he lifted his chin and with lips compressed spread his arms into a sign of furious impotence. Célestin returned the newspaper, whispering he did not wish his daughter to see it. "I also have children, and do I ever understand you. And these, they're worse than... No, wild beasts are good." Meanwhile, Célestin thought of Douglas—living miserably in Soweto with the constant fear his own children might necklace him on orders from their idol, the sixteen-year-old ANC comrade.

Strandfontein, although only eight kilometers to the east, looked much poorer than Muizenberg. Streets were in disrepair, houses run down, the beach filthy. Somehow they found a flower shop—the only one in town. Odile chose a bouquet for John's wife Laurel. The shop shared space with a pharmacy, and one person, a woman in her thirties, was both a florist and pharmacist. "A clever idea, though on second thought..." he mused. The lady owner of the diversified business told him: "You should have bought the flowers in Muizenberg. It's called 'Mouse Hill,' and we're supposedly 'Spring on the Beach,' yet everything is better where the mice live! I buy everything there, flowers and pills, and resell here to make a tiny profit. Our town receives no subsidies from the authorities, and we know why: Almost all of us here are mongrels, mixed-race, officially Cape Coloureds." When he inquired further, the intelligent, educated woman explained, with bitterness and resignation: "Skin color is almost inessential. I, for example, would be a white woman in Paris, or would at least be able to 'pass' as white, whereas here I'll forever be a Cape Coloured—because I have one Zulu great-grandfather and one half-Bushman grandmother!"

John Glott's smallish two-story house sat on a street corner with a narrow grassy area in front. On the threshold, Laurel cheerfully received the bouquet and hugged Odile. John grasped Célestin's extended hand with both of his, and they lied to each other about their unchanged appearance since the congress in Paris five years earlier. Laurel and John had three children: son Jeroen, eighteen years old, and two daughters, Mona and Luise, thirteen and nine. Odile and the younger sister became instant friends. Before they disappeared together, Luise sweetly told Laurel she would serve lemonade to her guest. But Mona suddenly informed her parents she would miss lunch because of a meeting of the arts group at the school. Laurel and John did not wish to argue in front of visitors but were visibly upset because they sensed Mona had been cunningly waiting for an opportune moment.

Jeroen had a serious, expressive face and wore black-rimmed spectacles with thick lenses. He immediately asked the guest if he liked classical music. After the affirmative answer, strains of solemn eighteenth-century music resounded. Jeroen ceremoniously announced: "Christoph Willibald, Ritter von Gluck! Overture for one of his operas." Célestin smiled and nodded, pleased with the young man. "Jeroen is committed to classical music; he's been studying clarinet for seven years," John said and continued in a different voice: "He's inherited the talent from his uncle Bruce, Laurel's brother, who now lives in Chicago and works as a conductor of a chamber orchestra."

They all sat down and chatted amiably, although the hostess often went to the kitchen. Célestin and John had a couple of glasses of a South African fruit apéritif. The meal was outstanding and abundant: Six fresh oysters with lemon juice per person; a complicated tuna salad à la Niçoise, except better; the main course of salmon with rice and vegetables, expertly prepared and spiced; excellent cheeses, even some French; tasty homemade cake; and fruit. Odile sat next to her father, and Luise by her mother, so both received help regarding fresh oysters and blue cheese. Célestin was happy to note that his daughter secretly observed Luise's progress and pretended to be as inept as the adorable, one-year-younger girl. The worldly Odile had long been familiar with oysters and mussels from Nantes and with the Roquefort cheese in tiny quantities. As for Laurel, upon receiving praise from her guests, doting husband, and loving son, the kind lady glowed with pleasure.

Only over coffee, after Luise had again enticed Odile to her room, were thorny topics addressed. It began harmlessly enough, at least on the surface, with John saying it had been "quite a job" squeezing the visitor's phone number out of Rose Jenkins. "Yes, she told me she'd hesitated, I couldn't understand why," replied Célestin. "Because..." John temporized but was helped by Laurel, "... because Rose doesn't like John!" After a moment's reluctance to continue, came sharp words, "... doesn't like him because he's black, black a little, ha, ha, *that is, colored*—as is our whole family, we're all colored!" Célestin preferred to listen rather than say something indelicate.

John explained: "Yes, the color of my skin is the way it is because my paternal grandmother was born in Gujarat, in the northwest of India, next to Pakistan; she's no longer living. Her maternal tongue was Gujarati: It's interesting linguistically because of the numerous Arabic, Persian, and Portuguese words in it. Of course, the people also speak Hindi and Urdu. In part because of her, I became a linguist specializing in those languages. As you know, Hindi and Urdu speakers can understand each other, but the two languages use different scripts.

"To return to Rose. Laurel spoke heatedly, but she was right. Since we're pursuing this knotty theme, I've no choice but to be direct: There's no doubt Rose has a racist disposition. What's surprising to us is she's a South African of English extraction, and such people more often than not successfully pretend to favor racial equality."

Laurel took over: "I know from a reliable source that Rose will soon leave South Africa forever. She'll move to England. Something must have happened that's made her cup of distress, hate, and fear overflow. Maybe it's the ever-increasing crime rate; even here, in tiny Strandfontein, it's bad. Or she's identified violent political changes on the horizon. Listen, a person like Rose doesn't want to live in a country ruled by blacks—which she'd tell you herself. She'll escape like a rat from the sinking white ship! Sorry, but that's the way it is."

Jeroen abruptly got up and asked if he could play another record. The Piano Concerto by Francis Poulenc soon began, and Célestin wondered if the young man had been so considerate as to choose music by a French composer. With no connection to Jeroen, he realized that Laurel's words explained why Rose had been so gloomy in her office the day before. Perhaps she had just received the papers about an irreversible decision to depart from the country of her birth and youth. And John and Laurel? They were a well-rehearsed team, though probably often without listeners. He did not mind, being always willing to learn.

He heard John's voice; it was measured at first, but soon the pitch shot up: "When it gets hot here, the British will escape but won't forget the money. They can go wherever they want because they've perfidiously convinced the whole world they appreciate and even like us blacks and coloreds. They hate apartheid, and they're helping us—outrageous lies for John Lennon's *Imagine*-loving naifs. In comparison with Afrikaners, the British are parasites. They came here long after the Boers—for gold, diamonds, and other resources. And they'll leave with everything portable, whereas the Afrikaners have nowhere to go. The whole world hates them because of apartheid, especially Holland, due to its phony guilt complex and its extreme, insincere liberalism. Remember the crimes they committed in Indonesia? Almost as horrible as those of the Belgians in the Congo."

Célestin responded calmly: "I've heard similar opinions from many people in South Africa—black people, the so-called Cape Coloured people, and white ones. But I'd very much like to hear from a teenager. Jeroen is at hand, and Poulenc won't mind. So, what does the young gentleman think?"

Jeroen accepted the invitation and spoke in a poised, rarely trembling voice, seldom gesticulating. "Thank you, Sir, for wanting to hear me, although mine is certainly a minority opinion. I'll speak candidly, based on my experiences in high school, music school, and elsewhere. Personally, I regard Afrikaners as more honest than white people of English and Scottish descent, less duplicitous and calculated. They're real Africans, even though they don't have black or brown skin. They truly love this land they've been cultivating and irrigating for hundreds of years with their Dutch skill, care, patience, and persistence. I think the rest of us South Africans—and other Africans—should learn from them, including deep love toward one's native country."

His parents were neither shooting him disapproving glances nor contradicting him. Because of his intelligence, courage, and talent for music, he was undoubtedly their pride and joy. Célestin used the brief lull after Jeroen had spoken to bring up similar views he had heard from a Zulu ranger in Kruger Park and the owners of Groot Constantia. Three pairs of eyebrows were lifted at the mention of Constantia, but it was all.

The young man continued: "I adore my country and will never leave. Each time Uncle Bruce—whom I love and hugely respect—calls from Chicago, he offers, gently but insistently, to apply for a U.S. student visa. I thank him from my heart but stubbornly repeat I would never part from my parents and sisters, from the Indian Ocean, and this destitute little town full of delinquents and other unfortunate people.

"I'm different from many in my generation. I can't stand ANC methods. I worry non-stop about my sister Mona, whom you haven't had the chance to get to know because she used your arrival to leave and meet her ANC mentors. Our parents forbi..."

Unlike John, who was looking at his son with admiration, Laurel yelled: "Jeroen! Leave Mona alone! We don't need to display our dirty laundry."

Jeroen got up, apologized to the guest and his parents, and kissed his mother on her flushed cheek. "I'm going for a walk," he said. John accompanied him to the front door and advised him in a low voice, but still loud enough for Célestin to hear: "Please, son, don't go spying on her in the schoolyard. Those wicked villains might beat you up severely—or kill you."

Célestin walked to Luise's room and knocked. A chirpy voice exclaimed: "Come iiiiinn!!!" The girls greeted him joyfully. They were sitting on the floor and playing delightedly, just as boys would, with a small electric train and a construction crane. He left the room and reached his armchair at the end of a dispute between Laurel and John.

Without beating around the bush, John said: "We didn't wish to talk to you about Mona because... it's awfully hard for us. You can imagine what happens in families when their daughter who's barely a teenager is seized by the ANC junior rogues. Mona—we simply don't know what to do with her. And Jeroen, we dread what those ruffians might do to him because he loves his sister and is always trying to protect her." Célestin told them in detail what he had heard from Douglas in Joburg. Laurel and John kept nodding their heads with sheer horror in their eyes, and finally he said: "It's good you've heard it from someone else as well, so you don't think we're a family of freaks."

Laurel had calmed down and changed the topic: "You haven't heard from Jeroen what we've endured and how much we've suffered as a colored family under this regime! And look at us: John is the way he is, slightly brown in the Indian style. I was born officially white, albeit with olive skin, but by law, I'm no longer white: I'm colored because I've married a colored man. The problems the two of us have had! My brother Bruce is officially white by birth, like I was, but is politically undesirable. So he escaped from South Africa just before he would be arrested. He can't come back even for a brief visit. And then: Our children are all automatically classified as colored, even though Jeroen is brownish like John, Mona is the darkest in the family, and our little Luise is the color of milk chocolate."

John found the strength to laugh: "I told you on the phone you'd find my family interesting." Célestin was sad and silent.

Laurel was not amused: "We should tell you what happened after Bruce's escape via Lesotho. One evening, two types in civilian clothes came here. They pretended to be apologetic about interrupting our meal and showed us the order of the Examining

Magistrate by which the family was required to present all the documents and information pertaining to Bruce—'who had broken the laws X, Y, and Z.' Then they turned everything upside down in our closets, sideboards, kitchen cabinets, and the garage. They worked methodically for hours. Before finally leaving, they uttered empty apologies, nasty smirks on their faces."

Célestin forced himself to say what he was thinking: "My friends, I commiserate with your whole family. But I must ask you: What now? You don't need me to remind you what might happen if Mona becomes involved in anything, even very minor, with ANC members."

Laurel and John gazed at him. With a resigned, downbeat look in his eyes, John spoke softly: "You've stated everything succinctly. Laurel and I owe you a heartfelt thank you. I knew whom to invite to my family circle—a kindhearted but objective man. And thank you for bringing your girl along. How nicely she played with Luise! It's sweet to be nine or ten years old." Laurel added: "But not thirteen!"

Managing to extract the girls from Luise's room, he helped Odile get ready. At the door, they thanked the hosts for the superb lunch and asked them to convey greetings to Jeroen and Mona. John walked them to the Rover. "Jeroen is a special young man, I'm sure Laurel and you are very proud of him," Célestin said. Some locals walking on the opposite side of the street stopped to stare. John whispered: "They're not hostile, just surprised to see white people visiting a colored family. I told you on the phone that we haven't had any colleagues from Linguistics as guests in a long time. Apartheid rules." While they were driving back to Caypee, Odile chatted about Luise: "Isn't she sweet, Papa? And so pretty, with her kind round face!"

It was a Friday afternoon, but they managed to park near a music record store downtown. Célestin knew what he wanted: Clarinet Concerto in A major, K. 622 by Mozart and Clarinet Quintet in B minor, Op. 115 by Brahms. Then they drove to Regent Road, where at a small post office a lady they knew packed the records and mailed them. The recipient was Mr. Jeroen Glott, Strandfontein 7785.

8.

The following morning at eight, Nelius Boshof phoned: "Sorry, I wanted to catch you before you disappeared somewhere. You see, having heard so much from me, Viola would love to meet you both. Could you possibly come tomorrow around four to tea plus this and that? Apologies for inviting you at short notice." Everything was quickly set.

Before a leisurely walk on the Promenade, Célestin and Odile went for breakfast at Little Tel Aviv, a restaurant in Sea Point. While serving a tasty Middle Eastern meal, the Israeli owners introduced themselves as Eitan and Ariel, Sabras from the same village. Both were in their mid-thirties, alternating visits to the guests' table. Odile proudly enumerated the cities she had visited in Israel, adding she had a girlfriend, a student of law in Jerusalem called Osnat. The Israelis mentioned the wars they fought for their country but without visible pride. Then, having first agreed with each other in Hebrew, they confided to Célestin that they liked the denizens of Caypee because they did not loudly chomp food, talk with their mouths full, and yell during meals—like many Sabras. But they did complain about certain experiences. "Here, in our modest eatery, sometimes two or three black guys arrive, order nothing, and come to the counter rudely demanding money for the 'Congress', as they call the ANC. They can't scare us, we kick them out... In a few years, who knows? We'll have to leave, go to Britain, as so many Anglo-Scottish types are already doing, ha, ha!"

At Clifton № 4, the waves were too wild in Célestin's estimation even in the protected corner of the beach. "Neither Luuk nor other surfers are here. The ocean is too agitated—high tide and strong currents." It was still hard to convince her that swimming was out of the question.

In the evening, they went to the nearby hotel President, the best in Sea Point. The hotel café-bar was an elegant place with discreet lighting, walls with dark wood paneling, and deep-buttoned plush upholstery. Before sitting down, Célestin walked with Odile to the toilet and said he would wait. A passing man with refined looks overheard them: "Excuse me, Sir, *ou Monsieur*, are you *par hasard* from France?" They began chatting in the hallway. It turned out the gentleman was an Afrikaner from Cape Town who spoke French fluently. He was in the company of a Parisian colleague who was on a brief visit to the city. When Odile came out, Dr. Adriaan Momberg politely greeted her and requested they join him at the table where he was sitting with his colleague.

The Frenchman and the Afrikaner were cardiac surgeons—Dr. Jean Bataille at the renowned Paris hospital *Hôtel-Dieu*, and Dr. Momberg at Groote Schuur in Cape Town, perhaps the most famous hospital on the African continent. Célestin was certainly not an ignoramus regarding those hospitals and major achievements in cardiac surgery. An intriguing discussion in French on medical and linguistic subjects ensued among the three courteous, cosmopolitan men.

Odile could not be included in the trialogue, but the surgeons were in any case about to leave. Célestin and Dr. Bataille exchanged addresses, agreeing to go horseback riding at the Metz estate or in the Bois de Boulogne with their daughters. But Célestin felt truly honored that Dr. Momberg invited him to visit the hospital—the following Saturday suited them. After all, Groote Schuur was the place where Christiaan Barnard performed the first successful man-to-man heart transplantation in 1967.

At the Helmsley, a message from Mary Goode awaited, asking for a return call. On the phone, her voice was gleeful: "I hope you're free on Thursday. Paul very much wishes to meet you and has learned from a colleague that there will be a Pinot Noir harvest at the exclusive Meerlust winery in Stellenbosch. He even received a recommendation for the cellar master. So, he's freed himself from obligations at Sociology and suggests we all drive in his car to that town of vineyards. Thus, you and I will be able to taste the wines while Paul, who rarely consumes alcohol, will keep Odile company with juice!"

9.

The Boshofs' house was on Pinewood Road in the sedate Newlands Quarter, about two and a half kilometers south of the university campus. It sat almost at the bottom of Table Mountain's eastern slope, near the entrance to the nature reserve Newlands Forest. Viola, Nelius, and a tender ten-year-old girl came out of the house to welcome guests. Nelius was delighted to receive a bottle of Cognac from Célestin, while Viola exclaimed joyfully when Odile gave her a large bouquet. She kissed the girl and introduced her to Nicolette, her niece. Odile apologized: "I'm sorry, Nicolette, I didn't know you'd be here, so I don't have flowers for you." Nicolette gratefully nodded. "No problem at all! I'll give half of my bouquet to Nicolette," said Viola gaily. The men privately concluded harmony would rule.

Before the girls and Viola went out to the splendid garden, they all sat in the living room, drinking tea and chatting. Three white Angora cats sat in the room, each in its distant corner. Nicolette picked one up, but the cat soon escaped from her lap. "Ankara's independent and conceited," the good-natured girl smilingly complained to Viola, "always running away!" While Odile was giving her Caypee report, Célestin noticed she was talking more tentatively than usual. The probable reason was the presence of an age-mate born in the city. "That's how it should be," he thought contentedly.

But when Viola asked her about Table Mountain, Odile had a lot to say: "We fell in love at first sight with the 'long dining table,' as Papa called the mountain in fond fun when we saw it the first time. It was evening, we were driving from... Kimberley and had just begun to descend from the high hills to the city. The mountain suddenly showed up—what a unique sight! And later the same evening, we were looking at it from the garden of our hotel. Papa promised me on the spot we'd climb it together, and just today, we decided to do it tomorrow. Right, Papa?" He nodded with a smile, correctly anticipating what would happen next.

Viola exclaimed: "That's wonderful! Views from the top are incredible. The cable car leaves, I think, every half hour from seven in the morning and ascends rapidly." The guests looked at each other, and she wisely let her father respond: "Thank you for the cable car information, but we'll climb on foot. She will now blush, but the fact is that Odile is resilient, in fine health, and rarely whines. From a young age, she liked to finish what she'd started. In the Sinai, she gained some climbing experience in hot weather. And four or five days ago, when we climbed Lion's Head, she managed the affixed steel ladders and chains. So I think with a little help, she'll endure four hours of climbing without problems—from what I've read, that's how long we'll need. And then, well, I can imagine how excited and happy she'll be to have conquered Table Mountain on foot."

The hosts and Nicolette looked serious as he continued: "However, we'll come down by cable car. Often descent is much more dangerous than the ascent, notably on steep slopes and with tired legs." After an interval, Nelius said: "It's an excellent plan. Odile is a brave girl, as expected from the daughter of a mountaineer and world traveler. You won't need more than three and a half hours unless the heat near the summit becomes hellish. But Célestin, you probably know there was a fire in the middle part of Table Mountain about six weeks ago." He did: "Yes, I read a few days ago in *The Argus* that sprouts and even shoots have already appeared amidst all the soot. It'll be lovely to see how quickly nature restores itself. Of course, we won't wear white socks and pants!"

Viola spent some time in the garden with the girls and then went to prepare snacks, letting them get to know each other. Nicolette was a pensive child of fragile health, a dreamer with huge eyes and golden locks. She spoke trustingly about school, girlfriends, music, and drawing, not envying Odile on her travels but on Pasha and swimming in the ocean. In a despondent voice, she revealed: "Because of my health, the doctors have forbidden me to take part in certain sports, most of all riding, and I love horses."

Odile had never before been in the position to console a girl of her age—in fact, to console anyone except, very rarely, her papa. She was unsure what to say, so she spontaneously took Nicolette's hand and placed it on her cheek.

Nelius and Célestin spent a long time discussing Israel and the Arab countries. The host, an expert in Hebraic studies, knew many people whom his colleague had befriended: Jakob Shmotkin, Shalom Yinon, and Hila Bellin. As Nelius was also a specialist in Dutch and Afrikaans, Célestin learned interesting details about the gradual separation of Afrikaans from Dutch and Flemish and its development as a separate language. He also found that Muslim schools in South Africa switched in 1815 from instruction in Malay to Afrikaans, but using the Arabic script; the transition lasted until 1850.

Somehow they got onto the subject of John Glott and Rose Jenkins. "It's poor form to discuss colleagues, but I must admit John is right regarding Rose. You must've also heard Laurel's opinion; she's quite outspoken. But Rose has not always been the way she is now. After all, horrendous things have been happening here. And it's better for her to go to England as soon as possible. At least with Rose, it has nothing to do with money, as is the case with so many escapees of English, Scottish, and Irish descent. It's also better for us Afrikaners and the country in general that people with Rose's current racist attitudes are no longer here. I'm sorry to say it, I've known her for a long time. She has many estimable qualities. But our public life and atmosphere at the university have been poisoned enough."

Around eight, when Célestin and Odile were leaving, the girls' eyes were teary. Viola said: "Your daughter is always welcome. With or without you and regardless of whether Nicolette can also come."

10.

Before ten in the morning, they again drove up to Kloof Nek but turned left on Tafelberg Road and soon arrived at the parking area by the Cable Car lower station. The thermometer was showing thirty degrees. They were prepared: sunblock; shoes with good traction; arms and legs covered by light clothes; white hats. Célestin's rucksack contained the Table Mountain trail map, compass, Nikon, binoculars, water, nuts, and raisins. Odile's little backpack weighed only about half a kilo.

They started at 10:45, and it took twenty minutes of climbing up a steep stony slope before they reached Contour Trail. They turned eastward and after a while crossed the First Stream, as was written on the map. It did not take long before they saw signs of the fire, but there were indeed green shoots protruding out of the black remains of bushes and shrubbery. They kept walking uphill and after crossing the Fourth Stream, found the beginning of a very steep trail that led into Platteklip Gorge. On some tricky sections, Célestin helped Odile and occasionally carried her on his back a dozen or more meters. Still, despite the heat and the acute angle of the slope, the pair passed several other climbers, exchanging greetings with each person.

Farther uphill, there was a massive smooth rock beside the trail. On its face, in giant black-green-gold lettering, "ANC" was inscribed. The same or different hand, friendly or hostile, added a large red hammer-and-sickle. He took a photo of the rock in its austere setting.

By a narrow picturesque trail, they finally arrived on top of the gorge at 1:45 p.m. and needed another quarter of an hour to reach the Cable Car upper station. The temperature was thirty-four degrees and the elevation one thousand eighty-four meters. The view from the summit was sublime, worthy of yells of delight. To the north, they saw Lion's Head, Devil's Peak, Sea Point, and Robben Island, whereas in the south, False Bay was already hidden by the billowing, swirling fog rolling in from the Cape of Good Hope and the Indian Ocean.

The pair drank icy-cold Platteklip Gorge water and laughed at the sooty attire. Nearby, there was a tall pillar from which arrows pointed toward various cities on the globe. Odile counted sixteen arrows and dutifully wrote down the cities and distances in her notebook: Paris 9,344 km, Berlin 9,624 km, Tel Aviv 7,540 km, and so on. Her father sniggered: "Did you notice there's no arrow toward Moscow? Undoubtedly, the official attitude doesn't allow it because the ANC likes that direction! Ha, ha."

In the small cafe, they ate sandwiches and drank South African white-currant juice. Odile wrote in her diary, while Célestin reflected on the ANC inscription he had photographed—powerful and indestructible. He became certain ANC would win and the movement was dauntless and unstoppable. However, other thoughts also crossed his mind: "What will black Africans in this country accomplish with the hammer and the sickle? What will happen to the Afrikaners, white people who have been Africans for over three hundred years and have nowhere to go—as even the 'coloured' sufferer John Glott admits?"

Something else in the ANC sign kept grating on him, and Célestin finally realized what it was: Proud, pure mountains must not be defaced by politics! On one side of the philosophical chessboard stood the earthly, almost always selfish idea of justice; and on the other, the God-given eternal beauty of a mountain that needed defending from arrogant hands. He gazed at his daughter's tranquil visage and did not wish, was not able, to disturb her by controversies involving politics—or God.

They entered the cable car and through the fog quickly embracing Table Mountain reached the Rover.

* * *

In a corner of the elegant *salon* at the Helmsley, father and daughter were watching the fireplace with raging flames and reviewing their successful ascent. Odile was ecstatic and exhausted. Her leg muscles hurt, but she referred to the discomfort as her well-deserved trophy.

Célestin decided it was the moment to present his Devil's Peak plan. "When we went to the university on our first day in Caypee, Mrs. Rose took us to an office and from there showed us Devil's Peak. Remember? We also saw it today and a few days ago from Lion's Head. The peak is part of Table Mountain, yet to get there requires a separate, especially perilous ascent. Well, I want to climb it. Unfortunately, it must happen without you. Even though the elevation of Devil's Peak is only one thousand meters, it's a more demanding and dangerous place than Table Mountain. I know you never want to prevent me from doing something important to me and not appropriate for your age. Isn't that so, *ma douce?*"

"*Bien sûr, cher Papa*, climb without me, although I'm afraid you may be doing something really, really dangerous!" They talked about it until Célestin was able to convince her he would be safe. "*Alors, si tu es d'accord*," he proposed, "I'd like to do it on Wednesday morning, the day after tomorrow. It occurred to me it would be best if you spent time again with Viola, Nicolette, and Nelius. You have an invitation to visit them whenever you wish."

Since Odile liked the suggestion, he called Nelius. First, they talked about Table Mountain: "My daughter managed superbly and continues to enthuse about it. You were right, our climb took three hours and fifteen minutes. And yes, we were sooty." When he asked Nelius whether she would be welcome for another visit, Viola came to the phone and instantly agreed: "I hope Nicolette can also come, although Wednesday is a school day. Most likely, my sister will decide to bring her anyway because Nicolette is at the top of her class, doesn't have many girlfriends, and likes Odile very much."

11.

Célestin wished to spend the day between the climbs quietly with the girl. They slept late, had a leisurely breakfast, and she swam in the heated hotel pool where the warm water comforted her leg muscles. Around noon, they went for a long drive along the coast south of Sea Point. They passed the Clifton beaches and reached the semicircular Camps Bay where small restaurants were nestled under palms. At a cafe, they watched volleyballers skillfully playing two-against-two games on the sand. The highway abandoned the coast and took off into the hills from which they spotted a beach with the Welsh name Llandudno. The road then swerved deeper into the woods before plunging to the port of Houtbaai with sailing boats and fishing vessels. From the bay, serpentines again took them high up, all the way to Chapman's Peak, from which the magnificent coastline could be experienced by several senses: Mediterranean vegetation, mists here and there, and a breeze singing on the steep wooded slopes that dived into the Atlantic.

Farther on, some fifty kilometers south of Cape Town, they arrived at Noordhoek. Célestin shared with Odile his immediate thought: They were at the most perfect beach he had ever seen. Flabbergasted by the exceptionally wide half-moon of blindingly white sand, she believed him. The beach was surrounded by luxuriant subtropical trees and empty, except for a lone woman on her horse. They both wished to speak to the rider and stroke the horse's neck, but the woman had ridden far away while they stood still, gazing at the ocean as if bewitched.

Back at the Helmsley, the elderly concierge gave them a message from Viola he had painstakingly jotted down: "Nicolette will come at ten tomorrow and can't wait to see Odile again!" They happily read the message, but the curious girl sweetly asked the man: "How did you know to write my name correctly, Sir?" He smiled equally sweetly: "Well, I asked the lady to spell it; and then she asked me to add the exclamation mark at the end of the message!"

In the evening, they went to the pub Cape Sun because he had read in *The Argus* that the well-known local singer and guitarist André de Beer was performing. It was still early when they arrived, so there were few customers. The musician was indeed outstanding. When he took a break, Célestin went to the small podium to congratulate him and invite him for a beer. He was an educated, handsome man in his thirties. Born in Cape Town, he had lived for years in New York, Paris, and West Berlin. With Célestin, he soon established excellent rapport, while with Odile he managed to be humorous in so-so French. It turned out his repertoire was broad, so after the break he gladly fulfilled requests, singing Bob Dylan's and Bruce Springsteen's songs.

He returned to their table and ordered three lemonades, as one beer was his limit when performing and Célestin's when driving. In answer to the singer's question why he had not requested any song by Leonard Cohen, he said: "I didn't because you'd probably have chosen 'Suzanne.' I love that ballad, but it saddens me. The first time I heard it was in Cologne with Odile's mother, a year before our daughter was born." He stroked the girl's cheek. "And about a year ago in Paris, a lady acquaintance of ours who didn't turn out quite... played it in her apartment." She interrupted: "You're thinking of Tante—of Mathilde, Papa, right?" "*Oui, mon bijou.* But André, I do like the song. To prove it, I'll sing the beginning for you." He sang softly in his tenor:

Suzanne takes you down to her place near the river
You can hear the boats go by, you can spend the night forever
And you know that she's half-crazy but that's why you want
to be there...

André and Odile applauded, also softly. Célestin added: "If you'd like to do something by Cohen, please sing 'So long, Marianne'." André sang it sensitively, in a voice the Frenchman preferred to Cohen's. Later he told the singer about the great talent and sad life of Vladimir Vysotskiy to whose music Olya had introduced him in Moscow. Sometimes one couldn't go on without sorrow, he thought—but snapped out of melancholic musings by remembering that the following month he would be meeting Dima and Lyudmila on Cape Soya. Maybe the news would be good. But Odile could not yet know about their trip to Japan.

12.

At eleven the next morning, Célestin began to climb the wicked Devil's Peak. The weather was cold and cloudy, with rain and strong wind. "These are precisely the conditions when smart mountain people don't climb," he castigated himself. "But Odile is with Viola and Nicolette, so I prefer not to back out. Of course, that's when mountaineers have accidents—when they're stubborn and feel omnipotent even about Mother Nature. Yes, I'm being ridiculous and must be extra cautious." By very steep, sharp serpentines he arrived at a gully where the wind was bending several pine trees to their waist. Then, on an even steeper goat track, he reached a big rock in the saddle of the mountain and was met by a cold fog. From there, pursuing the long, bare Oppelskop ridge, on which the wind carved raindrops into his face, he climbed up to a bulge jutting out of the mountainside, a stony protrusion called Pulpit Rock. Célestin saw he would be killed if he fell from three of its sides and prudently negotiated the climb farther up to a gorge where precision was also needed in taking every step. It remained to clamber up the steep slippery rocks routinely using hands.

On top, his face was aglow with excitement, even though visibility was virtually nil: It depended on the play of strands of fog and gusts of wind mercilessly chasing them. He was delighted to see clouds fly below him into the gorge through which he had climbed minutes earlier. Naturally, nothing could be seen of Cape Town, despite the Peak being celebrated for the extraordinary 360-degree views. "It's not important; Odile and I saw it all from Table Mountain," he consoled himself. To his mind, the climb of the unholy peak in dreadful weather created a radically different species of beauty: The sublime feeling he was like King Lear alone in wild nature, surrounded by tempestuous wind, opaque fog, dark rocks, and gray clouds.

The descent was steep and slippery. He knew Devil's Peak had claimed the lives of many people, sometimes because the weather would suddenly worsen. Those were the devil's nasty whims—revenge on fate for being only a thousand-meter-high shorty.

When he parked in front of the Boshofs' house, the door opened immediately into the raging storm. Odile ran out and threw herself at her wet father. She did not say anything, only held him tightly. As they were entering the house embraced, the girl whispered: "*Tu es arrivé, mon cher Papa…*" Indoors, she helped him take off the wind jacket. Nicolette was also at hand to hang the soaked gear. Viola arrived with hot tea, and they all sat near the fireplace, Odile with an arm around his shoulders.

Nelius gazed at Célestin and said with a smile: "Dear colleague, you've wisely chosen the day for climbing Devil's Peak! Today's papers and television news are talking about nothing but the storm. So, was it crowded on the summit?" He grinned: "There was no one anywhere, and the city was invisible. So what? One doesn't climb only for attractive views in mild weather but also to feel the mountain when nature goes wild."

"I agree. It's a very special, dangerous climb. Viola, who is a passionate nature lover, has never done it and doesn't want to..." Nelius said. "So, how much time did you need? Four hours?" "No, altogether three: An hour and forty minutes for the ascent, an hour and twenty for the descent. Only at the summit did I spend any time not climbing up or down, which was no more than ten minutes. The bad weather was driving me on. I took two or three photos that might be interesting as studies in pure gray, brown, and white—although I used color film!"

13.

Cape Town awoke to blue skies and a fresh salty wind from the Atlantic. Only broken branches on trees around the hotel pool testified to the fierce temper of the storm the day before. Odile spoke about the time she had spent with the Boshofs: "When I saw the weather in the garden, I became worried about you, but Mr. Nelius reassured me. Mrs. Viola and Nicolette did everything to make my stay nice. I enjoyed it most when Nicolette and I were drawing together. We sat in front of a big window and drew the same two drenched trees lashed by the wind."

* * *

"On this road N2, we'll travel thirty-five kilometers to the southeast and then take R310 for another twenty to Stellenbosch," Paul informed Célestin, who was sitting beside him in the old Toyota. He was a lanky and talkative man with smiling eyes and glasses. For seven years, Mary and he had failed to get married, but it was evident they loved each other.

"By the way, Célestin, weren't you surprised that I, who as Mary told you, almost never drink alcohol, including wine, would find out about today's grape harvest at the Meerlust winery? Well, I have a colleague in whom *joie de vivre* is better represented than in me—even though, believe it or not, he's also a boring sociologist," he winked at Mary. "I told Lissandri—he emigrated from Italy—about Odile and you. And he, as soon as he heard you were French, suggested that Mary and I take you to Stellenbosch. She was delighted, and I asked Lissandri to cover my lectures. Odile will also love Stellenbosch; it's very pretty and a historic place."

"Many thanks to you, Paul, and to Mary and *signore* Lissandri, for the invitation," said Célestin and tried to be witty: "At the wineries, while Mary and I are tasting the wines, Odile will draw us and you can take photos! And thank you for driving. But tell us something about Stellenbosch."

"Paul and I are from Joburg," began Mary, "but we've read a lot and been to Stellenbosch frequently. The town was founded by Simon van der Stel in 1679 and later named after him. He was also the first Governor of the Dutch *Kaapkolonie* near the Cape of Good Hope. Like his father Adriaan van der Stel, the Governor of Mauritius in the Indian Ocean, he was an important officer of the powerful, outrageously rich *Vereenigde Nederlandsche Oostindische Compagnie*, the Dutch East India Company."

Célestin nodded and contributed what he knew: "Yes, I read about the *VOC*, or just the 'Company.' In large part because of it, the Dutch Golden Age took place. In the seventeenth century, Amsterdam was the most affluent city in the world. Nowadays, when tourists flock there, they do it mostly because of the extraordinary architecture and painting of that period lasting almost a hundred years."

"You won't believe it, but Mary and I've never made it to Amsterdam, although we've stayed for two weeks in Paris. Even to us, it's unclear why pharmacy and sociology, the university career, etcetera, are so important," said Paul pensively. Mary leaped in: "Wonderful, today we'll start afresh! You'll often cancel your lectures, we'll get married, travel to Amsterdam and Metz, you'll never be promoted to full professor..."

She realized those words were not funny and went on quickly: "Van der Stel acquired a sound knowledge of botany, agriculture, and viticulture. Under his management, many oaks were planted in Stellenbosch—it became the City of Oaks. Some are still living giants and have become national monuments."

Odile asked if she would be able to see those trees and mentioned that at home in Metz there were four ancient giant oaks. She also recalled the enormous baobab near Kruger they had seen. Célestin added: "Yes, we have two-hundred-year-old oaks with documents in their pockets! But the baobab was incredible, a memorable sight fitting an official 'national tree.' It beautified the town of Louis Trichardt, south of Musina. Sorry, we've interrupted you, Mary."

"Don't worry. Your manor must be quite something. Paul, we ought to go again to Kruger Park. You see, we've both been there on high school excursions but never together. And Odile, we'll be able to see some great-great-great-great-grandfather oaks in Stellenbosch because the first wineries were built next to them. Our brilliant and industrious Simon also planted the first grapevines in both Caypee and Stellenbosch. To top it all, he became an irrigation expert. With his Dutchmen, he built a system of ditches and canals through which water from the Eerste River flowed to the first mills and vineyards."

"Since our arrival in your fabulous country," said Célestin, "Odile and I were on numerous occasions amazed by what the African Dutchmen had accomplished in the seventeenth century." "We are glad to hear it," replied Mary. "As you know, Paul and I aren't of Dutch or Afrikaner descent, but we admire those people. They brought their knowledge and the habit of day and night toil. Of course, Hottentots and Bushmen had for centuries worked for minimal pay, yet they did receive incomparably more money than what they would've managed by themselves in these arid, inhospitable regions."

"Indeed," Paul exclaimed impatiently: "Without Dutchmen who became Afrikaners in the seventeenth century, there wouldn't exist either the gradually acquired fruitfulness of the land or the superb Cape wines. One would have global agribusiness and anonymous owners who would not be deeply rooted Africans."[2]

Célestin was relieved he could talk openly about his new friends, Groot Constantia's Olivia and Petry, without his exceptionally positive impressions leading to a vexing debate and ill feelings—which would have perhaps happened if these two were tendentious types. As if he had heard that internal monologue, Paul said: "You've no idea how I quarrel with my stubborn, allegedly leftist colleagues at the university, with many of whom I'm otherwise on reasonable terms. However, I doubt Mary and I could stay together if we didn't have similar opinions on this matter."

Everyone was quiet as they approached Stellenbosch. Southeast, a bare mountain with painterly nuances of gray on its rocks loomed above the town. Mary explained it was Simonsberg, with the elevation of a thousand three hundred meters. She then resumed bitterly discussing Paul's colleagues: "They refuse to speak about work and achievement—only about race and race, and so never tire of repeating that Simon van der Stel was of mixed race. Which is true. You see, his mother Maria Lievens, Adriaan's wife, was the daughter of an Indian lady, Monica of Goa, who'd been a freed slave but later married the merchant Hendrik Lievens. However, one needs to be aware that at the end of the sixteenth century, one could become enslaved regardless of race, wealth, and social position. The Indian Ocean and all the seas around it were infested with pirates, freebooters, and marauders. The kidnapped captive would be released after a huge payment."

---

2. Precisely when I began writing the novel in February of 2020, I learned that in accordance with the new South African law, Afrikaners would be forced to leave their centuries-old vineyards and their land would be divided and distributed. The politically correct Western globalizers remained silent.

Just then, Paul was parking the car at the Uiterwyk winery. A splendid giant oak stood by the entrance to the white Cape Dutch building. Odile could hardly wait to touch its bark. But Célestin pointed to the steep slopes of Simonsberg and told her: "*Regarde, ma fille*... In this crystal pure air, those sharp peaks seem so close, as if one could reach out and touch them." The sky resembled the insanely blue color one sees above Capri, the Adriatic, and the Aegean Sea.

14.

Their guide through the winery, and a courteous host at the tasting, was one of the middle three sons in the Afrikaner family De Waal, as the urbane young man described himself—there were five sons! He told them something they already knew: Almost all the owners of wineries in Stellenbosch and the entire Cape were Afrikaners. The young Mr. or *meneer* De Waal had received a degree in enology from the University of California in Davis and then spent a year at Robert Mondavi's winery in the Napa Valley north of San Francisco. "But in California, beautiful as so many things there are, you can't find something like this," he said proudly in the elegant Uiterwyk tasting hall: There were cut-glass chandeliers, a gorgeous French-style parquet floor, and doors and ceiling made of the traditional yellowwood in different shades. He added their *pater familias* had a fixation with authenticity. Not long before and without a real need—despite the opposition of his spouse and three sons, and ignoring the steep price—he ordered the modern roof on the main building to be removed and the traditional dark thatched roof placed there again. However, the young miser admitted, a new reliable method for protecting thatch from fire had been invented. At the end of the enjoyable tasting, they bought several bottles of Blanc de Noir 1978 and Riesling 1977.

Following the young man's advice, they went to have lunch in D'Ouwe Werf, The Old Wharf, a rural-style restaurant that had existed since 1802. They ate Greek salad and various cheeses and sausages with homemade bread. The wine lovers shared a half bottle of excellent Shiraz from the old winery Simonsig. Paul did not look envious and drank mineral water from Matjiesfontein with Odile. After lunch, they walked along Dorp Straat, Village Street, taking photos of many jewels of Cape Dutch architecture. Every house displaying a brass National Monument plaque had a thatched roof.

They visited other estates. The touchingly unpretentious winery Muratie had original cellars, barrels, and utensils from the beginning of the eighteenth century. A tall and wide oak tree had for more than two hundred years benevolently overseen the Muratie winemakers. They bought Chenin Blanc and drove southward to the Delheim estate, a large commercial wine business in the stunning setting of Simonsberg's foothills. The aesthetician in Célestin waxed poetic: "I've never seen dark conifers so close to vineyards. Consider the contrast in color, height, and *meaning*—and how the pines and grapevines are silhouetted against those gray, sharp, broken-up hills: Sheer beauty!" However, when an employee in the winery tried to sell them cheap Delheim glasses and winetasting coupons, Paul immediately took the guests out. "It's a question of principle," indignantly said the righteous sociologist.

A narrow red-earth track, some four kilometers long, led to Hartenberg, a wine estate founded in 1692. The road meandered through a picturesque landscape. Paul occasionally had to crawl because people of all ages were walking along the edges, many in colorful clothes. Almost every woman, with a child or two in tow, carried a sizable load on her head, which was not the case with a single man they passed. As usual, Odile's attention was drawn to children, but her father warned her: "Please don't gaze too intently. You always mean well, but those women may think you're arrogantly staring at them and their loads, not at their cute children." Mary visibly approved.

Parkland, a long *allée*, and an easygoing dog welcomed the visiting quartet at Hartenberg. Through the tall windows of the perfectly proportioned main building, one could see the lit chandeliers in the reception hall. A young vintner greeted them and led the way to a separate building where he showed them modern winemaking equipment. Afterward, he brought them to the tasting hall with its graceful chandeliers.

At a long yellowwood table on which bottles were lined up, several couples were seated far from each other. A gray-haired lady in her seventies, who barely mumbled her name—probably "Hartenberg"—was in charge, but it was obvious her heart was not in it. As she was limping, carrying bottles from guest to guest surely caused her pain. The other visitors were Germans who whispered to each other. Maybe the awkward, almost tense atmosphere influenced Mary and Célestin to consider the wines mediocre, particularly Zinfandel Primitivo. Or, they agreed, the better ones were not on offer. In any case, they left as soon as they could do it politely.

Beside the narrow track leading from Hartenberg, they found a spot to park and walk into the vineyard. The air was warm, fragrant. Around them were grapevines loved and treasured like babies. "What a climate, what a region, what soil, what vineyards," enthused Célestin again while hugging his daughter. He put a single grape in her mouth and then one in his own. "Thank you, dear friends, for bringing Odile and me to paradise!"

* * *

About twelve kilometers southeast of Stellenbosch, near the intersection of highways R102 and R310, there was a small dam creating a lake from the Eerste River's water. Several kilometers farther, a long shady driveway led to the imposing Cape Dutch building dating to 1693 at the Meerlust estate. That famed winery was not mentioned in the brochure Stellenbosch Wine Route, which meant it was not open to tourists for winetasting.

Nonetheless, a casually dressed elderly gentleman who was passing by greeted them amiably at the main entrance of the striking white edifice. On hearing they were looking for Mr. Cellarmaster, he led them down a long staircase to an office near the cellars. To a shortish dark-haired man in his forties, who immediately got up, he said in English: "Giorgio, it's your lucky day. A sweet girl of about ten, with three companions, is looking for you!"—at which he playfully winked at the wide-eyed Odile and disappeared up the stairs.

With a friendly chuckle, Giorgio welcomed them all. "Sent by Lissandri, but where is he?! I thought *signor professore* would also show up?" Paul looked at his watch: "Right now, at half past three, he's giving a lecture on the sociology of media—instead of me!" After introductions, the conversation soon centered on wine-making. Giorgio dalla Cia was the supreme master of the Meerlust cellars. He was from Udine in the Friuli region in the extreme northeast corner of Italy—as was Lissandri. On the wall, there was an impressive, framed certificate: Giorgio had been nominated *Cavaliere* by the president of Italy.

Elsewhere, Célestin noticed another framed certificate, the format of which seemed familiar. It resembled the award for Sauvignon Blanc he saw in Constantia. However, the certificate in Giorgio's office was for a wine called "Rubicon," awarded in 1980 to Meerlust proprietor Nicolaas Myburgh and cellar master Giorgio dalla Cia.

Célestin cuffed himself on the forehead: "Giorgio, listen, I must tell you something, perhaps you'll find it interesting. Two years ago, I heard from Marcel Sauveterre, a friend from Bordeaux and merchant dealing with Médoc wines, that an excellent new wine had been produced in South Africa, a blend by the name of Rubicon. I remember Marcel telling me Rubicon was 70% Cabernet Sauvignon, 20% Merlot, and 10% Cabernet Franc. Of course, I had no idea the wine originated in a winery called Meerlust nor that I would be invited here for the Pinot Noir harvest by your friend Lissandri, via Mary and Paul."

Everyone present gazed at him with amazement, most of all Giorgio, who said: "And I, of course, had no idea Lissandri would be sending me, unannounced, such a wine connoisseur as you are, Monsieur Célestin. Nor that he would do it via a colleague, Mr. Paul, who—it's hard to imagine—doesn't drink wine at all! You're now even more welcome. Anyway... The grape varietals and their proportions in Rubicon that you stated are correct. Your friend in Bordeaux is well informed. You see, the Meerlust boss Nicolaas Myburgh—the silver cup mentioned in the certificate you were reading is in his office upstairs—Nico and I had experimented for two years until we achieved something we were pleased with. You'll try it!

"As chance would have it, Nico is the gentleman who brought you down here. That's the way he is, always modest, witty, and direct, and his wife is the same. He is the seventh generation of Myburghs, who are one of the oldest Dutch families on the Cape: They've owned Meerlust since 1756 without interruption. God willing, Nico's son Hannes will inherit Meerlust as the eighth generation. Young Hannes speaks French and English and has spent a fair amount of time at Château Lafite in Médoc. You probably know the place." "Yes, I was there long ago," Célestin answered, "and also in the nearby Château Margaux and Château Latour."

Mary remained curious: "Giorgio, Paul, and I are delighted we've brought you a connoisseur, especially because we are simpletons about wine. But do tell us, why the name Rubicon?" Giorgio laughed: "The naming went like this. In Bordeaux, they've long been making blended wines, which was not the case in South Africa. Nico, however, having stayed several times in Médoc, reasoned they had breezes from the Atlantic and the Gironde estuary, but we had the Eerste River and the cooling breezes from the Indian Ocean: The terroir was comparable. We talked and experimented. When we finally decided to try it here, it was an irrevocable mental and financial choice after which we could not easily go back."

Giorgio abruptly addressed Odile: "*Cara signorina,* are you thirsty? I have fruit juices, please look in the fridge." While the girl was deciding, Giorgio addressed Paul: "Excuse me, Mr. Wino, I've forgotten you: Pellegrino, Evian, or Vichy?" They moved to a cozy tasting room and sat at a solid old table. Giorgio brought out Meerlust Rubicon 1980 and Meerlust Pinot Noir from the same year, explaining: "The formal, quite magnificent, tasting room is upstairs. It's for major customers and business partners. This one in the cellar is intimate, for my soul. Friends and connoisseurs from around the world come here."

Célestin asked Giorgio: "I'm thinking about the origin of the name Meerlust. Would you please tell us?" The cellarmaster recounted: "The first owner of the estate, Henning Hüsing, a settler probably from Germany, chose the name in 1693. According to the Myburgh lore, Hüsing intended to express something like 'craving or longing for the sea,' which is in keeping with our belief that cool breezes from the ocean are crucial for this terroir." The Frenchman smiled: "If he wished to express that, then he indeed was a German, not an Afrikaner—because '*meer*' means lake in Afrikaans, and '*lust*' is '*wellus*' in Afrikaans." Giorgio again stared at Célestin with bewilderment, whereas Odile enjoyed everything. Encouraged by her father's mini-lecture, she said: "Signor Giorgio, my papa is a *comparing* linguist!"

Both wines were exceptional in several respects, but he did not wish to impose by asking questions about aroma, color, and taste. Meanwhile, Odile was happily sipping the white-currant juice she chose because she had drunk it on top of Table Mountain. Their travel in South Africa was fascinating even after Kruger, she thought, mentally reviewing the variety of sights and occasions: A high mountain with steep sides and a flat top; a very deep hole with a phenomenal green lake at the bottom but no diamonds; and the rather sour-smelling wine cellar. There was so much talk about the "blended" wine on the table: The bottle had an almost black label. As for its name, she learned in school about the Rubicon River in northern Italy close to the Adriatic Sea and knew the meaning of Julius Caesar's exclamation, "*Alea iacta est!*" But what did it have to do with wine?

Giorgio had more to say about Rubicon. "Bergkelder, a major wine merchant, is now selling Rubicon 1980 for eleven rands, which is a bargain. It suits us because our plans and hopes are long-term. We're certain the twenty percent Merlot content will cause the wine to age handsomely and eventually yield an enviable price. But my friend, even though it's getting late, let's look at what's still happening in the winery, or else your daughter will fall asleep."

He took the guests to a separate building where many people were at work. A mass of Pinot Noir grapes, to which some green, unripe ones were added to increase freshness, was continuously sliding into a machine that broke the skin of the grapes and released the juice but without crushing the seeds, which would have produced a bitter tang.

Odile, Mary, and Paul were fascinated by the sight and Giorgio's explanations, but he liked best to talk to Célestin. The two got along swimmingly and managed, despite frequent interruptions, to carry out a long private conversation. Giorgio first came to South Africa as a quality control inspector for Stock, a company from Trieste that sold apéritifs, digestifs, and brandy. Having fallen in love with Cape Town and Stellenbosch, he had decided to stay but became increasingly troubled by the political situation.

The oenophile spoke to Giorgio about the wine-growing regions in France. He described the cellars at Château Margaux and the ancient winemaking implements at Château Palmer, both in Médoc. Opening up further, he mentioned Patrizia and how they climbed a wooded hillock next to the Loire, afterward enjoying the local goat cheese along with the driest Sauvignon Blanc from the nearby Sancerre estate. He remembered Veronique Quénard, owner of the bar Chablis, situated in the heart of the same-named village in Burgundy, three hundred kilometers west of Metz. Veronique was Patrizia's girlfriend from school but was born in Chablis where she knew everyone. She took them to taste wines at the best estates. How dry the world-famous Chablis was, with the taste, as was said locally, not of fruit but of gunflint! To avoid any effect of oak barrels on wine, fermentation was carried out in casks of stainless steel.

When it was time to leave, Odile had the difficult job of separating Giorgio from her father—and was the only one who dared to do it. Célestin received two bottles of Rubicon and a bottle of Pinot Noir as gifts. Mary and Paul got two bottles, of which one was for Lissandri. The girl did not leave empty-handed and carried off several bottles of white-currant juice in her very own wine tote bag.

She dozed on her papa's shoulder while Paul drove to Caypee. Mary suddenly said: "It's good news that at least some wealthy Afrikaners don't consider this country dangerous. You saw how we just strolled into the resplendent building in which there must be valuables and money in addition to wine. No trace of guards, steel gates, heavy iron locks, or Doberman Pinschers." Célestin agreed: "The situation in Groot Constantia, the home of the Van Schiltes, is similar." Knowing Mary and Paul much better by the end of the day, he could truthfully depict the visit to Olivia and Petry.

* * *

Jeroen Glott called: "Dad gave me your number and permission to call. I want to thank you wholeheartedly for the exquisite records you sent me. I'd heard that marvelous music before but only on mediocre cassette tapes at the music school. I was extremely surprised and happy when I received the package! Also, thank you for what you said to Dad about me."

"Nice of you to call," Célestin replied, "I was hoping you'd like my choice. But Jeroen, may I ask candidly: How are you?" After a few moments of silence, a tremulous voice was heard: "I suppose you're thinking of that Friday afternoon and my leaving home to find Mona. Well, she was behind the school with her group. It wasn't easy, but I brought her home after you and Odile had already left. She and I fought bitterly the whole way, and we've been arguing every day since. Mona, who's still a naive little girl, has managed to set all members of our family against each other. Sides switch hourly as harsh words are exchanged. She has endangered all of us. Dad most of all... Sorry, I didn't mean to vent, but you deserved a full explanation." Both voices were hopeless when saying goodbye.

Later, they went to a wine store because Célestin wanted to inspect Bergkelder's brochure. He discovered that in 1980, in addition to Rubicon receiving the First Prize Award, Nicolaas Myburgh was declared Champion Estate Wine Maker and Champion South African Wine Maker.

15

Before leaving for the hospital Groote Schuur, the "Big Barn," he made sure Odile had everything she needed at the Helmsley, as she studied, drew, and called Nicolette for a goodbye chat. From the windows, there was a lovely view of Table Mountain and Lion's Head.

A few minutes before eleven, he parked at the hospital. It was set near the center of Cape Town, about two kilometers north of the university. Devil's Peak stood guard behind it. By agreement a week earlier, Dr. Adriaan Momberg was waiting in the main reception area.

In that hospital fourteen years earlier, on the 3rd of December 1967, Dr. Christiaan Barnard had transplanted the heart that used to beat in the chest of Denise Darvall, who had died in a car accident, into the chest of Louis Washkansky, a Jewish man who had emigrated from Lithuania a year earlier. Fate! Célestin had long known of the epochal medical, philosophical, and religious significance of the event. Talking to Dr. Momberg, a cardiac surgeon at Groote Schuur, was an opportunity to learn something extraordinary. Cape Town meant much more than the South Atlantic, mountain climbing, and vineyards.

On seeing the Frenchman, Dr. Momberg quickly stepped forward to shake his hand with a welcoming smile while a nurse came running with a white coat. The two men smoothly agreed to be on a first-name basis. As they walked toward the elevator, the surgeon said: "Since you're not a medical doctor and—as far as I can tell—there's nothing wrong with your heart, I think two things are probably of the greatest interest to you here..." Other people were in the elevator, so Adriaan waited for the third floor where Cardiology was located. "Let's go to my office and later have some tea. We have a decent café on this floor."

After greetings from Adriaan's secretary, Célestin was seated in the surgeon's office: *"Ergo*, two things," his host continued. "Above all, the first man-to-man heart transplantation and what followed it. And second, hmm, the controversial racial issues—

let's put it that way—concerning the people involved in those surgeries and also more generally in this hospital. Am I right?" The visitor studied the courteous, dignified Afrikaner about seven or eight years older than himself. Despite penetrating blue eyes, his countenance and voice were kind and cultivated. "Yes, you've summed up my curiosity better than I could've done," he said after a brief delay.

Adriaan smiled: "All right, you're obviously aware of the two transplantations Dr. Barnard carried out. I was present at both—not in the main operating room, for I was still a young cardiac surgeon, whereas Christiaan had his brother Marius and a team of about thirty most experienced men—but in one of the support rooms. However, do you know about the unseemly debate, a truly nasty quarrel, which took place in the country after the second case?"

"Yes, I've read about it. In the first transplantation, both the donor and the recipient were white people. But in the second, the donor was a so-called Cape Coloured person, and an ugly argument broke out. Am I right?" Adriaan did not hesitate: "That's right. In the second transplantation, at the beginning of 1968, the donor was Clive Haupt, a 'Kaapse Kleurling' young man, only twenty-five years old, who had collapsed on the beach, and the recipient was a middle-aged white dentist by the name of Philip Blaiberg. The so-called public opinion was often hideous, and there were highly unfavorable criticisms of South Africa around the world. Meanwhile, Philip Blaiberg—I spoke to him many times—lived for nineteen and a half months during which a 'coloured' heart kept ticking in him."

They quietly gazed at each other. "I and the other Afrikaner surgeons—but most of all Dr. Barnard himself—were horribly embarrassed by the quarrels and the disgusting insinuations," Adriaan continued seriously. "Christiaan spoke very bravely about it! But the truth of the matter was best expressed by Edward Darvall, the father of Denise. After giving consent for her heart to be transplanted into Louis Washkansky's chest, he said: 'Help for someone who suffers doesn't know racial prohibitions.' At that time, poor Mr. Darvall, a good man who even wasn't a religious believer, didn't dare to utter much stronger words to the journalists interviewing him, but the vast majority of us at Groote Schuur felt them and spoke them."

Lost in thought, Adriaan softly drummed on the table and at last said: "Things have changed somewhat since then, at least in our hospital. For instance, only several years ago, it was unthinkable for a Cape Coloured and a white person to have beds in the same room—regardless of the urgency of the situation and even if the white patient was under deep sedation. Now it's different. All of us here hope it's different because it's more humane, not because of practicality."

The host walked to the long shelves filled to bursting with medical books and brought to Célestin a massive leather-bound volume. It was a Groote Schuur photo album commemorating the first two successful heart transplantations in the world: Operating rooms, equipment in detail, donors and recipients, and all the surgeons, anesthesiologists, nurses, and technicians. Christiaan and Marius Barnard were the first among the surgeons, and a very young-looking Adriaan Momberg among the last. The guest took twenty minutes looking through the album. He was honored to see the photographic record of such a significant event in medical history and gratefully said so.

They went to the café with a view of Devil's Peak and talked for a long time. At parting, Adriaan walked out with the visitor and conveyed greetings to Odile. Célestin said: "In a few days, we're returning to France. Once there, I'll call Dr. Jean Bataille about a visit to Metz. I don't know how to thank you for this candid dialogue, but here's a token." A bottle of Rubicon emerged from the car.

16.

It was time to say goodbye to the people they befriended. Odile called the Glotts and asked, to Laurel's delight, to speak to Luise, while her father telephoned Carl Goode in Joburg and described the time they had spent in Stellenbosch with Mary and Paul.

The following day, a Sunday, they spent swimming and relaxing, but in the evening went to hear André once more and invite him to Metz. He was delighted: "Perhaps I can even get a pub engagement as a stand-up comedian? I've seen Odile in stitches listening to my French." He offered to drive them to the airport on the 10th of February, which Célestin declined. The Paris flight left at six in the morning—a taxi would do.

During his next break, André asked his new friend: "Are there things in Caypee and South Africa you wish you'd seen or done?" After an exchange of glances with Odile, he said: "Yes, there are many things we haven't managed to do. This unreal, astounding country gave us a lot but kept even more out of our reach. The Kalahari Desert remains a dream. We haven't returned to Kruger to stroke our Lady Giraffe again and send a kiss, across a stream, to our graceful monsieur Cheetah in Mozambique—or mademoiselle?" Célestin smiled at Odile and went on: "I even had an invitation from Casper, a ranger in Kruger, to fly in his helicopter over the Oliphant and Limpopo Rivers. But regarding the Cape region, there's also much we haven't seen: Paarl, Bloubergstrand, even 'Crossroads.' But the least excusable omission we'll certainly avoid: Tomorrow we'll be off to the Cape of Good Hope! *D'accord, ma princesse?*"

* * *

From Sea Point, they drove south along the same coastal road that had enchanted them a week earlier—all the way to the incomparable Noordhoek Beach where the mysterious horseback rider was absent. They continued farther south reaching Kommetjie—with its unsightly houses inhabited by poor black families and an occasional white one. After the village of Scarborough, the road again climbed into the hills where they soon entered the wild Cape of Good Hope Nature Reserve.

Over the next eleven kilometers, Célestin noted the same sequential change of scenery he had observed during his approaches elsewhere to *finis terrae*—ends of the land. He remembered Cabo de São Vicente, the southwestern corner of Europe in

Portugal, an important Cape with a similar climate: Trees gradually became smaller, then dwarfish, until they disappeared altogether; shrubs were crooked under the assault of the winds, fighting for life; and at the end, there were only rocks. A touching, brutal sight.

There were no living creatures anywhere, except for an occasional family of stunted Cape baboons. The small animals were joylessly chewing orange peels they had found in knocked-over trash cans. Several kilometers from the Cape, Célestin drove a short distance off the road and stopped in front of a cross dedicated to Bartolomeu Dias, who was, in 1488, the first navigator to sail around the Cape of Good Hope. Dom Bartolomeu was a nobleman from the Portuguese royal family, but a courageous sailor: He called the cape Cabo das Tormentas, Cape of Storms.

Near the cross, Célestin found an even narrower track. The steep slope ended on a dune about a hundred meters above a deserted, gorgeous, westward-looking beach. It was tiny, with startlingly white sand. They came out of the car and for a long time gazed, with arms around each other, at the agitated waves. "Look how perfectly, but in an always different form, they're inexorably breaking," he whispered. "And they're doing it all over our incredible planet at this moment."

Dressed in T-shirts and shorts, they romped down to the beach and frolicked on the soft sand. "It's ice-cold," laughed the girl joyfully, teeth chattering, after they had stepped into the ocean to her knees. "Naturally it's icy. This is still the Atlantic, and now we're even closer to the Antarctic than when swimming in Caypee." They walked out of the water, but after a few steps, he turned again toward the ocean: Aquamarine waves with frothy tops; deep blue sky; a heavenly day; the famous Cape so close... "It's dangerous to swim here, who knows what the currents are like, one could be carried around the corner into the Indian Ocean!" he exclaimed almost cheerfully. "But you know me, *mon bijou*, I must get my whole body and head wet." Odile was not surprised; on the contrary, she remembered Baikal: "I want to do it too!"

So off came their simple clothes, and they ran into the ocean naked. When the water reached Odile's chest, they grabbed each other's hands and merrily bounced up and down—she squealing and shrieking, he yelling and roaring. Then they jumped out onto the beach and cavorted to get dry. Still out of breath, they got dressed and holding hands silently surveyed the ocean.

There was hardly enough space on the dune, but Célestin managed to turn the Rover around and crawl uphill, back to the track, where driving south they soon reached a sign that read, "3 km to the Cape." At the end of the road was a small parking area and a dilapidated kiosk. Its door banged forlornly, and more paint seemed to peel off with each gust of wind. It was a woebegone, disconsolate landscape devoid of life. Even for the baboons, the place was too desolate.

They quickly climbed a stony hillock and then a steep metal staircase. Once on top, their astonished eyes encountered an endless horizon. The next continent, under its gigantic shackles of ice, was the Antarctic. Utterly alone, they were at the bottom of Africa, the majestic green-black continent—although those colors were absent on the Cape. Odile and Célestin again held hands for several minutes. It was a solemn moment for them, as it would have been for all living souls who adored their planet.

However, they wished to be even closer to the spot where two grand world oceans collided and mingled. Gingerly, albeit still foolishly, they climbed down the steep slope until any progress became suicidal. Creeping under a rocky overhang, they found space for three—but their Olya was inexpressibly far. In the abyss, the oceans boomed and leaped up high. They inhaled the salty spray for a long time...

PART ELEVEN

Ice on the Wine-Dark Sea

1.

After their return from the Cape of Good Hope, Célestin and Odile had only one day to say adieu, in their thoughts, to the incredible country and a city like no other. Both had fallen headlong in love with South Africa and Cape Town, the Dutch-Afrikaner Kaapstad. They were feeling almost at home, but there were nevertheless diverse conflicting emotions in their hearts, including stormy ones.

In the late morning of the last day, they went to the university. They could not say goodbye to Rose: After her strongly worded resignation, she did not reappear. Nelius and John proposed driving them to the airport, but their offers were cordially declined. While having coffee at the student cafeteria with the forever-engaged happy couple, Mary gallantly but uselessly claimed to be willing to arise before daybreak...

They returned the car to the Avis office in the city center. The handsome vehicle, their "doggie Rover," served them loyally for six weeks and one day. "It seems to me we'll buy our Rover's brother in Metz. It will be perfect for negotiating tracks on our estate and elsewhere in Lorraine," Célestin said. Odile was delighted to hear it because she could resume driver education on an old chum.

Because Avis did not have an office at the airport, an agency driver returned them from the city office to the Helmsley. The company also booked a cab for the next morning at 4:15 a.m. and paid for it. The Air France flight took off precisely at 6:00, landed in Zurich for an hour and a half, and arrived at Paris Charles de Gaulle at 9:00 p.m.

Three days later, Célestin went to the Air France office in Metz without anyone knowing it. He bought two tickets for the night flight from Paris to Tokyo, departing on the 5th of March and arriving on the 6th at the new Tokyo airport in Narita, which opened only four years earlier. From the thirteenth of February, when he purchased the tickets, there remained only a month to the fourteenth of March, the rendezvous with Dima and Lyuda at Cape Soya on Hokkaido Island in Japan. "Little time is left: February is short and 1982 isn't a leap year," he calculated nervously.

It was high time to tell Odile they would be traveling to Japan. He did it gently, minutely explaining why it was essential for the fates of not just Olya, but also Dima, Kolya, and their spouses, that she be given as little time as possible to reveal accidentally the trip to anyone: No chatter about the trip with her girlfriends, please! The temptation was understandable because Japan is so exotic, but... There would be plenty of time for entertaining stories after their return. Since the absence would last only two weeks, the school would be informed at the eleventh hour. In Paris, the following Saturday, they would buy clothes appropriate for the severe Hokkaido winter. "You'll see yourself in a fur coat and hat," he promised.

2.

The 1982 winter brought an abundance of snow to Lorraine, so the manor grounds were covered. Riding was impossible, but Odile spent time with Pasha in the stable gently talking and grooming her. Gilles and the people from the estate fought frequent blizzards by cleaning the paths diligently. Célestin often joined them. The track from the garage was the most important because he insisted on driving Odile to school himself. As the end of February approached, he regularly monitored the state of the Paris airport and was relieved that until the beginning of March, not a single flight had been canceled. No problem arose with school—neither the grades nor permission to be absent.

On Friday the 5th of March, Célestin and Gilles were waiting at the school for lessons to finish. At three o'clock, the girl flew into the car exclaiming, "*Japon, nous arrivons!*" During the three-hour drive to Charles de Gaulle, she changed from school uniform into travel clothes. At the airport, Gilles was entrusted with the school bag and received kisses on his cheeks. They easily completed airport formalities before their twelve-hour Air France night flight to Tokyo, which departed on time, at eight p.m. Odile slept like a baby throughout the flight, dreaming of herself not in a kimono, but a fur coat: An authentic *fille européenne*.

He woke her up when the plane was circling above Tokyo—that stupendous, gloomy, winterish, and for the two of them utterly incomprehensible megalopolis. Due to the seven-hour time difference, it was three in the afternoon on the 6th of March in Narita. They passed smoothly through passport control and found the gate from which the Japanese company JAL would take them to Sapporo, the capital of Hokkaido. The DC8-82 plane on which they would fly in an hour was within minutes of arriving from Hawaii. All airport employees spoke poor English, successfully compensating with exceptional courtesy. There were no languages other than Japanese and English at the by far biggest international airport in Japan.

They awaited the boarding call, barely comprehending they were after two years again in Asia—but in a country they did not know at all. After a short while, the murmur of passengers arriving from Hawaii brought father and daughter to a fully awake state. The arrivals were Japanese but many had tanned faces, quite unlike the gray of those waiting to board the flight. The majority were young couples, some with arms lovingly around each other, others walking wide apart. But happy or not, each person, male and female, wore a flower necklace. Célestin answered Odile's question: "Most of them seem to be returning honeymooners, but other passengers are also wearing what is called a *lei*. I've read they give them at Honolulu airport to all passengers, arriving and departing; it's a clever tourist move." "*Mais Papa*, the flowers seem wilted!" observed Odile.

During the two-hour flight to Sapporo, he was occupied by

various thoughts, not all pertinent to the meeting at Cape Soya. One was that the young Japanese tourists, born long after the end of the war in the Pacific, undoubtedly had no problems with Americans in Honolulu—especially because Japan had obtained and kept a privileged semi-vassal status. But what would happen if a Japanese man in his seventies arrived in Honolulu as a tourist? On the 7th of December 1941, when over three hundred fifty dive bombers, fighters, and torpedo bombers attacked Pearl Harbor, that septuagenarian would have been around thirty. Some persons on Oahu Island might think the skinny elderly tourist was a hated pilot bombardier responsible for the deaths of their family members. Nevertheless, exhaustion overwhelmed Célestin's irksome speculations.

Late in the evening, they were resting in their suite on the ninth floor of the hotel Aspen. It was in the center of Sapporo, three hundred meters east of the University of Hokkaido and its botanical gardens, and equally far north of the main train station. Even though many Japanese elements were included in the design of the foyer of the hotel, their two rooms and bathroom were in the Euro-American style, except for a few graceful details. That was precisely what Célestin wanted. For him and Odile, it was the beginning of a crucial business trip, so to speak, rather than an opportunity to discover a high-level traditional *ryokan*.

3.

While taking a shower and dressing the next morning, he watched the news on a Japanese television station; in their suite № 915, there were no less than four TV sets. Famished, father and daughter arrived for breakfast at eight.

The *maître d'hôtel* and several waiters, all in European-style black-and-white suits and shirts, made Japanese bows when the pair entered the elegant restaurant on the third floor. They were shown two ellipsoid tables, one with Japanese dishes, with the addition of some Chinese and Indian items, and the other for the Euro-American taste, where French cuisine was well represented. The maître d' looked worriedly around the dining hall and deeply bowed again, saying there was no free table at which they could sit alone. Would they mind waiting a short time at the bar? Or should he ask one of the chefs who was from Paris to apologize in French? Or would they mind joining the gentleman sitting alone at a table for six? In that case, would they wait a minute for him to obtain the guest's consent?

When Célestin immediately chose the last option, the maître d' trotted to a large table next to a window and bowed whispering to the occupant. Soon he returned saying the guest would be delighted to share the table with a gentleman from France and his daughter. In an undertone, he added that the guest was a famous artist who spoke English fluently. While they were approaching the table, the man stood up and waited for them with a broad smile. He was in his late seventies, distinguished-looking and balding, with a slender body and erect posture. His face was ascetic and seemingly a mélange of Japanese and European. The Frenchman was certain he had somewhere seen photographs of the man from an earlier period.

"Isamu Noguchi... or since we're in Japan, Noguchi Isamu," the gentleman said politely, offering his hand to Célestin, who introduced himself and Odile. The sudden recognition in his mind's recesses of an ancient memory produced shivers in the back of his neck.

"I know who you are, Mr. Noguchi! My daughter and I are honored to make your acquaintance. You may not believe it, but you and I have a long history, if one can say so. You see, when I was about sixteen years old, my grandfather Olivier de Quernevelle, Odile's great-grandfather," he looked fondly at the girl, "took me from Metz to Paris to visit museums. One day, we found ourselves near Champ de Mars from where one could see the UNESCO building. My grandpa, who was a passionate gardener, remembered reading that a Japanese Garden had been opened nearby. He didn't know who the designer was or the landscape architect. Needless to say, we were curious about Japan, the land of mystery. Not to bore you, Grandpa and I took a long walk in your superb garden. That was the first time I read your name. Your birth year, 1904, was also written on the plaque. Olivier chuckled—you were exactly ten years younger than him! It was also stated you were born in Los Angeles, which hardly fitted with either your name or the Zen garden. Anyway, I never forgot it. Subsequently, I read descriptions of your accomplishments in many journals of art and design. I know you've worked throughout the world."

Noguchi gazed at Célestin reflectively, then glanced at Odile, and again looked at her father. He was moved—moved as an artist, not as a teary old man. "That's a touching story, Sir, thank you! There's no artist, nor any creative person, who wouldn't be honored to sit with you in my place... Listen, I'm busy this afternoon, and I'm flying to Tokyo in the evening, but right now I'm not in a hurry. We can have a leisurely talk. Please get something to eat first, the food on both tables is outstanding."

After ladling *miso* soup into bowls, they added dried seaweed and soy sauce. The sticky white Japanese rice required an egg to be cracked over it. Célestin had seen all that in a movie and liked it, without having a good idea what the taste would be. To have something to eat in case the seaweed proved unpalatable, they took brioches and croissants from the European table. And several madeleines: The French chef certainly used the pastry's original recipe from their Lorraine.

"Mr. Noguchi, if you don't mind, are you in Sapporo for a professional reason?" Célestin asked. "I am—and will explain later," the artist replied. "Besides, I love Hokkaido. It's a wondrous island, there's nothing like it in Japan. Stunning nature! And there are numerous traces of the aboriginal Ainu people, which modern Japan is destroying systematically. I even love Sapporo, although it's the least traditional and historic of all Japanese cities. The centenary was celebrated only about a dozen years ago: It was born in 1868 with the modern Meiji Japan."

"What you say about Sapporo is interesting. Your Zen sensibility in design is well known, yet you love this city. It's certainly handsome and modern, but... Already yesterday, coming by taxi from the airport, I noticed that major streets formed American-style rectangular city blocks. I admit I 'know' it only from films, for I've never been to America."

"You're not mistaken. Sapporo owes its plan to an American who was invited here to establish an agricultural college in the seventies of the last century. He gave lectures with a Bible on the lectern and imposed rectangles on the unsuspecting fledgling city as something desirable. Still, he founded a college that grew into a solid university. The fabulous botanical garden was also his idea. You must visit it. The ground will be under snow, but the trees are remarkable."

"And yes, it is a little odd that I like Sapporo so much. There are two reasons. The first is that I am full of contradictions," Noguchi said with a self-deprecating smile. "After all, my father was a forbidding Japanese man and my mother a wild Irish woman. The second... Well, you see, I adore human voice in music, most of all in opera, and it so happened I came to Sapporo for the first time in 1974 to attend an unforgettable vocal performance. City fathers had sent me an invitation and paid for my trip—already at that time they had a project in mind, but more about it later. The performance was by the operatic diva Maria Callas in front of two thousand people. It was her last concert in public, and I remember it took place on the 11th of November. Something magical and unforgettable. I had the opportunity to talk to madame Callas alone for half an hour. What a lady, what a woman she was!"

Odile ate slowly, listening to the conversation. A new side to Papa was emerging. He had many well-known friends, but they were all in the same profession and on par with him. However, with Mr. Noguchi, she saw Papa for the first time in a dialogue with someone whom he—judging by his words and small gestures—genuinely admired. More to the point, the Japanese man was twice her father's age and world-renowned for something Papa greatly appreciated. That something was art: He loved it but did not engage in it. Except for photography, she remembered. In any case, the gentleman treated her father with much respect, which had to be, she decided, because of Papa's other qualities.

The observant Mr. Noguchi thought his interlocutor might be worried about his daughter being bored, although that certainly was not the conclusion he reached looking at those bright eyes. Nevertheless, not knowing what would come from the girl, Noguchi innocently asked where she had traveled before coming to Japan. The response was calmly worded: "Well, Mr. Noguchi, we were in China, Mongolia, Russia, Israel, Kenya, and South Africa—but during the entire time, I never had to repeat a class!" Isamu and Célestin laughed, and Odile talked about the Cape of Good Hope, her freshest African adventure. When Noguchi asked the girl about Table Mountain, he received detailed instructions for climbing it.

"I notice you love capes, ends of the earth. They are indeed an amazing geographic phenomenon," Noguchi said. "I also love them. Here on Hokkaido, there are two of great interest. One is Cape Soya at the extreme north end of the island, only about forty kilometers from Russia—across the sea, of course. But I don't recommend it at this time of year: Snow, winds, bitter cold." Father and daughter covertly glanced at each other. "The second is Kamui *misaki*, Cape Kamui," the artist went on, "where you could go. Gales may be blowing there too in this season, but Kamui isn't Soya, and it's even more beautiful. It's about a hundred kilometers from here, to the northwest. The mountains, the sharp rocks, the Sea of Japan—all prepossessing! If you're lucky for the sun to show up, you'll see a divine color of the sea, such that doesn't exist anywhere. It's called Shakotan blue. The concierge in our hotel will tell you how to get there, the road is good."

"Thank you very much, I think we'll do it, won't we, Odile?" She was overjoyed. It would be wonderful to see a new cape, maybe covered by snow, and surrounded by a Japanese sea of an unusual, marvelous color. Célestin said: "But please, Mr. Noguchi, don't forget to tell us what you have twice postponed. If it's not a secret, are you working on a new project in Sapporo?"

Noguchi analyzed his new acquaintance with the wisdom of his seventy-eight years, most of them spent swimming in the piping hot lava on three continents called "the artworld." Soon he decided to describe his project to the sophisticated cosmopolite he had fortuitously encountered. He felt the need to talk to someone like Célestin before the final meeting that afternoon with the Mayor of Sapporo and his team. The widely traveled French linguist knew much about art and aesthetics but was not an artist. The thought he would blabber to a member of some rival international art clique was ludicrous. And so, Noguchi Isamu took out a map of Sapporo, a sketchbook, and a black felt-tip pen from his bulging briefcase. "The same sketch pad I have," Odile thought proudly.

4.

"Well before 1974, the Sapporo city fathers were planning a new park as an important segment of the green belt," Noguchi began while spreading a detailed map on the table. "Apparently, I'd been their prime design candidate from the start. Just a day after the farewell concert by the magnificent diva, they offered me a vast tract of almost two hundred hectares some ten kilometers northeast of the city center," he showed the location. "I was in Sapporo several times during the seventies, and they continually upped the pressure. In the respectful Japanese manner, naturally."

Noguchi continued, deep in thought: "First of all, they dried the marshlands and regulated the course of the Fushiko River. By 1977, they had purchased land that did not belong to the city and turned it into a garbage dump as I had proposed. You see, I've long been dreaming that a couple of cute hillocks would eventually arise in the park. And scheming! Heaps of trash are a convenient and cheap substrate."

Célestin used a pause in Noguchi's exposition to show Odile the locations of their hotel and the future park on the map. The artist followed her questions with a beatific smile. Looking somewhere far through the window, he went on: "The park will be called 'Moerenuma.' In the Ainu language, 'moyre pet' means 'slow-flowing river,' while 'numa' is 'swamp' in Japanese. I insisted there be at least something symbolic for the Ainu people. By the way, as Japanese bosses go, the mayor is young. He appreciates art and artists and is ambitious and hard-working. For instance, he called a meeting of his entire team with me for today, a Sunday."

"Very interesting, so what's next?" asked Célestin. "Today, the whole thing will probably be finalized, although my formal appointment, for budgetary reasons, will not happen until the beginning of 1984. In my briefcase here, I have sketches and diagrams of almost all the objects that will be erected; their team has seen them." One by one, Noguchi took out the completed designs, lining them on the table. For a long while, they studied the drawings, some of which had enigmatic names: *Mountain Moere, Sea Fountain, Children's Hill, Top of the Amphitheater, Cherry Orchard, Moere Beach,* and *Tetra Hillock.*

Noguchi closely observed their faces and could not decide who was more delighted—the child or the adult. That was precisely what he wanted for the park. The artist was happy.

Because Odile was not shy, she and her father alternated praising the designs and asking questions. Noguchi then returned the drawings to his briefcase, leaving only the sketchbook on the table. One could not divine what would happen next.

"I've kept you in the dark about the most important object in the park—you and the mayor! He knows there'll be another large-scale, expensive structure but will find out only today what it is. Some background information is necessary. You, Mr. De Quernevelle, have certainly heard of the eminent American architect of Chinese descent Ieoh Ming Pei, or I. M. Pei, as he usually introduces himself in the West. I know him personally and respect him. You see, three years ago, the Presidential Library of John F. Kennedy was opened in Boston, an excellent building for which I. M. Pei was the chief architect. However, I and others familiar with the politics and other goings-on behind major architectural events knew that Ieoh Ming had first unsuccessfully proposed a glass pyramid for the Library.

"Still, the glass pyramid undoubtedly remained in his head. And as the unfailing architect gossip soon enough revealed, your

President Mitterrand, hmm..." He hesitated, smiling: "I don't know if he is 'yours,' or not, but you are, after all, French—well, it emerged monsieur Mitterrand would in 1984 announce the result of a competition, or an alleged competition, for the design of the new entrance to the Louvre Museum. And the winner will be, mark my words, I. M. Pei with his glass pyramid!"

As the end of the complicated story loomed, Célestin and Odile were excited. With elbows on the table and arms calmly crossed, Noguchi pressed on: "But *I've* had a glass pyramid in my mind's eye for over ten years and have recently decided to place it in Moerenuma! I'm certain both the Ainu people and the Zen-inclined Japanese will be thrilled because the pyramid will be full of sunshine and have an irregular shape." He opened the pad and sketched his pyramid with lightning speed. It was a croquis featuring a cherry orchard—"hommage to Chehov," Noguchi smiled gently—and a bend of the Fushiko River in the background. The pyramid was in the foreground: Transparent and with parts cut off at unpredictable angles, it looked highly imaginative, unique.

"I believe Ieoh Ming's pyramid at the Louvre will have a regular shape. He'll most likely use the design he developed for the Kennedy Library, which simply had to have the classical pyramidal form. That's because something irregular would have insinuated a lack of respect for the assassinated president in the puritanical eyes of many Americans. Zen, in contrast, freely and unpredictably twists and wriggles; remember my Japanese Garden in Paris.

"There's another important thing. The pyramid Pei will erect in Paris is only the Louvre's entrance. A memorable decorative entrance... but only that. In contrast, my glass pyramid will be multifunctional. There'll be space for a small library, for sculptures, and a chamber music hall—as well as areas in which children will play unimpeded and wedding ceremonies and visitors' picnics take place. There'll be water and greenery throughout." It was becoming clear that Noguchi Isamu was a prophet of the future of design.

The designer cum landscape architect was not finished: "I don't know where exactly the glass pyramid will be. I have, you see, a diagram in mind of the whole park, with everything in place, but I've so far avoided putting the plan on paper. I keep moving the objects around like chess pieces. Much depends on the location of the entrances to the park—I'd like there to be only two—and on how the nearby traffic will be regulated. But I'm not an expert on urbanism."

"Take a look at Odile," said Célestin. "You can see she's enchanted. And I don't doubt you've always envisaged your park as a place where children of all ages would be playing. So, there's advance proof, right at this table, you'll succeed. But may I ask you something much more prosaic and yet very important: Once the plan is bureaucratically formalized in 1984, when will they begin to build? And when do they expect to finish?"

Absently, as if hypnotized, the great artist kept clinking his empty teacup against the saucer. He was becoming older with each passing moment. After a minute or two, he said in a suddenly lifeless voice: "They promised to start in 1988, work as fast as possible, and finish in ten years. Even though they're Japanese—usually industrious and well-organized—who knows? In any case, I'll not live long enough to see the result. Moerenuma Park is my swan song... one I will not hear."

5.

While ambling through the modern center of Sapporo, they dwelled on Noguchi and Moerenuma Park. "Papa, couldn't we visit the area where the park will be? Wouldn't that be interesting?" He thought otherwise: "*Non, ma chérie*, we won't do it. Didn't you hear there's still a garbage dump there? Not to mention the recent rain, snow, and muddy ground. I think the place as it is now would leave an ugly picture in our minds. We'll wait until we return to Sapporo in about fifteen years when you're twenty-five!"

Snow was removed from the main paths in the Botanical Gardens Isamu had recommended, but under the trees, it was ample, perhaps twenty centimeters deep. In a distant corner, they came to a fenced-off oval area with a sign in Japanese and English that read "Zen Rock Garden." However, the entire Zen creation was covered by snow and thus could not be distinguished from a neglected ice hockey rink. When Célestin made a joke, Odile objected: "But Papa, don't you see the big white rock protruding from the snow over there? It doesn't look like a frozen goalie!"

The collection of trees included specimens from the whole world, but mostly China, Korea, the Philippines, and every corner of Japan. All were a feast for the eyes, even the bare deciduous ones.

* * *

The morning was windless, with the temperature around zero and cloudy skies. They inquired at the front desk of the Aspen about Cape Kamui, so passionately recommended by Mr. Noguchi Isamu, their fascinating new friend. The manager assured them Kamui was a special region and reachable in early March. Otaru, a town on the Sea of Japan about forty-five kilometers west of Sapporo, was at almost the halfway point, with many buses going there. Beyond Otaru, there were sixty-five kilometers to Kamui, and transportation was problematic. So Célestin booked a car with a driver for the next day. Twenty-five thousand yen, slightly more than a hundred dollars, would secure a comfortable vehicle with snow tires. They could communicate with the driver in English—although when he said it, the manager smiled timidly, implicitly asking for understanding.

Having firmly decided to travel to the small town of Wakkanai near Cape Soya already on the 11th of March, they bought tickets for the train leaving at 7:48 a.m. and arriving at 2:56 p.m. Even with few hours of daylight in the winter of northern Hokkaido, they would have two days to find their bearings and look into transportation to Cape Soya. Their caution when Olya's fate was in question had no limit.

From the main train station, it was only a dozen minutes to the heart of Sapporo, Odori Park. It was a hundred-meter-wide, though over a kilometer-long, ribbon with gorgeous greenery, sculptures, and playgrounds. The fountains had obviously been switched off, and there was no purple lilac in bloom that adorns Odori each May, but the playgrounds were full of shrieking children with red cheeks.

Near the park, they boarded a subway running westward on the Tozai Line and got off at Maruyama-Koen station. They found themselves in a handsome modern suburb and after a brief walk arrived at the foot of Mount Maru—a "*yama*" that would elsewhere, with its elevation of two hundred twenty-five meters, be only an average hill. Father and daughter were told there was a nice view of Sapporo from the top, but they did not feel like climbing through the snow to see a modern city spread out in the flatland.

Instead, they visited the Hokkaido Jingu, the first Shinto shrine in their lives. It was brand new, erected only three years earlier, although even the original one had been less than a hundred years old when it burned down. After they had climbed a dozen stone stairs to the *torii* of dark wood, Odile began to walk toward the tall gate, but Célestin took her hand and bypassed the torii. "Darling, I've read that the passage through the torii in Shinto shrines is reserved for gods. Also, one must not take photos of the shrine when standing in front of the torii, which seemed an arrogant newfangled rule: Nothing about photography could've been written in the original Shinto books from the eighth century."

While strolling along the broad stone walkway, he continued: "'Shinto' means 'the way of the gods'—in Chinese! Nevertheless, it's the only authentic Japanese religion. It contains many elements of animism and shamanism. You recall we talked about that in connection with Eskimos, or Inuits, and also the indigenous people in North America—Karl May's 'Indians.' In Shinto, there are hundreds of gods called *kami*, who are thought to be the spirits of forces or principles in nature, such as the sea, rivers, mountains, wind, and even courage and fertility. One of the four kami in this shrine, according to my book, to which the priests and believers bow and pray, is the spirit of Emperor Meiji. You read about Meiji just last night."

Before entering the shrine, Odile admitted she had difficulty understanding Shinto spirits. He kissed her on the head: "I can't accept the eccentric variety of their gods either. Moreover, whereas it would indeed be wonderful if the people to whom such diversity is dear lived in harmony not only with nature but also with people they consider different from themselves, the bitter truth is..." In the shrine, they encountered silence, otherworldliness, beauty, and aloofness.

Much later, when they were returning along Odori toward their hotel, he expounded: "I didn't want to tell you this while we were in the shrine, but precisely from the time of Emperor Meiji—from the seventies of the last century, and during the entire first half of our century, so about seventy-five long years—Shinto was Japan's State Religion. And an unabashedly chauvinist one. Remember our insufferable Frenchman Nicolas Chauvin? Yes, Shinto was heavily involved in all of Japan's wars, often very dirty ones."

6.

Katsura Katsumi, their fortyish chauffeur, was standing next to the open back door of a dark-gray Toyota when father and daughter emerged from the Aspen on the dot. He made separate bows to Célestin and Odile and gaily said: "Sir and Miss, please to call me Katsu!" Thus they departed for Cape Kamui.

A white silk curtain hung on the rear window. Katsu wore a severe dark suit and white shirt. His tie's color matched the car's. He wore impeccably white gloves, as did all cabbies and bus drivers in Japan. The black chauffeur's cap bore the name of the rental company in gold lettering above the brim. The only personal contribution Katsu had made was that his cap sat slightly askew.

He drove soberly, never exceeding sixty kilometers an hour. "This Mr. Katsu is driving too slowly; I'd prefer Papa at the wheel," Odile thought. It was out of the question for the driver to smoke, even though there was a half-empty pack of cigarettes below the dashboard. Katsu offered music only once and did not seem disappointed when the passengers declined. He never initiated a conversation but briefly responded to short questions, not taking his eyes off the road. "Papa, I just remembered our somber driver Pyotr on Lake Baikal. And Oksana, I must write to her soon." In his mind, thoughts of Baikal instantaneously flew to Olya in Kuybyshev. Soon he would know a great deal: Only five more days!

After twenty kilometers of tedious Sapporo suburbs, they emerged on the seashore. "It's called the Sea of Japan," Célestin announced. "And if you'd fly like a bird straight across the sea over there," he pointed to the northwest, "you'd arrive in Russia! It's four hundred fifty kilometers away. Last night I measured the distance on the map." During the remaining twenty kilometers to Otaru, the road hugged the sea, steel-gray like a warship. A proud pine forest stood on the left. It being early March, the trees still wore the long white fur coats of the feudal Russian boyars.

In Otaru, the main street sloped down from the train station to the port. Katsu asked his passengers what they wished to do. "We'll go for a walk; if your company rules permit it, please come with us." Katsu seemed surprised but parked the car and joined them, though constantly staying several steps behind. When Célestin asked something, Katsu quickly approached, answered as well as he could in broken English, and humbly retreated. Odile inquired about Katsu's behavior. "As you know," her father said, "in every country, there are customary manners and unwritten rules. As visitors, we shouldn't teach the locals how to conduct themselves."

In the small, almost empty port, they stopped several times on the docks to photograph the shabby warehouses—in part because here and there, among the gray, wooden storerooms, there was a shiny aluminum one, strikingly red or blue. Célestin commented: "Speaking of our driver, I suspect he thinks of us as silly Westerners since we're taking pictures of these run-down warehouses. Maybe he belongs to the rare sort of Japanese who aren't aesthetically inclined in intricate ways: I doubt he noticed our photos have been capturing subtle changes in the color of the sea... The weather is getting better just for us, *ma princesse*."

The winter sun peeked every so often through the clouds

above the snow-covered hill close to town. When asked about it, Katsu answered cheerily: "Tenguyama!" and wrote "533 ski" on the back of a business card. Célestin thanked him and said to Odile: "So Tengu is not a hill, but a genuine mountain of over five hundred meters. With binoculars, we'd probably be able to see a ski lift up there."

They strolled on an old iron bridge across a canal and found themselves in a street where stone houses looked as if they had been transported from Liverpool or Boston in the nineteenth century. The most conspicuous was a two-story building with a "Bank of Japan" sign. Katsu wrote "1912" on another business card and gave it seemingly with pride. Two small trees, bare and dejected, stood in front of the out-of-place edifice.

It was only half past eleven, too early for lunch. Still, on a corner stood a Lawson mini market with the characteristic blue sign with white lettering. Those stores could be found everywhere in Sapporo and all over Japan. Western-style sandwiches of mediocre quality but freshly packed were available. Katsu followed his clients into the store but then disappeared somewhere within. They ran into each other again at the checkout, where the driver let the pair go first. Célestin paid for their sandwiches and soft drinks, and then they waited for Katsu outside. "I'd be offending him by trying to pay for these Lawson trifles," he said.

Katsu soon appeared with a few cans of the type available in countless vending machines. For instance, one could buy both hot and cold coffee startlingly called "Viennese." When they arrived at the car, Katsu held the door open for Odile and then asked Célestin to look in the trunk, which contained a small paper bag. "My loonch," Katsu said smiling. Later, Odile heard in French: "Being considerate, our driver showed me the lunch he had brought—presumably so I wouldn't castigate myself for not offering to buy him something in the mini market."

After about forty kilometers, Katsu turned off the road into a small rest area by the sea and invited the passengers to join him. Sun-kissed waves were breaking against rocks while clouds that had been smashed by powerful gusts ran madly across the sky.

Glancing significantly at father and daughter, the driver pointed far into the distance. There was a row of steep, stony blocks plunging into the sea. At the end of the chain, through the sea mist, a solitary rocky hill was visible. With love and pride, Katsu exclaimed solemnly: "Kamui!" To convey the remaining distance, he raised both hands and stretched out all ten fingers three times.

Fishing villages left behind, the road climbed into snow-covered hills. Only then did they realize how barren and broken up the Shakotan coast was. "It reminds me of western Galicia in Spain when one approaches Cabo Fisterra," Célestin whispered. The car effortlessly defeated the steep road until a view of snowy peaks opened to the south.

Having negotiated a high pass a dozen kilometers farther, they sharply descended into a hollow where there was an empty parking lot and a modest tourist building. No one was in sight, so they mutely absorbed the scene. Finally, Katsu nodded toward a narrow gray-brick uphill path and respectfully said: "Kamui mi-saki." Tapping two fingers alternately on his palm, he indicated they would need to walk from that point. On yet another business card, he wrote "800."

Only after stepping out of the car did they detect the weather had changed since their stroll in Otaru. The wind was strong and icy even in the hollow. But whereas the sun had appeared only sporadically during the morning, at Cape Kamui it was unobstructed. Célestin said through chattering teeth: "We're lucky. What Isamu wished to happen here for our benefit is indeed happening. Winterish, the sun is shining!" Odile exclaimed: "And therefore the sea will be Shakotan-blue..."

They put on the clothes bought in Paris for Hokkaido: thick sweaters; fur coats to below the knee; woolen scarves; gloves with lining; and Siberian mink hats. Noticing the cafeteria was open, they drank hot tea and ate the Lawson sandwiches. Katsu had explained he would clean the windshield, windows, and headlights before having lunch.

Then they addressed the winding footpath with a moderate incline. Despite the absence of visitors, it had been meticulously cleaned. Japan! Elsewhere on the slope, there were banks of snow, but waves of white-yellow grass protruded from the drifts. At about halfway, they stopped and turned to look. The wind lashed them, yet they did not care. Mountains of about a thousand meters rose in the distance. The hilly terrain below the peaks abounded in colors: white, naturally; several nuances of green; brown and yellow. Trees had glittering crowns, while shrubbery led a secret winter life in secluded dells. Closer to the Cape, around the narrow valley with the parking lot and on the slope where they stood, there was no vegetation whatsoever, not even the crooked, stunted bushes of Cabo de São Vicente and the Cape of Good Hope.

Enormous disappointment awaited them on the exposed top of the path: The entrance to the Cape was closed. On the wicket gate consisting of thin vertical gray slats that reached Célestin's chest, there was a sign in several languages: "The approach to Cape Kamui is closed on the 9th of March 1982 due to dangerous winds." Exactly when they were irately reading the sign, a gust of wind so strong they barely remained standing hit them; they held onto each other and the barrier. It became easier to understand the ban, though they remained piqued and disappointed: Permitted to come so close to the Cape and not reach it... But after taking an impartial look around, they grasped how uncommon the spot was and how fortunate they were to be standing there.

"It doesn't matter, *ma douce*, this is almost as good as if we've made it to the tip of the Cape. It's lovely! To begin with, this simple gate has a rough-hewn mountain appearance, but a friendly Japanese roof sits on top of it—even if it's too narrow to serve any purpose as cover. Also, without being lifted by me, you can see, by peeking between the slats, what the path to the Cape is like. Well, you don't have to peek, I'll show you."

On the snowy uphill slope, which rose to the right of the roofed gate, there was a low fence reaching Odile's shoulders: It was constructed of thick round logs. Between gusts of wind and holding occasionally onto the smooth logs, they clambered a short distance up the slope. From there, they had an unimpeded view of the brick path to the Cape. Even without binoculars, they

could see not only the lighthouse but also the line of seven famous sharp rocks jutting out from the sea in front of the Cape.
The first three were small, the fourth one the biggest, and the last
three were of medium size. Waves perpetually broke against
them. "Those seven rocks... Long, long ago, they were Cape
Kamui," Célestin daydreamed. Odile did not respond. Perhaps
the wind carried away her father's words, or the girl was fright-
ened by the passage of eons of time.

The lighthouse was near the sea, at a level much lower than
the wicket gate. He estimated its height was no more than ten
meters. Its bottom and top thirds, including the small conic roof,
were brightly white, the middle third pitch black. Next to it stood
a tall antenna. It was obvious no one lived there. Everything the
lonely white-black structure was doing must have been controlled elsewhere. "Hmm, it wouldn't be very exciting to stand by
that lighthouse," he consoled Odile.

Had access been allowed, the gray-brick path, about a meter
and a half wide, would have been easy to negotiate. On both of its
sides, there was a fence about one meter high made of massive
logs—similar in kind and height to the one to which they were
clinging. In places where a steep hillside threatened, the path
was protected from falling rocks by a sturdy wire net. What effort
and skill it required, thought Célestin—like in Switzerland.

Starting from the wicket gate, the path descended to a lower
hill with two white, totally bare humps. Then it snaked along the
hill's contour on the right, north side, only to hide from view for
a short distance. It reappeared on the south side, where a few low
shrubs survived. The path next climbed onto the last, even lower,
stony hill and finally descended to its western edge. There, the
lighthouse stood sentinel above the sea.

When writing "800" meters, Katsu made a small underesti-
mate. From the parking lot to the gate, there must have been about
three hundred meters, and from there to the lighthouse, about
seven hundred. Father and daughter perceived that many places
on the path were completely exposed to the wind, so the ban was
understandable. "Adults and children of various ages come here,

which is why the gate was closed," Célestin said. He used the chance to explain the concept of the lowest common denominator by which authorities' decisions worldwide are guided to secure safety—and avoid millions of liability.

Returning to the path by which they had initially climbed to the gate, they discovered an almost untrodden trail in the snow branching off steeply uphill. It took perseverance to climb about forty meters in deep snow, bent low and often clutching clusters of yellow grass to keep balance in the wind. It was worth it. From the top, they could see the opposite, the north side of the most remote hill on the Cape. Incredibly, a small sandy beach was nestled far below. "The most inaccessible and dangerous beach in the world... Where we swam near the Cape of Good Hope was child's play in comparison. This one should be advertised as appropriate for crazy tourists like us." Odile grinned but managed to say between two gusts: "*Bien, Papa*, but you said many times we're not tourists but travelers. I don't want to be a silly tourist! That's what I say when I get into squabbles with envious classmates."

From such a height, well above the wicket gate and the lighthouse, there was a 360-degree view. To the south, the sharp black hills were inexorably surrendering to the vicious gale and waves. Close to the coast, rocks of monstrous shape protruded from the sea—all that remained of primeval hills. "A truly cruel land's end," they thought, yet conscious of the magnificence of the day. The wind whipped them forcefully under a sun shining from a brilliantly blue sky.

To the north, there was only the sea: Endless and of an unfathomably gorgeous color. Odile and Célestin realized they were gazing at the Shakotan-blue, Isamu Noguchi's divine color. Until that moment, they had been preoccupied with the powerful wind, the closed gate, the lonely lighthouse, and the seven somehow surviving rocks, but then, suddenly, they became enchanted by the magical color of the sea: God the painter had created an incredible blue with a touch of turquoise and a pinch of aquamarine.

With the sea of Shakotan color as the background, he took a photo of his daughter. Odile was beautiful and happy standing in the snow all in white: An ushanka of white Russian mink and a coat of white Canadian beaver. Because the snow was to her knees, the bottom of the girl's coat was bunched up, but that would not prevent either Odile or Célestin from loving the picture forever. Everyone else who loved the girl or will ever love her would also cherish it. Especially Olya.

7.

Content and agreeably tired, they were sitting in the living room of their suite in the Aspen. As white-currant juice was not available, she was drinking orange juice, whereas her father poured himself a glass of red wine from the bottle he had opened. The label stated in Japanese and English: "KAMUI WINE / Deep Red Grape Wine / Vineyard Hokkaido." He took a sip; it was very sweet, lots of sugar must have been added. "It's awful," he muttered, "which proves the Japanese can't be successful at absolutely everything."

At one point, when they were chatting about their adventure in wind and snow, Odile switched to a more serious tone: "While we were driving back from Kamui, I was thinking about something but didn't want to ask you—who knows how much Katsu understands—and to speak French constantly wouldn't have been nice, right? So, do you remember when we climbed the slope next to the closed gate and stood by the low fence with the thick logs? Even I could have easily gone over that fence, let alone you. From there, regardless of the wind, you'd be able to walk to the lighthouse without difficulty. I saw in your eyes you wanted to! I would've gladly waited for you by the gate. Nobody would've seen you. So, why didn't you do it?"

He laughed: "You're a perceptive psychologist. I also thought about the low fence while we were driving back, maybe at the same time as you did. But you know the answer to the key question: I would've never left you alone in those conditions! As you're aware, everything was different during my solo swim to Pharaoh's Island. However, what we might talk about now is how I would've behaved had I been alone today: So, everything is the same, except you're waiting for me in the hotel. The answer is also easy and negative, the reason being Olya. I wouldn't have risked breaching even the most trivial Japanese law when we're going to meet Dima and Lyuda in a few days."

He took one more sip of the wine, then frowned and decided to leave it alone—candied fruit was tastier. "But you could ask what I would've done if there was, God forbid, no Odile and no Olya. That wouldn't have been much of a dilemma either: I'm ninety-five percent certain I would've climbed over the fence and walked to the lighthouse. Going there and returning to the gate wouldn't have taken more than half an hour. And if the authorities discovered me? So what? For such a tiny misdemeanor, they certainly wouldn't have jailed me or expelled me from Japan. I'd have to pay a fine—you saw the long list of regulations posted on the gate—probably a hefty one, an amount in yen with many zeroes. They would claim that by putting my life in jeopardy, I'd somehow become a threat to public safety. Again, so what? It would be only money, and even though, as you know, money doesn't grow on trees, one could, for instance, equally nag about the high amount we paid today for a car with a chauffeur. We did it because we were able to, and it suited us. So, the probability is actually ninety-nine percent I would've climbed over the fence! Are you satisfied now, *mon rêve*?"

"I am, *cher Papounet*. The truth is that even before asking you, I knew what you'd say and why. I'm glad I can guess your thoughts, as you can mine!" She hugged him.

In the cafeteria back at Cape Kamui, Célestin had bought three identical bottles of wine. One he gave to Katsu with a decent tip when he brought them back. The second was intended for Lyuda and Dima in Wakkanai. The remainder of the wine in his bottle would go down the drain.

"As you know, the day after tomorrow we'll travel to Wakkanai," he said, "and tomorrow, we'll take a long walk and buy presents for our Russian friends. Let's think about the gifts before we go to the seven-story department store we've seen."

8.

Wakkanai, the northernmost town in Japan. Célestin and Odile arrived three minutes late, at 2:59 p.m., having been warned an hour earlier by a conductor who had passed through their half-empty carriage bowing and apologizing to each passenger. Japan!

Leaving Sapporo, there was not much to see as the train worked its way northward through the entire central Hokkaido. The winter scenery was monotonous: Fields under snow and an occasional low hill on the horizon. The most populous town along the way, two hours out, was Asahikawa: It was unattractive, with many factory chimneys. More picturesque, farther north, was Shibetsu; "*sipet*" meant big river in Ainu, according to Célestin's Japanese-English dictionary with an Ainu appendix. The river, in truth, seemed rather small, perhaps because most of it was covered by ice.

At the modest Wakkanai train station was a tourist office consisting of an articulate middle-aged Japanese woman—half-Ainu, as it turned out—and her small desk; there were also two uncomfortable chairs for clients. She introduced herself as Ayai and cheerfully added: "My name means 'baby crying' in Ainu, although my mom told me I hadn't bawled much as a baby. But I was the first child, plus a girl, so to my dad any sound from me was a nuisance!" They smiled uneasily, and Célestin wondered whether Ayai had the habit of confiding in strangers out of loneliness. As if reading his mind, she volunteered: "I was born here but have spent most of my life in the opposite, southernmost, corner of Japan near the city of Matsuyama on Shikoku Island. That's like a different country—the language and everything else. The people there are more open, emotional, and talkative than here and elsewhere in Japan." With a broad smile on her pretty

Ainu face, she added: "In Matsuyama, I managed to learn some English." And indeed, her fluency was enviable.

In the small remote town, Célestin and Odile were not going to be choosy about accommodation and immediately agreed to stay at the Watanabe Ryokan recommended by Ayai. "That's only seven minutes on foot from here. I know the owners, they're good people; not a word of English, but you'll manage. They have one spacious room on the upper floor, which has a Japanese part with tatami mats and a Western part with two separate beds. There's no other such room in the whole town. If you wish, I'll tell them to expect you, although in this desert," she waved both arms, "it's most unlikely someone would grab the room ahead of you."

"*Moshi moshi*," yelled Ayai into the handset and successfully finalized the booking within minutes. "Watanabe-san is a little deaf—or pretends to be," she explained, "but your daughter and you are welcome to stay in the room I described."

He thanked her and asked what most people in Wakkanai did for a living. Ayai looked at him wryly: "You mean, what do they do to survive in this wasteland? That's exactly what we, the locals, ask ourselves. Well, we go fishing when the weather is not too nasty and otherwise 'mine' for seaweed, which is called *kombu*. Put some seaweed into your miso soup tomorrow morning. That's our specialty, like frog legs in Italy and snails in France!" She laughed, pleased with herself, and was eagerly joined by the clients. To Célestin, it seemed admirable the lady used humor, with a forgivable scintilla of irony, to fight the despondency evidently pervading her life in Wakkanai and undoubtedly the lives of many other denizens. He hoped their depression was limited to winter months, enhanced by proximity to a *finis terrae*.

Before they left, Ayai stroked Odile's cheek, gave her a small chocolate, and added: "You should know, Sir, I won't receive any tip from Mr. Watanabe for my recommendation, no money beyond the tiny percent of the price of the room all guesthouses pay to the tourist office and not me personally. Oh, please take this brochure about Wakkanai." He took the mimeographed sheet with thanks. The text was trilingual, in Japanese, English, and Russian.

Ayai pointed the way to the ryokan. After helping Odile put on her coat, he placed a thousand yen note on the desk, saying: "Please, let me have a chocolate also and another brochure, I'm studying Russian!"

On leaving the train station, they encountered the weather of the extreme north of Japan in mid-March: Windy, cloudy, and cold, though only five below zero. "Let's hope there's no new snow since our friends will travel from Sapporo," Célestin said as they walked in a streetlet covered by well-trodden snow. All around, there were heaps of old but white snow: Maybe there were few sources of grime and soot. Still, the town exuded gloom.

The gray ryokan building could not have been older than five years. A sturdy wooden awning jutted out above the entrance—disproportionately large for the house but sized to accommodate all the desired text: The name in Japanese; Ryokan Watanabe in Latin script; and *Хотер Сахарин* in Russian Cyrillic script. "Hmm," he muttered, pointing to the Russian name: "I'll explain later why I'm surprised." The girl had long before learned the Cyrillic script and used it when adding a few words to her father's notes to Olga.

It was already half past five when they entered the ryokan, encountering an enjoyable homey smell of wood burning. The owners, husband and wife, stood next to each other smiling in welcome. Célestin and Odile wished them good evening with *komban wa!* The couple responded with the same words and an even broader smile directed at the girl. They were both in their sixties, the lady looking older but the gentleman more bone-weary. Before the hosts led their guests up the stairs, father and daughter—familiar with the elementary customs of Japanese ryokans—took off their shoes at the foot of the stairs and put on slippers that were lined up. Outside their room, they exchanged the ryokan slippers for those meant solely for their private quarter.

The unusually high ceiling and two windows caught his eye. "These people are generous with guests. It must cost a lot to heat all the space," he thought, noting the room was cozily warm. As Ayai had said, it was divided into two parts, with no partition. Tatami mats, a low Japanese table, and many small pillows for sitting and kneeling on the ground were in one part. Behind a screen with wax-paper panels on which pale, languid geishas sensually contemplated life, they saw futons and blankets. In the other part of the room, the floor visible around a small carpet was of a maroon-colored lacquered wood. There were two narrow beds with a nightstand between them. Four solid chairs surrounded a Western table on which sat a flowerpot. Discreetly pointing to it, he murmured: "Note the Japanese slightly off-center positioning of the plant—but it does seem sickly." A tall wardrobe with a mirror stood against the wall. Beside it hung a masterfully done graphite-pencil depiction of Cape Soya. Behind a bamboo screen, they saw a sink, miniature shower, and toilet. Watanabe-san took Célestin to the powerful heater and showed him how to adjust it.

"I think we'll be comfortable here. Shall we stay three nights, what d'you say?" Odile found the room intriguing so she nodded. He showed the owners three fingers for nights. Pleased, they nodded, saying *arigatō, arigatō!*

Out of season, in the far-away Wakkanai, the price was low and included breakfast. By law, a ryokan, unlike an ordinary guesthouse, had to serve both breakfast and dinner. While they were unpacking, Odile asked: "*Alors Papa*, please explain what's 'Хотер Сахарин' and why it's written in Russian?" He said: "Well, it's certain Dima and Lyuda won't be the first Russian tourists in this area. Others come to visit Cape Soya and see Sahalin Island from there. It's possible once in a blue moon in ideal weather, but Sahalin is far from Soya misaki—forty-three kilometers. *Bien*, that explains why it's written in Russian: It's welcome to tourists, which is important because the rich island had long been Japanese, then Russian, then again Japanese, and from 1945 Soviet."

Odile absorbed the information: "I understand; however, Russians don't say 'хотер' but 'хотел,' just like one does in English. And you, Papa, say Sahalin, not Saharin!" Célestin praised her perspicacity: "You're right, of course. But although the sounds, phonemes, 'l' and 'r' exist in Japanese, they are allophones of a single phoneme, or simply, they're merged into one sound. For this reason, Japanese people find it difficult to distinguish them and pronounce certain Western words correctly. It's not a genetic defect because the Japanese who grow up in Europe or America don't have this presumed problem; Isamu Noguchi, born in California, to an Irish mother, is a case in point. And so, when the Japanese raised in Japan try to pronounce 'l' and 'r,' that comes out, in both cases, like something in between. Many Westerners find it hilarious, especially in the case of some words. For instance, 'rice' sounds like 'lice', and 'Sahalin' like 'saccharine'—you know, the substitute for sugar in coffee and tea we never use."

Célestin knew what was missing in his story and was waiting for Odile to bring it up—and did not wait long. "*Très bien, Papa.* But that doesn't explain the sign 'Хотер Сахарин' on the awning: It's written, not spoken! Certainly they could've found how the words 'hotel' and 'хотел' in English and Russian are written and then copied 'l' and 'л'!" She was very pleased with her proof, while he experienced a rush of fatherly pride: "You're right again, which means the whole thing is intentional, a joke! We'll never know whether the sign maker wanted to make fun of the Watanabe couple as his small revenge for their alleged courting of Russian tourists or whether the owners themselves wanted to be witty, or..."

9.

"*O-hayo!*" father and daughter greeted a lone waitress when they entered the restaurant, as they did Watanabe-san, their elderly hostess, who appeared after several moments. In return, they received the same greeting and many other good-morning wishes, in addition to bows and smiles. The hostess then withdrew discreetly with another bow. The young Ainu waitress, with cheeks pink from good health and stage fright, repeated "dōzo" several times whenever she brought something to the table, which sounded more like "dōzō"—"bronze statue"—than like "please." She brought bowls and small ceramic trays of various sizes, shapes, and colors—exactly ten in number for each guest. The biggest bowls were for miso soup and white rice. They also received pieces of different types of fish, fried sea cucumber *namako* with dried shiitake mushrooms, two sorts of seaweed, thinly sliced and spiced daikon winter radish, two eggs—one hard-boiled, one raw—and a tiny cake. All was consumed with relish, except that he left half of his sea cucumber uneaten, and she did not touch hers.

The weather was cold and windy again. They walked briskly about a kilometer to the shore and found the sea gray and choppy, with ice floes. For Célestin and Odile the sight was new and exciting. "Do you remember," he said, "our visit to John Glott's family? We stood in the shallow sea on the beach in Muizenberg the evening before and stared to the south. Between us and the Antarctic, there was nothing except ice floes. And now, here they are in front of us in the northern hemisphere!" Odile looked at him pensively, needing a moment to recreate the sight in her mind: "Yes, I also remember the new moon appeared just then above False Bay."

There were huts with fishermen's nets and other sundries by the narrow beach, whereas the precious boats were kept upturned farther away. In the sea, close to the shore, piles of rough stones protected it. They soon noticed the tiny beach was far less exposed to the northern storms' waves than was the far longer stretch of coast perpendicular to it—and that exposed stretch, they could see from afar, was defended by an almost unbelievable stone structure.

The gigantic sea wall was perhaps half a kilometer long and fifteen meters high. In front of its whole length, one could see huge heaps of stones sticking out of the waves. "Half a quarry's quantity of rock!" he muttered. The entire side of the structure facing the sea was a continuous, convex, quarter-arc of stone. Since a port was not behind it, the sea wall defended the town itself, or rather an empty field in front of the first houses three hundred meters away. Striding fast, father and daughter were curious to discover how the inner side of the massive structure looked.

The top of the wall rested on numerous stone pillars about seven meters tall, with a gap of some six meters between them. Attractive contiguous arches connected the pillars. The distance between the pillars' pedestals and the bottom of the inner side of the wall was about eight meters, whereas the tops of the pillars were linked to the wall by exceptionally graceful, elongated half-ellipses. "Nothing less than a colossal arcade or colonnade in ancient Rome had inspired the architects of this work, although in Rome the arcade would've usually had pillars on both sides of the passageway. But this is the Town Defender, not a senators' promenade! I've never seen or heard of anything like it. It's perfect," he concluded when they arrived at the end of the magnificent arcade. The girl agreed: "It's gorgeous, Papa—and I counted seventy pillars." By then, he had determined the greatest height within the passageway was about eight and a half meters.

They returned to the beginning of the arcade to find if it were possible to walk along the top of the sea wall: It was, but not far. On the side facing the sea, they climbed up the steep stairs to a terrace about thirty meters long where pristine snow lay. In front of them, the gray sea dotted with ice floes reached through the billows of fog to the horizon.

The pair came down from the terrace and walked on the snowy field toward town. Halfway across, they turned to look again at the astonishing structure. Only then did they notice that along its whole length, above the arches, there was a low ornate pseudo-fence with tiny pillars. "Like a pretty border of stone lace," said Odile softly. "*Justement, mon bijou.* And altogether, this is not a sea wall, but a majestic work of art."

When they arrived at the tourist office to inquire about transportation to Cape Soya, Ayai greeted them affably. Feeling at ease with the Ainu lady, Odile asked her about the sea wall. Ayai grinned and pulled out from a drawer two copies of another brochure: "The stone marvel doesn't interest anyone here nor do tourists ask about it, which is why I didn't give you this brochure yesterday. I failed to realize a little girl can be smarter than other tourists and me!"

He scanned the text. The sea wall, built in 1936, was also the terminus of the railway line from Asahikawa. Odile was happy the colonnade had seventy pillars, confirming her count. "Listen," Ayai grumbled, "our town fathers, miserly as they are, have not bothered to print an up-to-date brochure praising the recent reconstruction of the 'North Breakwater Dome,' as they call it down in Sapporo. That job was finished a year ago."

Father and daughter decided they would make a trial run to Cape Soya before Sunday's meeting with the Russians—maybe even twice, by cab and bus. Ayai recommended a taxi man: "There is one Ikeda-san who's proven to be honest and has a four-door Mazda only two years old. To Soya, it's thirty kilometers on a good road. Snow is removed daily and gravel poured on icy patches. Ikeda knows twelve words of English and won't overcharge you. Should I call him?"

A gray Mazda arrived three minutes later, driven by a man wearing white gloves. He wore a cap on which "Taxi Ikeda" was written above the brim. In the meantime, Célestin had asked Ayai for another chocolate and left a thousand yen note.

10.

In the evening, they chatted reclining on pillows. It was not Cape Soya but the formidable sea wall that made their first day in Wakkanai unforgettable. The Cape did contribute, though in an unexpected sense.

Ikeda, whose first name they never discovered, could have been the twin brother of the Sapporo Katsu: Similar smile, courtesy, reticence, age, and slender build. He drove sensibly, did not smoke, and did not impose music. During the entire thirty-minute drive northeast to Cape Soya, the two-lane asphalted road hugged the sea, flat and with moderate curves. On the right-hand side, there were low, snow-covered hills devoid of trees and houses, except that halfway, they passed the airport. It was open, and one could fly to the south of Hokkaido with Air Nippon. However, he had found back in Sapporo that flights were often canceled due to inclement winter weather, which was why he believed Lyuda and Dima would arrive by train: But would they come?

The sky was moody during the drive and the sea agitated. A gust of wind would sometimes shake the car. After a long curve, while Célestin was staring at the ice floes thinking of Olya, Odile exclaimed: "Papa, look, our lighthouse!" The Cape Soya rendezvous lighthouse could indeed be seen in the distance.

At the Cape, they promised Ikeda to return within an hour. It was cold, eight below zero. The wind was strong but a breeze compared with Cape Kamui. Flanked by piles of stones in the shallows, stood a small white triangular monument. From the road, a path covered by flagstones, about twenty-five meters long, led to the sea and the monument. Beside the path, tiny empty fields were probably grassy in the summer. The parking area was surrounded by modest little houses: Two eateries, several souvenir shops, and the office of the bus company. The biggest house was the ugliest: A souvenir store painted a garish blue and constructed of wood, its shape pretending to mimic the monument's. Above the parking lot, some two hundred meters away, loomed a hillock with the lighthouse. And that was all to Cape Soya.

Célestin and Odile needed only minutes to climb to the lighthouse. They touched it superstitiously for good luck, absorbed in thoughts. The body of the lighthouse was square and about ten meters tall: In height, it was similar to the lighthouse at Cape Kamui and to an Olympic diving tower. The three and a half meters at the bottom of the structure were white, the next two meters red, then two white, and the final two at the top, under a little white terrace, again red. The wind was blowing fiercely as they wordlessly agreed that the lighthouse was unattractive.

Clouds prevented them from seeing Sahalin, yet his voice was optimistic: "Let's hope the weather will be nicer the day after tomorrow. Lyuda and Dima deserve it for their anniversary! I'll bring binoculars on Sunday, and Dima may have an even more powerful pair."

The view nevertheless took their breath away: Thousands of ice floes were spread out in the sea as far as the eye could see. While they were looking far to the north, Odile suddenly embraced her father: "I'm so happy these white floes look stunning on the dark-blue sea. I know what you like but this Cape... It's indeed something 'most'—northernmost—but not the most beautiful." Her sensitivity moved him again.

"Let's go down and look at the monument," he suggested. Erected in the sixties, it was of white marble and about five meters tall. Its triangular form was reminiscent of a hollow pyramid or a vertical slice of it. Five stone stairs led to a round platform in the middle of which stood the structure. On a black tablet at the foot of the triangle, the text in Japanese and English declared:

Cape Soya, Northernmost Point in Japan, 45°31'14" N.

They liked the monument only because it was modest but could not resist photographing each other in front of it—capturing, of course, ice floes in the background.

Back at the parking area, he said: "If you agree, we'll come here tomorrow as well. Hopefully, the weather will be better. We'll take the bus, so no one will be waiting for us, and spend more time on the hill and by the sea. All right?" They both wore thick gloves, but he nevertheless felt his daughter's hand firmly squeezing his in consent.

As soon as they reached the car, Ikeda came running from somewhere. Célestin asked him to drive to Ayai and step into the office with them. She readily conveyed the customer's requests to the cabby: Ikeda would pick them up at the Watanabe Ryokan on Sunday at ten in the morning; he would again drive to Cape Soya and wait for them there, maybe several hours; if he were to discover any problem with his Mazda, he was to send a reliable colleague on Sunday at all costs. To each of these instructions, Ikeda vigorously nodded and muttered "*Hai!*" In the end, pleased with the tip, he bowed deeply and exclaimed "*Hai! Arigatō gozaimasu!*" "Don't worry, Sir," Ayai said, "I'll ensure everything goes well." Two chocolates and three thousand yen.

11.

The next day was less gloomy, so they visited a park close to town and climbed a hill on which stood the 1978 tower commemorating a century of Wakkanai's founding, only ten years after Sapporo, as part of the Meiji penetration of northern Hokkaido. An elevator took them to the lookout terrace seventy meters up. Neither Sahalin nor the Japanese islands Rishiri and Rebun, west of Wakkanai and only half as far, could be seen. A bird's eye view of the North Breakwater Dome was their compensation.

Around noon, they traveled to Cape Soya by public bus, taking the seats in front. All of the driver's accessories were snow-white—the cap, gloves, and mask covering his nose and mouth. The day remained cloudy, but the wind had weakened, and it was six degrees above zero. Upon arrival at the Cape, they climbed the hillock to the lighthouse and from there strolled to a strange-looking structure of brown bricks, which they had noticed the previous day. It was an authentic military watchtower, about five meters tall, with a rooftop terrace. On a plaque it was written in several languages that the watchtower had been erected by the Japanese Imperial Navy at the end of the nineteenth century to "monitor the movements of Russian warships, the Imperial Russian fleet being considered the most powerful in the world at the time."

"This 'considered the most powerful in the world' is interesting and perhaps an expression of the Japanese secret exultation, even triumphalism, when one considers what happened later," thought Célestin. He talked to Odile about the Russo-Japanese War of 1905, which was a disaster for the Russian Empire and the reputation of Tsar Nikolay II. The catastrophic defeat of the Russian fleet near Tsushima Island, located between Korea and the Japanese southern island of Kyushu, was by far the most important element of the Japanese victory in that war.

Close to the watchtower was a modest restaurant in a single-story gray house with a dark-red tin roof. The interior was pleasant, with handsome tables and chairs of lacquered wood.

They were silent for a while, sipping tea. "Papa, you look worried, is it because of Olya?" "*Oui, ma chérie*, because of Olya; and I've also been thinking about something incomparably less significant but nonetheless troubling. When we meet Lyuda and Dima tomorrow, we could come here before we return to Wakkanai. But through this very window, the watchtower would be in front of their noses, as you can see. And I'm sure—all right, almost sure—the plaque by the watchtower is a painful reminder for every Russian of a horrific military defeat." With a serious expression on her delicate face, Odile looked at the watchtower for a minute and finally murmured: "They'll be sad..."

After another look at the watchtower and the lighthouse, they climbed down the hillock to the sea. Near the monument, there was a pedestal with a map, engraved in bronze, of northern Hokkaido and southern Sahalin. "I know this expanse of the sea in front of us—and look, here it's on the map—between Cape Soya and Sahalin is called La Pérouse Strait. It got its name from Jean-François, *comte* de la Pérouse, an eighteenth-century French nobleman who was a renowned seafarer. He was the first European known to have passed through this strait, but the expedition disappeared without a trace in the Pacific Ocean in 1788. Imagine! He was also the man who gave the name Cape Crillon to the place on Sahalin closest to us here—a piddly forty kilometers away. De Crillon, by the way, is the name of an old and famous family from our Lorraine," concluded Célestin.

"De Crillon? Isn't that the name of the wonderful hotel in Paris in which we stayed when we arrived from Cape Town?" Odile asked. "Yes, Hôtel de Crillon on Place de la Concorde. They know our family so we could get a room without a reservation," he replied. But her interest was piqued: "You told me then that some members of the family De Crillon had lived in that magnificent palace and also the last King of France, Louis XVI, and Queen Marie Antoinette, didn't you?"

He was not pleased with the drift of the conversation but had no choice: "François de Crillon, son of Louis, *duc* de Crillon, lived there from 1788, but the revolutionary government confiscated the building in 1791 and moved King Louis and Marie Antoinette there: It was the most luxurious prison in the world. You know what happened to those two." "Of course I do," the girl was offended. "The King and Queen were guillotined in Paris in 1793, but our teacher didn't tell us where." He unhappily specified the gruesome fact: "Both were beheaded, guillotined as you said, on Place de la Concorde in front of 'our' hotel. That's Paris, that's our bloody French history—though there's no country without a brutal past."

The Siberian-Canadian uniforms protected them as they paced near the inoffensive white monument. Those clothes had been bought on Rue du Mont Thabor, less than ten minutes on foot from the Concorde! When making the purchases, father and daughter fondly recalled Mount Tabor in Israel. But Odile had more questions: "*Bien, Papa,* did comte de la Pérouse or someone from the family De Crillon discover Sahalin Island?" After a moment, he said: "Listen, for who knows how many thousands of years various indigenous people have been living on Sahalin—the Ainu, but also the Nivh. There's no good answer even from a purely European viewpoint because it's unknown which 'foreigners' came there first. It certainly wasn't any De Crillon. I don't even know if De La Pérouse disembarked at Cape Crillon or only saw it from afar. One must also keep Japanese seafarers in mind."

Therefore, Célestin took his daughter to a life-size statue, not far away, of a Japanese nineteenth-century explorer with a samurai hair bun and a sword at his belt: He was Mamiya Rinzo, a vassal of the Tokugawa shogunate. "Yesterday, I got out of Ayai another brochure. According to the Japanese, he was the first man to determine that Sahalin was an island, not a peninsula. In 1809, he voyaged up the entire west coast of Sahalin and even entered the Amur River delta. The Japanese call Sahalin 'Karafuto'."

Cape Soya did not become beautiful, but it was much more interesting than they had thought the day before.

12.

Sunday, 14th of March 1982; 12:00 noon;
Cape Soya, Hokkaido, Japan

Either because sea cucumbers were not, for some obscure reason, eaten in Japan on Sundays or because Watanabe-san had observed that her guests did not sufficiently appreciate them, Célestin and Odile found two cakes instead of one on their breakfast trays—and no namako!

The gray sky did not promise much, despite occasional sunrays, but at least his wish for no new snow was fulfilled. After breakfast, they had time to check all the details before their third and final visit to Cape Soya. In Odile's rucksack was a carefully wrapped bouquet they had bought the previous evening at the train station. It was minimalistic yet expensive, having arrived by plane from Sapporo.

A separate shelf of the wardrobe was reserved for gifts. Dima would receive a bottle of the sweetened Cape Kamui wine with the advice to visit the magnificent place and look far to the northwest, where the closest point in Russia would be on the Ussuri River, halfway between Vladivostok and Habarovsk. Packages for Lyuda and Anya had little cellophane windows through which one could divine the contents. The presents were delicate silk yukatas, Japanese kimonos to be worn at home. Both were floor-length and had wide sleeves three-quarters long. They were open in front like a dressing gown and could be fastened at the waist by a silk obi. On one of them, there were hand-painted white cherry blossoms on a deep blue background, whereas on the other, there were pink and subtly yellow lotus flowers on a gray background, also hand-painted. Odile hoped she would one day have a yukata like one of these.

They busied themselves with trivia, trying not to look out every five minutes. But when she came to the window at a quarter to ten, Ikeda's gray car was there. On arrival at the Cape, everything near the monument was familiar, so they paced aimlessly for some twenty minutes. There were few other visitors and not a single tourist bus. An edge of the sun would appear for a few minutes and then hide behind dark clouds. "Maybe there'll be both snow and sunshine today—but in which order?" he mumbled.

At eleven fifteen, they climbed the hill and entered the small restaurant with the dark-red roof again. The hospitable owner brought a teapot with the best sencha he had. They nervously sipped the tea.

At twelve minutes to noon, they emerged from the restaurant and approached the lighthouse at a comical snail's pace. They both touched it, praying for Olya. Then they superstitiously walked around the lighthouse and stood in front of it facing the sea at three minutes before twelve. Already a minute later, their hearts began to pound even faster because a blue taxi had stopped at the bottom of the hill. Within moments, Lyuda and Dima exited the car and looked toward the lighthouse. The next second, a witness in the sky would see four jubilant faces and hear delighted yells emanating from four throats, in four voices. A man and a woman scrambled up the hill swiftly like youngsters while a little girl and her father ran downhill recklessly, holding hands.

Célestin and Odile had already sensed the news would be good. Exactly at noon, everyone was hugging and kissing everyone else on the slope below the lighthouse.

* * *

Sitting in the restaurant with the tin roof, they all spoke at the same time, except for Odile—and she was so happy for her father, for Olya, for Olga, and for herself, she wanted to cry. The words Dima uttered instantly by the lighthouse were: "Everything is all right, Tino, our friend! Olya will soon be free! And she'll get a passport for foreign travel!" He introduced Célestin to Lyuda, who embraced each other. Then Lyuda, although willowy and of average height, grabbed Odile and lifted her in the air, hugging her firmly in the Russian manner. Dima exclaimed in Russian: "Listen, Tino, *dorogoy*, when we're speaking Russian, we're switching to *ty*! All right?" Tino gladly agreed to the familiar 'thou.'

Without being asked, the elderly owner brought an elegant porcelain flask of saké and three matching *sakazuki*. On the white bottle with a thin neck, as well as on the tiny porcelain cups, there was a fine blue design. Smiling, the owner expertly poured the warm rice wine into the sakazukis. Before Célestin could say anything, Lyuda and Dima lifted their cups and emptied them, exclaiming "Long life!" for Olya and him. "Anya and Kolya are sending their heartfelt best," added Lyuda. Father and daughter seized the moment and congratulated the Russian couple on their anniversary. With delighted expressions, the two did not act like bashful teenagers but kissed each other long and hard on the mouth.

The friendly owner came to the table every five minutes to pour more saké. "Haruto-san knows us," said Lyuda, "we were here yesterday afternoon. But then the flask was earthen and of a nondescript color, not this refined blue porcelain. Today, he sensed we were celebrating something important." Célestin was surprised: "And we came yesterday morning! And also a day earlier, to reconnoiter. So the owner knows us too but never told us his name. Probably because Odile and I looked worried, he wisely figured we weren't in the mood for gay introductions." "That's possible," Dima replied, "whereas we had the advantage of knowledge and have been in a fabulous mood ever since we came to Sapporo." Lyuda, whose face had become pinkish, spoke excitedly: "As we walked around, we were amazed by the fantastic breakwater dome. Have you seen it?" Odile jumped in to praise the giant sea wall copiously.

"But have you seen the naval watchtower over there?" Dima suddenly asked. "We have," Célestin responded, glancing at the girl, "and were reluctant to sit here with you because you'd be looking at it through the window. When I mentioned it to Odile, she thought you'd be sad." Lyuda and Dima gazed at them. Then she said: "How kind and sweet you both are! Yes, seeing the plaque yesterday was the only jarring moment since we landed in Japan." Dima drank his cup bottom-up: "We immediately remembered the appalling catastrophe at Tsushima. You realize that for most Russians it's as if the battle took place yesterday. How well the defeat served the Bolysheviks; it's as if Japan fought for them." Hearing those words and sensing the powerful emotions behind them, Célestin privately concluded: "These people can't be communists."

Two hours later, when three tipsy individuals and Odile stepped out of the restaurant, all in heavy furs and ushankas, it was the sober girl who gleefully exclaimed: "*Papa, le soleil!* Can we now see Sahalin?" The men took binoculars from their bags and decided, without hesitation, to climb to the terrace of the watchtower, only a dozen steep stairs. Dima went first: Ignoring the warning in several languages, he stepped over the red-white chain and then helped Lyuda. To avoid Odile having to crawl under the chain, Célestin lifted her, fur coat and all, and placed her into Dima's arms. They fervently wished to use the interval of bright sunny splendor to see Sahalin and do it from a naval watchtower in the country that had sunk the proud Russian fleet—and still, after seventy-seven years, shrewdly exulted over it. Being on the watchtower was a symbolic act of revenge. And a way to see Sahalin...

And they saw it—with binoculars. Through the sea mist over La Pérouse Strait, the contours of Sahalin hills loomed. Although Lyuda and Odile claimed they could see the hills with the naked eye, the men refused to believe it. "*Cher Papounet*, I'm telling you I saw Cape Crillon!" she kept up a while longer to no avail.

Mutual mass photography of a mediocre caliber took place, with the Nikon, Dima's Russian Zenith-Zorkin, and the pocket Kodak all in use. In some pictures, the spot on the horizon where Sahalin had allegedly been observed served as the background; in other photos, it was the lighthouse, the Cape Soya monument, or their little restaurant. Odile thought she had spied someone watching them from a tiny window on the lighthouse, but the adults waved her words away. They were fearless!

The girl remembered Cape Kamui and the locked gate. No need to remind her father. It was much better at Soya: Her papa, the Russians, and she—everyone content.

Before they climbed down from the watchtower, they saw Haruto-san standing by the window waving. He liked those amiable Russian and French people, always generous. The foursome on the watchtower exuberantly waved back. They were certain old Haruto would not call the police; besides, they did not care…

At the bottom of the hillock, Dima and Lyuda canceled the blue taxi, giving the driver a tip exceeding the fare. Before they piled into his car, Ikeda took a photo of all four together. During the drive back to Wakkanai, they made sure not to mention Olya, Olga, or any prison. They did speak about Kolya and Anya who were sorely missed. Célestin mentioned Chehov and his visit to Sahalin in 1890. "Ah, yes," Lyuda said, "Kolya and Anya know much more than we do about Anton Pavlovich and his text 'Sahalin Island'."

Ikeda first drove Lyuda and Dima to their Kimura Ryokan, another recommendation by Ayai. The Russian couple would come to the Watanabe in an hour.

13.

"Olya will be pardoned on Friday, the 26th of March 1982. On the same day, her citizen rights will be restored and the internal USSR passport reissued. Mother and daughter will be able to embrace each other in front of the Kuybyshev prison on Saturday, the 27th of March, and together travel by train to Kazan on that day. Olya's passport for foreign travel will be issued in Kazan before the end of the month—by Wednesday, the 31st of March. If she feels strong enough, Olya can already on Friday, the 2nd of April, apply in person for a visa at the French Embassy in Moscow, while Olga seeks a short-stay visa. They were informed of this on Monday, the 8th of March—Women's Day in the USSR!"

Lyuda recited it all from memory as soon as she and her husband entered the large room at the Watanabe. Dima took over: "Because it's only the 14th of March, it remains for you to get in touch with Olga—but not too soon, you must minimize the chance of our meeting being discovered." Lyuda gave further instructions: "Only after your conversation with Olga—with eavesdroppers certainly present—only then you might try to expedite the visa issuance business at the Ministry of Foreign Affairs in Paris.

You must also send money via the ministry to the Moscow Embassy for Olya's and Olga's plane tickets; they obviously don't have that sort of money."

Father and daughter were deeply moved. Gazing at Lyuda and Dima, Célestin stuttered: "I can't find the words to thank all of you—you two, and Anya and Kolya." Dima said: "There's no need to go into details, but this proves there are good people even in the Soviet system. Anya and Lyuda succeeded in accomplishing everything with the help of their friends and colleagues, and they were all pleased to help Olya." Odile ran to Lyuda and embraced her around the waist, mumbling breathlessly: "You've done a lot for me too! I love our Olyechka very much..." She began to sob while the childless Lyuda hugged the girl's head and kissed her wet face. Odile then jumped up and came back with the gift for Lyuda: "I have these flowers for you, it's only a small bouquet. I forgot to give it to you in the restaurant." Lyuda smelled it and placed it on her chest, whispering tenderly: "Thank you, gentle girl, it's still fresh! How could you find flowers in Wakkanai?"

Dima took a bottle of vodka from his bag, and Célestin produced an Italian red wine the Watanabe couple had found somewhere in Wakkanai. Odile arranged plates, cutlery, and glasses that the waitress had brought. And Lyuda was busy with packages of French cheese and spicy Hungarian salami bought in a foreign-food store in Sapporo.

During these preparations for a modest festivity, Dima ceaselessly paced. Finally, he sighed gloomily: "You're both conscious of how dear you have been to Kolya and me. We got to know you well in Swaziland and Kruger. And through us, our wives have also become fond of you—Lyuda can confirm it." The couple looked at each other lovingly but forlornly when Dima uttered a devastating sentence: "So it pains us exceedingly to disclose that after this evening we can never see each other again."

Odile was in shock, whereas Célestin had suspected that something like it might happen. "To our huge regret, we won't be able to attend the wedding!" Dima said. "We can't even receive an invitation. Incredibly, we'll never meet Olya! All communication between us must end here in Wakkanai," Dima concluded dejectedly.

Father and daughter were speechless while Dima's words were sinking in. With lips trembling, Lyuda empathized: "It's not easy for us and the two of you, nor will it be for Olya and Olga, but you'll understand. The four of us, as well as some other people who don't know you and Olya at all—well, we're in considerable danger of being discovered. The agencies have a long memory and numerous tentacles. That we who are involved believe it's humane to help great love win means nothing; nor does it go in our favor that we did everything altruistically, with no personal gain. We are sand in the machine, irritants, guilty!"

"And we'll remain guilty until there's a change of regime," added Dima. He stared at them sorrowfully. Then he forced himself to cheer up and poured vodka into three glasses, exclaiming: "Tino, let's celebrate freedom and love! And you, Odilichka, our golden girl, drink your juice for the same reason."

Soon after, Odile went to the window. It was getting dark. Never in her life did she feel happy and sad to an extreme degree at the same time. She was maturing daily and beginning to understand that life was seldom easy. While gazing through the window, she noticed the first snowflakes falling reluctantly.

"Snow!" she exclaimed in a child's ringing voice.

* * *

After recovering from the shock, they shared the snacks and sprawled on pillows around the low table. They were comfortable with each other as if they were a closely-knit family. It remained unimaginably hard to comprehend that they would never see each other again.

Lyuda and Dima thought the yukatas were alluring. However, she was in a quandary. The initial inclination was not to open the packages until she was with Anya, but that would be unkind to the gift-givers. Or to open only the one she liked better? But which one, for the cellophane windows revealed only the color and design? So, to open both packages and then choose the garment? No, that would be unsisterly to Anya. Besides, she liked both colors equally: To decide, she would need to put a yukata on and feel the silk. "Anya and I are both brunettes and have the same skin color, so..." Lyuda mumbled almost inaudibly, a little embarrassed.

Seeing his wife perplexed, Dima proposed a solution: Odile would play the role of the Judge, and he would be the Witness. Taking a 100-yen coin from his pocket, Dima asked Odile to throw it in the air. "If it's 'heads,' Lyuda gets the yukata with the blue background, and if it's 'tails,' she gets the one with gray. All right? Everyone agrees? I hope Anya will believe me," he chuckled. Odile gaily threw the coin. It naughtily rolled far off, but the girl got to it and showed "heads" to everyone. Lyuda seemed pleased, immediately opened the package, lovingly stroked the deep-blue yukata with white cherry blossoms, and walked to the tall mirror. She peered at herself holding the garment: "How lovely and elegant. Thank you so much, dear friends! Anya will also be delighted—she loves lotus flowers and gray." After taking off the thick sweater, she put the yukata on and tied the obi. Everyone thought Lyuda and her yukata were exceptionally pretty.

Suddenly, during the picture taking, a disturbing thought crossed Célestin's mind: "Dima, I doubt Lyuda and you haven't thought about this, but I'll bring it up anyway. These photos you just took of Odile and me and those at Cape Soya, what are you going to do with the films? Is there even a minimal chance for your films to be examined at the Moscow airport? I know how interested they were in my films at the Finland border, although that was quite a different situation."

Odile understood her father's concern. She remembered the disagreeable experience with the rough Solyony and sly Nataliya on the day Olya was arrested. "We've thought about it, Célestin," Dima nodded gravely, "and made a plan. While we're still in Japan, for almost another week, we'll have the films developed in Sapporo and obtain prints. Then we'll destroy the films. After enjoying the photos, we'll keep only those that don't compromise either you or us. Heartbreaking but...

"Tino, you'll make prints for us and safeguard them until... And, naturally, photos from the wedding. Sooner or later, we'll find out how your Olya looks—the Russo-Tatar beauty with whom you fell in love head over heels!" He promised with tearful eyes.

"The only other possibility would be for us to send the films to an address in Maputo, but that's dangerous," Lyuda went on. "What's secret today is not tomorrow. Besides, the Japanese may be curious about films sent to Mozambique, a country with communist leanings." She thought aloud: "Regimes treat people like chess pawns. By forcing us to destroy our cherished photographs, they hope to wipe out our memories."

Célestin looked at the Russian couple, then at his girl, and again at Lyuda and Dima, before saying almost cheerfully: "Cherished photographs matter, but they're only paper. Odile and I wholeheartedly hope all four of you will one day see Olya and Olga together with us—face to face! In Metz or Moscow!"

* * *

They spoke long into the night, but Odile did not allow herself to fall asleep: She wished to spend every possible moment with those two extraordinary people. They were so genuine and warm with her, and she knew how brave they had been. There was talk about Cape Kamui to which she could contribute. To mark the couple's decision to go there, Dima's bottle of Kamui red wine, overly sweet or not, was opened and finished off.

"It seems Kamui is incomparably more beautiful than Soya," said Lyuda, while looking tenderly at her husband, "but to us, Soya is unique and we'll never forget it—because of our ten happy years together and the two of you at the lighthouse. And we saw Sahalin even with the naked eye, didn't we, Odilichka?"

At half past one, father and daughter saw Lyuda and Dima to the door of the ryokan. They were hugging each other and crying. The snow was already ankle-deep and falling Russian-style.

14.

In the morning, Mrs. Watanabe called the airport and found that all the flights had been canceled, so they took the 10:24 a.m. train to Sapporo. Before leaving, they exchanged friendly good-byes with Ayai and received chocolates for which she smilingly declined compensation. After arriving in Sapporo at 6:00 p.m. and checking again into the Aspen, Célestin called Air France and changed their reservation from Tokyo to Paris for an earlier date. It was essential to follow the Russians' instructions to the letter.

With a lame excuse, he left his daughter to unpack and shower, then dashed to the department store where they had bought the yukatas. For Olya, he chose a beige silk one with pink lotus flowers. Since silk yukatas were not available for young girls of Odile's height, he picked out a cotton one with carefree wild-flowers. Before going to bed, blushing in the new yukata over her nightgown, she stood at the mirror listening to her father's compliments. The fourteenth of March had to be celebrated!

* * *

They arrived in Paris in the evening on the 16th of March in-stead of the 19th. Célestin chose De Crillon again so they could swim in its splendid pool the following morning. Around half past two, Gilles was waiting for them at the Metz train station. In the car, he reported the most significant event: A Russian lady named Olga had called a week earlier. "Did you tell her where we were?" Célestin asked worriedly. "No, of course not! I said only what you'd told me to say to everyone—you'd be returning on the nineteenth of March. I repeated 'in ten days.' A telegram arrived from the USSR within forty-eight hours. It's waiting for you."

The devoted people at the estate sensed something vital was in the air when father and daughter, barely exchanging greet-ings, rushed upstairs to the study. Thanks to the inevitable but harmless gossip involving Lucien the mailman and even Gilles, they all knew a telegram from Russia was awaiting the master.

Célestin kissed the small envelope and hurriedly tore it open. Olga had detailed all the facts and dates with no attempt at concealment. Everything matched what they had been told in Wakkanai. At the end of the telegram, which must have cost Olga her weekly wages, she added: "Olya loves you immeasurably and is beside herself with joy! I'm too!" They breathed a sigh of relief and hugged each other. Without music, they energetically danced something like a waltz around the study.

Around eight in the evening, ten in Kazan, Célestin phoned Olga. In the happiest of voices, she exclaimed his name affectionately. He told her they were in Metz and thrilled to find out from the telegram that Olya would soon be free. Then he asked with bated breath if Olya still wanted to come to France to marry him. The tremulous answer arrived immediately: "*Da, da, da!* Yes, yes, yes!" His voice also shook when saying he was relieved and ecstatic. Odile realized all was well and insisted on speaking. But a dozen seconds later, Célestin grabbed the handset and promised Olga he would call his "finally free Olya" in Kazan on the evening of the 28th of March. He suggested that mother and daughter travel to Moscow on the 2nd of April to apply for French visas and begged Olga not to worry about plane tickets, as he would make arrangements. She was deeply grateful.

The next day was Thursday, the eighteenth of March. Before driving Odile to school, he sat her down and spoke in a weighty tone: "What I've to tell you is crucial. It's not easy for me to ask you to be deceptive—it goes against everything I've tried to teach you. But I've no choice. At school, as before our trip, you mustn't tell anyone a single word about Japan. If you have to explain your absence, say you went to Koblenz with me. We also won't mention Japan to messieurs Gaubert and Marceau." She fully understood the reasons for secrecy and promised solemnly not to divulge anything to anyone. He felt sorry for her but had no choice: Not only Olya's freedom and future, but the careers and possibly lives of at least four amazingly selfless and courageous Russians were at stake.

That morning, he walked into the school together with his

daughter, which he did rarely. She went to her classroom and he to the teachers' lounge. Cheerily, and pretending to be in a hurry, he greeted Michel and Philippe. They thanked him for returning Odile within the promised two weeks.

* * *

"To hear again her dear, silvery voice, what could be more magical?" he thought, while Olya was thanking her Tino for the loving words. "*Bozhe moy, Gospodi!* Dear Lord! How insanely happy I am to hear you! To be free, free—and to know you want to marry me!" They spoke at the same time, Olya often cried and he stuttered. She had suffered, suffered much but had prevailed over evil because the boundless love she felt for Tino gave her the hope and strength to survive.

"Do you remember the little book of poems supposedly authored by a Katarina Sepuhova you read in Leningrad? Well, I never gave up! Yes, I was freezing but never tore my hair and didn't allow it to turn gray. I lost a lot of weight but slowly recovered with the help of packages Mamochka, barely eating, was sending me... How is my tender, sweet Odilichka, does she still remember me?" The time stopped, distance disappeared: They were together, profoundly in love.

"Olga told me, Olyechka, you will both get Soviet passports for travel abroad within the next three days. So on Thursday, the 1st of April, please take the train to Moscow and go with her to the French Consulate the following morning. Submit separate visa applications, yours for marrying a French citizen and Olga's for a visit of one month. Meanwhile, I'll send to the consulate in Moscow via the ministry in Paris the plane tickets Moscow-Paris for Monday, the 26th of April. They'll give them to you with the visas."

Olya had been rapturously happy even before Célestin added: "We'll get married on the 11th of May in the Russian Orthodox Cathedral in Paris! It's a Tuesday, but that date is important. I hope, my love, you have nothing against this plan..."

EPILOGUE

Tuesday, 11th of May 1982:
Cathedral of Saint Aleksandr Nevskiy in Paris

Monday, 17th of May 1982:
De Quernevelle manor near Metz, Lorraine, France

On a gloriously sunny morning, two women, a man, a child, and a middle-aged mare were walking through a lush meadow on the gorgeous estate of an old noble family. The manor and parkland were situated fifteen kilometers from the city of Metz and belonged continuously, for almost four centuries, to the family De Quernevelle. An observer resting in a grove on the nearby hill would notice that all the promenaders, including the horse, were content. Beyond them, in a dell, he would see four giant oaks in front of the spacious ancient edifice. The sight was idyllic, resembling the landscapes Berthe Morisot and Mary Cassatt painted in the 1880s.

Madame Olya-Dinara Alimova de Quernevelle turned twenty-four on that seventeenth of May. Strolling up the gentle slope, she eagerly inhaled the fragrant spring air. One of her arms was tightly wrapped around her husband's waist while the other hugged the shoulders of her stepdaughter—a girl she would love forever as her own child. Olya thought: "If God blesses Tino and me with children, Odilichka will nevertheless always remain our firstborn and dearest." The young woman's face was radiant and lightly sunburnt, gracefully framed by chestnut hair that fell to her shoulders. With a sylphlike body and erect bearing, she was as light-footed as Odile.

Ahead of those three, Olga and Pasha were walking serenely like old friends. More out of affection than need, she held the lead rope, but the mare knew all the trails and walked where she pleased. The back of Olya's mother was bent, and her face etched by wrinkles of fifty years of hard life in Kazan, but she had not been as happy since the first years of marriage and the birth of her only child. Olga did not mind returning to Kazan in less than two weeks: Her daughter was walking on air, free and madly enamored of her husband, while God had given her a marvelous son and granddaughter. Tino had invited her back for the next Russian Christmas and Odile's eleventh birthday, the dates falling close to each other. In Kazan, she would give her parents good news and presents—and announce Odile was tickled and happy to have living great-grandparents.

Meanwhile, the girl's heart rejoiced: "How wonderful everything is... I feel on top of the world, and so does Papa!" She loved Granny Olga and her face filled with goodness. Every day, Olya was dearer and closer to her—and her papa, she had never seen him happier. Her schoolwork was going well, and only the previous day, a Sunday, a dozen friends enjoyed her party. Admittedly, she had to continue hiding her yukata and staying mum about Japan.

Because Célestin had suggested to his daughter that she organize her little event on the day Olya's birthday would be celebrated, the manor house was packed to the gills with a hundred guests. Friends who lived out of town—Paris, Koblenz, Bordeaux, Berlin—were to stay for a long weekend.

Some invitees were not aware of Olya's birthday and came to congratulate the newlyweds, knowing they had been married five days earlier at the Russian Orthodox Cathédrale Saint-Alexandre-Nevsky in the Eighth arrondissement in Paris. Although Kliment, the Metropolitan of Paris and Nice performed the formal ceremony, the wedding was private and intimate.

How miraculous, preternatural it all was. Olya received a pardon thanks to Célestin's chance meeting with two warmhearted Russians in Swaziland, a remote tiny country, and his subsequent friendship with them. Trust first developed over chess and South African wine, and grew deeper in the proximity of amiable Zulus and Xhosas, not to forget Kruger's astonishing animals. The valiant spouses of the Russians, twin sisters—another bizarre stroke of luck—knew influential people in Moscow. Olya, an Orthodox Russian, married Célestin, a Catholic, in the grandest Russian Orthodox Cathedral in Western Europe. The groom's Catholicism was tolerated: After all, he was baptized, never divorced, and came from a family with centuries-old connections to high circles in France. A concrete expression of his benevolence toward the Cathedral contributed to a permit for a private wedding being issued—and quickly.

Walking embraced with her husband up the green slope, Olya suddenly remembered her tormented, despairing words in front of the *Bronze Horseman*: She refused to live in the West; Moscow and Kazan meant the whole world to her; Russia was her only country. Then she begged her beloved to come to Kazan with Odile to meet Olga, her mother, and help the girl acquire a loving granny. She had felt terrible saying it on the 27th of October, Tino's thirty-sixth birthday. But the true nightmare began the next day—she was seized by ruffians at Finland Station.

"They threw me into a horrible prison and everything changed," she thought bitterly, yet soon rallied: "My lives before Tino, after Tino, in prison, and now with him again—it's as if I've existed as four different human beings!" In Metz, with Tino and Odile, she had a new life, and her mother would be visiting often...

But what about Moscow, the Gnessin, and musical theatre? And Kazan, Lena, and Ilysiya? And most of all about her grandparents who had suffered to support their daughter and granddaughter? Guilt and sorrow grabbed, then pierced Olya's throat, as she weakly muttered inwardly: "Things will change, this hateful régime won't survive." She knew how feeble that was and could only hug Célestin and Odile even tighter, lovingly and desperately.

In the grove on top of the hill, they breathed in the verdant beauty of Lorraine. The Moselle shimmered in the distance. Turning from the tranquil view, Olya asked: "Darling Tino, on the day after Mamochka and I'd arrived from Kuybyshev to Kazan, you phoned to give me the thrilling news: We'd get married in the Russian church in Paris on the 11th of May—an important date, you emphasized. I thought about it from time to time, but because of the exhilarating whirlpool I found myself in, I never asked you about it."

"I should've explained it earlier, but I've also been in a delightful swirl." He invited Olga and Odile, who were a short distance away smelling wildflowers with Pasha, to join them. "All right, my love, please translate for Olga. First, why the Cathedral of Saint Aleksandr Nevskiy in Paris? I chose it because its patron was Tsar Aleksandr II—and he endowed it in 1861, the same year he'd abolished serfdom in Russia. I consider him a great man, a genuine martyr. You took Odile and me in Leningrad to the Church of the Savior on Spilled Blood, Aleksandr's blood.

"I said Leningrad, but it'd be better if we call the stunning city something else—not even Sankt-Peterburg, but Petrograd, as Tsar Nikolay II did in 1914 eliminating the German 'sankt' and 'burg.' It will happen sooner or later. Our Russian friends, whom we sorely miss, think so."

The rapt listeners nodded as he continued: "That's about the cathedral of the two great Aleksandrs living six centuries apart—a holy place which will always be ours also. Now the date. Since high school, I've admired Roman Emperor Constantine the Great, not because he became a Christian, but because he ended their brutal persecution. However, I also respect him for founding the New Rome, Constantinopolis. And what do you think, my dears, on which date was that city solemnly consecrated? Well, it happened on the 11th of May in the year 330 after Christ, *Anno Domini* 330. True, it wasn't a Tuesday like our wedding, my darling wife, but a Wednesday, one thousand six hundred fifty-two years ago…"

Three pairs of female eyes fondly gazed at their father, husband, and son-in-law. Pasha too? Célestin finished: "And the recent past? A year ago, on the 11th of May 1981, our beloved cathedral in Paris was included among Historical Monuments—as PA88807. France should be ashamed to have done it so late. Let's point it out, Odilichka, to messieurs Gaubert and Marceau... courteously!"

Odile agreed. But then she mentally toyed with a wish that tied her past and a future she dreamed of. She would travel, travel far with Olya and Papa. Perhaps again to Mongolia? There, sitting on the wooden train seat and peering through the dirty window, she would determine if the Ferris wheel among the yurts was still stuck.

THE END

AFTERWORD

About the author

Vladimir J. Konecni (the family name is spelled Konečni and pronounced "Konechny") was born in the war year 1944 in Belgrade—then Yugoslavia, now Serbia—where he graduated in psychology and philosophy at the University of Belgrade. From a young age, he wrote stories and poems in Serbian, French, and English. The prestigious Serbian publisher *Prometej* has brought out four collections of his poems and short stories, which have also appeared in the highly regarded literary journals in Serbia, including *Letopis Matice srpske*.

Konecni has also written performance texts for the theatre, which have been staged in several European countries and the USA. In some productions, he functioned as director, and in others as set and costume designer. His multimedia play *Duality/Dvojnost* was performed in a renowned Belgrade venue in 2003. And while four of his plays were published in the Belgrade journal *The Contemporary/Savremenik*, *Apostrophe* bound two others into a book.

In 2011, the Belgrade *Licej* produced a bibliophile edition, limited to ninety-nine numbered and signed copies, of Konecni's *Autobiography – Literary and Artistic Experiments 1986-2011* (http://vladimirkonecni.net/books/Autobiografija.pdf).

For over four decades, Konecni has pursued art photography, with solo exhibitions in La Jolla and Los Angeles, California, and Belgrade. He also participated in several group exhibitions in the San Diego area and had his artworks presented in curated collections.

The novel's author has also had a distinguished scientific career. After earning a doctorate in cognitive and social psychology from the University of Toronto in Canada in 1973, he has been a professor of psychology at the University of California, San Diego, from then until now (professor emeritus since 2008). He was a John Simon Guggenheim Fellow in 1979 for research in Brazil, Australia, and Papua New Guinea. The scope of his scientific work is very broad: the psychology of emotions, psychophysiology, quantitative analysis of legal decision-making, as well as the philosophy and psychology of art and aesthetics (music, theater, painting, architecture). He has lectured on his research at nearly two hundred universities on all continents.

About the novel

In 2022, Konecni crowned his prose work with a masterpiece, a great classic novel. He wrote it in Serbian Cyrillic. Released by one of the leading publishing houses in Serbia, *Prometej*, the title of the novel is *Жудећи заОљом*. It has been very well received (https://www.prometej.rs/prodavnica/proza/zudeci-za-oljom/).

Already a year before the publication in Serbia, Konecni had begun translating his novel into (American) English. As with any translation, especially by the original author, there are modifications. For example, the title was changed to *A Dreamer's Fervor*. The book now in the reader's hands is the result of four years of work.

* * *

In early 1980, a father and his daughter, Célestin and Odile de Quernevelle, embark on a two-year challenging and sometimes dangerous journey. With powerful brush strokes and painterly precision, their extraordinary experiences and several astonishing human destinies are laid bare in Asia, Europe, and Africa.

Célestin, a thirty-five-year-old French aristocrat from Metz, a city on the Moselle River in Lorraine, northeast France, is a highly educated comparative linguist and polyglot. His eight-year-old, multi-talented daughter Odile is of Franco-German descent; her mother was from Koblenz, an old town on the banks of the Moselle and Rhine. She had died giving birth.

After a stunning romantic episode early in the odyssey, Célestin's pressing, crucial goal, with Odile's wholehearted support, becomes the release from the Soviet penal system of Olya Naratovna, a young poet of Russian-Tatar origin, with a controversial past, who is languishing in a strict prison on the Volga.

But through all the later mind-altering, surprising events, the profound love of Olya and Célestin insistently touches the travelers' and readers' hearts.

* * *

The author has written elsewhere: "This novel is 70% pure fiction, 15% documentary, and 15% based on my diaries—but I am not Célestin!" The authenticity of countless locations in the novel is partly achieved by skillfully introducing the writer's diary entries into the consciousness and behavior of the characters.

In addition to the literary qualities of the novel, there is another notable feature: A versatile, educated French voice directly addresses readers with an independent, yet convincing, point of view regarding both world wars, the Soviet system, the cruelties of the French and English colonialism, Japanese militarism, apartheid in South Africa, and the difficult Jewish-Arab relations.

Joseph Nalven, Ph.D.